I0788198

GAMES THRILLER SERIES

By

J.E. Taylor

J.E. TAYLOR
SUPERNATURAL SUSPENSE
& DARK FANTASY AUTHOR

Fallen Chapter 1

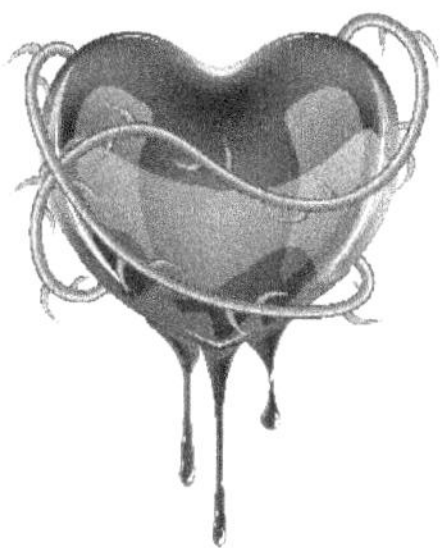

THE GUNSHOT FILLED THE small bank lobby, echoing off the marble pillars.

Lieutenant Thomas Patrick Ryan looked down at the red stain spreading on his chest, not understanding what had just occurred.

"What the...?" Before his eyes rose to his assailant, the world went black.

He died before his body hit the ground.

TY RYAN SAT ON the couch where his mother instructed. Her bloodshot eyes and shaking hands left a chill, and he shivered, pulling his shirtsleeves tighter over his dimpled skin. He flicked his gaze to Anna, his older sister flanking him on the right and got a half shrug in response, but her pale features just hammered home his terror.

His younger brother bounced next to him, unable to sit still, even with their mother's chiding.

When she sat on the coffee table in front of him and took Anna's hand, he swallowed the fear and stared into her sorrow filled eyes. Her mouth opened and closed once before she closed her eyes and drew in a deep inhale.

Ty held his breath, waiting.

When the words tumbled from her mouth, Ty's world spun. He blinked as his brain wrapped around what she just said and then he reacted, ripping his hand out of hers and darting away.

"No!" he yelled, denying what his mother had revealed. "No," he whispered as he settled into his favorite hiding place under the kitchen table, wrapping his arms around his knees, lowering his forehead as tears blurred his vision. A painful sob built in his chest, and he didn't recognize the sound as it wound from his lungs.

His father was never coming home again.

THEY FOLLOWED THE HEARSE to the cemetery and memories overtook Ty. He took a deep breath and closed his eyes, getting a grip on the tumult inside him. When the car stopped, he opened his eyes to a full view of the cemetery plot.

The door swung open, and the smothering summer heat enveloped him. He stepped out of the car and fidgeted in the dark suit. He would have preferred shorts and a t-shirt, but his mother insisted on the monkey suit, clothes fit for a funeral.

The aroma of freshly rolled dirt filled the air and the gaping hole waited to swallow the casket. Pallbearers brought the casket, laying it on the brass-plated stand straddling the grave. Ty scanned the crowd as they gathered, recognizing many of the faces from the Albany police force as well as some of the hospital staff his mother worked with.

When the folded flag was handed to his mother and the coffin lowered into the ground, she broke down. Maria Ryan grasped the flag to her chest and sobbed. The sound drifted over the quiet crowd.

Ty reached out, taking her hand, startling her. She turned toward him. The sob hitched in her chest as her bright blue eyes met his. "It will be okay, Mom." He squeezed her hand.

His mother squeezed back.

THE KITCHEN TABLE OVERFLOWED with dishes, from casseroles to cookies, and Ty maneuvered through the sea of people packing their house to the buffet. He fought his way between an overweight officer and the nurse the cop flirted with to grab a handful of cookies. Instead of mingling, he ducked under the table and sat down, munching on the semi-sweet confections and watching the legs come and go, picking at the desserts and pastries. The conversations ran from the morbid death of his father to some more humorous subjects, like how excruciating it was to wear nylons in this summer heat.

Chris looked under the tablecloth and slid beside Ty. "What cha doing?"

He held up the last cookie, snatching his hand away before his brother could grab it from his grasp.

Chris pouted, hanging his head, and slid a sideways glace at the cookie.

Ty sighed and sacrificed the dessert, handing it to his brother. The five-year-old shoved the entire cookie into his mouth, chewing without attention to the crumbs tumbling from his lips. He sent a chocolate smeared smile toward Ty and shot out from under the tablecloth.

He smiled despite himself. Chris was just so happy-go-lucky. He really didn't know what the loss of their father meant. He just thought Daddy went away for a while. Crushing despair bowed him over and the tears came, hot and silent. He wrapped his hands around his legs and rocked, keeping the sobs locked in his chest, but the tears flowed like the driving rain of a thunderstorm.

He didn't notice when Anna pulled back the tablecloth and scooted underneath with him, pulling him into her arms. Nor did he realize his arms transferred from his tightly balled legs to around her, clinging as his body vibrated with unvoiced sobs.

"Shhhh," she cooed.

Slowly, Ty became aware of Anna's voice of comfort, and he buried his face further into his sister's shoulder, hugging her and sniffling. When they separated, her bloodshot eyes met his, and she offered a grimace that was supposed to be a smile of support, but it failed.

"I'm okay." He wiped his face on the sleeve of the suit.

"I don't know if I'm ever going to be okay," Anna whispered and tears sprung, sliding down her cheeks in slow motion.

Ty nodded. He knew the feeling. There was no logic to the situation and his child genius brain just kept misfiring into emotional turmoil, leaving him unable to focus for any length of time. His father permeated every waking moment, and the loss crept up on him in subtle ways, like the unfinished chess game in his room and the Kevlar vest hanging in the front closet or sharing his last cookie with his brother.

"I'm sorry. I'm supposed to be strong for you," Anna sniffled.

Ty's eyebrows rose. "You don't need to hide your feelings around me," he said.

"How'd you get so grown up?" She messed his hair and smiled through the tears.

He shrugged. "What do you think will happen now?" he whispered.

It was Anna's turn to shrug.

Fallen Chapter 2

LEARNING TO COPE WITHOUT his father had been tough, but Ty focused on school and excelled beyond even his father's highest expectations. The conversation at the end of sixth grade hadn't surprised his mother at all, but it sure surprised the daylights out of him. They recommended he jump to ninth grade or find a school for gifted children because the level he was at was well beyond the children in his grade and he had already skipped from fourth grade to sixth grade the prior year.

Anna had taken the news in stride, but Ty knew it had to be tough for her to swallow. He was now invading her territory and having a freaky brainiac as your little brother was one thing, but the idea of having him in the same school when he's five years younger must be unbearable, but she didn't show any signs of the cringe he expected.

Instead, she just grinned and gave him a hug and told him they could study together. Ever since their father died, Anna leaned on him for everything, and this was no different. She seemed to cling to the idea like it was a piece of salvation.

Ty woke to a strange noise downstairs, and it took a few minutes to get his bearings. He blinked when the sound filtered through the floor and glanced at the bed beside him. Chris didn't stir, but then again, nothing woke him except a nightmare.

A quick glance at the clock alerted Ty that he had at least an hour before he had to get out of bed. The first day of the school year loomed and his stomach clenched at the thought of a new school. The middle school was a known he was used to, but going to high school left a big hole of scary behind.

At least he'd be there with Anna.

The noise repeated, bringing him out of his reverie. Ty slipped out of bed and pulled on his jeans before stepping out of the room. Hushed voices filtered up the stairs and Ty descended slowly, his heart pounding in his chest and his grip on the railing was one bound by nerves. He turned at the bottom of the staircase, staring at the glow coming from the kitchen.

His mother's soft laugh drifted in the air, and it sent a shiver of surprise through him. This was the first time he heard a genuine laugh from her since his father had died. When a deep timbered voice joined her, Ty froze.

The shock tingled over his skin and after a beat, he found his footing again and walked to the kitchen entrance. They sat at the kitchen island sipping from coffee cups, and Ty cleared his throat.

His mother's head snapped in his direction and the cup nearly teetered over, but the man reached out and steadied her hand before turning his gaze in Ty's direction.

"What are you doing out of bed?" his mother asked.

Ty stared at her and then glanced at the man. "Who are you?"

"This is Jacob Aris. I met him at the hospital a couple of nights ago," his mother answered. "Jacob, this is my son, Ty."

Jacob nodded in Ty's direction. "It's nice to meet you," he said.

Ty narrowed his eyes, studying the two of them. "Why are you here at five in the morning?"

"Ty, don't be rude. Jacob is a guest in our home."

Ty huffed. He may only be nine, but he understood more than his mother gave him credit for. He also knew if he kept up the attitude, his mother would give him a world of grief when this man left.

"Nice to meet you, too," he said, his voice flat and unwelcoming. He shifted his gaze to his mother. "Why is he here?"

"He invited me out for a cup of coffee," she answered and waved at the glasses on the counter.

Ty pressed his lips together, sending her a cross look before turning and heading back to bed. He didn't like this at all.

Fallen Chapter 3

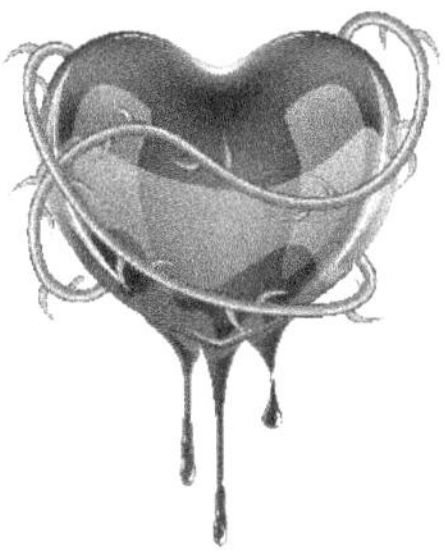

WAKING TO LAUGHTER BECAME a ritual over the next two months and each time their voices drifted up the stairs, it sent an icy fear through Ty's body, a fear he couldn't comprehend.

Jacob Aris seemed nice enough, but a wave of alarms sounded in his mind every time he crossed paths with the man. It was almost as if his father was trying to warn him from the grave.

Ty waited until Jacob left the house and then he headed into the kitchen, catching his mother cleaning up the breakfast dishes. She turned when he pulled out the stool and sat at the counter.

"Jacob has asked us to dinner at his house tomorrow night." The smile she delivered it with left no doubt what her answer was.

Ty didn't say anything, but his teeth clamped together in derision. His jaw ached from the pressure, and he slid off the stool, heading back toward the stairs.

"Ty?"

His mother called after him, and he stopped, but didn't turn around.

"Did you ever love Dad?" he asked in a quiet voice filled with all the anger building in his young frame.

"Of course I did," she said, crossing and stepping into his field of view. "But don't you think he'd want me to be happy?"

"It's only been a year." Ty met her gaze.

"I know, but Jacob is such a sweet man." She sighed. "I didn't plan on this so soon, but I think your father would approve of him."

Ty couldn't argue with his mother's logic, and he wanted her to be happy, but those warnings were on high alert. It was almost as if this moment was a turning point and if he could convince her to let this go, his life would take an entirely different road.

"Isn't he rich?" Ty asked, raising an eyebrow.

Her arms crossed. "Where did you hear that?"

Ty shuffled his feet and looked at the ground before glancing back at his mother. "Doesn't he own Aris Technologies?" he asked. He had done his homework. There were enough stories about Aris Technologies in the papers and the local library had slews of stories stored on microfiche.

His mother nodded.

"So, he is rich." Ty crossed his arms.

Her arms dropped to her sides. "I suppose," she said. "But that doesn't matter to me."

"I remember Dad saying money corrupts." Ty stared her down.

"Your father was a police officer. He was conditioned to think that way," she said. "But it isn't always the case. There are some wonderful people who also happen to have money."

"Like who?"

"I don't know? Oprah?" his mother said, exasperated, and then sighed. "Ty, I know you loved your father. I did too. With all my heart and Jacob knows exactly what I'm going through. He's been kind and patient, waiting for me to come to terms with your father's death. He wants more, and I think I'm ready, even if you aren't. Just give him a chance."

Ty's internal debate continued, and he stared at the floor. It was only when his mother said, "For me?" that he looked up and nodded. He couldn't help the chill that settled over him, like a door to a bright future had closed forever.

Fallen Chapter 4

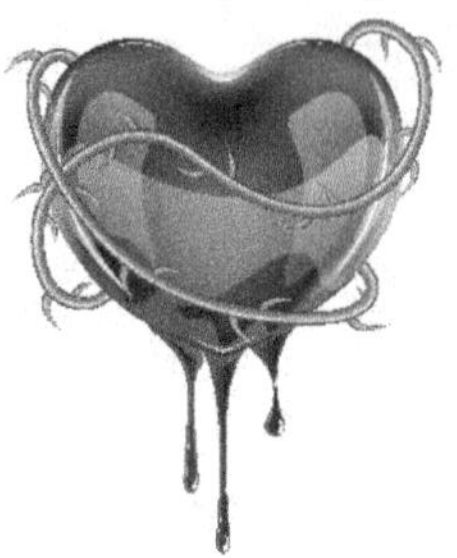

IT WASN'T UNTIL THEY rounded the bend on Orchard Street that the nest of upscale mansions came into view and Anna gasped, pulling Ty out of the book he was reading. He glanced at the looming houses and pristine lawns with skepticism. He liked their neighborhood better than this, and he dropped his gaze back to the story.

The turn onto Capricorn Lane drew his attention again. As much as he didn't want to be, Ty was impressed with the architecture of the majestic homes and when they pulled into the single driveway off the cul-de-sac, he actually sat up straighter at the behemoth in front of them.

The clean lines of the structure appealed to him, and he put the dread in the pit of his stomach away. Maybe they weren't so bad and the glance his mother gave him in the rearview mirror left him no choice but to behave.

When the car stopped, Ty unhooked Chris and helped him out of the car before taking his hand and falling into step behind Anna and his mother. He stopped on the top step, his gaze lifting up the pristine bricks and the notion of turning and taking flight overcame him enough for him to retreat a step. The fear that gripped

Ty was overwhelming in a way he'd never be able to describe.

It was a life-flashing moment. One minute he was a carefree ten-year-old genius, and the next he was in a mental prison that would crush him if he let it.

"Ty?" Anna asked.

Ty's gaze shot to hers, breaking the spell. "Yeah?" he replied, meeting her gaze.

"You looked like you just saw a ghost," Anna whispered in his ear. "Are you okay?"

"I'm fine," he mumbled and sent her a shy smile.

The door swung open and a man in a suit waved them inside. "Mister Aris will be right with you. You are welcome to wait in the library," he said, motioning toward a warmly decorated room to the left of the entry.

Ty studied the architecture of the atrium, especially the ornate banister curving up to the second floor, and then his focus fell on the walls of the library. Bookshelves lined the walls from floor to ceiling on three sides and an enormous picture window graced the front wall. Ty had spent enough time at the city library to understand that the collection of books lining the walls wasn't just for display. Most of the books had crease marks, which meant someone in the house was as veracious a reader as he was.

He scanned the titles; some of them he knew, like Jack London's *Call of the Wild* and some he didn't, like *The Stand* by Stephen King. A throat cleared behind them and Ty turned and stared at a girl that was at least five years older than Anna. The girl's dark hair was cropped short, making her face rounder than what would be considered attractive, and the coke-bottle glasses perched on her thin nose didn't help. Her gaze flitted from Ty's mother to his sister and then landed on him, completely passing over Chris.

Ty shifted under her direct stare. She kept her gaze locked on him as she stepped into the room.

"You must be Marian," Ty's mother said, stepping forward and extending her hand. "My name is Maria."

Marian stared at her hand and moved her gaze from the offering to the woman attached to the hand like she had viewed a particularly disgusting bug. Without acknowledging the salutation, her gaze jumped back to Ty.

"Is that the Mensa kid?" she asked, jutting her chin in Ty's direction.

Ty met her gaze and narrowed his eyes. He didn't like the way this girl dismissed his mother. "Perhaps you should learn some manners," he said, squaring his shoulders toward her.

She huffed at him and turned, marching out of the room without comment, and Ty traded an amused gaze with Anna before his mother turned on him.

"That was rude, Ty," she snapped.

He knew better than to talk back to his mother, so he met her cool stare and shrugged. "I'm sorry," he mumbled and shoved his hands in his pockets. He dropped his gaze and stepped closer to his younger brother, who seemed to find the most valuable things in the room. His little hands went to grab one of the statues and Ty intercepted him.

His brother's bright blue eyes looked up at him in surprise.

"No touching," Ty whispered, reciting the same words his mother said over and over to him.

"It's okay," the baritone voice announced from the entry, and Ty glanced at Jacob Aris as he strode into the room and took his mother's hands, planting a warm kiss on her cheek before returning his attention to Ty and Chris.

"He can explore. There's nothing in here that is irreplaceable, except maybe your mother." He grinned in her direction.

Her cheeks bloomed. "Oh, Jacob," she whispered, flustered at his attention, and then she recovered and cleared her throat. "You've met Ty before," she started, waving in his direction, "but you haven't met Christopher or Anna." She pointed the two other children out. "Kids, this is Jacob Aris," she added after the silent stares continued.

"Hello," Anna and Chris said at the same time.

Ty's gaze moved beyond Jacob to the entryway, where Marian stood with a boy that might have been her twin.

Jacob turned as well, waving them in. "This is my daughter Marian, and my son Frank." The two sent cool nods toward his mother before moving their critical gaze to Ty and his sister.

Ty shifted under their stony stare and lifted his hand in a wave before it dropped by his side. It wasn't Marian's gaze that left him squirming; it was Frank's. The kid had a darkness about him that made Ty want to put a protective arm around Anna and Chris. Hell, it made him want to bolt from the vicinity, like he was the devil in human form.

Instead, he plastered on a smile. "Nice to meet you," he said, taking the lead and the relief on his mother's face made him sigh inside.

Fallen Chapter 5

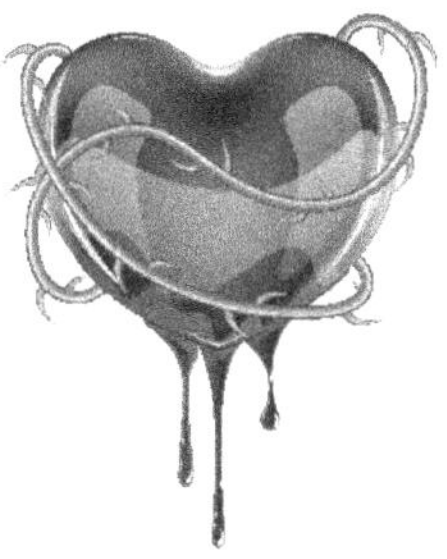

THE NEXT COUPLE OF months were filled with dinners at Jacob's house, where Ty smiled and nodded at all the benign conversations, his insides turning every time Jacob touched his mother's hand or placed a kiss on her cheek. But she beamed at the attention.

Ty sat in the living room waiting for his mother to get home. His school notes were spread all over the coffee table as he furiously crafted the end of a school paper that was due in the morning.

He glanced up when the front door opened, and Jacob walked in with his mother on his arm. "You could get at least a hundred and fifty for this place," he said.

"I'm not sure about that," Maria said, her face flushing as her gaze fell on Ty. "What are you still doing up?" she asked after a quick glance at her watch.

"I have a paper due in the morning," he answered.

She narrowed her gaze. "How long have you known about this assignment?"

Ty leaned his elbows on his knees and straightened out the disparate piles. "I don't know, two weeks?" he answered her question and glanced up when the papers were all in a neat stack.

"And you waited until the last minute, again?" She crossed her arms and tapped her foot, waiting for his answer.

"I had other things to do," he said. High school had proved to be a harder than he imagined, but it wasn't the advanced classes. School was the easy part—it was the other kids that were a problem. They didn't like having a ten-year-old, smart-mouthed genius in the school with them. And the ones who were nice just wanted to add Anna to their friend list. He never said a word to his mother about it, either. She would have marched into the school and demanded justice, which Ty knew would make things so much worse than they were now.

"Give the boy a break."

Maria turned, leveling a gaze that Ty recognized, even in profile. It was her shut up look and then she turned those eagle eyes back on him.

"Ty," she started, and he put his hand up.

"I know. I should have started a little earlier."

"Yes, you should have." She sighed. "But I'm glad you're up. Is Anna still awake?"

Ty shrugged. He hadn't paid much attention to anyone tonight. For all he knew, Chris could have eaten all the cookies in the kitchen and Anna could have gone out with her latest boyfriend for the night, but he knew better. Anna was more responsible than he'd ever be. His gaze dropped to his mother's nervous hands, wringing each other like they were in a wrestling match.

The hesitation in her features broadcast to Ty, and his gaze bounced between his mother and Jacob Aris, suddenly uncomfortable with the heavy silence. Something prickled his intuition, and he sat up straight, giving his mother his full attention.

"We have some great news," she started and stepped farther into the living room.

Out of all the items he would qualify as great news, what she said next didn't fall into the category at all.

"Jacob and I are getting married," she announced and beamed in a way that made Ty's stomach roil, and then their earlier conversation clicked.

"We're moving?" Ty asked, his voice breathless with shock.

"Yes. Jacob's house is so much bigger than this, and it's closer to the hospital." She didn't seem to notice Ty's jaw-dropping stare. "And Jacob wants to adopt you all. He wants to become your father," she added.

"I have a father," Ty said, sending a glare that would pierce armor.

"The Aris name holds a lot of clout in this town," Jacob said. "And I want you kids to have the same opportunities that my children have." He glanced at Maria.

Ty stared and said nothing. Instead, he stood and headed up the stairs without so much as a congratulations. He pushed open Anna's door, and she turned from her desk.

"Mom has something she wants to tell you." He crossed to his room, slamming the door closed on the world. Ty stared at Chris sound asleep in the adjoining bed and wondered what their life would end up being like living in a mansion with wait staff to do their every whim.

The thought left a dirty taste in his mouth, and he opened his window and spit, but the bitterness wouldn't go away. He lay on his bed and stared at the ceiling, wondering if this weight on his chest would ever lift.

Anna opened his door some time later and ducked inside. Ty met her gaze in the dark room, and she sighed, taking a seat next to him on the bed.

"Mom said you didn't take the news very well."

He let a huff out and turned away from her. He didn't need her to convince him everything would be just fine. He knew better. A black shroud had blanketed over his life, his future, and all he could see was devastation and horrors that he had no name for, and it was all wrapped up in the Aris name.

"Ty?"

"Leave me alone, Anna," he said.

"Mom's happy."

He rolled and met her sympathetic stare.

"She may be happy right now, but it won't last long. As soon as he gets us in his house, tagged with his name, he'll start treating us like possessions, and everything will fall to pieces." The conviction in his voice brought a rash of gooseflesh on Anna's arms and Ty dropped his head, rolling back on his side. "It'll be the end of everything, Anna."

"No, it won't. You'll be able to go to Harvard or Yale or even Oxford if you want and there won't be the worry about where the money comes from."

Ty closed his eyes, doubting he'd ever see the halls of an Ivy League school now, despite what Anna was mumbling on about.

"Can't you just be happy for Mom?" she whispered.

Ty didn't respond and eventually Anna got up and left him alone with his swirl of doom.

Fallen Chapter 6

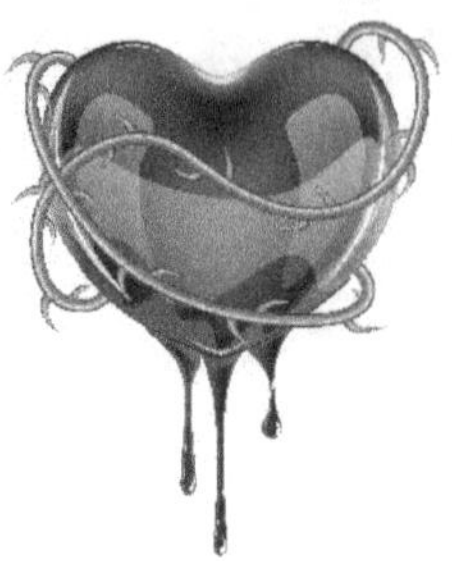

THE WEDDING WAS AS much of a blur as Ty's father's funeral, but only a fraction of the size. Maria wanted small and private, and Jacob obliged. They grinned and caught kisses at every opportunity, looking every bit the epitome of the happy couple.

The wedding included marriage certificates and adoption papers and as soon as everything was signed, Jacob's lawyer folded the paperwork neatly away and raised a glass in a toast for a long and happy marriage.

As soon as they got to the mansion, Chris and Ty were shown to their room. All of their belongings had magically appeared during the wedding. Same with Anna's, and Ty was glad to at least have his own bed in this strange place.

Frank stalled in front of Anna's open door, staring into the room at Anna as she sat down on her bed, pulling the heels off her feet. Ty hesitated, uncomfortable with retreating into his room until Frank had passed her by. He gave Ty an uneasy feeling and when he glanced over his shoulder, sending a creepy smile in his direction, Ty nearly closed the door on him, but the underlying need to protect his sister kept him in place.

"Don't you have to go to bed?" he asked.

"No. I've got homework, and I need Anna to look it over." Ty shifted at the ease with which the lie rolled off his tongue.

"I'm sure Marian can look at it for you," he said, but the tone was not one that made Ty comfortable.

"I'm sure she could, but I'm more comfortable with Anna looking my homework over. She's used to my style."

A shadow passed over his face and he glanced back in her room before disappearing down the hall. Ty had a feeling he had just dodged a bullet, or more accurately, he saved Anna from one.

He crossed the hall and stepped into her room just as she came out of her private bathroom dressed in a nightshirt and shorts and gave him a tired smile.

"I guess we're no longer Ryans."

Ty nodded, but kept his opinion to himself as much as he wanted to relax and be happy in this new life, something bit from the inside out, keeping him leery of everyone and everything around him.

THINGS WERE RELATIVELY EASY for the first six months, enough so that Ty let his guard down. He still kept both Marian and Frank at arm's length, which was easy considering they were both in college, but Jacob had a way of getting under his skin. There was something disingenuous about the man and one day, when everyone was out and even the house staff seemed to be scarce, Ty picked the lock to Jacob's study.

The computer presented little resistance to Ty's hacking knowledge, and he stared at the assortment of icons and folders. Most had to do with Aris Technologies, but there were a couple that were more of a personal nature, and Ty's gaze kept moving to the one labeled private.

He glanced up at the door and bit his lip.

"Screw it," he whispered and clicked. The file was protected, and Ty chuckled, pounding out commands in DOS that eventually unlocked the file.

The file opened to a document listing dates and times and corresponding names of women. The most recent date was just a few days ago. Ty closed the file and logged off the computer, focusing on the file cabinets instead. He debated on whether or not to leave it alone, but curiosity got the best of him.

He stepped to the cabinets, glancing at the door again before testing out each drawer. He didn't bother with the ones that opened freely. There was only one that was locked, and he kneeled, pulling the pins he used to unlock the study door out of his pocket, and went to work on the lock.

In a matter of minutes, he had the drawer open and stared at the names tagged on each label. He knew he was crossing a line, but he needed to know what the only locked cabinet held, and he reached in, pulling a file out.

The minute he opened the file, he knew he was in deep shit. The pictures collected inside displayed a naked woman in all manners of positions and she wasn't alone. The absent look in her eyes gave Ty the chills. Some kids at school had shown him a *Playboy* magazine once, and these photos were much worse than the centerfold spread.

He leafed through the folders and each one contained a new girl in the same lewdly compromised positions. Ty was so focused on the file contents, that he never heard the door open.

"What are you doing in Jacob's office?" his mother's stern voice broke through and Ty turned, wide-eyed and dry-mouthed.

Being caught doing something wrong was one thing, but being caught looking at porn was a whole different ballgame, and Ty couldn't get the files back in place fast enough. His mother crossed and grabbed one out of his hand and when she flipped it open, a shadow of shock crossed over her face.

Ty went to close the drawer.

"Leave it open and go to your room," his mother said in a tone he had never heard before. He scrambled up, and left her crouched on the floor, peering into the files with one hand clamped over her mouth.

Fallen Chapter 7

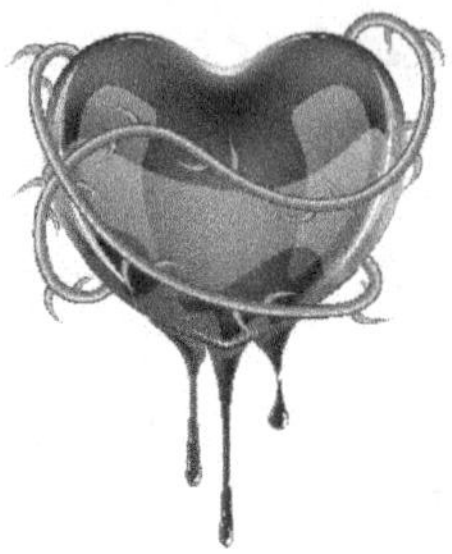

TY SAT UP IN bed, blinking and getting his bearings as the angry voices echoed through the marble foyer. Chris snored lightly, oblivious to the surrounding noise. The kid could sleep through anything, but not Ty. Ty woke to any unusual noise, and over the last year, there were many strange noises in this mansion.

Instead of slinking lower into the sheets like most eleven-year-olds, Ty sought the source of the noise. On one occasion, he found a mouse in the corner of his closet. After trapping the rodent, he set it free in his stepfather's manicured garden, hoping the furry creature would ruin the man's award-winning roses.

The argument raged and Ty slipped out of bed, sneaking to the top of the stairs and hiding behind the thick banister, peering around the fine-grained wood.

"Jacob, I want a divorce!" his mother yelled.

"Maria, be reasonable," Jacob argued. He grabbed her arm, and she spun away, breaking his grasp, still clutching the prints Ty had found earlier that day. She waved them in his face before heading for the door.

"I didn't sign up for this. What you're doing is wrong and I want no part of it!" She threw the stack of pictures across the foyer at Jacob.

"I swear, Maria, if you leave me..." Jacob's hands curled into tight fists, and Ty almost stepped from his hiding space. His heart pounded in his throat and raw anger flashed over his skin at the thought of his stepfather laying a finger on his mother.

"What are you going to do, Jacob? Tie me up and photograph me like your little whores? Or are you going to do something more permanent, like kill me?"

Jacob's face turned crimson. He said nothing, and Maria slammed the door behind her on her way out of the house.

Ty slipped back into bed and stared at the ceiling. It had been almost two years since his father died, but he couldn't ever remember a time his mom and dad yelled at each other: At him and Anna, sure, and occasionally at Chris, but never, ever at each other. The spackling blurred as tears filled his eyes and his heart ached.

He missed his father.

THE NEXT MORNING, JACOB lined them up on the couch while his kids stood in the entryway, whispering to each other. Ty looked from his stepfather to his step-siblings and back, the setting morbidly familiar as the man sank to the coffee table in front of them. Ty knew, even before the old man spoke, Ty knew and his heart froze, shutting off all feelings save one: anger.

"Kids, I have some bad news." He stared at his hands, unable to look up.

"It's Mom, isn't it?" Ty leaned back, crossing his arms. His mother caught him with Jacob's pictures yesterday and now this. A more visceral reaction toward Jacob radiated from her yesterday and last night's argument was just another illustration to Ty that his mother made a mistake by marrying this man.

Jacob wore the same somber expression his mother had all those years ago, just before she told them their father had died. He prayed he was wrong, but he knew better. He had seen his stepfather's face when his mother walked out the door. Ty's stomach knotted.

Jacob nodded. "There was an accident last night." His voice cracked, and he raised his eyes.

Ty ground his teeth together as he met his stepfather's gaze. *You killed her.* Mist covered his eyes, and he blinked the thin layer of tears away. Anna's trembling arm thread into his as she buried her head on his shoulder. The fabric of his shirt absorbed her tears, becoming tacky against his skin. Chris just stared at Jacob, not comprehending what he was telling them.

Ty turned to Chris. "Mom's not coming back."

Chris looked up at his older brother, his lower lip trembling as tears welled, filling his eyes before they tracked down his cheeks.

Fury raged within Ty like a ball of hot lead ricocheting off steel walls in an attempt to break free, and Ty slowly turned his angry glare to Jacob. "You killed my mom."

The table slid back a fraction from the pressure Jacob's legs suddenly exerted. "I loved your mother. Why would you say that?" he asked, with eyes as wide as saucers.

Liar! Ty pursed his lips, and narrowed his eyes, staring down Jacob while the blood boiled in his veins. He wrapped his free arm around Chris, pulling him close, leveling a glare that would have stopped Jacob's heart if it had any power behind it.

Jacob ran his hand over his face and glanced toward the doorway. "Don't you have somewhere to be?" he said to Frank and Marian. They disappeared from view.

Anna pulled away, wiping her face and looking up at Jacob. "What happened?"

Jacob turned toward her voice, and the spark in the man's eyes lit more of a rage in Ty's bones. The same flare of hunger he used to see in Jacob's face when he looked at his mother was now there. His mouth opened to speak and then closed again.

"What happened?" Ty barked, catching his attention.

"A tractor-trailer hit her car," Jacob answered, and visibly shuddered when he met Ty's blatant stare.

Fallen Chapter 8

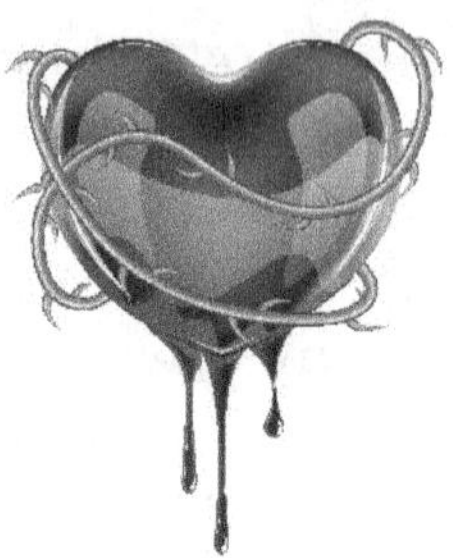

THE FUNERAL WAS ANOTHER blur that left Ty as cold as the winter wind, and he stood stoically as they lowered his mother's casket into the ground. His hands threaded in Anna's and Chris's grip as they both held on, sobbing.

Ty leveled his glare at his teary-eyed stepfather. The man looked as devastated as he professed to be, but Ty knew better. He knew the sickness in the man's heart had nothing to do with his mother.

At the house, he withdrew from the crowds, opting to sit outside on the patio with the chill penetrating through his clothing, numbing his skin in the same manner as everything had numbed his heart.

Jacob stepped outside and crossed, standing over him.

"It's cold out. You should come inside."

Ty refused to acknowledge his presence.

"Did you hear me?" Jacob's voice rose with aggravation lacing each word, and Ty looked up.

"You killed her." He crossed his arms.

"I swear, I didn't," Jacob said softly, and crouched down next to the chair, his eyes conveying hurt and confusion, but Ty didn't buy it.

"She wouldn't have gotten angry and left if it wasn't for those pictures I found."

A shadow passed over Jacob's face. His lips thinned and his eyes narrowed, and he stood with clenched fists. "You're responsible for showing her those pictures?"

"Damn straight," Ty said, but didn't expand further. He turned his attention back to the vista behind the house, not caring about Jacob's reaction.

The door slammed and Ty glanced at the packed house and Jacob's back as he navigated through the crowded space. Ty shivered and wrapped his arms tightly over his chest.

It wasn't until Anna came outside that he listened to reason. The warmth of the house hit, making him feel dizzy and nauseated, and he nodded as everyone he passed offered condolences.

In the quiet of his room, he lay down and let the sadness overwhelm him. The tears came and Ty rolled, burying his face in his pillow to stop the sobs from reaching the door. An empty dread scratched at his skin and overtook the sorrow, leaving him hollow and exhausted.

Hours later, Ty opened his eyes to the darkness. Chris was asleep in the bed next to him, and the house was silent. According to his clock, it was a little after two in the morning. Ty blinked, straining his ears for any signs of the funeral guests. Silence had settled over the house and Ty's sorrow gave way to a raw anger.

Fury swept through him at the injustice of what had happened, and he stood in his crumpled suit and climbed downstairs to the dining room with the need to destroy racking his young form. A stack of clean china sat on the table, and he picked up the top one, studying the pattern his mother adored.

He hurled it like a Frisbee across the room where it smashed on the wall. It felt good to break something, and he took another and another and another, the fury in his system escalating with each shattered dish.

He didn't stop when the lights switched on, or when Jacob stormed into the room. It was only when Jacob's hand grabbed a fistful of his shirt and hauled him out of the chair, yelling, "What the hell do you think you're doing?" that he stopped, and turned his angry glare at the man.

"Playin' Frisbee, what's it look like?" Ty answered, his voice as frigid as the night air outside. Jacob flung Ty across the dining room table in the same direction as the shattered plates.

Ty yelped when he landed in the pile of broken china and he scrambled to his feet, the hardness in him replaced with a hot plume of fear. He tried to back away, but Jacob wasn't about to let him get away this time. He converged, swinging a fist that connected with Ty's chest, sending him another four feet through the air.

Air forced from his lungs on impact and shards of glass embedded in his back from the first toss, gouged deeper. Ty fought for air, fear dulling his senses. His eyes pulsed in their sockets, and he stared at Jacob.

Jacob took another step and stopped, pointing his finger at Ty, his face the color of the burgundy wine he drank with his steak. "I swear..."

"You swear what?" Ty gasped, anger returning. "What are you going to do, kill me?"

The blood drained from Jacob's face, and he turned and stormed into his den, slamming the door.

Ty's chest burned just as bad as his back and he rolled onto his hands and knees, pressing his forehead onto the hardwood floor, closing his eyes against the pain. The distinct creak of the door rang out, and he looked up into Anna's shocked gaze.

"Ty!" Anna ran to his side, falling to her knees next to him.

"I'm fine," he said, his senses now returning and with them came the pain. "Just take the glass out, please."

"What happened?" she asked as she pulled significant debris out of his back.

Ty shook his head, still stunned by Jacob's actions. He knew the man was bad news, but he never guessed Jacob would resort to violence where his hands were the ones that got dirty. A new fear crawled through his bones. What if he turned his fists on Anna or Chris? "Don't worry 'bout it." He pushed himself up.

Anna studied the destruction and turned a questioning gaze to Ty.

"I broke the plates." He bit his lip and dropped his gaze to the floor. "I slipped on my way out," he added, hating himself for the lie, but it was better than the alternative.

"I need to clean out your cuts." Anna led Ty up the stairs and into the bathroom. Ty took one last look at the demolished china before he let Anna take care of dressing his wounds.

JACOB STUMBLED OUT OF the den for breakfast. He took the seat at the head of the table as his inebriated eyes scanned the five children. His gaze lingered on Anna longer than it should have and then stopped on Ty. His jaw tightened and the drunk stare turned into a glare before he refocused on his food, digging in without a word.

Ty picked at his food. His back stung every time he leaned against the chair and his eyes kept drifting to the smashed china still on the floor. No one had picked up the gleaming shards, and he wondered how long it would take to be cleaned up.

"You're cleaning that up," Jacob said, his voice a belligerent slur.

Ty turned toward his stepfather and uttered a sharp laugh at the finger pointed in his direction. "That's what you think."

Jacob slammed his hand on the table, making all the children jump except for Ty. Ty expected the outburst, almost welcomed it, and suppressed a smile of triumph at getting under the old man's skin. He crossed his arms, leaned back in the seat, and cocked his head to the side in a silent challenge.

"You really want to tango with me, kid?" Jacob's eyes blazed into Ty.

Anna elbowed him, pulling his attention away from the stare-down in progress. "Don't do it," she whispered so only he could hear.

Ty turned back to Jacob. "Guess not," he mumbled and dug into his food.

After breakfast, Frank brought a broom and dustpan into the dining room. "Dad said to give you these."

Ty nodded, taking the broom from his stepbrother. Remorse colored his vision with each scraping sweep of the bristles. He stared at the broken bits of his mother's favorite china, knowing she would be so disappointed in him.

35

Fallen Chapter 9

T HE CHINA INCIDENT ESTABLISHED a new pattern for Jacob, one that purged his daily frustration in the form of a fist, and Ty was the recipient. Every time Jacob's gaze landed on him, Ty's stomach clenched, unsure of whether the hatred in the man's expression would erupt beyond a backhand or a punch.

Until Anna's sixteenth birthday, Jacob never turned his aggressions on either Anna or Chris. Ty saw to it that whenever the old man got irritated with Chris, he was there, stepping between the two in a protective reflex. He wasn't sure if it was just the action or the defiance he displayed that always ended with him in pain, but he didn't care, as long as it wasn't his innocent little brother.

On Anna's sixteenth birthday, Jacob brought home a cake to celebrate. He asked Ty to carry it into the dining room and instead of saying no, Ty picked it up, wincing from the prior day's beating and he nearly made it to the table. The cake slipped out of his grip, landing on the floor face down next to Jacob's chair, and his heart leaped into his throat.

Jacob reacted, backhanding him across the face in front of Anna and Chris and pain flared in his cheek and eye where Jacob's hand connected. All lighthearted conversation ended, and shocked silence settled over the room.

Anna burst into tears and fled to her room, and Jacob locked himself in his den.

Ty and Chris followed Anna upstairs and stepped into the room.

"I'm sorry, Anna," he said, and she turned from the window, crossing to him, and wrapping her arms around him. He winced, and she pulled back, lifting his shirt. Her eyes widened at the bruise on his ribs and when they met his, more tears escaped.

"Oh, Ty," she whispered, her fingers fluttering to the bruised skin near his eye, and he pulled away from her touch.

"I'll be fine," Ty said. "I'm sorry I dropped your cake."

"I couldn't care less about the cake. How many times?" she asked.

"How many times what?"

"How many times has he hit you?" she asked, cupping his cheek, and forcing him to meet her gaze.

Ty shrugged. He didn't know. His life had become a progression of schoolwork and beatings and it kept his siblings safe and until tonight, Anna hadn't been a witness to Jacob's wrath. Chris had seen a few occurrences, but never more than a slap. Jacob kept his punches for a more private setting.

Her gaze moved to Chris. "Did you know about this?"

Chris stared at the bruise on his brother's side and shook his head. "I've seen Jacob slap him before." He looked at the floor when Anna's eyebrows creased.

She turned back to Ty. "You should have told me."

"There's nothing you can do," Ty said. "He said he'd send me to juvenile detention if I told anyone."

"Bullshit." Anna started toward the door.

Ty grabbed her arm. "Don't," he said, suddenly afraid for all three of them. She tried to break his grip. "Anna, he'll kill me," Ty whispered, trying to convey that it wasn't just an expression of speech.

"If he so much as..." She stopped and closed her eyes. "Tell me if he hits you again, okay?" She opened her eyes and met Ty's gaze.

He nodded, but he had no intention of enlightening her if Jacob used his fists on him. Not with the various threats the man issued in the fit of anger. He blamed Ty for losing Maria and he was hell bent on destroying any future Ty had and promised if he opened his mouth, he'd never see his sister or brother again.

TY WOKE TO VOICES in the hallway.

He slid from the bed and cracked the door. Anna was in her room, arguing with Jacob. He turned an angry glare toward the bedroom door and Ty ducked back into the darkness of his room. Anna's door closed, and Ty heard the distinct sound of the lock. He couldn't hear anything but hushed whispers, some sounding more like growls, and then a muffled cry rose before it cut off.

Silence settled, and then a soft creak cropped up. Rhythmic and steady, and Ty couldn't imagine the source. It reminded him of the sound the beds made when he and Chris jumped on them. When the noise stopped, Ty slid his gaze around the edge of the open door, peering out into the dimly lit hallway in time to see Jacob stumbling out of Anna's room, fumbling with his pants. His sister's soft sobs cut off when Jacob closed her bedroom door.

What the hell did he do to Anna?

He waited and when her crying continued; he slipped out of the bedroom, keeping an eye out for any sign of Jacob. When he pushed Anna's door open, the sob hitched in her chest.

"Anna?"

"Go back to bed, Ty," she said, sniffling.

"Are you okay?" Ty stepped into the room despite her request.

"Yes, now go back to bed," she whispered. "Before he comes back."

Ty stiffened and shot a glance over his shoulder, the sudden shudder of fear captivating his attention. The last thing he wanted was another beating. He nodded and snuck back to his room, wondering what Jacob had done to his sister.

Fallen Chapter 10

TY'S VISITS TO THE doctor became more frequent. A broken arm here, a broken rib there, and Jacob paved the way with his wealth and clout. No one raised the flag beyond a raised eyebrow.

Jacob's visits to Anna's bedroom perpetuated the routine. Beat Ty, drink, and then a taste of Anna before retiring.

Ty watched him leave Anna's room every night, the hatred building in his bones with each of her quiet sobs blackening his heart as much as the alcohol altered Jacob's. He wanted his stepfather dead, and he knew without a doubt, if Jacob caught him spying, he would be the next one fitted for a casket.

IT WAS RARE FOR Ty and Jacob to be alone together at the house, never mind bonding in any fashion; however, this particular Sunday was different. They found common ground watching an intense match between the Buffalo Bills and the Denver Broncos. Both cheering for the Bills and adding colorful commentary to the game. It was fourth quarter, and the Bills were trailing by a field goal with less than two minutes on the clock.

Buffalo was making a run down the field when Jacob said, "Get me a beer."

Ty hesitated, his eyes still glued to the television, wanting to see the end of the game.

"Go get me a beer!"

The fun of the day ended abruptly as Ty glanced at his stepfather. The mean-spirited glare told him this wasn't a request that could wait. Ty bolted to the kitchen as fast as he could to grab the last beer from the refrigerator. In his hurry, the beer slipped from his hand, smashing on the hardwood floor and capturing Jacob's attention.

"You stupid son of a bitch!" Jacob shot out of the chair and swept the broken bottleneck off the floor, approaching Ty, his hand curling into a fist as the fury turned his face red.

Ty saw the swing coming and ducked.

Jacob stumbled forward, his fist catching nothing but air, but his second attempt was more focused. It caught Ty in the chest, sending him onto the floor.

Ty's head bounced with a thump on the hardwood and stars filled his vision. When he regained focus, his eyes widened at the sharp edge of the bottleneck less than an inch away from his eye. Terror filtered through him, almost letting his full bladder loose.

Jacob's knee pressed against his chest kept him pinned and helpless on the floor.

"You little shit! You broke my last beer!" The sharp point of the bottle moved closer to Ty's eye with every angry word.

In the past, Jacob always stopped before he went too far, before he left a permanent mark on Ty. But this time the glint in his eyes was different, sadistic and crazed, and Ty knew there was no stopping him. When the glass dagger ripped through his skin, his breath caught in his throat. Searing agony, like a brand from hell, burned down the side of his face in the path of the jagged bottleneck. Pain silenced his scream at first and then, like a light switch, his vocal chords sprang to life, giving voice to the wail locked in his chest.

"Shut the fuck up!" Jacob bellowed as he stood and paced, pointing a blood covered finger in Ty's direction. "Next time you'd better not drop my drink."

Ty pressed his hand to his burning cheek. Coppery slick blood filled his mouth, oozing from the gash in his severed cheek. He pulled his hand away and his vision tripled at the amount of blood dripping from his palm. His stomach lurched, and he rolled, gagging on the bile rising in his throat.

"Don't you dare throw up on my floor, boy," Jacob warned. His pacing slowed and stopped altogether. The bottleneck dropped on the floor next to Ty. Quiet permeated the room, and Ty lifted his gaze from the growing red puddle to Jacob's face.

Jacob stared at him, blinking like a man just waking from a long nap. "Oh shit," he whispered and hustled out of the room.

THE DOCTOR GLANCED BETWEEN Ty and Jacob, his gaze stating more than words could at the sorry situation, and he placed his medical bag on the kitchen counter before peeling the bloody rag away from Ty's cheek.

"Jesus, Jacob, he really should see a plastic surgeon for this," Dr. Adams said, glancing over his shoulder before he began the slow process of stitching Ty up.

Ty remained still and silent, with eyes bloodshot from crying. Hatred kept his tongue in check, and he knew whatever he said would be ignored. Dr. Adams was on Jacob Aris's payroll, and he kept what happened at the Aris mansion a secret.

No one lifted a finger to help. No one stepped in to stop the beatings. No one stepped in to save Anna from Jacob's advances. The one time he tried to step up and protect his sister, he landed in the hospital, and she begged him not to say any more, not to put himself in the path of hurricane Jacob.

Ty understood the futility of their situation. Money bought silence and turned help away and as long as they lived under Jacob's roof, they would be subjected to his twisted idea of justice. He glared at Jacob, scheming, devising a plan to get his sister and little brother out from under the man's sadistic thumb.

"WHERE WOULD WE GO?" Anna asked. She sat perched on the edge of Ty's bed long after the household had gone to sleep.

"I don't know. Anywhere's better than here," Ty whispered. His hand absently grazed the bandage on his cheek.

"We'd never make it out there, Ty. I'm only sixteen and I don't have enough money to take care of myself, never mind the three of us."

"What he's doing is wrong," Ty said, his eyes darting to the door and back to Anna.

Anna hung her head, nodding. "But he's got those fancy lawyers and all that money, Ty.

Going to the police won't work. He'd pay them off and it would only get worse. It's just a couple of years. I can handle it if you can." She raised her eyes, meeting his sad gaze.

Ty nodded, but he wasn't sure they'd be alive in a year, let alone two. Not with how violent Jacob had become.

"If we run, Jacob will find us, and he'll make what we're going through now seem like a trip to Disney. Believe me, he's made it clear exactly what will happen if either of us opens our mouth." Her gaze shifted to the bed where Chris slept soundly.

Ty followed her gaze and a chill bit at the recesses of his stomach, shifting outwards until his entire form was numb. Jacob hadn't laid a finger on Chris yet and the thought of him taking his frustrations out on their younger brother turned his stomach. He'd do anything to protect Chris from the bastard's wrath.

He turned back to Anna and tears made slow tracks down her cheeks.

"I'm sorry I wasn't here to stop him," she whispered, bringing her dainty hand up to the bandage.

Ty closed his eyes and hung his head. He wanted to say he was sorry for not stopping Jacob from his nightly visits to her room, but the words wouldn't form. Instead, the bitter tears choked him, burning his throat.

"I will get you out of here, Ty. When I turn eighteen, I'm going to take you and Chris away from this hellhole. I promise. But in the meantime, just stay out of his way as best you can, okay?"

"Okay."

Fallen Chapter 11

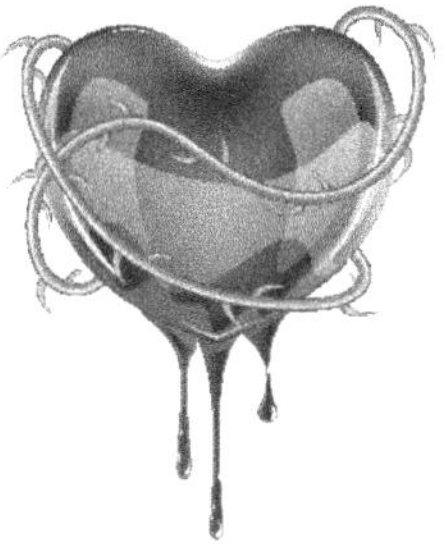

TY STEPPED OFF THE bus and strolled down the road, kicking rocks as he shuffled along. When he got to their house, Anna's car was in the driveway as usual, but the sight of Jacob's shiny silver Mercedes stopped him cold. Jacob was never home at this time of day. Ty's mouth dried up like the desert floor after a rainstorm. Something was wrong, and he dropped his backpack on the porch, pushing open the front door.

Anna's books and papers were strewn in the foyer and up the stairs, like someone dragged her up and her backpack emptied, leaving the ominous trail behind. His heart hammered above the silence of the house and each step Ty took reverberated fear, leaving a taste in his mouth like biting on tin foil.

Ty stepped into Anna's open doorway and stopped breathing, his heart plummeting into his stomach. Jacob sat on the side of the bed, his head down and his hand resting on Anna's bare, blood smeared stomach. Jacob's shoulders shook, and small pathetic noises of grief escaped, filling the room.

A blood-soaked knife lay on the carpet, and Ty stared at it. His eyes darted from the knife to Anna. Sudden and overwhelming confirmation of what had occurred hit him harder than any punch Jacob had doled out.

Fury took hold, and the switch that kept the morals his parents taught him before they died intact tripped, pushing Ty into a silent, murderous rage. He rushed the room, sweeping the knife off the floor and planted it in the middle of Jacob's back, burying it all the way to the hilt.

Jacob's breath hitched, and his head turned slightly, just in time for Ty to glimpse recognition in Jacob's bloodshot gaze before death arrived. Jacob slowly collapsed on top of Anna.

A combination of righteousness and panic filled Ty, paralyzing him in place for a second. His eyes shot to the clock.

Gotta get Chris off the bus.

The thought catapulted him into action, and he stepped forward, lifting a small piece of clean bedspread. He wiped the handle of the knife and backed out of the room, assessing his clothing and shoes before he slipped into the bathroom and washed his hands.

He deserved it; he killed Anna!

Ty's mind screamed, justifying his actions and burying the guilt along with the rest of his humanity.

Ty stepped out of the house, hauling his backpack on his shoulders, and jogged to the bus stop. He took a seat on the familiar oversized rock like he had every day for the last four years, but today he felt nothing.

No fear.

No remorse.

No compassion.

Nothing, just an empty husk of his former self.

The high-pitched whine of brakes filled the neighborhood and Ty looked at the approaching bus, wondering what would happen now.

Fallen Chapter 12

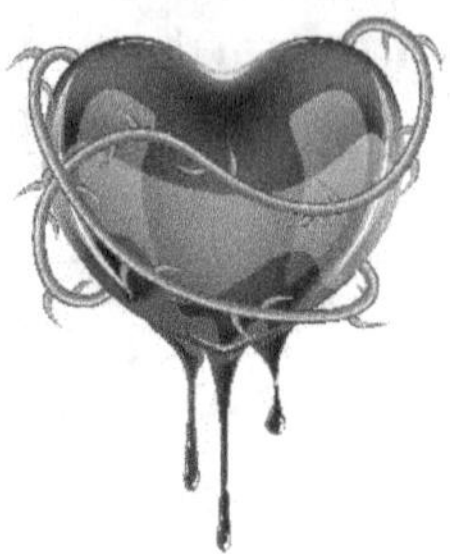

TY AND CHRIS APPROACHED the house, slowing to a stop at the police lights. Ty hadn't seen the cop car come into the neighborhood, or any of the other cars sitting in the driveway. He had been preoccupied, staring at the ground in front of him for the last forty minutes.

Anna's boyfriend sat in the back of the cop car and Frank stood to the side, jabbering with the police and pointing between the house and the cruiser in animated fashion. Seeing Frank screwed Ty up. He wasn't supposed to be back from school yet, and a layer of guilt reared up at him.

As much as he didn't like Frank or Marian, the reality was their father was dead and he was responsible. Ty stared with Chris's hand in his and Frank's gaze turned in Ty's direction. All the animation left him for a moment and his hands dropped by his sides.

Frank said something to the officer and trudged in Ty's direction just as a body bag was carried out the front door. One too small to be Jacob and Ty suddenly had difficulty swallowing.

"Ty," Frank said as he approached, his voice softer than he had ever heard it, and Ty tore his gaze from the body bag to Frank's. His eyes carried red bloodshot lines along with a healthy sheen of tears. "There's been a situation," he started and glanced over his shoulder before returning his gaze to Ty's. "There's no easy way to say this... Anna's dead and so is my father." He shifted his weight before adding, "It looks like her boyfriend killed them both."

Ty blinked, and his gaze dropped to the cop car. "Are you sure?" he asked, surprised that his voice was steady and carried the appropriate level of shock. It wasn't a stretch. The shock of her boyfriend being blamed for both deaths rode through his blood like a wildfire signaling freedom.

"They caught him with the knife in his hand and her blood all over his clothing. Bloody footprints are all over the room, the hall and up and down the stairs. They think he had a breakdown of some sort." Frank ran his hand through his hair and met Ty's gaze. "Ironically, he was the one who called the police." Frank let out a laugh and glanced at the house.

Ty closed his mouth as the second body bag was carried out. Anna's boyfriend must have driven by while he was at the bus stop.

"Anna?" Chris said, looking at Ty and then Frank.

"She's dead," Ty whispered, and the swirl of noise banged his eardrums. The world spun, and he dropped to one knee, resting his head on his arm, still holding Chris's hand. He didn't know if it was grief or raw relief that threaded through him, dropping him to the ground, but he knew he had been handed some sort of reprieve from hell.

It was Chris's sniffle that brought him out of it, and he glanced at his little brother, pulling him into a hug. The human contact helped him break the numb barrier, and he looked up at Frank through a sheen of tears, his vision warping as the flood let loose.

The innocent kid in his arms was all he had left, and he didn't know where they would end up now. Frank still had another year of college and Marian was off at medical school, which left him and Chris alone.

Frank crouched down and put his hand on Ty's shoulder. "Don't worry. Marian and I will figure this all out, okay?"

Ty nodded and covered his face with his hand. Hot tears choked and he let out a cough, just enough to clear the wedge lodged just below his tonsils. Frank helped him to his feet, and the three of them approached the house.

"This is an active crime scene," the cop said, putting his hands out to stop the three boys from entering.

"Can I get some clothes for these guys?" Frank asked, waving toward the entrance and the swarm of cops.

The cop mumbled into his walkie-talkie and then nodded as a plain-clothed cop appeared in the doorway. They disappeared into the house, and Ty slung his arm around Chris while they waited.

Another car pulled in and Ty turned, meeting Marian's horrified gaze. She nearly ran across the lawn, her eyes crazed in a way Ty knew all too well. Grief and disbelief traded places in a circus of expressions on her face.

Fallen Chapter 13

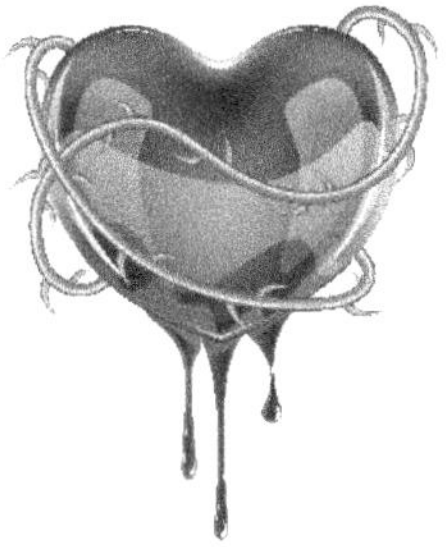

TY HATED FUNERALS AND this one more than any of the others because it was a dual funeral, and in his heart, he was screaming at the injustice of having the service for the man that murdered Anna combined with hers. But he had to remain stoic, unaffected, neutral because if he opened his mouth, he might confess and then Chris would be at Frank and Marian's mercy, with no one to stand for his rights.

Ty knew any future would be severely crippled if he landed in juvenile detention until he was eighteen and he didn't trust either Frank or Marian to do right by his little brother. While they had been warm and accepting of both him and Chris in the aftermath of the deaths, he couldn't let his guard down again with any Aris.

Ty hoped to be out of college by the time he turned eighteen and then he'd take Chris and scamper off into the sunset as fast and as far away as possible.

Frank and Marian were just as quiet as he was as the four sat in the front row for the service. High school kids and Aris Technology staff packed the church as most of Albany mourned for the dead.

Frank was named successor of Aris Industries and Marian took her father's post on the board. Neither Ty nor Chris were named in the will, but both Frank and Marian agreed to dual guardianship.

All four of them moved back to the house and things quieted down for a while. Ty threw himself into schoolwork and working out, pumping his body up so no one would ever mess with him again the way Jacob did. He finished high school right before his fifteenth birthday and Marian got her medical degree the same year.

While Ty could have chosen any college, he stayed close to home and worked for Aris Industries during summers and holidays, especially with the proposal Frank laid at his feet. When Frank found out Ty added a bachelor's degree in film production to his list, Frank took him down to the old dusty basement of Aris Industries.

"I always envisioned this sub-floor as more than this," Frank said, waving at the dank basement. "I think you could engineer a fantastic network of rooms for making movies down here," he added and slid his gaze to Ty.

"What kind of movies?" Ty asked as he scanned the dust-ridden hole, his mind already turning over a complex structure of rooms and equipment. When Frank didn't answer, he turned, meeting his stepbrother's gaze.

"The kind my father used to make," Frank said with a smile.

Ty's mind jumped back to the pictures he found, and he turned his gaze back to the concrete, shocked at his reaction. Intrigue fanned a heat inside him. He had never been with a girl. Not with the ugly scar marring his face, and the thought of filming some of those lewd scenes wasn't as horrifying as he expected it to be.

"And whatever you decide, this is between you and me. I don't want anyone to know this is down here."

"Is that the only way in?" Ty asked, pointing at the outdated elevator that was in the executive garage, and Frank nodded.

"Okay," Ty agreed, not because of the type of movies Frank suggested, but more because the development of a secure and hidden network intrigued him.

CONSTRUCTION WAS SLOW, ESPECIALLY with Ty's college course load, but by the time he finished his first year, he had a single room completed. Frank wanted it all done faster, but the reality of Ty being the only one doing the labor made it hard for him to press for a faster delivery.

On Ty's sixteenth birthday, Frank gave him a rare break, taking both him and Chris boating on Lake Champlain. It had taken years, but Ty had learned to relax around Frank, and this day of fun really dropped his guard.

He even chuckled at the razzing both Frank and Chris gave him after he thought he saw an angel on the observation deck when they docked for gas. Ty didn't even realize he had whispered, "Angel" until they started ragging on him.

ON HIS EIGHTEENTH BIRTHDAY, Frank left Chris in Marian's hands and took Ty to the nearly completed complex. The upgraded elevator made the smooth ride down, and Frank led Ty through the short hall into the finished room.

"I've got a birthday present for you." Frank flipped on the bank of switches, flooding the room with harsh light. A chair sat in the center of at least a dozen video cameras and beyond it hung a sheet, blocking the rest of the room.

"Have a seat," Frank said, leading Ty to the chair.

Ty hesitated, his gaze cataloguing all the hardware in front of him.

"Sit," Frank said, his voice rising into the tone of a demand, and Ty obeyed.

Frank stepped beyond the curtain and the click of switches filled the room and all the cameras' red lights went on. Ty shifted, uncomfortable at being the focal point of the cameras, until Frank's hand yanked the sheet and it drifted to the floor.

He stood a few feet away with a leather mask hiding his face and a handful of blonde hair in his hand. Ty's mouth went dry, and his gaze met the wide gray eyes of the kneeling girl. Her hands were bound behind her back and a gag silenced her. She trembled in Frank's grip.

Ty turned to Frank with a million questions running through his head.

"You said you wanted to make movies," Frank said with a grin.

"Yeah, but..." Ty's voice trailed off as his gaze traveled over the girl's naked form.

Frank crouched next to the girl, still holding a handful of her hair. "Ty's a virgin," he said, and her eyes bounced between Frank and Ty. "By the end of the night, I want him to be a porn star, understand?"

She blinked.

"I don't know," Ty said, but his hormones were singing a different tune. She was beautiful. Pouty lips, perky breasts and an hourglass figure he wouldn't mind exploring.

"I can always repeat our last performance," Frank whispered in her ear and Ty caught the fear in her eyes and she shook her head.

Her gaze traveled back to Ty, and she studied him for a moment. What he saw made him shift in the seat. It wasn't fear as she looked at him; it was almost pity, and Ty stiffened.

"She's my birthday gift to you." Frank reached down, caressing her breasts.

She tried to jerk away, but he held her in place. "Ty needs a proper birthday blow job," he said, pulling the gag from her mouth.

"Frank, if she doesn't want to..." Ty started, and her eyes widened with a silent warning he didn't understand. He stood from the chair, but the admonishment in Frank's gaze was clear. Ty glanced back into the gray eyes and shifted, offering what he hoped was an acceptable smile. Just being near a beautiful naked girl made him horny.

"Unzip," Frank said, and Ty's eyebrows rose. Frank pulled the girl closer. "Her hands are tied—unzip for her," he said, and the girl stared at Ty. Her gaze dropped to Ty's open shirt and slowly lowered to his lap, and she actually licked her lips before returning his gaze.

"Are you sure this is okay?" Ty asked, but his fingers were already busy unthreading the button of his cutoffs.

"She gets off on bondage," Frank said. "Right, hon?" he asked, and her gaze flitted from him to Ty and then she let out a nervous laugh along with a nod.

Ty unzipped, and Frank pulled the girl's face into Ty's lap.

"Blow him, bitch," he growled and before Ty could argue, her mouth was around his stiff member. All logic ceased, and he closed his eyes, threaded his hands into her hair, and guided her movements.

Her muffled cry brought his eyelids open in time to see Frank kneeling behind her, banging her from the back. Something about this lewd scene snapped in his head, but his mind wasn't making connections. It was too preoccupied with his body's pleasure.

Ty's first sexual experience was not what he envisioned, but after she sucked him dry, he didn't care. Frank arranged her in a sex swing next and took the spot in front of her mouth, slamming his full length down her throat and she struggled against it, but with her body ensnared in the bonds, she couldn't do anything against his deep throat action.

"You're hurting her," Ty said, and Frank smiled. The reality of the situation hit, and Ty felt all the heat drain from his face. It wasn't the girl that got off on bondage. It was Frank.

"Fuck her," he said, staring at Ty.

Ty stammered and stared at the widely spread legs. An open invitation, and he looked up at Frank. Frank moved out of her mouth.

"Tell him you want him to fuck you," he said to the girl.

After a few haggard breaths, she said, "Fuck me."

Frank resumed pounding her mouth and Ty stepped forward, touching her and teasing her with his fingers while he let the urge build. She actually moaned under his touch, and he smiled at the power it created inside. He hadn't played with the female body before, and he engaged everything he had learned from Frank's hidden porn stockpile, sinking to his knees and using his tongue until she cried out, her body flushed, and wetness rushed from her.

When he slid inside, it was like entering a new stage of heaven. He didn't ride her hard; he preferred the slow burn, enjoying this because he wasn't sure he'd get the chance again for a while. After all, this was his birthday gift.

By the time he ramped up, Frank had already finished and stepped aside to watch through one of the camera lenses and the girl was staring at Ty, crying 'yes' as he brought her around again. Sweetness settled over him with each stroke until all his energy pooled and shot out like a volcanic eruption.

Ty stumbled back, falling into the chair as his muscles trembled.

The girl gasped for breath. "Holy shit," she whispered, her voice filled with a reverence that made Ty grin.

Frank repositioned her, this time with her legs spread wide and her bound wrists hanging behind her in the air, forcing her head down. The height of both her face and her ass was a clear invitation, and Ty watched as Frank pushed a vibrator in her, making her moan.

He left it inside her, crossing to the table beyond the cameras and bringing back a contraption that he fitted in her mouth, holding it open no matter what, and then he turned to Ty.

"Time to fill her up." He waved Ty toward her ass.

Ty blinked, and his gaze dropped to the vibrator. "But," he started and stopped as his member jumped to life again at the alternative. "Really?" he asked, unsure of what his stepbrother was asking.

"Her ass is tight. You'll love it."

Ty pressed his lips together. "I don't know," he whispered.

"Do you want Ty to fuck your ass?" he asked her and while her eyes held trepidation, she nodded, and Ty wondered what the hell Frank had done to her before that would make her so submissive now.

"Do it," Frank demanded, and Ty stepped into position as unsure now as he was when he first saw her, but his body was already responding, already hardening at the thought of sliding inside her in such a taboo manner.

"Are you sure?" he asked, meeting her upside-down gaze. She swallowed and nodded her assent.

When he breached her ass, her eyes squeezed shut, and she gasped. Ty stopped, afraid to move any further. She slowly relaxed and opened her eyes. Her brow creased in pain, but the moan coming from her mouth was mixed with pleasure and Ty started the slow grind again until her eyes rolled back in her head and her body trembled under his touch.

"Fuck her with the vibrator, too," Frank said, reminding him he was not alone with this bound girl.

He obliged, and the reaction was met with a gush as she nearly screamed from the orgasm tightening her muscles around him. Her pleasure fueled him, making him feel all-powerful over her form, in control of the heightened levels and the number of times he brought her over the edge.

Ty closed his eyes, reveling in the feel of her, the wetness of her and the sound of her. When her moan cut off, his eyes opened, and he stopped his artful penetration.

Frank filled her mouth again, fucking it with bravado, but that's not what slowed Ty down. The necktie wrapped around her neck and straining in Frank's fists did.

"Keep it going, Ty." Frank smiled as he pulled the ends tighter.

Her body bucked with the lack of oxygen and Ty stopped.

"What are you doing?"

"Sexual asphyxiation," he said. "She'll cum like a fucking fountain," he added. "Keep going," he ordered when Ty didn't continue.

Ty resumed his slow stroke, unsure of Frank's wisdom. Her body convulsed, and he went faster until her muscles tightened and cum sprayed out from around the vibrator. Her orgasm triggered his, and he plunged deep inside her as his muscles seized in ecstasy.

Ty pulled away from her and dropped into the chair, his breath ragged and harsh as his heart settled back in his chest.

She was still bucking in the chains and Frank tightened the noose, speeding up his assault of her mouth.

"Stop." Ty stood, zipping his shorts back up. The look Frank gave him froze his blood in his veins. "Stop, you're killing her." Ty stepped closer, just as Frank shoved his entire cock down her throat with a groan and the vibrator shot out of her along with a plume of cum. All the fight in her ceased. Frank delivered a smile that made Ty want to turn tail and run, but Frank dropped the fabric, and it unraveled from her throat.

"That was the idea." He pulled out of her slack mouth. Her chest rose and fell with each wheezing breath, and Ty exhaled in relief. She was still alive, and his legs gave out. Ty sat down hard in the seat, running a shaky hand through his hair.

"I really thought you were going to kill her." Ty met Frank's gaze.

Frank zipped up his pants and walked to the controls, switching the cameras off.

"Once we edit that tape, it will be worth a fortune." Frank pointed toward the camera and peeled his mask off before crossing to the unconscious girl. With a smile, he put his hands on either side of her face and twisted. The sickening snap of bone filled the room and her breathing ceased.

Ty scrambled to his feet, knocking the chair over as he stared at her contorted head.

"What the hell?" he said as a fresh fear laced his mouth.

Frank's eyebrow rose. "I couldn't exactly let her go."

"What?" Ty's skin crawled, and he pulled his discarded shirt on against the shiver. His stomach roiled, and he clamped down on the bile burning his throat.

"I kidnapped her to make a few videos," he said like it was the most natural thing in the world and Ty stared at the girl and then moved his horrified gaze to his crazy stepbrother. "That's what I want this complex for," he added, waving at the concrete walls.

"What?" Ty asked again, his brain not allowing Frank's ideas to fully form.

"Porn and snuff. There's a big need in the black market for these types of videos, and we're going to fill it."

Ty blanched, every muscle in his body became numb. "We?"

"You and I and Marian," he said.

Ty swallowed, his gaze traveling to the cameras, to the room he built and back to Frank.

"You need to finish this place and we're going to set up a state-of-the-art editing suite for you. I've seen what you can do with the simplest tools, and I think between the videos I want to make, and your skills, we can make a killing."

The particular use of words wasn't lost on Ty, and he just stared, dumbfounded. "What if I refuse?" he said when he found his voice.

"Then I will strangle your brother while you watch," he said, delivering the line with all seriousness and enough venom to make Ty as stone cold as the dead girl hanging from the chains.

The dead girl filled with his semen. And the full scope of his duplicity hit.

Ty was trapped, and this time, there was no escape.

The End

Continue Ty's story with SURVIVAL GAMES on the next page.

Survival Games Chapter 1

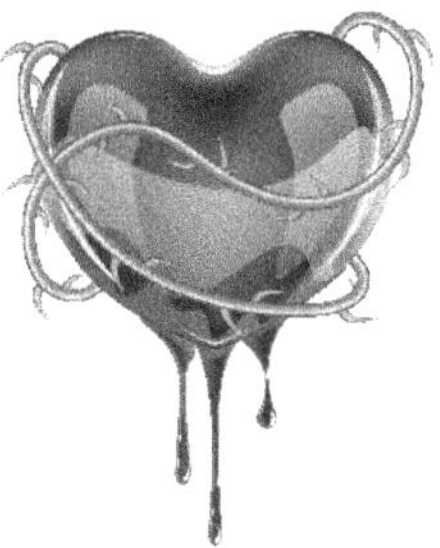

JESSICA CONNOR WOKE CHAINED to a chair in a dark room. Her heart thundered in her chest. She strained to look around, but her head refused to move. The lights slowly brightened, revealing a video screen.

Hands descended onto her shoulders, and a low voice whispered, "Relax and enjoy. I think this is my finest work yet."

A video remote appeared, and with a click of a button, the screen filled with a highway scene.

Her little Scion XA rolled into the camera view and then zoomed by and cut in front of an eighteen-wheeler. The front tire burst, and the little car swerved out of control. The truck driver had no time to react before he barreled into the little car, sending it rolling down the highway where it skidded to a stop on its roof.

Jessica glimpsed brown hair covered with blood against the driver's side window. The scream of brakes filled the room, and the truck hit the demolished car again. The little vehicle exploded, and the truck pushed the flaming car another hundred yards before both came to a halt.

People swerved to the side to view the wreckage. Sirens wailed in the distance. The car taping the accident passed by the excited crowd gathering on the highway, and Jessica caught a glimpse of charcoaled remains of the driver in the wreckage before the video faded to black.

"Oh God." She glanced down at her legs, fully expecting to see burned skin. Her legs were bare and unmarked, with no sign of harm from the fire or from the accident she had no recollection of. "I-I-I don't understand."

She twisted her wrists in the iron bands holding her to the hard chair. Straps held her head in place, and when she tried to move her legs, hard cold metal around her ankles stopped them.

She stared at the screen in confusion. "I… I…" The memory of being attacked at her car came flooding back. Jessica's heart rate tripled, and uncontrollable tremors gripped her bound frame.

"Mmm, the death of Jessica Connor." The smooth edge of his fingernails trailed down her bare arm. "They all believe you died in that crash. It was all over the news this evening." The husky voice laughed, and he came around the chair to stand in front of her.

The man frightened her more than the video had. He squatted down from a height of a little over six feet to her level and rested his arms on his knees. He was fit, like a quarterback, lean and powerful, with light chestnut hair slicked away from his face. When he smiled, his perfectly straight teeth seemed unnaturally white in contrast with his eyes, which looked black in the dark room—black and devoid of any hint of humanity as they breezed over her. A hideous scar ran from just below his eye to under the jawbone, breaking the left side of his face. Under normal circumstances, she would have described him as handsome, even with the scar on his face, but the lack of emotion in his eyes made Jessica recoil farther into the chair.

"Unfortunately, that's not how your life will end," he said. "But until that time comes, we are going to have a world of fun!" He sat back on his haunches and smiled. Their gazes finally met.

His eyes flashed, revealing striking blue irises, becoming almost iridescent in the dark room. Something clicked deep inside her, and she couldn't catch her breath. Her skin screamed as if doused in flames, and terror gripped her, along with something else much more frightening.

She yanked her mesmerized gaze away from his, bringing it back to the blank screen. Understanding slowly seeped in and her fear turned to rage.

"You bastard!" She struggled to free herself.

He put his hand on her bare leg and slid it up her thigh. "You will beg me to fuck you before this is all over," he said, his breath hot and foul.

"Never!" She squeezed her eyes shut.

The man laughed and pulled his hand away. He stood. "That's what everyone says at first, but I always win."

Her eyes snapped open, and she clenched her jaw in defiance. "Not in a million years."

He stepped back and pressed a button on the remote.

Burning pain filled every cell. She screamed through a clenched jaw, her body rigid from the electricity passing through her. Her eyes rolled up to the ceiling and her body convulsed in the restraints.

"I always win." He released the button. "Always."

His declaration followed her into the darkness.

Survival Games Chapter 2

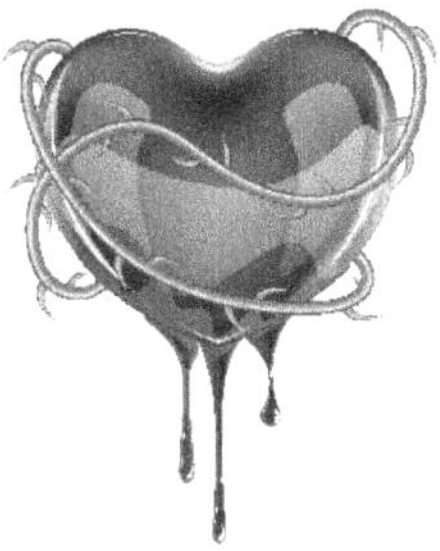

AN URN, A PICTURE, and dozens of yellow roses graced the altar. The organ played solemnly as people shuffled into the church.

Daniel Connor sat in the front pew, staring into space with his arms around each of his children. His daughter, Emily, cried softly while his son, Eric, played with little Star Wars figures. But he sat stoic, his emotions locked inside since that first phone call, the words yanking the air out of his lungs and turning his bones to gelatin. The wall supported his slow descent to the floor, the explanation of the officer jumbled, warbled in his ears like he was submerged in water. When he regained the ability to breathe, he realized his heart had been torn from his chest, and what remained was an endless cavern.

"Shhh," Daniel cooed into his daughter's hair.

A hand touched his shoulder, and he looked up to find his in-laws entering the row. They shared the same shell-shocked look. Daniel could relate. His world had plummeted into turmoil with that phone call, and the hole in the center of his chest blasted a hundred times wider when he had to identify his wife's burned remains.

They sat in silence, and the memorial service began. The priest shared inspirational words for the family about their loved one being at peace with God, but it did nothing to fill the hollowness in his soul. He didn't want to know Jessica was in heaven—he wanted her here to help raise their family, to watch them grow, to rejoice and celebrate year after year together. He wanted his wife. As family and friends shared stories, Daniel listened with a bitter and empty heart.

Twenty years together.

Twenty years gone in the squeal of tires and exploding gas.

Twenty years, and now, he was alone.

A tug on his sleeve caught his attention as they were walking out of the church. He looked down at his son.

"Daddy, don't be sad. Mommy's just sleeping. The bad man isn't hurting her," he said and then resumed playing with his Luke Skywalker figure.

His son's innocent words struck hard, slicing through the bitterness. The empty cavern in his chest flooded. Hot burning tears choked him, and for the first time since getting the call, Daniel cried, a harsh rasping sound like sandpaper on steel.

"Eric, your mom isn't coming home." The words croaked from his throat.

"Yes, she is." Eric smiled and went back to playing with his toy.

Daniel stared at his son, catching his breath and wiping the tears from his face, aware of the people filtering around to pay their respects. He wished he shared the same delirious oblivion. He swallowed the bitter taste that filled his mouth and burned his throat, blinking the last of the stinging tears away and focused on the people in front of him, extending their hands and condolences.

Survival Games Chapter 3

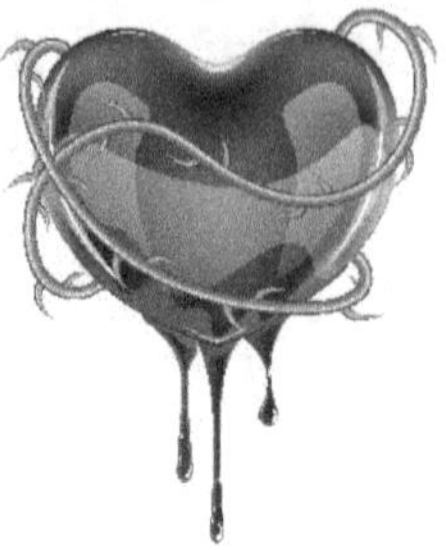

TY ARIS PACED BACK and forth, watching his stepsister work on his latest acquisition. His bright blue eyes swept over his prisoner's body. Anticipation thrummed through his veins. He licked his lips and checked the IV in her arm before resuming his hunter's pace.

"When can we have her?"

"Be patient," Marian snapped and continued the tedious task of administering electrolysis to Jessica's legs. "You want her to be perfect. That takes time. Besides, you don't want to give someone else a razor, now do you?" She diverted her eyes from the magnifying glass to meet his gaze.

Ty shook his head. The last time they gave someone a razor to shave, they found her dead in the bathroom.

Marian let out a huff. "I probably would've done the same, considering the alternatives."

Jessica stirred, her eyes fluttering open, and she struggled against the bonds.

"Shit!" Marion dropped her tools and seized a needle.

Ty grabbed Jessica's shoulders and held her still on the table. Just touching her skin sent a shockwave through him. Need like nothing he'd ever felt filled every pore, creating an inferno inside him he didn't understand.

Marion fit the syringe in the IV line and slowly released more sedative into Jessica's system.

Jessica's eyes closed, and the taut muscles relaxed once again.

"You're going to have your hands full with this one. She's a spitfire," Marian said. "Any time she is remotely conscious, she fights." Marian went back to permanently removing the hair from Jessica's legs.

He studied the slight form, inhaling. Her last defiant words echoed in his ears. *Not in a million years.* "We'll just see about that," he muttered under his breath.

The first time their eyes had met, it jolted him, like the surge from a bolt of lightning. Every sense heightened, tingling, overwhelming him like nothing he had ever felt before. His heart stopped beating, his lungs closed for the fraction of a second their eyes had locked, and then a rush of pure liquid fire engulfed him. He wanted that instant high again and couldn't wait until she was conscious.

This one, this little wildcat, was his and his alone.

"When will you be done?" Ty asked again.

"Another month or so."

He reached for the soft mound of her bare breast, drawn to her like the opposing sides of two magnets.

"Go play with your other toys," Marian barked and slapped his hand away. "I'll let you know when she's ready."

Ty nodded and gave their latest acquisition a last glance as he slipped out of the procedure room. Locked steel doors periodically broke the gray concrete halls. Strolling past the doors and into the control room of the complex he had built from a large underground bomb shelter, he glanced up at the monitors and grinned.

Who am I going to play with today?

Survival Games Chapter 4

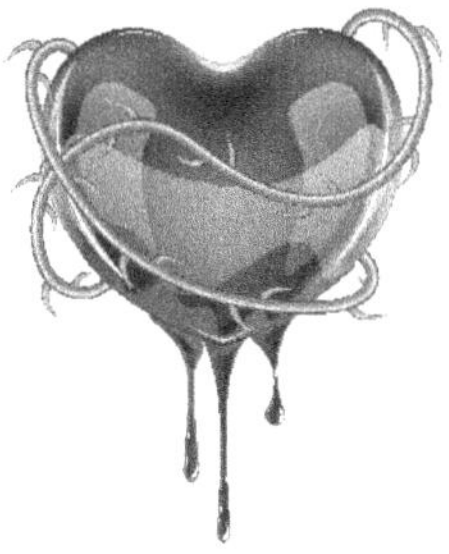

JESSICA VAULTED OUT OF a nightmare, sitting up with her hands covering a scream that never quite made it out. Her entire body ached, but she thankfully had clothes on, unlike the last time.

Random images flashed through her mind. *Walking through the shadowy parking lot at work and shivering from the cold with the feeling of being watched. A cloth covering her face, then darkness. The terrifying encounter in the electric chair. An IV bag. Being strapped to what looked like a hospital bed and feeling pain in her face, arms, and legs.* She shook her head, erasing the images, and glanced around.

The room was a perfect rectangle made of gray concrete except for a single mirrored wall. Cold. She shivered, catching her reflection before studying the lumpy mattress she sat on. It certainly had seen better days, but at least there was a sheet on it. A treadmill sat in the far corner, facing a screen attached to a swivel platform, allowing a view from any angle in the room. And right smack in the middle of the room was the electric chair.

A short wall beyond the monstrosity caught her attention, and she stood, crossing and entering a small private bathroom that included a separate tub and shower, along with the standard toilet and sink. A closet adorned the corner, and she opened it, finding towels, shampoo, soap and feminine products, but no razors or anything that could be used as a weapon and no medications of any kind.

Stepping out of the bathroom, she inspected the ceiling, noting three cameras and wondering if there were any more she couldn't see. Slow, icy fingers tapped their way up her spine, and she shuddered.

He was watching.

Panic threatened, so she took a seat on the mattress with her back to the mirror, bringing her knees to her chest and resting her forehead on her folded arms. Her long brown hair cascaded around her, shutting off any view of her face. She didn't want him to see. She didn't want him to know how unnerved she was. She closed her eyes, willing the terror away, willing herself to relax.

She inhaled and exhaled, continuing to take deep cleansing breaths, concentrating on counting each one, taking herself into a state of meditation.

The room slowly evaporated around her, and she went deeper into herself. When she opened her eyes, she was sitting on her son's bed in her house.

"Hi, Mommy." Eric's voice filled her mind even though his lips remained in the closed smile she adored.

"Hi, baby." She reached out to touch his face.

The physical sensation of touching his skin startled her, and her eyes flew open to the barren jail.

She stared at her fingertips in awe. Her heart raced, throbbing in her ears. Her fingers still carried the sensation of his soft skin. Uttering a startled laugh, she glanced around the room and back at her hand. If she could reach her son with her mind, she would eventually reach him with the rest of her being.

"Get up!" a voiced boomed through the room.

Jessica jumped. She hopped to her feet and turned toward the mirrored wall, unwilling to show a hint of the fear tainting her veins. She flipped her hair, squaring her shoulders, and glared at the mirror. She stared at her reflection: deep brown eyes, high, graceful cheekbones, full, soft lips, and the shocker that made her blink a couple of times—a perfect hourglass figure accented by the faded remnants of a deep summer tan.

She hadn't looked this good in years. The small bulge at her belly that she'd carried since her son was born was gone, along with any hint of extra weight she carried on her hips and thighs. When her eyes locked with her reflection, she shook the shock off her face.

"What?" she barked at the mirror.

"It's time for your workout," the voice thundered in the room.

"Yeah, right. And if I refuse?"

"We will have another turn in the chair," the voice said.

Jessica turned her head toward the chair and then at the treadmill, trying to keep the fear at bay. "Fuck you." She returned her gaze to the mirror.

"That can be arranged."

The low purr of his voice terrified her. Heat flushed her cheeks, and she glanced back at the treadmill, rubbing her arms against the chill in the air. She cast a wary glance at the mirror before heading toward the exercise machine.

Sitting on the floor next to the treadmill were a pair of running shoes in her size. She slipped them on her feet and inspected the machine. There were metal wrist shackles on the handgrips. Her heart jumped into her throat and her gaze shot back to the mirror.

"You're out of your fucking mind."

The cackling came over the speakers. "Perhaps. Now I'm going to give you to the count of ten to get on the machine, or we'll be having another unpleasant session in the chair."

Jessica's gaze alternated between the chair in the middle of the room and the treadmill as she debated. She made her choice and stepped onto the machine.

"Now, put your right wrist in the restraint."

"I don't think so." Jessica shook her head.

There was silence for a moment. "Then I guess it's the chair."

Goose bumps glided over her skin, and she shivered. "Shit," Jessica said under her breath and begrudgingly put her right arm in the restraint. The shackle closed painfully around her wrist.

"That a girl," the voice said. "Now the other one."

Jessica glared at the mirror, muttering a ream of curses, and put her left arm in the restraint. The shackle closed around her wrist with the same painful grip. The treadmill moved slowly at first and then increased, pulling on her wrists painfully as she tried to keep up the pace.

"Not so fast." She gasped. "I can't...keep up...this pace."

"You will keep up the pace," he commanded through the loudspeakers. "Here are some motivational tapes to help."

The screen lit up, and she watched in horror.

An array of videos assaulted her senses, alternating between scenes of such sexual heat that she could feel the burn radiating from the screen, to those of people being tortured, maimed, and murdered. This wasn't Hollywood. These were real, and the blood that spurted from the victims wasn't some red syrup. It was someone's life bleeding out. The blue-eyed man with the scar was never in the violent videos. That was reserved for someone with the most gleefully evil dark eyes. Eyes that made her skin crawl.

Jessica struggled not to vomit at the glimpse of what her future held.

Her heart slammed in her chest with the frantic beat of her feet on the tread. Her thighs burned like red-hot irons stabbing her with each step. Buckets of sweat rolled off her, making the treadmill slick in the spots where it stained the belt. The metal shackles cut into her wrist, and she fought to catch her breath, to keep pace. Her eyes filled with tears, tears of frustration, tears of pain, tears of fear and she caught herself, violently shaking her head, blinking them away.

I will not cry!

She clenched her teeth, determined not to let her captor see her falter, focusing instead on the videos, studying her captor's habits. His repeated signature was requiring the females in the videos to beg. And they did, eagerly. It was as if he had the same effect on them as he had on her. They nearly fell over to comply with his wishes, and when they did, he complied with all their pleas, taking them to heights that produced the burn of jealousy under her skin.

His power play was for the gratification of hearing them beg.

That was the thing she would never give him.

After the last horrifying image scrolled off the screen, the treadmill slowed enough for her to keep pace without the frenzied pounding in her chest leaving her breathless and terrified her heart was going to explode.

She closed her eyes and ran, thankful for the silence.

The door opened, and he walked in. His steel-blue eyes studied her, and he approached the front of the treadmill and leaned his crossed arms against the monitor displaying her speed. His gaze dropped to her bloody wrists and back up to her face, then his lips twitched into a boyish grin.

"Bastard," she said breathlessly. The son of a bitch was enjoying her pain.

He laughed and straightened. "Beg for me. Beg me to stop the treadmill."

His reasonable smooth tone struck a match inside Jessica, and she jutted her chin out in defiance. "No."

"Do you know how long you've been running?"

She had no idea. It seemed like forever, and every muscle in her body screamed for her to give in, for her to beg him to turn off the treadmill. She shook her head.

"Over an hour," he said. "You haven't exercised in months. How much longer do you think you can last?"

Jessica shrugged, not daring to speak for fear of giving him what he wanted.

"When you fall, and you will, those shackles will tear the skin off those pretty hands and your lovely knees will be ripped to the bone by the treadmill." His blue eyes sparkled, and he tilted his head a little to the side. "I would really hate to see that." He shook his head slowly, feigning pity, and then his expression changed. "Now, let's hear you beg."

"No," Jessica whispered, willing herself not to cry. She turned away from him and ran on.

He grabbed her face and yanked it toward him, almost knocking her off balance on the treadmill. "You will," he said through clenched teeth.

"Not in a million years!" Jessica thundered and yanked her face out of his grip.

Frustration turned his blue eyes dark, and he stormed out of the room, leaving her running.

She stared at the treadmill, shaking with rage, not daring to sound the sob building in her chest. Locking it down, she blinked, and her tears splattered on the machine.

Her heart skipped a beat. Metal lined either side of the continuously moving strip. If she could jump and catch the edges, she could stop running. That would give her the break she desperately needed. It was a risk, but at the pace she was going, her legs would give out any minute.

She had nothing to lose, so without hesitation, she took a deep breath, jumped up, and spread her legs the distance that she thought was correct. When she came down with both feet on the edges, she let out a yell of triumph and shuffled until she could lean over on the front of the treadmill. She hit the off button with her chin. Her legs were wobbly but able to sustain balance on the small area while the treadmill slowed to a stop. She closed her eyes in relief.

TY, ALREADY INFURIATED WITH her defiance, went over the edge when she let out a yelp of triumph and clicked the treadmill off. He stormed back into the room.

His fury made her recoil, and the part of him used to being in this prison rejoiced at her flinch. But the other side, the one that wanted her, cringed. He slammed a button with his palm, and the wrist shackles opened, freeing her. She took another wobbly step back, but he grabbed her arm, tossing her onto the ground, towering over her while his chest rose and fell, the air audibly filtering through his flaring nostrils.

A burst of laughter escaped her lips.

This would not do. None of the women treated him like this. She needed to learn she was not in control. He climbed on top of her, sitting on her chest, pinning her to the floor. He fumbled with his belt buckle and unzipped his pants, intending to make her choke on her laughter.

"You put that in my mouth, and I will bite it off," Jessica said. Her jaw clenched, and her glare conveyed she was dead serious.

His eyebrows rose, and his lips parted in disbelief at her audacity. He blinked, weighing his options. He was partial to his member, and the thought of her teeth severing his skin sent a chill through him, cooling whatever thoughts he had of teaching her a lesson.

He slowly zipped his pants and stood. Without a word, he stomped out of the room.

81

Survival Games Chapter 5

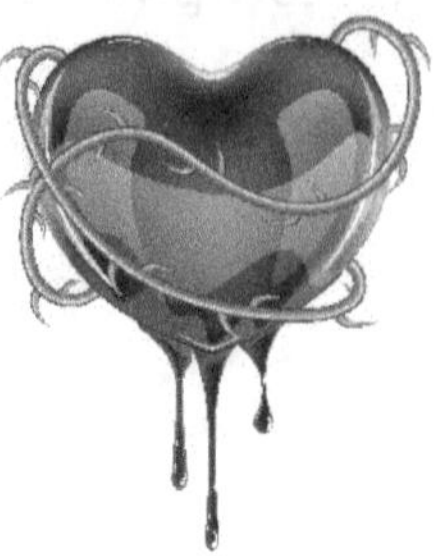

TY STORMED INTO THE control room and paced back and forth like a caged animal, watching Jessica lying motionless on the floor.

"I will get what I want!" he snarled at her image.

Wildcat. He ran his shaking hands through his hair, wondering what the hell had possessed him. He never got this agitated.

Not only was Jessica a fighter, but she proved to be resourceful as well, and she had the balls to laugh at him.

No one had ever done that before, and maybe that was the reason his heart was knocking around in his chest like a fucking loose cannon.

The others took an interest in him after their initial scare. It was like he was an aphrodisiac compared to Frank, whom they all recoiled from, as if they could sense the twisted evil of his mind.

But not Jessica Connor, not the one woman who set his skin on fire and made his entire frame tingle with desire. Not the one woman he would give his left arm to hear whisper his name. The one woman who drove him absolutely mad, and he hadn't even been with her yet.

He needed to tame her, and the sooner the better, because he wasn't sure how long he'd be able to resist the storm brewing below the surface.

He slumped in the seat and scanned the monitors. Four of the fifteen monitors had occupants—a man and three women, including Jessica. The rest of the monitors displayed empty holding cells, hallways, and the filming rooms for the movies they made.

A master at editing, Ty crafted some of the finest underground movies from the footage captured in the complex, and with the public's appetite for black market videos, they consistently sold out as fast as he could produce the twisted motion pictures under the Dark Dreams label.

The only camera free area besides the control room was the prisoners' bathrooms. Ty fought long and hard for that right, finally winning out over his stepbrother's will based on money. That crusade ended up biting him on the ass, and neither Frank nor Marian let him live it down.

Money wasn't his driving factor; he enjoyed the game, especially the perverse sense of power he got from hearing them beg. It was the only true control he had ever experienced in an otherwise powerless lifetime.

Frank pushed him early on to understand why so many wouldn't comply with their wishes, why they fought even when their lives were in peril. It wasn't until they brought in someone else, someone the person cared about, that he found the catalyst to break their spirit and make them readily comply. Guilt was a powerful leverage tool, and once their will broke, they became puppets, doing anything either he or Frank desired.

And the sex... The sex was unbelievable, especially when they begged. That was the ultimate high for him.

Or at least it had been until now.

His eyes snapped back to Jessica's monitor.

Even with the devious vocation Frank threw him into, he had a strict list of rules he played by. There were many instances his stepbrother insisted he break them, but Ty refused.

Until Jessica.

He wouldn't go a mile near anyone with kids.

Until Jessica.

The moment he saw her, he was drawn to her in a way he could not explain, and he caved to his brother's will.

He always got rid of the significant other. If the prisoner had a relationship, girlfriend or boyfriend or husband or wife, that person was doomed when the kidnapping occurred.

Until Jessica.

In her case, Ty refused to kill her family. Hurting children? No way in hell, and he was not leaving them without parents, either. He had been there and suffered the consequences.

Frank had been livid, but he got over it when the news reports died down into obscurity.

He watched her on the floor and wondered if bringing her in had really been a wise decision, especially considering the tornado sweeping through him every time he looked at her. He shook the thought out of his head and swiveled his gaze to Mike's monitor.

If she knew he was here, would that be enough to break her?

That could make the game interesting.

Ty's gaze kept returning to her asleep on the floor.

Frank wanted to film tomorrow. He said she'd be hot in the black market, whether or not she wanted to perform, and Ty had no doubt about that. Yet the thought of her with his brothers made him shift in the seat and he moved his gaze again.

Mike.

The thought of making him more uncomfortable than he already was brought a smile to Ty's face, and certainly any video of Jessica would do that.

That would drive Mike farther over the edge.

The moment Mike saw her, he'd crumbled. She was his weakness. Mike had cried and screamed pitifully when they electrocuted Jessica. He begged them not to hurt her again and said he would do anything they asked. Anything.

Frank took him up on the offer.

One of the other women in the complex bored Frank, so he'd concocted a particularly brutal way to get rid of her, insisting Ty create a masterpiece from the footage.

The video had become one of their hottest black-market sellers, despite the gruesome outcome.

He stared at the master library and shook his head; there were some sick folks out there, and Frank topped the list.

Ty controlled the different cameras for long shots and close-ups in the editing suite, his teeth clenched against the bile that seemed to line his throat any time they killed one of the prisoners. He didn't have the same issue masterminding an explosion or a car accident that took lives. Killing from a distance was less personal, less hands-on.

But Frank... Frank liked to carve his victims. He liked to hear them screaming in pain, gasping, begging him to stop, and eventually begging for death.

When it was over, it was his job to clean up the mess and create a video that would sell.

He closed his eyes, remembering how Mike had collapsed to the floor when he unchained him. The poor bastard was still semi-catatonic from that episode.

He rubbed his face with his hands, the images still playing in his mind.

His eyes drifted to Jessica, her chest rising and falling in sleep, her sweat-dried skin glistening under the dim lights. Her peacefully slack face sparked his libido, and when he turned to act on his longing, he stopped at the door, closing his eyes and taking a deep breath.

Not yet.

Survival Games Chapter 6

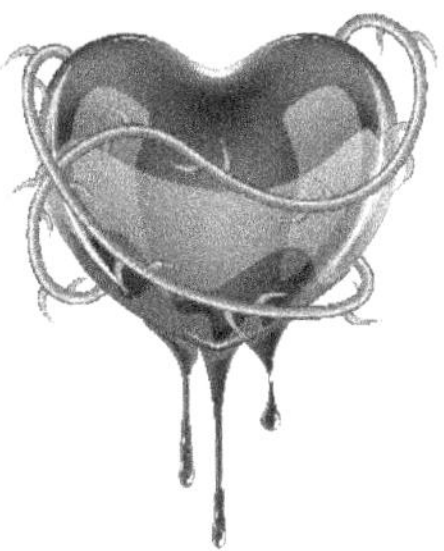

JESSICA DRAGGED HERSELF INTO the bathroom. It took every ounce of energy she had to haul her tired body into the bathtub. She turned on the spout and sighed when hot water came out, filling the tub. She soaked with her eyes closed.

Bedroom eyes. Where the hell have I seen them before?

The question ate at her, gnawing, percolating, unanswered.

She sat up, frustrated, and snatched the shampoo bottle from the small shelf, lathering and rinsing before the water cooled down completely. When she pulled herself out of the tub, she reached for a towel and hesitated. Laid out on the closed toilet lid were clean clothes, a nightgown, and underwear, all of which were her size.

She dried off and dressed, brushed her hair and teeth, and stumbled on wobbly legs back into the room. Sitting next to the mattress was a little tray of fresh fruit with some bottled water. Jessica sighed in gratitude. She didn't know how long it had been since she last ate, and she devoured every bite. After she finished, she crawled to the bed, pulled the sheet up to her neck, and curled up in a ball. The lights went out, and for a while, Jessica stared into the darkness, sure he was going to come and do unspeakable things to her.

Slowly, she relaxed into a state of meditation, and the room dissolved around her, once again replaced by her son's room.

"Are you okay?" Eric inquired, his eyes squinting with concern.

"Yes," Jessica said.

"Did the bad man come?" His eyes widened, making his whisper ominous.

Jessica didn't know how to respond, so she inhaled, thinking of her captor's blue eyes.

Eric shook his head. "The bad man's eyes are black."

Before she could ask what he was talking about, he took her hands, studying the cuts and bruises surrounding both wrists.

"You're hurt." He leaned over and pressed his lips to her palms. "That should make them better."

Jessica's eyebrows arched. Tingling overtook her hands, and the bruises faded, the cuts healed, leaving her skin perfect again. She couldn't believe it.

"See."

"How?"

Eric looked over her shoulder. "Be careful. He's watching!"

Jessica turned her head, and her reflection stared back.

Survival Games Chapter 7

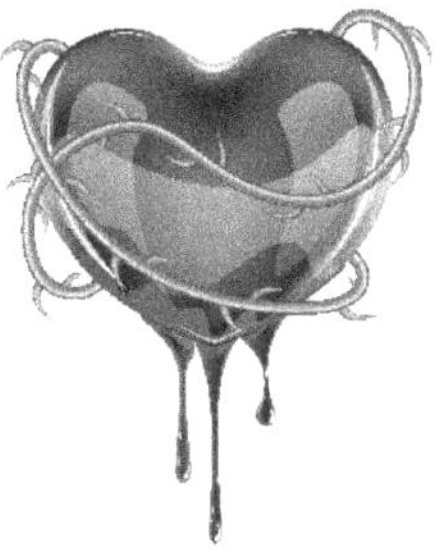

ERIC WAS TALKING IN his sleep again, and Daniel walked into the room to find him sitting up with his hands in front of him, as if holding hands with someone he couldn't see.

Fear filled Eric's face, and Daniel stepped toward the bed.

Eric looked at the wall near where he stood. "Be careful. He's watching."

"Eric?" Daniel sat on the bed.

Eric focused on his father. "Mommy got hurt," he said, and tears welled up in his eyes. "I made her better, but he was watching."

Daniel looked at the floor. Inhaling, he chewed on the inside of his lip before meeting his son's gaze. "Honey, your mother died in a car crash."

Eric looked straight into his father's eyes. "No, Daddy, she didn't."

Daniel took a deep breath, the weight of his son's denial pressed on his chest. He nodded, not knowing what else to say to the boy. "Good night, Eric." He leaned forward and kissed his forehead, tucking him into bed before he headed to his own room.

Sitting on the edge of his own bed, he studied his room. Jessica's things still occupied the space they always had. Her clothes, her jewelry, her knickknacks, her books, all still where she had left them. He reached under her pillow, pulled her nightgown out, and put it to his nose, closing his eyes and inhaling the remnants of her scent like he did every night since she'd died.

He pulled the silk away, realizing he shared some semblance of Eric's denial.

"Damn it, Jessie, why'd you have to go and die?"

The ceiling had no answer for him, and neither did her knickknacks.

They needed some help, Eric for his complete denial, Emily for her anger issues, and he... He just needed someone to talk to. He remembered the priest gave him a card, and he dug through the nightstand drawer and set it next to the phone for the morning.

With a deep breath, he scrounged through the storage closet, finding a couple empty paper boxes, and began the tedious job of packing her things. He held each item in his hands, turning it over and over before slipping it into the box. Jewelry was placed in two piles—one for Emily and the other in the storage box. The knickknacks were the easiest items. The clothing was infinitely harder to put away. Each item carried with it a hint of her scent, just like the nightgown. With each item stored away, another piece of his heart broke. Tears no longer came, just an all-encompassing emptiness that he never thought he'd fill again.

When all the closets and drawers and counters were clear, he sat and stared at the collection of boxes representing her life. His jaw tightened, and he blinked back tears. "Damn you for leaving us."

He deposited the boxes in the basement storage space. He couldn't bring them to the Salvation Army. Not yet. He stripped and lay on his back, staring at the ceiling, sliding the silk nightgown through his fingers as the clock ticked off the hours.

The next morning, after Daniel put the children on their busses for school, he grabbed the card off his nightstand and studied it. LeAnn Sheehan, Grief Counselor. He dialed the number, and when a soft, sweet voice picked up, he closed his eyes.

"Hi, my name is Dan Connor. My pastor gave me your card after my wife died."

"When did she pass away?"

"Three months ago. I'm calling for my kids. They aren't adjusting very well." He sighed.

"And you?" the voice asked.

"I'm surviving," Daniel said. "Barely," he added, thinking of the nightgown stashed under his pillow.

"Would you like to come to my office, or would you like me to come to the house to see them?"

Daniel thought about this for a moment and looked around the tidy kitchen and family room. "I think the house would be better. The kids are comfortable here."

"I can fit you in either tonight or tomorrow. Which is better for you?"

"Tonight would be good. My son hasn't accepted my wife's death at all. He is in complete denial. My daughter is just angry, and I think it would be good for her to talk to someone." He paused. "To a woman."

"And what do *you* need, Dan?"

Daniel looked out the window of his house. "I need my wife," he whispered, and the bitter taste of tears filled his throat. He closed his eyes and squeezed the bridge of his nose, fighting for control of his emotions.

The line was silent for a moment. "Where do you live?"

DANIEL SAT AT THE dinner table. "Someone is stopping by tonight to help us."

"Help us with what?" Emily pushed the food on her plate around with a fork.

"With dealing with your mother's death." He looked from his daughter to his son.

"Mommy's not dead." Eric took a bite of food.

"Shut up, you stupid jackass!"

"Emily, don't talk to your brother like that!"

"You always take his side!" She stormed away from the table.

Dan sighed and hung his head for a moment. This had been a recurring theme at the dinner table for the last three months.

The bell rang just as Eric finished his homework. Daniel opened the door, unprepared for his reaction to the woman standing on the doorstep. Blonde and curvy in the right places, with smoky green eyes that reflected the smile on her lips. The combination caught his voice in his throat and the muscles in his stomach fluttered.

"Um, hi. You must be LeAnn?" He stumbled over his words and waved her inside.

She nodded and crossed toward the back of the house. Eric looked up from the table, closing his math book and tucking it away in his backpack.

"Eric, this is, um, Mrs.... Miss Sheehan?" He looked at her for help.

She smiled. "Ms. But you can call me LeAnn," she said to Eric and sat down. "Do you mind if I talk with you for a while?"

"Sure," Eric said.

Daniel just stood there.

"I'd like to talk with Eric alone for a bit. You said you also have a daughter?"

Daniel nodded.

"I'll sit down with her after Eric and I talk a while." She smiled and tilted her head for him to leave.

"Oh," Daniel said, getting the hint. He left the room.

LEANN LOOKED AT ERIC. "Tell me about your mom?"

Eric looked up at her with his sweet brown eyes inherited from his mother. "She's sleeping now," he said. "The bad man was watching her again today."

"Where is she?"

Eric studied the tabletop for a minute, and his brow furrowed, trying to best describe the concrete prison that held his mother. "I'm not sure, but it looks like the basement before Dad made rooms down there."

LeAnn nodded. "What does the bad man do?"

"He likes to hurt people." Tears blurred his vision. "He wants to hurt my mom." His brow creased, and he got a hint of LeAnn's thoughts.

Jesus, this is a little more detailed than any other denial fantasy I've encountered. How do I handle this? LeAnn put her arm around his shoulder. "It will be okay, Eric."

He raised his eyebrows, looking at her as if she had two heads. "No, it won't."

Not unless I can get her to open that door. However, he wasn't about to tell a stranger about the door deep inside his mother. Somehow, her capture had triggered his abilities. His ability to hear other's thoughts had been supercharged the minute she was grabbed in the parking lot. Now he didn't need to concentrate to hear what people were thinking. It was a constant background noise in his head, and he could open the door in his mind at will, like he had with his mother's hands the other night. His door didn't scare him the way hers did. She possessed both the power to heal and a much darker, more dangerous power.

He lowered his eyes and studied his knuckles.

LeAnn took a deep breath. "Eric." She tilted his chin so he was looking at her. "Your mom is in heaven now, and I know this is very hard for you to understand, but eventually, you will need to accept it." She touched his face. "This fantasy that you have concocted in your mind may seem real, but it isn't, honey."

"I don't want to talk with you anymore." He got up to leave the room.

"Eric?"

He turned. "What?"

"I'm here anytime you need to talk."

He nodded and walked out of the room.

LEANN DREW A DEEP breath. Eric was only seven, yet he seemed to hold the world on his shoulders. When reality set in, it would be very

tough on the little guy. Her heart went out to him.

Daniel walked in with Emily.

"Emily, this is LeAnn. She's a grief counselor, and I thought it would be good if you and Eric talked to her." He pulled out the chair for his daughter and pushed it in to the table after she sat. Then he nodded and left the room.

Emily sat with her arms crossed, her lips pressed together in annoyance.

"Tell me about your mother."

"She's dead." Emily glared at LeAnn.

"I know, but tell me the things you remember about her."

Emily's eyes softened a little. "She used to laugh a lot. She was a lot more fun than Dad." Her chin quivered. "I miss her." The tears came.

LeAnn covered Emily's hand with her own.

"When will it stop hurting?"

LeAnn closed her eyes. "Honey, it never does completely stop. It just gets easier with each day that passes. And as it gets easier, you can cherish the time you had with her more and more."

"Dad finally packed her things yesterday." She looked down at her hands. "I used to go into the closet and run my hands over her clothes. It made me feel better. Now there is nothing left of hers to do that with."

"Did you talk to your father about that?"

"I can't talk to him about anything," she said, her eyes filled with pain.

"You can talk to me anytime you need to." LeAnn smiled and handed Emily her card.

Emily took the card. "Thank you," she whispered. "Can I go now?"

LeAnn nodded. "Send your father in, please."

Daniel walked into the kitchen. She motioned for him to sit, but he ignored the invitation.

"Would you like a cup of coffee?" He headed over to the coffeepot and poured himself a cup.

"Sure."

"How do you take it?"

"Cream and sugar," she said.

"Do you mind flavored creamer?" He pulled the vanilla creamer from the refrigerator and showed it to her.

"My favorite."

Daniel mixed the coffee. "Jessie didn't drink coffee." He put LeAnn's cup in front of her, taking the seat across the table. "I live on the stuff."

"Me, too." LeAnn took a sip. "Tell me about her."

Daniel leaned back in his chair and looked out the back door. "Jessie and I... We could talk to each other about anything, and she certainly knew how to make me laugh." He paused and allowed a smile to form. "I can't imagine never seeing her again." He looked back at LeAnn, and his smile faded away. "I miss her."

LeAnn nodded. "I understand completely. I lost my husband almost two years ago, and I still feel the things you're talking about. It gets easier with time, but..."

Daniel laughed bitterly. "Aren't you supposed to tell me I will get over it? I will live again and love again? Isn't that your job?"

"Not really," LeAnn said. "I'm here to help you accept her death so you can move forward with your life."

Daniel stared into his coffee, then back up at her, and nodded. "How are the kids doing?"

"Emily is doing amazingly well. Sure, she's angry, but that's healthy, and understandably, she misses her mom. She was very upset with you for cleaning out your wife's things. They were a comfort for her," LeAnn said.

Daniel closed his eyes and lowered his head. "I thought that would make it easier."

"It was the right thing to do." LeAnn took another sip of her coffee and set the cup down.

Daniel stared at the lipstick mark on the inside of the cup, and something stirred inside him. He pushed the inappropriate thoughts out of his mind and looked back into her green eyes.

"But Eric is another story. While it is normal for younger children to make up fantasies when in denial, I'm just a little worried at the vividness of his fantasy. He seems to think a bad man has your wife and is going to hurt her. That is a tough fantasy to stomach, especially since he already knows how it ends."

Silence blanketed the kitchen. Daniel's coffee cup stalled halfway to his mouth as the reality of her words set in. He slowly lowered the cup, staring at her. The horror of the accident would be nothing compared to his son's final fantasy.

"Jesus."

LeAnn inhaled. "I'd like to come by a couple times a week to talk to them for the next month or so, and then we can assess how often you need me after that. Does that work with your schedule?"

Daniel thought it would be good for his children to have someone to talk to. He nodded consent.

Survival Games Chapter 8

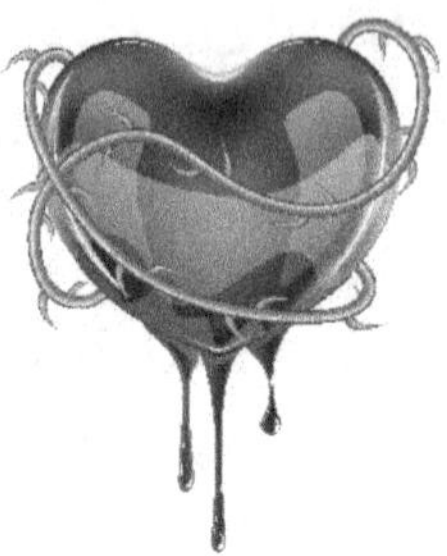

JESSICA MOANED. HER STIFF muscles protested, reminding her she'd overexerted yesterday. She rolled off the mattress onto the concrete floor and crawled to the bathroom. With a gargantuan effort, she hauled herself onto the toilet and then stumbled into the shower. She dialed the water to the scalding point with the hopes it would loosen her muscles. Water pulsed on her shoulders and drizzled down her back and legs. After close to an hour, she stepped out, her muscles a little looser, enough so that each step wasn't drawing a wince. She wrapped a towel around herself and brushed her teeth before looking around for clothing. No clothes anywhere. Her heart leaped into her throat.

She tightened the towel and limped back into the room. He was leaning against the wall waiting for her, holding a slinky black dress. His blue eyes scanned her in a way that made her heart palpitate.

Bedroom eyes.

The words pinged through her brain, trying to locate the source of the déjà vu.

"Put this on." He tossed her the dress.

Jessica caught the garment and looked from him to the black fabric and back. All the hussies in the videos he showed her wore garbs like this. "I don't think so." She tossed it back.

He grabbed the dress out of the air and stormed to where she stood, towering over her. "Put it on," he bellowed.

"No," Jessica growled up at him, doing her best to keep the thread of fear from her voice.

He dropped the outfit and grabbed her by the throat, slamming her against the wall.

The towel slipped, and she kept it in place with one hand despite the fury welling, drowning the fear. She swung her other fist at him, but he caught her arm mid-punch and pinned it to the wall.

His bright, angry eyes flashed when they locked with hers, and the air between them shifted, heating to the point Jessica broke out in a light sweat. Having him this close was like standing a foot from a raging forest fire.

Her breath labored against the grip around her throat, and he let go. She gasped, inhaling much needed oxygen. He snatched the hand holding the towel and slammed it to the wall by her head, mirroring her other arm in his grasp.

The towel fell, and the smile that spread over his lips made Jessica shiver. He stared her down before his gaze dropped, appraising her. When he met her defiant glare again, a jolt as strong as the electric chair raced through her.

He pulled her arms over her head and clamped down on her wrists with one hand. She struggled to pull free, but his grip was too strong. He ran his free hand down her arm as desire flared in his eyes.

"Beg," he demanded.

"It's not like you're *Smallville* and I had reason to beg," she spat at him. "Get your hands off me, you twisted freak."

His eyes narrowed and his nostrils flared. Enraged, he flung her toward the middle of the room.

The shock of the hard concrete meeting the curve of her hip ripped a yelp from her chest, along with the air from her lungs. She rolled on her back, willing her body to move, to breathe, to get the hell away from the determined set of his jaw.

He swept the dress off the floor and towered over her within seconds, frightening her into action.

Jessica swung her feet and kicked him squarely in the balls. She rolled away before he collapsed to his knees, a low groan emitting from his lips. His eyes filled with tears that he blinked back.

She stood. A nasty plum-colored bruise covered her hip. She launched herself at him with a roar, her fist swinging.

He moved quickly, much quicker than she expected, parrying to block her punches and spinning her around. His elbow caught the side of her face, dazing her as he swept her feet from under her, bringing her to the ground hard.

He pinned her to the floor and glared at her with his lips clamped together into a tight, thin line. "Cut the shit." His deep voice was as menacing as a hungry lion shredding his prey.

Jessica paused, but the change in his eyes renewed her efforts. He hauled her to her feet and dragged her toward the chair.

She clawed and kicked at him, but could not break his grasp. He slammed both her wrists into the shackles on the arms of the chair, strapping her in. She kicked, connecting with his shin.

"Fuck!" Muttering under his breath, he overpowered her and locked her feet in the straps before stepping back.

Her breasts heaved as she tried to catch her breath. Screaming in frustration, she struggled to break free. Her guttural cry echoed in the concrete room.

He glared at her through tousled hair and lowered his gaze to his arms, inspecting the gouges she'd left behind. He closed his eyes and tilted his head to the ceiling, sighing before he met her angry stare. "Why couldn't you just put the goddamn dress on?"

"I'm not one of your slutty sex toys!"

His eyebrows rose, and he broke out in a genuine smile. A laugh trickled out, full and musical, the kind of laugh that would catch her attention on the street and produce a smile of her own, but not here. Not now. She gritted her teeth, staring at him.

His laughter wound down, and he reached out to touch her reddening cheek where his elbow had hit.

She jerked her head away from his hand, flinching. The last thing she wanted was for him to touch her. The good humor in his eyes faded, and he paused, his fingers inches from her face. She could feel the heat radiating from them, the electrical current buzzing between his skin and hers. His fingers grazed her cheek, and he slowly sank to his knees in front of her. His hand traveled slowly down the line of her neck, his fingers tracing her skin lightly, enough to create a lava flow that ran from his fingertips to between her legs.

"Get your hands off me, you son of a bitch." Her voice shook.

Dimples formed in his cheeks. He pressed his lips together, suppressing what she assumed was the beginning of a smile. Instead of heeding her warning, his hand glided down to her nipples, pausing to run his thumb gently around the tip. She growled when it hardened under his touch. He leaned forward, taking her breast in his mouth.

Her breath quickened, curses pouring out from between her lips. She stared up at the ceiling, unwilling to respond to the inferno burning inside her. The inferno he created with the touch of his hands and the gentle suckling of his lips and the swipes of his tongue. Her hands balled into tight fists, nails digging into her palms as his mouth traveled lower, playing with her belly button, rolling the tip of his tongue inside the small indentation.

His blue eyes glanced up at her, sparkling with mischief. He chuckled, sliding his hands up her thighs and pushing them apart. "Wildcat, you *are* my sex toy."

His breath tickled, then his tongue found her, and she clamped her mouth shut on the moan that wanted to escape. His technique was exquisite, and her body responded, despite her best efforts to squash the growing fire in the pit of her stomach. She could not let him win. That would be as good as a death sentence.

She leaned forward and then threw herself back in the wooden chair, hitting the back of her head hard enough to see stars.

He looked up with wide blue eyes and his mouth dropped open.

"Not in a million years." She threw herself back again. This time, darkness enveloped her.

TY SAT BACK ON his haunches, tilting his head and staring at her slumped unconscious form in the chair.

The blooming color in her cheeks faded.

She knocked herself out. What the fuck?

He stood and retrieved the dress off the floor while he mulled this recent development over. He unlocked her wrists and ankles and dressed her in the silky fabric. Without overthinking, he picked her up, carried her limp body into one of the studio rooms, and set her on the couch.

He stared at her for a moment and then turned, grabbing a brush from the shelves. He took a seat next to her and gently worked the knots out of her hair.

God, she is beautiful.

Ty blinked at his random thought. He ran his fingers along the line of her jaw, relishing the smoothness of her skin. When his thumb crossed over her supple lips, an impulse overwhelmed him. He leaned forward and pressed his lips to hers. Her slack lips molded to his.

What the hell am I doing?

He yanked away from her and shook his head.

She is a prisoner here, not your girlfriend. Get a grip.

He took a deep breath and climbed to his feet. He crossed the room and unlocked the cabinet with all their good drugs. He scanned the contents and grabbed the smelling salts.

He studied her, and an uncomfortable chill caressed his skin. A twinge of something he couldn't place nagged at him. Building discomfort bloomed in his belly, but he dismissed it. He waved the smelling salts under her nose, jolting her back into consciousness.

Jessica sank deeper into the couch and looked around, her eyes wide and confused.

The door opened, and his brother and stepbrother walked in. Chris Aris was the epitome of the all-American boy with light brown hair, sharp blue eyes, and an enviable bronze tan despite the long, cold winter. If it wasn't for Ty's scar, people had told him he and Chris could pass for twins.

Ty's stepbrother, Frank, was an entirely different story. When Jessica's gaze landed on his dark Italian face, she squirmed in the seat. Ty glanced at him, seeing Frank's particular brand of cruelty reflected in his nearly black irises.

Ty dumped the smelling salts into the garbage and pointed her way. "Chris, Frank, this is Jessica."

"She looks a little knocked around already," Chris said.

"She put up a fight." Ty turned toward them.

They both winced at the scratches covering his arms.

"Damn."

Ty sighed, glancing between his brothers and his prisoner. His stomach tightened with emotions he didn't understand. The bottom line—he didn't want her there with them. He scoffed, ignoring the warning bell inside him, and turned away, focusing on making this as pleasant for her as he could.

He crossed to the cabinet, pulled out a clean syringe, and filled it with liquid X. He turned and gently plucked the side of the needle with his middle finger to ensure no air bubbles remained. When he raised his gaze, Jessica's complexion was nearly green, and she trembled. Her wide eyes were glued to the needle in his hand. She wrapped her arms tightly around herself and curled her legs up.

Ty glanced at the needle and back at her, surprised at the manifestation of fright in her features. "You guys might want to hold her."

Frank and Chris grabbed her off the couch, peeled her arm from her chest, and held it out to Ty.

She whimpered as he stepped closer, and he paused, meeting her frightened gaze. Annoyed at his own hesitation, he tightened his jaw in determination, slid the needle into her vein, and injected her. When he pulled the needle out, she struggled from their grip and took an unsteady step back.

THE WORLD WENT FUZZY. She swallowed, trying to satiate a mouth gone dry. She blinked, focusing on the two men crowding her before she turned toward him.

"What did you give me?" She stumbled back onto the couch.

He leaned close, his blue eyes intense and bordering on irritation, but his voice was just as smooth as the silk dress caressing her skin. "Just a little something to help you relax and enjoy."

He nodded to his brothers and took a seat at the table. He picked up the video camera and pointed it in her direction, one eye planted in the scope and the other squinted closed, his jaw clamped tight.

The drug settled into her skin, numbing her, making her movements sluggish like the components of a nightmare and a wet dream smashed together. Hands caressed her, sliding the skirt up, rubbing her, and plunging into her wetness. The slinky dress was soon in tatters as mouths and hands satisfied her.

Out of the corner of her eye, she caught him staring over the top of the camera at the lewd scene, his eyes blazing daggers in her direction. She laughed, taking full advantage of the drug running through her system and the sensations the two men were creating in her body.

THEY HAD HER ON her hands and knees, Chris in front of her and Frank behind her. And she was playing it up, moving, writhing, moaning, sucking, and sending sly glances in his direction all the while. Ty watched with growing anger. She was enjoying this just to spite him. He was sure of it.

His aching member throbbed against the fabric of his jeans. His stomach clenched with envy. He wanted what his brothers were getting. His skin burned with the injustice, and his chest constricted. He clenched the camera tighter, refocusing the lens, zooming in on her face as her lips serviced his brother.

Anger did not begin to describe the liquid poison boiling through his veins. *She knocked herself out when I touched her and they… they get this sexy vixen?*

After they finished with her, Ty dropped the camera on the table and walked over, oblivious of his two brothers dressing behind him. He kneeled in front of Jessica on the couch, tilted her chin, and unzipped his pants. "My turn."

She looked up at him in a drugged haze. "Not in a million years," she slurred and passed out.

Rage overwhelmed him. He hopped off the couch, grabbed a chair, and smashed it against the wall. Splinters flew, and he rammed it again and again and again until all he held were two twisted rails that were once the frame of the chair.

Tossing those away, he turned to Chris and Frank's wide stares and snarled, "Get her out of here!"

He stormed away before he used his clenched fists on someone's flesh. In the control room, he paced like a caged lion, trying to get a grip on his temper. Movement on the screen caught his attention. His brothers slipped Jessica into a nightshirt and left her sprawled on the mattress. He caught the way Frank glanced at her before he left the room, and Ty's fury overflowed. He swung his fist at the closet door and cracked the fiberboard.

The flare of pain tempered his anger a notch, and he shook his hand, rewinding the room video to earlier today.

Frank and Chris walked into the control room.

"What the hell is wrong with you?" Frank asked.

Ty ignored the question and turned on them, pointing to the screen. "Who is *Smallville*?"

"Huh?" they both said in unison.

Ty pressed play on the disc, and the screen filled with her pinned to the wall.

They watched as he said "Beg," and her response was, "It's not like you're *Smallville* and I had reason to beg. Get your hands off me, you twisted freak."

Ty stopped the tape. "What is that?"

Frank shrugged, narrowing his eyes as he studied Ty.

Chris stared at the screen, his brows creased. "I think she's talking about a television show."

Ty's gaze swiveled to Chris. "What?"

"There's a show on TV called *Metropolis*," Chris answered, looking from one brother to the other. "C'mon, you haven't seen it?"

They shook their heads.

Chris looked at Jessica on the screen and then glanced at his watch. "I'll bring you a copy the next time you give me a call. If you want some of my buddies for the next video, let me know. I'm sure they'd love to have a piece of that." He nodded toward the screen with a smile.

Frank glared at him. "You'd better not be blabbing about this operation to anyone. I wouldn't want to see them get into an accident or something." He stepped toward his youngest brother.

Chris took an involuntary step backwards. "Just giving you a hard time, Frank."

Frank reached out, grabbed him by the arm, and pulled him so they were face-to-face. "If you so much as breathe a word of this," he said, pointing to the screens. "There's no telling where you'll end up." He smiled and let Chris go.

"Back off, Frank," Ty warned and stepped between Frank and Chris like he always did.

They stared each other down, but Frank conceded, stepping away.

"He's not going to say a thing." Ty shot a glance over his shoulder and received a nod in return from Chris.

Chris looked at the monitor and back to Ty. "I gotta go." He walked out of the room.

Ty watched the monitor as his little brother lumbered to the elevator. "He was just trying to get a rise out of you."

Frank grunted as he watched the other monitors. He glanced at Ty and swatted the back of his head. "What the hell is your problem today?"

Ty shot to his feet, ready to plant his fist in Frank's face, but pointed at the monitor where Jessica slept. "It's her fault." He bit back the rest of the response, suddenly aware of the way his stepbrother was ogling her. Frank was dangerous, and if he had an inkling of what Jessica did to Ty, he would kill her with his own hands. "She laughed at me." He slid his hands in his pockets and returned his gaze to the monitors. "It pissed me off, that's all, especially since she knocked herself out when I tried to touch her."

Frank's eyebrows rose, and he looked at the monitor again. "Make sure that part gets in the video, too." He smiled at Ty.

Oh great. He wants to showcase MY humiliation.

Ty nodded and turned back to the monitors. Frustration simmered below the surface as he began the task of editing the scenes with his brothers.

Survival Games Chapter 9

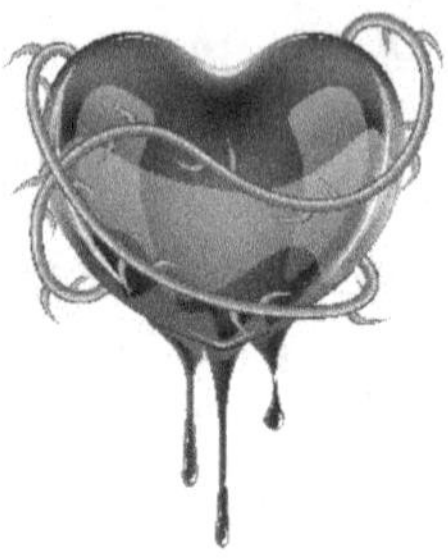

ERIC'S LITTLE HAND RAN over her hair and bruised face.

"Oh, Mom," he said, and tears ran down his cheeks. "You're hurt."

She slowly opened her eyes and looked at her son. "Angel boy."

"You're hurt," Eric repeated.

"Not so bad," Jessica whispered and tried to smile. Stiff and sore, every muscle in her body hurt.

Eric leaned over her and kissed her cheek where Ty had elbowed her. The bruise faded, and his tears fell onto her upturned face.

"Don't cry, baby," she said. "Lie down. It's past your bedtime."

"Mommy," he cried and lay down, snuggling in her outstretched arms.

She closed her eyes and hugged him, smelling the sweet scent of his shampoo. "Shhhh," she cooed and fell back asleep.

Survival Games Chapter 10

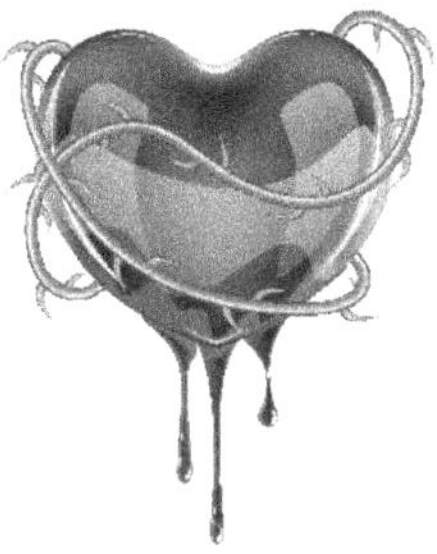

TY CAUGHT MOVEMENT OUT of the corner of his eye and looked at the monitors. Jessica moved. He couldn't quite hear what she was saying, so he turned the volume up and zoomed the camera in.

"Not so bad," she said.

A second later, there was a weird light on her cheek, and her bruise faded. His jaw dropped.

"Don't cry, baby. Lie down. It's past your bedtime," she whispered, and a moment later wrapped her arms around the air next to her. "Shhhh," she said, and her eyes closed with a peaceful smile on her face.

Ty stared at the monitor.

Normally, he'd chalk it up to talking in her sleep, but the absence of the black and blue bruise on her cheek snuck under his skin, festering until he got up to investigate with his own eyes.

He opened the door soundlessly and stepped in. She was sound asleep. Ty rolled her onto her back to get a closer look at her face. The bruise was gone, and her cheek was wet. He gently wiped the wetness with his finger and tasted it.

Tears.

"Huh," he grunted aloud.

She didn't stir at either his touch or his voice.

He looked at her for a long time, wondering again about the wisdom of snatching her from her nice, quiet life.

He sighed and stood, heading back to the control room to finish the new video. He played what he'd edited so far. He toggled between her with his brothers and her knocking herself out, flipping back and forth between the two shots at least ten times. He turned the editing suite off in disgust as her words echoed in his ears.

"Not this time," he mumbled. He stood and crossed to the toy drawer. He pulled out four pairs of handcuffs, some rope, and a pair of scissors. Swiping the lighting and camera remote for her room from the counter, he headed back to her room.

Jessica lay partially on her back, her right arm out on the bed and her left hand on her stomach. One leg curled and the other straight. He stood over her and inhaled, scanning her perfect form and licking his lips. The burn of her being this close caressed his skin.

He leaned down, put one set of cuffs on her wrist, and closed it gently. He didn't want her to wake just yet. He slowly lay her arm so that it was shoulder height and at the edge of the mattress. Then he hooked the other side of the cuffs to the loop he had made at the end of the rope. He tied the rope to an anchor in the floor next to the mattress. He repeated this with her right hand and looked down at her. She looked like a cross. He pulled her legs straight down, pausing as her head tilted to the side.

After a moment, he cuffed each ankle, securing her legs to the corners of the mattress. Spread eagle, like the outer reaches of a snow angel.

He smiled, unbuttoned his shirt, and rolled up his sleeves before settling on the bed next to her, waiting.

He ran his hands over her nightgown, feeling the soft mountains of her chest beneath. His hand wandered down to her bare legs, and he slowly ran his fingers up the inside of her thigh, testing, teasing.

Her gasp caught his attention, and he looked into her wide brown eyes, chuckling as he reached for the remote. He gradually increased the lighting in the room and leaned on his elbow next to her.

"Not in a million years?" he asked, putting the remote down and cocking his eyebrows. "And then you had the audacity to show my brothers the time of their lives?" He reached for the scissors without breaking eye contact.

Jessica's eyes widened. "Brothers?"

"Mm-hm." He nodded and ran the scissors over the nightshirt. "Brothers. But I get 'not in a million years' from you?" He hesitated, gliding the scissors over her underwear. "Twice?"

He slid between her outstretched legs, getting on his knees. Grabbing the hem of her nightgown, he cut it straight up the center and swept the torn fabric aside to reveal her breasts.

She licked her lips, and her breath quickened. The color in her cheeks bloomed, and her pupils dilated as she stared at him. He read all the unspoken signs that matched the increased beat of his heart.

He smiled. "It looks like a million years is today, my dear." He took her breasts in his hands and leaned over to kiss her neck.

Jessica twisted her head sharply away from him, just as he'd expected. "No," she whispered and struggled against the bonds.

He kissed her ear and ran his tongue down the side of her throat. Her skin broke out in gooseflesh, and her nipples hardened in response to his gentle caress. Everything about her belied her words, and while a part of him screamed for him to back off, he couldn't, not with the way she had willingly mocked him last night.

"Mm-hm," he purred and moved down her body, his hands sliding over her like silk. His mouth found her nipple, rolling it around the hard nub before moving on to the next one.

TEARS BLURRED HER VISION as he continued his exploration of her body. When he looked up at her, his eyes sparkled with delight, positively smoldering. Jessica turned her head away; the look in his eyes drove her over the edge as much as the feel of his hands did. The feel of him, the smell of his cinnamon toothpaste, the sharp blue eyes framed by those ebony lashes, and his velvet voice all ran through her like a poison, setting her skin on fire. Her soul cried out for him to take her, to own her, but she refused to give in, to give him what he wanted, to lose this battle of wills, because losing meant the end to her survival.

"This is only the beginning." He chuckled. He shifted back on his knees and leaned over, licking her stomach. His hands, his velvet fingertips, ran up the inside of each of her thighs and over the front of her underwear.

"No," she whispered desperately, his touch igniting her.

His innate magnetism tingled through her, turning her on to the point that if he stopped, she was sure she would beg. She prayed he wouldn't do that, that he wouldn't call her bluff. The only word she allowed herself to utter was the sheer denial of him.

"Oh, yes." He smiled and seduced her completely with his expert touch.

He played her body like a fine concert pianist, slowly building the fire up to an inferno that flashed, peaking in a rush of hot liquid.

She gasped, betrayed by her body, betrayed by the hint of a moan. "No!" The word was a complete lie. Her body ached for him and wrapped around the motion of his fingers, trembling for more, slick with wanting...and he knew it.

"Yes," he said, licking and repeatedly bringing her to the next climax, and the next, and the next until she was dripping with sweat and sex.

She tilted her head back and twisted her wrists, grabbing the metal chains that held her in place. She gasped for breath, praying for relief from the sheer pleasure of his seduction. The betrayal was complete when the moan slipped from her lips.

"Beg," he whispered. "Beg for me."

"No." Her entire frame quivered. "Never!" she screamed.

THE DEFIANCE IN HER eyes enraged him. He pulled away slowly and hesitated, closing his eyes for a moment to gain control. Her mouth said no, but her body... Oh, her body sang a different tune. He opened his eyes and gazed into what was left of her fawn irises. He licked her again, smiling in satisfaction at the moan that escaped and the slight arch of her body. Oh, she wanted him. Whether or not she said it, it was written in the slickness of her, in the stiffness of her nipples, and in the flush of her cheeks.

He moved his way up her body, kissing, licking, and gauging each of her reactions.

"Tell me you want me," he whispered, meeting her gaze.

She shook her head. "No," she whispered.

He settled on top of her, jeans the only barrier between them, and he circled his hips, grinding slowly, watching sweat trickle down her forehead. The muscles in his arms ached from the strain, and yet he continued, relishing the slow burn, relishing the desperate plea in her eyes. The muscles strained in her arms, too, as she gripped the chains, pulling with each arch of her back. He wasn't sure she was aware of her body's flow, its natural arc in sync with his, meeting each of his motions with the curve of her hips.

This was a sweet torture he could fall into for the rest of his life. It was like having one foot in heaven and the other in hell.

Her eyes spoke to him, pleading in their own right, even as her lips refused to acknowledge his carnal appetite. Her eyes drew him in, taking the breath from his lungs and the reins over his power. He squeezed his eyes closed until he regained control. Drawing a deep breath, he opened his eyes, his arms now trembling, threatening to collapse under his weight. He looked down at her, taking what he could from the small win. She didn't beg, but she certainly came for him.

"Million years, my ass." He rolled off her onto his back.

Her jaw clenched, and a sheen of tears glazed her eyes. "Get away from me."

He rolled on his side and ran his fingers between her breasts. "Is that what you really want?"

She closed her eyes and looked away. "I have to go to the bathroom."

The handcuff key wedged into his hip when he sat up and he fished it out of his pocket and unlocked her ankles. But he didn't untie her wrists. Instead, he untied the ropes from the floor anchors and nodded toward the bathroom.

"Go," he said.

She stumbled around the wall separating the two areas and he closed his eyes, hanging his head, shaking it slowly back and forth.

How stupid can I be?

Playing with her was one thing, but the way she consumed him... That was something he would have to keep in check. He glanced toward the bathroom, the feel of her still with him, knocking down the walls surrounding his heart.

The flushing of the toilet didn't quite drown the sound of vomiting. He straightened, suddenly irritated. *I couldn't have read her wrong, could I?*

"No way," he whispered, and stormed around the partition.

KNEELING ON THE FLOOR, she glanced in his direction, wiping her mouth with a piece of toilet paper. Whatever he had given her last night made her stomach roll the moment she'd stood, and she barely reached the toilet. "What the hell did you give me last night?"

The lines in his forehead smoothed as he exhaled. "Liquid X. It sometimes does that." He waved toward the toilet.

"What the hell is liquid X?" On shaky legs, she pulled herself to the sink and rinsed her mouth.

"Something like ecstasy."

She huffed, and before she could reach for a towel, he grabbed the rope, yanking her back toward the main room.

She glared at him. He had stripped her of all her dignity, and she was as angry with him as she was with herself. Wanting him in this hell hole did not make a lick of sense, and craving his touch was wrong on so many levels. But she did. When he was near, it consumed her and made her forget where she was. In that respect, he was far more dangerous than the electric chair in the center of the room.

She stood tall, defiantly yanking her arms down by her side, ignoring the heat in his eyes. Neither of them said a word.

He cocked his head to the side and let a grin surface, sliding the rope through his hands and then pulling her toward him. This time, she resisted, and he hauled her across the floor. Her struggle was no match for his strength, and he grasped the handcuffs and wrapped an arm around her, reclaiming his power.

"The things I'm going to do to you."

The promise of those words sent a rash of gooseflesh over her entire body.

He moved to the treadmill and tied the handcuffs to the bar. "But in the meantime, I think these will do today." He stepped back, appreciatively scanning her naked body. He turned and left the room, then came back with a tub of Vaseline. He leaned down and applied a healthy layer to each side of the treadmill. He straightened, smiling and snapping the top back on the container.

"You won't be able to do what you did yesterday. You'll stop when *I* say you can." He swatted her ass and turned the treadmill on.

Her wobbly legs moved, picking up the pace until she hit a moderate jog. He dialed the speed down a notch and turned on his heel, leaving her staring after him.

Ty stepped into the control center, and Frank swung the chair around, smiling.

"That was quite the show." He reached over and held up a DVD package containing the complete fifth season of *Metropolis*.

Ty raised his eyebrows, plucking the set from his brother's hand. He opened it and pulled the first disc out, then put it in his DVD player and pressed play. He also pushed the router that would send it into Jessica's room.

He flipped the microphone on. "For your viewing pleasure," he purred and flipped the speaker off, watching to see her reaction.

Jessica winced at the screen, but when the *Metropolis* logo appeared, she let out a small laugh.

Ty watched the transformation as Jessica went into autopilot, running and staring at the screen in tandem.

He focused his attention on the show, and when one of the secondary characters referred to the main character as *Smallville*, he smiled at the thought of Jessica bending to his every whim.

He turned to his brother. "He's next." Ty pointed at the screen.

Frank laughed. "It's too big of a risk. We've never had that kind of high-profile target here. I don't feel like seeing everything I've worked for all these years blown away by an idiotic move like this."

Ty smiled and looked at Jessica and then back at the screen. "Sure, it's a risk. But think of the payoff." He turned back, knowing what made his stepbrother tick. Knowing greed drove the bastard, even though he had more money than he could ever spend. Throwing it out there would paint dollar signs in front of his eyes. "Didn't you say our clients want to see some names in the videos?"

Frank studied him and then glanced at the screen. "How?"

Ty bit his lip. "I don't know yet," he said. "It could take a while." He looked down at the set and filtered through the pamphlets.

Frank nodded, leaving him to figure it out.

He set the disc so it would continuously loop and then connected to the Internet to research the show, the filming locations, and where exactly the star lived when he was not on set. He leaned back, the plan already forming.

He looked up to see Jessica stumble and catch herself. He slowed the treadmill down to a moderate walk. He did not want to hurt her, especially after today. She continued to walk, her eyes locked on the monitor, and he flipped the switch, turning the DVD off before heading to her room.

Her eyes glazed with exhaustion. When he turned the treadmill off, she faltered. Like lightning, he was at her side, catching her before she collapsed. He unclasped the handcuffs and carried her to the bed, concerned with her pale cheeks and shallow breathing.

"Damn it," he muttered to himself, closing her door and then running to the kitchen. He grabbed a bag full of water bottles and threw together a tray of fruits and vegetables for her. He paused, taking a Gatorade from the refrigerator and adding it to the bag. She needed hydration and nutrients, and he hoped she wouldn't need an IV.

Returning, he set the tray down and then sat on the edge of the mattress, twisting the top of the Gatorade off. He put it to her lips, holding her, helping her drink until the bottle was empty.

"That a girl." He covered her with the bed sheet before he headed for the door.

"Thank you." Jessica closed her eyes.

Ty looked at her and shut the door. No one had ever said thank you to him, at least not here. Her words touched him. He leaned his head against the door for a moment and went back to the control center.

He continued editing the tapes of Jessica, including his seduction of her this morning. It was tasteful and sexy and torturous at the same time, making this one of his best. When he was done, he played it back for Frank.

"That, my friend, is a gold mine." Frank nodded toward the monitor rolling bogus credits. His eyes flicked from the dark screen to Jessica, and he licked his lips. "She is one hot fuck."

Ty caught the look on his stepbrother's face, the sadistic blend of wanting and violence, and a shiver played low on his spine. "No one is to touch her."

Frank turned to Ty, his eyebrows raised and his mouth slightly parted. "Are you telling me what I can and cannot do?"

He inhaled and nodded. "No one touches her."

He popped the disc out and put it in the holder, glancing at the bank of monitors. His interest in the family business had come to a sudden end the moment his lips touched her skin, and now all he wanted was her. The rest of the captives held no substance. They weren't even in the same league as Jessica.

But he had to play this smart with Frank, appeal to his sense of drama. Otherwise, Jessica was as good as dead, and he probably wouldn't be far behind.

Frank cleared his throat. "That's a little extreme."

Ty turned. "It is. But she isn't like the others. She didn't cave when we showed her the accident that left her dead in the real world. She didn't cave when we showed her our videos. It is going to take a little more to break her. So we wait until we have him." He pointed at the video case on the counter. "Otherwise, she'll fight us every step of the way, and while that will sell a few videos, the buyers will get bored with that pretty quickly."

Frank bit the side of his lip. "We've got him." He pointed at Mike's monitor.

"He's not the one who will push her buttons." He turned, studying the monitors and wondered if what he'd said was true or not. Would she bend to his every whim if she knew? He glanced over his shoulder. "Think of the money that will roll in when she's willing to do multiples."

Frank pursed his lips. "She already did a multiple scenario."

He was running out of excuses. "Just let me handle this one my way, and I promise it'll be worth your while." He picked up the disc. "In the meantime, I think it's time our boy there sees this video. That should snap him out of it." He smiled in Frank's direction, waving the video he'd just finished. "Send Lisa in once I get everything set up."

Ty grabbed a chair and walked out of the control room with the disc. He entered Mike's room, set up the chair, and slipped the DVD into the player. "I've got a surprise for you," he said, crossing to where Mike was curled up. He hauled him to his feet and dragged him to the chair.

Mike continued staring aimlessly into space.

Ty strapped his wrists and ankles to the chair and stood, looking down at him. Mike had an uncanny resemblance to the actor Ed Harris, and that had pleased their benefactors.

He crossed to the screen and pressed the play button before taking the seat next to Mike. Jessica's face filled the screen, and Mike blinked. He was no longer staring aimlessly. He was staring intently as the highlights of the last three days rolled before him. It was the first reaction he'd had since the day they killed Mary.

The video opened with her sprawled on the couch and Chris and Frank mauling her with their hands and mouths, and her dress soon fell in tatters on the floor.

MIKE'S EYES NEVER LEFT the screen. He didn't notice Ty getting up or Lisa crawl in front of the chair. He watched Jessica, and his heart pounded between his legs, hard and raw and wanting. How he wanted to be one of those men, to feel her skin under his fingers, to taste her sweet nectar, to stick his member in her mouth. He dreamed of her, of doing everything these bastards were doing and more. The fire of jealousy burned under his skin. At least it wasn't the coward sitting next to him.

Hands on his groin jerked his gaze from the screen to the blonde unzipping his pants. A low groan escaped when she slipped him into her mouth. His eyes shot back to the screen, playing out the fantasy in his mind.

Jessica.

"Ah God," he whispered.

The scene on the couch faded with her collapsed and staring with glazed eyes, a spiteful smile plastered on her lips.

"Bastards," Mike breathed, partially lost in the feel of Lisa's mouth.

"Wait, there's more."

He shot a glare in Ty's direction and then returned his attention to the screen as the picture faded up with Jessica tied to the bed.

"Shit!" Mike gripped the arms of the chair, his desire now swarming with envy and anger.

Ty leaned over. "Nectar of the gods, I swear," he whispered as the screen showed his face buried between her legs. "I lost count of how many times she came."

Mike sent him a sideways glare and returned his attention to the screen.

Jessica cried, "NO!" but her body sang a different tune, reacting to Ty's touch like they were lifetime lovers.

"She was so wet," Ty said when the video showed his fingers slipping into her.

"Son of a bitch," Mike growled. He was hard and throbbing. "Son of a BITCH!" He couldn't help it. He spewed his load with a groan, and the screen faded to black.

He stared at the black screen as Ty led Lisa out of the room. His heart pounded in his chest, and his skin burned with jealous rage.

When Ty returned, he grinned at Mike. "I'm wondering how good she'll be when she finally begs."

"You really are a sick son of a bitch."

"Did she ever beg for you?"

The burn of his words sent a heated flush into his face. "I never had her, you son of a bitch."

Ty laughed. "Poor bastard." He got up to leave. He folded the chair, ejected the DVD, and walked out.

"Let me out, you coward! I swear if I ever get my hands on you, I'm going to rip you to pieces!"

Survival Games Chapter 11

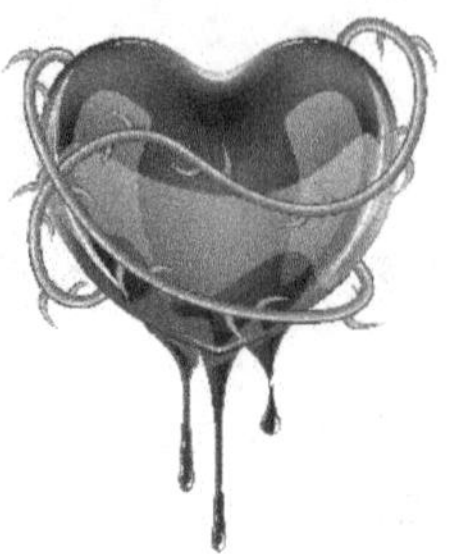

PAIN PENETRATED HER NIGHTMARES. She sat up in the dark room. Her muscles trembled as the dark vision clung to her like the scent of a skunk. Her gaze shot around the room, looking for the source of her fear.

He stepped out of the shadows, his dark, sinister eyes catapulting her to her feet. She backed into the wall as he approached her. Frank smiled. The cobwebs of sleep cleared as if a hurricane had blown them away.

"My brother likes his women compliant and moaning his praises, but I get off on the smell of fear and pain," he said, stalking towards her.

The hint of steel reflected under the light caught her eye, and her heart stuttered at the sight of the blade in his hand.

"I like it when they bleed." He stepped close, running the dull edge of the blade down her arm. His other hand clasped around her throat in a tight grip, shutting off the air to her lungs. "I just want you to understand who is really in charge here," he said. "Now go lean over the arm of that chair so I can give you a proper introduction."

"Fuck you," she wheezed, glaring at him despite the fear wracking her form.

He smiled. "That is the plan." He nicked her chin with the knife and threw her across the room.

Jessica stumbled and fell, scraping the skin off her palms and her knees. She climbed to her feet and spun, wiping her chin with the back of her hand. Blood smeared her skin.

He twirled the knife in his hand as he approached. His maniacal grin caught her breath in her throat.

Oh my god, he's going to kill me!

He stopped, cocked his head and looked at the camera in the ceiling with a nod. He moved his deadly glare to her with his lips thinning. He pointed the blade at her. "Until next time." He turned, stalking out the door.

She trembled and reached out, steadying herself against the electric chair. She glanced at the mirrored wall and wondered what had stopped him. She glanced at her raw palms and turned, heading into the bathroom to assess her wounds, thankful they hadn't been worse. Whatever he'd had in mind for her promised the kind of pain she wouldn't walk away from.

She shivered, trying to shake off the fear. She reached into the shower and flipped it on, dialing it to the hottest setting. She stepped in, hoping the hot water could warm the ice that filled her veins. While Bedroom Eyes set her on fire with a desire she couldn't fathom, Frank scared the daylights out of her.

Stepping out of the shower, she wrapped one of the plush towels around her and crossed to the sink. She wiped a clean swath over the mirror with her hand, wincing against the sting. She shot back a step, blinking at the clear mirror, the steam slowly filling the space again, but it wasn't her that was in the reflection. It was Eric.

She grabbed a face cloth and wiped the mirror again. Her little boy stared back at her, his wide eyes locked on her chin. His gaze shot to her eyes.

"Mom." His eyes filled with tears.

She reached her hand toward him, expecting the glass to stop her progress, but when her palm cupped his warm cheek, she gasped. He turned his face into her hand, pressing his lips to her palm. A tingling sensation started on the scraped skin and traveled up her arms, through her body, concentrating on her chin before fading.

Jessica stared at her unblemished palms. "How?"

"It doesn't matter right now." He took her hand and placed a small metal object in it. "I can show you what this opens, but not right now. Hide it in a safe place." Then he was gone.

Jessica stared at the key in her hand and back up at her own reflection. The cut on her chin was gone, leaving only the memory of the nightmare. If she didn't have the old skeleton key in her hand, she'd seriously doubt her sanity. Twirling it in her fingers, she glanced around the room for a place to hide it. There was a lip at the top of the shower stall, so she climbed up on the edge of the tub, stretched her hand up and placed it out of sight.

Survival Games Chapter 12

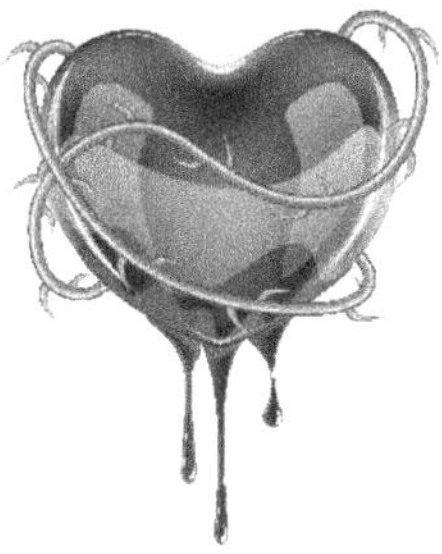

DANIEL HEARD ERIC IN the bathroom. He came around the corner as Eric said, "Hide it in a safe place." And then he turned to leave.

"Who you talking to, Sport?"

Eric looked up at his dad and shrugged. "No one," he answered nonchalantly.

He knew how upset his father got when he told the truth. Daddy didn't believe Mom was alive, and neither did his sister. They said it was in his head, and the sooner he accepted she was gone, the better he would be. Therefore, Eric kept quiet. He knew he needed to help his mom get out before something terrible happened. She was special, but he needed to show her the way to get out. If he could get her to open the door, she could stop the bad man and get out.

Their therapist LeAnn lost her husband a few years ago and said she knew how hard it was to let go.

But she didn't know.

She didn't understand, so Eric just stopped talking about his mom altogether. He needed to save her, not forget her.

Survival Games Chapter 13

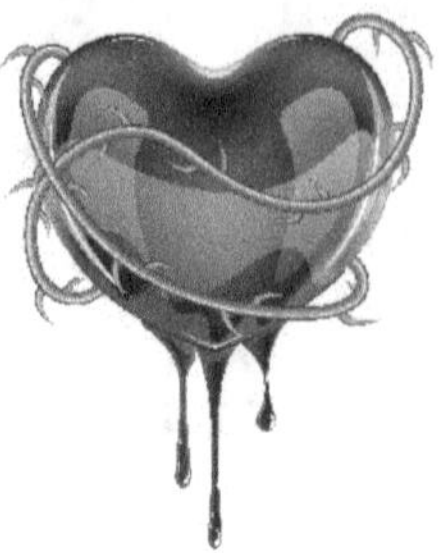

THE NEXT MORNING, JESSICA stepped out of the bathroom, dressed in a pretty cotton sundress, and then stopped in her tracks.

He set the tray of food down, turning his head in her direction. His blue eyes caught hers before they made a quick scan, and then he straightened. Hunger sparked in his eyes as he started toward her.

Bedroom eyes. The phrase jumped into her head again. She stepped back, feeling the wall behind her. Flashes of his hands gliding on her body, tainted by Frank's brutal promise, snapped off in her head. She panicked. His slight laugh shattered the silence, and her eyes darted between him and any escape route.

He cornered her, and the phrase *fight or flight* ran through her mind. She stepped toward him and threw a right hook with the power of her weight behind it. Her fist connected with his chin and sent him back a step. Pain flared in her hand. She darted under his arm around to the center of the room, where she took the stance of a boxer waiting for her opponent to advance.

He rubbed his chin where she'd hit him and stopped laughing, spinning in her direction. Stalking toward her, he easily sidestepped her next punch, grabbing her arm as it passed him.

He yanked her toward him, clasping the bicep of her free arm and holding her in place with her back against his chest. She squirmed in his grip.

Her bare heel slammed down on his Nike-clad foot, but it was not enough for him to loosen his grip. He leaned into her ear, but before he could speak and kill the fight in her, she slammed her head into his nose.

"Shit!" He let go of one of her arms.

When she swung away, he yanked her back. She rammed her elbow into his chest using inertia to her advantage.

THAT WAS ENOUGH. TY was no longer amused. He picked her up by her arms and threw her toward the bed. She landed on the mattress, rolled, and was up on her feet seconds later.

He started toward her again. She charged full into his stomach like a linebacker and knocked him to the floor. He grabbed her, bringing her down with him, and then rolled, pinning her to the hard concrete with his body. Her hair fanned out under her as she struggled, and he was able to get a hold of her arms, holding each one by her head and keeping her there until she stopped struggling.

"Are you finished?"

"No," she growled and tried to bite him.

He kneeled on her thighs, pushing them open with sheer force, pressing all his weight on his knees onto her pressure points. Charlie horses flared in both of her thighs.

"Are you finished?" he growled down at her.

She spat at him.

He grabbed both her wrists in one hand and wiped the spit from his face, glaring at her. "What the hell is wrong with you today?"

"You're hurting me," Jessica snarled.

"That's the point." The part of him she had awakened cursed himself out for causing her pain. That was the last thing he wanted to do, but he didn't know how to diffuse her otherwise.

"Get off me," Jessica said, trying to buck him off. Her breath caught in her throat, and she winced.

"I just came in to bring you food," he explained.

Jessica stopped struggling. "Then stop hurting me."

Being this close to her, even with her struggling and fighting, was as intoxicating to him as a gram of heroin was to an addict. He straightened his legs, settling between hers, and his free hand ran down the length of her arm.

"Stop," she commanded softly.

He stopped but remained on top of her, studying her face, the flush in her cheeks, her wonderfully dark eyes. He hesitated, tracing the outline of her jaw with the fingers of his free hand. *God, you are beautiful.* A deep sigh passed his lips, and he went to kiss her. But she turned her head away.

Sudden overwhelming anger engulfed him. Anger at his stupidity, anger for her insolence, and anger because more than anything, he wanted this woman to admit she felt the same heat, the same wanting, the same need throbbing in his veins.

He grabbed a handful of her hair and pulled her head back. She cried out, and he took the opportunity, covering her mouth with a powerful, unwanted kiss. Her teeth clamped down on the soft tissue of his tongue. He yelped, yanking away. A hot, coppery taste filled his mouth, and he swiped his finger on his tongue to find red tinged saliva. She had bit hard enough to draw blood.

He narrowed his eyes. "God damn it! I just came in here to bring you something to eat."

She looked up at him defiantly. "Then get off me."

"You're the one who started this," he said, looking down at her.

"You cornered me," she shot back.

Ty closed his eyes for a moment. She was right. He had cornered her. Inhaling, he opened his eyes. "Maybe," he said, conceding with a half grin, letting his simmering anger cool.

"Let me go," she said.

He was certain she wasn't talking about this moment, and he shrugged an apology. He released the handful of hair and put his hand on her cheek. Energy buzzed between them as he ran his thumb over her lips. "I can't do that. Besides, I don't think you really want me to."

"Please," she whispered.

"Sorry, babe." *But I couldn't let you go if I tried.* The silent admission troubled him because it had nothing to do with this prison. He studied her face, moving his hips gently, circling, teasing, grinding, throbbing against the fabric of his jeans.

"Jess, what am I going to do with you?" He scanned her face, the flush in her cheeks, the alternating heat and plea in her eyes. Gaining control, he laid his forehead on the concrete next to her, closing his eyes.

"God damn it," he whispered, tasting his own blood. He lay on top of her until his heart rate slowed to a normal pace.

"Damn it," he said, and rolled his head so he could see her face. She was looking away from him, but he could still see the curve of her neck and the smooth skin of her cheek. For a second, he understood completely why Mike was so in love with her.

This cannot happen.

It just can't.

He shot to his feet and left the room.

JESSICA ROLLED, GETTING TO her hands and knees, and glanced at the tray. A bountiful breakfast of fruit decorated the plate and a glass of fresh-squeezed orange juice sat next to it. Her head dropped, and she blinked back the tears blurring her vision.

Damn him!

The way he looked at her was different, like she was no longer a possession, and God help her. When he'd said her name, it melted her to the core. That worried her. Worried her a great deal, but the fact he'd stopped gave her a sliver of hope.

She needed to work this, to milk it for all it was worth, and maybe, just maybe, she could walk out of here alive. Maybe Bedroom Eyes was her ticket out of this hellhole.

She crawled into the bathroom, but instead of a shower; she filled the tub and slid into the hot water. She leaned her head back against the ceramic lip. A quick glance toward the hiding spot of the key and then she closed her eyes, mulling over how she could manipulate him into helping her.

He'd stopped, and he didn't ask her to beg. Both significant, if the videos he played for her were a real representation of his attitude. Today, he didn't follow that path; today he softened and tried to kiss her.

Her brow creased.

In none of the sultry film scenes had he give any indication of warmth. Passion and sexual prowess, oh yeah, but warmth and depth, no. No sign of that in the videos he took part in. She sighed, opening her eyes and reaching for the soap, and froze.

He stood in the doorway, his arms crossed, his head held low, glaring through those long, dark lashes. His biceps strained in the gray T-shirt he wore.

If she didn't think he was dangerous before, she sure did now. She shrank back in the tub, curling her legs. Her heart jumped in her chest, and sweat broke out under her damp hair, tickling her scalp.

"Get out," he commanded.

"I'm not ready to," she challenged, ignoring the metal taste of fear in her mouth.

His hands curled into fists. "Get out," he said through clenched teeth.

"I don't think so." Jessica braced herself against the back of the tub.

In one stride, he was next to the tub. He kneeled down, grabbing a handful of her hair.

Suddenly, her head was under water. She flailed. Her hands slipped off the smooth lip of the tub, and she reached for the hand holding her under. Panic filled her. Her lungs burned for air. Just as suddenly, she was yanked back out of the depths. Water spewed from her lips with the power of her cough.

"Get out." He let go of her hair and stood.

Jessica met his crazed glare and decided the most prudent route would be to do as he'd said. She reached for a towel, but he stopped her.

"Just like you are." He pointed toward the room.

She crossed her arms over her breasts and walked into the main room, dripping wet.

He followed her.

"Sit down and eat."

Jessica obeyed, kneeling down and eating, shivering from the cold concrete under her knees. She refused to look at him. His agitation scared her; he seemed just as pissed off with himself as she had been with herself yesterday. She stopped mid bite at that thought, but then finished the food and drank the juice.

He reached down to grab the tray.

"Thank you," she whispered.

He hesitated but wouldn't look at her. He scooped up the tray and left the room.

Survival Games Chapter 14

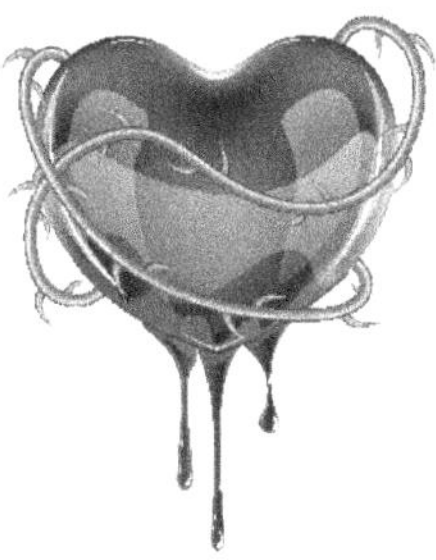

TY WALKED INTO THE control room and stared at her monitor. She clutched the bathrobe, her arms wrapped around her legs and her cheek resting on her knees. Her hair hid her face.

He inhaled. "Shit."

Today was the second time he'd wanted to kiss her. He never kissed them. Ever. It was just too personal. But this... this differed from anything he'd encountered before. She took his breath away every time their eyes met. Her defiance, the stubborn set of her jaw, completely frustrated him, especially with the heat burning in her eyes. It was a contradiction he didn't understand. A contradiction he wondered if it would change if someone else's life rode in the balance. If he had that leverage, would he ever have the luxury of hearing her cry his name in ecstasy?

"I need some fresh air." He turned away from the monitors and headed out of the complex.

He stuck his head in Frank's office a few minutes later. "I'll be back in a few."

He hopped into his little Nissan, undid the convertible top, and drove out of the private garage. Speeding down the access road, he skidded onto the street moments later, trying to outrun the feelings coursing through his veins.

The sun shone down, melting the remaining traces of snow. Ty tilted his face, feeling the renewing warmth. It took twenty minutes to get to his studio apartment and another ten minutes to grab a couple of shirts and a couple pair of jeans from his closet.

He hadn't bothered with much in the way of decorating. He sighed as he took a second to look around the near empty apartment.

Empty, just like my fucking life.

He wanted a life of his own, not this horrific crap Frank had him doing. Closing his eyes, he hung his head and drew a deep breath before turning back the way he'd come.

He didn't drive as fast on the way back, taking his time and enjoying the sun on his face and the wind in his hair for a change.

Survival Games Chapter 15

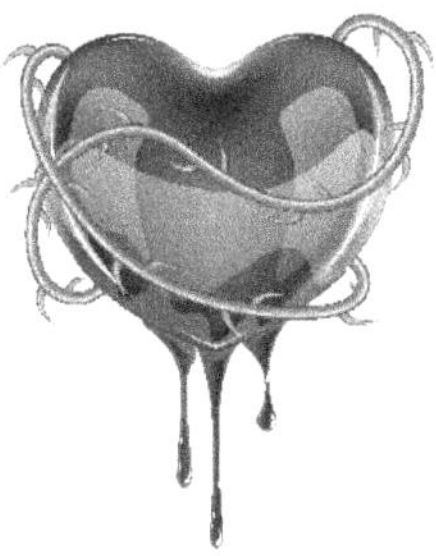

JESSICA LOOKED UP AS the door opened. Frank walked in, leering at her as if she were his next meal. He held a workout outfit in his hands this time instead of a knife, but the sadistic glare in his eyes made her blood cold.

"Where is he?" Jessica held her bathrobe tighter, hoping her question would diffuse whatever horror this freak had in mind.

"Out, and you need a workout today." He pointed to the treadmill.

"No."

The clothing dropped. He crossed the room and backhanded her. His knuckles collided with her cheek, sending blooming pain through the side of her face. With a handful of hair in his fist, he dragged her to the treadmill and tossed her onto the machine.

"I can still make you bleed without a knife," he growled. He ripped the bathrobe off her and slammed one of her wrists into the shackle.

It closed tight, pinching her skin.

She swung her free fist at him. He caught it and forced it into the other shackle, leaving her exposed and vulnerable. Her heart drummed, and fear tainted her veins, stinging with the force of the adrenaline.

"You will scream for me today," he whispered in a sinister voice. He grabbed the back of her neck and slammed her down against the console.

The descent of a zipper renewed her futile struggles, only aiding the pain in her wrists from the odd angle the shackles held her. His weight crushed her forward. Pain like she'd never experienced spiraled through her, the least of which was the sickening crack of both wrists as the bones snapped. She screamed.

He laughed in her ear.

Harsh gasps accompanied each of her exhales because she couldn't gather enough oxygen to produce another scream. Tears streaked her face as she prayed. Prayed for this vile rape to end, prayed she would pass out, and prayed for Bedroom Eyes to save her.

When he finished, he set her on the treadmill and started the machine with little more than a snarl.

Waves of dizziness accosted her, and she stumbled, the shackles tearing at her already mangled wrists. She cried out, catching herself. Wetness drizzled down her legs. The thought of her blood mixed with his semen crawling on her skin caused her stomach to roll. She forced the vomit back down her throat.

He stood, staring at her, biting the side of his lip, inspecting her like a mean kid inspected bugs.

After a while, he glanced at his watch and stopped the treadmill. He slid on her shorts before restarting the machine and then left her alone with her exquisite pain.

Survival Games Chapter 16

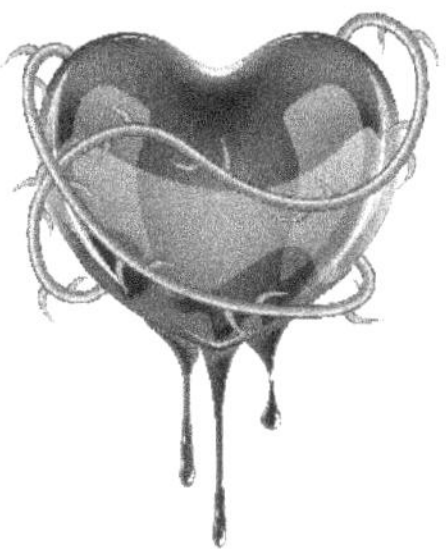

TY WALKED INTO THE control room to find Frank and Chris watching the monitors. Jessica was on the treadmill with only shorts on and crying. His gaze snapped to the video playing on the screen in her room.

The video they'd made of her. "What the hell!"

Both Frank and Chris jumped in their seats.

He reached over and shut off the video feed to her room.

"Are you out of your fucking minds?" He grabbed both of them by the scruff of their necks and hauled them out of the room, throwing them to the floor in the hallway.

"Chill," Chris said, looking up at his brother. "We were just waiting for you. Frank said we were filming with her again today."

Ty glared at him and went back into the control room. He popped in a *Metropolis* DVD and pressed play, piping it into Jessica's room. Then he turned his attention back to his brothers.

"No. We aren't taping anything with her today." He stormed to the door. "You don't fucking get it."

"Do tell," Frank said sarcastically, getting to his feet.

"It's about timing, and you just screwed it up." He took a deep breath and looked at Frank. "I thought we were clear that there would be no more games for a while with her. She works out, eats, and that is it until I say so. She only watches this as long as she is on the treadmill. Otherwise, nothing, especially the videos we make. Understand?"

Frank and Chris exchanged a look.

"She's here to make videos. Isn't that the deal?" Chris asked.

Ty glanced at the bank of screens, careful with his next words. While Chris was aware of the sex part of the business, he had no clue of the dark side of the business, and Ty wanted to keep it that way.

"She doesn't have a reason to give us what we want," Ty said, hoping that would be enough.

"She certainly worked out the other night," Chris countered.

"We drugged her, and she didn't know we were brothers then. I bet even if we drugged her again, she wouldn't repeat that mistake," Ty said.

Frank pursed his lips, narrowing his eyes at Ty.

"I disagree. If we doped her up again, I bet she would be just as good," Chris challenged, crossing his arms in that cocky manner that irritated Ty.

Ty looked over his shoulder at the screen and took a deep breath. He didn't enjoy betting on her. "Okay," he said. "If she doesn't, then we do things my way, and if she does, you two get to do whatever you want, and we do things your way."

Frank looked at Ty. "Maybe it should just be Chris."

"Two-on-one sells better than one-on-one," Ty stated. He sensed Frank's hesitation, but didn't know why. "Go set things up, and I'll bring her in."

Ty grabbed a red dress and walked into the room. Her bloodshot eyes locked with his. The red bloom on her cheek sent his heart into a heavy drumbeat in his chest. Her wrists were not at the right angle. He rushed to the side of the treadmill and slammed the buttons to turn off the machine.

"Jesus," he whispered and dropped the dress. He unclasped her battered arms.

She flinched away from him, crossing her arms over her chest. Her eyes were empty and almost listless.

What did they do to her while I was gone?

He glanced down at her legs. The vague rust streaks on her skin made him glance at her shorts. There were no other signs of that time of the month, but the faded blood weighed heavy on his heart. He brought his gaze back to hers. She wouldn't look at him. The bloom of anger simmered inside, and he pressed his lips together.

"Let me look at your arms," he said softly.

"I'm fine." She finally met his gaze.

"You don't look fine."

Her eyes narrowed. "Since when do you care?"

He blinked, unsure of how to respond to her. He swiped the dress off the floor, offering it to her. "Go clean up."

She took it with a wince and disappeared into the bathroom. The shower went on. He stared at the treadmill and the discarded exercise top in the middle of the floor.

Frank.

He was the only one capable of putting the fear of God into the prisoners, and that was what he saw in her eyes. Anger bloomed, tightening his chest, and he started across the room.

She stepped into his view, and he sucked in his breath. The redness was gone from her cheek. The dress clung to her sensuous curves, instantly lighting his fire. When she ran her fingers through her wet hair, he didn't dare move a muscle for fear he'd grab her and bolt, taking her out of this place to disappear into obscurity.

Neither of them moved right away. With an almost imperceptible shake of his head, he dismissed the initial shock of seeing her.

"Come with me." He wrapped his hand around her upper arm, staring at the barely visible bruises around her wrists and wondering if his eyes had played a trick on him. He met her gaze before leading her out of the room and down the barren concrete hall.

She didn't resist, and she didn't speak. Her bare feet made the lightest of swishes compared to his squeaky sneakers. It wasn't until he opened the door to the room that she tried to pull away.

"Uh-uh." She shook her head, her eyes wide at the sight of the two men.

Ty clenched his teeth and yanked her into the room. He wanted her here about as much as she wanted to be here. His mood darkened.

He threw her toward them. "Hold her!"

Ty filled a syringe and walked to Jessica. She trembled, staring at the needle with wide, scared eyes. It didn't take long for the drug to take effect. She sank to the couch, crossing her legs and arms, her eyes glossy as she traded hostile glances with the three of them.

Ty stepped back and took a seat at the table, watching the dynamics between Jessica and Frank in particular. The way her body tensed when her gaze landed on Frank set off his internal alarms, and he felt his body react in a similar fashion. Muscles clenched, and his heart thundered in his chest. The anger that had started in her room threatened to explode.

Chris sat down next to Jessica on the couch and ran his hand up her leg.

She slapped it away. "I don't think so," she snapped and looked from Chris to Frank and back. "Not goin' ta happen," she slurred with attitude. She looked at Frank. "You already ripped my ass to shreds today." She looked at Chris, then beyond him at Ty. "And I'm sure you derived some kind of twisted pleasure from filming it."

The volcano erupted.

Frank launched at her. Ty moved like a shadow, intercepting Frank before he could touch her again. In one motion, he catapulted him across the room. Storming after him, the only thought that filled his mind was *I am going to kill you!*

Frank's restricted hiss of pain satiated his volatile need for violence. His teeth clenched as Frank's eyes bulged. Chris tried to pull him off his stepbrother. His brain caught up with his actions, and he loosened his grip. He had no escape plan, and if he killed Frank right now, like every fiber in his body demanded, they might never leave this prison.

"We had an agreement." Ty squeezed for good measure and then released Frank, stepping away. He crossed to Jessica, took her arm, and gently pulled her to her feet. Meeting his brother's gaze, he hissed, "I won. It's my way."

Ty walked her to her room, flipping between triumph and fury. Even though he'd witnessed their little ménage the other night, the thought of his stepbrother taking advantage of her, hurting her, turned his stomach.

She weaved down the hall, stumbling occasionally from the drugs, but each time he caught her. When they entered her room, he sat her down on the mattress and met her glazed stare.

"I'm sorry about Frank. I didn't know," he said, and the flash of sorrow in her eyes cut deep.

Tears brimmed, sliding down her cheeks, and she tilted her head into her hands, cradling her face as the sobs ripped from between her fingers.

He gently stroked her silky hair and pulled her into his arms, holding her as she cried. Long, deep sobs shook her frame. He closed his eyes, kissing the top of her head between the soft "shh" repeating from his mouth.

Escape scenarios played over and over in his mind, but in each case, he ended up behind bars, or worse. There was no happy ending to this fairy tale, and he knew it.

When she stopped crying, he put her gently back on the bed and stood to leave.

"Can you play some music?"

He paused. "What do you want to hear?"

"*Calling all Angels* by Train."

"Okay." He walked out.

In the control room, he popped in a CD he had made months ago, set it to loop, and piped the music into her room. He typed commands into the computer, bringing up the feed for the times he had been gone, and scrolled through. He stopped when Frank walked into the view of the camera with one of his knives. When the knife cut her chin, Ty's fists clenched. He fast forwarded to the time he was gone today, and the brutal rape rolled across the screen. Murder filled his heart, and he flipped the feed off.

He inhaled and exhaled, counting his breaths, dialing back the rage so he could think. Frank would never allow him to take her out of here. If he somehow managed it, Frank would use Chris as a bargaining chip. He had done it before, and Ty wouldn't put it past the bastard to kill his little brother out of spite.

Movement on the screen caught his attention. She stood and swayed to the music; the drugs doing their magic in concert with her natural grace. She twirled and sang in the red dress, her voice soft and sexy and her movement downright seductive. He watched, breathless, and carnal hunger filled every fiber of his being.

He had to find a way.

He turned at a noise behind him and swung the chair around to face his brothers.

"God damn," Chris whispered, his eyes glued to the monitor.

"She's different," Ty said, toeing the line that he prayed would buy him time.

They looked at him.

"This is going to take time." He glared at Frank, barely keeping his temper in check.

"What about our conversation made you think what you did today was okay?"

"This is my business. I call the shots," Frank said.

Ty stopped his hands from clenching and took a deep breath. "Yes, but you don't have the same level of editing talent that I do."

They stared at each other. The tension in the room kicked up.

"I'm making this call because we need to treat this one differently. If we can't agree about this, then I'm walking." Ty pressed his lips together.

Frank's eyes narrowed into slits, and his jaw tightened. "Are you really sure you want to do that?" His gaze slid to Chris and then back and he cocked his head, silently conveying his threat.

"No, but it should tell you how serious I am about this plan and how sure I am it will work," he said, praying his bluff wouldn't be called.

Frank blinked, and his eyebrows rose. He glanced at the monitors and then back at Ty. "Are you sure there isn't anything more going on here?"

"No. But if you fuck it up again, I might just have to castrate you." he allowed a smile to surface, like he was cracking a joke. Although the idea of castrating the sick fucker was appealing.

Frank burst out laughing. "Fine. We will do this your way."

Relief swept through Ty. Somehow Frank believed him, and he thanked whatever guardian angel had given him a break.

Survival Games Chapter 17

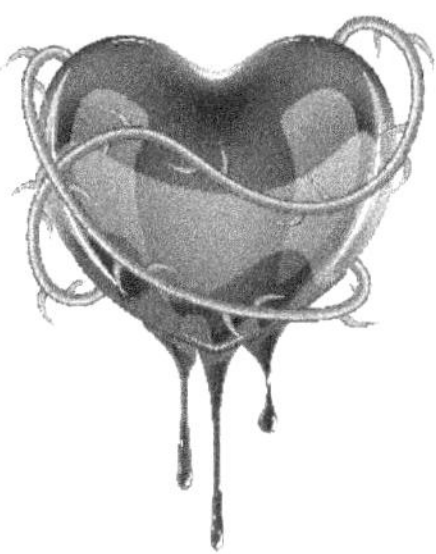

AFTER CHRIS AND FRANK left, Ty walked into Jessica's room. She saw him but kept dancing and singing as if she didn't have a care in the world.

He leaned against the wall with his arms crossed and watched her. The rage at what Frank had done settled back a notch, replaced by his desire for her.

Sighing, he wished the heavens would open up and deliver the angels to her. He wished he'd met her in another time and place, under different circumstances. He huffed. She probably wouldn't have given him the time of day.

She stumbled and caught herself, her soft voice cracking and going off key for the briefest instant. He smiled, catching her attention. She stopped and looked at him, and the song began again.

"That's a nice smile," she said. "It's not mean or sadistic or sarcastic." She pirouetted over to him. "Lean over."

He leaned over as she asked, and she messed his hair up with her hand. His bangs fell onto his forehead instead of slicked back the way he usually wore it.

"That's better." She smiled and danced away.

Ty looked at himself in the mirror, still smiling. He didn't look so serious or threatening with his hair tousled; he actually looked more like his brother Chris.

He grunted at his reflection and looked back at Jessica. "Girl, you got moves," he said over the music.

She laughed and twirled by.

No wonder Mike loves you.

Jessica stopped dead in her tracks. She turned and stared at him, her eyes dark and wide. "He's here?" she asked incredulously.

"Who?"

"Mike."

Ty's jaw dropped. *How the hell?* He snapped his jaw shut.

Jessica walked toward him—her eyes no longer brown, but a strange, deep, dark violet, and still glossy from the drugs. "You just said, and I quote, 'No wonder Mike loves you.' Oh, and another thing, I'm not different. I'm special." She stumbled into him and then passed out cold.

He caught her and stared at her limp body. *Did she just read my mind?*

"No fucking way," he whispered and picked her up. He stood with her cradled in his arms, staring at her slack features. His gaze lifted to his reflection, weighing his chances of an escape. With Chris still in the crosshairs, he couldn't chance it.

He crossed to the mattress and laid her on it. Then he covered her and went back to the control room to replay the video.

He chewed on his lip, fiddling with the controls as he watched the scene multiple times until he yawned. With no more answers, he switched the review monitor off.

He stared at her sleeping form. For someone who calculated everything like he did, this was something new, something he couldn't control, and as much as he hated to admit it, he wanted to be near her.

In a rare, impulsive move, he returned to her room and stretched out on the bed, wrapping his arms around her. He allowed himself to drift off.

Survival Games Chapter 18

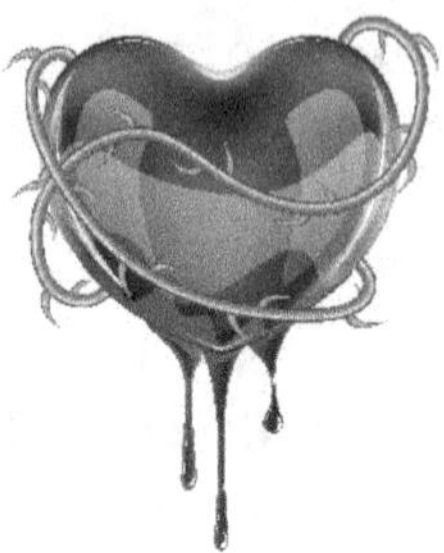

TY WOKE A FEW hours later with Jessica still securely in his arms. He closed his eyes and smelled her hair; the mango shampoo scent still clung to it. Begrudgingly, he slipped his arm from under her and left the room.

He stood in the hall with his back to the closed door and ran his hand through his thick hair. "What the hell am I doing?"

He shook his head and headed to the bathroom beyond the control room to shower quickly. Instead of slicking his hair back like usual, he shook his head and just let it fall where it wanted, achieving the same look she'd liked last night.

How the hell am I going to make up for what Frank did?

With a clean pair of jeans and a crisp blue button-down oxford that matched his eyes, he stepped into the kitchen. Scanning the contents of the refrigerator, a slow smile spread on his lips.

He set up a plate of grapes and strawberries and then scooped a healthy dollop of Cool Whip into a bowl on the side. On his way through the control room, he pulled a couple pairs of handcuffs from a drawer and slid them into his back pocket.

She woke as he entered with the tray. "May I?" She pointed to the bathroom.

He nodded and waited for her to come back. When she did, he motioned for her to sit on the bed.

She crossed the room, her head cocked to the side, studying him as she sat on the mattress. "You changed your hair."

He put the tray down and looked at her through his bangs. "Lie down."

Her eyebrows rose, but she made no move to obey.

He gently took her by the shoulders and laid her back on the bed. She didn't fight until he pulled out the handcuffs, but he was faster, had the cuffs around her left wrist, and attached to the anchor on the floor in a flash. He pushed her back down and quickly flipped the handcuff around her right wrist as she swung at him. He looked around for a place to hook it and realized there was nowhere close by to put the other end of the handcuff.

"Shit." Ty closed his eyes, shaking his head at his lack of forethought.

"Quite the predicament," Jessica said, her voice laced with a hint of humor.

"Not really." He attached the other handcuff to the same anchor and left the room. When he came back, he had three long pieces of rope.

Jessica's smile disappeared, and his got wider.

"Please don't do this."

He sighed and unhooked the handcuff holding her right hand. Then he tied the end of the rope to it and walked to the other side of the bed, where he anchored it to the floor. He put the remaining rope next to the tray and sat down.

Trembling, she planted her feet firmly on the mattress, her knees bent and her arms straining against the binds.

"I'm not going to hurt you." He reached over to the tray, plucked a grape off the vine, and popped it in her mouth.

Her eyebrows arched, and she ate the grape, warily watching him. He repeated this until the grapes were all gone. Then he dipped a strawberry in the whipped cream and held it to her lips. She hesitated with her eyebrows still scrunched together. She took the strawberry in her mouth, careful not to bite his fingers.

An act as simple as eating a strawberry moved him. He took a deep breath, tossing the top of the strawberry back on the tray. He repeated with another strawberry. When he picked up the third strawberry, his hand shook. He changed tactics, dipping the strawberry in the whipped cream and dragging it from her neckline to between her breasts, leaving a trail of cream. He popped the sweet strawberry in his mouth and dropped the top on the tray. Without a word, he leaned down and licked the whipped cream off her.

Jessica closed her eyes, arching into his touch.

He sat up slowly and took another strawberry, dipped it, and slid it down the side of her neck and put it to her lips, leaving a hint of whipped cream on them. He ate the strawberry and leaned over to kiss the cream off her lips, hesitating when she turned her head away. Instead of licking the cream off her lips, he ran his tongue along the line on her neck. Her skin quivered under his touch.

He smiled as he sat up, meeting her pained gaze. "Tell me you want me."

"I don't."

Ty cocked his head, running his fingers back and forth along the neckline of her dress, pushing it farther open with each pass. "That so?"

"I don't want you." Her husky voice belied her words.

Ty took a deep breath and closed his eyes, gaining control again. When he reached for the whipped cream, Jessica's feet connected with his ribcage, knocking the wind out of him, and sending him sailing off the mattress.

He stood and flexed his hands into fists. She smugly raised her eyebrow in a silent challenge.

He turned his back to her and took a few deep breaths, needing the admission, needing to feel her skin against his, her breath in his ear, her heart pounding against his. He needed her to say the words. He ran his hands through his hair and turned around again, more determined than before.

He walked over to the tray and picked up the rope. Then he tied a slipknot in each strand before grabbing her kicking ankles and anchoring her legs. He kneeled between the spread he'd created and grabbed her dress, tearing it open. Silently, he picked up the Cool Whip and traced her breasts with the sweet confection. Her eyes held both ecstasy and apprehension as he leaned down to suck the cream off, rolling his tongue around each nipple. They hardened under his mouth. He smiled and sat up again.

"Tell me you want me," he said again, his voice smooth and low. He dipped his finger in the whipped cream and trailed a line along her stomach.

"No." Her voice wavered with passion.

Ty continued his slow seduction with the whipped cream. He lined the inside of her thigh from her knee to just shy of her underwear and licked it off slowly. He repeated with the other.

Her breath came in thready bursts. Sweat shined on her skin.

"Tell me you want me," he said, looking straight down into her eyes, his arms holding him above her without touching her. He fought for control, fought the urge to peel his clothing off and make love to her.

She still had cream on her lip, so he leaned down and sucked it off and then pulled away with his eyes closed. Slowly, he opened them.

"I can't," Jessica said with a voice barely audible. She shut her eyes for a second. "I can't," she repeated, as if trying to talk herself into believing it.

He hung his head, consumed with so many emotions at that moment that he didn't dare move. Lust, anger, and futility combined to dangerous levels within him. He opened his eyes, took a deep breath, and kneeled back.

Again, he dipped his finger in the cream, traced a line from her belly button to the band of her underwear, and licked it slowly and deliberately downward. He looked up at her again, and for a brief instant, he forgot to breathe.

"Say you want me," he insisted. He lapped at her belly button, rolling his tongue slowly around and ending with a wet kiss. He kissed the inside of her thighs, her stomach, her breasts, her neck, and her lips as she trembled beneath him. His whole body ached, and he pulled inches away from her, staring into her eyes, and breathing hard. He leaned down and kissed her tenderly.

Jessica's lips parted, allowing him to explore her mouth.

The sweetness of her tongue dancing with his sucked the air out of his lungs. He pulled away slowly and sat back on his knees. He looked at her for a long time and ran a shaky hand through his hair.

He untied her and unlocked the cuffs. She wrapped her arms over her belly, pulled the remnants of the dress around her, and rolled on her side, her face buried in the pillow.

He spun away, storming out of the room, and slammed the door behind him. Anger welled up from the bowels of his soul. He spiked the handcuffs on the hallway floor, pacing back and forth as the fury grew. His gaze landed on another door halfway down the hall, and he darted to it, yanked the door open, and glared at the bastard who had brought all this on.

Mike scrambled to his feet, his eyes narrowing in hatred as he charged.

Ty sidestepped and swung an uppercut, catching Mike under the jaw and sending him sideways. He grabbed Mike, slamming him into the concrete wall with his hand locked around the bastard's throat. "You son of a bitch, you knew!"

He threw Mike across the room and stalked out, leaving Mike baffled on the floor.

His frame shook with barely contained emotion, and he went back to the source, entering her room and listening to the shower. He paced, frustration brewing to unprecedented levels within him.

Survival Games Chapter 19

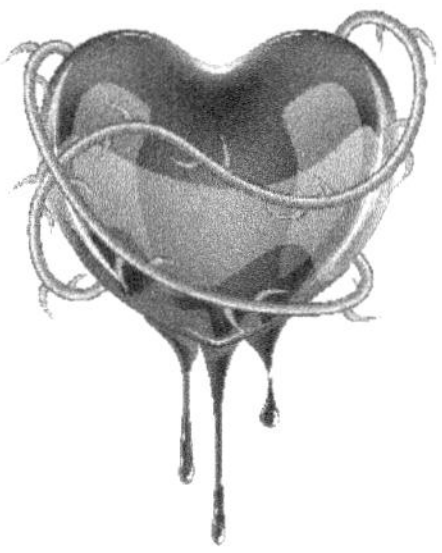

JESSICA LAY ON THE mattress and shook with anger, frustration, and fear. She turned her head to the tray still holding a half-eaten bowl of strawberries. She stood and kicked it across the room, heading toward the bathroom and relief from her burning skin. After Frank's assault, she hadn't thought she was capable of desire. At least not this soon after that horror, and certainly not while within these walls. But in a matter of moments, Bedroom Eyes had seemed to heal all the scars on her soul as if by divine intervention.

That frightened her more than Frank did.

Stepping under the cold water, she yelped, arching her back from the frigid spray. She forced herself to stay under until all hints of the heat he'd created disappeared. The cold water brought clarity, and with it a truth that tore her right down to the core. She wanted Bedroom Eyes almost as much as she wanted her freedom.

That could not happen, not if she wanted to see her family again.

God help me.

She shivered as the frigid water bit at her skin, cooling her down and letting her gain control.

Her teeth chattered, and she flipped the water off, grabbed a towel, and dried the cold droplets from her goose-pimpled skin. The room tilted, and she grabbed the stall door.

Visions slammed into her consciousness hard enough for her to collapse from the weight of them. She dropped to the floor as past and present collided.

She had seen his face before.

Long before her children were even a thought, she'd had an unsettling dream. Her memory of that dream sharpened, and she saw herself sitting up in bed afterward, shaking as her husband consoled her. She'd never led on that it was one of those crystal-clear dreams which reminded her of her occasional glimpses of the future. It was of Bedroom Eyes crouched in front of the chair she'd been bound to. His blue eyes flashed recognition of some sort. It had been the exact circumstances of the first time she'd seen him in this godforsaken place.

The next memory cut her deep. She folded over in the bathroom, unwilling to accept it as another glimpse of her future. Those sincere blue eyes had looked up at her as he kneeled on a snow-covered lawn, the words he'd uttered impossible.

"Oh my God," she whispered and climbed to her feet. She stared at her reflection with dread. She dressed, dismissing the thought, along with the gnawing fear gripping her every cell, and focused on running until she dropped.

Still shivering, she walked into the room to him pacing back and forth like a caged animal. When his enraged gaze landed on her, she shuddered from more than the chill in the air.

"Tell me you want me," he bellowed at her, his face a mask of fury.

Jessica said nothing. She continued to shake.

He shot over to where she was standing, picked her up, and pinned her to the wall so they were face to face. "Say it," he said through clenched teeth.

"No." The word came out of her throat in a low growl.

"You kissed me," he growled back.

"A lapse in judgment!" The second dream flashed before her eyes again. *Impossible.*

He let her slide to the ground and stepped back. Then he walked to the center of the room and glared at her over his shoulder. "Do you have any idea, any idea at all, how fucking frustrating you are?"

"No, why don't you tell me?" Jessica snapped. "You ripped me from my life to bring me to this hellhole. What do you expect?" she yelled. Her fury now matched his. "You brought me here to kill me, but first you expect me to perform in your little sex shows. Bullshit." She walked around to face him. "And what? You have the audacity to think you have a shot with me? Go to hell!" She started walking toward the treadmill.

He grabbed her arm, threw her on the mattress, and was on top of her before she could move. He grabbed her arms and slammed them down. He held her pinned as they glared at each other. "You have no idea what I'm capable of," he sneered.

"No, you have no idea of what *I* am capable of."

"That's because it's just your ass on the line. What if I pull someone else in the mix, someone *you* care about? Would you be this obstinate then?" He let this sink in. "Who is it, Jess? Who would *you* beg to save?"

She fumed. "Bite me."

He shifted, pressing his hips into her, the fabric of his jeans restraining him from doing exactly what he wanted to her. "I can have you any time, any way I want!"

"You will never *HAVE* me," Jessica screamed at him.

"I promise you, I will," he whispered. "And next time, I won't stop like I did earlier. That was *MY* lapse in judgment," he breathed bitterly in her ear. He hopped to his feet, leaving her shaking on the mattress.

Survival Games Chapter 20

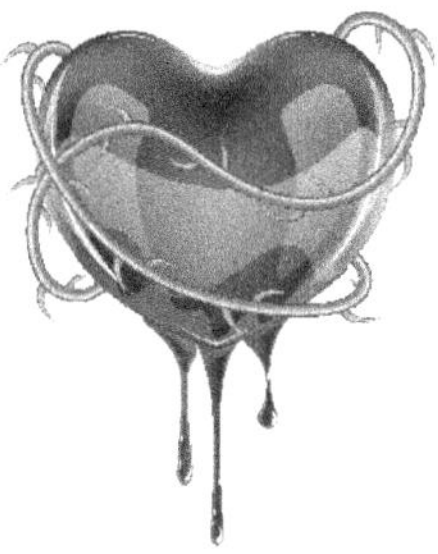

JESSICA COVERED HER FACE with her hands. The memory of that second dream-glimpse flashed in her mind. She knew he would eventually make her eat her words, like he had before.

When the tears dried up, she headed into the bathroom, splashing her face with water. She reached for a towel, voicing the mantra that began in her head. "I need to survive."

Movement out of the corner of her eye tripled her heart rate. She glanced at the empty doorway. *Oh God, what if it's him again? What if he decided to make good on his threat?* The thought produced a trembling fear. She waited, but nothing stirred, and she looked back at the mirror.

Eric stood in a room she didn't recognize, smiling at her.

"Don't give up, Mom. I'll show you what to do with the key when he isn't watching." Then his reflection faded away.

The realization of where he had been slowly dawned on her. He was in school, in the school restroom, looking at her in the mirror. A small sound escaped her, and she touched the mirror. She wasn't imagining seeing him. She would have never placed him there, and he could see her and touch her and the key. He had really given that to her.

She stared in the mirror and tilted her head to the side. The night before was a blur—a flurry of jumbled memories, sporadic at best. She couldn't help but feel something significant had happened after he drugged her, but the labyrinth of her subconscious was shut tight. While studying her reflection, his words echoed ominously in her ear.

Who would you beg to save?

Her kids flashed through her mind first and then her eyes closed as the only other name that came to mind escaped her lips. But he had died in a horrible house fire with his wife.

Survival Games Chapter 21

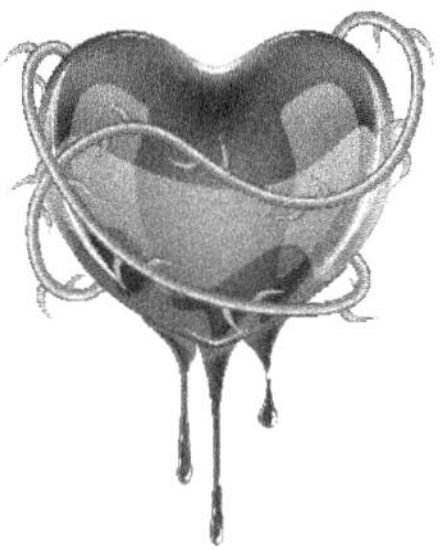

MIKE PACED IN HIS room, watching the screen as the video played. Jessica danced and sang in her room and was obviously high as a kite. The fact that Ty was standing there watching struck both fury and terror in Mike's heart. Mike stopped moving when Jessica messed up Ty's hair and stood back, smiling at him.

The tape suddenly fast-forwarded through the next part, showing Ty crawling next to her on the mattress, holding her through the night, and leaving before she woke. Mike watched with his mouth hanging open as the most terrifying thought since he was brought to this hellhole passed through his mind: *He's in love with her.*

Mike sat down hard on the floor, the morning scene unfolding on the wide screen before him and confirming his greatest fears. The monster who ruined his life was in love with the woman of his dreams, and she'd kissed him back. His heart plummeted into his stomach, and he closed his eyes, slowly shaking his head. *She couldn't, could she?*

TY SMILED WITH SATISFACTION at the devastation etched in Mike's face. "Yep, she certainly kissed me back, lapse of judgment or not."

He switched the monitor in Mike's room off. Leaving him to replay it over and over in his mind, the sheer joy of torturing the son of a bitch who prompted him to bring Jessica here was bittersweet.

It was time to do his job. He collected the discs of Jessica and wandered into the observation room overlooking her cell. He paused, staring at her jogging on the treadmill of her own free will.

He grunted and then inserted the discs in the timeline order in the editing suite, along with a blank disc. Before he began the task of editing the scenes together on the software, he piped music into the feed to her speakers.

"Unwell" filled her room, and she jumped.

Ty smiled. He went through each of the tapes, thirteen in all that interested him. He strung the scenes together with all the different camera angles onto one disc to work from and then began piecing each scene meticulously together with intertwining camera angles from last night's events.

THE MUSIC CONTINUED IN the background, and Jessica stared as the feed came up on her monitor. The starts and stops, along with the seamless integration of scenes, left her breathless. She recoiled and nearly stumbled on the treadmill when Frank walked in the room on screen. The video froze, rewound, and jumped to her stepping into view in the red dress. It was almost as if Bedroom Eyes wanted to erase that from memory. The fact it wasn't added to this sensual composition sent tingles of hope through her.

Her expressions when he was near were more telling than she wanted to admit. Any dimwit on the street could tell she wanted the man. It turned her stomach sour. She kept running and watching the editing of the exceptionally hot video.

The scene in the filming studio room unfolded, and Jessica's jaw dropped. While the drugs they gave her nearly wiped her memory of the entire ordeal, seeing Bedroom Eyes nearly kill Frank after she outed him sent a piece of her soul soaring. His rage came through on the screen. His eyes darkened, becoming deadly daggers aimed at his stepbrother.

Her intuition that he was a dangerous man compounded when he crossed the room in a split-second and caught Frank in midair. Jessica shivered as she watched him beat his own brother. She'd apparently passed some test of his. The video switched from that room back into hers as he brought her back in.

When his soft voice whispered, "I'm sorry about Frank. I didn't know" on screen. Her heart clenched, aching for his tender touch. She craved the way he held her with such care while she cried out her pain.

She didn't remember any of it.

Music piped in the room on screen and suddenly the tape returned to her stepping out of the bathroom and then transitioned to her swaying to the music. She shot her gaze to the mirror, irritation itching at her skin. He edited out any record of him displaying kindness.

Jessica's brow creased, and she studied him on-screen. The way he casually leaned against the wall, relaxed and in his element with a natural smile on his face, not the one he flashed for show. It was damned sexy. Her dancing image took no notice of him at first, continuing her oblivious twirling pirouettes and singing at the top of her lungs to the music filling the room.

While the words from "Calling All Angels" echoed on the screen, she saw herself dance over and comment on his smile, ask him to lean over, mess up his hair and dance away. The screen went blank after he said, "Girl, you got moves."

"No!" Jessica yelled at her reflection. Unwanted tears slid down her cheeks, and more than just her running regiment kept her breathless.

The video came on again at the point she fell, the two scenes seamlessly edited together. Bedroom Eyes caught her easily and laid her on the bed gently. The scene faded. The tape then fast-forwarded through the night. She saw him come in, lie next to her, and wrap his arms around her before the screen went black again.

Jessica turned her gaze to the mirror, swallowing the lump in her throat. She knew she would need all the angels in heaven to help her, because he was in love with her, and that made him much more dangerous.

The full irony of the song hit her like a blow to the stomach, and she wondered if he even caught the significance of the choice.

"God almighty," Jessica whispered, and looked at her reflection.

The dream she remembered was still dancing around in her memory. She closed her eyes and the ring he held up for her in the snow-covered yard sparkled in her memory.

I can't, she thought and opened her eyes.

The scene rewound from the fade of her on the bed to the fade up of him walking into the room with the tray of fruit and then sitting next to her. The morning seduction unfolded before her eyes. When the scene faded, she had no more doubts. Her vision blurred.

HE FINALLY GLANCED UP from the editing suite after the last fade to black. She was still running, but tears streamed down her cheeks. His gaze jumped to the screen with his heart in his throat. He rewound and when the screen in her room jumped to life, he quickly tuned off the feed.

"Shit," he whispered.

She had been privy to his private editing session. He ran his hands through his hair, debating on his next step. He slowly made his way to the room and stepped inside.

They looked at each other without a word, and tears streaked from her bloodshot eyes.

He approached the treadmill tentatively. She shut it down but stayed in place, leaning on the console. Her gaze flicked to the black screen.

"You weren't supposed to see that." He shoved his hands in his pockets.

She let out a high-pitched laugh and wiped her face. "What do you expect me to say?"

That you feel the same things I do. "That you want me," he said very softly.

Jessica hung her head, and she dropped to the treadmill, a sob escaping while she shook her head. "I can't," she whispered, her voice barely audible. "I can't."

"Why?" he asked with a voice laced with bitterness.

She looked up at him. "Because you're a monster."

Ty stepped back as if he'd been hit with a powerful blow. He backed out of the room and slammed the door behind him. He sank to his knees in the hall, struggling to catch his breath, the weight of what she'd said crashing down on him. He closed his eyes and leaned back against the door. With a shaky hand, he slowly wiped his face.

"What the hell am I doing?" he asked the empty hall.

She's wrong. I'm not a monster.

But he knew well enough that she'd hit the nail on the head. He looked around, knowing he'd live up to that label by the time this was all over.

Survival Games Chapter 22

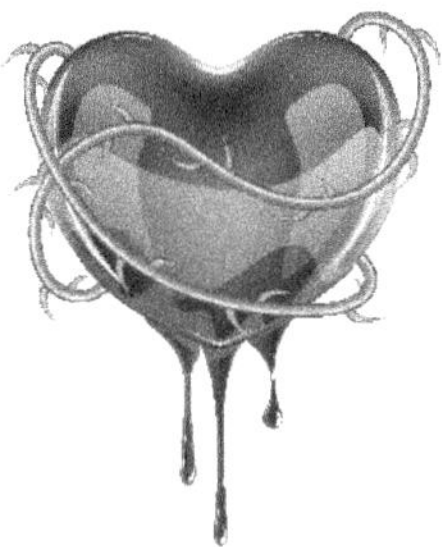

MIKE LAY ON THE mattress, and as Ty had predicted, the images looped in his mind in a sick cycle, replaying again and again whether or not he wanted it to.

He closed his eyes, escaping into the past, to the first time he saw her, roughly seven years before. He had been assigned a project that was out of his realm of expertise, so he called the players into a meeting to get up to speed. Jessica was one of the major knowledge foundations, and when she'd walked into the room, she set him on fire. He remembered the disappointment when he'd looked at her left hand. *Damn,* she was wearing a wedding band.

Jessica was smart. She also was an amazing flirt, and she knew how to use her assets to her advantage. She even had rendered him speechless once, which was not an easy thing to do.

He had scheduled an offsite for the group, and she called him to ask if everyone could wear jeans and be comfortable. He had said he didn't care, and her response was, "As long as we wear something, right?" He'd smiled at the memory. She insisted it was an innocent slip; she was just trying to be cute. He could still hear her laughter when he replied, "I don't know how to respond to that."

He would kill to hear her laugh like that again. His eyes flew open. He had killed for her. He ran his hand over his face, shoving that thought aside, and slipped back into the past.

The offsite increased his appetite for her; just seeing her operate a room full of people was awe-inspiring. She had an interesting combination of freedom and intelligence that was sexy as hell. He would have given anything to take her up to one of the rooms in the hotel and do to her what Ty had done.

Soon after the offsite, a heat wave had hit New England. Mike smiled, recalling the day he found out she felt the same. She had emailed asking if he wanted to go for a walk, but it was too hot out for his tastes. He had declined.

Her email back had sent a shock through him.

Some like it hot, she had written.

He had looked at the computer screen, weighing how to respond. He took a chance and sent back: *Are you talking about the weather?*

The next words that had flashed on the screen made his jaw drop.

Perhaps. Are you familiar with chemistry?

With those words prompting him, he flew over to her desk. "We need to talk."

She swung her chair around and smiled, reducing him to a mass of overactive hormones. He just wanted to take her in his arms, but instead, they went for a coffee in the cafeteria.

When they sat down with their drinks, she told him she didn't know quite what to do with their situation, but couldn't ignore it anymore.

Being that close to her drove him crazy. He wanted her so bad he ached.

Mike opened his eyes and looked at the blank monitor. He stood up in frustration and screamed. "You son of a bitch!" He paced the room again and threw a punch at the wall. The pain vibrated up his arm, but he punched again, scraping the skin off his knuckles. "If I EVER get my hands on you, I will tear you apart!"

Survival Games Chapter 23

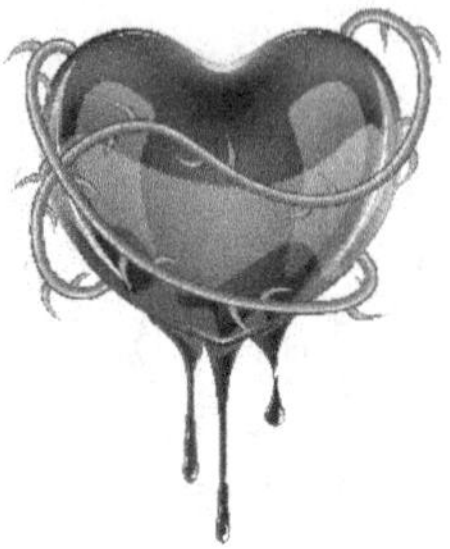

JESSICA LAY WITH HER eyes closed, thinking about the images she'd seen. Heaven help her, every fiber of her being wanted him. That low husky voice of his, along with his seductive hands and velvety lips, got to her. His smile could melt armor, and he could be downright sexy when he wasn't trying, despite his scar. He was falling in love with her, and that terrified her to the core.

She wasn't sure if the first deluge of videos he'd shown her was a blessing or a curse. If she hadn't seen them, she never would have known what a monster he really was. She wouldn't have been able to resist without the knowledge that they got off on humiliating, torturing, and killing.

Even though he only appeared in the hot videos with what seemed like more than willing participants, he edited everything. He saw everything. And he did nothing to stop it.

That made him a monster.

No matter how much she physically wanted him, she would never say what he wanted, because that was giving up her power. Once that happened, it was all over.

The complete irony of her song choice made her smile. She sang softly.

"In a world that what we want is what we want until it's ours..."

She had one hope, one bet, and if she played her cards right, she'd get out of this mess alive.

Survival Games Chapter 24

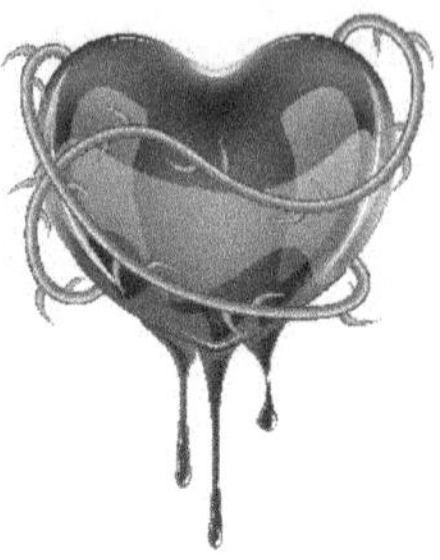

TY DECIDED TO FOLLOW his own orders where Jessica was concerned. No one touched her, including him. He brought her food and clothing each day, but didn't talk to her. She ignored him at first, but then, after a couple of weeks, she said hi when he entered the room. He just nodded, acknowledging the salutation, and as always, she said thank you when he put the tray down for her. She surprised him each day by getting on the treadmill of her own free will and running. He had got all the seasons of *Metropolis* and played a disk for her when she ran, and when she wasn't running, he piped in music.

He watched her, planning the diversion that would get her the hell out of this place. The diversion she said she would beg for.

"I don't know your name," Jessica said one day when he brought her lunch. "What's your name?"

Ty looked at her for a moment, debating on whether he should answer. "Ty." He started to leave.

"Ty," she whispered his name, causing him to turn back.

He was not prepared for the impact of hearing her say his name. The world disappeared, and there was only her. His heartbeat thundered in his ears, and he stared, silently counting to ten before he dared move a muscle. He inhaled and blinked the room back into view.

"Is it possible to have a book to read?" she asked sheepishly, surprising him.

"Um." He cocked his head a bit. "What kind of book?"

Jessica shrugged. "I don't know. Something good."

Ty smiled. "What I think is good might not be the same as what you consider good. What genres?"

"Thrillers, suspense, horror. You know, things that go bump in the night kind of books," she said, and her cheeks flared red.

"Wow, no sappy romance novels?"

Jessica laughed. "I hate those things."

Ty nodded. "I'll see what I can do." Then he left the room.

"Thank you, Ty," she said softly before the door closed.

Ty stood in the hallway with his hand on the doorknob, fighting the internal need to go back in and wrap his arms around her. He wanted her so bad it hurt, and today when she'd said his name, he had almost given in. Patience was not a virtue he possessed, but he forced himself to be patient this time.

He took a deep breath and headed out to get her what she had asked for.

That evening, he came back with her dinner tray and then returned a second time with a stack of books for her. She lit up like Yankee Stadium when someone on the home team hit a grand slam.

"Thank you." Jessica smiled and took the stack from him.

Their hands touched, and an electrical charge raced through his cells just like the first time their eyes had met.

He smiled, mumbling, "No problem. Gotta go." Then he slipped out as fast as humanly possible. If he stayed, he'd do something he would regret, and it wasn't time yet.

He went back to the control room and breathed deep. He looked at the plan he had devised over the last few weeks to obtain the target. It would be a hell of a challenge, and he would need the company's contacts to pull strings to get him on the set. That wouldn't be too hard, considering the company supplied most of the wiring for sound and video equipment for the entertainment industry. He placed a call and waited.

Frank arrived a few hours later, and Ty mapped out the strategy.

"What do you think?" he asked when he finished.

"It's risky," Frank said as he studied the written plans. He chewed on his lip and rubbed his hands together. "You are going to need someone to help you with this one."

All he needed was Frank hovering over him on this. He opened his mouth to object, but Frank beat him to it.

"It's time to bring your brother in on this side of the business," Frank said.

Ty's stomach dropped. He had done his best to keep Chris out of the killing side. To protect him from Frank's brutality.

"It's the only way this is going to go down," Frank said.

Chris was an adult, and he would have to make his own decisions where the business was concerned. There was only one problem—if he didn't make the right one in Frank's eyes, it would be the last decision he made.

Ty's gaze traveled to Jessica's monitor. For the first time in his life, someone else besides blood trumped his protective reflex. Ty nodded, agreeing to Frank's terms.

Frank set the wheels in motion, and they waited for the call to come in.

Survival Games Chapter 25

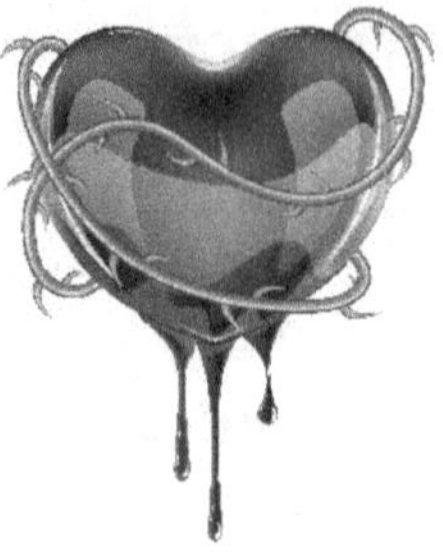

JESSICA WAS ENGROSSED IN one of the scarier novels when the door swung open. She jumped a mile and glanced up at Ty, blushing at her reaction to the interruption.

Ty suppressed a laugh. "You really like that scary shit?" he asked, setting the tray down near her.

"Yeah, don't you?" she answered, folding the corner of the page over and setting the book on the mattress. She looked at the food on the tray and sighed. It was a salad again. She would kill for a good steak.

"Sure, but I'm twisted," he answered with a smile.

Jessica laughed. "Not that I'm complaining, but don't you know how to make anything other than salad?"

His smile faltered. "Like what?"

"I don't know. Something in the realm of protein would be nice for a change," she said, keeping eye contact.

Ty nodded. "I'll see what I can do." He went to leave.

As always, Jessica said, "thank you."

He paused in the hallway, leaning against the door and fighting his desire. He wanted to feel her beneath him and hear her whisper his name as he made love to her. He took a deep breath and headed for the bathroom off the kitchen. He needed a shower to cool down.

JESSICA STOOD AND APPROACHED the door. She wrapped her hand around the doorknob, silently wishing for a miracle.

"Open," she whispered and turned the knob.

The latch unclasped, and the door swung open. *Holy shit, he forgot to lock it this time!*

Warily, she stuck her head out in the hallway and looked in both directions before stepping out of the room. Her heart slammed in her chest, flitting like a Mexican jumping bean with every step she took.

She glanced to her left. She had been down that way before. That was where the taping room was. She swung her head in the opposite direction. The hallway took a sharp turn to the right where she envisioned her room ended. Tentatively, she started in that direction.

Her heart pounded so loud that it drowned out all other noise. She kept glancing behind her, making sure Ty didn't come from that direction. Jessica leaned against the wall at the corner and closed her eyes for a moment. She opened them and took a peek. An elevator stood at the end of the hall, and she took the turn, walking faster toward her escape.

Her gaze darted down the hallway behind her and then to her right as she stepped in front of the elevator and pressed the button. Her heart jumped into her throat, hammering, pulsing in her ears.

The doors slid open, and she turned, staring into dark, twisted eyes.

"Looking for a ride?" Frank asked, and then his fist connected with her eye.

Jessica stumbled back, hitting the wall, but didn't fall. The liquid fire of freedom froze in her veins, turning to a fear that constricted her throat. Her internal alarms blazed at his murderously cool stare.

He barreled down on her. She turned to flee.

Frank grabbed her and slammed her into the wall face-first, pushing himself against her back, ripping at her clothing. "You just made a big mistake," he whispered in her ear.

His fist slammed her kidney, and the air rushed out of her lungs. She jammed her elbow into his midsection. He slammed her head against the wall. She saw stars as panic raked across her skin. The pain she remembered from their last encounter froze her muscles in place.

His hand wrapped around the front of her, squeezing her throat as he continued his assault. Frank seemed hell-bent on killing her in this cold hallway. She closed her eyes, silently screaming the only name that could save her from this horrifying ending.

Ty!

His name blasted through her conscious mind with the power of a freight train.

Survival Games Chapter 26

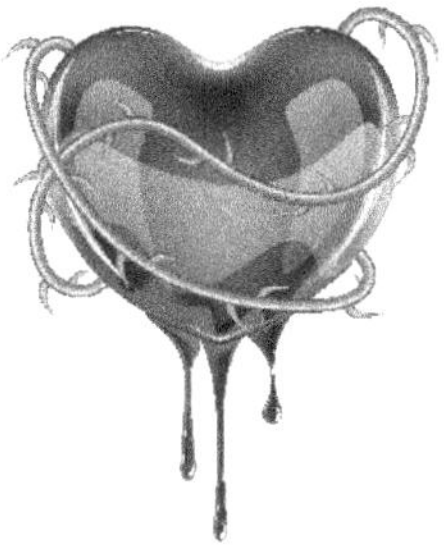

TY STOOD UNDER THE stream of water. His eyes closed and his hands rinsed the shampoo out of his hair, when her scream drowned out all other thoughts.

The terror in her voice shot him into action. He bolted from the shower, grabbing a towel as he ran by the rack. Sprinting into the hallway, he wrapped the towel around his waist and rounded the bend by the elevator. He slid to a stop less than ten feet from where Frank was raping her against the wall.

"Let her go," he growled.

Frank glared his way. "You let her out of the room," he shot back, but did not show signs of stopping what he'd started.

Ty launched himself at Frank and tore him off her. He tossed him onto the floor. Jessica crumbled to the ground, coughing and wheezing.

Ty grabbed her by the upper arm and hauled her to her feet, leading her back toward her room while holding onto the towel so it didn't slip off. The water dripped from his body, leaving a trail of wet footprints all the way back.

He threw her into the room and shut the door behind him, staring at her.

Remnants of shampoo slid into his eye, and he pressed his palm to it to stop the stinging. "Shit!"

"Why did you stop him?" She hitched her breath in as she attempted to wrap her ripped clothing around herself.

Ty shrugged. His gaze landed on the black and blue around her throat. "I heard you scream, and I reacted."

What the fuck are you thinking?

He couldn't articulate why he had saved her. It was instinct. The same need to protect her put her above his only brother, and it left him feeling raw and exposed. He headed into the bathroom and stepped into the shower, letting the water wash the soap from his eyes. It drowned out all thought for the moment. When he stepped out of the shower, he dried his body, toweled off his hair, and ran his hands through it to get some semblance of order before he wrapped the towel around his waist and stepped into the room again.

"How the hell did you get out of this room?" He stood as far from her as possible, not daring to get any closer.

"The door was unlocked."

"Bullshit!"

"It was." Jessica glared.

Ty took a threatening step toward her and thought better of it. He turned to leave.

"Why did you stop him?" she asked again.

He looked at her. "I told you, I reacted."

"You said you heard me scream."

He nodded and reached for the doorknob.

"I never screamed out loud."

Ty stopped and stared at the metal before him. He slowly turned his head to look at her.

"I know what I heard," he replied, his eyes going hard. *What kind of game is this?*

Jessica pressed her lips together, blinking the tears away. She curled up on the mattress and brought the sheet up. "Thanks for stopping him," she said, tightening her jaw and blinking the sheen from her eyes.

Ty gave a slight nod and left the room.

Frank was waiting for him in the hallway, seething.

"You let her out," he said.

"No, I didn't." Ty glared at Frank as he headed to the quarters off the kitchen where his clothes were. "I'll check the program to make sure there isn't a glitch." He shot a glance over his shoulder. "You weren't supposed to touch her, Frank." He slid behind the door and pulled on his clothes, then came out a few minutes later buttoning his shirt.

Frank leaned against the wall with his arms crossed. "She was trying to get out of here," he said. "She needed to be taught who's in control, and you haven't been doing that lately."

Ty shook his head. "We had a deal. Now we are back to step one." He took a breath and forced himself to focus on Frank. He was on dangerous ground, and if he played this wrong, he would take a fast and hard fall into oblivion.

"What the fuck are you babbling about?"

"She was getting comfortable, almost trusting, and now I have to build that all up again."

"Why? She's just another whore to be used," Frank snapped.

Ty clenched his fists. "Because it will be much more devastating to her when we pull the rug out from under her feet. When we reveal our secret project, it will crush her spirit."

Frank's eyebrows arched, and his mouth popped open. It took a moment, but then his face broke out in a broad grin. "You are one evil son of a bitch." He slapped Ty on the arm.

Ty shrugged and smiled back. "I learned from the best." He glanced at the monitors. "You want me to set up one of the girls for you?"

Frank nodded. "Both of them this time," he instructed. He looked over at Ty. "Don't you want to see the three girls together?"

Ty looked at the monitor and slowly shook his head. "That wouldn't help the situation you just screwed up." He didn't want to share Jessica with anyone. "Come on."

Ty strode down the hall and opened Angela's door. She jumped, pulling her hand out from between her legs. Ty offered her a knowing smile.

"Come with me." He took hold of her arm as she approached him, trembling. He brought her to the room with the couch and left her handcuffed to the wall, where she couldn't get into anything. He opened Lisa's door and repeated the command and the short walk to the room, bringing her in and sitting her on the couch.

Frank was already at it, running his hands over Angela. Ty tossed him the keys to unlock her and went to leave.

"Aren't you staying?" Frank asked in surprise.

"No." He closed the door behind him. He had more important things to do, like getting a look at the hallway footage.

Inspecting the tape over and over, with the sound cranked, he repeated the crunching punch to her cheek through to when he slid onto the scene. He tapped the speakers, shaking his head. He clearly heard the punch and Frank's voice, but no sound emitted from her. In each pass, Jessica didn't utter a word.

He took a deep breath and stared at the monitor for a minute before he got up and headed to her room. He stepped in, walked over to her sleeping form, and kneeled beside her. He reached out, moving the hair from her face, gently tracing the bruise Frank left on her cheek.

How the hell did you do that?

Jessica's eyes fluttered but didn't open.

Ty stood and left the room before he woke her.

JESSICA HEARD HIS SILENT question and opened her eyes as the door closed.

I have no clue.

Survival Games Chapter 27

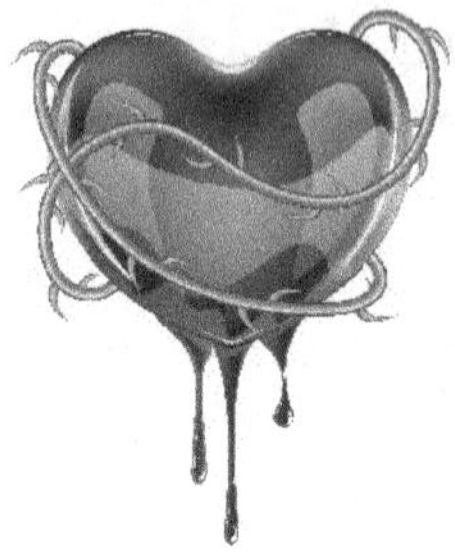

TY ADDED SOME VARIATION to the salads he brought her, including chicken Caesar or cob salad, giving in to her request for protein. He watched and waited as Jessica tore through the remaining stack of books he brought her. Each time she finished one, she would hand it to him with a small smile and a "Thank You, Ty" as he put down her tray. He would nod, take the book, and leave the room.

Neither Ty nor Jessica spoke about what happened in the hallway.

Jessica handed him the last book and looked up at him. "Do you have a deck of cards?"

"Yes." He left the room. He came back a few minutes later with a deck of cards, handed them to her, and went to leave.

"Do you know how to play Rummy 500?" she asked as he reached for the doorknob.

He slowly turned back toward her. "Why?"

"Want to play?" she asked.

She had no idea what that question did to him inside. He hesitated. He wasn't sure he could be in the room with her for any length of time without doing something he would regret.

"Come on." Jessica shuffled the cards from her position on the mattress.

He laughed. "I'm not playing cards with you on your bed." He slipped out of the room.

He stood in the hallway, taking a few deep breaths. He had no videos to edit today, and Frank was busy with board meetings, so he wouldn't have any quick interludes to tape either. In the past, he would busy himself with the women prisoners and have lots of footage to pare down, but since Jessica came into the complex, that well had dried up.

"Fuck it," he mumbled to himself.

In the kitchenette, he grabbed the card table stowed in the corner, along with two of the four foldable chairs, and headed back to her room.

Jessica's eyebrows rose in surprise.

"I'm bored." He set up the card table. "And this should prove to be entertaining." He took a seat in the chair closest to the door, pulling a pad and pencil out of his back pocket. He waved at the opposite chair with a small smile.

Jessica stood, walked to the table, and continued to shuffle while her gaze moved over his face like she was looking for the key to unlock his mind. She dealt the cards, and they played in silence.

"Why do you do this?" she asked, picking up a card from the deck.

Ty glanced at her and pressed his lips together. The rationale for his participation in Frank's venture wasn't something he was going to discuss with her, especially when he constantly questioned it himself. He looked back down at his cards without saying a word. She discarded, and he smiled a little. The card she'd dumped was the one he needed. He picked it up and laid his entire hand down, then placed a discard facedown on the pile.

"You don't talk much, do you?"

"Not a whole lot to say," he said, dealing the cards.

"What's your favorite color?" she asked, picking up her cards.

Ty raised his gaze to her. "Now why do you want to know that?" He organized the cards in his hand.

"Work with me," she said, furrowing her brow at the cards in her hand. "What's your favorite color?"

He laughed, amused by whatever game she was truly playing. Her cheeks flushed.

"All right," he said, picking a card from the deck. He glanced at it and discarded. "Blue."

"What color blue?" She picked up most of the cards he had discarded and laid an ace, king, queen and jack of hearts down, as well as three fours.

"Blue," he repeated, drawing his eyebrows together. Blue was blue.

"There are a lot of shades of blue. Which one?" She bit her lower lip, studying her cards.

Ty took a deep breath and tried to concentrate on his cards and her question, analyzing both. He glanced back up at her as he discarded and honed in on a proper description. "Late afternoon sky when you have sunglasses on."

Jessica slowly looked up at him as goose bumps covered her exposed arms.

"What?" he asked, observing the slow bleed of color from her cheeks.

"That's word for word the way I described my favorite color," she whispered.

A shiver started at the base of his spine, but he crushed it with a smile. The irony in the fact they described it the same way was not lost on him. "It is what it is." He laid his cards out again with the familiar discard facedown.

"Damn it," she said. "I hate losing."

"I never lose," Ty said, making her look up sharply at him. He rubbed the back of his neck.

"That so?" she retorted.

Ty leaned back and grinned, trying to loosen the knot in the back of his neck with his fingers.

"Sore neck?" She shuffled the cards.

"A little," he said.

"What happened?"

Heat filled his cheeks. "I fell asleep in a chair watching you."

"Ah," Jessica replied and shuffled the cards again. "Am I that boring?"

He laughed and tilted his head. "No, you are anything but boring." He rolled his head back, still working at his stiff neck.

She continued to shuffle. "I'll tell you what. Since you never lose, why don't we play a hand of poker? If you win, I'll fix your neck; if I win, you let me go."

He raised his eyebrows and laughed at both the proposition and her audacity. "That's hardly a fair bet."

"For someone who is so sure he always wins, that sounds a little like waffling to me."

"Make it sweeter," he said, "and I'll consider it." He leaned back in the chair and crossed his arms. *Check*, he thought.

"I'll give you a massage," she said. "*If* you win."

Checkmate.

He smiled. The thought of her hands willingly on his body sent a delicious thrill down his spine. "Still, a massage versus your freedom?"

He held his hands out like a balance, moving them up and down as he cocked his head. "Mmm, I don't know. Still seems a little unbalanced to me."

"I give a killer massage." Jessica slowly smiled. "Someone once said I had magic hands." She wiggled her fingers and went back to shuffling.

That little nugget intrigued him. He took a deep breath, nodding. "Deal the cards."

"Five-Card Stud." Jessica dealt five cards to both of them. She picked up her cards.

Ty glanced at his cards, pulled two out, and put them facedown on the table. Just in case she didn't already get the cue from his cards, he held two fingers up, keeping his expression neutral as his heart picked up speed.

Jessica dropped two cards as well and then dealt each of them two cards from the deck. Her lips spread in a grin. Ty glanced at her cards as she spread them on the table. She had two pair, ace high.

"Not bad." Then he unleashed a smile of his own. Her smile faltered as he slowly fanned his cards out on the table. "Full house." He stood and turned the chair around, taking a seat with his arms folded over the back of the chair. "I told you, I never lose." He peeled his shirt off. "Pay up, babe."

"First of all, I'm not your babe," she said.

He cocked an eyebrow. "Reneging on the bet already?"

She sat back in her chair, silent at first, and then an incredulous laugh escaped. "No." She dragged her chair and set it down behind him.

He glanced over his shoulder at her. The smile was gone, concern replacing it. Her fingers gently traced his scars. The evidence of his childhood was still visible in the welts on his skin.

Her gaze moved to his, questioning him without words.

"That isn't a discussion for today," he said. "Pay up."

She sighed and nodded, sliding her hands up to his shoulders. Her thumbs began the painful task of working out the kinks. Her fingers were strong and demanding, but gentle at the same time. Hypnotic. He allowed himself to relax under her mastery.

"If I had won, would you have let me go?"

Ty's eyes fluttered open, and he glanced back at her. "I don't know," he said in all honesty. He put his head down on his folded arms, and she continued rubbing his back, neck, and shoulders.

He turned his head to the side. "You do have magic hands." He closed his eyes, allowing himself to drift off as she continued her slow, deep massage.

HIS EYES WERE THE same color blue that she loved.

Jessica broke out in a light sweat, the temperature rising with every stroke of her hands on his skin. She traced the scars on his back, kneading the muscles as she studied the traversing pattern. Despite the disruptions to the perfect skin, it was smooth and warm, and the muscles underneath well defined. After finding the kinks in his neck, she gently massaged them out. A small rumble of pleasure formed in his throat.

Jessica watched him sleep on the table with a sweet smile on his face. She sat down in the chair, reluctantly pulling her hands away from him.

His eyes fluttered open, and he straightened, turning toward her, his eyes that deep, penetrating blue that capture her soul.

"I really should be going." He put his shirt back on.

She nodded and stood, pushing her chair back and stepping aside. "Thank you."

He paused and looked down at the table, a hint of regret tracing his features. With a slight shake of his head, he reached for the deck of cards and notepad, handed them to her, and then folded up the table. He folded the chairs next, picked them all up in one hand, and opened the door with the other.

The game was just beginning for her. As the door latched, Jessica smiled. If he had seen the grin on her face, he probably would have taken her on the floor just to spite her. She was hell bent on winning the game she played with him, and regardless of how much he melted her core, she wanted her freedom more. She wiped the grin off her face and turned back toward the cameras.

Survival Games Chapter 28

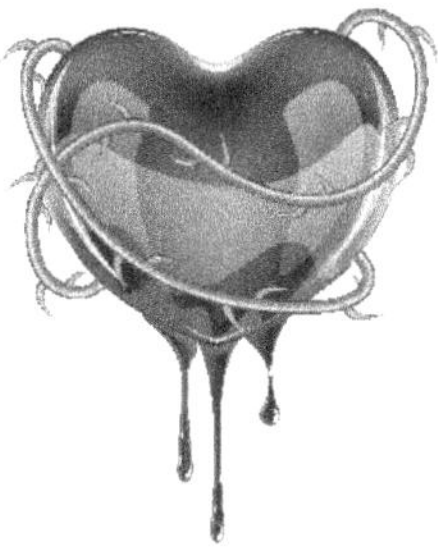

THE NEXT MORNING WHEN Ty came in with breakfast, Jessica held up the cards. "Rematch?"

Ty smiled and waggled his eyebrows. "Strip poker?"

Jessica laughed and shook her head. "No. Rummy."

"Sure," he said, although the prospect of playing strip poker sounded much better to him, especially considering the stupid bet he'd made the day before. His brain had rolled that around all night, wondering if he would have honored the deal had she won. It didn't even occur to him he could lose, and he recognized that as a reckless, impulsive decision. Thankfully, it went his way, but the what-if scenario clung to him.

He collected the table and chairs, wondering what the hell kind of game she would bring forth today. He stepped into the room, set up the card station where he had yesterday, and took his designated seat near the door.

Jessica shuffled and dealt the cards. Her brow furrowed.

"What's going on in that head of yours?" he asked before he looked at his cards.

"Why have you left me alone?"

He waved to the card table and raised his eyebrows.

She rolled her eyes at him. "You know what I mean." She leveled a look that shot right through him.

He bit his lower lip. Such a complicated and extremely direct question. He did not know how to answer her, so he turned the tables. "Would you prefer I don't leave you alone?"

"No. I was just wondering what you are up to."

She discarded, and he dropped his cards, grabbing her hand as his frustration rushed to the surface. He yanked her towards the table. "I've been wondering the same. You see, I recognize a game when I see one."

Jessica pulled her hand away and sat back in her chair, out of his reach.

"Do you really think I'm that stupid?"

"One could only hope."

Her answer caught him completely off guard, tempering the boil down to a low simmer. He burst out laughing. "I'm far from stupid," he said. "Let's finish the card game." He straightened his back, picked up his cards again, and stared at her expectantly.

Jessica reached for a card. This time she went out, happily placing the discard facedown on the pile.

"Have you ever played chess?"

"No."

"Really?"

"Nope, never played it."

"It's a game of strategy. It would be very interesting to see how you do." He smiled and shuffled the cards.

She studied him. "You're much more talkative today."

"Rummy isn't all that challenging. But I've got a better game for you." He put the cards down. "Come here."

Her complexion paled.

He turned his chair and pointed to the spot in front of him. "Bring your chair over here."

Jessica hesitated.

"It's a game of how well you can read people," he said.

She cocked her head as interest sparked in her eyes. She dragged her chair over the concrete and sat facing him.

He reached out and grabbed the front of the chair, pulling her until their knees touched. "You can't be yards away for this one." He shifted in his chair, getting himself set. "Put your hands out like this." He put both hands out, palms to the floor. Jessica did as she was told. "This is the game of flinch. Have you ever played it?" He put his hands palms up under hers.

Jessica shook her head a little.

"You have to anticipate your opponent's next move," he said, and like lightning, slapped the back of her hand lightly. "You need to move the hand away the instant that your opponent makes his move. If you flinch and move it away before he actually moves his hand, then you lose."

"Kinda like chicken."

"Precisely."

"Bring it on." Jessica watched his eyes instead of his hands.

The first time he made a move, she pulled her hand away, and he slapped nothing but air.

She grinned. "This is easy."

"Oh, really." He laughed and then, on the next move, he caught her. A measure of triumph filled him.

"Ouch." She shook her hand. She put them back out a little more hesitantly this time.

He suppressed a smile. He flexed his arm without moving his hand, and Jessica yanked her hand away in anticipation of the slap. "You just lost."

"That's not fair. You cheated." Jessica pulled her hands away.

"No, I didn't. Faking you out is part of the game, and you flinched."

"My turn." She put her palms up.

He obliged, putting his above hers. The first time she slapped his hand, his eyebrows rose at the sting. He sucked air through his teeth and shook it out before putting his hands back in play. Jessica tried to move her arm just like he had, but he anticipated that, and didn't move. Humor filled him, and he smiled.

The third time, she caught nothing but air. Her lips pursed, and then she tried again, catching him the next three rounds until the skin on the back of his hands burned from the slaps. His smile faded.

Jessica laughed after she tagged him a dozen times, but to his credit, he never flinched when she tried to fake him out.

Ty grabbed her hands the next round. The connection was something alive and real, almost sending sparks into the air. He stared at her, his smile fading. "I want you." The words tumbled from his mouth before he could stop them.

"I know," Jessica answered, dragging her hands away from his.

"No, Jessie, you don't know." He backed away from her before he did something he would regret. He stood and folded the table and chairs.

"I'm sorry if I upset you," Jessica said, her eyes wide and sincere.

"I don't want to play games with you." He went to leave, but took a second to glance over his shoulder as he opened the door.

"Then let me go."

He paused, meeting her gaze, but said nothing. He closed the door behind him and walked into the hallway, heading straight for the control room and the bathroom beyond. Looking at his reflection, the stark truth hit him like a brick in the face.

"I love her," he whispered and closed his eyes. All this buying time crap he fed to Frank had sealed his fate. Either way, he was screwed.

He leaned on the sink with his head hanging over and took a deep breath. He had no clue of what to do now.

"God damn it," he whispered in frustration, and headed back to the control room.

Survival Games Chapter 29

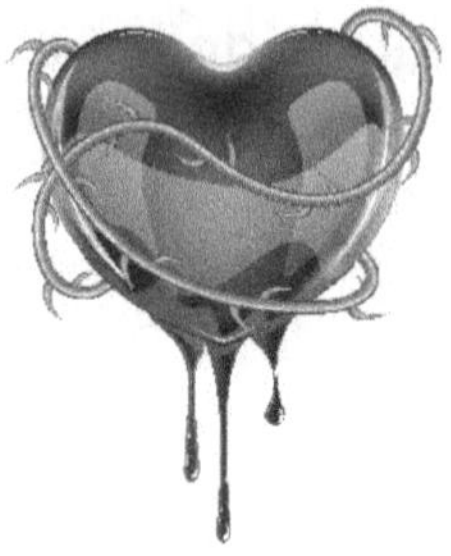

TY SAT IN THE control room, rolling a pencil through his fingers and staring at the monitors with his feet resting on the console. His mind replayed every encounter with her, every glance, every spoken word, every nuance of her body language. He shook his head. Why the woman wouldn't admit to the feelings he saw in her eyes frustrated the shit out of him.

He focused on her monitor where she sat, idly playing solitaire.

She had no clue.

No clue that he hadn't touched anyone since the day he first put her with Chris and Frank.

No clue that he had no inclination to find another release for the pent-up sexual energy boiling in his blood.

No clue that he constantly turned escape scenarios over in his head, trying to find a way to get her out of this place without losing her.

And she had no clue how dangerous the game he was playing would become if Frank ever doubted his actions.

He grunted. If Frank found out what he was trying to pull, he would bury him alive.

On more than one occasion, Frank had tried to coerce him into joining the festivities, but each time, he declined with a lame excuse. He caught the sideways glares Frank sent his way, but up until now, he'd gotten away with it because he edited some first-rate footage of Angela and Lisa and Mike. He wondered just how long that would last before Frank insisted on his participation, or worse, insisted on Jessica's participation.

While he wasn't interested in the sideshow sex with the girls, tormenting Mike still held a certain thrill. He'd occasionally play the video for him as a reminder, smiling when Mike freaked out and screamed at the camera.

He glanced at the pile of *Metropolis* discs and sighed. If he could get that acquisition in the door, it might be enough to distract Frank and get her the hell out of here.

The phone rang, and he snatched it off the hook before the second ring. "What?"

"I'm bored with Angela and Lisa," Frank said.

Ty took a deep breath. *Oh shit!* "What do you want to do?"

"I want you to take care of them."

Ty raised his eyebrows. "Me?" He was used to watching the killing, not carrying it out, at least not personally. He was the planner, the idea man, rigging explosions that killed from a distance, not a hands-on kind of guy. While he didn't have issues cleaning up after the fact, he had only taken a life with his own hands once, and that was years ago.

"Yes, you."

Ty hesitated and looked at the monitors. "You don't want to help?"

"I've got a board meeting, and I want one of them gone today. Think you can handle it?"

"I can handle it." He hung up the phone and stood, glancing at the monitors and trying to formulate how he was going to do what Frank had asked. His gaze landed on Jessica's monitor, and he shook his head. This was Frank's way of gaining more leverage, and the next thing he'd be asked to do would involve her.

Shit, shit, shit!

"Which one?" He put his hands on his hips, still looking between the monitors, frozen in indecision. "Fuck it."

He collected both Angela and Lisa and brought them into one of the performing rooms. A bed sat in the center of the floor, with nothing else in the room. Both of them scanned him hungrily, licking their lips, thinking their next sexual encounter would include him.

When he returned with a butcher knife, both women's brows creased in confusion.

"Choose." He put a knife on the bed between them.

He stepped back, far enough that if one of them turned the knife on him, he could react.

The girls looked at each other and back at him.

"Choose what?" Lisa asked, her voice shaking. She glanced at the knife.

"Who lives and who dies." He leaned against the door, waiting. His stomach clenched at the words, and he swallowed the remnants of acid that crawled up his throat.

Angela looked at him. "What if we don't?"

He sighed, his gaze bouncing between the two of them. "Then you both die." He didn't know if he could follow through on that threat, but it was exactly the kind of thing Frank would say.

Lisa grabbed the knife off the bed and stood holding it with both hands in front of her. The blade wavered as tremors overtook her lithe form. "I don't want to die."

"Then kill her." Ty nodded toward Angela.

Lisa looked at the blade in her tight grip, at him, and then at Angela. Her eyes filled with tears. "I'm sorry," she said to Angela, and then she advanced. As she rounded the end of the bed, Angela backed up against the far wall.

Lisa hesitated and turned toward Ty.

He saw the flash of realization in her eyes as they traversed from the weapon she held to his empty hands. When her gaze met his, he knew he'd made a mistake.

She lunged at him. He parried, blocking the knife with his forearm. The blade raked through his flesh, sending burning hot pain up his arm and into his shoulder. He grabbed the back of her neck and smashed her into the door, knocking her unconscious. The knife dropped from her hands. He slammed her face against the door again, smashing her nose and cheekbones, sending bits of bone into her brain, which killed her instantly.

Adrenaline rushed through his veins. He tossed Lisa's convulsing body across the room toward Angela. "Stupid bitch!" His roar filled the room.

His angry glare landed on Angela. He swiped the knife off the floor and stormed across the room, pointing the blade at Angela. She pressed herself against the wall, trying to dissolve into the concrete away from him. He stopped when he towered over her, the knife centimeters away from her throat. The tip of the blade vibrated from the fury encompassing him.

Angela cowered. "P-p-please d-don't k-kill me."

He ground his teeth and spun around, tossing the knife on the bed, and stormed out, followed by Angela's wail.

Survival Games Chapter 30

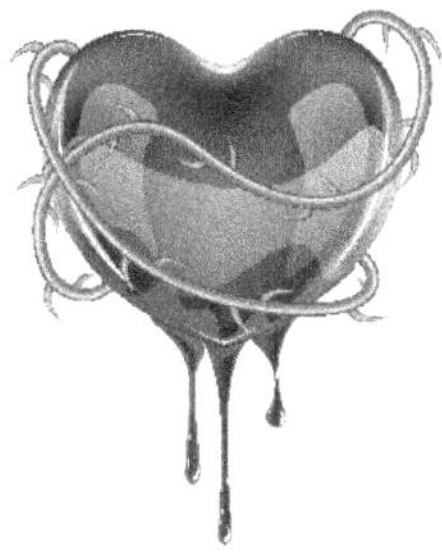

TY MADE IT TO the bathroom beyond the control room and threw up the meager contents of his stomach. He trembled as he rinsed his mouth and splashed water on his face. Blood dripped into the sink, reminding him he had taken a direct hit with the blade. He peeled his shirt off, concentrating on it as opposed to what he had just done.

The cut was deep enough to require stitches, but not deep enough to be life threatening. He closed his eyes and stepped into the doorway, staring at the monitors. When his gaze landed on Jessica's, he followed the pull that gripped his heart.

"It's all about you," he mumbled under his breath, giving in to the need to be near her. He pushed open her door and walked in, shirtless and still dripping blood.

She jumped when the door banged shut behind him.

"Oh God, you're bleeding."

He nodded and walked to her, leaving a trail of red droplets. She started to get up, but paused when he shook his head and kneeled on the end of the mattress.

"Do you believe in redemption?" he asked.

Jessica raised her eyebrows and cocked her head, searching his eyes before focusing on his arm. She reached out and took his bloody hand, turning it slowly so she could see the wound. She sighed and looked up at him, still not answering his question. Then she led him into the bathroom and motioned for him to take a seat on the closed toilet lid.

Ty watched her, and with every beat of his heart, his arm answered with a throb. When she dropped a washcloth in the sink and turned on the water, he raised an eyebrow. He hardly felt the swipes of the washcloth. Her gentle touch stirred his need, taking it to the edge of boiling over.

"Do you believe in redemption?" he asked again.

She said nothing at first, continuing to clean his wound. "I don't know."

"Why are you doing this?" he asked, pointing his chin at her.

She shrugged. "Because you're hurt, and it's in my nature to help."

"My nature is much darker."

She nodded.

He reached his good arm around her waist, closing the minimal distance between them. "Much darker." he crushed his mouth to hers.

Her lips parted, allowing him access to the sweet depths. He plunged his tongue inside, tasting her, relishing the slow circles of the exquisite tongue dance. Pulling her closer, the kiss deepened, stirring the molten lava flowing through him, his bloody arm forgotten in the wake of the building sensual heat.

Breathless, she yanked herself away and backed against the wall to the shower stall, her eyes wide with surprise, her chest heaving. "I can't," she whispered.

"Yes, you can." He stood.

She moved out of his reach into the shower stall.

Ty blocked the entrance to the shower and slipped his clothes off, never breaking her wide-eyed stare. He flipped the water on, drenching the nightshirt she wore, and he stepped under the warm stream.

"I know you feel the same things I'm feeling. I see it in your eyes." His mouth found hers again, and his hands glided down the wet nightshirt toward the hem.

"God help me," she whispered, and the nightshirt slid up and over her head.

He kneeled, trailing kisses down the front of her as he tore her underwear off. His hands slid up the inside of her thighs, spreading them enough for him to find the spot that made her moan.

She gasped, running her hands through his hair, tilting her head back against the cool tile as he teased her. His lips glided over her skin, reveling in her, sucking, biting, licking, kissing until he found her mouth again.

"I need you," he whispered against her lips. The admission sent shock waves through his body.

Her palms slid down his chest to his sides, and she squeezed, digging her nails into him, and pulling him closer. It wasn't the spoken words he wanted, but it was enough.

"Oh, God!" she breathed.

He picked her up, wrapping her legs around his waist and thrusting his hard member inside her. This time, her lips crushed his, taking his breath away.

"Tell me you love me," he whispered and kissed her neck, pushing deep into her.

She arched, letting a soft moan escape. Her hips circled slowly, seductively with him, and she sucked his earlobe. "Tell me," she said in a low, husky voice.

"Jess," he moaned and tore his lips away from her neck so he could see her eyes.

She gently traced the line of his shoulders with her fingertips, her other hand embedded in his hair. She arched, pushing her hips into him and throwing her head back. Her body tensed with the climax rippling through her. The moan of pleasure escaping her lips pushed him over the edge and he plunged deeper, his own orgasm exploding inside her.

He gently set her down on her feet and caressed her cheek. The blood dripping from his arm caught his attention. He needed to address his wound and the mess he'd made in the other room before he could think about what had just happened.

He stepped out of the shower and toweled off, pulling his pants back on before he turned to her. She wrapped herself in a clean towel, meeting his gaze.

"You never said it," he said.

"Neither did you," she responded, leaving them at a stalemate.

What the fuck am I doing? He wrapped his arm in the blood-streaked towel and left the room. When he got to the door, her voice stopped him.

"Ty?"

He paused and looked at her standing wrapped in a towel, her hair tousled, and her cheeks flushed, and he realized there wasn't anything he wouldn't do for her.

"I'm hungry. Is there any way I can get a steak in here?" She sheepishly looked down at her feet.

At least she didn't ask me to let her go. He smiled and nodded. "I can do that, but only if you let me join you."

She hesitated and glanced up at him. "Okay."

"It may take a little while. I have to take care of this," he said, showing her his bloody arm.

She nodded, and he closed the door behind him.

While he would rather relish the last half hour in his memory, he had work to do, like getting rid of the body in the warehouse incinerator. Ty crossed to the room where he had left Angela with a dead body.

He opened the door, and she looked up from her vantage point on the floor, the knife clutched in her hand.

Her swollen red eyes found his. "You killed her."

Ty nodded.

Her lower lip quivered.

"Put the knife down."

She stared at him, then lowered her eyes to the knife. "You almost killed me."

Ty sucked air in through his nose and slowly exhaled with another nod. "Put the knife down," he repeated, closing the door behind him.

She looked around the room, and her eyes landed on Lisa's broken body. "Do you think it hurts?"

"Do I think what hurts?"

"Dying."

He bit his lip. Death in this place was always accompanied by screams of pain and terror. Lisa was the first casualty of theirs who had died a quick and relatively painless death. "Yes. Now put the knife down."

Angela stabbed the point of the knife to her throat and threw herself forward, sending the blade through her neck.

Ty pressed his back against the door, the horror of her suicidal death clenching his stomach and overriding all the recent images in his mind.

She gasped and gagged, bucked and twisted on the floor, grasping the knife and yanking it sideways. It tore her throat open further as death rode her slowly into oblivion.

His gazed moved from one dead girl to the other as his veins turned to ice. He'd just put Jessica within Frank's sights.

I need to get her out of here.

He backed from the room, rattled by what he had done. He headed into the bathroom off the kitchen and splashed water on his face, studying his reflection in the mirror. Haunted blue eyes stared back from a trembling form. "Get your shit together," he snapped at his reflection. There was no time to freak out. He had to go about business as usual until he could put an alternate plan together to get Jessica out.

He shook the images out of his mind and opened the medicine cabinet in search of a bandage to cover the cut on his arm. He found a box of butterfly Band-Aids, antibiotic ointment, as well as a good-sized bandage he could cover the entire cut with. When he was finished dressing the wound, he picked up the phone and called Frank.

"In a meeting," Frank said.

"I need to take the trash out," Ty said.

"That's fine," he said. "The cleaning crew isn't expected for another hour. Does that give you enough time?"

"No problem. I'll be out of their way by then," Ty replied. That meant he had less than an hour to get this done.

Ty grabbed a dozen dark green garbage bags and a pair of plastic gloves and walked into the utility room. Looking around, he decided on the quickest tool to do what he needed. He grabbed the chainsaw. He also grabbed a dolly to transport the full bags to the incinerator. There was always a risk of being seen, and the timing needed to be coordinated.

He covered the bed with plastic and went about the gruesome job of cutting the girls up and placing their parts into the bags and then onto the dolly. Once he was done, he took off his clothes, stuffed them into a bag, and switched on the overhead sprinklers to clean the blood off his body and the concrete floors.

A thick trail of gore poured down the drain in the floor, and he almost gagged. He closed his eyes to get his stomach in check.

He rubbed his arms, face, and chest with disinfectant and stood with his head tilted back as the spray cascaded down on him. When the water ran clear, he switched the sprinklers off, stripped the bed of the plastic tarp, and left the room.

He pushed the dolly toward the elevator, stopping long enough to wipe himself with a clean towel, change the soaked dressing on his arm, and put on a jumpsuit and a hat that would label him as a member of the janitorial crew if he were seen. As he walked out of the room, he grabbed a key off the wall. He stood in front of the retinal scan and waited for the elevator doors to open. Once inside, he put the key in and pressed the button leading to the basement of the warehouse.

He got to the incinerator without incident and heaved the bags in. He closed the door, and they melted in the heat. He didn't wait to see the rest. They would be ashes in a matter of minutes. He walked back to the elevator, turning his focus back to Jessica and the question he'd asked her.

After today, there was no redemption for him.

He thought about just making Jessica her usual dinner and leaving it at that, but the sheepish way she'd asked for steak crawled under his skin. He couldn't deny her a nice dinner, despite his total lack of appetite.

Now that both Angela and Lisa were gone, Frank would be on his ass regarding Jessica. He closed his eyes, leaning against the back of the elevator. Mike would only satisfy him for so long, and he had to figure out a way to keep his stepbrother's attention on anything but Jessica. His eyes opened with the whoosh of the elevator door opening.

But first, he had a steak dinner to deliver.

He changed into another pair of jeans and pulled out a black button-up dress shirt, slipped on socks and sneakers, and placed a call.

He put the phone down and looked at the monitors. Something about bringing the card table into her room for a special dinner didn't sit right with him. He looked at the room with the sex couch and decided against that as well. He walked into the kitchen and shook his head. This wouldn't do either—too many sharp objects for her to get ahold of.

That left an array of empty cells to choose from. His gaze landed on the only room in the place without an electric chair or mattress included. It was small, nothing more than an oversized supply closet, but it had the mirrored wall and cameras, so he could have a memory of this night if everything else went to shit.

He grabbed the card table, two chairs, a tablecloth he found in one of the kitchen drawers, along with a couple of wine glasses, and headed to the empty room. He set the table and stepped back, scanning his work. Something was missing. He turned, heading to the kitchen, and rifled through all the drawers and cabinets but came up empty.

How can we not have candles here? He grabbed the ice bucket, filled it, and placed it on the table in the room.

He glanced at his watch and headed up to the ground floor. Frank's eyebrows rose when he stuck his head in the office.

"Everything okay?" he asked.

"Yep." Ty headed to the garage. "Just going to grab some dinner. Be back in a few."

True to his word, he was back within fifteen minutes, carrying a large takeout bag and a bottle of wine. Ty set the plates out on the table, put the bottle in the ice bucket, and went to get her. He swung into the control room, dropped the CD in, turned it on low, and flipped the switch to feed it into the room.

He hesitated and looked at the screens. She sat on the bed with the towel around her. While he would love to have dinner with her only wearing a towel, he was sure she wouldn't appreciate that at all. He turned and looked at the selection of dresses in her size and picked his favorite, along with a pair of matching sandals.

His gaze landed on Mike's monitor. He wanted the bastard to know he'd won the game, that she belonged to him. He flipped the live feed from the mock dining room to his monitor.

"This'll kill him."

Ty left the control room to collect his date.

Survival Games Chapter 31

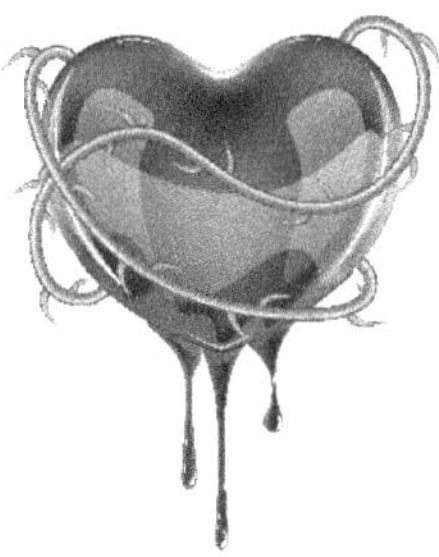

MIKE LOOKED UP AT the screen and saw a beautifully decorated table with two plates, wine glasses, and silverware. A bottle opener lay on the table next to the ice bucket, which held a bottle of Zinfandel. The plates were covered with warmers you would find in an upscale hotel, and music played softly in the background.

When Ty escorted Jessica into the room, Mike stopped breathing. She was wearing a floor-length white gown with a slit that came up to her hip. She had her hair up in a clip, and she was stunning.

Ty held her chair, pushed her into the table, and pulled the warmer off in a grand gesture. She looked down, taking in the delectable meal on the plate before her, and then smiled at him.

She fucking smiled at him!

He opened the wine and filled their glasses. When he put the bottle back in the ice bucket, he looked into the camera. He slowly smiled directly at Mike.

Mike approached the monitor and punched it with everything he had, shattering it to pieces. The image shattered with it.

He paced the room, oblivious to his cut hand and broken wrist. "How could she?"

Survival Games Chapter 32

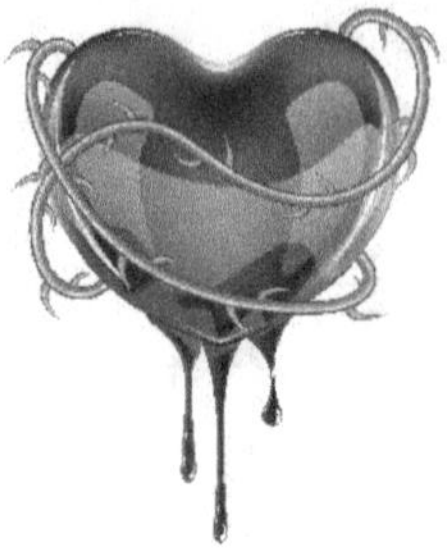

JESSICA STOOD WHEN HE walked into the room. He held an amazing dress, sandals, and a hair clip, offering them to her.

"Your dinner awaits," he said, waving toward the door in a grand spectacle.

Irritation and attraction fought for control in her blood. "I'm not Cinderella, and you're certainly not Prince Charming," she replied, making sure he was clear about where she stood, despite what had happened earlier.

She took the dress and the hair clip and headed to the bathroom to put it on. The white silk fabric caressed her skin, and she smoothed it over her abdomen, loving the way it felt. It reminded her of his hands. She had to take a slow breath to remind herself this wasn't a date; she was still his prisoner.

She brushed her long hair and twisted it into a bun, putting the clip in to hold it in place.

When she walked into the room, Ty dropped one shoe and fumbled with the other one.

Even though she was amused by his reaction, she didn't give any hint of it. Her face remained stoic as she glanced in the mirror, appraising herself, pleased with what she saw. She turned back to Ty, reaching for the shoes.

He brought them over, and she held onto his arm with one hand while slipping them on. She did the once-over in the mirror a second time and then turned back to him.

"It's a beautiful dress," she said.

"Mm-hm." He escorted her out of the room, glancing her way, and his bangs fell into his eyes. He ran his hand through his hair, pushing it out of his face, and smiled down at her.

Damn him. That smile transported her to another place. Everything switched to slow motion. The door swung open to a table decorated like it came from a restaurant. He held her chair and pushed it in as she sat, just like a true gentleman. He pulled the warmers off their plates with the same bravado a magician would have, and she grinned. Filet mignon with béarnaise sauce drizzled over it, along with bright steamed vegetables, awaited them. Her mouth watered, and she glanced up at him, seeing the need to please her reflected in his eyes.

She put the linen napkin on her lap and picked up her fork and knife as he sat down. She paused and studied the sharp steak knife in her grasp.

He picked up his wineglass, but it froze midway to his mouth. The smile on his face faded, and she caught the flash in his eyes.

Please don't. His thought echoed in her mind with all the fear she saw in his gaze.

"You trust me with this?" she asked, holding the steak knife, and ignored the shock of hearing his voice in her head.

He said nothing and brought the wine to his lips, taking a sip.

She smiled and cut her steak. The meat melted in her mouth, and she closed her eyes, relishing the taste. "This is amazing," she said. She couldn't remember the last time she had a steak. "How long have I been here?"

He took a bite and said nothing.

"How long?"

"Over five months."

Jessica stared, her next bite halfway to her mouth. She thought about how much had happened, but it still didn't add up. "Really?" She took another bite.

He nodded. "You weren't awake for the first six weeks."

That explained the time gap, but it still didn't feel like five months. Yet it felt like forever. She ate slowly, savoring the meal. When she finished, she drained the rest of her glass and held it out for more. The wine was going straight to her head like it always did.

"Thank you," she said. "For all of this." She waved at the table, then drained the glass again and offered it to Ty for another refill. The wine was doing its magic, relaxing her muscles and throwing her filter right out the window.

He sat with his hands folded on the table with a hint of a smile that softened his haunted eyes. Her insides twisted at the sight of him enjoying himself, and the spell that suspended reality for a few moments crashed down around her.

"I'm not getting out of here, am I?"

He didn't answer her.

"I have kids," she said.

"I know, two of them. A girl and a boy."

Her mother bear reflex roared to life. She picked up her knife, pointing it at him. "I will kill you if you go near them," she hissed.

"I wouldn't do that," he said. "Going after kids is wrong."

Jessica slowly put down the knife. *At least he has some scruples.*

"But your husband." Ty raised his glass, cocking an eyebrow.

Jessica paused and looked at Ty, narrowing her eyes. "My kids need their father."

"Do you love him?"

She blinked and sat back in the chair. "I've been with him for almost twenty years. He's the father of my children."

"That's not what I asked. Do you love him?"

"Of course," she answered, but there had never been the spark that existed between her and Ty. "But my kids need him."

He nodded slowly. "Kids shouldn't grow up without their parents."

She raised an eyebrow and finished the glass of wine, the effects of the alcohol warming her hands and cheeks. "And yet you have me locked up in here."

Ty shrugged a little and looked down at the table.

"I'm not getting out of here, am I?" she asked again.

He sighed and leaned back in the chair.

She knew just by his physical cues—she would not get an answer to that question. "What happened?" She pointed at his scar.

He put his hand up to his face self-consciously and then looked at her.

"I'll tell you my story if you dance with me." He slipped his shoes off and stood, then crossed to her side of the table with his hand extended.

She stared between his hand, and his eyes, and curiosity won out. She took his hand and let him lead her to the middle of the floor. He slipped a remote out of his pocket and pressed the button before dropping it back inside. Music encompassed the room.

When he pulled her close and started the slow sway with her in his arms, her heart swelled at the sensation of rightness filling her. It was as if the gods demanded their union, and she shivered, nestling farther into his shoulder. His arms tightened around her, and for a moment, she felt invincible.

HAVING HER IN HIS arms felt right. The same thoughts he had earlier echoed in his mind, especially now that Frank had no one else to play with.

I have to get her out of here.

She looked up at him. "What happened?" She traced the scar on his cheek.

He closed his eyes at her touch and sighed. "My stepfather," he answered. "He used to beat the crap out of me regularly. One day, I dropped his beer bottle when I was bringing it to him, and he decided to teach me a lesson."

"Jesus," Jessica whispered. "Where was your mother?"

He stiffened and looked at her. "She was dead. My stepfather killed her. Made it look like an accident."

Jessica put her cheek back on his chest.

He pulled the hair clip out, tossed it toward the table, and ran his hand absently through her hair as they danced. He kissed the top of her head and looked at the mirrored wall.

She had her eyes closed against his chest. Dressed in white with her long dark hair falling over her shoulders, she looked like an angel.

"Did he hit your brothers, too?" She stroked her fingers back and forth on the back of his shirt.

Ty squeezed her closer. "I did my best to protect Chris. Pissed the bastard off whenever I stepped between him and my brother." He inhaled. "The other one, Frank, he's my stepbrother. The sun rose and set on him. We were the old man's punching bags. He never laid a hand on his own kids." He stopped and pulled away from her. He hadn't ever talked about his past and didn't really want to talk about it now. "This is really not the subject I want to end our—" he twirled his finger around "—momentary escape from reality on."

He took her hand and walked her back to her room. Then he reached out and touched her face. "You really look beautiful tonight." He gently kissed her. Pulling away from her lips took everything he had. He turned and left her alone for the night.

SHE CROSSED TOWARDS THE mirrored wall, studying her reflection as her mind reeled from the last half hour. Her brain knew it was all kinds of wrong to be allowing him into her heart, but her heart had other ideas. He had already cut a piece of her and claimed it as his own, and she could not deny the electricity between them.

It went beyond chemistry. It was deeper than a physical connection. The fact she read his thoughts on multiple occasions unsettled her.

Movement out of the corner of her eye caught her attention.

Her chest squeezed, and fear wiped all thoughts from her mind.

Frank walked out of the bathroom dressed in a sleek three-piece suit, looking sharp and even scarier than when he was in jeans and a T-shirt. His glare was enough to make her bladder heavy. "What the hell have you done to him?"

"Nothing." She stepped back as he advanced.

"I beg to differ. A dinner date? That has never been part of his job description, unless, of course, he is fucking someone while feeding them." He cocked his head and narrowed his eyes. "And I did not see you bent over that table with his cock down your throat or pounding that pussy of yours."

She crossed her arms over her chest, trying to quell the shakes that had started. She backed into the mirror with her heart clamoring.

"Unfortunately, I do not have the time right now to dole out the proper punishment for turning one of my best money makers into a lovesick, googly-eyed boy." He glanced at his watch and then pointed at her. "I promise you, we will settle this score when I have the proper time to dedicate solely to you. And when I'm through, I'm sure he will think twice before he acts this way again."

He slipped out of the room as quickly as he'd appeared.

Survival Games Chapter 33

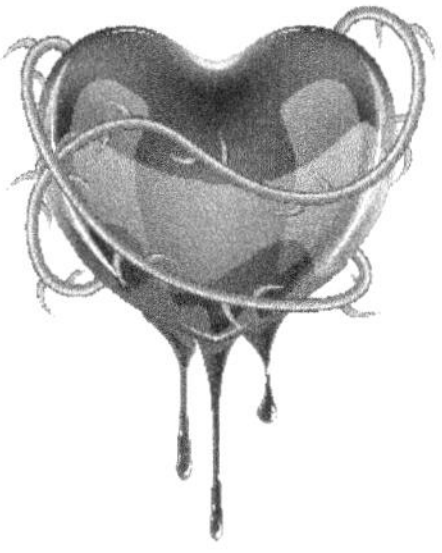

AFTER TY CLEANED UP the room, he found himself standing in front of her door. He turned away, taking a step toward the control room and stopped, turning back. He leaned with his hands on the doorjamb, fighting the urge to enter and just take her, take her in bed and take her out of there.

He reached for the doorknob and hesitated. He wanted to be with her tonight, and that urge won out. He stepped into the room and gently closed the door behind him.

He met her guarded gaze, blowing the air out of his lungs. Silently, he crossed the room like a lion cornering his prey, took her face in his hands, and kissed her.

She put her hands on his wrists and pulled away. "Don't," she whispered.

"I want you," Ty said. He slowly moved the straps of the dress off her shoulders and kissed her neck. The dress drifted to the floor, and he ran his hands down her arms.

"Please don't."

He kneeled down, slipping her heels off one foot after the other, and ran his hands up the outside of her legs, over her hips and behind her back as he stood. He leaned in to kiss her.

"He's watching," she whispered.

Ty stopped. "Who?"

"Frank."

"He's in a meeting." He went to kiss her again and paused, pulling back, searching her eyes. Fear lived in her irises. "I promise, no one is watching, Jess."

"Then turn the cameras off," she whispered.

He glanced up at the ceiling. The green lights flashed. He had left them on. Sighing, he brought his gaze back to hers. "I'm the only one with access to the tapes," he said. "Do you really want me to leave?"

She licked her lips as color bloomed in her cheeks. "Damn it." She reached out, grabbing the front of his shirt, pulling him to her.

This time, when their lips met, she kissed him like he was her lifeline. He took full advantage, deepening the kiss. Her fingers fumbled with the buttons on his shirt, and he joined her in trying to get the fabric between them out of the way.

Her hands slid along his chest, and fire burned deep in his soul. He ran his fingers along her sides, shifting his lips to the line of her graceful neck as he sought the spot between her legs that made her breathing hitch. He ran his tongue down the line from her ear to her collarbone, and her skin transformed into a landscape of goose bumps, followed by that breathy sigh that he could listen to for all eternity.

He swept her off her feet, bringing her to the mattress on the floor. "Tell me you want me," he said, holding her in his arms.

"You know I can't do that." She slid her hand up his chest.

"Tell me..."

She put her finger on his lips, stopping him. "Shut up and kiss me."

Ty leaned in, pausing a breath away from her lips, allowing a brief smile, meeting her hungry gaze with his own. "You want me to kiss you?"

Without saying the words, she took his lower lip between her teeth and sucked it gently before kissing him full on the mouth, playfully flicking her tongue and drawing his into her mouth. A low rumble of contentment formed in his throat as he laid her out on the mattress without breaking the kiss.

Passion, hot and urgent, pulsed through his skin, her body molding to his, her arms wrapping around his neck, and the kiss... God, her kiss stopped time. He ran his hands into her hair, increasing the intensity of their tongue dance, eliciting a soft moan in response.

Shifting, he shimmied out of his pants with her help, tossing them aside, and settled between her willing legs. He slid inside her already wet canal, her legs entwined with his. Then heaven's door opened, blinding him with unusual emotions.

Emotions long forgotten. Joy. Bliss. Ecstasy.

He stopped the slow grinding of his hips and broke the kiss, pulling away far enough to stare into her soulful brown eyes. Words alone could not express the tirade of feelings sweeping through him. He sighed, slowly curling his lips in a smile, letting passion take precedence once again.

"Roll," she said.

He tilted his head, the smile morphing into a grin. "You want me to roll?"

"For the love of..." She squeezed her eyes closed. "Just roll over."

He let out a light laugh and wrapped his arms around her, rolling over on the mattress. Jessica tossed her hair aside and stared into his eyes. Her gaze sparked a heat so consuming he forgot she was his captive in their prison.

She grabbed the front of the silk dress shirt he still wore and yanked him into a sitting position, stripping the garment off, and slipping it on herself. With his shirt on, she was even sexier than she had been in the dress. Smiling, she rolled up the sleeves and swung her hips in slow circles.

He leaned back on his elbows, his gaze locked with hers, and a playful smile flirted on his lips. When he reached for her, she caught his wrists, pinning them on the mattress by his head and smiled at his sudden inhale.

HE PRESSED HIS LIPS together, closing his eyes as he blew a slow stream of air before he opened them again. This time they were no longer smoldering—they flashed into an inferno.

"I kind of like you being in control," he teased, his low, raspy voice adding to the roaring fire consuming her.

Her lips trailed down the line of his neck, nipping at the salty, sweet taste of him. Smiling at the nuance of change in his breathing and the muscles flexing in his arms, she moved to the other side of his throat, licking her way up the line of his neck. She chuckled at his low moan when she gently bit down on his earlobe.

"Jess," he whispered, with eyelids at half-mast. He surrendered completely, allowing her to set the pace, matching her rhythm, their bodies in sync like lifetime lovers.

She found his mouth, nipping at his lower lip, tasting remnants of the wine from dinner before swirling her tongue with his. Her hips quickened, a tsunami of pleasure cresting until the wave broke. She arched, pulling away from his lips as she moaned his name.

The wave abated, still churning, waiting to reform and overtake her. She moved her grip and laced her fingers in his. A light sheen of sweat stood out on his forehead, evidence of his desperate need to keep control and make this last. His eyes searched hers, and he broke her clasp, sliding his hands down the length of her sides, his hot palms a sharp contrast to the cool fabric settling in the wake of his touch.

She shivered, flipping her hair out of the way again, studying the intensity of his gaze. Her entire life forgotten, the images of her dreams prevailed, converging to the moment with him kneeling in the snow before her, the diamond sparkling in his shaking hands, the cold ocean breeze filtering through her hair. Overwhelming joy encompassed her.

"Tell me you love me," she said.

He wrapped his arms around her and rolled, pinning her under him. He held her face, kissing her passionately, slamming his full length into her over and over. She arched into him with the same force each time. He pulled away from her lips and whispered in her ear the words she wanted to hear.

"Oh God," she cried.

The tidal wave overtook both of them until they lay spent and trembling in each other's arms.

HE ROLLED AGAIN, CONTENT to let her snuggle on his chest while he smoothed the hair away from her face. The suspension of reality that captured them came crumbling down, their situation as dire as the concrete walls surrounding them. They both exhaled.

"Ty," she sighed, closing her eyes.

He ran his hand over her back, back through the fabric of his shirt she still wore, trying to find words to the feelings overwhelming him. Feelings he had locked up for years. Emotions behind walls she'd chipped away at daily until that wall exploded to dust. Now, he couldn't escape the weight of them.

When she lifted her head, he pressed his lips together in contemplation. "You really are an angel sent to save me, aren't you?"

"I'm not an angel, Ty."

"I never knew..." he started and stopped, struggling to form words. "I never thought..." He closed his eyes in frustration, because he couldn't find the words. He drew in a shaky breath.

She lazily drew circles on his chest with her fingers, waiting patiently for him to continue.

He opened his eyes and tried again. "When my mom died, there were just the three of us." He took a deep breath. "And I was helpless to stop anything that happened to us. My stepfather beat the shit out of me regularly, and occasionally hit Chris, but the things he did to Anna were worse. I used to hear her cry at night after he left her room." He closed his eyes and squeezed her tighter before he continued. "She was sixteen when he killed her." A tear slipped out of the corner of his eye. He absently wiped it away.

"When I came home from school, he was sitting on the side of the bed next to her body. I had never seen so much blood. It covered the bed, the walls, even spots on the ceiling." He shook his head and bit his lower lip, meeting her gaze. "I killed him, Jess. The knife he used was on the ground near the foot of the bed, and I picked it up and planted that sucker into his back all the way to the hilt."

Ty trembled as the memory came flooding back. "I kind of freaked out. I was only twelve, but I was smart enough to wipe the knife. I made sure I didn't have any blood on me and left the house. I went to Chris's bus stop and waited like I did every day."

He paused, looking at the ceiling as a tear slid down and pooled in his ear. "The police pinned both murders on Anna's boyfriend. That's the day I became just like the son of a bitch." He blinked the sheen covering his eyes away and looked at her. "Everything that was good in me died that day," he said. "I didn't believe I was capable of feeling anything but anger until..." He inhaled. "Until you." He pulled her lips to his and kissed her. "Until you," he whispered again.

JESSICA TOUCHED THE SCAR on his face and looked into his eyes, breaking away from the kiss. Tears blurred her vision, and she pulled away, getting to her feet. "I'll be right back," she whispered and headed to the bathroom.

She put her fist to her mouth, silencing the sob that threatened and turned on the water to splash her face and wash the tear tracks. When she took the towel away from her face and glanced at her reflection, her son stared back.

Eric's eyes widened. "You need to fix him before the bad man comes." He pointed behind him towards the concrete bedroom. "He will protect you. Tell him not to go, Mom. Make him stay."

"Ty?"

Eric nodded. "Fix him. He'll protect you, but you have to make sure he stays." He held his arms out for a hug, and she leaned in, feeling his butterfly kiss on her cheek.

"Please," Eric whispered, and he disappeared.

TY PUT ON HIS jeans on and sat on the edge of the mattress with his head in his hands. His mind went over every option again and again. *How the fuck am I going to get her out of this building, away from Frank?*

His head snapped up. *Frank. Fuck. I need to get to the tape before he does.* He was halfway to the door when she stepped back into the room.

His heart skipped another beat at her pale cheeks, and he stopped, turning toward her. "Are you okay?"

She nodded, but her eyes... Her eyes had changed to that dark violet from the night she'd danced, and when she looked down at his arm, he followed her gaze to the bloody bandage. In one fluid movement, she ripped the dressing from his skin and leaned forward, pressing her lips to the oozing wound.

Pain, searing and furious, snaked up his arm. He sucked his breath in, yanking his arm away from her grip.

"Jesus Christ!" He shook his arm, droplets of blood springing off and splattering on the floor. He tore his gaze away from her bloody lips and haunting eyes to the fading burning sensation in his skin. He froze, his eyes popping in their sockets at the vision before him. The cut closed like a zipper, mending, healing, until nothing was left, not even a faint scar under the bloody sheen.

"Jesus, Mary, mother of God." He looked up at Jessica.

She took a step toward him and fell in a dead faint. Ty caught her, staring at the stark contrast between his blood smeared on her lips and her pale, corpse-like face. Fear, feral and savage, ravaged him, turning his legs to liquid. He sank to the ground with her in his tight grasp.

"Jess?" He shook her. "Wake up. Please wake up." He leaned down and sighed with relief when her light breath grazed his cheek.

Her eyes fluttered open, still that unearthly violet, and they locked with his. "What happened?" she asked. She ran her tongue ran over her lip and grimaced, then wiped the tacky blood away with the sleeve of his shirt.

Dear God, whatever she did changed her eyes.

He shook the thought out of his head and glanced down at his arm. "I have no idea." He widened his eyes in disbelief. He helped her to her feet, speechless and in awe.

He blinked and glanced at the ceiling, specifically at the cameras recording their every move, their every word. "Jess, I have to go erase the tape. I'll be right back."

Jessica's brow furrowed, and she glanced up at the cameras. She nodded slowly. When her gaze dropped back to his, fear lived in her violet irises.

"I promise I'll be right back."

He had to get to that tape before anyone else did. He didn't even glance back when he left and was in a full sprint by the time he rounded the corner.

Survival Games Chapter 34

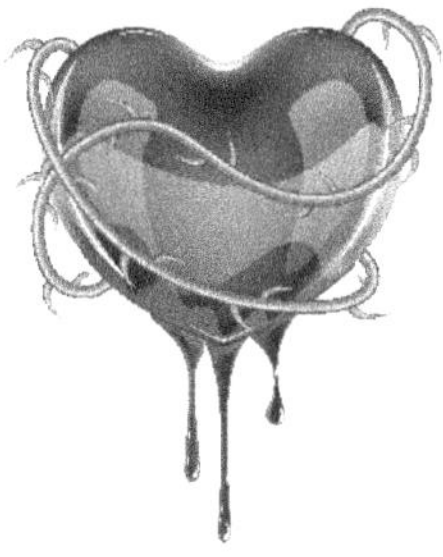

DANIEL WALKED INTO ERIC'S room to see his son opening his arms and hugging the space in front of him. He kissed an invisible being, and the air filled with sparkles before whispering a desperate plea.

Eric looked at his father, and tears welled, cutting wet paths down his cheeks. "He needs to protect Mommy, and I don't know if he can!"

Daniel put his arms around his son. This was the first time since they saw LeAnn that Eric had talked about his mother. "It's okay, Eric. Your mom's all right. She's in heaven now."

"No, she's not! And the bad man is going to hurt her if he leaves her." He was breathing heavily. "I need to help her open the door!"

"What door?"

"The door in her mind."

Daniel hesitated, a shiver sliding down his spine. "What's behind the door, Eric?"

Eric swallowed hard. "It's the only way."

"What's behind the door?"

"The power of heaven." He paused. "And hell," he added in a voice almost too low to hear.

Daniel looked at his son. LeAnn had said Eric was playing out a fantasy to deal with his mother's death and that it was a healthy reaction, but this... This didn't sound healthy at all.

Survival Games Chapter 35

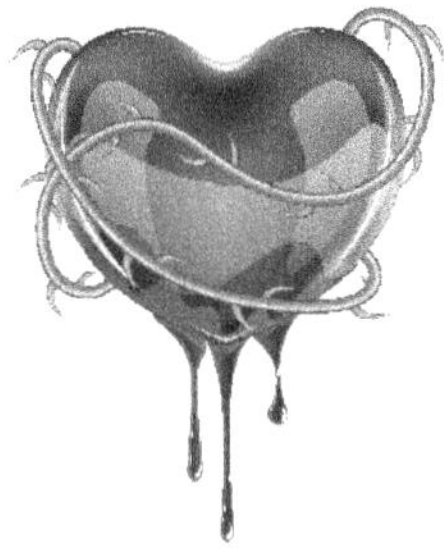

TY BOLTED TO THE control room, stopped the disk, and found the place that he wanted. He backed it up a few seconds and pressed record again, forever overwriting his confession and the miracle Jessica had performed. He closed his eyes, relief flooding through him in a dizzying whirl, and he sat down in the chair.

If Frank ever found out about either the confession or her ability to heal the wounded, Ty wasn't sure if either of them would get out of the building alive.

"How in God's name did you do this?" He pulled the butterfly Band-Aids off his perfectly unmarked arm.

When he finished, he glanced over at Mike's image. Pieces of the shattered monitor embedded in his ruined hand, and he paced back and forth, muttering under his breath, looking every bit as insane as Ty set out to make him.

An icy hand wrapped around his heart, and he moved his gaze back to the monitor overlooking Jessica's room. He swallowed hard, his palms suddenly slick with sweat.

What would she think of me if she knew?

He looked from monitor to monitor, frozen with indecision.

The phone rang, snapping him out of it.

"The call came. The package is ready to collect," Frank said.

Ty paused. "I'm not sure that's necessary."

"Look, Ty, you said yourself this will bring in a healthy profit. Everything's already in place. We've been contracted to deliver to the set, and I've got a truck waiting at the airport. The jet's gassed up and waiting to take you and Chris. You'll need to bring your passport because you're driving back."

"Frank, the risk."

"You said yourself, the payoff would be sweet. From the inquiries I made, you are absolutely right. But if you want to pass this up, I'd be glad to film with your girl tonight."

He could almost see the grin forming on Frank's lips. A shiver cascaded down his spine.

Not on your life.

He took a deep breath. "You have everything I asked for?"

"It's in a bag up here just waiting for you."

He closed his eyes and hung his head. With a heavy sigh, he nodded. "I'll be up in twenty." He was met with a click, followed by a dial tone.

He approached her room, apprehensive and kicking himself for the damage he would do in the next few days, all for a distraction to get her the hell out of there. And he had to make sure Frank would keep his distance while he was out of town.

Ty stepped into her room.

"Don't leave." She stood, her fingers nimbly unbuttoning the shirt, and she crossed, sinuous and seductive. She pushed him against the door and ran her tongue across his chest while tugging at the button on his pants, her violet eyes on him. "Don't leave."

He grabbed her upper arms and pushed her away. *How does she know?*

"I just know."

He hadn't spoken.

"Sometimes I just know things, especially…" She looked down and circled her toe on the floor. "Especially when it's accompanied by a powerful emotion," she explained. "So, don't leave." She caught his gaze out of the corner of her eye.

He listened to the song playing and closed his eyes. Ironically, it was "Angel" by Sara McLaughlin. He reached out and pulled her to him.

Frank could wait.

"Angel," he said, carrying her back to the bed. He took the shirt off and made love to her again, relishing the feel of her as if it were the last time.

HE SLAMMED THINGS INTO a duffel bag, and with each stitch of clothing, his mood worsened. *What the hell am I doing?* He glanced at the monitor in the control room yet again.

His black shirt was still wrapped tightly around her as she sat in the middle of the mattress, staring at the mirror. Staring at him. He could almost feel her exercising her will, demanding he stay.

Almost.

His gaze flicked to the monitor next to hers, and he sighed, the momentary spell broken.

Stalking to the elevator, he shook his head, clearing his thoughts, and stood in front of the eye scan, waiting. As soon as the doors opened, he slid inside, set his access key in the slot and turned it. He closed his eyes at the feel of her still with him as he headed upstairs.

Chris sat across from Frank, swiveling the chair back and forth in the oversized office. "What took you so long?" he asked, getting to his feet.

Ty shrugged and dropped his bag. He turned to Frank, half hidden behind the large mahogany desk.

"I won't be in the office for the next couple days, but I will have my cell with me if anything goes haywire," Frank said, keeping eye contact with Ty. "I'll be back before you get here with the package."

"Where are you going?" Ty asked.

"To a conference in the city. Marian is all set to watch over the complex." He pointed to the bag in Ty's hand. "Everything you asked for is in there, and the town car is waiting outside. I will let you bring your brother up to speed."

Ty picked up the bag and nodded. He wasn't thrilled about confessing his complicity in this part of Frank's business, or dragging his brother into the position of accomplice to the death he planned on doling out in the next few days. But perhaps his brother would be a valuable asset in his plan for escape.

Survival Games Chapter 36

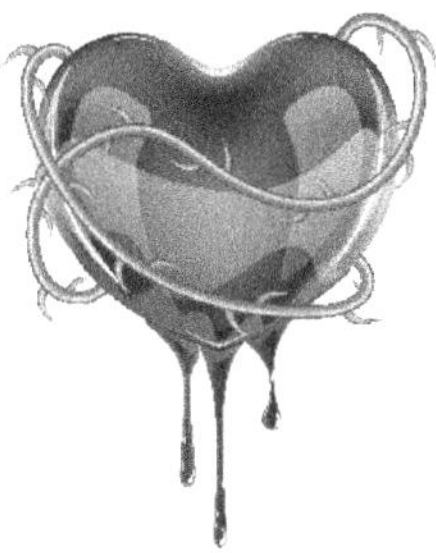

JESSICA SIGHED. THE CONNECTION she'd had with Ty severed, leaving her cold and alone in the concrete prison.

Please, God, please don't let that bastard come down.

She shivered, pulling the sheet tighter around her, laying her forehead on her bent knees. Closing her eyes, she drifted, counting her breaths and going deeper into herself until she stood alone in an unfamiliar hallway, the key turning precariously in her fingers. A noise caught her attention, and she glanced over her shoulder. Eric walked up to her and took her hand, leading her through the halls of her mind, turning this way and that until they reached their destination.

A huge door lined in white light stood at the far end of the corridor. The old-fashioned keyhole was easy to spot even at this distance. Jessica dropped her gaze to the key clutched in her hand.

Eric smiled as he pulled her forward, then stopped before the door. "You have to unlock it, Mom."

Her hand shook, and it took a couple of tries to get the skeleton key into place. Unlocking the labyrinth of her mind was not a simple task. The key barely budged at first, but with more pressure, it turned centimeter by centimeter until the telltale click filled the small space. She put her hand on the doorknob and hesitated. Fear gripped her muscles, cutting off the command from her brain telling her hand to turn the damn knob.

"What's behind the door, Eric?"

Dread etched into his features, furrowing his brow and pressing his lips into a tight, thin line. "It's the only way." He swallowed hard. "The *only* way."

"What's behind the door?" She crouched on one knee to look into his tiny face.

He kissed her cheek and whispered, "The power of heaven and the power of hell."

She experienced a fraction of the divine power tonight when she'd healed Ty, but it was the darker side of the equation that drove fear into her heart—the power to unleash hell. "I'm scared."

"So am I, but it's the only way." His eyes widened, and he spun away from her. "Mommy, he's coming!"

Her eyes flew open, and her head snapped toward the door. The terror in her son's voice echoed in her heart. She shot to her feet, her hands curling into fists and her eyes narrowing in a defiant glare. When the door opened, she was ready for the fight of her life.

Frank laughed at her, slipping a Taser gun from the back of his waistband.

She couldn't dodge fast enough. The talons hit her in the right shoulder. Pain seized her muscles, the debilitating shock crumpling her to the ground. A hiss of pain escaped her lips. She kept him in focus as he crossed the room.

Spasms racked her body in concert with the electrical surges. "Son of a bitch!"

"I promised you we would have this little coming-to-Jesus." Frank crouched in front of her, his dark eyes contemplating. "I should just kill you now." He clasped his hand around her throat and dragged her to the electric chair in the center of the room.

The shackles around her wrists and ankles clamped painfully into her skin. If she had any control over her muscles, she would have fought back, but she was still suffering the aftereffects of the taser.

He yanked the hooks from her skin and reconnected them to the gun before setting it aside. Then he inspected his handiwork.

"But if I killed you now, that just wouldn't be enough of a punishment to either of you." He turned and left her chained to the chair. When he came back, he carried a chair and a stack of discs. His cool composure frightened her even more. He set the discs down on the seat, and peeled his jacket off, and carefully folded it over the back of his chair.

He rolled up the sleeves of his designer oxford and leveled his dark gaze at her. He grabbed the first DVD and popped it in the slot below the television, then produced a remote from his pocket and took the seat next to her.

"I've got at least three days with you, sweetheart. But before I settle our score, there are a few things I want to get off my chest." He pointed the remote and hit play.

The screen transformed to another room with two women and Ty. When Ty set the knife on the bed and said "choose," she gasped, and the next words out of his mouth hit her like a blow to the stomach. When one grabbed the knife and turned toward Ty, just for an instant, Jessica silently cheered for her. However, the complete transformation of his face from resignation to a mask of rage drew her breath from her lungs. The violence in which he took her life shook her to the core. She knew he was dangerous, but this... this confirmed she was right on the mark with her earlier label of monster.

Frank stopped the video on the full shot of Ty's enraged expression. "Ty's a cruel son of a bitch."

She let out a laugh that bordered on hysterical. "Look who's talking."

His fist came out of nowhere. It slammed into her cheek, pain flaring even before her head hit the wood behind her. The laugh caught in her throat, and she squeezed her eyes closed until her breath returned.

"As I was saying, Ty can be a cruel son of a bitch, but I really didn't think lover boy had it in him." He stared at the screen before shooting her a glance. "Don't get me wrong, Ty has no issues blowing someone up or cleaning up after my adventures, but to actually kill someone with his bare hands?" He shook his head and then shrugged. "But then again, I didn't have all the pertinent information when I gave the order." He pressed the play button, and the scene jumped from the first death to the second and then the subsequent cleanup.

When it was over, she trembled, knowing exactly where the cut she'd healed came from and exactly what Ty was capable of. Eric's words echoed in her mind: *He will protect you.* She cursed under her breath, her vision warbling from unshed, unwanted tears. He had left anyway, and now she was at the mercy of the madman sitting beside her.

He stood to switch DVDs and then took a seat, pressing play to illustrate his point. Mike, staring at a screen in his room, his expression horrified, pained, devastated. He strained against the chains holding him in place, bellowing "NO" as the electricity flowed through her body on the screen before him.

She gasped. "No." *Not him. Not here.*

The video flickered to another scene, and Frank leaned back, stretching in the chair with his arms crossed and a smile on his face. "I'm not as good an editor as Ty, but I think this captures the gist of what we do."

Another violent death flashed across the screen, along with Mike's resulting catatonia. Her stomach churned, the steak fermenting into a rotting boiling ball. She swallowed the bile lining her throat, stifling a sob as well. Even the echo of Eric's words claiming Ty would protect her could not erase the humiliation.

Another rough edit jump and then there was Ty lounging next to Mike, watching the tape of his first seduction. The first time that bastard had made her eat her words, the first time his hands created magic in her skin, the first time she feared for her soul. And Mike watched it all—-the anger in his eyes sparked a fury in her aimed at the man taunting him.

She would never forgive him for this.

Ever.

The video jumped, and Mike was alone, staring at the screen. Even though Jessica had never seen the expression of betrayal firsthand, she recognized it in his eyes when she kissed Ty in Technicolor. Another jumbled edit. Again,

Mike's room. But this scene... This one sent her over the edge. Ty had set up a camera for their dinner and smiled that sly ha-ha-she's-mine smile into the camera, right before Mike smashed the monitor to pieces.

She bucked in the chair, a scream barreling from her mouth. No words, just a guttural cry of despair and fury, echoing off the concrete. The scream left her chest heaving and her breath raspy and harsh. "You fucking bastard!"

This time, when his fist shot out, she reacted, moving her head out of the way. She sent a dagger of a glare at him. His hand plowed into the wood headrest, and he yanked it back, shaking the sting from it. He wound up and shot his fist into her abdomen, folding her over in the chair.

Jessica fought for breath. Her stomach throbbed, threatening again to dump its volatile contents on the floor. She closed her eyes, willing both her body and her mind to ease up and relax, ignoring the pain for the time being.

But her anger... her anger she reigned into a state of controlled fury.

"I hate Ty. I've always hated him since the day his whore of a mother moved them in with us." Frank glanced sideways toward her. "After my father died, he was so easy to coerce into doing things like this gig." He waved his hand at the concrete walls. "Poor bastard didn't really understand the scope of my vision until it was too late, and by that time, I already had him believing this was the best he could do. This was where he belonged." He scoffed at her. "Gullible shit. Always following orders and trying to please me, like he had some debt to pay that I didn't know about."

Frank's jaw tightened, and his eyes went a shade darker, the anger blistering through. When he turned the glare at her, Jessica sank back in the seat. "Of course, all of that went straight to hell when he brought you through the door.

"He obviously doesn't know I have a backup recording system upstairs. I have my own collection. Not the edited versions, but the raw deal. So, any time a camera is live, I get a secondary recording in my office that I can look at any time I please. He's not the only one who's been watching you."

He shook his head and blew air out of his nose in disgust. "Your little games... He never really caught on, but I saw that satisfied smile every time he left your room. I saw you try the doorknob every day."

Another punch spun out, catching her in the side of the face, dazing her and drawing a moan of pain. Her eye swelled, and she shook her head, trying to focus on the blank screen in front of her.

Jesus, oh Jesus! He's going to kill me.

In that brief thought, the last encounter with Ty flashed in her mind, and her heart sank, spiraling her down into an abyss of despair.

I'm never going to see him again.

"At first, I thought he was playing you, too, but the look in his eyes when he threw me off you in the hallway... You can't fake that."

"Fake what?" she inquired, her voice hoarse, stalling the pain she knew was inevitable.

Frank turned, reached behind him, yanked out the Taser, and shoved it between her breasts. He pulled the trigger.

Her body went rigid. Spasms racked her, and the scream wavered in time with the shock pulsing through her.

"Shut the fuck up!" he bellowed in her face and let the trigger go.

Pain like tiny stabs covered her skin, dissipating slowly, but the terror... The terror grew, creating a mist of tears over her wide eyes and uncontrollable tremors throughout her frame.

Frank changed DVDs again, and the screen filled with her and Ty making love, her in control, riding him, holding his arms to the mattress. "In all my life, I've never seen him give up control like that." He pointed the remote at the screen, fast-forwarding to the conversation afterwards. "I knew I was in trouble and had to get him out of the complex, but then he confessed."

His hands curled into fists again, and she cringed away from him. "The bastard killed my father." The words hissed out between his clenched teeth. He turned his hateful gaze on her, tilting his head. "And you know the funniest part?"

Trembling, she shook her head and waited for his answer without looking at him.

He leaned in a fraction. "Ty killed the wrong person."

Her head snapped toward Frank, her mind reeling with the insinuation.

"I killed his sister." He let that hang in the air for a little while. "I've got plans for him now. The kind of plans this place was built for." Turning his dark eyes toward her, he reached out and grasped a handful of hair, yanking her head back. "And you. You're the pinnacle of my revenge.

"You see, I'm going to destroy everything he cares about, which, lucky for me, is limited to his brother and you." He slammed his fist full into her nose.

The snap of bone followed by the spray of blood filled her world. Debilitating pain caught her breath in her chest behind the river that flowed down her throat. She gagged, turning and leaning over the arm of the chair. Both blood and vomit shot from her mouth between harsh sobs.

"Three days." An evil, sadistic smile found his lips. "I'm betting he won't recognize you when he gets back." He let go of her hair and rewound the tape, watching her with him again. "I'm going to kill Chris, and then I'm going to make Ty watch the things I'm going to do to you." He slid his hand up her thigh and she shivered. "I'm toying with showing him exactly what I did to his sister."

He said nothing for a few minutes and then said, "I want to see his face when the last thing he loves on earth dies."

She braved a glance in his direction. "What makes you so sure he loves me?"

Frank fast-forwarded the tape, increasing the volume, and stopped just as he rolled her over. His husky, sex-laden voice rang through the room. "I love you, Jess."

She closed her eyes, and despite the betrayal and humiliation she felt, her heart ached for him. She couldn't stop the tears.

Frank stood, retrieved the last DVD, and tossed it on the small stack before turning his attention back to her.

She stiffened, aware that he'd stopped in front of her. She raised her eyes, daring to meet his angry gaze. "Is Mike still alive?"

The smile that formed chilled her as if she'd stepped outside naked in the middle of a Siberian winter day. "Oh yes, but you're going to kill him." He hit her again.

Her head snapped back, hitting the chair hard enough for blackness to drown her senses.

Survival Games Chapter 37

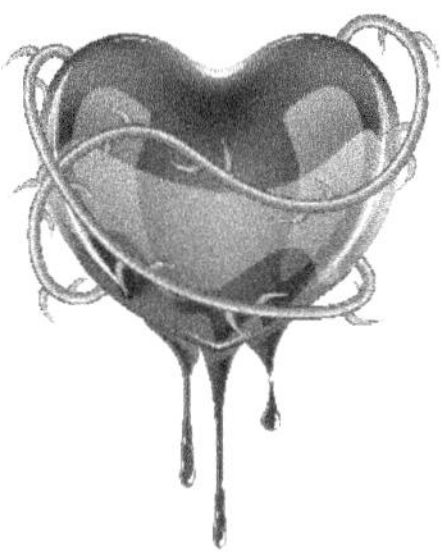

TY WATCHED THE CLOUDS pass by the window in silence. He hadn't said much since they'd left, and he couldn't shake the feeling that something was wrong. Very wrong. He sighed and glanced at Chris.

"What's eating you, bro?"

"There's a lot you don't know about our side business." Ty looked down at the floor. They were alone in the belly of the company plane. "Stuff I've kept you out of."

"Beyond kidnappings and making sex tapes?" he asked, his expression serious.

Ty nodded. "Sex is one thing, but Chris, I swear, if you ever saw the things Frank did... I purposely kept you out of that side of the business."

Chris's eyebrows furrowed.

"Where the hell do you think all those people went?"

Chris shrugged, blinking like his mind couldn't wrap around the information he was being fed.

"Did you think we just let them loose?"

"I don't know. I never really thought about it."

"No one we ever brought in left there alive." He measured his delivery for maximum impact.

Chris leaned back in the seat as his face paled. "I-I thought those were digitally enhanced, or you did some fancy work with computer graphics."

"No, every single video produced was real. Frank killed all those people, and I filmed it and cleaned up after him." He inhaled. "And this trip we are going on is another kidnapping. People are going to die. So, you are taking part in a premeditated murder."

Chris's eyes widened, and he pushed back in his seat. "Why are you telling me this now?"

"Because..." He stopped and glanced out the window. "Because Frank ordered me to." Both his jaw and his hands clenched. "Because he's trying to make sure I don't make a run for it by involving you in this side of his insanely fucked up addiction." The venom spilled out, wrapping around the words and putting a growl into them.

Chris studied him. "Why? Why did you go along with him if you hate it so much?"

Ty leveled a stare at his brother. It took a few seconds, and then Chris closed his eyes and leaned his head back against the headrest. "He threatened me, didn't he?"

"Yes. And to be honest, it wasn't all Frank. Once he coerced me into this, I got so I liked the sex part a little too much, and I'm a decent editor."

Chris huffed. "You're a fucking master at editing."

Ty's face heated at the compliment. "Well, I enjoyed having power over someone. It was quite the change from everything else in my life, so between that and some hot-as-shit sex, my moral code got truly fucked up. I did nothing to stop Frank and his violent fetishes, and I cleaned up his mess every time, so I'm just as culpable as he is."

Chris was quiet for enough time that Ty shifted in his seat. The admission of his part in all Frank's dirty dealings left him craving the sanctuary of Jessica's arms.

"So why the change in heart?" Chris asked.

Ty sat back in the seat and didn't answer right away. He chewed on his bottom lip, returning his gaze to the clouds, debating on how to broach this subject, which seemed infinitely harder than telling his brother he was party to murder. He decided head-on was the best route. "I'm in love with Jessica." His cheeks warmed, and he picked at a hangnail.

"You're in love with someone you kidnapped to make perform in sex tapes and someone Frank eventually will kill."

"That pretty much sums up the shit that my life has become." He looked at his brother. "This stunt is a diversion to get her out. And when I do, we need to disappear." He pointed between the two of them. "Because Frank is going to come after us with everything he's got."

"You know I love you, bro, and I'll do what I can to help, but are you sure she won't just turn you in?"

"I don't know. But it's a risk I have to take. Before I kidnapped her, I felt nothing. Empty. I have felt nothing since Anna died."

Chris's brow creased.

"How do you think I could do all this shit?" Ty asked and leaned back. "Our parents would be so disappointed in me. I mean, seriously. Dad was a cop. He put scumbags like me behind bars."

Chris reached out and put his hand on Ty's shoulder. "You've always tried to protect me, and I'll never forget that." He glanced out the window. "I'm not comfortable at all with killing, though. But sitting here and looking back, I can't say the thought didn't cross my mind when I saw some of the things you were editing. So, I'm not an innocent victim in all this either." He laughed. "And man, I looked forward to those calls. The sex was out of this fucking world."

Ty chuckled. "You don't have to help me with this. Just chill in the trailer while I do the bait and switch and make sure no one looks for him afterwards." He continued, detailing as much of the plan as he was willing to share.

Chris glanced out the window, wringing his hands. "Is she worth all this?"

Ty waited until Chris swung his gaze back at him. "Yes, she is worth it." *I'd walk through a roaring inferno for her.*

"Is it mutual, or will we be running from the law for the rest of our lives?"

"I don't know. I'd like to think so, but I'm not sure I would bet on it." He pulled out his phone and stared at the one snapshot he'd uploaded of her before he left the complex. "But I have to get her out, regardless of the consequences."

"Okay, when we get back, I'll help you get her out and we'll disappear."

"If either Frank or Marian are around, we'll have to play it cool and wait for an opening."

"Okay." Chris inhaled and looked out the window with a troubled expression.

The plane landed in Vancouver, and as Frank promised, there was a utility truck waiting for them. Ty inspected the truck, making sure everything he needed was there, including the sub floor holding area. Frank hadn't disappointed him.

They headed off toward the taping site and arrived late in the day, delivering the cables and equipment to the crew just in time for sunset. They were scheduled to stay on through the following day and transport the equipment back to New York.

The site director brought them to their accommodations, one of the less luxurious travel trailers that was dwarfed by the utility truck they drove. Ty noted the luxury lines were just on the opposite side of the lot. His target slept less than fifty yards from where he stood.

He slipped to the luxury end unit and picked the lock easily, then snuck inside and set up his equipment—a small explosive charge, a camera, and a sensor that would trigger chloroform mist. Quietly shutting the door behind him, he stepped out unnoticed, shoving his work gloves in his pocket.

While watching the taping from the wings, a man tapped Ty on the shoulder. He turned, getting a good look at the secondary target. Same height and build as the primary, but not a pretty boy. *Frank got good intelligence.*

They were having an issue with the equipment and needed his help, just as planned. Their path took them close to the primary's trailer. Ty jabbed the small syringe in the man's back, depressing it and catching the dead weight as he fell. He was able to roll him behind the wheel well, hiding him from view before returning to give direction on the equipment. No one took notice of the man's disappearance.

Ty and Chris headed back to their trailer before the scene wrapped up. Darkness settled over the lot as Ty opened his laptop and linked to the surveillance frequency. He didn't have to wait too long before the target entered his trailer, saying goodnight to his co-workers. The door shut, and Ty switched the feed to the interior camera in time to see his target undress and crawl into bed. Ty pushed a button, and an invisible vapor streamed from above the bed, settling over him and dragging him into unconsciousness. Ty pressed the button again, and the vapor stopped.

Ty tapped into the lot cameras and set the two-minute recording he had of the empty parking area between the trailers on a loop, faking out the feed.

"Our boy's not a night owl." Ty looked at Chris. "That's much better for me."

"I'm helping you, remember?" Chris said.

Ty sighed and stood, crossing to change into a black outfit, a black cap, and black gloves. Chris did the same; they needed to be invisible tonight.

They crept through the maze of trailers unseen. Ty picked the lock and pointed under the trailer. Silently, they pulled the man Ty had curled up under the wheel well and carried him into the trailer. They stripped him down to his underwear and put him on the bed, switching him with the target. The return trip carrying two hundred pounds of dead weight was more challenging, but they made it to the truck, pulled open the doors, and got in.

Ty opened the floor and tossed him into the space. He then removed the target's wedding ring and headed back to the trailer. He slipped it on the man lying on the bed, covered him, and picked up the discarded clothing. He lifted the bed up to reveal a small storage space and threw the clothes in after carefully removing the wallet the man had in his pants. The small propane tanks he'd planted earlier were still there. He turned them on, and the propane hissed out as he pushed the bed back down.

Then he plucked the chloroform mister that he had on the ceiling and placed it in his pocket. He also removed the small camera before inspecting the room for anything he may have left behind.

Next was the stove. He reached under the stovetop and pulled the main propane connection, severing it from the controls. More propane hissed into the room. He left the trailer and headed back to the truck, where Chris was setting up the IV drip that would keep the target unconscious for the remainder of the trip. They covered him with a battery-operated electric blanket and closed the flooring in the truck.

They slunk back into their trailer and changed clothes, then packed away the night gear in their bags and cut the feed to the lot cameras. One glance at the clock told him they had moved quicker than he'd expected. It took a little under an hour to make the switch. He waited and watched as another hour passed. The man in the trailer was most likely dead by now from CO_2 poisoning, but Ty had been instructed to wait for something else.

The car pulled up around 2 a.m., which was what Ty had been expecting, and a woman climbed out. She unlocked the door to the trailer and swung it open.

That was the last thing she ever did. Ty pushed the button, and the electronic device he had in the trailer sparked, igniting the escaping propane. The entire trailer blew to bits.

Chris gasped.

Ty switched off the feeds and closed his computer. "Time to act." He messed his hair up and did the same to Chris.

They went running out of their trailers like all the others to see what had happened. Flames had transitioned from the target's trailer to the one next door. Ty grabbed the fire extinguisher out of their truck and ran toward the commotion with the crowd.

Screams came from inside the burning trailer. Ty dropped the extinguisher, bolting to the door, and yanked. The door didn't budge. He snatched up the discarded extinguisher and smashed the side window.

More people had gathered, and someone hoisted him inside. The female star of the show was rolling around on the floor screaming in pain as flames licked her hair and nightgown.

Ty aimed the extinguisher and pulled the trigger. White foam covered the woman, dousing the flames. He dropped the now empty canister and swept her into his arms, then kicked the door open, getting her out of the trailer before the fire flashed in the small space.

The site became a nightmare of firefighters and a media circus that lasted throughout the night. The ruling by the fire department was that it was a tragic accident—a propane leak that was ignited when Mr. Whitman's wife entered the trailer and flipped the light on.

Several witnesses were interviewed, and footage of the rescue effort splashed the airwaves, including footage of Ty saving the girl. Microphones were shoved into his face as reporters attempted to interview him. He sheepishly rebuffed them all. He was dubbed a hero by the media, and it was plastered all over the news coast to coast.

The truck was loaded and ready to go before the sun came up. Both Ty and Chris begged off offers of staying on site for the remainder of the day, telling the crew they were a little gun shy with publicity, and headed back home with all the excitement still brewing.

The moment they hit the highway, Ty blew a stream of air out of his lungs. "Jesus." He glanced over at Chris, and the shakes began. He pulled over to the side of the road and put the truck in park until the shakes stopped. He stepped out on the side of the road and leaned over, his hands on his thighs, and his eyes squeezed shut, wondering if he was going to throw up this time.

"You okay?" Chris asked once Ty got back in the truck.

He nodded. "Thank God that's the last time I have to do that." He put the truck in gear and headed home.

Survival Games Chapter 38

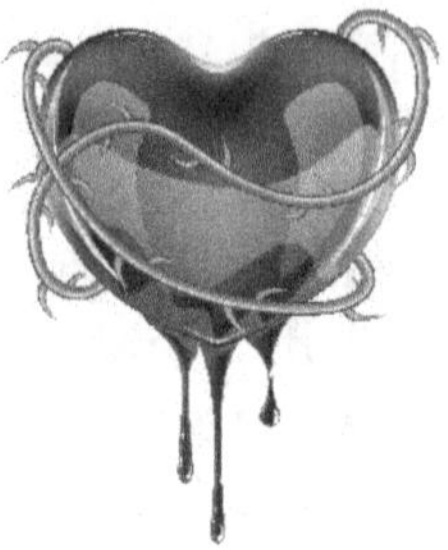

ERIC WANDERED INTO THE kitchen and mumbled "Good morning" to his father. He climbed up on the island stool to dig into the cereal waiting for him. As always, his father had the news on instead of cartoons. Eric sighed, focusing on his meal.

Jessie would be so devastated.

His father's thought invaded his mind. Eric looked up at the television and froze with a spoonful of cereal partway to his mouth. Footage from the rescue scene rolled across the screen, including a reluctant interview with the on-site hero. Eric dropped his spoon and ran to the upstairs bathroom.

"Mom! Mom, where are you? Mom!" he screamed at the glass, but only his reflection stared back.

Eric's vision clouded, blurring. He couldn't reach her. He couldn't see her, and even more terrifying, he couldn't *feel* her.

"Mom!" His voice sounded hoarse from his choking tears.

THE COFFEE CUP SLIPPED out of Daniel's hand and smashed on the tile floor, but he paid no attention to it as he ran toward his son's frantic screams. Sliding into the bathroom and falling to his knees, he grabbed Eric's arms, turning the flailing boy toward him.

"I can't see Mom anymore!" Tears streaked his face, his chin trembling. There was fear—fear deeper than Daniel had ever seen in anyone's eyes.

The pain of Jessica's death shot through him yet again, knocking the wind out of him. He wrapped his arms around Eric, pulling him against his chest, holding the child as he fought to break his grasp.

Eric wiggled, screaming, "You don't understand!" over and over and over.

"Don't understand what?" Daniel asked once Eric stopped moving. His heart, pounding double-time in his chest, nearly shattered at the look on his son's face.

"You don't understand. He left. He didn't stay, and now I can't see her!" Eric pointed toward the hall.

"Who left?"

"The man on the TV. He was supposed to protect Mom. Now the bad man has her, and I can't see her."

"You mean Clark?" They had shown the actor's face on the TV, and both the kids knew the show was one of their mother's favorite. It made sense that Eric's fantasy included Superman.

"No, Dad, the one who saved Lois. He was supposed to protect Mom."

Daniel was dumbfounded. He pulled Eric to his chest again. "It's okay," he said.

Eric pulled away. "No, it's not, Dad." He yanked out of his father's grip and disappeared downstairs to finish his breakfast, glaring at the television as the news cycled around again.

With the front door open and kids congregating on the corner for the school bus, Daniel handed Eric his coat. "Are you okay?"

"Yes." Eric offered a half-hearted smile.

Daniel watched him get on the bus and then closed the door, heading straight to the phone. His hand shook as he punched the number he had gotten so used to calling when grief overwhelmed him. This time, when LeAnn answered, his voice uncharacteristically trembled. The aguish was clear in every word as he walked through the morning episode.

"I'm on my way." She hung up the phone.

Daniel sat at the table staring into his coffee when the doorbell rang. He crossed to the door and held it open for her. Her green eyes searched his, and he shook his head, waving toward the kitchen where a hot cup of coffee sat on the table waiting for her.

Daniel slumped in the chair next to her, his eyes filling with tears. "I know you said the fantasy was normal, but it's hard. I thought by now he would have accepted her death. I can cope with a lot, but this"—he laughed a little to himself—"I don't know how to deal with this."

LeAnn took his hand and squeezed.

He squeezed back and held it, sending her a sideways glance. They had grown very close over the past few months. She was easy to talk to, and he was so lonely without Jessica.

On impulse, he pulled LeAnn toward him and kissed her. Her lips soft and inviting, she kissed back, leaving a slight berry taste under the coffee.

He licked his lips and leaned back in his chair for a moment, staring at her. "I'm sorry," he said after a moment's hesitation.

"Don't be," LeAnn replied and reached out to touch his face.

Her fingers wiped the stray tear off his cheek, the light touch igniting him, making him forget his dead wife for an instant. He closed his eyes. The maelstrom inside him created jitters in his stomach, a feeling he hadn't had for close to twenty years. When he opened his eyes again, the depth of her green ones pierced his, reflecting the same raw need flowing through his veins.

"Think five months is too soon?"

"Probably," she responded, but she didn't stop him when he leaned in to kiss her again.

Survival Games Chapter 39

TY LOOKED IN THE rearview mirror and nearly drove off the road. A little boy stared back at him, and he looked angry.

"You were supposed to protect her," the boy said.

Ty blinked, and he saw the road behind him again.

"What the hell was that?" Chris asked as Ty swerved back into the lane, jolting him awake.

"I don't know," Ty answered. "I think I may have drifted off."

Ty took the next exit, filled up the truck, got a cup of coffee, and climbed back in. He looked at the map, tracking where they were. Chris settled into the passenger seat.

"We're doing great on time. Cutting through Canada like this saved us close to a day. We'll cross over at Niagara Falls and head south from there." Ty handed Chris the map. "Let's roll."

"Do you want me to drive?"

Ty looked over at his brother and smiled. "What, you don't trust me?"

"I trust you. I just don't think we will make it home if you continue. You haven't slept since the plane ride out west, and you really can't sleep and drive at the same time."

"I've been okay to this point…" A yawn interrupted the conversation, followed by Ty's light laugh. "Maybe you should drive." He handed Chris the coffee.

Even before they were on the highway, Ty had drifted off.

Sometime later, he narrowed his eyes, turning around in the bathroom. Standard for any educational institution he had ever seen, right down to the beige tile, white urinals, and the smell of stale piss hanging in the air. When he was done with his casual survey, he glanced at the boy standing in front of him. The anger in the kid's eyes caused Ty to take a step back. The boy's words rang through the room, echoing on the ceramic walls.

"You were supposed to protect her."

Fire and fury and something else reflected in the boy's face. It took Ty a second to recognize the underlying emotion. Fear. But not fear of him. Some other nameless fear that spread into his bones and clenched his stomach. His mouth went dry.

Ty hunched down to eye level with the boy, wiping his clammy, cool hands on his jeans. "Huh?"

"My mom. You were supposed to protect her."

The boy's deep brown eyes penetrated his, familiar in a haunting way, the same intense doorway, the same soul-searching gaze. His knees weakened, almost dropping him to the floor.

Even though he knew the answer, it still took him two tries to ask the question. "Who… Who's your mom?"

Quiet permeated the room, settling between them before the child spoke. "Jessica," he said.

"Now the bad man has her, and I can't see her anymore."

Ty felt his heart stop and his breath hitched in. He swallowed and licked his lips. "Eric?"

The boy nodded and took his hand.

"You had a cut on this arm. She made it better, like I made her better."

Ty stood and stepped back, but there was nowhere to go. *If this is a dream...*

"It's not a dream," Eric said. "You left her, and I can't see her anymore." A tear slipped down his face. "You have to help me save her."

Ty stooped down again. "What do you mean 'save her'?"

"The bad man, he has her. He's going to hurt her."

Ty shook his head, meeting the boy's sharp gaze. "He's out of town."

"No, he isn't, and *you* left her alone."

The kid's whisper caused a bone-deep chill. "I'm sorry, but..." Ty didn't know what else to say. How could he explain his actions to a little kid? The stunt last night was all to provide a distraction. A distraction to get this boy's mother out of that hellhole. But then what? Then where would that leave him? His head dropped, and he stared at the little Nikes on Eric's feet.

"You and my mom were meant to be together."

He raised his eyes. "Excuse me?"

"She fixed your heart. You're meant to be together."

Ty raised his eyebrow. "She fixed my heart?"

"Yes, you aren't mean or angry anymore."

He sighed, thinking of what he did last night. "Yes, Eric, I am still mean."

The boy shifted uncomfortably, his gaze dropping to the floor. "You saved Lois."

Ty assumed he was referring to the actress in the trailer and nodded.

"What is redention?"

Ty scrunched his eyebrows together.

"You asked Mom if she believed in redention?"

"Redemption. I asked her about redemption."

"What does that mean?"

"Redemption is when your soul is saved."

"Mom can do that. She's special."

"She can't save me."

"Yes, she can." Eric looked over his shoulder and then back at Ty. "You have to tell her to open the door. Tell her that Eric said so. I gotta go." He turned and disappeared.

Ty sat up like a rocket in the passenger seat.

Chris was laughing at him. "You still talk in your sleep, and let me tell you, you have some really weird dreams."

"Huh?"

"Who is Eric anyway?"

Ty glanced out the window. "Eric is Jessica's son."

"Dude, you've got issues."

Ty grunted and rubbed his eyes, the vision of the boy still as clear as the scenery racing by them.

"Get some more sleep."

He nodded and closed his eyes, drifting off into sleep again. This time his dreams were fragmented, bordering on nightmares. Flashes of blood and bruises, of Jessica screaming his name in agony, of him not being able to reach her, all careened through his restless mind.

Ty opened his eyes to a small rest area. Chris wasn't in the driver's seat. Behind him, toolboxes and cable equipment covered the hidden space to prepare for the border crossing. He turned his attention toward the building they were parked in front of. Chris crossed the parking lot and opened the passenger door, dark circles of exhaustion framing his eyes.

Ty looked around. "Where are we?"

"Ten miles from the border," Chris answered.

Ty did the math, and his mouth dropped. "You let me sleep for fourteen hours?"

Chris smiled. "You needed it."

Ty slid out of the passenger seat and stretched his aching muscles. "I'll be right out."

Turning, he trotted quickly toward the building. The cool water from the sink felt good against his tired skin. After he'd sopped the remaining sheen on his face with a paper towel, he opened his eyes. Instead of seeing his own reflection in the mirror; the boy from his dream was staring at him. Ty whirled around. No one else was in the bathroom with him. He turned back to the mirror.

"I'm losing it," he said. The conversation with the little boy came flooding back.

"Promise me," Eric whispered.

Ty just looked at him, his mouth hanging open.

"Promise me you'll protect her," he whispered again, more urgently.

Ty nodded and looked around the room again.

"Say it," Eric said.

"I promise," Ty answered.

Eric reached through the mirror and put something in Ty's hand. "Give this to her."

He stared at the metal as if it were from outer space. When he raised his gaze to the mirror, his slack-jawed, wide-eyed reflection stared back. He closed his mouth and twirled the old-fashioned key in his fingers before depositing it in his pocket. His stomach growled, and he headed to get something to satiate his hunger.

"I'm really losing it," he said as the bathroom door closed behind him.

Survival Games Chapter 40

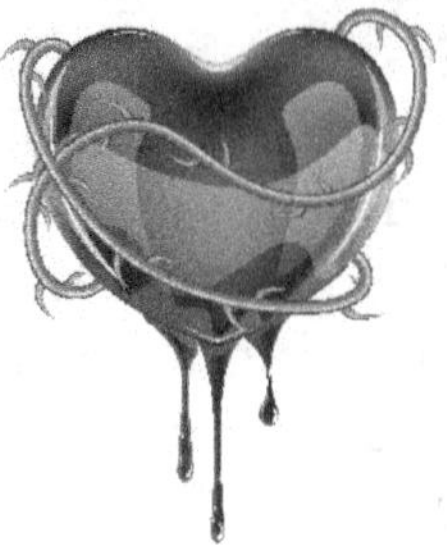

THE DOOR SWUNG OPEN, and Mike shot to his feet, meeting Frank's gaze.

"Back up," Frank commanded with the Taser pointed at him. He bent down to grab something that lay in the hallway beyond Mike's field of vision.

It took a moment to recognize the battered, unconscious body that Frank dragged into his room, but when he did, his fury at Ty transferred to the sadistic son of a bitch in front of him. He launched at Frank. The Taser shot hit him in the chest. Pain exploded through his body as he crumpled to the ground.

Frank hauled him into the chair and chained him in place before yanking the Taser hook out of his skin.

He left the room, and Mike lowered his gaze to Jessica. Her face was still beautiful despite the black and blue tones covering her skin. A swirl of emotions overcame him—relief, jealousy, hate, guilt—and each negative emotion was tainted with the love he felt for the woman. He looked up at the broken monitor, his mind whirling, and he gritted his teeth. His gaze snapped back to her, specifically to the black dress shirt draped over her frame. The shirt Ty wore last night.

Frank returned, setting a portable DVD player in front of him, and pressed play. The screen filled with her room as Ty entered. He couldn't pull his eyes away from her standing in the white dress, and then the dress was gone. She was in that bastard's arms. The betrayal was complete.

"I begged for her," he said, as all his illusions shattered. "I-I killed for her."

"I'm leaving her here for you. But I want her alive. Understand?" Frank said as he pressed a remote.

The cuffs holding Mike in place released. The door clicked closed behind Frank.

Mike glanced between the video and back to Jessica. "Fucking bitch." He rubbed his wrist, wincing at the sudden pain that traveled up his arm from the shattered bones. He returned his gaze to the video, her riding that fucker, the black fabric of his shirt covering her back. The playful smile on her face taunted him. He crossed to her, staring down as fury raged underneath his skin.

Ty's words from weeks ago rang in his ears. *Nectar of the gods*. Mike saw red.

PAIN BROUGHT JESSICA OUT of the dark nothingness. She groaned, her eyes cracking open and her hands pushing on the bare chest above her. Mad ramblings filled her ears as he muttered and muttered with each violent slam of his hips.

"I begged for you and killed for you. And you fucked *him*?" Mike screamed.

Jessica blinked at the face above her. Recognition set in, and she pushed harder. "No!"

The volume of her cry gave him pause, enough so she could buck him off and roll away. Scrambling to her feet, she yanked the ruined shirt tight around her and backed away from him.

He came after her. "I would have given my life for you, you bitch!" He lunged.

She sidestepped. "Stop!"

"I will not stop until I get what he got," Mike said, pointing to the screen.

"I didn't know you were here!" She didn't look at the video playing behind her because she knew the moment she moved her gaze, Mike would pounce.

He lunged at her again, knocking her into the concrete wall.

"You don't want to do this," Jessica begged.

He pinned her with his body, his eyes crazed with fury, his hands rough and brutal in their quest. "I've waited for seven years for this," he growled and threw her to the floor. "Don't tell me what I want!"

Jessica scurried to her knees and crawled across the cold concrete until he slammed into her back, his elbow piercing the space between her shoulder blades. She dropped to the ground under his weight.

"And you wanted me for seven years," he whispered in her ear.

"Not like this," she said, crying. "Not like this." She closed her eyes and put her forehead on her hand, sobbing into the concrete. This place had reduced the man she'd once loved to this ugly version of a warped, muttering monster.

He pulled away and stumbled to the bathroom.

She remained on the floor, her chest tight enough to choke the sobs, holding them in place as she trembled. Retching sounds came from the bathroom, followed by louder, harsher sobs. She rested her cheek on the cool concrete and stared at the bathroom doorway, lacking the strength to move.

Mike didn't come out.

Sobs filtered out after the sounds of the flushing toilet dissipated. Jessica found the strength to get to her knees, pulled Ty's shirt around her, stood on wobbly legs, and walked toward the noise. She sat down next to him on the floor.

"Get away from me," he whispered.

She leaned back against the wall and closed her eyes, holding her knees. The tears kept coming. "I'm here because of you," she whispered.

He nodded, staring at the far wall.

"I didn't know you were here," she whispered. She put her head down on her knees, tightening her grip and trying to stop the shakes that took hold. "I thought you were dead. I went to your funeral. I watched as your coffin..." She couldn't finish, and she turned her head, meeting his still-angry gaze. "Part of me died that day, Mike." Her own anger pushed past the humiliation and devastation. "And just now, out there"—she pointed to the other room—"*you* crushed what was left of me."

She stood up and left him staring after her. She took a seat in the far corner of the room, her back to the mirror. Eric called, his small voice crying for her, but she shut him out, consciously turning off the connection. She didn't want to hear his promises, his pleas to hang on.

Her head dropped to her knees, and when she closed her eyes, it was Ty's face she saw. His hair was speckled with melting snowflakes, his blue eyes hesitant and unsure as he held out the sparkling diamond for her. His breath came in white plumes, and his perfectly fitted black suit shimmered against the winter landscape.

Her eyes snapped open, the vision holding even against the gray concrete. His face, his beautiful, *unscarred* face, and one word echoed in her mind.

Impossible.

Even so, the image tore through her, ripping her soul apart as effectively as a hollow-point bullet. She knew. She knew she would beg to save his life, but she didn't know if she would for the man in the other room.

Mike ventured out some time later. "Why?"

"Why what?" Jessica asked.

"Why him?"

Jessica shook her head as her eyes locked with his, and a slightly hysterical laugh escaped. Why? That was as good a question as any, and there was no reasonable answer for Mike. None that she expected him to understand, anyway, especially since she didn't understand it herself. It just was.

"I don't know," she said.

He kneeled in front of her. "I'm sorry, Jessie." His green eyes glossed over with tears.

"You raped me."

He winced at the words and looked at the floor. After a few seconds, he nodded.

"He never did."

Mike's gaze snapped up to hers and his eyes narrowed. "What do you call chaining you to the bed and... and..."

Jessica tilted her head. "That was his attempt at seduction."

"You said you didn't want him."

She met his blatant stare. "I lied. I'm good at games, remember?"

His jaw dropped.

"It was a game. A game I had to play in order to survive." She leaned forward. "A game that worked, but then again, I didn't have anyone else riding on it, and frankly, if I had known you were here, I'm not sure things would have turned out the same." She sighed, leaning back and glancing up at the cameras.

Mike half smiled. They had played cat-and-mouse games for years. "Games, huh?"

"Yes, and despite what you think, Ty never raped me. He manipulated me, seduced me, and coerced me, but the man never raped me."

"I'm sorry." He reached out to touch her face with his good hand.

Jessica grabbed his wrist. "No. You don't get to do that now." Her eyes flashed a warning.

"You look like hell," he said after a moment.

The absurdity of his statement caught her off guard, and she burst out laughing. It was the first time she had laughed, really laughed, in months.

He laughed too. He moved, so he was sitting next to her and took her hand in his good one. She stared at the gesture, but didn't pull her hand out of his soft grasp.

The laughter wound down as they looked at each other.

"Thank you," Mike said, leaning his head back on the glass.

"For what?" She wiped her tears and winced. Her face hurt.

"For laughing. I missed your laugh," he said.

She glanced sideways at him. "That had to hurt," she said, pointing her chin toward his hand. She giggled again.

He joined her. This time they continued laughing, leaning into each other until tears streamed down their faces.

Frank slammed the door open, and their laughter died. "That's the best you can do?" he yelled at Mike. "That isn't making someone pay."

They stood up slowly, still holding hands. Mike stepped in front of her to shield her from Frank's wrath.

"You don't want to make him pay for everything he has done to you?" Frank seethed.

Mike nodded. "But not by hurting her. I've already done enough of that to last a lifetime."

"Mike, don't," she whispered from behind him.

"It's okay, Jessie," he replied. "I got to hear you laugh again." He fell to the ground in front of her, the Taser embedded in his chest.

She charged at Frank. She wanted to claw his eyes out, to hear him scream in agony. He moved faster. The sharp crack of bones snapping filled the room and sent her flying into the wall. Pain exploded in her side, and her breath locked in her chest. Her ribs throbbed where his fist had connected, and she crumpled to the floor, holding her side and concentrating on drawing air into her shocked lungs.

He grabbed Mike and strapped him into the chair, hooking the electrical conductors to the metal. He pointed the remote and Mike cried out as his body went rigid.

"Stop," Jessica said. "STOP!" she yelled, getting to her feet unsteadily.

Frank complied.

"I deserve a blow job." Frank swept the DVD player off the chair and sat down. "C'mon, bitch, let's see what that mouth can do."

"No," she said, holding her side and gasping.

"Then he dies." Frank pointed the remote again.

"Okay. Okay," Jessica said quickly before he pushed the button again. She stiffly crossed the room and dropped to her knees between the two men. Unwanted tears slid down her cheeks, and she inhaled, wincing as the expansion of her lungs pushed on her cracked ribs.

"Don't," Mike whispered. "We're going to die, anyway. Don't."

"I can't watch you die." She turned, laying her head on his leg, shaking with silent sobs.

His fingers grazed her cheek the second before Frank grabbed a handful of her hair and pulled her toward his lap. His hard member was out and ready for her mouth.

"Don't, Jessie. Not for me."

"Suck or he dies!"

Jessica opened her mouth to protest, and he plunged the tip of his member inside. A slightly salty taste made her gag. He pulled her further down his hard shaft.

"Now suck me." His dark eyes glared at her, and half closed when she pressed her lips over his skin. Then he smiled at Mike.

Raw fury consumed her. She snapped her teeth closed, locking her jaw together, and yanked away as violently as she could.

His smile morphed into a grimace, followed by a high-pitched scream. Blood, thick and metallic, filled her mouth around the chunk she'd bit off. She turned, spitting the mess onto the floor and then gagged as the hot copper taste coated her throat. But that didn't stop the near hysterical laughter that bubbled up. She turned to glare at Frank. His hand clasped tightly around his ruined member, his scream still filling the room, but his other hand descended fast and struck her in the temple.

Everything went black.

Survival Games Chapter 41

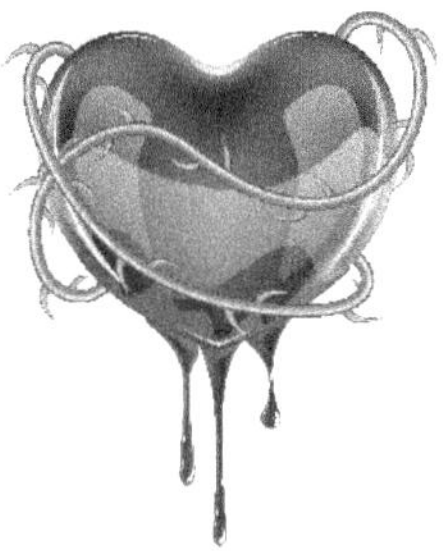

MIKE SAT HELPLESSLY LOCKED in the chair while Jessica lay unconscious on the floor. Frank hadn't killed him yet, but the promise, the threat he'd issued when he stormed out of the room hung over him like a black cloud. His body still twitched from the brief electric shock that had punctuated Frank's words.

Mike's ears buzzed, and he slumped, his head tilted against the wood. His eyes closed. For a minute, he wanted to remember what his life had been like before he was snatched out of it. He wanted to remember what she looked like without the black and blue hazing. He wanted to remember *her*.

The chemistry between them had always been intense from day one. He would walk into the room, and if she were there, it was as if all the hair on his body stood on end.

He remembered sitting next to her in a meeting one day, and she had this short dress with her legs crossed. He couldn't help himself—he'd grazed his hand over her bare knee. She'd taken a slow deep breath, half smiled, and looked sideways at him. That always killed him. She'd recovered before anyone else in the meeting took notice.

After the meeting, she leaned over to him and whispered, "You are so bad." Smiling, she'd walked away.

Later that same week, in a separate meeting, she slipped her shoe off and ran her foot up his calf under the table while he was trying to explain something to the group. He ended up forgetting where he was in the explanation and had to start over. She was highly amused by his reaction.

Any time they touched, his entire body burned for her. Every now and then, he would whisper something dirty, and she would give him the same deep breath, half smile, sideways look that made him have to go splash his face with cold water. When she added a very sexy lower lip bite as well, it had driven him completely nuts. It was a cat-and-mouse game they played well, but unfortunately, they were both taken, so they never actually did any of the things they insinuated.

The only time he'd crossed the line was a memory that came back time and time again over the past seven years. He thought about her more often than he should, and that day was always where his mind wandered to. They were alone in her car going to a goodbye lunch for a co-worker, and he'd pointed her the wrong way. She pulled into a driveway to turn around. When she reached over his seat and looked over her shoulder to back out, he planted a kiss on her. It was impulsive and caught her completely off guard, so much so that she almost got in an accident.

After she collected her bearings, she sent that sideways look at him with a small shake of her head and a musical laugh that all but asked: *Are you insane?*

Lunch had been a blur. All he'd wanted to do was get back in the car with her. While she pulled out of the parking lot, he slid his hand up her skirt, grazing her stockings and smiling at her flustered expression. She again made a wrong turn and let out a slight laugh, shifting her gaze to him as she spun the car around. But she didn't stop his gentle exploration.

"You're wet," he'd whispered, and he was rewarded with her blooming cheeks and a slight nod. Her eyes locked on the street before them but glazed over with a lust so strong he'd felt the electrical connection in the car. "Take your stockings off."

She laughed. Her eyebrows rose, and her gaze flitted between him and the crowded road. "I'm not Houdini."

He continued to rub her gently while he took her right hand and placed it in his lap. A small, sweet sound escaped her lips, and her hand slid the length of his hard shaft before she pulled it away and grasped the steering wheel.

She'd looked at the clock in the car, at the hotel they were about to pass, and then at him. Uncertainty filled her features.

"What do you want, Jessie?"

"Everything." She looked at the road. "Nothing. I don't know."

They looked at each other. The hotel passed by, and so did the opportunity to act on their attraction.

Now, he opened his eyes as she stirred on the floor. "Jessie," he whispered and closed his eyes again, going back to the day she'd left.

She said she had a great job opportunity closer to home, but he always suspected he had a lot to do with why she was leaving. It was close to a year after that car ride, and they had continued playing the cat-and-mouse game the entire time. The heat between them was still as intense as it was that day in the car, as the day they'd met.

She'd found him between meetings, gave him a hug, saying goodbye. He trembled as he held her. He still remembered her coconut shampoo and the way she felt in his arms. He didn't want her to go, and he didn't want her to see him lose it, either. He told her to keep in touch and walked away as quickly as possible. He could still hear her sobbing as she told a good friend she had been fine until she said goodbye to him.

He still remembered how she made him feel when she was near him, when she laughed, when she cried, and when she said goodbye.

Mike opened his eyes, looked down at her beaten and battered body, and cried, because he didn't want to say goodbye to her ever again.

Survival Games Chapter 42

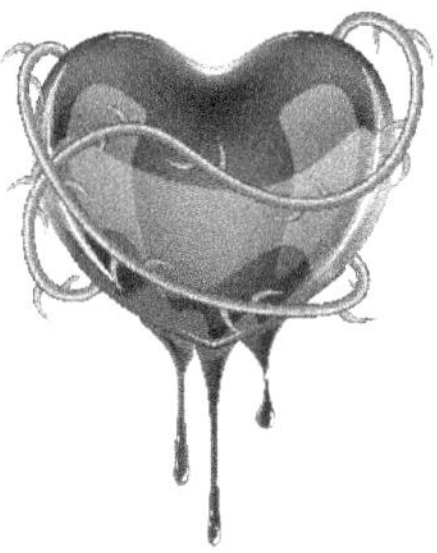

MIKE LOOKED UP WHEN Frank entered. He walked slightly tilted, pain etched into his features. A small iota of satisfaction gripped him, pushing away some of the devastation wrapped around his heart.

"Don't hurt her," he said, his voice raspy with emotion. "Please, don't hurt her anymore."

Frank gave him a sinister smile. "Oh, what I'm going to do won't hurt her, but I can't say the same for you." Frank heaved Jessica over his shoulder and left the room.

A while later, he returned, walking a little straighter and whistling. He reached into his pocket and pulled out both a cloth and vial, a devious smile playing on his lips.

Mike struggled against the shackles, holding him firmly to the chair, ignoring the flaring pain in his wrist. However, even with his thrashing, Frank was able to get the cloth over his mouth and nose.

Blackness was swift and complete.

Survival Games Chapter 43

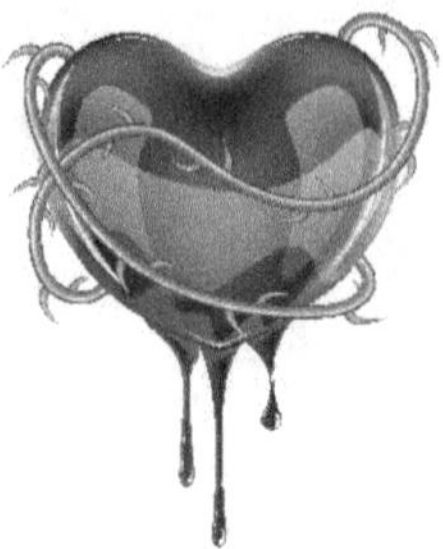

JESSICA WOKE TO THE foul stench of smelling salts being waved under her nose. Frank leaned in close, and as her eyes cleared up, she head-butted him before he could say a word. Stars colored her vision as he leaned back, holding his bloody nose and cursing.

"Bitch," he began, waving the salts under her nose again. "Have I got a present for you."

Frank flipped a switch on the monitor next to her. She stared in horror as a thick metal dildo slid between her legs. The modified vibrator slowly fucked her, sending electrical currents through her lower half that were enhanced by strategically placed conductor pads. The result— a thrill of pleasure through her body, much like the electricity therapy she received on her back after an accident. Her entire lower body tingled from it, especially where Frank had placed the conductors. He turned the dial up so as the vibrator went in, the tingling strengthened to levels dangerously close to pain and then weakened as it slid out.

Frank stood watching her. "My ex-girlfriend loved that machine. She came and came and came until she begged me to stop it. To say she was disappointed when we broke up is an understatement." He tilted his head. "I've always wondered just how long a woman could last before she died of pleasure." He tapped his lips, studying her.

"No," she whispered in horror as her body responded.

"But I'll have to test that theory some other time." Frank smiled and stepped away, revealing Mike behind him.

He was suspended in the air, chains shackled on his wrists and ankles, all pulling in opposite directions. A semi-conscious moan escaped his lips.

Frank crossed and waved the smelling salts under his nose. Mike yanked his head away from the pungent odor, his eyes blinking open and the moan turning to a groan of pain. The groan silenced as his gaze fell on Jessica. Or, more appropriately, the contraption Jessica was strapped to.

Frank stepped back and smiled. "Wonderful little toy. It guarantees she will have orgasm after orgasm, whether or not she wants to." He walked behind her, grabbed her breasts, rolling the nipples around with his fingers, and smiled up at Mike. "Much better than Ty ever was," he whispered in her ear and then licked her face.

She cringed.

"And every time she has one, those chains get shorter and shorter." He let the situation sink in. "Basically, she's going to tear you apart."

"No!" Jessica screamed as the first orgasm gripped her.

Mike cried out as the chains stretched him farther in opposite directions. Frank laughed and stepped away.

She sobbed and struggled against the bonds holding her in place, but the more she struggled, the more she slid into the horrid machine, enhancing the experience. With each stroke, her body burned hotter and hotter, building to that plateau, building her to the brink with exact science. There was nothing she could do. No image she conjured stopped her body from responding. She screamed a high-pitched, tortured wail, and her body arched. The strength of the orgasm rippled through her muscles and triggered the chains to recede.

Mike's cry filled the room, announcing the agony gripping his wrists and ankles and every bone in between.

She threw her head back in an attempt to knock herself out and was met with a soft backing behind her.

Frank laughed. "I thought you might try that, so I padded the chair."

"Please." Jessica gasped between sobs. "Please. I can't. I can't." She put her head down, willing her body not to give in. It was futile as the third orgasm built.

"I can't watch him die. Please," she sobbed.

Frank kneeled down next to her. "He is going to be torn apart because of you, and you have a front-row seat."

"Jessie," Mike snapped. "THIS IS NOT YOUR FAULT!"

Her breath hitched in and out of her chest, panting, sobbing, cursing—all as the heat between her legs built to a stronger crest than before. Her throat, raw from the flow of air, forced in and out, stung with the scream that barreled out of her mouth, her body rigid and trembling with the enhanced current.

A loud popping sounded. Mike screamed. His shoulder pulled at a funny angle, and his head suddenly lolled on his neck, his eyes half closed and only showing the whites.

Frank opened another smelling salt under his nose, and Mike came screaming into consciousness.

"You bastard, can't you let him be? Let him stay unconscious!" Jessica screamed, glaring at Frank, her body bathed in sweat. The machine continued its slow, steady movement, her body betraying her, reacting, building with each electrical crest.

Mike gasped in pain. "Jessie."

Jessica nodded.

"Look at me," he said.

She looked up at him with her head low, concentrating. Her face was hot, too hot. She held her breath against the burn in her lungs. She prayed it would work, prayed for darkness, and it paid off. Blackness engulfed her, but the smelling salts brought her back.

Mike gasped. "Look at me."

She did, and tears blurred her vision, spilling over the edges and cooling her hot skin.

"You are here"—he gasped, forcing himself to stay conscious long enough to say what he needed—"because of me." The words hissed out of him, and then he passed out again.

Jessica peaked, sobbing as the chains receded again. The skin on his shoulders tore.

Frank waved the smelling salts under his nose again, yanking him back into a world of agony.

"Not...your...fault." Tears streamed down Mike's face from both the physical and mental agony.

Frank flipped a switch, turning the machine on high.

The chains pulled him farther in different directions. Mike gagged, choking the scream, constricting it with a low groan. For an instant, his eyes went wide, almost to where she thought they might explode out of his skull. Then a crack shattered the room and his head lolled back. His right leg pulled at the same odd angle as his shoulder. The skin on his stomach stretched too far and tore. Small bursts of blood shot beyond the torn skin.

Frank waved the smelling salts under his nose again.

"Jessie...love... you," he labored, his chest hitching with each difficult breath.

"I'm sorry." She kept repeating this over and over as the next release built up. She sobbed as it racked her body.

Mike screamed, and his arm tore from the socket, ripping away from his body and dangling from the chain. Blood pumped out of the wound in a torrent. His screams silenced to whimpers, and before silence finally descended and he let go of life, he sent his last coherent word her way. "Goodbye."

The light faded out of his eyes.

She sobbed. The next release tore his broken leg from his torso.

Frank smiled, watching until Mike's body was torn in half.

Gasping for air, her eyes locked on the dead dangling form that once was Mike, hardly aware that Frank turned off the machine and removed it from between her legs. Awareness came when his fingers penetrated her. She lowered her gaze to his insane grin, and then to his hand, following the lead of the vibrator and sliding in and out of her in quick thrusts.

She opened her mouth to tell him to get his hands off her, but the bile was quicker. Vomit spewed out of her lips and splashed his face and shirt.

He shot away from her, cursing and spitting, wiping the bile off his face. Then he stepped in, throwing a punch with his full weight behind it.

Jessica welcomed the blackness when it overcame her.

Survival Games Chapter 44

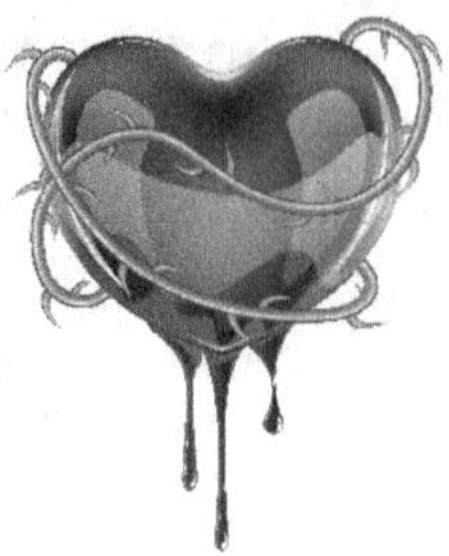

TY PULLED THE VAN up to the gate at the border, handing their passports to the guard. Then he smiled as the border disappeared in the background. In less than six hours, he'd be back, showered, shaved, and enacting his plan to get Jessica out of the building. He tempered his impatience, pulling his foot back from the gas pedal and falling to within ten miles of the speed limit. A ticket would be a terrible idea right about now. They didn't have the time to monkey around with a traffic violation regardless of the worry gnawing on his bones.

Chris snored in the seat next to him. It was the kind of snore that grated on nerves as it wheezed in his nose and thundered out of his mouth. Ty looked around for something, anything, to throw at him so he would shut up. He reached down, grabbed a discarded cup, and tossed it over. It bounced off Chris's head, but he didn't stir, and continued snoring.

Ty grabbed one of the fast-food containers within reach, crumpled it up, and tossed it at him. It bounced off his head. Chris continued to snore.

Ty grinned; it was all he could do not to laugh as he leaned over quietly. "Chris," he yelled as loud as he could.

Chris jumped a mile out of the seat and banged his head against the window.

Ty burst out laughing.

Chris sulked. "That wasn't funny."

Still chuckling, Ty said, "Yeah, it was."

Chris looked away, trying to hide his laugh.

Ty swatted his head. "You should have seen your face."

Chris glanced at his brother, laughing with him. "You really are a son of a bitch."

"Don't talk about our mother like that," Ty scolded, and they both laughed harder.

"Ty?"

"Yeah?"

"It's nice to have my brother back."

Ty looked over at Chris.

"Don't give me that look. It has been way too long since you've let loose. We used to laugh. When we were kids, we used to laugh a lot."

Silence filled the cab as he considered Chris's words.

"I don't know what that girl did, but I've got to thank her. She gave me my brother back." Chris watched the trees pass by. "I'll do whatever you need me to."

Ty nodded. He didn't say anything for a while.

"I don't think I've really laughed since before Anna died," Ty said, looking over at Chris. "It's been that long."

Chris whistled. "Christ, Ty, that's what, twenty years ago?"

Ty nodded. It was actually eighteen years, almost to the day. "Something like that." He took a deep breath and looked over at Chris. "I killed him."

Chris hesitated. "Killed who?"

"Frank's Dad."

Chris stared at the road ahead of them, quiet. When he turned his gaze back, he offered a shrug. Ty knew neither of them had grieved over his death, but the lack of compassion in Chris's eyes signaled the same type of contempt he held for the old man.

"What happened?" Chris finally asked.

"I got home from school, and the old man's car was in the driveway. He was never there when I got home, so I knew something wasn't quite right. When I walked in, I saw Anna's books and school papers scattered over the stairs like someone had dragged her and they fell out of her bag on the way. I snuck up and peeked into her room, and there the bastard was, sitting next to her on the bed. There was blood all over his hands, and the knife was on the floor." Ty stopped and looked over at his little brother. "I just lost it. I picked up the knife and planted it in his back. I think he saw me before he died. At least, I like to think he did. Then I wiped the knife handle with the blanket and walked out of the house to meet you at the bus stop."

"If Frank ever finds out, he'll kill you."

"I know."

They drove in silence.

"What's going to happen to this one?" Chris pointed his thumb over his shoulder.

Ty sighed. "I'll figure something out."

Survival Games Chapter 45

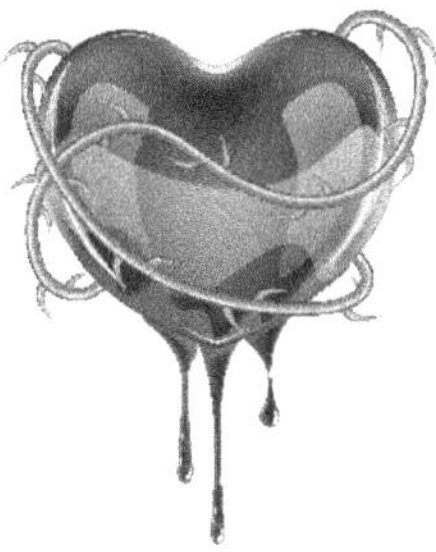

BURNING, RIPPING PAIN GRIPPED her back, and she screamed herself awake. Her hands were clasped to the front of the treadmill, on the wrong side, her bare back facing the room. She glanced at the mirror in time to see the business end of the whip tear her back again.

Her mind reeled, accepting the punishment, feeling as though she deserved this for killing Mike. She persevered in silence through each crack of the whip and the resulting pain that flared as it dug into her skin. Twelve, fifteen, twenty times, she lost count, but the blood flowed from her back, hot and sticky down her legs and splattered on the floor.

Her breath hissed in her chest, and she lost her balance. Then he was there, the whip wrapped tightly around her throat, his hot, foul breath in her ear.

"When I'm through with you, you will beg me to kill you," he whispered in her ear as he yanked the whip from around her. He undid the handcuffs from the treadmill, leaving them on her wrists.

She collapsed to her knees, not even looking up when the door closed.

Survival Games Chapter 46

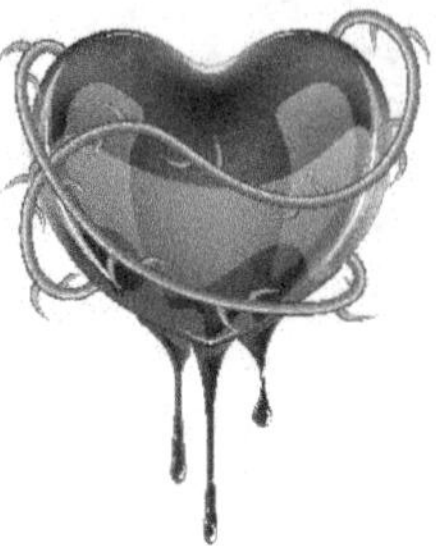

TY FLIPPED HIS PHONE open as he pulled onto the dark access road. "Hey, Frank, are you back yet?"

"I got back a little while ago. Why?"

"We're just pulling onto the access road. Is it clear?"

"Yes, the cleaning crew is already gone. I trust things went well?"

"The package is fine." He hung up, turning the last corner to find the garage door slowly opening. Frank waved them in.

Both Chris and Ty got out of the truck and stretched.

Frank shot his gaze from one to the other and shifted his weight impatiently. "Come on, come on." He looked over his shoulder at the open office door and back.

"Just hold your horses, will you?" Ty snapped. "It's been a long ride. He'll keep for another minute or two."

Ty and Chris opened the truck, moved away the equipment they had strewn over the floor to cross the border, and opened the compartment where their guest was stored. He was still unconscious, thanks to the I.V. in his arm, but he was a mess. They would have to clean him up. Chris backed away in disgust.

Ty looked over at him. "Come on. What'd you think would happen after a little over two days in a cargo hold?" He pulled his prisoner out of the truck and started inside. "It's a shitty job, but someone's got to do it." He chuckled at his tasteless joke. "I'll get him. You get the truck," he said over his shoulder to Chris.

"Fabulous," Chris said dismally.

"Hold up, Ty," Frank said. "I'll go down with you." He turned to Chris and handed him a piece of paper. "Before you do that, can you run to the store and pick up this stuff for me? We are running low on supplies."

Chris looked at the paper. "Sure. Can I take the BMW?"

Frank hesitated like he always did when Chris asked to take his car for a spin.

"Come on, he deserves it. This guy is getting heavy," Ty said from the door.

"Okay." Frank flipped the keys to Chris, heading inside with Ty.

"Sweet!" Chris slid into the driver's seat and opened the garage door behind him. As he pulled out of the garage, he grinned.

"You know, he might just disappear with that BMW," Ty joked as they entered the elevator.

"I know, but it's got GPS tracking, so I can find him anywhere," Frank said, patting his pocket.

Ty laughed. "And sure as shit, you'd go collecting, wouldn't you?"

Frank nodded. "Payback's a bitch."

They walked into the room that Frank had set up, and Ty took their prisoner into the bathroom, dumping him in the bathtub. He started the shower and poked his head around the corner. "Frank, you mind getting the clothes out of the truck and a pair of jeans for me? I need to get cleaned up, too. Might as well do it in here."

"Sure thing." Frank headed out of the room.

"Frank, you back yet?" Ty called after a few minutes in the hot shower, scrubbing their newest prisoner clean.

"Yep," Frank replied and walked into the bathroom.

Ty handed him the unconscious and clean body of Tom Whitman, the star of *Metropolis*. "Can you get him dressed, or do you need my help?"

"I've got it covered." Frank grabbed a towel to wipe him down.

Ty nodded, stripped the wet clothes off his back, and stepped back into the warm shower. He couldn't wait to see Jessica, but he also needed to feel clean. He hadn't had a shower since the morning before the explosion, and he really needed it. He leaned with his arms against the wall as the water and exhaustion rolled off his body.

He closed his eyes. *How am I going to get her out?*

Ty sighed, turning the water off. He grabbed a towel and dried off, then pulled on the clean jeans Frank had left before rummaging through his wet clothes and transferring the key, a Swiss army knife, his wallet and the loose change from his wet soiled clothes to the clean, dry jeans. He pulled his shirt on as he stepped into the room.

A jolt knocked him to the ground. He stared at the Taser embedded in his chest in confusion. His gaze shifted to Frank as shackles closed around his wrists and ankles.

Frank yanked the Taser shard from his skin and replaced it with a vicious blow from his foot.

Ty coughed, trying to pull air into his now seized lungs.

Tom stirred in the chair.

Frank leaned close to Ty's face. "Payback *is* a bitch," he seethed and stormed out of the room.

Survival Games Chapter 47

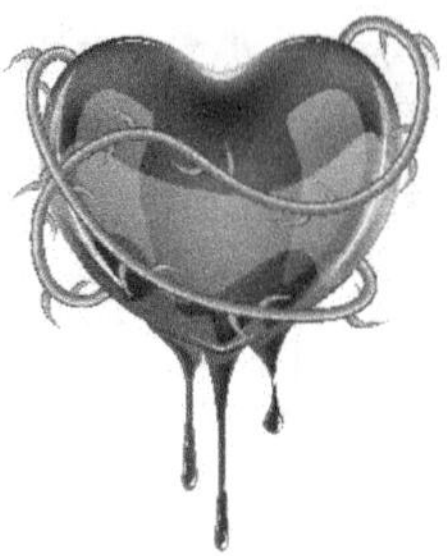

JESSICA CRAWLED TO THE bathroom after he left. Her back felt like a thousand claws had ripped into her flesh, and it looked that way, too. She turned the shower on low and stepped into the water, turning the knob so cold water ran over her body. She shivered. The stream of red coming off her back turned to pink and eventually cleared as the cuts clotted.

She dialed the water to hot, turned to face the stream, and absently ran the soap over her body. The normal daily functions were mechanical and calmed her. Since Mike had died, she'd existed. That was it, and showering was a necessity of existing.

Eric was calling, but she tuned him out. She dried her body and wrapped the towel gingerly around her, limping back into the bedroom. She curled up in the chair in the middle of the room.

She was still there, staring aimlessly into space, when Frank walked in. The white dress was still crumpled on the floor where it had landed when Ty took it off.

Frank pointed to the dress. "Put that on."

Jessica stared right through him as if he wasn't there, so he crossed the room, swept the dress up, and shoved it at Jessica in the chair.

She still didn't move, so he took the dress, and slipped it over her head, and threaded each arm through the garment. He grabbed the handcuffs still bound to her wrists and clasped them together, yanking her up. He pulled the towel off her as the dress slid down over her legs.

He dragged her from the room, and she stumbled behind him. The room he brought her into was unfamiliar, but the two sets of eyes staring at her were. Frank threw her on the mattress, and she winced in pain, bringing her back to reality from wherever she had been hiding.

Jessica looked at the man in the chair, and her mouth dropped open.

Tom stared at her and whispered, "Sweet Jesus."

She shifted her gaze to Ty, chained to the far wall, agony visible in his eyes as he looked at what Frank had done to her.

"You are a dead man," Ty snarled and stood.

Frank flipped the monitor on and smiled at Ty. The screen filled with a picture of Chris with the radio on in the BMW, and he was singing badly to the music as he pulled onto the access road.

"Choose," Frank said to Ty, removing the remote from his pocket.

Ty looked at him in disbelief.

"Who lives? Who dies?" Frank asked, pointing at Jessica as he slowly advanced.

Ty looked between the screen and Jessica, who stood. "No." He knew how this game ended. *At least Chris is safe for the moment.*

Jessica brought her finger to her lips to keep Tom quiet and stepped behind Frank.

Frank held up the remote. "GPS tracking." He shook his head and pushed the button.

Ty had a split second to see the tracking screen in the car say Boom, and then the entire car blew to pieces, along with his little brother.

He stepped back against the wall. "You son of a bitch," he whispered and glared at Frank. His face hardened as rage filled him. "You know."

Jessica threw her arms over Frank's head and yanked. The handcuffs settled around his neck.

Frank threw an elbow, ramming it into her ribs. He smiled at her scream of pain as he flipped her onto the floor and ducked through her arms, out of her reach. He grabbed her by the hair and slammed her head on the concrete, knocking her out.

"NO!" Ty thundered.

Frank dragged Jessica back to the mattress and tossed her onto it.

Tom watched in stunned silence.

Ty struggled against the chains holding him in place, and then he stopped. The reflection in the mirror caught his attention. A patch of red spread over the fabric of the back of her dress, spinning out onto the white silk like little crimson snowflakes. He slowly fell to his knees.

Beyond the reflection stood Eric.

Please, God, please help her.

Eric nodded and leaned down over Jessica's reflection.

Not her face. Ty lowered his gaze to the floor in front of him. Frank couldn't know about Eric. *He will kill her if he finds out, so you cannot fix her completely. Just the inside. Okay?*

Eric nodded and looked nervously at Frank. He kneeled down, putting his hands on Jessica's head and her side. He leaned over and kissed her shoulder.

Speckles of light flowed over Jessica's body.

Tom's mouth slowly fell open.

Jessica groaned softly as Eric did his magic.

Ty changed his focus to Frank, letting fury fill his eyes again. "I swear to God that if you touch her again, I will tear you to pieces."

"Funny you should say that. I've got some things for you to see." He popped in the DVD and looked from Ty to Tom. "Hey, pretty boy."

Tom's head snapped toward him. His eyes were wide.

"They're the reason you're here," Frank said, pointing toward Jessica and Ty.

"Where is 'here'?" Tom said, his voice hoarse and dry.

The weird light around Jessica was gone. She was moving.

Ty glanced back in the mirror. Eric was no longer there.

Jessica's eyes slowly opened and focused on him.

I hope Eric was strong enough, Ty thought, and her eyes went wide.

"All in good time." Frank pressed play. "First, I think you need to understand WHY you are here."

The screen filled with the scene in Jessica's room, and when her image snarled *It's not like you're Smallville and I had reason to beg,* Tom exhaled, shaking his head as he continued to watch the screen. He winced as she lashed out, kicking Ty in the balls.

"Damn," he whispered when she knocked herself out and the screen went black.

"You see, my boy there fell for this bitch," Frank began. "It was a good thing because I got this little tidbit because of it." He pressed play again, and Ty's confession filled the screen.

Ty kneeled on the ground with his head low as Frank walked behind the chair toward him and squatted just out of reach.

"It's too bad you killed the wrong person." Frank laughed as Ty's eyes widened.

Ty lunged and one of the chains holding his arm gave enough for his hand to graze Frank.

Frank shifted back. "That's right. She never wanted me. I found out about Dad's little nightly adventures and decided to have one of my own. Bitch was a wildcat. I cut her up while I fucked her." He smiled sadistically as he looked over at Jessica. "I plan on doing the same to her." He looked back at Ty. "And you are going to watch."

Ty shook with rage and something else, something foreign since the day he'd planted the knife in Jacob Aris's back. He was afraid.

"I'm sorry," Jessica said to Tom.

Tom shook his head a little as if to say don't be.

"Now, since you left, we have had some fun." Frank stood and grabbed Jessica's cuffs. Then he brought her to the opposite corner and attached the cuffs to a hook in the wall over her head, high enough so she had to stand on her tiptoes. "Figured now that you're awake, you'd want to see this again as well."

Jessica said nothing, but a tear slipped from her eye as she looked from Tom to Ty and back.

"I don't need to see this," Tom said.

Frank turned on him. He walked up to the chair and threw a right hook at Tom's cheek.

"I think you do," Frank said.

The screen filled with Jessica in the chair, watching all the horrible images that Frank had put together for her. Ty saw the change in her, his heart sinking at the betrayal in her eyes. He glanced at her, momentarily forgetting how to breathe. She was a goddess in that white dress, even with the bruises. Ty put his head in his hands. First his mother, then Anna, and now Chris. He could not lose her, too.

He looked back at the monitor as Frank knocked her out with a punch and then screwed her unconscious body.

A small sob escaped Jessica, making all the men in the room look at her. Frank walked over and ran his hand down her side. She moved away from his touch, but he stepped closer. Her breath hissed in and out in anger.

"Get away from her!" Ty and Tom yelled at the same time, causing Frank to turn a little, just enough to leave him vulnerable.

Jessica's eyes flashed as she lifted her knee. It connected with his crotch. His scream sounded like a little girl's, high and shrill, as he dropped. She wound her hands around the cuff chains and used them as leverage to dropkicking him in the face. He rolled away as her second foot connected with the side of his head.

Ty lunged toward Frank and was stopped within inches of reaching him by the chains. His cry of rage filled the room as he strained to get free. Every muscle in his chest and arms quivered. He stepped back and lunged again. "I'm going to kill you, you mother-fucking son of a bitch!"

Frank backed away from Ty, still holding his crotch in pain. He limped out of the room, glaring at Jessica. She glared back as the door slammed. On screen, Mike was raping her.

"Jess?" Ty said.

SHE LOOKED OVER AT him, willing herself not to cry as she tried to figure a way to unhook herself.

Ty dropped to his knees again. The pain in his eyes cut right into her heart, and she could not hold the tears back.

Jessica looked at the hook holding her arms in the air with determination. She jumped a couple of times but wasn't able to release her hands from the hook.

Laughter drifting out of the speakers caught her attention, and she glanced at the screen. She was laughing with Mike. The tears came again.

"What was so funny?" Ty asked, watching the screen.

"He said I looked like hell." Jessica shook. Her eyes shifted to her reflection in the mirror across the room. Her face was still the black and blue shading, but it no longer hurt. Neither did her ribs or her back.

Ty smiled a little. "You still had my shirt on."

Jessica nodded. She flipped her hair to the side and tried to turn to see her back. It was, for the most part, healed. All that was there were red welts, no more open wounds.

She looked at Ty. "How?"

"Eric." Ty shrugged. "He was scared because he couldn't get to you. He said I had to protect you. Bang-up job I'm doing at that."

She softened a little.

"Will someone please tell me where I am, and what the hell is going on?" Tom said in frustration.

"I'm not sure where here is, but I am sorry that you're here. You shouldn't be." Jessica glanced back at Ty. "What the hell were you thinking?"

She jumped again, and this time she almost got it. Her heart thundered in her chest. *Just a little higher!* She jumped again, and the chain came free. She leaned back against the wall with her arms lowered in front of her. Her eyes were on the screen.

They both followed her gaze. Frank was grabbing her by the hair, pulling her into his lap. The air whistled between their teeth, and they both winced with what followed. Both sets of eyes swiveled in her direction.

A hint of a smile found her lips. "He isn't going to do anything for a while." She walked over to Ty.

When Jessica slipped her chained arms over his head, he wrapped his arms around her. Tears made slow tracks down his cheeks.

"He killed Chris." Ty laid his head on her shoulder, shaking to contain the sobs he had locked in his chest. He squeezed her tight and when he pulled away, her shoulder was wet from the flow of his tears. He removed her arms from around his neck and wiped his face with his hands. "I'm sorry I left you," he whispered and grazed her cheek with his lips.

Both of them jumped as Tom cried out, rigid in the chair as an electrical current flowed through him.

Frank stepped back into the room. "I thought that would get your attention." He shut the door behind him. Brass knuckles shined on both hands as he approached Ty.

TY HAD SEEN THAT look in Frank's eyes many times before. He grabbed Jessica, pushing her behind him in a protective reflex.

Jessica buried her face in the back of his shirt as the next chapter in her horrifying week rolled across the screen.

Ty glanced up. His eyes slowly widened, and his jaw dropped.

Frank laughed.

Ty could feel Jessica shaking behind him. His eyes drifted to his stepbrother as the screams from the monitor echoed off the concrete walls.

"Oh, Jesus, I think I'm going to be sick," Tom said.

"Suck it up," Frank replied as he passed by the chair.

"You touch her, you die," Ty growled.

"Who's going to stop me?" He swung, connecting with Ty's jaw.

Ty took a small step back. Jessica moved against the wall and pulled him back another step, drawing Frank closer. The next punch caught him full in the nose, sending him backwards.

Frank had miscalculated the length of the chains. Ty stopped the next punch. His hand closed around Frank's throat, cutting off his airway in a death grip.

The growl that escaped Ty reminded him more of a Rottweiler's snarl than a human.

Ty didn't react to any of the punches Frank threw at his midsection, even with the sharp crunching sound of his ribs breaking under the blows. He was hell bent on squeezing the life out of Frank, regardless of the pain racking his body.

NEITHER TY NOR JESSICA saw Frank reach for the Taser until it was too late.

Frank rammed it into Ty's chest and pulled the trigger. Ty's grip tightened for a moment, and then he went down hard, leaving Jessica standing unprotected. Frank glared at her and then beat the life out of Ty as he lay helpless.

Jessica backed away, slowly inching her way across the room. She trembled, watching Frank hit Ty over and over again with the brass knuckles. The sound of pummeled flesh and bone drowned out the audio from the video still rolling on the screen. She passed within inches of Tom, who was staring at the screen, his eyes wide and glossed with tears. She turned to see a woman opening the door to a trailer, followed by a flash as the trailer blew up.

Tom looked at her as she passed. "My wife," he whispered. "They killed my wife."

Jessica stopped, and just for a moment, her fear transitioned to heartfelt sorrow at the devastation in Tom's eyes. She shifted her gaze back to Ty, who was unconscious and bleeding on the floor. Frank kept punching, and each time his fist connected, Ty's body flopped as it absorbed the blow.

Her fear came crashing back. "Stop!" she yelled.

Frank stopped mid blow and turned, meeting her wide-eyed stare. He advanced on her, and she took an involuntary step back. For each step forward Frank took, she stepped back.

Tom could not help her. Their eyes met for a second as she felt the wall behind her. There was nowhere else to go.

She saw movement out of the corner of her eye. Eric's reflection appeared next to Ty, and the little boy leaned over, sending some of his miracle healing power into him.

Everything went black as Frank's fist connected with her face.

Survival Games Chapter 48

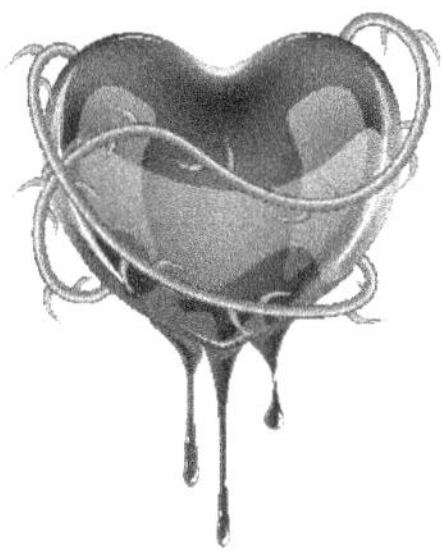

DANIEL WALKED BY ERIC'S room. Eric's eyes held more worry than a child of his age had a right to feel. He kneeled on the floor with his arms spread wide and his hands flat on an invisible being. Then he leaned over and kissed the air.

Daniel's eyes went wide as the air below Eric's hands sparkled.

Eric looked up and saw his father standing at the door. "The bad man really hurt Mommy," he whispered, and tears fell from his eyes.

Daniel was speechless. He walked in and kneeled before Eric. "What just happened?" he asked softly.

"I fixed Mommy, but Ty told me to only fix her on the inside. I had to leave the booboos on her skin, so the bad man doesn't kill her," Eric answered.

LeAnn walked around the corner and popped her head in the door. "Is everything okay?"

Daniel turned to her and shook his head.

LeAnn kneeled down in front of Eric and took his hands. "Are you upset with your father and me?"

Eric blinked up at her, his tears drying up, replaced by confusion. "No, why would I be upset with you?"

"Because we're dating," she said. "And maybe you weren't ready for that."

"It's okay that you're here."

"Then what's the matter, honey?"

He blinked again, switching his gaze from her to his father and back. He rubbed his eyes and yawned. "I think... I think I just had a nightmare." He climbed back into bed, shuffling under the covers, and smiled when his father kissed his forehead.

Daniel and LeAnn glanced at each other as they tucked Eric in.

Once they were downstairs, LeAnn spoke. "Maybe it's too soon for this."

Daniel took her in his arms. "No, it's not." He kissed her. "I didn't think I would feel this way about anyone else ever again, and then you came along."

LeAnn smiled and kissed Daniel. "I feel the same way."

"Then marry me," Daniel said.

She gazed into his eyes and sighed. "It's too soon, Danny."

He nodded, disappointed at the rebuttal.

ERIC KNEELED OVER TY, sending his magic flowing into the nearly dead man on the concrete floor. He left the bruises on the skin just like with his mother, but the broken bones righted themselves, mending to where not even an MRI would show a break had occurred. The cuts, contusions, and internal bleeding stopped as light danced over his body.

Eric pulled away and stood, glancing at his reflection in the bathroom mirror of the house. He needed to get some sleep, because they were going to need him again. Next time, he wasn't so sure he would be able to fix them.

Survival Games Chapter 49

JESSICA WOKE WITH HER arms tied to the bed. Tom paced back and forth like a caged lion, trying the door, then continued pacing.

Ty opened his eyes, wondering why he wasn't in excruciating pain. The beating he'd taken should have landed him in the morgue, or at the very least the ICU at the nearest hospital, but that wasn't the case. He glanced at his reflection. The bruises were still on his skin, but as he shifted position, there was no pain.

Holy shit! Eric? His eyes found Jessica's.

She creased her eyebrows and nodded slightly before turning her attention back to Tom.

He stopped pacing when his gaze caught hers and sighed, taking a seat on the edge of the mattress facing Ty. "I'd like to kill him." He nodded his chin in Ty's direction.

"Don't," Jessica said.

Tom turned and looked at her. "He killed my wife."

"I know," Jessica began and swallowed. "It's my fault, and I know it doesn't make sense right now, but he'll protect us."

Tom shrugged with a look on his face that said 'so what?'.

Jessica tilted her head. "We need him to get out of here."

"That psycho wanted me to hurt you. He wanted me to do whatever I wanted to you, but I had to make sure he was awake."

"Did you?"

"Did I what?" Tom asked in annoyance.

"Do what he said."

"No," he answered, as if that were the worst thing in the world.

Jessica knew firsthand that it wasn't. "Maybe you should."

He looked sharply at her. "Should what?"

"Do what he says."

"*You* didn't," he objected.

"And look where that has gotten me. I've been beaten, whipped, humiliated, and raped, and then I had the pleasure of watching someone I once loved literally ripped to pieces. For some godforsaken reason, he's in love with me, and oh joy, I'm the reason you're here and your wife is dead." She took a breath, tears streaming from her eyes. "Now I'm tied to a bed, with very little hope of ever seeing my kids again. And I have to pee. I'd say resisting has done one hell of a job for me."

Tom wiped the tear off her cheek.

Ty closed his eyes. "I'm sorry," he said, loud enough for both of them to hear.

"What the hell were you thinking?" she snapped.

"I was thinking of how I could get you the hell out of here," he answered. His steel-blue eyes bore into her, willing her to look at him.

Jessica did. Her eyes were purple now, no longer the deep violet.

Eric said you need to open the door. Ty pushed the thought, transmitting loud enough to make her wince. She sent a slight nod in his direction, but her fear was the only thing that tingled through him. For some reason, whatever Eric was talking about scared her more than Frank did. He shivered at the thought.

"Frank is going to kill me, Ty."

"Not if I can help it."

She brought her gaze back to Tom. "Can you let me up?" she asked. "Nature is calling, and I don't know how much longer I can hold on."

Tom raised his eyebrows and glanced at the handcuffs holding her wrists in place. He shook his head.

"Catch." Ty tossed a small pocketknife to Tom.

"What am I supposed to do with this?"

"Pick the goddamned lock."

Tom looked at him and shrugged. "How?"

"Are you really that fucking useless?" Ty took a deep breath and walked Tom through the art of picking locks.

Tom let out a small laugh as the first cuff clicked open. He repeated with her right hand, and as soon as the remaining cuff fell off her arm, she got up and ran to the bathroom.

"You'd better not hurt her," Ty said when she was out of sight.

Tom folded the pocketknife and slipped it in his pocket instead of returning it. "There is nothing you could do if I did," he said bitterly. "Just like I had no say in whether or not you killed my wife."

Ty propped himself up. He tried to do a good job at pretending to be hurt, enough to fool the actor in the room. "I'm sorry," Ty said as Jessica walked out of the bathroom.

She squatted and slapped him. "Sorry doesn't cut it. You had a choice," she said, her eyes bright with disappointment. "You made the wrong one." She sat next to him anyway and allowed him to put his head on her lap. She ran her hand through his hair and looked up at Tom.

His impossibly blue eyes returned her gaze.

The door opened, and a woman walked in with a tray of food, surprising all of them.

Ty shot up next to Jessica, meeting the hostile stare of the woman.

She set the tray on the floor and backed out of the room without saying a word.

When the door closed, both Jessica and Tom swiveled their gaze to Ty.

"Who was that?" Jessica asked.

Ty closed his eyes for a second and let out a small breath of relief. "My stepsister. We sometimes ask her to help when we can't be here, so the prisoners..." He looked at the chains, realizing that he was one of them now. "So we don't starve."

"Which means?" Jessica asked. Her eyes were hopeful.

"Which means he probably won't be back for a while."

Tom's stomach growled. He had gotten up and crossed to the tray, taking a plate and water and settling on the floor on the opposite wall facing Ty and Jessica.

"You might want to go easy on that. You have had nothing in your stomach for almost three days," Ty said.

Tom wolfed the food down and drained the water bottle, glaring at Ty. A few minutes later, he turned a little green and closed his eyes, breathing slowly, visibly trying not to throw up the meal he'd just scarfed down. After a couple of deep breaths, the color returned to his cheeks, and he opened his eyes.

Jessica got up, brought the tray over to Ty, and set it down between them. There had only been two plates on the tray. Sighing, she ripped the sandwich in half and handed the bigger portion to Ty.

He stared at it for a moment and slowly took it from her, humbled by this simple act, because the intent of only two plates was perfectly clear. Frank had told Marian that he would not get any food. He ate the sandwich in two bites, and Jessica handed him the water bottle to wash it down. He only drank half and handed it back. She finished it and then went into the bathroom to refill it with the water from the sink. She came back and handed the full bottle back to Ty without saying a word.

TOM WATCHED THIS EXCHANGE quietly, and when Jessica gazed over at him, he understood. The contrast of her elegance and beauty with the black and blue tones of her beaten face gave him pause. He could not fathom it, but somehow she forgave Ty for all he had done.

He closed his eyes and leaned his head back against the wall as the events of the day slammed into him hard. The reality of never seeing his wife again hit, and tears burned the corners of his eyes.

JESSICA TOOK A STEP toward him. But Ty grabbed her arm. He dropped his hand at her warning glare.

She kneeled in front of Tom, hesitantly reaching out to wipe his tears. His eyelids shot open in surprise at her touch.

"I am so sorry," she whispered.

He shook, allowing her to pull him into her arms as he silently cried, mourning the loss of his wife.

"I'm so sorry." A tear slipped down her cheek as she turned and looked at Ty.

TOM CLUNG TO HER like a child as the silent sobs quaked inside him. After a while, he pushed her away and headed toward the bathroom.

Bastard!

He sucker punched Ty in the face on his way and shook the sting from his hand, feeling a little better at taking out some of his aggravation on the target of his hatred.

In the bathroom, he splashed water on his face and leaned on the sink.

I want him dead!

Anger brewed. The rage in his reflection caught him by surprise, and he straightened up, taking a step back, his eyes widening a fraction. He shook his head.

"You're better than that," he said to his reflection, feeling the fury die down to a low simmer. He splashed another handful of cold water on his face and grabbed the hand towel hanging from the rack.

As he walked out of the bathroom, Jessica brushed by him, her hand grazing his. And that

simple touch was enough to give him the strength he needed not to kill the man chained to the wall.

JESSICA WANTED OUT OF the soiled dress she was in, so she walked into the bathroom. She rummaged through the closet for anything but found only towels.

"Shit," she mumbled, coming out into the middle of the main room. Staring at the camera, she spoke loud and clear. "May I please have something else to wear? And something for them as well?" She pointed to both Ty and Tom. Her gaze dropped to Ty. His shirt was bloody and ripped from the beating, and she sighed as she scanned him, her gaze landing on the iron shackles on his wrists and ankles. She crossed to Tom and put her hand out. "Give me the knife."

Tom reached into his pocket and handed it to her.

She walked over to Ty.

"It's not the same as handcuffs," Ty said. "Believe me. We lost a key once and had to cut a prisoner's foot off."

Jessica stared at him for a moment, debating whether he was exaggerating. He gave her a shrug and dropped his gaze in shame. She kneeled down and picked up the shackle on his wrist, turning it this way and that. She pulled the metal toothpick out of the pocketknife and stuck it in a little hole in the side. She frowned and closed her eyes, feeling the metal with her fingers, slipping the toothpick blindly into the hole again and willing it to open.

Click! The sound filled the room.

She opened her eyes, letting a small laugh escape. "I'm not so fucking useless after all."

He stared at the open shackle and rubbed his free wrist. It wasn't possible. He raised his eyes, slowly extending his other wrist to her. A few moments later, another *click* filled the room. Ty uttered a laugh and shook his head. She obviously had something on him in the realm of picking locks.

"Where'd you learn to do that?" he asked, offering her his ankles.

She furrowed her brow.

"Pick locks."

"I've never done this before," she answered. *Click, click* in quick succession, and he was free.

Ty shot to his feet and made a run for the bathroom. When he came out, Jessica had a pair of clean clothes for each of them. Ty glanced between the camera and Jessica, taking a deep breath. She was a piece of work.

With a clean dress and undergarments in her arms, she headed toward the bathroom. Hesitating at the doorway, she turned. "Don't even think about it."
The warning glance she shot in Ty's direction was clear. And just like that, she disappeared out of sight.

THE GENTLE WHOOSH OF the shower being turned on filtered out into the room. Ty and Tom traded a glance.

Ty stepped toward the bathroom.

"She said no," Tom warned.

Ty looked back at him in surprise. "What?"

Tom approached him, and they stood eye to eye. "No," he said again.

Ty snorted at him in a half laugh. "Bullshit." He took another step.

Tom moved quicker and blocked Ty's path, crossing his arms over his chest. He planted his feet firmly. When Ty tried to sidestep, Tom countered, blocking his every move.

"Leave her alone," he warned. They stared at each other. "Haven't you hurt her enough?"

The air went out of Ty as those words sank in, and he winced at the flare of pain they produced.

"Hurts, doesn't it?"

Ty nodded and backed down. "Like hell." He looked at Tom. "Are you always such a boy scout?"

Tom nodded slowly. "I should really kick your ass right now."

"What are you waiting for?"

"That's what *he* wants," he said, pointing at the cameras. "And I've concluded that it's his fault my wife is dead."

Ty sighed. "Not entirely," he confessed. "I was the one who pushed the button."

Tom slowly lowered his arms, his hands balled into fists as Ty's confession hit home. He swung, but Ty grabbed his arm and bent it behind Tom, pushing him against the wall. Even though they matched in height and weight, Ty was much stronger.

"I don't want to hurt you," Ty snarled in his ear as he held him against the wall.

"Let him go, Ty," Jessica commanded.

They both looked at her, and Tom's jaw dropped. Water rolled off her legs, pooling on the floor, and the bath towel barely covered her. Droplets slowly drizzled from her hair, but the most striking thing about Jessica was her perfectly unmarked skin. The bruises and cuts were all gone, and her eyes had changed to a strange combination of lilac and blue.

Ty let go and stepped back. As she turned, they both stared at the unbroken skin of her back.

Tom looked at Ty and then walked toward the bathroom as she slipped a dress over her head.

She turned to see him staring—his jaw hanging open—and smoothed the dress self-consciously. "You can catch flies with that mouth," she said.

He snapped it shut, stepped closer, and reached out to touch her face. "Your face?" he asked. "Your back?"

"She's special," Ty said from behind him, making him jump.

Tom put his arm out, stopping his forward progression. "You have hurt her enough," he growled. "Back off."

"Okay, settle down you two," she scolded. "Now get." She waved her hands at them. "Go," she said a little louder.

When she walked out of the bathroom, she stumbled and her eyes rolled back.

Ty moved quicker than Tom and caught Jessica before she hit the floor. He swept her unconscious body into his arms, glancing at Tom as he laid her out on the mattress.

Her eyes fluttered open as Ty wiped the hair from her face. Tom stood over his shoulder, wearing a look of pure concern.

"You can't keep doing that," Ty said.

"I'm tired," she said, her eyelids fluttering closed. Sleep grabbed hold and dragged her into the dark.

They covered her with the sheet and each of them sat on the floor next to the mattress with their backs to the wall, watching the door and waiting.

"We're gonna die, aren't we?"

Ty shook his head. "No. You two will walk out of here." He leaned his head back, closed his eyes, and drifted off.

Survival Games Chapter 50

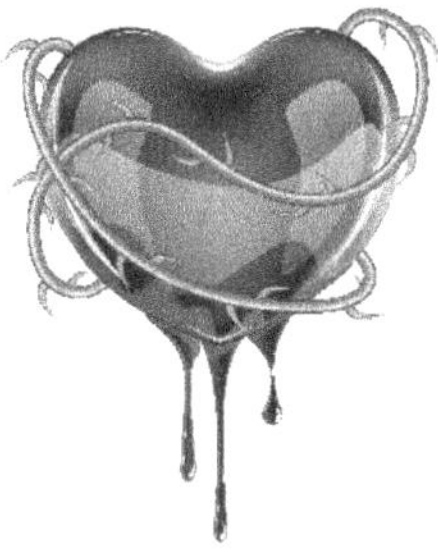

TY APPROACHED THE CENTER of the room where the coffin sat, each step almost as loud as the beat of his heart. Terror gripped him, and he couldn't draw a breath into his lungs even though they burned for oxygen.

Blood dripped from the edges of the casket. He didn't want to see what was inside, but his feet kept moving and his heart thundered against his rib cage, almost hard enough to rattle his bones. His lungs screamed for air, but he couldn't pull any in.

He took another step closer, and he could see a hand, a small hand, holding the side of the coffin. As he stepped around the side, he saw Jessica's face immersed in blood.

The boy looked up, tears tracking down his cheeks. "You killed her," he whispered.

Air rushed into Ty's lungs, enough to bellow, "No!"

Ty sat up, his eyes wide and his breath coming in quick bursts as the nightmare held on. His eyes darted around the room, the sight of the familiar concrete walls calming him enough so he could catch his breath.

Jessica woke with a start to his scream. She reached out, touching him, and he turned her way with wide eyes.

"Shh," Jessica whispered.

Tom was lying on the outer edge of the mattress on top of the covers with his back to them, sound asleep and snoring lightly.

Jessica moved back and pulled the covers up. She motioned for Ty to join her.

He slid under the covers, putting his arm under her head, and lay on his back with his eyes open. The dream still haunted him, even with her warm, decidedly alive body against him, her head cradled in the nook of his shoulder. Her breath evened to the sleep pattern he'd memorized over the last six months. He didn't sleep. Instead, he did something he hadn't done in years.

He prayed.

Survival Games Chapter 51

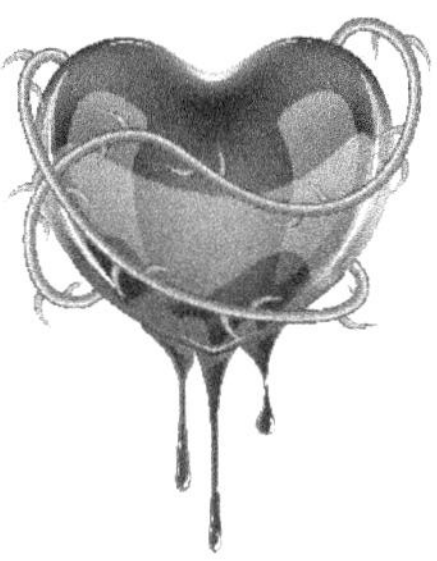

TY SLID JESSICA OFF him, grabbed the clothes that Marian had brought, and went into the bathroom. He started the shower and stepped in under the hot water, leaning with his hands against the front wall as the water rolled over him.

How the hell am I going to get us out of this?

His mind wandered back to Chris. "I'm sorry, bro," he said. "I messed up."

The pain came, and with it, the tears. He sobbed quietly as the water pounded down on the back of his head.

HE DIDN'T HEAR HER come in the room. Jessica stood and watched him cry. She wanted to put her arms around him and comfort him, but she couldn't. Not with all that had happened. She walked back into the room and sat down on the edge of the mattress.

Tom rolled over and looked at her, wiping the sleep from his eyes. He looked around the room and closed his eyes. It wasn't just a nightmare. This was real.

"Morning," he said.

Jessica nodded and studied her hands.

"You okay?" he asked.

Jessica let out a small, hysterical laugh and turned her tear-filled eyes in his direction.

Tom moved next to her, putting his arm around her shoulders, and pulled her closer. They sat quietly.

"You have a son?" Tom asked.

Jessica nodded. "And a daughter."

"Tell me about them," he said, still holding her next to him.

"Eric and Emily," she began and smiled. "Em is thirteen. She is a handful. Smart, too smart for her own good, but she is also a bit sly, so we have to watch out for her. If she is anything like I was, we are in for a wild ride." She sighed, wiping her eyes. "Eric... Eric is my angel boy. He is seven and has such a good heart. He is going to be a different type of handful, because he is such a little cutie. All the girls love him. He is going to break hearts when he gets older." She started to cry. "I'm not so sure I'm going to be there to see it."

He pulled her closer as the hum of the shower ceased.

"I miss them," Jessica whispered and covered her face, turning into him, burying her head in his shoulder, trembling with unshed tears.

He wrapped both arms around her.

TY WALKED OUT, AND his heart dropped. Tom looked up, still holding her tight. His eyes warned not to come closer, and Ty heeded the warning.

The door opened, tearing his attention away from Tom and Jessica. He met Marian's glare. Her swift placement of the tray and subsequent scramble out the door didn't give him much of a chance to reason with her, but he tried anyway.

"Wait."

She hesitated, with her hatred on display in the sneer on her face. "You killed my father." She closed the door.

Tom stood and retrieved the tray. He brought it over to Jessica.

"Ty needs some too," she said.

"Why?" Tom asked.

"Because," Jessica answered and looked at him. "Whether we like it or not, he is stuck in here, just like we are, and I'm not going to just sit here while he starves to death."

"I can't forgive him as easily as you can. He killed my wife."

"I haven't forgiven him, and I certainly don't expect you to," she said. "But that doesn't make it right to hurt him, either."

Tom stared into her eyes and nodded.

Ty slowly sank to the ground at her words. "I'm sorry," he said again.

Jessica brought her portion of the breakfast over to Ty. "I know you are." She sat next to him with the plate. She ate a small portion and handed him the remaining food.

"You need more than that, Jess."

"I'M GOOD." SHE GOT up and started pacing, lost in her own thoughts. Thoughts of Ty. Thoughts of Mike. Thoughts of her life before all this.

Both Ty and Tom watched her with rapt attention, for lack of anything else to do.

It was way too quiet in the room. She looked up at the camera. "Any way we could get some tunes?" she asked and continued pacing.

Music filled the room, and she stopped, sending a nod of thanks toward the camera. The track was familiar—it was what Ty had played for her every day. Her lips curved in a sad smile.

Her hips swayed softly to the tune, her skirt swishing with each about-face. Her hands floated by her side, graceful arcs motivated by the tune. "Calling All Angels" started, and she stole a glance in Ty's direction as the melody escaped her lips. She twirled, tilting her head back, feeling more like Dorothy Hamel twirling on the ice than a woman in a concrete prison.

The effect on Ty was immediate. He stood up and had her in his arms in a matter of seconds, his hands in her hair and his lips pressed to hers. She pushed him away at the same time Tom yanked him from her.

"No," Tom said, inserting himself between the two of them.

"It's okay." Jessica put her hand on his shoulder.

"No, it isn't." Tom looked at her. His blue eyes warned her not to push, but there was something else there, too.

Ty glared at Tom, his eyes narrowing. "You want her, too," he said in disbelief.

Tom looked back at Ty but didn't say a word. "I told you not to go near her. You have done enough."

Ty took a threatening step toward Tom, but it was Jessica who stopped him.

"Don't," she warned, stepping around Tom. She looked back and forth between them. "Just stop this." She put her hands on both their chests, holding them at bay.

"I can take care of myself," she said to Tom.

Ty smiled smugly at him until she turned and looked at him.

"You don't get to do that anymore," she said.

His smile vanished.

It was Tom's turn to smile.

"Go clean up," she said to Tom, catching the smug smile on his lips.

He looked down at her and back up at Ty.

"Go," she whispered, and he did.

He left her alone with Ty.

They watched him leave the room and heard the shower turn on. She looked back at Ty; her hand was still on his chest. Just touching him made her ache for him. He stepped closer.

"Ty," she sighed and looked up at him. He went to kiss her, but she pulled away.

Anger flashed in his eyes, and he yanked her close.

She had seen that look before. It had come with the words, *I can have you any time, any way I want.*

She flinched and pushed him away. "No."

"Yes." He pressed her up against the wall. His lips crushed hers, and he tangled his hand in her hair, the other sliding between her legs.

Instead of fighting him, she just stood there, unwilling to respond to his touch, even though every fiber screamed for him, every cell wanted him. She swiped his hand away, mumbling "no" under the pressure of his lips.

He slowly pulled back, taking a step away from her. "I lost you, didn't I?"

She shook her head, and a single tear slipped out of her eye. "You can't lose what you never had."

THE CRUSHING BLOW OF her words buckled his knees. He dropped in front of her, hanging his head in defeat. His shoulders shook. Hot tears burned his throat, and what remained of his heart died, sealing itself in a gray tomb, much like the concrete prison surrounding him.

Devastation clouded his mind.

Jessica stepped forward, wrapping her arms around him, and slowly ran her fingers through his hair.

In that moment, in her arms, Ty Aris ceased to exist in his solitary self-centered world. He knew without a shadow of a doubt that he would die for her if that was what it took to save her.

WHEN TOM CAME OUT of the bathroom, Jessica was back to singing softly and pacing, and Ty was lying on the mattress with his eyes closed.

"This is surreal," Tom said.

Jessica stopped and looked at him. His hair was wet and hand-combed back. He had rough stubble from not shaving, and the combination with his blue eyes looked really good. He was wearing a white button-down shirt he hadn't bothered to button and jeans that Marian had brought for him. As he walked toward her, he rolled his sleeves up.

"I need to move," Jessica said. "There was a treadmill in the room before. I got used to running."

"Mind if I join you?"

"It's a free country," she said, as if the question were absurd.

He started pacing with her, and after a while; she cracked a smile.

"What?" he asked, smiling as well.

"This *is* surreal," she said.

Ty opened his eyes. "Do you know how stupid you look?"

"Fuck off," Tom snapped, his smile evaporating.

"My restlessness is your fault." Jessica pointed at him.

Ty sat up, shrugging with his arms out. "How is it my fault?"

"Uh, the daily run you made me do."

Ty laughed. "For the last few months, you've been doing that on your own."

Jessica sent a glare in his direction. "What else did I have to do?" She turned and disappeared into the bathroom.

TY SIGHED. HE GLANCED at Tom for a second, then back to the bathroom doorway, reminding himself that he would never have her again. His smile vanished slowly.

"If you love her that much, tell me how to get her out of here."

Jessica came back into the room.

Ty took a deep breath. "You can't get out of here," he said. "Doors operate on fingerprints, and mine are obviously not ones that are in the system anymore. I've tried the door." He paused. "The elevator has a higher level of security. Retinal scans, and once you are inside, you need the key to operate it. There were only four scans that were approved for access. Chris, Frank, Marian, and mine. There are cameras in every room and in the hallways, so monitoring activity didn't require more than one of us at a time. The only places there aren't cameras are the bathrooms and the control room." He closed his eyes. "The editing suite in the control room is top of the line, and that's where I created the magic out of whatever brutality Frank dreamed up." He shook his head to clear his thoughts and opened his eyes, scanning the room before he brought his gaze back to the two of them. "I designed the place. There is no way out unless you have someone's eyeball and a key. The only other way is to get access to the security system, and that isn't happening either."

Jessica and Tom looked at each other.

"Why not?" Tom asked.

"Because the security system is in Frank's office, which is three stories above us on the ground floor of the warehouse. No one but the four of us knew this was down here, and no one we ever brought down left alive."

"How many have there been?" Jessica asked.

Ty shrugged and studied his fingers, picking at a hangnail.

"How many are here now?" Jessica asked.

Ty held up three fingers, raising his eyes to hers.

Jessica looked at him for a long time. "Where is this place?"

"Just outside Albany. Ever hear of Aris Technologies?"

Aris was one of the most successful privately owned communications companies in the world. She had worked with several companies who wanted to buy it.

"Yes." She nodded. "Why?"

"Frank owns it."

"Holy shit," Jessica said, gaping at him.

"What? Holy shit what?" Tom asked.

"Frank is richer than God," Jessica said. "Which means you aren't hurting either." Her face hardened a fraction.

Ty laughed. "No. Chris and I weren't accounted for in the old man's will, but Frank took care of us, anyway. At some level, we were grateful, but now, looking back, I guess we would have been better off somewhere else. Money and power, that's what it's all about. At least that's what my stepfather and Frank grilled into us. I never cared about the money." Ty closed his eyes. "But power." He laughed. "Power. That was something I wanted. Maybe it's because I was so powerless growing up. This little side venture gave me ultimate power." He opened his eyes and looked at Jessica. "Frank told me what the customers wanted, and until you came along, I was just fine with providing them with their black-market videos. I have to admit being in control, having that level of power, was such a rush."

"You're a sick bastard," Tom said.

Ty nodded and smiled a little. "Yeah, well, being on the other side sucks." He looked around the room.

"There has to be a way," Jessica said.

Ty looked over at her. "I'm working on it," he said. "I'm working on it."

Survival Games Chapter 52

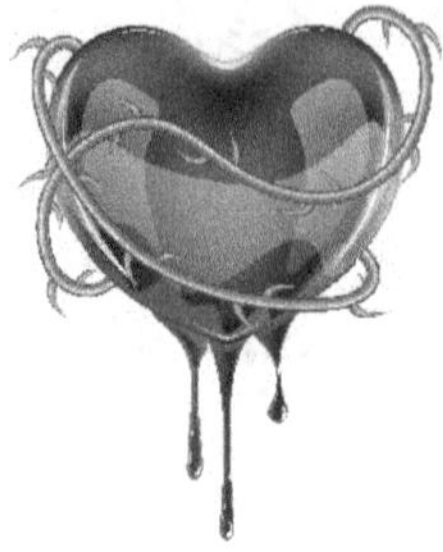

THE NEXT MORNING WHEN Marian opened the door to bring in the food, Jessica was standing nearby. Marian jumped in surprise and pulled out the gun she usually hid behind the tray.

The men were still asleep.

"Back off, bitch," Marian said, leveling the gun at Jessica.

Jessica stepped back. "Um, I need something," she whispered.

Marian stared at her as she set the tray down.

Jessica tilted her head and widened her eyes. "Period?"

Marian's face slowly registered understanding, and she nodded.

"Could I also have a couple more outfits for us, too?" Jessica pushed.

Marian nodded and closed the door. A few minutes later, she came back with what Jessica had asked for.

"Thank you," Jessica said.

She took the items and went into the bathroom, showered, and dressed in the shorts and T-shirt Marian had brought. When she came out, both Ty and Tom were awake. Tom had taken his half of the breakfast and left hers.

Ty hadn't touched anything. Jessica walked over, took the apple off the plate, and handed Ty the rest.

He closed his eyes. "Jess, you need more than just an apple." He handed back the plate.

"Not today," she said. "I'm not feeling that great." She had killer cramps and didn't want to eat. "I need to move." She began her restless pacing.

"Will you stop that?" Ty snapped at Jessica.

"This is your fault, so just shut up," Jessica snapped back.

"How is you not being able to sit still for five minutes my fault?" Ty inquired as he dug into the food.

She shot a glare in his direction.

Ty finished the breakfast sandwich and got up to put the empty plate back on the tray by the door. He stretched and turned, watching her pace. "Stop." He grabbed her arm as she passed him again.

Tom shot to his feet.

Jessica looked at the hand on her arm and back up at Ty. "Let go."

"Stop pacing," he warned.

"Or what?" Jessica ripped her arm from his grasp and continued to pace.

TY LOOKED AT THE ceiling, silently asking for patience. He glanced over at Tom, who looked like he was ready to pounce if he made the wrong move. "Cool your jets, scout," he shot at Tom. "I'm not going to touch her."

"You'd better not." Tom sat back, keeping his gaze on the brewing storm.

Ty looked at the mirrored wall and then around the room. When his gaze landed on the tray, he glanced back at the mirror. He leaned down and picked up the tray, dumping the empty plates on the ground, and wondered if what he was thinking would work. He crossed the room and walked along the mirror, counting out his steps. When he was three quarters of the way down the wall, he stepped back and pitched the tray with everything he had. The tray bounced off the mirror and hit him in the shin.

"Shit!" He hopped away and limped off the sting in his shin.

Jessica stopped pacing and just stared at him.

Ty picked up the tray again, and this time swung it like a baseball bat at the mirror. The impact echoed through the room, and it vibrated all the way up Ty's arms.

"God damn it!" He stared at the undamaged glass. He turned and pitched the tray at the door, the anger and frustration getting the best of him. "Marian, let me the fuck out of this room," he bellowed at the camera.

"Not on your life," she boomed through the speakers.

"Fucking bitch!" Ty glared and then strode into the bathroom.

He leaned over the sink with his head down, and when he caught movement out of the corner of his eye, he turned his head, meeting Jessica's concerned gaze.

"What?" he snapped.

Jessica put her hands up. "Just wanted to make sure you're all right."

Ty looked down again. "Well, I'm not. I'm about as far from all right as you are." *And it's my fucking fault. If I hadn't said anything, we wouldn't be here right now.* The muscles in his jaw tightened, and his teeth ground together in frustration. He stood up straight.

"You don't know that," Jessica said.

"The hell I don't. I would have gotten you out, Jess," he stated.

Jessica's mouth dropped.

"I was going to get you out of here," he said again, his anger ebbing away at the look on her face.

"Ty," she said, her eyes filling with tears.

Ty walked to her and looked down into her strange eyes. "Happy birthday," he said. "I'm sorry this isn't the gift I planned for you." He leaned down, kissed her cheek, and then retreated into the main room, leaving her standing with her mouth hanging open in the entrance to the bathroom.

JESSICA WANDERED TO THE sink and splashed cold water on her face. She looked at her reflection and back at the doorway. "If you were going to get me out of here," she began as she walked out of the bathroom. "Why the hell did you yank him out of his life?" She pointed at Tom.

"I needed a diversion."

She balked. "Do you honestly think I would have let you sacrifice an innocent man to get me out of here?"

He sighed. "You wouldn't have ever known he was here."

Jessica's jaw tightened as she looked at the man who'd destroyed her life. "You son of a bitch." She launched herself at him.

Ty grabbed her swinging arm and swiveled her around, taking hold of her opposite arm as she struggled, screaming in his grip with her back to him. All the frustration, fear, and anger that had built up over the past six months blew out in a snarling wail. Jessica thrashed in his grasp until her throat was raw and her snarl turned into a sob.

TY SENT A WARNING glance at Tom, stopping him from coming any closer. A strange blend of remorse and sorrow gripped him as she struggled furiously in his arms, growling and spouting the foulest of curses.

Jesus, I did this to you.

Jessica sobbed, and Ty let go of her arms. She spun around and buried her head in his chest, surprising him. Hesitantly, he wrapped his arms around her, closing his eyes and kissing the top of her head. He swallowed the lump that formed in his throat.

"I'm sorry." He combed his fingers through her hair.

Jessica pushed away, wiping the tears from her face. "This is unforgivable." She turned and began her restless pacing again.

Tom sat back down in the corner, glaring at Ty. "You killed my wife as a diversion?"

"Yes," Ty answered and dropped his gaze. "I would have never gotten the chance to get her out without some kind of diversion." *And I would do anything for her.* He looked back at Jessica.

Jessica stopped and turned back toward Ty.

"Anything," Ty whispered as his eyes met hers.

JESSICA PACED UNTIL HER breath evened out and the pounding in her head subsided. With each step, her anger diminished, and she focused on what they would need to survive. Sitting on their asses waiting for the inevitable wasn't doing any of them any good. She stopped at the far side of the room and leveled a glare at the two men.

"Get your ass up," she barked at Tom. "And both of you get over here." She pointed at the floor in front of her.

Surprise registered on both their faces, but neither one moved.

"If you want to walk out of this place, you'll get your asses over here *now*," she commanded and waited while they slowly approached her. "When I'm through with you, you're gonna wish you never met me," she said to Ty.

Ty half smiled and stood before her, looking down at her angry features.

"We can sit on our asses and wait to die, or we can build our resistance and possibly survive this place." She looked between them. "Tae Bo or hip hop?"

Ty laughed.

"Do I look like I'm laughing?" Jessica shot at him, and that shut him up.

HER BARK OF AUTHORITY surprised Ty. This was a different side of Jessica Connor, one that he never would have guessed. It reminded him of his old karate instructor.

He couldn't help but smirk. "How about calisthenics?"

"No, we need aerobic exercise, along with strength training and stretching. Not just calisthenics. That alone will not help with endurance," she answered, shocking him. "I taught dance on the side before my son was born."

"I gotta see this." He crossed his arms and raised an eyebrow in a silent dare.

Jessica clenched her jaw. She might as well have said 'fuck you' because it was written in her glare.

She looked at Tom.

Tom shrugged. "Whatever."

Jessica nodded and waved them back a few steps. She pounded out a complicated hip-hop routine.

Ty dropped his arms along with his jaw. She was channeling again, and he shook his head to clear the sound of her internal hip-hop beat repeating over and over in his mind. A song that she was perfectly in sync with.

Jessica finished and looked at the two of them.

"Maybe Tae Bo would be better," Tom said, bringing a smile to her lips.

Ty glanced at Tom and then returned his gaze to Jessica. "I can do that."

"Prove it." She stepped back and crossed her arms.

Ty closed his eyes and let the song flow back into his memory. Then he repeated the moves Jessica had just done, finishing with his arms crossed and staring down at her. "Good enough?"

"You screwed up a few times."

"Bullshit."

The tension between the two of them teetered on ignition.

Tom cleared his throat, reminding them he was in the room. "I can't do that."

"Sure you can." Jessica glared at Ty. "Keep doing it," she commanded.

Ty pointed at his chest.

"Yes, you," Jessica snapped. "Until *I* say you can stop." She gave him a mean grin, turning the tables on him. She turned her attention to Tom and started a step-by-step instruction.

Ty repeated the routine.

Patiently, she walked Tom through all the steps between barking orders for Ty to keep repeating the routine. A couple of hours went by before Tom finally could repeat the steps she instructed.

Ty's muscles ached. "Can I stop yet?" Ty asked, out of breath. He hadn't stopped, even to watch the last repetition of the steps with Tom.

"Keep moving," Jessica ordered.

"Only if you do it with me."

TOM STEPPED BACK. DANCING did not come easily to him, and his thighs were burning. Muscles he didn't know he had hurt. He sat down on the cool concrete to watch.

Jessica's skin was lined with sweat as she pounded out the routine with Ty. Tom inhaled. Even though the routine was hip hop, she still exuded a grace that stirred him, a grace that made the concrete prison disappear. And Ty mimicked the moves just as flawlessly as she did, in time with a beat Tom couldn't hear. Flawless, as if they were connected in some bizarre manner, like their movements were two halves of the same person, like they were destined to be together. Tom broke out in goose bumps and blinked the train of thought away.

He didn't believe in destiny, and as long as he still had a breath in him, he would not let that happen. He wasn't going to let the bastard win.

"Go again," Jessica said to Ty when they'd finished.

Ty looked at her with wide eyes that said 'are you kidding?'. Sweat covered his body, making his shirt cling to his muscular form. "I can't." He leaned over with his hands on his knees, out of breath. "I didn't think someone your age could do that."

"Fuck you." She walked into the bathroom to clean up.

"Gladly," Ty said as she disappeared around the corner. He grabbed one of the bottles of water and downed it. "Goddamn. I don't think I'm gonna be able to move for days." He was still panting.

"How old is she?" Tom asked.

"Forty-two today."

Tom's eyebrows shot up, and his mouth dropped open.

No way! I thought she was my age or maybe a couple of years older, at best.

Ty laughed. "I was surprised, too. She is one hot ticket." He looked at the bathroom where the shower was running and took a step toward the sound.

"Don't even think about it," Tom said, and he stood, wincing as his muscles screamed at him.

Ty closed his eyes, then looked at Tom. "C'mon, man, I am in love with the woman."

Tom shook his head. "I don't give a damn. You hurt her enough and I'm not letting you near her." He positioned himself between Ty and the bathroom.

Ty glared at him, his chest still rising and falling heavily from the workout. "You have no idea how much..." he began and stopped, frustrated.

Tom raised his eyebrows. "How much what? How much you want her?" he snapped. "Any idiot can see that. But I don't care. She doesn't want you, and you are not touching her."

"She wants me. She's just pissed off because I brought you into this mess."

Tom thought about that for a minute. "She may want you," he conceded. "But she doesn't love you."

"You're both wrong," Jessica said, making them jump. She went back into the bathroom with no further explanation and then came out a few minutes later in jeans and one of their button-up shirts.

Ty sighed, raking her with his eyes, and then he headed in to clean up.

While the shower was running, Marian came with their lunch.

"You were watching?" Jessica asked.

Marian nodded. "I'm surprised he can move after the beating my brother gave him."

Jessica shrugged and stepped back as Marian put the tray on the floor.

Marian looked toward the bathroom. "I've never seen him so accommodating."

Jessica glanced toward the bathroom as Marian closed the door behind her. She reached down, picked up the tray, and headed over to Tom.

"What did you mean we were both wrong?"

Jessica took a deep breath as she sat next to him. "I know this is so cliché, but there is a fine line between love and hate." She took a bite of food. "No matter how I feel about Ty, I can't give him what he wants. It isn't right." She paused. "If I were to admit to wanting him..." She looked at Tom. "Then I would have no power over him."

Tom leaned back and absorbed that, but it did nothing to ease the feeling of being a third wheel around the two of them. "What about me?"

Jessica laughed. "I'm sorry. I don't mean to laugh. It's just that you've been my fantasy since I first saw you on TV. My kids teased me relentlessly because I once said you were my eye candy." She blushed and looked over at him. "And you are just as sweet in person."

Heat tingled in his cheeks, and he smiled. "Eye candy. Yeah, okay, thanks." He rolled his eyes. *Just what I wanted to hear.*

A dimple appeared in her crimson cheek. "Sorry, but you are."

"And that translates to what?" He took a bite of the sandwich, enjoying seeing her squirm a little.

"You already know what it means."

He feigned innocence, raised his eyebrows, and cocked his head.

She waved her hand at him. "Even all sweaty and such, you are one fine looking man."

He laughed. "And?"

"And any woman in her right mind would want you." She took a sip of water, blushing and glancing away from him.

He chuckled, satisfied with the answer. His wife used to tease him about the way his fans stared at him, both female and male, but in his mind, he was just an average guy who happened to land a terrific role in a popular series.

Eye candy, who would have thought?

Jessica saved more than half the plate for Ty and handed it to him when he came limping out of the bathroom.

"Thanks." He inhaled the food. Sighing, he leaned back against the wall and studied her. "Aren't you the least bit sore?"

Jessica shook her head. "Perhaps it was the three- to four-hour run you had me doing daily." She tilted her head as if to say 'so there.'

"Ha-ha," Ty replied.

"Have to admit, you got rhythm," she said.

"Nothing compared to your moves. I still can't believe you can dance like that." He pointed to where she taught him the routine.

"You've seen me dance before," Jessica said.

Ty smiled. "Yes. That's what started this whole mess."

Anger flashed in her eyes. "No, Ty, this mess started when you yanked me out of my life in that parking lot." She flopped onto the bed with her back to him.

Ty went to say something and closed his mouth.

Tom took advantage of the situation and moved next to where she lay. He gently ran his hand through her hair. It was the kind of thing his wife used to like when she wasn't feeling well. She always said it relaxed her, and if anyone needed to relax, it was Jessica. Her hair was silky and damp on his fingers.

Jessica looked over at him for a second, then rolled back. "Don't stop," she said when he pulled his hand away.

He sent a smug smile in Ty's direction and continued combing her hair with his fingers.

"Son of a..." Ty whispered and looked away, keeping his temper in check.

THE TENSION MELTED AWAY under Tom's gentle combing. For the first time since she woke in this hellhole, she felt safe. Like he was appointed her guardian angel, and nothing could hurt her while he was here. She knew how false that sense of security was, especially in this place, but she was grateful just the same. And with the continued strokes of his fingers, she drifted off.

The next morning, Jessica continued the exercise regimen, alternating between Tae Bo and the hip-hop routine she'd taught them the day before.

"Come on, I can't move like this today," Ty groaned.

"Do it!" She pointed at the floor, unimpressed by his whining.

TOM KEPT HIS MOUTH shut. His muscles and joints screamed with every move she asked of him. His personal trainer was demanding, but this was beyond anything he put him through. While he would like nothing more than to collapse on the concrete, he pushed harder, trying to get the rhythm, the same natural ease Ty had, even though he knew it was impossible.

She let them stop for the day when Marian brought lunch. The food had never tasted so good. He wolfed down his plate, watching Jessica split her lunch with Ty. A small pebble of guilt edged into his stomach, and he looked at the crumbs on his plate. He was the only one in the room getting a decent meal. He set the plate aside and stretched on the cool floor, regulating his breathing and ignoring the cramping in his muscles.

Both their heads swiveled when Jessica stood.

"Wuss," she said to Ty, but her eyes flicked to Tom for a moment and then she turned, disappearing into the bathroom.

Neither of them spoke. Tom sighed, his hatred toward Ty alive in his skin, but it didn't seem as acute as that first day. He still had reservations every time he left Ty and Jessica in the room alone, but he'd learned quickly that she was serious about not giving in to his advances.

When she came out, Tom stood and headed to take a shower.

"YOU STILL HAVEN'T GOTTEN up?" She laughed.

Ty dragged himself into a sitting position, wincing. His lower back and hips felt like Frank had taken the brass knuckles to them again. He met her amused gaze. "You're going to kill us, you know."

"It's a matter of survival." She leaned close. "He is going to come back, Ty. I want us all to be ready, and maybe we can get out of this alive." She lay back on the floor, keeping eye contact.

Ty felt the sudden rush of lust and had to resist the urge to take her right then and there. He wanted her so damn much.

He took a deep breath. "I hope you're right." And while hope played a big part of his existence right then, it wasn't placed on his life. That was something he planned on sacrificing.

No, his hope centered on her living, her surviving, and getting out of this place.

He was still staring at her when Tom came out of the bathroom.

They exchanged a nod, and Ty went to rinse the sweat off his aching body.

TOM STRETCHED OUT ON his side next to Jessica, propping himself up on his elbow. He brushed the hair out of her face and smiled.

"You didn't do that bad today," Jessica said, and he laughed. "Really."

"I don't have a natural ability like he does." He glanced up as the shower turned on and then slowly grazed her with his eyes. "Or like you do."

"You're not that bad."

He chuckled and placed his hand on her stomach. Her warmth radiated through the shirt. He sighed, meeting her questioning stare. The crease between her eyes deepened, and she shot her gaze to his hand and back.

On impulse, he leaned in to kiss her.

She stopped him, putting her hand on his chest and shaking her head. "Tom, your wife just died."

"But *I* didn't."

Her hand dropped.

He kissed her softly on the cheek and pulled away. "Thank you," he whispered.

Her hand touched the spot his lips had, and she stared at him with wide eyes. "For what?"

"For making me forget where I am, even if it was only for a moment."

"You shouldn't be thanking me, Tom. You're here because of me."

He didn't say anything right away, thinking about the video Frank had played for them. "You didn't know they would act on what you said," he finally replied. "And besides, you referred to a character in a television show. Not me."

"Don't you wish..." She looked over at him with a silly smile.

He knew where she was headed. He played the infamous Clark Kent in the show *Metropolis*. Superman before the cape and tights, and now that she mentioned it, he wished it were more than fiction.

"Wish I was Superman? Hell yeah." He smiled back. "That would come in real handy right about now. We would be out of here so fast his head would spin." He motioned toward the bathroom.

Her smile faded, and she followed his gaze. "I wouldn't let you leave him behind," she said. "He thinks he has to die to save me."

He didn't want to discuss Ty Aris at the moment. He wanted this suspension of their situation to last a little longer. "What's your favorite episode?"

Jessica chewed on her lower lip as the blush heightened in her cheeks. "I don't know. I guess I like the episodes where Clark is exposed to red kryptonite the best."

It figures. He grinned. "Ah, you like bad boys." He tickled her side.

She turned crimson and pulled away, laughing.

Survival Games Chapter 53

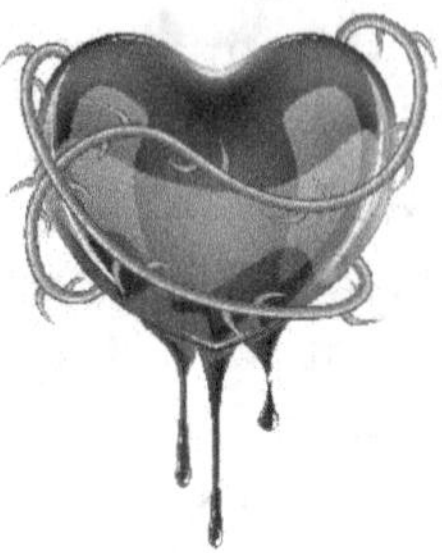

JESSICA MADE THEM WORK just as hard every day for the next several weeks. Each day they lay on the floor, exhausted as she cleaned up and emerged revived by the workout.

"What is she, the fucking Energizer Bunny?" Ty mumbled after seven weeks of her boot camp.

"She's a sadistic version of the Energizer Bunny," Tom agreed. "Better than any personal trainer I've ever had."

Ty chuckled and glanced at Tom. "I'm sure she's a hell of a lot better to look at, too."

Tom smiled and nodded. Seven weeks had diminished his hatred to what he would categorize as dislike. Ty wasn't all that bad. He was quiet most of the time and had a wicked sense of humor when he talked, which wasn't much. He was more content to sit on the sidelines and watch Jessica rattle on about her family or let Tom babble about working on a television show. But now and then, he interjected comments, almost like he was reminding them he was in the room. But Tom knew damn well Jessica never forgot his presence. Even when they spoke, her eyes drifted to wherever he was, like a magnet to steel.

Ty stood and started toward the bathroom.

"Don't even think about it," Tom said, jumping to his feet. He had done this same routine for seven weeks at various times, putting himself between Ty and wherever Jessica was.

Ty sighed and looked at Tom. "Don't you ever stop?"

Tom shook his head. "Afraid not." He had a bigger reason to stop him now than he did in the beginning. Ever since the eye-candy conversation, he had taken notice of her more and more. Her funky sense of humor, her drive, her grace, her faith in people, all combined with her raw sexuality, was intoxicating.

He'd asked her once about her husband, and she'd said very little, just that they had been together for twenty years and that he was a good man and a great father. No admission of love, of missing him like she did her kids, and Tom wondered if they got out of here, would she run back to the life she had?

He hoped not, because after seven weeks of being locked in the same room with her, he had fallen in love.

Ty backed off and stretched out on the floor again, and Tom joined him, waiting for Jessica to return.

"She's your miracle," Ty said.

Tom's brow furrowed. "What do you mean?"

Ty looked at him. "Don't fuck it up."

"Fuck what up?" Tom's heart hammered in his chest. Did Ty know?

Ty stared at him and tilted his head knowingly, then returned his gaze to the ceiling. "You know what I'm talking about. I've seen the way you look at her." He turned back toward Tom. "Don't try to bullshit me, either."

Tom glanced toward the bathroom and then back, offering a slight nod.

"She'll get you out of here." Ty took a deep breath. "*She* will be your miracle."

Tom was quiet as he digested the babble Ty was feeding him. He couldn't see how what he was saying was true, but he knew one thing—if they got out of here, he would still protect her from Ty. Regardless of the way the bastard felt about her.

"You really love her?"

Ty nodded. "Enough to die for her. So, you'd better damn well get her out of here while that happens. Understand?"

Jesus. What melodramatic crap is that? "How? How is she going to get me out of here?"

Ty looked toward the bathroom and shook his head. "I don't know, but you'll know when it happens."

She walked out, and both pairs of eyes drank her in, wanting her to be theirs.

Ty hopped to his feet and went to clean up, leaving Tom alone with Jessica.

She smiled at him and sat down. "What's up?"

Tom listened for the shower and looked down at his hands. "You're amazing."

Jessica laughed.

"I'm serious," Tom said, locking eyes with her. "Most people would have given up under the circumstances."

"I've got kids," she pointed out. "The thought of seeing them again is what drives me." She offered him a smile. "If I didn't have my angels, I'm not sure I could do this day after day."

It was Tom's turn to smile. "Sure you would, and that's why I love you."

HIS WORDS LEFT HER speechless, along with the sincerity in his blue eyes. He meant it, and a sweet sensation gripped her stomach, like butterfly wings riding along the lining. She reached over and caressed his face, his beard soft against her fingers.

He closed the distance, his hands sliding into her hair and his palms holding her cheeks. His kiss melted her, and the butterflies became heated syrup, warming through to her soul. He kissed her slowly, seductively, rolling his tongue with hers, exploring the depths of her mouth, his sweetness overpowering.

Ty. Oh my god. Ty.

She yanked away from Tom's lips, her eyes darting toward the bathroom, and her heart fluttered with panic. The shower was still running, and she exhaled, glancing back at Tom.

Tom rolled on his back, his eyes scrunched closed and his lips tight, like he knew what had interrupted the kiss. He opened his impossibly blue eyes and stared at the ceiling.

"I'm not sure it's such a good thing for you to care about me."

"Why's that?" Tom sat up again, his eyes a little cooler and his jaw tight.

She looked toward the now quiet bathroom. "If Ty knew, he'd kill you," she whispered.

Tom laughed. "Ty knows."

Her gaze snapped back to Tom, and he stood, crossing to the bathroom just as Ty stepped out.

"WE NEED A BREAK, Jess," Ty said the following morning, and for once Tom nodded in agreement. "You are more than welcome to work out, but I'm sitting this one out."

She came out of the bathroom in a little red dress with a flare skirt. It reminded Ty of the dress she'd worn the first time she'd danced. Jessica moved gracefully around the room, showcasing her ability to execute a perfect ballet pirouette. He sat up straighter, riveted, and the time bomb in his head exploded.

He stood and felt the grip on his wrist. After tearing his gaze from her, he met Tom's glare. The Boy Scout was shaking his head no.

Seven weeks had passed since Frank left him on the floor for dead. Seven weeks was long enough to heal, and he knew it. He was running out of time, and he had to do something. He glanced at the monitor, remembering the videos Frank had played that first day back from Vancouver.

When he returned his gaze to Jessica, he knew what he had to do. Acting quickly before he lost his nerve, Ty balled his fist and slammed it into Tom's temple, knocking him out cold.

Jessica's eyes went wide, and she froze mid twirl. "What are you doing?"

He swept her off her feet, bringing her to the mattress, and ripped her underwear off. She struggled under his weight as he unzipped his pants, pushing her legs apart even as she cried, "No!" It wasn't the same seductive protest she insisted on in the beginning. This was a cry for help, a cry that blasted his heart to a thousand tiny pieces.

He grasped her wrists and pinned them to the mattress. With one thrust, he buried his hips to hers, regardless of her wishes. Feeling both the passion that burned any time he was near her mixed with a level of self-loathing he never thought he'd experience, he ignored her pleas. He lined her neck with kisses and closed his eyes, remembering her the night he left for Vancouver. The night she broke down every defense he had. It didn't take long, playing the memory instead of this brutality. He released with the force of a volcano, her name rolling off his tongue, and her sweet smiling face still lining the back of his eyelids.

He collapsed onto her, burying his face in the nook of her neck, her sobs breaking through his fantasy. He glanced at his reflection in the mirror, hating himself for what he'd just done. He deserved whatever painful death awaited.

He rolled off her, stood, and zipped up his pants, crossing to the other side of the room. Then he took a seat on the concrete floor. He kept his face neutral under the flurry of feelings assaulting him.

Jessica pushed the dress down around her, silently sobbing. She rolled onto her side, wrapped the sheet around herself, and curled into a ball.

He didn't want to see her cry. He didn't want to see what his brilliant plan did to her. Ty put his head on his knees.

TOM STIRRED ON THE floor, his eyes fluttering open and falling on Jessica curled in a ball on the mattress. He scanned the room and halted a few feet from the mattress. Her torn underwear lay crumpled on the concrete. His eye was swollen almost shut where Ty had hit him, but he was coherent enough to understand what had happened while he was unconscious. Fury filled him, and he shot into a sitting position. His sight became hazy, and he swayed, dizzy and nauseous from more than just the concussion.

"Son of a bitch." He crawled to Jessica and put his shaking arms around her, pulling her into the safety of his lap. Sobs ripped from her, muffled against his chest, and her entire frame trembled, fueling his rage.

This time, he could do something about it.

"Son of a bitch," he growled louder, glaring at Ty and peeling Jessica from his arms. He stood, ignoring the small plea of "don't" coming from her lips, and stormed across the room.

Ty stood up, and Tom swung, his punch connecting with Ty's nose, the feel of it satisfying. He drew back again. The second punch doubled him over. Tom grabbed Ty in a headlock, dragged him across the room, and threw him to the floor. He reached down, grabbed a shackle on the floor, and clamped it around Ty's ankle before he could react. Ty was on his feet moments after and threw a punch, but Tom ducked and sent an uppercut into Ty's jaw, sending him back against the wall.

Tom glowered and stepped out of Ty's reach. In a rare display of crudeness, he growled, "Mother fucker" at Ty and spun back toward Jessica. He sat down and wrapped his arms around her. "He won't hurt you again," he stated, watching as Ty sat slowly on the ground while looking at the chain around his ankle.

"I need to feel clean," Jessica whispered. "Can he reach in there?"

"Yes," Tom answered. He thought Ty could reach at least the sink, but maybe not the shower.

Jessica put her head against his chest. "I don't want to be alone where he can reach me," she whispered, and then looked up at him, the tears still sparkling in her eyes.

He nodded and helped her up, leading her past Ty and into the bathroom. He stood in the doorway with his back to her as she undressed and showered. He could hear her sob from time to time, but remained standing guard until she said okay.

He turned to look at her; she had one of their shirts on.

"There was nothing else to wear," she said, wiping the continuous stream of tears with sleeves that were too long for her petite arms.

"No problem," Tom said, even though it was anything but. The blue button-down shirt reached her mid-thigh, and she looked sexy as hell without trying. He put the toilet lid down and took a seat while she brushed her hair.

"I can't seem to stop crying," she said.

He reached for her and pulled her into a powerful hug. "I'm sorry." His voice quivered, and he blinked back the sudden mist that blurred his vision.

"Why are you sorry?" She sniffled and pulled away.

He met her gaze. "I wasn't... I couldn't..." He hung his head, unable to articulate his failure.

Jessica tilted his head back up so she could see his eyes. "That was not your fault."

Tom uttered a soft laugh, looking away from her. "If..."

Her hand stopped the rest of the words, covering his lips while she adamantly shook her head. "Please don't." She shifted her gaze and moved her fingers to the bruise capturing his right eye.

He winced.

Jessica rinsed a washcloth with cool water, folded it, and placed it on the swelling purple skin.

Cool relief flooded the fiery burn of the bruise. He covered her hand with his, closing his eyes and sighing. Only when she removed the cloth, did he open his eyes, meeting her concerned gaze.

She leaned forward, tenderly kissing the sore flesh. Instantly, a tingling sensation overtook him, localized to the bruise and the surrounding skin, like he'd had a shot of Novocain and it was just now wearing off.

She took a shaky step back, swaying just before her eyes rolled back in her head. He caught her as she collapsed in a dead faint.

"Shit!"

Tom laid her down gently on the hard floor, tapping her cheeks. Her eyes fluttered open, and she stared at him, blinking rapidly.

"You okay?" He swallowed, staring at her open eyes. Eyes that had drastically changed in the last few minutes—taking on the qualities of a stormy sky instead of the blue-lavender they had been. Now, swirling patterns of lavender, blue, green, and gray swirled in her irises. A brewing storm, beautiful but dangerous. A chill caught him off guard, rattling through the bones in his spine.

"Yeah." She studied his face, reaching up and stroking where she had just a few minutes before.

This time, he didn't wince. He raised his eyebrows and helped her into a sitting position before turning to the mirror. "No way," he whispered. The bruise was completely gone.

He reached out and put his hand on her face, her stormy eyes looking back at him. "How?"

"I don't know."

Tom looked back in the mirror and took a deep breath. Ty's words came back to him: *'She's your miracle.'*

He looked back at her. "Fair enough." He led her back into the other room.

JESSICA GAVE TY A wide berth, scooting around him and ignoring his cool stare. She sat on the mattress and waited for Tom to bring the tray that Marian had left by the door. She couldn't bring herself to look directly at Ty and was thankful Tom took a seat on the edge of the mattress closest to him, blocking her view.

Tom handed her a plate. Out of habit, Jessica tore the sandwich in half, laying the larger of the two on the plate before digging in herself.

Looking at the second half, she debated. She was still hungry. The spiteful half of her wanted to eat it, but she couldn't, not even now. Not even after his blatant disregard for her. She hung her head and took a shaky breath before getting to her feet.

"You've got to be kidding," Tom said, stopping her from taking another step toward Ty.

She met his bewildered eyes and exhaled. "I still can't watch him starve." She grabbed the plate, crossed, and handed it to Ty as she finally met his hard stare.

TY'S GAZE BOUNCED TO the plate and back, and then he slowly took the food, his mouth parting in disbelief. He had intentionally done the one thing she swore to Mike that he'd never done, the one thing that separated him from Frank. He had taken her without consent, raped her to drive a wedge the size of the Grand Canyon between them, and it had backfired.

"Why?" Her eyes expressed her pain and tore at his gut.

He shook his head and shrugged. "Because..." Rape wasn't enough to make her hate him, for her to wish he were dead, and he needed her to feel both those things. He mulled over his choice of words. How he played this was important, and he was silent for a few minutes, contemplating the lie. "Because I could." He narrowed his eyes and gave her a small, evil smile.

Jessica's face reddened with anger as she squatted in front of him. "You will never touch me again," she hissed. "Understand?" The colors swirled in her eyes.

Ty shrugged with the same small smile on his lips. "I've heard that before."

Survival Games Chapter 54

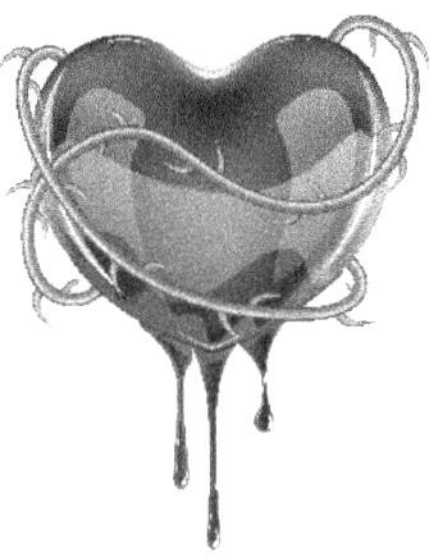

"YOU WANT TO WHAT?" LeAnn asked.

"Elope. Let's elope this weekend," Daniel said. "The kids are at my in-laws for the next few days. We can go out on a boat and have the captain marry us, or hop on a plane to Vegas. Either way, I don't want to wait."

"Danny, we haven't really talked about marriage. Why the rush?"

"I want you to be my wife." He grinned and took her in his arms.

LeAnn kissed him. "Are you really sure?" she asked. "All of this happened so fast. I don't want there to be any regrets."

"No regrets. I loved Jessica very much, but she's gone and she wouldn't want me to be alone and miserable. Her passing was hard, but ended up being a blessing. I met my soul mate and I don't want to go another day without you by my side," Daniel said.

LeAnn took a deep breath. "Okay. Let's do it."

"Vegas or the ocean?"

She looked out at the sea through the window of the cottage in Maine. "The ocean."

He smiled. "The ocean it is!"

THE CEREMONY WAS SIMPLE and beautiful, and they even had a couple of whales in attendance, to everyone's delight.

Daniel kissed LeAnn as the boat pulled back in the harbor, grinning like a schoolboy. He thanked the captain and walked her to the car.

"Well, Mrs. Connor, what next?"

LeAnn laughed and leaned over, whispering in his ear. Daniel blushed as he drove faster to their cottage and carried his new wife over the threshold.

Survival Games Chapter 55

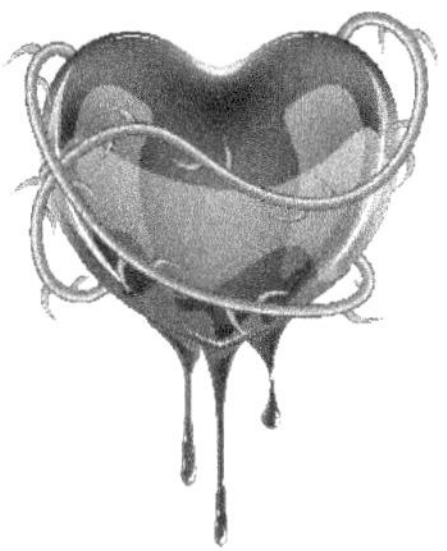

“WHERE IS HE, MARIAN?” Ty stood as Marian set down the breakfast tray.

“He's healing quite nicely. He should be back any day now.” She smiled. “And when he does, I can't wait to see what his plans are for you.” She went to close the door.

“I thought he killed Anna,” Ty said.

She turned and looked at him. “I don't care. It just gives me a reason to hate you more.” The door closed behind her.

“What did you do to her?” Jessica asked, startling him.

Ty snapped his head in her direction, pressing his lips together and stepping back into character.

“Well?”

Leave it alone. He shook his head.

Jessica opened her mouth to say something.

“Drop it.” He wandered into the bathroom as far as the chain would allow.

JESSICA CLOSED HER EYES for a moment. Tom still had his arms around her, and she wrapped hers over his and nuzzled closer.

"Morning," he whispered and stretched. "I haven't slept that good since I got here." He yawned and rolled onto his back.

"It was the first time I really felt safe." She rolled toward him. "Thank you."

"I try." He looked around. "I see the son of a bitch is already awake."

Jessica's smile faded. She rolled onto her stomach and propped herself up on her elbows.

He looked back at her with those impossibly blue eyes and pushed her hair out of her face, running his fingers behind her ear. She leaned her head into his touch as her eyes closed.

"Do you know what you do to me?" Tom whispered.

"Looks like the same thing she thinks she does to me," Ty said. He was leaning against the wall with his arms crossed.

Tom glared over at him. "Drop dead," he snapped.

Ty smiled bitterly. "All in good time."

Jessica shivered and looked over at Ty. She didn't want him to die. She just wanted him to leave her alone. She stood, got the plates off the tray, handed one to Ty as she walked by, and brought the other one to Tom.

"You need to eat," Ty said.

"As much as I hate to admit it, he's right." Tom handed her his plate.

"Enough!" She shoved the plate away. "If I don't feel like eating, I don't have to." She stormed into the bathroom, sat on the floor, and started rocking gently.

TOM GOT UP TO follow, but Ty scrambled to his feet and grabbed his arm. "She needs time to think."

"You don't know what she needs!"

Ty grabbed Tom by the throat and slammed him into the wall. He leaned his arm across Tom's chest, holding him in place. "She needs to think," he growled and leaned closer. "She needs to hate me. Otherwise, what my stepbrother will make her do will destroy her," he said softly in Tom's ear. "Do you understand?" He clenched his teeth, locking eyes with Tom before loosening his grip. Then stepped back. "Let her think."

Survival Games Chapter 56

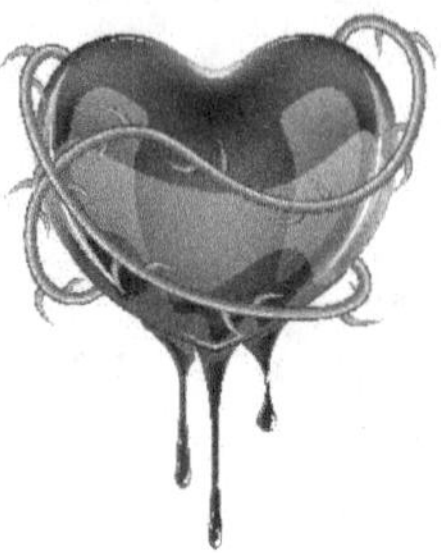

JESSICA CONTINUED ROCKING WITH her head on her knees. *How could he?* The thought kept echoing in her mind as the events of the previous day caught up with her. She wanted to hurt him. She wanted to hate him, but she couldn't. The slow realization of why made her stop rocking. She leaned her head back against the wall.

"Oh God," she whispered. "Oh God." Her breath hitched in and out of her chest. And tears came as the terrible truth hit.

I love him. God help me, I'm in love with a killer.

The dream resounded in her head, his beautiful blue bedroom eyes looking up at her as he held the engagement ring, waiting for her to answer in the cold, snowy yard. The impossibility of that ever happening brought a fresh bout of tears, blurring her eyes, stinging her throat. It wasn't because he raped her. It wasn't because he was a kidnapper. It wasn't because he was a murderer.

The tears streamed because she wanted that vision. Despite everything, she still wanted that vision, and she knew they would never leave this place alive. She crawled over to the toilet and threw up.

She pulled herself up to the sink and rinsed her mouth, brushing the vile taste from her teeth, still sobbing, still shaking. When she turned the water off, she dropped to her knees, leaning her head against the cool ceramic of the sink.

Arms wrapped around her, and she stiffened, glancing over her shoulder. Tom's concerned eyes stared back, but she turned away, feeling guilty for the sharp stab of disappointment. He rested his chin on her shoulder and squeezed a fraction tighter, telling her he was there for her in his own way.

Jessica turned to face him. She loved him for making her feel safe, but it wasn't the same as the impulsive, all-consuming emotions that Ty drove into her. Tom was a good man and deserved so much better. Tears slid down her face, pooling in the corner of her lip, the saltiness settling there gone with a flick of her tongue as she raised her eyes.

Tom reached up and took her face gently between his hands. He wiped her eyes with his thumbs and leaned in, kissing her gently.

When his tongue ran against her lips, they parted, tasting him, melting into the sweetness of his kiss. When his arms wrapped around her and the kiss progressed into the urgent zone, Jessica pushed him away. "Tom, I can't do this right now." Tears filled her eyes again, and she put her hand on his cheek.

"Okay." He kissed her again, took a deep breath, and drifted away from her. "I need to cool down, so if you don't mind." He nodded toward the door and stood to turn the water on in the shower.

Walking out of the room, she glanced over her shoulder, glimpsing his backside as he stepped into the shower and out of sight. She ran smack into Ty.

He had been standing just beyond the doorway. He grabbed her by the arms, swinging her around, and slammed her into the wall. His sharp eyes penetrated hers, making her squirm under his stare.

"Let me go," she said.

"No." Those bedroom eyes scanned her, and he licked his lips. He dropped to his knees before her and slid his hands up her shirt.

She shifted, trying to skirt out of the way, but he pushed her back against the wall.

"Ty, please," she pleaded as she swiped his hands away from the buttons on her shirt.

"Please what?" His hands grazed her thighs, and he parted the shirt, leaning in and rolling his tongue in her belly button.

She tilted her head back against the wall as his velvet hands slid over her body, his touch leaving a trail of burning skin in its wake. "Please," she whispered. She wanted to say stop, but she couldn't as she trembled under his touch.

His mouth found her breasts, and his fingers slid to the spot that drove her wild, slowly circling, easily setting her on fire.

"Oh God, please."

"Please what?" He smiled up at her as he moved his hand expertly, arousing her to the point of no return.

"Please, Ty." She gasped and ran her hands through his hair.

He moved to kiss her, running his hands up her body until they held her face. When his lips grazed hers, she found the strength to push him away.

"Please what?" he asked yet again.

She planted her hand firmly on his chest. "Let me go," she whispered, her voice shaking.

In the bathroom, the shower turned off.

"Not in a million years." The words growled from his chest and his eyes hardened. He flashed a sadistic smile.

She gasped and crept away from him. Her heart banged against the walls of her chest cavity. The heat he had created in her body rushed to her cheeks and pooled.

He casually leaned back against the wall, crossing his arms. Then he blew on his fingers and shined them on his chest. "I still got it."

Her mouth slowly dropped. "You think this is a game?"

Ty laughed. "Babe, I play games for a living, remember?"

She stepped back, and her eyes went wider. "But…"

"But what? You actually thought I cared? That I loved you? That I would have let you out of this place?" Ty shook his head. "That's just priceless. This is the game I've played for years, babe, an elaborate ploy to tear you down to nothing, and from the look on your face… I've just reached my goal."

Jessica's hands flew to her mouth, his words slicing a hole in her chest. She couldn't breathe.

He leaned forward a little. "As I told Mike, you're just a really good fuck."

Jessica fled into the bathroom, passing by Tom and into the shower. She blasted the water on, turning it as hot as it would go. She wanted to burn the feeling of his hands off her skin. She didn't realize she was screaming until her breath hitched in her chest and turned to sobs. She slowly sat down on the shower floor, the water scalding her skin, but she didn't care. She hated that bastard, hated him more than she hated Frank. He'd played her, took her will and crushed it as callously as a child crushes an ant.

TY SLUMPED AGAINST THE wall. Every muscle in his body trembled, and his legs gave out as Tom rounded the corner. Her screams crushed him more than anything Frank could ever dream up.

Tom glared. "What did you do?"

"I played the game." His voice cracked, and he put his head on his knees.

Jessica went silent in the bathroom.

TOM SPUN ON HIS heels, bolting back into the bathroom and finding her on the floor of the shower. The water created red welts on her skin. When he reached in to turn it off, he instinctively snatched his hand out of the scalding water, and it turned red where the water connected.

"Jesus!" He gritted his teeth and reached beyond the water, switching the handle to the off position.

Jessica stared aimlessly into space, her face slack and her eyes distant.

Jesus, she's catatonic. What the fuck did he do to her? He wiped her hair out of her face and tilted her chin toward him. "Jessie?"

His heart hammered in his chest as she looked right through him, not showing that she saw what was in front of her. He grabbed a bath towel and wrapped it around her, scooping her up in his arms. He carried her to the mattress, setting her down, and covered her with the sheet.

Only then did he turn his attention to Ty. The transformation was incredible. Ty was leaning against the wall with his legs crossed out in front of him, his arms across his chest. He wore a small smile that sent a tremor of fear down Tom's back. His eyes were dark and had no indication of warmth or mercy.

He swallowed the dryness in his mouth. "What the hell did you do to her?"

Ty shrugged nonchalantly. "I just played my final hand in the game," he said, and his smile widened. "It's taken months, but I finally got what I wanted. You know, it's a hell of a lot of fun to watch what happens to people when they're pushed over the edge." His eyes sparkled. "It's such a rush." He hopped to his feet.

Tom roared and launched himself at Ty. The next thing Tom knew, he was facedown and Ty had his arm bent at an alarming angle, pinning him to the ground.

"Don't fuck with me," Ty growled and released his arm, stepping back.

Tom stood and faced Ty. His anger raged through every fiber of his being. His hands clenched and unclenched. He turned as if he were going to walk away, but threw a right hook. Ty moved back, and he caught nothing but air, tilting off balance enough so that Ty could get an arm lock around his neck.

"Stop," Ty commanded, but Tom threw his elbow into his side. Ty tightened his hold. "I told you not to fuck with me," he growled. "I could snap your neck as easily as snapping a wishbone. So just cut the shit and leave me alone." He shoved Tom away.

Tom stood in the middle of the room, glaring, his chest heaving with fury. "You really are a sick son of a bitch."

"You have no idea." Ty smiled.

Tom shivered. He felt like he was looking at the Angel of Death himself. He moved closer to Jessica on the bed in a protective reflex.

Ty disappeared into the bathroom.

Tom let out a shaky breath, still furious, but at least he was in control now. He kneeled next to Jessica and wiped the hair out of her face. Fear gripped him, turning his stomach to ice.

God, I need her. What if she never snaps out of this?

Her eyes closed, and she turned her head away.

"Please, Jessie," he whispered in her ear. "I need you." He pressed his lips to her cheek, but she didn't stir.

Tom stood and started pacing like a caged animal, trying to rein in the fear and anger into something manageable. He didn't know what to do, didn't know what would snap her out of it, and that terrified him. Time was running out. He knew it as well as Ty. Marian had said Frank was due back any day now. That was why the bastard did this to her. He glared over at Ty, who was coming out of the bathroom, watching him like he was an exhibit.

"Stop looking at me," he finally burst.

Ty laughed. "You're the entertainment."

"Fuck you."

"Nah, I'd rather fuck her." He pointed at Jessica and sat against the wall.

Tom moved to go toward Ty but thought better of it. If he gave in to that urge, he wouldn't stop until the man was dead. Turning everything over in his head, he couldn't decipher which was the game and which was reality.

Which was the act?

He continued pacing.

Marian opened the door. Tom approached her, but she pointed a gun at him. He stopped, watching as she put the tray down, her eyes never leaving him.

"Mar," Ty said, coolly acknowledging her presence from where he sat.

"Shit for brains." She closed the door.

Tom stared at the door. If it were a game, they would have let him loose the second Jessica broke. His anger diffused a notch. The sick bastard must really love her.

Tom picked up the tray and brought it over to Jessica. Putting it down on the floor, he gently shook her. Her eyes blinked open for a second and then closed again.

"Come on, Jessie, you've got to eat something," he said.

She opened her eyes and looked at him without moving. "Why? What's the point?"

Alarm drowned his hammering heartbeat. He leaned close. "Because I need you," he said, soft enough, so Ty couldn't hear him.

Tears filled her eyes. She blinked them back and slowly sat up, holding the towel to her. She meekly took the plate and broke the sandwich in half. She ate slowly and didn't look at either Tom or Ty.

She finished her part of the sandwich and looked at the remaining half. She reached down and picked up the plate, and then to the surprise of both men, she heaved the plate across the room like a Frisbee at Ty. It smashed against the wall where his head had been moments before. She took a sip of water, lay back down, and closed her eyes.

THE SILENCE IN THE room was deafening. Ty stared at the sandwich that was strewn on the floor amidst the broken glass. He wasn't very hungry, anyway. He brushed the glass and the sandwich into a pile with the back of his hand and left it there, then retreated into the bathroom to get a drink of water from the sink.

He glanced at the mirror as he wiped his mouth with the back of his arm. Eric stared back at him.

"He's coming." Eric faded away.

Ty felt the weight of those two words crash down on his chest. He gripped the sink to keep steady. "I'm not ready," he whispered at his reflection. Steel-blue eyes stared back. He studied his face. He didn't look that bad with a beard. It made the scar seem less severe. He wondered what he would look like if, by some miracle, he survived this. "Game on," he whispered and headed back into the room.

The door opened, and Frank stepped into the room.

Tom was on his feet and charging within seconds. He didn't make it too far. The Taser hit him, and he went down mid step.

Frank hauled him into the chair and strapped his wrists in. He looked over at Ty and then at Jessica. She still had her eyes closed.

Frank crossed and grabbed her by her hair, lifting her to her knees. "I have been waiting for this for eight weeks," he purred and unzipped his pants.

She looked up at him as if drugged.

"Leave her alone," Tom bellowed from the chair.

Frank turned and pressed a button on the remote he held.

An electrical buzz filled the room, the lights dimming a fraction. Tom went rigid in the chair.

Jessica's face changed. "Okay, just... just don't hurt him anymore," she pleaded.

Ty tried to keep his expression neutral, even bored. A far cry from the tumultuous emotions filling his body as he watched her open her mouth and service Frank. If Frank had been within reach, the man would be dead in a matter of seconds, but he was well beyond Ty's grasp. The game had to be played, regardless of his fury.

"Now that was worth the wait," Frank said, tossing her to the concrete floor.

JESSICA GAGGED, AND FEAR left her shaking and nauseous. She attempted to get to her feet. Frank was going to hurt her, maybe even kill her today, and all she could think about was Ty and his goddamned game. Was this part of it?

Before she could consider the question, Frank grabbed a handful of her hair and dragged her to her feet.

"Is this part of your sick game?" she asked Ty. The smile and half shrug he sent her way was worse than the fist that connected with her ribs, lifting her off the ground and knocking the wind out of her.

Frank leaned close to her. "Make no mistake, my stepbrother is in love with you, and this little façade he's put on for the last couple of days is solely for your benefit."

Jessica saw the flash of emotion in Ty's eyes before he suppressed it.

Frank backhanded her, sending her sprawling onto the concrete. "And every single punch, every single cut, every single whimper of pain is killing him beyond words."

The chuckle that escaped Ty sent shivers down her spine. "Are you so sure about that?"

Frank grabbed Jessica by the hair and swiveled in Ty's direction, yanking her head back until she gasped in pain. "You really think it's wise to test me right now?"

Eyes devoid of emotion stared back. "I don't give a shit what you do with her as long as you let me the hell out of here."

Frank laughed. "That's not going to happen. I've got something special planned for you." He looked at Jessica. "But in the meantime, this bitch owes me." He snapped her toward the wall.

"Stop!" Tom bellowed, struggling against the shackles that held his wrists in place.

Dazed, Jessica crumpled to the ground, gritting her teeth so the cry of pain wouldn't escape.

Frank squatted in front of her. "Pretty boy wants to fuck you. Did you know that?"

Jessica winced, shying away from Frank. Her gaze traveled to Tom and back.

Frank stood, pulling a switchblade out of his pocket. "But that just isn't in the cards right now." He pushed a button, and a long, jagged-edged blade popped out.

Jessica scuttled backwards until she hit the concrete wall. Her breath was ragged with fear and her heart pumped so hard that the sound drowned out the shuffle of his footsteps as he approached her.

"I'm wondering if either of them will want to fuck you when I'm done with you."

She tore her gaze away from the knife and met Ty's. For a fraction of an instant, blazing fury filled his eyes, but then he blinked, and the icy, neutral expression returned. He inhaled and tilted his head, twisting his lips into a sadistic smile.

Tom struggled to break the bonds holding his wrists to the chair, his roar echoing off the concrete. "Don't you dare!"

Frank turned, raising an eyebrow at Tom, and then returned his attention back to Jessica, switching the blade from his right hand to his left. "Like you could stop me."

Jessica stood, pressing herself against the concrete, her eyes now riveted on the knife. The game of flinch that Ty had taught her came barreling back. She blew a slow stream of air between her lips, calming her nerves, waiting for him to strike. She didn't have a great deal of maneuverability, but she hoped it was enough. When he flicked the blade toward her, she turned, blind to his attack.

Frank grabbed a handful of hair with his right hand and yanked her toward him, bringing the knife up and slicing a line down her face.

Jessica could not speak, could not scream at the pain and terror that gripped her, immobilizing her to the point of inaction. Tears blurred her eyes and hot liquid dripped onto her shoulder and chest. It took a second or two to realize it was her own blood, and then the tremors started.

Frank twirled her toward Ty. "Now she matches you."

Ty shrugged, his gaze locked on hers.

Frank brought the tip of the blade to her left eye, toying with her and both men. Tom gasped, his struggle forgotten, but Ty remained unimpressed.

"I thought you wanted her to *see* me die?" Ty said with another tilt of his head, punctuating it with a raised eyebrow.

Frank paused, pressing his lips together, debating. Slowly the knife lowered, but he didn't sheathe it. With another flick of his wrist, he sliced her left nipple. Then he tossed her toward the mattress, where she fell with a gasp. Crossing the room before she could react, he slammed the knife into Tom's thigh just above the knee, leaving it embedded to the hilt.

"No!" Jessica screamed, jumping to her feet and charging Frank.

Frank back handed her, knocking her to the ground and then advanced again, this time unbuckling his pants.

Tom inhaled sharply.

"They might not want to fuck you, but I certainly do." Frank's pants dropped, showing her he was more than ready for her.

Jessica tried to maneuver away, but he was on her, slamming her on the hard concrete and shoving inside her as she struggled. Her screams mixed with Tom's empty threats as Frank's brutality rained on her.

TY, ON THE OTHER hand, looked on silently, his face bordering between neutral and amused. But inside… inside, a dangerous cocktail brewed. *I swear, if I ever get my hands on that bastard, I will kill him as slowly and painfully as humanly possible.* It took all his concentration to not let the fury or the hatred show on his face, and not to lunge at Frank.

When he was through, Frank stood, towering over her and pulling his pants on. He laughed and traded a glare with Tom. "I love it when they fight."

"Sick fuck," Tom hissed, his face covered in sweat, his blue eyes sparkling with a fury that matched Ty's unseen wrath.

Jessica rolled onto her side, curling up into a ball of pain and humiliation. She tilted her head in Ty's direction, blinking the tears from her eyes. His gaze flicked to hers and then back to Frank.

"That'll make one hell of a video." Ty slowly grinned. "But don't they want her fucking a star?" He framed the word star with finger quotes.

Frank's jaw tightened, and he looked between Jessica and Tom, debating.

Ty knew it was a long shot, but if he could create that kind of diversion, maybe Frank wouldn't kill her today. Maybe Frank would bite and make him edit one last video. Maybe.

When Frank looked back at Ty, his eyes narrowed, and Ty could almost see the dollar signs register. Frank grabbed a handful of her hair and pulled her to her knees, dragging her to where Tom sat. He yanked the knife out of Tom's thigh, wiped it on his pants, and closed the blade. It disappeared into his pocket for the time being.

"YOU STILL WANT TO fuck this whore?" Frank tugged her hair, so Tom could see her face clearly.

Tom's eyes watered, but he blinked, and they cleared. "She's..." His voice cracked, and he swallowed. "She's not a whore."

"Do you want to fuck her before you die?"

A sob escaped Jessica, and Tom's eyes found hers. With an almost imperceptible tilt of his head, he nodded.

"Now the million-dollar question." Frank pulled her head back further, staring down into her eyes. "Do you want to fuck *him*? Or is Ty the only one that has that market cornered?"

She flinched at the use of his name, her insides a tumultuous mess, and she didn't know how to answer the question. If she said yes, would Frank hurt him again? If she said no, what would he do then? Instead of answering, her chin trembled, and tears welled and poured down her face. Her eyes lowered to Tom's. His silent pleading squeezed her heart, sending a spindled web of pain through her chest.

She swung her gaze to Ty, and his eyebrow rose as if saying, 'Well, are you going to answer the question?'. The absence of humanity in his stare clinched her decision. She brought her eyes back to Tom, nodding.

"So, little slut of mine, are you going to grant the man his dying request?"

"Yes."

THE WORD WHISPERED FROM her lips silenced the scream in Ty's head. While this was his intention, the idea of her willing to give herself to anyone else was maddening. Almost to the point of breaking down his solid defenses, but he knew the second he screwed up, Frank would carve her to pieces in front of him.

"GIVE US A SHOW." Frank released her hair. He stepped back, crossing his arms, almost matching the posture and expression on Ty's face.

Jessica moved mechanically, at first crawling to Tom, wincing as she stood on bruised and battered legs. Every inch of her body ached. Her face and breast burned where he'd sliced her. She stepped between his legs, meeting Tom's gaze.

"You don't have to do this."

"Yes, I do. He'll kill you if I don't."

TOM MANAGED A LAUGH as she fumbled with his belt. "He's going to kill me, anyway." The words were laced with agony as she peeled his pants off, scraping the gaping wound in his thigh.

He wrung his wrists against the restraints, wishing he could wrap his arms around her, wishing he could run his fingers over her skin. But this would have to do. This was all he would be allowed, at least in this life. He closed his eyes, willing himself to concentrate on only her,

her skin, her legs, her hands, her lips, and her stormy eyes. He gasped, his breath hissing under her lips.

His thigh flared. Burning pain far worse than the knife wound gripped him and he groaned. His eyes squeezed shut until the burn faded to a dull tingling, and his eyes snapped open, meeting her intense stare.

"Tom," she whispered, straddling him, circling her hips on his lap and wrapping her arms tightly around his neck. Then her eyes rolled back in her head, and she slumped into his shoulder.

"Jessie.," His whisper matched hers. He closed his eyes, nuzzling his head against hers and brushing her ruined cheek with his lips. He prayed Frank wouldn't figure out she had passed out.

She stirred a moment later. He shrugged his shoulders to simulate a hug. His relief was short-lived, because she was violently yanked from his lap and tossed on the floor.

"I CHANGED MY MIND." Frank turned and punted. His foot connected with her rib cage and flipped her onto her back.

She gasped, then froze, unable to draw back in. Her cracked ribs screamed at even the smallest infusion of air.

Frank stepped toward her. She rolled on her hands and knees, barely able to crawl a foot before he was on her. He drew his foot back and connected with her side in a vicious kick, the snapping of her bones echoing off the walls.

Debilitating agony ripped through her with each blow. She fell forward, landing on her elbows, unable to draw the strength to attempt escape. Her muscles seized, locking her in place throughout the brutal assault. Pained weeping ripped from her chest, and her mind teetered on the edge of an abyss.

Through it all, the man who professed to love her watched with almost a bored expression. Tom, on the other hand, was raging in the chair, thrashing and swearing, promising vengeance through the sobs that racked him.

Frank finished his beating and straightened out his clothing. "I've got some things to do." He smiled. "But I'll be back." He practically skipped out of the room.

As the door closed, the wrist restraints holding Tom in place snapped open.

TY DISAPPEARED INTO THE bathroom. He took a piss and then closed the toilet lid. After taking a seat, he put his head in his hands. Without making a sound, tears flowed, and his shoulders shook. His chest felt like someone had put the muzzle of a shotgun to it and pulled the trigger, leaving a gaping, bloody hole where his heart once was. That hole filled with a hatred so black, so complete that it over took every cell of his being. He swore Frank would pay. One way or another, that bastard was going to get his due.

Ty came out of the bathroom to the sight of Tom cradling Jessica in his arms and rocking slowly, her head buried in his chest and his cheek pressed to her temple. Tom glared at him.

"Is this what you do here?" His raw voice shook. "Is it?"

Ty blew a huff of air through his nose, keeping in character. "Yep, and we do it pretty goddamn well, too." He chewed on his lip for a moment, gauging Tom's temper. "However, I am surprised he interrupted your..." He waved to the chair, unable to bring himself to say the words. "Because that would be worth a mint." He leaned on the wall with his arms crossed.

Tom shifted.

"Don't."

Jessica's command stopped him, and he looked down at her.

"He's not worth it."

Her voice, devoid of strength, devoid of hope, clinched it. Tom ignored her, setting her gently on the floor. He grabbed his jeans and slid them on, then took a few steps towards Ty.

Ty's arms dropped. "Do you really want to tango with me right now?" Some of the fury locked inside bled through into his voice.

TOM PAUSED. INSTINCT TOLD him he might get a couple punches in, but then Ty would lose control of whatever beast he had caged inside. This was a man who had been pushed beyond the edge of reason.

He backed off, stepping away and returning to Jessica's battered, barely conscious form. He scooped her up and carried her into the bathroom, then set her gently on the toilet before turning on the shower. He pulled her under the balmy stream and just held her to his chest as the warm water cascaded on his back.

Eventually, her arms wrapped around his waist. The warmth of the shower did nothing to quell either of their tremors.

"I couldn't stop him." His voice was raw with emotion and trembling as much as the rest of him was. "Jessie, I couldn't stop him."

"It's okay," she whispered in his arms as the water fell over them.

"No, it's not," he said, kissing the top of her head. "There was nothing I could do while he…" He swallowed hard. "While he…" He couldn't say the words. Rape didn't cover the brutality he'd just witnessed.

"That's not the worst thing that can happen in here."

Survival Games Chapter 57

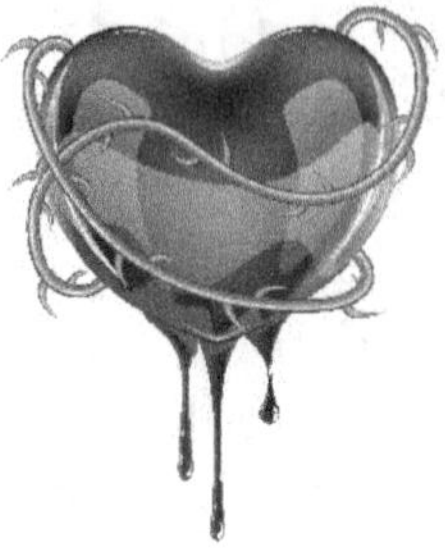

TY HEARD THE WATER go on and closed his eyes, leaned his head back against the wall, and took a shaky breath. He wondered just how much time they had left.

His thoughts were answered by the creak of the door.

Frank leveled the tranquilizer gun and pulled the trigger.

Ty looked at the dart in his chest and back up at Frank as he fell over into blackness.

THE BLACKNESS TURNED GRAY and the smell... Ah, God, the smell. Ty yanked his head away and blinked. His vision righted itself and his heart jumped into his throat.

How much time passed? Shit!

His hands were even with his head, suspended in the air by painfully tight shackles attached to heavy-duty linked chains. The same with his ankles, but for now, he stood barefoot on the cold concrete. He looked beyond Frank at the two very familiar chairs. One was an electric chair that almost every room in the complex housed, but the other one made his head snap back at Frank.

"You son of a bitch!"

"As I said before, payback's a bitch," Frank said. "I thought long and hard about how I was going to kill you." He stared up at the chains and waved to the room. "This ended up winning out because it's slow enough to see you in agony, but fast enough to let me hack that little bitch to pieces before you die. I'm just sorry she has to derive any pleasure from it at all." He turned, starting the contraption. "Ironic that the bitch gets to die coming."

"You were right about her eyes. I want her to see you suffer, and see her pretty boy suffer. I'm still not sure if I'm going to kill her first or not. I don't know who I'd get a greater pleasure out of destroying after what she did to me."

Frank walked over to the table and picked up a knife. Twirling it in his hand, he advanced on Ty. "On one hand, I can almost understand what you did to my father. I contemplated what I would have done if the tables were turned, and Marian was the one your father screwed every night." He stopped in front of Ty. "But you still killed my father."

He ran the blade down the unscarred side of Ty's face, ripping the skin open. Ty jerked back as far as he could, but it wasn't enough to get away from the knife.

Ty glared at him as the blood dripped down his chin onto the floor.

Frank smiled. "If you had come home an hour earlier, you would have gotten a look at quite a different scene. If I had to make a comparison between your sister and your whore, I would say they fought with the same grim determination. Unfortunately, in both cases, it was a waste of precious energy."

"You bastard." Ty's voice shook. A second later, he realized the chains were vibrating with the tremors that racked him.

"Tsk, tsk, tsk." Frank waggled his finger. "I thought she meant nothing to you." He put the knife down and headed out of the room, whistling.

Survival Games Chapter 58

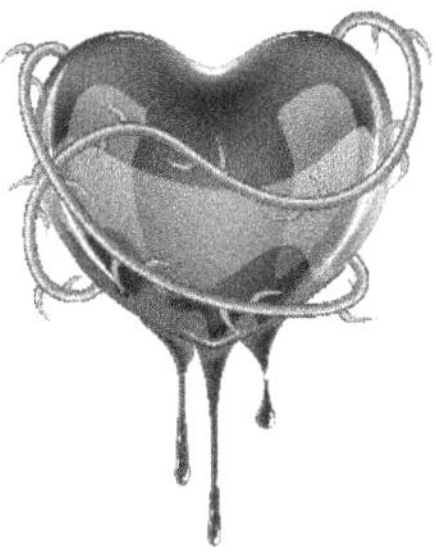

TOM STEPPED OUT OF the shower and grabbed a couple towels, one of which he handed to Jessica. He noted two things—the clothes he had discarded were gone and a new set was placed on the lid of the toilet.

A shiver snaked down his spine. Someone had entered the room while they were in the shower, and neither of them had noticed.

Jessica stepped out next to him, wrapping a towel around herself gingerly. The cuts on her face and breast still oozed. She was still listless until she saw the choice of clothing. Both items were crimson red and highly inappropriate, given the last hour.

He picked up the silk pajama shorts, scrunching his eyebrows together before he dropped them back on the skimpy pile. He stepped to the pantry and rifled through the towels in a futile attempt to uncover hidden clothing.

"There's nothing in there." Jessica stared at the crimson outfits. "Silk and lace. Jesus." She wrapped her arms around herself, warming her goose-bump-ridden arms.

Tom closed his eyes and wrapped his arms around her. He couldn't promise that nothing would happen to her. He knew that now. He snapped upright, staring at the clothing and then the doorway. The room outside the door was unusually dark. If Ty was out there, how the hell did they get the clothes in here?

"Just... just put the clothes on." He picked up the shorts and slid them on, absently handing her the lace ensemble, his eyes still on the door. He swallowed despite his dry mouth.

He glanced at her when she moved to his side, lacing her fingers in his, staring at the darkness as well. Her face still bore the jagged, oozing scar, but it paled compared to the fear in her eyes, which were riveted to the doorway and the darkness beyond.

"I feel like I'm walking the green mile," he muttered, taking his first step toward the door.

"You and me both."

THE ROOM WAS DRENCHED in shadows, but one thing was clear—Ty was no longer chained to the wall. The *'thump'* of an air gun filled the room. Tom staggered back a few steps, his hand slipping from Jessica's. They both stared at the tranquilizer dart sticking out of his chest.

He went down, hard.

And all she could think about was yelling "Timber!" The sudden silly thought brought a hysterical fit of giggles, but they were cut off by the second *thump*. Then darkness descended.

Survival Game Chapter 59

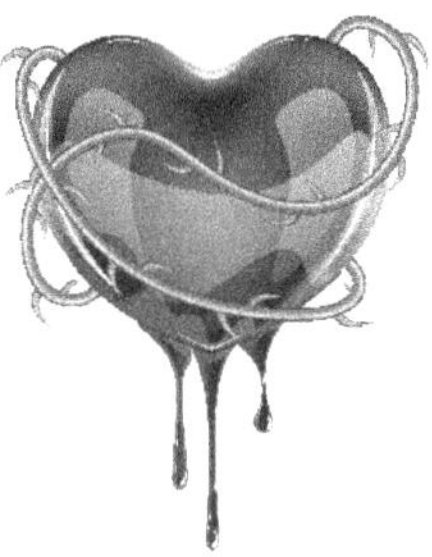

TOM JERKED HIS HEAD away from the god-awful smell and blinked in confusion. When his eyes found Ty, they widened.

Frank laughed. "I'll let him explain while I go get your whore." He walked out of the room.

Tom looked around. "Jesus," he said at the sight of the other chair. The contraption that they had seen in the video was attached to it. He shot his gaze back to Ty. "Sweet Jesus."

Ty nodded. "Now you get it," he said as the blood continued to drip from his face.

Tom glanced back at the other chair and followed one cord across the concrete. He had been zapped enough times to understand what Frank had planned for them. He started to shake.

"Get your shit together," Ty said harshly.

Tom took in the chains that would eventually tear Ty to pieces. "How can you be so calm?"

"I told you I would die for her," Ty responded. "You... You need to be the one to get her out of here."

Tom looked down at the shackles holding his wrists to the chair and the strap around his chest. "How the hell am I supposed to do that?"

Ty shrugged. "You'll know when it happens."

"What if it *never* happens?" Tom asked.

"Then we all die today," Ty said calmly.

They stared at each other in silence.

"Do you love her?" Ty asked.

Tom nodded.

"When you get her out of here, will you tell her?" Ty closed his eyes. "Tell her I loved her? Will you make her understand?" Ty opened his eyes. They shined with tears, and he blinked them back.

Tom nodded again.

"Thanks, man," Ty said.

Tom nodded slightly.

"Game on." Ty hung his head for a moment. Then he lifted his head back up, transformed. His dark, soulless eyes looked out from his bloody, bearded face.

Tom was glad chains secured the man. The sight of him was enough to set him quaking again.

The Angel of Death was already in the room with them, and his name was Ty.

MOMENTS LATER FRANK WALTZED in with Jessica on his shoulder. He dumped her into the chair and threaded her legs through the arms, securing her like he did before.

He glanced over his shoulder at Ty and shoved his fingers between her legs.

"Get your filthy hands off her," Tom growled. He struggled against the bonds that held him in place, searching for a weakness, for an escape, but he might as well have been sealed in a tin can and dumped in the Atlantic. It was now just a matter of time... and pain.

"Wouldn't you just die to be inside this sweet cunt?" Frank moved his fingers in and out a few times, relishing Tom's struggles. "Oh, wait, you are going to die!" He cackled, removing his hand, and replaced it with the metal vibrator. He placed the sensors in the same strategic locations they had seen in the video, and then he stood, glancing between Tom and Ty.

With dramatic flair, he turned the machine on, displaying the mechanics like he was the girl from *The Price is Right* displaying a showcase item.

TY WANTED TO SCREAM. He wanted to struggle in the chains the same way Tom was in the chair. He wanted to wipe the sick grin off Frank's face, but that would only prolong his torture, so he remained silent.

"Time to wake up sleeping beauty." Frank waved the smelling salts under her nose.

JESSICA CAME TO, THE electrical pulses between her legs aiding in her sudden alertness.

The feel of the slick, cool metal enhanced by the slight electrical current overtook her. She tilted her head back, the shakes starting as well as the tears.

"No, please, no," she whimpered.

"What's the matter, baby? You don't like to cum?" Frank ran his finger between her breasts and slid his hand under the lace, squeezing her cut breast.

He stepped out of the way so she could see both Ty and Tom. "Today you get to kill them both."

Jessica's chin quivered, the heat already building between her legs. She was as helpless to stop that as she was to stop the chains from tearing Ty apart. She glanced at Tom in the electric chair. His sad eyes met hers. So many unspoken feelings, so much love in that gaze mixed with the hopelessness that she felt.

"I'm sorry," she whispered.

She swiveled her gaze to Ty and inhaled. A jagged cut slashed through the skin of his cheek, dripping blood through his light beard. His blue eyes were stone cold, revealing nothing. Nothing at all, but she knew better. She felt the inferno of emotions raging inside him in time with the hellfire. None of these things was the reason her gaze locked with his and stayed there. No, it was his silent plea, his repetitive mantra that filled her head with a voice so racked with agony, she wanted to cry.

Please, please don't let him kill her. God, please. Don't take her. You can have me. Do anything you want to me, but don't take her. Please, God, I love her.

He prayed over and over again, pleading, making promises he couldn't possibly keep all for her. But not one iota of emotion reached his eyes. The only indicator of the depth of his feelings was his riveted stare mixed with the death-like silence.

Only an act of God, or that of a small child, could tear his gaze from hers.

Jessica tilted her head, silently trembling from the force of the orgasm the machine enacted, but she never broke the connection to Ty, not even when Tom cried out in pain. A tear slid slowly down the unmarked side of her face.

That tear broke through the iron wall surrounding Ty. His face transformed. The agony broke through, visible in the sudden softening of his eyes, his trembling lips pressing tightly together so the rumbling of despair building in his chest would not be freed. Agony, not borne of physical pain, but of the anguish that accompanied losing her. Losing her to Tom was one thing. He could fight that, but losing her to death… That reality bowled him over, sucking the air from his lungs even as the chains lifted him off the ground.

Tom screamed again, and a hint of singed hair permeated the room.

"I told you he loved you," Frank whispered in her ear, sliding the sharp edge of the knife between her breasts. With a flick, the front of her bra broke open. He flipped the blade over in his hand so the serrated side faced her skin. With a slow, deliberate stroke, he sliced, shredding her skin and performing an impromptu partial mastectomy. "That's for tearing the tip of my cock to shreds."

A high, thin whine escaped between her lips, but she didn't break eye contact with Ty. The pain gripping her chest didn't discourage her lower body from hurdling over the next peak. She concentrated on the blue set of his eyes, going deeper into them, deeper into a meditative trance, concentrating on each breath, losing herself, losing the connection to this godforsaken room.

The familiar hallway filled her vision, and she jumped as a warm hand slid into hers. She looked down at her son, his once brown eyes now swirling with colors, swirling like a storm.

TY'S BREATH HITCHED, THE chains creaking, now pulling him in different directions. He blinked, still concentrating on her. The colors in her eyes started swirling slowly, sparking hope. He broke her gaze, swiveling to the mirror at the back of the room.

The reflection of the room was there, but superimposed over it was a hallway that Jessica and Eric were walking through. At the end was a door with blinding white light spilling around the edges. Raw power. Awe-inspiring miracles resided behind that door.

And the key was clasped in her image's hand.

Come on, come on, come on. Ty repeated it over and over in his mind, no longer caring about the pain racking his joints. All he cared about was that she got to that door before Frank got bored carving her body, especially with the lack of reaction. Even the sudden snap in his shoulder didn't dissuade his intense attention. The only one in the room that voiced pain was Tom, and his cries were getting weak.

The key slid into the lock, and she turned, glancing down at Eric as a new bloody welt ripped open her abdomen. Her hand dropped to the doorknob, but before she could turn it all the way, Eric spun, his eyes widening. Ty's vision cleared and shot to Frank.

In unison, three voices screamed, "NO!" Two men and a boy, shattering the near silence of the room.

Ty squinted at the flood of light. She had opened the door. Eric threw himself in front of his mother, blocking the arc of Frank's knife.

The knife stopped, lodged in nothing but air over Jessica's chest, and yet blood covered it, dripping from the tip. More blood than just the cuts on her body would warrant. Ty's gaze snapped back to the mirror, and he understood the wail that escaped her lips.

THE TRANSITION BETWEEN THE halls of her mind, Eric's bedroom, and the hellish prison where her physical self was suffering took just the blink of an eye. The sight of her son lying across her chest with the butcher knife buried in his chest pushed her over the edge. The power escaped full force. The room went white. She grasped the hilt of the knife, cutting her fingers on the sharp blade below the smooth black handle, desperate to pull the blade from the image of her son.

Only one purpose overtook her mind. *Save my son!*

THE SHACKLES BINDING TY'S wrists and ankles blew off in a blinding spray of metal. He fell. The same acute pain he felt when Jessica healed his arm flashed over his body, and in the time it took to fall six feet, the tingling set in. He landed on his hands and knees.

An overwhelming purpose overtook him. *Save Eric.* Like a stealth rocket, he charged.

He hit Frank like a linebacker, his shoulder hitting him square in the ribs, launching both of them a few feet in the air. The impact dislodged the knife from Eric's chest and sent it clattering across the concrete.

"MOMMY, IT HURTS," ERIC whispered.

Jessica leaned over and planted her lips on his forehead, closing her eyes and channeling all the healing power she had into her son. Light flared brighter, and as it dimmed, Eric faded, his stormy eyes at peace and his chest fully mended.

Jessica blinked, and the room came into clear focus, the chains hanging with no captive locked in the shackles. Tom slumped in the chair, his chest still rising and falling, but his face displaying the slackness of unconsciousness.

Behind her, she heard the unmistakable sound of fists hitting flesh. "Ty?"

The sound paused, and the rustle of jeans approached. Ty kneeled next to her, taking her hand and scanning her unmarked torso. The machine still hummed, bringing her closer to the next climax. He glanced back toward Frank, and after kissing her hand, he lowered it and locked it in the shackle before she could protest.

Survival Games Chapter 60

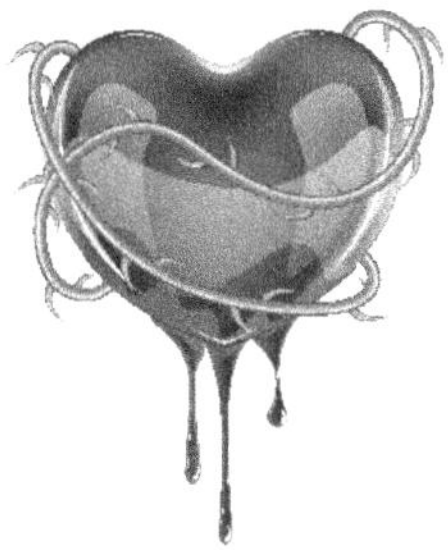

A SCREAM SHATTERED THE silence of the house. Daniel shot to his feet, disoriented in the darkness of their bedroom. Then he pinpointed the sound at the far end of the hall. Gasping and sobbing—the usual nightmare noises. He shuffled to Eric's room, rubbing his eyes and muttering under his breath.

He flipped on the light, and any remnant of sleep vanished. Eric lay arched on his bed, his breath coming in forced gurgles with blood everywhere. It covered the boy's bare chest, dripping down his sides and staining the sheets. A gash the width of a standard butcher knife marred his skin just below and to the right of his heart.

"Mommy, it hurts."

His pain-filled words broke Daniel's paralysis, but before he could complete the few steps to his bedside, white light encompassed Eric, blanketing his skin. Tendrils drifted like smoke, seeping into his nose, ears, and mouth, filling his small form until his skin glowed with it.

Daniel blinked. It was only Eric. Eric, covered with blood, but no sign of the ugly gash he had seen when he first entered the room.

Eric stared up at him with wide, strange calico eyes, the colors swirling like clouds caught in a vortex.

Daniel blinked again and scanned the filthy bed, still unable to understand. This had all the characteristics of a dream, but the unmistakable metallic stench of blood did not fit neatly into that theory. "Wha–What just happened?"

A gasp sounded in the doorway. Daniel turned in time to see LeAnn scurry past.

"Oh God, a bloody nose! Eric, you need to lean forward and pinch the bridge of your nose to stop the bleeding!" She tried to manhandle Eric, to sit him up and push him forward.

What she said made perfect sense, although there wasn't a trace of blood on Eric's face.

"I'm okay," Eric said, pushing her away.

"Let me see!"

Daniel cleared his throat. "I think the bleeding has already stopped."

LeAnn tilted Eric's head a little to make sure no geyser waited in his nostrils, and then she nodded. "He seems to be okay now." She scanned the bed. "But I can't say the same for his bed. You want to get him cleaned up and I'll change the sheets?"

Daniel nodded and helped Eric to his feet, leading him into the bathroom and turning on the shower. He still couldn't find words to voice the questions flurrying through his head. He waited until Eric turned the water off and opened the shower curtain, wet and clear of any trace of blood.

"Is LeAnn going to find a knife in your bedroom?" The question flowed out in nothing more than a whisper.

Eric raised his eyebrow and shook his head slowly.

"Then would you care to explain what the hell just happened?"

"I saved Mom, and then she saved me." He took the towel that Daniel handed him and wrapped it around his shoulders. "She should be home in a few days."

It was Daniel's turn to raise his eyebrows. "Eric, your mother died in February. It's almost September. She isn't coming home."

"You'll see." Eric ran the towel over his body and dropped it on the floor before heading back to his room to find clean underwear.

Daniel followed, tongue-tied. He traded a glance with LeAnn as she tucked in the new sheet and then held it up so Eric could climb underneath. She tucked him in and gave Daniel a peck on the cheek as she headed to put his soiled sheets in the wash.

"You'll see," Eric said again, and his eyes closed, leaving Daniel alone with no real answers.

Survival Games Chapter 61

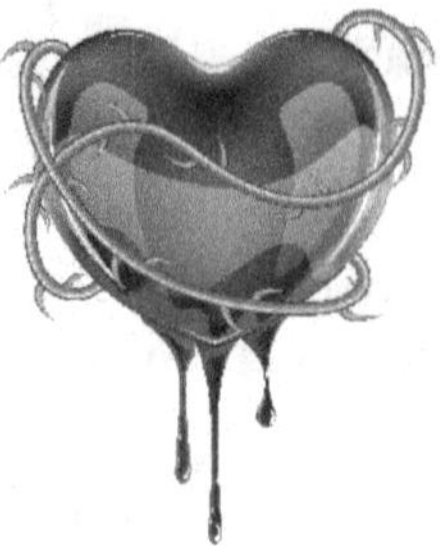

TOM WOKE SCREAMING. THE electricity buzzed in his ear again, his body arching with the current one second, and the next, the flow cut. Ty stood holding the cord, the frayed edges skating across the floor, spraying small sparks in an arc.

Tom stared at him and then swiveled his gaze to the chains. The last thing he remembered was Frank raising the knife above Jessica and then a flash of white light. He assumed that was the end of everything, but here he was, relatively unharmed, and Ty was free.

His heart hammered as he turned his gaze to Jessica, expecting the worst. His jaw dropped. Jessica stared back at him without a scratch, the ugly cut on her face gone. Her breasts were intact and not a slice on her perfect skin. Ty wasn't kidding when he said she could perform miracles.

When the wire stopped sparking, Ty crossed and pulled the other end out of the monitor, cutting the charge completely. Then he cranked the chains down and crossed the room to rip the clothes off Frank's unconscious form. He dragged him across the floor and clasped the shackles tightly around his wrists and ankles.

TY IGNORED BOTH TOM and Jessica, concentrating on the task at hand. He manually cranked the chains until Frank was hanging listlessly in the air.

"Get me out of this, Ty." Jessica gasped, the tremor of the last release rippling through her body.

"Not yet." The images of everything Frank had done to her flashed like a slide show. He crossed to the table and studied the array of items meant for producing pain. One particular item caught his eye, and he picked it up, turning it over in his hand. He looked at his reflection. He had never been the one to execute torture. Sure, he had watched it a thousand times through a camera lens or a monitor, but he had never entertained the notion of doing the things Frank had.

Until now.

He grabbed the smelling salts and trudged back to his stepbrother, cracking them open and then waving the foul salts under Frank's nose. His eyes blinked open, and his head moved away from the stench, but Ty followed his jerking path, making sure he was wide awake before he tossed the salts on the floor.

"You seem to have forgotten what I told you I'd do if you touched her again," Ty said, his voice a low growl. He gripped the tool in his hand, not revealing it to Frank. He wanted the bastard to remember first.

Frank stared at him and blinked before his gaze shot around the room, landing on Jessica. His eyes widened and snapped to the machine. The rattle of the links shortening again filled the silence. Panic spread over his features, and he swallowed, glancing back at Ty.

Ty waited patiently, but Frank seemed too paralyzed by fear to speak. He tilted his head and brought the utensil within his line of sight.

Frank started blubbering and jerking on the chains.

"I told you that if you touched her, I'd castrate you," Ty said. He placed the item between Frank's legs and squeezed.

Frank screamed as his member and his scrotum fell to the floor.

Ty reached up, plucking Frank's eye out of the socket, yanking it free without crushing it. "I'll need this for later." He walked back to the table.

The chains shortened again, making Frank scream louder. Frank's screaming continued, and Ty ignored him, wiping his hands on the towel.

"Please, Ty, please let me out of here!" Jessica gasped.

Ty closed his eyes and took a deep breath. The chains retracted again, followed by Frank's high-pitched scream. He crossed to Jessica, kneeled next to her, and ran the back of his fingers across her cheek. "Not yet."

"Don't make me do this," she pleaded. "Don't make me kill."

"You aren't. You're just my vehicle for justice," Ty replied, and she climaxed again.

Frank screamed, and something broke.

"Ty." She met his gaze, her eyes crazed with the build-up of the next orgasm.

"I'm sorry," he said. "I'm sorry about everything back in the room. I didn't expect to live, and I thought..." He hung his head. "I thought it would be easier if you hated me."

The next wave overtook her. She tilted her head back, gripping the arms of the chair, and she closed her eyes, tears squeezing out of the corners and sliding in slow motion down her flushed cheeks.

Frank's scream turned to a gurgling choke, and the wet ripping of flesh pulled Ty's gaze away from Jessica's face. His single eye rolled into his head as blood gushed from both his torn shoulder and torn hip. The choking ceased with the slowing flow of blood. The flesh ripped, and his leg fell to the floor, his arm dangled, and the left half of his body sagged, the sudden release of tension swinging it in a slow arc.

Ty reached over and flipped the machine off. He unlatched the shackles and pulled her trembling body from the chair, wrapping his arms around her in a tight bear hug. "I'm so sorry," he whispered in her ear.

Tom yelled out. Ty dropped Jessica, both of them spinning toward him. The buzz of electricity filled the room, and Tom's body went rigid, his teeth and eyes clamped shut.

"Turn it off!" Jessica bolted across the room.

The door burst open, and Marian stepped in, leveling a gun at Ty. She emptied four rounds into his chest. By some miracle, none of them hit his heart.

JESSICA REACHED THE CHAIR, grabbing the primary power source with one hand. The second her other hand touched Tom's shoulder, the restraints blew off him, and she pushed him out of the chair. With her hand on the conductors, the flow of energy burned through her palm, and she absorbed it, like a battery renewing itself.

Marian swung the gun in her direction.

"Don't!" Ty yelled and fell to his knees.

Another round discharged. The force of the bullet knocked Jessica back into the wall. The bullet tore clean through, but the path behind it immediately healed, leaving only a trace of a scar.

The sudden onslaught of pain sharpened her focus. Her gaze fell to Ty. His blue eyes locked on hers, relief flooding his features. He moved his gaze back to Marian and the gun swinging back in his direction.

She was going to plant a bullet in his brain.

Jessica shook her head. "I don't think so," she whispered and lifted her burned hand to her head as if it were a gun.

Marian's eyes widened in horror as her hand mimicked the motion of Jessica. The gun pressed to her temple, and she squeezed the trigger.

Ty's gape transitioned from Marian's falling body to Jessica.

The sound of the gun still rang in the quiet room.

Jessica spread her arms wide, hands in fists, and tilted her head back, uttering a guttural cry that echoed on the concrete. The cry of a warrior. Her hands shot open, and he felt the power ripple through the room, leaving a slight ozone odor. The door blew off its hinges, and not just their door. Every door in the complex lay in a heap of twisted metal across the hall from where it had originated.

Ty fell forward, whispering, "Angel."

The echo of metal on concrete was dimmed by the sound of the door slamming in the halls of Jessica's mind. It rattled on its fame and fell silent. Jessica lowered her arms and her gaze fell from the ceiling to Ty. Her breath hitched, and she stumbled toward his still form.

"Ty," she cried and turned him over. "Oh God, Ty!" She scanned him, lingering on the bloody bullet holes, and then she leaned forward, pressing a kiss to his forehead, wishing the wounds away.

Nothing happened. No overwhelming magical sparks, no white light, nothing.

She tried again, with the same result.

A sob escaped her. She held his slack face between her hands, her eyes filling up with tears and blurring her vision. "Oh God, I can't fix you!"

She turned to Tom. "I can't fix him."

Tom tilted his head, scrunched his eyebrows together, and then looked around the room, still dazed.

Ty's eyes fluttered open. "Jess," he whispered, coughing up blood.

"I'm sorry. I-I can't. I don't... I can't fix you," she stammered through the tears. "I don't have it anymore."

Ty raised his hand, gently cupped her cheek, and wiped the tears with his thumb. "It's okay, Jess." Before she could say anything, he swiveled his gaze to Tom. "Get her out of here," he commanded in a voice too strong for his condition. A coughing fit followed, racking his body and spraying drops of blood everywhere.

Tom stared at him, his eyebrows slowly rising, and the silent question of "How?" covered his face.

Ty blinked, bringing his focus back to Jessica. "Get out of here," he started and coughed again. "The eye. There is a bag under the control board, has money and keys to my car. There are clothes in the closet. Your sizes." He closed his eyes for a moment. "Go," he whispered. "Please, just go."

Jessica nodded, kissing his palm before he let it drop to the ground. His eyes closed. She leaned forward, pressing her lips to his. She didn't know if he would hear her or not, but she needed him to know. She needed to say the words before it was too late.

"I love you," she whispered in his ear.

She turned toward the table, getting to her feet and crossing to the array of weapons. Frank's eye rested on a towel, and she gathered the edges, folding them together over the ghastly item that was the key to their freedom. She reached down and took Tom's hand, helping him up and out of the room.

She paused at the door, looking back at the carnage. Ty's chest still rose and fell as the puddle of blood surrounding him slowly expanded.

She turned and led Tom down the hall, his hand still clasped in hers as they skirted around the twisted doors and quickly looked in each open entry for the control room. At the end of the hall, right after the fully equipped kitchen, stood a room with several monitors and an entire bank of controls. All the cameras were live, including the one in the room they'd just emerged from. Setting the towel on the counter, she reached out and flipped each master switch. One by one, the feeds went black. She hesitated at the last monitor, staring at the wide shot, staring at Ty.

Tom reached past her and shut the camera off.

She nodded, shifting her gaze to the considerable closet and the neat rows of clothing marked by Post-it Notes with size and prisoner name. She grabbed a pair of jeans under the sticky that indicated her wardrobe and slid them on. The sticky with Ty's name caught her attention, and a black dress shirt hung among the collection, clean and pressed. Instead of grabbing a shirt under her label, she grabbed the dress shirt and put it on, buttoning it nimbly and rolling up the sleeves.

Tom had slipped into a pair of jeans and was just finished buttoning up his shirt. His gaze slid over her and jumped to the section that she'd taken the shirt from. He inhaled and met her stare. He turned away and grabbed a couple pairs of pants, underwear, and shirts from both their sections, placing them on the chair.

"He said something about a duffel bag. I figure we're gonna want more clothes than what's on our back," he said.

She nodded, grabbed a bra, and then opened the cabinet under the control board. As promised, there was a duffel bag. She pressed the back of her hand to her mouth, stifling a sob when she looked at what was inside. It was full of cash. A pair of car keys sat on top of the crisp hundred-dollar bills.

Tom peeked over her shoulder. "Jesus."

Jessica recovered from the initial shock, grabbed the keys, swept the clothing into the bag, and handed it to Tom. Gingerly, she picked up the towel and led the way out of the control room. At the elevator, she fished the eyeball out of the towel, gritting her teeth against the squishy ball in her hand. She punched the button and held the eye in front of the scan bed, holding her breath. She prayed for it to work.

The door opened with a whoosh, and she dropped the eyeball, stepping inside quickly, like the elevator would change its mind. A sob escaped at the sight of the key in the slot. She turned it and pressed the only other button. The doors slid closed, and the elevator ascended.

Jessica's heart beat so hard she shook. The last time she had tried to use this elevator was so very vivid in her mind, and the idea of what lay beyond, the unknowns, what else would they have to fight through to get free, froze her breath in her lungs. The doors silently whisked open.

Presented with a choice of two doors, they looked at each door and then at each other. Jessica decided, reaching for the closer of the two doors, and they stepped into a private garage. She looked at the keys she held and the limited choice of cars. A silver Nissan 350Z Roadster, a Black BMW, and a beat-up Ford Taurus. She pointed the remote at the cars and pressed the unlock button. The Nissan's lights flashed, and the locks released.

She exchanged glances with Tom, and then they bolted to the car, she taking the driver's seat, and he the passenger seat after tossing the duffel bag in the space behind them. On the visor was a door opener, and she pushed the large red button. She burst into a fit of hysterical laughter as the garage door whirled to life, slowly rolling up. Darkness greeted them, and Jessica sped out into the open night, pressing the button once again before they drove out of range.

Tears blurred her vision as the bright headlights carved a path down the access road. She didn't dare speak until they hit the crossroad. "Which way?"

Tom inhaled, and after studying the landscape, he pointed to the left. "Let's go that way."

The massive warehouse receded in the rearview mirror, and she began to cry. Tears for Ty, tears for Mike, tears for Tom's wife, and tears because the taste of freedom was as sweet as she had dreamed.

Tom reached over and took her hand as she drove. "Ty was right. You were my miracle."

Jessica shook her head slowly as she cried. "No, Tom, Ty was the miracle. He let us go."

Survival Games Chapter 62

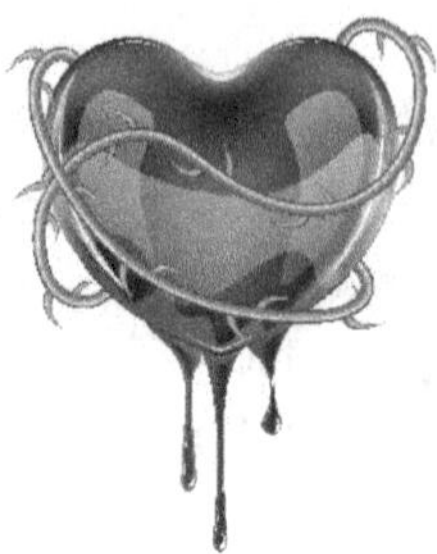

JESSICA REACHED FOR THE doorbell, hesitated, and pulled her hand away, suddenly filled with trepidation. "I can't," she whispered and looked into Tom's impossibly blue eyes.

"Yes, you can." He turned her back toward the door. "This is what kept you alive all that time."

"I know. I know. It still doesn't make it any easier." She rang the doorbell and held her breath.

Running feet and muffled voices approached the door, voices she'd longed to hear for the past seven months.

The door flew open, and a young teenage girl gasped at the couple standing on the doorstep.

A boy flew down the stairs. "Mommy!" He flew past the girl into Jessica's arms.

Jessica leaned over and wrapped her thin arms around Eric. "Hi, angel boy," she whispered in his ear. "Hi, Em," she said, looking up at her daughter through tear-filled eyes.

Emily looked up at the man standing behind her mother, and the remaining color drained from her face. Emily shook and sat down on the stairs in stunned silence.

"Who's there?" Daniel called from the back of the house.

"Mommy!" Eric announced with excitement. "And Clark!" he yelled and looked up at the man. "Daddy, it's Mommy and Clark!"

"Mom," Emily whispered, finally finding her voice. Tears dripped down her cheeks in thin rivers.

Daniel Connor walked around the corner and stopped in his tracks. "Holy shit," he uttered, his gaze bouncing between Jessica and Tom in astonishment before landing on her and gawking. "But you died," he whispered as if he were talking to a ghost.

Jessica stood up straight. "Danny." She squeezed the word out of her constricted throat. The relief washing through her was tempered by Tom's presence. She stepped into her house for the first time in months and threw her arms around her husband's neck.

"You died," he whispered again into her hair, and then he wrapped his arms around her. "Oh my God, I buried you." His voice shook, laced with long buried emotions.

"I told you she'd be back!" Eric danced around his mother and father. "I told you!" His voice filled with triumph.

Jessica smiled down at her son and then up at the man in the doorway. She pulled away from Daniel's grasp. "Please come in," she said to him. "Danny, this is Tom. He's the reason I'm still alive."

"It's actually the other way around." Tom stepped across the threshold.

Eric tugged at Jessica's leg. "Where's Ty? He made the bad man disappear. Where is he?"

Jessica and Tom exchanged a look. The last time they saw Ty, he was lying on the floor with four bullet holes in his chest. That was days ago.

"Honey, who's there?" a female voice called from the back of the house.

Jessica looked at Daniel. "Who's that?" she asked as a beautiful blonde walked around the corner.

Daniel answered both questions with two words. "My wife." He looked from one to the other.

Jessica's eyebrows shot up, and she went to say something. No words came, and she clamped her mouth shut, glancing at Tom. His face registered a measure of relief, and on the same level, she felt like a weight had been lifted from her chest only to be dropped on her foot.

"You certainly didn't waste any time." She looked between Daniel and the woman standing next to him, voicing the shock she felt.

"How?" Daniel asked. "How are you alive? How are you here?"

Uncertainty crossed the woman's face, and she put her arm around Daniel.

"We were kidnapped, our deaths staged." Jessica moved closer to Tom.

"Why?"

"You don't want to know." Jessica peeled off her tinted glasses.

Daniel recoiled. "You're not Jessica. Her eyes were brown."

Jessica's eyes were now a conglomeration of blues, greens, and grays, surrounded by an outline of brown that matched her original color.

"Opening the door changed her eyes, Dad, just like mine," Eric said from in front of her.

DANIEL LOOKED AT JESSICA and then down at Eric, and the connection between the two slammed into him. Eric had been with her in some way through this entire ordeal. "I need to sit down." He headed to the back of the house.

Everyone followed.

"You mean I'm married to two women?" he asked after a few minutes of awkward silence, trying to push the connection and what that really meant far out of his mind.

ERIC AND EMILY SAT on Jessica's lap, and Tom took the spot on the couch next to her.

"Looks that way," Tom said, looking from Jessica to LeAnn and back.

They all looked at him.

"Sorry," he apologized, holding his hands up.

Jessica squeezed her children, looked up at Tom, and then over at Daniel and LeAnn. "Danny, what do we do now?"

There was sadness in Daniel's eyes as he spoke. "I let you go, Jessie. As much as I loved you, I let you go." He drew a shaky breath. "I know this marriage..." He looked at his hand clasped in LeAnn's and held it up to bring his point home. "This marriage is where I belong. I'm in love with LeAnn. So, I'm not really sure what the next step is here."

Jessica nodded, and fresh tears streamed down her cheeks. As much as she didn't want to admit it, she knew he was right. She knew this was not where she was meant to be, either. She loved Daniel, but it wasn't the same as what she'd experienced with Ty, and it wasn't the safe harbor that Tom provided. Yet the rejection hurt.

She took Tom's hand and attempted to smile. "I can't be away from the kids right now. I need them."

Tom pulled her close and stared dumbfounded at Daniel. "You have got to be kidding?"

Daniel looked at him. "What?"

"If Jessica was my wife, and she came back from the dead, it wouldn't matter who I was with. I would thank the heavens above." He leveled a sharp stare at Daniel.

"I thought she died," Daniel said. "I moved on."

"Well, then you couldn't have loved her that much, now could you?" Tom challenged.

"Stop. Please." She looked over at Daniel. "After everything I've been through, I can't come back anyway," she said. "You would never fathom the hell we went through." She closed her eyes for a moment. "Tom understands. He lived through it, too, saw what I saw and protected me when it counted." She sighed and looked over at the television. It was on but muted, and she froze, the blood draining from her face, leaving her dizzy.

Tom followed her gaze, and his jaw dropped.

"Turn up the sound," Jessica whispered.

The news story unfolded on the screen.

"Holy shit," Tom whispered.

Eric looked up at him and laughed. "Clark said a bad word." But no one in the room heard him.

"Eric, Emily, leave the room now." Jessica said. It wasn't a request—it was a command delivered in a sharp, stern tone—one neither of them questioned.

They left the room, glancing back only once in her direction, but she pointed, and they disappeared down the hallway.

Daniel gasped, recognizing Jessica in the video. He turned up the sound.

"Aris Technologies CEO Frank Aris ran an underground pornography and S and M ring with sister, Marian Aris, and stepbrother Ty Aris over several years, which included shooting videos of various sex acts, mutilation, and murder. We believe their last two victims escaped after the Aris's self-destructed. The following video is disturbing and not suitable for children. If anyone has any information regarding the whereabouts of the witnesses, please contact the following number."

Jessica gasped as the view of the room came on the television and the last few minutes of their horrific ordeal rolled across the screen.

When the screen changed back to the news anchors, Jessica and Tom were both shaking, and Daniel was deathly pale.

"You were shot?" Daniel sent his wide-eyed gaze in her direction.

Jessica laughed. "That was the least of what was done to me, Daniel." She moved her shirt so he could see the scar. "But this is the only physical scar I have."

The screen filled with a man who had an uncanny resemblance to Ty, with one exception—his face was perfect, unblemished, scar free. He apologized to the families of those victimized.

Jessica watched him closely. He played a good part, just the right tremor of indignation and pain in his voice punctuated by tear-glossed eyes. The caption said his name was Christopher Aris, but she knew better.

Her son's question in the foyer reared in her mind. She hadn't fixed Ty, but he certainly had the power to do such a miraculous thing. The man droned on, and her attention snapped to his words.

"Never in a million years could I have fathomed this was going on, and I deeply regret the pain it has caused so many families. I will do my best to make this right for those who have lost so much." The man paused. "Again, I am truly sorry."

She stared into the eyes of the man on television, and his name flashed in her head like a beacon.

Ty.

Her dream blazed to the forefront of her mind, and Jessica knew it was only a matter of time before he came looking for her.

Survival Games Epilogue

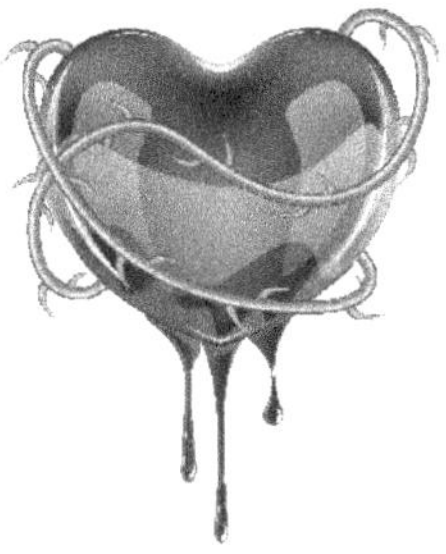

"TY?" THE LITTLE VOICE in the mirror called.

He looked up to see Eric. "Hey," Ty managed to say.

"You don't look so good." Eric leaned down over him.

"Don't feel too good." Everything faded to black.

Eric put his little hands on Ty's chest, closing his eyes and concentrating, pushing, projecting, sending every ounce of healing mojo he had into Ty's body.

Pure white light enveloped the room. Ty gasped, his body arching in response to the burning sensation filling his chest. Not quite pain, but nothing like what he felt earlier when Jessica released her magic.

Is this heaven?

"No. It's just me fixing you," Eric said sleepily, and the light died down around him. "You saved my mom. Thank you." Eric removed his hands from Ty's chest.

"No, Eric, thank you." Ty reached up, messing Eric's hair.

He blinked, and he was alone in the cell. He sat up, running his hands over his chest, feeling nothing but smooth, perfect skin under his hand. He hopped to his feet and turned toward the mirror, expecting to see his torn cheek. But what he saw sapped the strength out of his legs and he collapsed. With his wide, shocked eyes locked on his reflection, he crawled forward until he was within an inch of the glass.

His image reached up with both hands, running his fingertips over his bearded face. His perfectly unscarred bearded face. The scar he had lived with for so many long years was no longer there, even on close inspection. Only perfect, unblemished skin. He blinked and looked around the room, again wondering if he might be dead and in heaven. The thought produced a quiet laugh. He wasn't heaven bound, not in a million years.

"I'm alive. Holy shit, I'm alive." *And damn if I don't look like the spitting image of Chris.*

The first thing he did was take a shower, washing the blood and gore from his skin. He wiped the mirror and scraped the scrappy beard off his face. Clean shaven, he studied the reflection, and a thought tingled through him.

Could he pull off one last switch?

"Jesus." He sprang into action.

He cleaned every surface in the entire place, including turning on the sprinkler system in the room where his blood soaked the floor. Then he sat down at the control center, choosing four discs from the archives and dropping them into the duffel bag on the floor.

He pulled down the archive discs that had Chris in them and lined them on the counter, including the bit with Jessica. Then he accessed the original feeds based on the catalog dates and deleted every one of them. Erasing any record of Chris's involvement.

The control panel, console, and keyboards were all wiped down. He rummaged through the control room, gathering every item of Chris's and threw it into the duffel bag with all the discs, filling it to the brim.

Ty looked at the ceiling and exhaled. He needed to find Frank's back up. After a last look around, he headed to the elevator. On the floor next to the elevator was Frank's eye. Ty picked it up with a Kleenex and pressed the elevator button. He held his breath as the scan light rolled over the eyeball and let it out as the doors opened. He dropped the eye where he had found it, turned the key, and left behind the carnage and pain.

He opened the back door, looked around the garage, and smiled. Chris's car was still right where he'd left it. He tossed the bag inside and returned to Frank's office.

He opened the computer and found the last item that had been on it. It was the view of the room, the feed that Marian must have pulled up before she came barreling down with the gun.

Marian had royally fucked up. He sped through the electronic backup, deleted the same records he had in the control room, and erased the keystrokes in the computer memory. The last vestige of Chris was the fingerprints and retinal scan in the permissions file. With a few keystrokes, Chris's name was replaced by Ty's. Only three people now had access to the sub-basement according to the file—Ty Aris, Frank Aris and Marian Aris.

He went deeper into the program, making sure his fingerprints and retinal scan were not even shadows in the memory. Nothing the cops could trace back. When he was satisfied, he closed down the permission module and left the last gruesome shot on the computer. He unplugged the keyboard and cleaned it, careful to not leave prints when he reattached it.

He chuckled. This would give the secretary a hell of a start when she came in to turn his computer on and the authorities would have access to the backup.

The ambient time of day—between darkness and light—covered the landscape, and he took it all in, driving away in his brother's Ford Taurus after finding the spare keys under the floor mat. Some things never changed, and as he drove away into the ever-lightening day, he tasted freedom for the first time in years.

He had roughly twenty-four hours before Frank's secretary turned on the monitor. Twenty-four hours to complete the identity switch. The lock on his apartment didn't slow him down. He, like his brother, had back up. Under an overgrown bush sat one of those fake rocks. He picked it up and slid the key panel, dropping the single key in his hand. He wiped the rock with the tail of his shirt, dropped it into the dirt, and then, with the toe of his shoe, he pushed it back in place.

Once inside the apartment, he closed the door and reached into his pocket for the latex gloves. With a deep breath, he slid them on and went to work. The first place he went was the bedroom closet. He pulled open the doors, removed a couple of floorboards, and twisted the combination on the safe beneath the floor. Passports, licenses, and IDs were stored away for both him and his brother. He pulled anything with Chris's information, dropping them in a bag, and then wiped down every piece before he put them back in the safe. Then it was time to wipe out any record of fingerprints. He covered any and all surfaces, including all the dishes in the kitchen, praying he didn't miss anything.

The computer was next, and he accessed his special network—the national database of dental records—his playground for almost a decade, forging, changing, and switching records to suit his needs.

He found his records, temporarily changing the name to Ty Ryan before searching out his brother's files. A few keystrokes and he replaced Chris's name with Ty Alexander Aris. The mouse hovered over the save button and he exhaled.

"Sorry, Chris." With the press of his index finger, his brother's records transformed, leaving a trail to the death of Ty Aris in the event the authorities ever found his brother's remains.

Another flurry of activity across the keyboard brought him back to his records, and his hand shook as he stared at the last update. The pointer poised on the save button, and he bit his lower lip, staring at the name now attached to his files.

Christopher James Aris.

With a deep intake of air, he clicked the command, forever altering his life.

Before he closed the database, he erased any trace of the changes, any audit trail that would lead authorities back to his door, and then he did the same on the hard drive, wiping out the memory of the day's transactions. Even the most brilliant of computer geniuses wouldn't be able to trace his actions.

Standing at the entry and glancing around his cold empty apartment, he blinked back the sudden onslaught of tears. Sorrow gripped him, wrapping a tight fist around his heart. Losing Anna and Chris and now himself diluted the overwhelming sense of freedom flowing through his skin. He sighed, turning away from the memories.

"Goodbye, Ty."

CHRIS RYAN STARED OUT the window overlooking the Manhattan skyline of his brand new apartment. Months had gone by since he'd left Albany.

He had been cleared of any wrongdoing in the scandal and was named the sole heir to the Aris family fortune. That kind of inheritance was heady, to say the least, and with more money than he knew what to do with, he tried to make good on the damage he'd caused.

He sold the company to the highest bidder and earmarked a sizeable chunk to a trust fund—a victim's fund—doling out checks to the surviving families as the feds uncovered the identities of the captives from the tapes they'd found.

He legally changed his name, reverting to his original surname, and escaped into obscurity, leaving the Aris family legacy and the publicity that came with it far behind.

He could see the reflection of the video playing on the screen behind him, her voice seductively flowing from the speakers.

"Tell me you love me," she said.

He sipped his scotch and exhaled, watching snowflakes drift from the night sky.

"Someday."

The End

Continue Ty and Jessica's story on the next
page with MIND GAMES

Mind Games Chapter 1

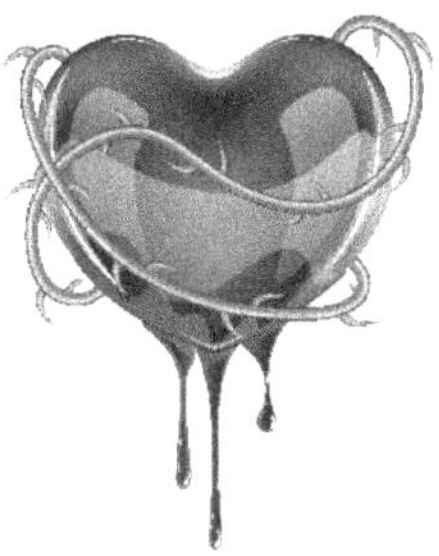

AFTER ADJUSTING THE ZOOM on his camera, he panned, scanning the beach until he found her. His heart skipped a beat. She was alone and still as beautiful as he remembered. He wondered if seeing her up close would have the same effect it used to, a rush of sudden electricity, followed by consuming heat drowning all his senses to the point he forgot to breathe.

God, I miss her.

A quick click of the shutter captured her image, and he tossed the camera back in his car.

He stretched, waiting until she took the turn at the rocks lining the end of the beach and jogged by where he stood. When he moved onto the sand, he sprinted until he was a few feet behind her. A few more strides and he jogged alongside her.

JESSICA WHITMAN BECAME AWARE of the shadow matching her stride, but didn't look over. Instead, she sped up a little. The shadow kept pace.

She pulled the earphone out of her ear. "You a reporter?" she asked without looking at him.

"Not in a million years," he said.

That phrase stopped her beating heart for a moment, then the pounding resumed, tingling through her skin with frantic pressure. She put on the brakes, skidding to a stop in the sand, her eyes plastered to his form.

He ran a few steps ahead and turned, his sunglasses reflecting a sharp glare in the midday sun. Edges of dark hair curled around the backwards baseball cap, and the smile... God, that smile made her bones melt to molten jelly. She stumbled back a step.

He reached up and took his glasses off, revealing the deep blue eyes she saw every night in her dreams.

"Ty?"

"Chris. Chris Ryan," he said, and approached her, extending his hand.

She stared at his outstretched hand and then scanned the beach. Relief settled in her at the sight of other winter beachcombers, giving her bones a more solid feel. His intense gaze captured hers, and she offered a slight smile, but didn't shake his hand.

She needed to give her reeling mind time to think, so she jogged again, putting the earphone back in her ear.

He jogged beside her.

After a few measured yards, she popped the earphone out again. "Where have you been?"

"New York City."

Her heart raced faster than usual; it had been over five years since she last set eyes on him. She never expected to see him again, alive and so vibrant, not after leaving him bleeding to death in that hellhole.

"Are you okay?" he asked.

"I've been worse," she lied, and glanced at him.

The silence enveloped them, and they continued jogging down the beach.

"How'd you know?"

"Tabloids," he answered. "Where's Tom?"

"California."

"Is everything I read true?"

The loaded question stopped her in her tracks. She walked toward the water. The tabloids capitalized on her pain, splashing her daughter's death and her impending divorce all over the rags. Her chest squeezed tight, and she scanned the horizon.

"Tom couldn't deal with it. He doesn't have a clue of what losing Em did to me. She wasn't his daughter. He thinks I should snap out of it, get on with life, and he just gave up trying. So yes, he left."

"I told him not to hurt you," he said, reaching to wipe a strand of hair out of her face.

Jessica nodded slowly. "He came back for the funeral, but..." She shook her head, listening to the waves hitting the sand. "But he said it was over when he left this time."

"How's Eric?"

"Devastated, just like me." The imaginary strap tightened around her chest, trying to close the endless empty hole. "We couldn't fix her." Tears burned her eyes, and she turned toward him. "We couldn't fix her."

He reached out and pulled her close, kissing the top of her head. "I'm so sorry, Jess." His voice wavered, filled with pangs of guilt.

The hole in her soul faded a fraction with his arms around her. Warmth radiated through the thin sweatshirt, and she nuzzled closer, letting the sobs she'd locked in for so long have free rein. His hand ran idly over her back, creating ripples of electricity through her muscles with each lazy pass.

She pulled away and wiped her face, looking up into his eyes. "Why now?"

"Thought you might need me." He shoved his hands into his pockets and looked out at the whitecaps.

Jessica followed his gaze, squinting at the glimmers of sunlight reflecting off the ocean's surface.

"I missed you," he said.

Without saying a word, she sent a glance in his direction before heading toward her beach house.

"Do you want me to come with you?"

She hesitated, not ready for him, not ready to let the overwhelming storm circling her to rain down. "Ty..."

"Please, call me Chris," he said, cutting her off. "Ty died on the floor that day."

She inhaled, scanning him. He was even more handsome without the scar, and the flood of feelings she'd denied for the past five years overflowed the levies she'd built around her heart.

Her eyes filled with new tears, and she nodded. "I need you."

His lips spread into a smile that twinkled in his eyes. "My car's over there." He pointed to a beautiful red vintage Corvette Stingray.

The flashy car brought a smile to her face.

"You like?"

She nodded.

"It's yours." He handed her the keys.

The shock of his statement unhinged her jaw, and her eyes danced between the dangling keys and the red sports car. Candy-apple red. Unbidden, her hand reached for the keys, stopping just short of the glinting metal.

She pulled her hand back, letting it drop to her side before she raised her gaze to his bright blue eyes. "I can't take this."

"I've got more money than God, remember?" He smiled, sliding his sunglasses back on. "You can have anything you want."

"You can't give me what I want."

He reached out and pulled the hair tie out of her hair. The wind swirled her long locks around her face. "What do you want?" He stepped closer.

"I want Emily back."

"You're right. I can't make that happen. But I can give you everything else you need." He ran his hand into her hair and leaned over, gently kissing her.

His touch ignited that flame inside her, filling the void with heat and smoke. When she opened her eyes, she let him lead her to the car, where he propped open the passenger side door for her. She slid inside, watching him trot to the driver's seat and smile at her as he turned over the engine.

He navigated the car through the winding streets, then pulled into her driveway a few minutes later without any instructions.

"You knew where we lived?"

"I kept tabs over the years."

Jessica fumbled with the keys, then unlocked the front door and swung it open for him, following him inside. "Eric's with his dad for the week." She closed the door behind them.

He removed his hat and ran his hand through his hair, scanning her home. He walked to the windows that overlooked the bluff and the most photographed lighthouse on the East Coast. "Hell of a view."

The storm inside her brewed, and a tornado of feelings gripped her, the most pronounced being lust. She had forgotten how strong the bond between them was. Not just the depth of their love, but the raw power of his physical proximity, the sinuous tingle to the air, the magnetism, the heat, the electricity.

"Ty," she whispered and flew toward him.

He met her in the middle of the room, wrapped his arms around her waist, and picked her up. Their lips met, unleashing the passion that had been bottled up for five years. He swept her off her feet, breaking the kiss to look at the layout of the living room, choosing the hallway to their left when she gave a nod of affirmation.

Seconds later, he kissed her, laying her out on the bed and running his hands through her hair, holding her face, his tongue dancing with hers. Heat enveloped her, leaving her breathless.

"Tell me," he whispered in his smooth, sexy voice, moving his lips to her neck. His hands glided down her body.

She trembled under his touch, pulling at his sweatshirt.

He leaned up so she could strip it off.

She ran her fingers over his perfect chest and gazed up into his eyes. There were no scars. Not the ones on his face and back that were already there before he'd kidnapped her. Not the one Frank carved in his cheek. Not the ones from the four bullets that ripped through his chest. Nothing. His skin was as perfect as a newborn's, and she understood the extent of the power her son had unleashed. The power she now felt in him.

"Say it, Jess." He propped himself over her, staring down, his eyes intent and pleading.

His game, his need to hear the words took precedence over his passion, and she crumbled, giving herself to him completely. "I want you, Ty."

The change in his eyes, the longing satisfied, transitioned to an emotion so pure it owned her body, heart, and soul. He made love to every inch of her with his hands and mouth, and she savored the feel of him, the smell of him, the sound of him, whispering his name over and over until he found her lips again, cutting off her need-laden voice.

"I love you," he whispered and slid inside her.

JESSICA WHITMAN SAT UP in her bed, calling his name. Her chest heaved, and she looked around the empty room.

Tom stuck his head out of the bathroom, toothbrush in his mouth. "You okay, babe?"

Jessica stared at him and then around the room again. "Yes." She nodded, falling back on the soft mattress, staring at the ceiling, still feeling his hands on her body.

Mind Games Chapter 2

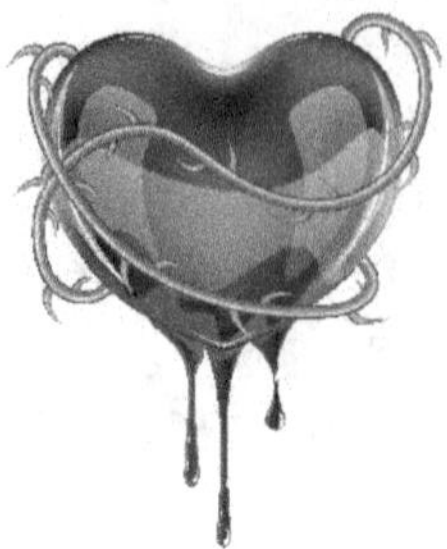

CHRIS SHOT UP IN the bed, his heart pounding, her voice still ringing in his ears.

The dream.

Again.

Profound sadness filled him, pressing down on his chest like an invisible hand reaching in and brutally yanking his heart out.

"Jess." He stared at the ceiling, concentrating on breathing in and out, counting each breath until his seized muscles relaxed.

"Damn it." He threw the covers off. He shook his head clear and made his way into the bathroom.

He splashed his face with cold water and glanced at his reflection. He sighed, his gaze moving to his perfect scar-free cheek, and he traced a line with his index finger. The line where the scar once broke the skin, from just below his lower eyelashes stretching all the way under his jawbone, jagged and angry.

After five years, he still wasn't used to his blemish-free profile. Every time he looked in the mirror, his reflection reminded him of her. And every time the ache returned, the itch to waltz back in her life crawled under his skin. The dream didn't help; it just made the itch all that much more insistent.

"I have to see her," he said to his reflection.

Blue eyes looked back, telling him that wasn't a good idea.

Irritated, he grabbed his toothbrush and walked into the bedroom while polishing his teeth and flipping on the television to catch the morning news. Nothing relevant or noteworthy scrolled across the bottom of the screen, so he retreated to the bathroom and spit in the sink.

The dream grated on his nerves. The satin of her skin under his hands and lips fanned the fire that had been in his belly since the day he'd first laid eyes on her. And now this... this blatant carrot dangling in front of him, all because he still had the healing power simmering in his veins.

Chris walked out on the terrace of his penthouse apartment with his coffee and leaned on the balcony wall, looking down at all the people rushing around like ants, amazed at the activity for such an early hour. The morning skyline, a mixture of reds and yellows reflecting off the high-rises, did nothing to quell his restlessness.

A new thought dawned on him, stopping the coffee cup midway to his mouth.

What if the dream is real?

What if her daughter is dying?

A layer of arctic air brushed his skin, forming bumps along his exposed wrists, and he shivered. If it were real... Dear God, if it were real, he had to fix it, even if that meant losing his freedom.

Looking beyond the buildings at the water in the distance, Chris made a decision.

Mind Games Chapter 3

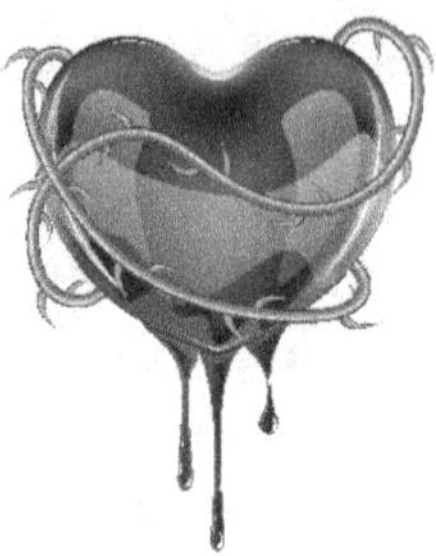

JESSICA STOOD ON THE deck of their cottage overlooking the choppy ocean, the cool breeze whipping her hair away from her face.

Where is he?

"You had another nightmare?" Tom stepped behind her and wrapped his arms around her waist.

She nodded. Even though she would not quite categorize it as a nightmare, it was disturbing.

"You're having them a lot. Is everything okay?"

She turned and kissed him. "Yes. It's perfect now that you're back. I hate it when you leave."

"You can always come with me. I could see if they'd give you a walk-on part on the show. You're certainly hot enough," he teased, knowing Jessica hated the spotlight. She would much rather be here on the quiet coast of Maine than in Los Angeles.

Jessica laughed. "I'm not one of the pretty plastic people." She batted her eyes, heading to the door. "Like you," she said over her shoulder.

He chased her inside around the living room like a teenager, laughing as he caught her and tickled her, dragging her to the couch. His tickling quickly drifted into foreplay, and he kissed her, peeling off the bathrobe she wore.

"I missed you." He pulled away from her lips. "I wish you would come with me. The thought of you here alone, of what could happen…"

"It can't happen twice." She went to kiss him.

He pulled away. "Jessie, they never found his body. If he's out there…"

"He hasn't come collecting. If Ty was alive, he would have already tried." She lied to appease him, to keep the pretense of their marriage as solid and sure.

If he knew Ty was alive and masquerading as Christopher Aris, his insecurity would barrel back to the forefront, and she didn't want that. He hated Ty with a passion that the years had not erased. There was no forgiving the murder of his wife. No forgiving the fact Ty had hurt her in ways Tom deemed unforgivable, no matter what the reasoning. If he ever found out she knew Ty was alive, Jessica didn't know what he would do. And she did not want to find out.

Tom nodded and looked down at his hands. "And if he did?"

Jessica reached over and gently cupped his chin, turning his face toward her. "Tom, I am in love with you. Nothing can change that."

"Then come with me next week."

"I've got the kids next week. April vacation."

He closed his eyes and leaned his head back. "I forgot." He took a deep breath, and she straddled his lap, running her finger down his bare chest.

"Now, where were we?" She leaned in and kissed him with a fraction of the passion her dream had produced, hell-bent on forgetting the feel of Ty's hands, focusing only on Tom. She smiled under the kiss as he stood, carrying her into the bedroom to finish what he'd started.

Mind Games Chapter 4

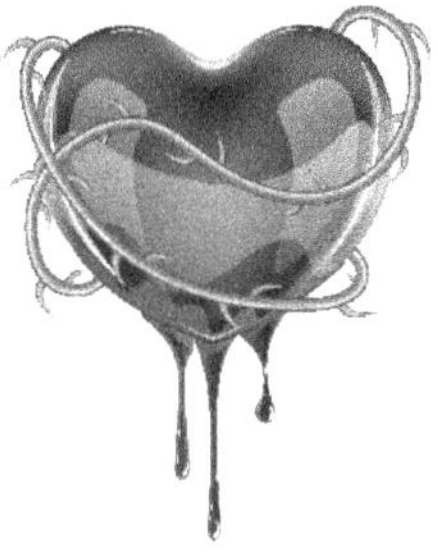

THE LATE MORNING SUN glistened on the Piscataqua River as Chris crossed the bridge into Maine. With the top down, the unseasonably warm, early April air whipped his hair. He glanced at his speedometer, keeping his speed in check, resisting the urge to open her up on the nearly empty road ahead.

"What am I going to do when I see you?" he asked the road ahead of him. "What the hell am I going to do?" He didn't have an answer, but his stomach growled, prompting him to take the Kittery exit in search of a late breakfast. His GPS squawked at him, repeating the command to turn around and get back on the highway in order to reach the programmed destination. He flipped off the sound and pulled into a restaurant between the shops lining U.S. Route 1.

The row of local real estate magazines in the restaurant's entryway caught his attention, and he grabbed a couple before following the hostess to a seat overlooking an inlet. Flipping through the pages, he stopped, studying an oceanfront estate with good acreage and a security gate enclosure, remote enough to provide the privacy he craved and not far from where Jessica lived. The price wasn't listed in the magazine, and by the look of it, Chris figured it was in the double-digit-millions range. He smiled and folded the page, then rolled up the magazine and slid it into his back pocket.

After scarfing down breakfast, he punched in the address for the realtor's office, then followed the pleasant voice of his GPS right into their parking lot. Everything about York was quaint, even the realtor's office, and he strolled inside.

"I'd like to see this property," he said to the perky receptionist.

A few moments later, a pretty blonde agent with the nametag "Betty" stepped out into the small lobby area.

"I understand you want to see the Carrington property." She looked him over, and a skeptical crease appeared between her brows.

"If you wouldn't mind." Chris offered a smile, dripping with sincerity.

She nodded and escorted him to her car, waving him into the passenger seat, and promptly took him to the estate. She attempted to engage him in conversation, and he avoided more than the congenialities but that didn't dissuade Betty from aimlessly rambling about the estate and its history.

The Carringtons apparently owned the entire outlet at the end of Roaring Rock Lane, along with the modest 5,000 square-foot English Tudor on a bluff overlooking the ocean. The grounds were impeccably maintained, with an iron gate surrounding the entire thirteen acres. According to Betty, this was a rare find, and it included a lovely in-ground pool.

He stood at the thigh-high rock wall that bordered the cliff, scanning the ocean and the marina at the mouth of the York River, and inhaled. Sea air, salty and refreshing, blanketed the backyard, and he couldn't imagine anything more perfect.

"I'll take it. All of it, as is, including the furniture," he said, spinning around and locking eyes with Betty.

"Um, Mr. Ryan, th-this is a sizable estate," she stammered.

He walked to her car and slid into the passenger seat without another word. Betty followed on his heels, rattling on about other properties that may suit him better.

"I have no interest in other properties," he said, ignoring her chatter and looking out the window until she pulled into the parking lot.

"Mr. Ryan, I don't think you understand. The Carrington estate is... sizable."

"How much?" he asked as they walked into her office.

Betty floundered. "The listing is for thirteen and a half million, but I need to talk with the owners about the contents."

He almost laughed at the pittance. His penthouse cost almost twice that figure, but then again, this wasn't New York City or the Hamptons. This was Maine, and that figure was probably considered outrageous here.

"Offer them fifteen million for all of it and tell them you will have the money tomorrow," he said, smiling and taking a seat. "When can I move in?"

Her jaw dropped momentarily, but she quickly recovered, handing him the forms. "If you would be so kind as to fill out these forms, I'll give the sellers a call."

She returned a little while later. "They accepted the offer, and you can move in as soon as the funds are verified and the paperwork is settled. That will take a few days."

Chris nodded and handed her the completed paperwork. "I assume you have an escrow account, so where should I have the money wired?"

She nodded. "I'll need to verify the availability of the funds."

Chris pulled out his wallet and handed her a business card for the firm that managed the majority of his money.

Betty dialed the number on the card and asked for the contact. She explained the situation and handed Chris the phone.

Chris authenticated his identity and gave the directive to verify the funds and wire fifteen million dollars to the realtor's escrow account for the purchase of a home. He handed the phone back to her, and she listened to the banker as he disclosed Chris's account balance, verifying the availability of the funds.

Betty slowly sat down and smiled up at Chris as she fumbled through her desk. She gave the routing and account number for the wire and hung up. With a strained smile, she called the realty firm's bank to let them know what was coming and to notify her once the wire was confirmed.

He stood to leave.

"Thank you for choosing Stanford Realty," she said, and her eyes twinkled with a whole new level of interest. They dropped to his ring-less fingers, and her smile widened when her gaze returned to his. "The paperwork will be completed by the end of the week. Where can I get in touch with you?"

"You can get in touch with me through the number on that card." He never gave out his private numbers for any reason. His banker and his lawyer were the only ones who knew how to get ahold of him, and he liked it that way. Chris glanced at his watch. It was almost one. "Will Friday be acceptable to sign the papers?"

She nodded, and he walked out of the office, leaving her holding the business card in awe.

Mind Games Chapter 5

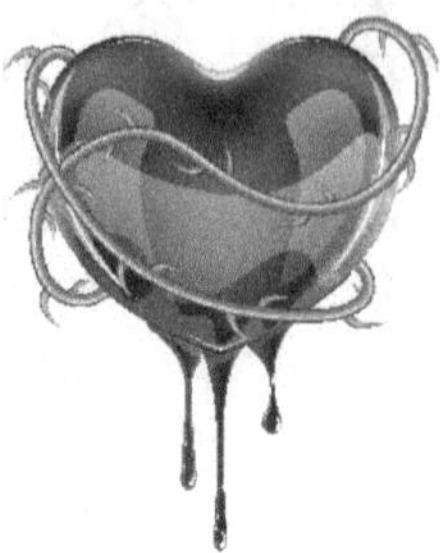

JESSICA LAY ON TOM'S chest while he lazily ran his hand through her hair.

"What do you have going on today?" he asked.

"Nothing until later this afternoon. I've got a couple of dance classes scheduled. You should come watch. There are some talented girls up here."

"I'll pass. You know what watching you dance does to me. I'm not sure that's appropriate for the kids to see."

She laughed and climbed out of bed, then pulled on her jogging shorts and top. "You coming?" she asked and twirled her hair into a clip.

"Not today. I'm still a little jet lagged."

"It's almost one in the afternoon." She kissed him and left the room. "Lazy shit!"

"You wiped me out," he called after her.

Jessica walked briskly to the beach and trotted down the stairs. She needed her daily routine, jogging on the hard-packed sand, losing herself in the music filtering through the tiny speakers in her ears. But it wasn't enough to lose the dream. The slight chill in the air penetrated to her bones, and she shivered.

What if he really did show up?

HIS HEART DOUBLED DOWN, jumping in his chest at the sight of her, causing his hands to tremble. Swallowing with a mouth suddenly devoid of saliva, Chris took off his leather coat and threw it on the passenger seat, along with his sneakers and socks.

This is it.

He walked to the middle of the beach, right in her jogging path, and waited, with his thumbs hooked into his back pockets, to keep the shakes in check. The cool, salty breeze grazed his cheeks. He stepped forward at the sound of her footfalls.

So intent in her quest, she almost bumped into him, and recovered with a stumbling sidestep, mumbling an apology.

"Jess," he said before she could get back into her stride.

Her body went rigid, her eyes widened, and her mouth parted in disbelief. She took a few steps back, her cheeks losing all color before suddenly blooming red.

Chris took his glasses off. "We need to talk."

Jessica closed her mouth. *This isn't how the dream went.*

"No, it isn't." Chris answered her thoughts and took a step toward her. "Not at all like the dream."

She reached up and slowly removed her sunglasses. "You can read my thoughts now?"

"I guess." He shrugged. "You and Eric changed me."

"I can see that." Now that she was face-to-face with him, she didn't know what to do.

"Me neither." He smiled and looked down at the sand. He brought his eyes back to hers after a moment.

"What?" she whispered, shifting her weight from foot to foot.

"Now that I'm here, I don't know what to do either." He stepped closer. "I just needed to see you again."

Jessica stopped moving. "I never thought…" She looked toward the bluff where she lived. "Tom and I got married." She looked back at him.

"I know. I kept tabs on you."

"Then why are you here?"

"I'm not sure." He studied the sand again and shoved his hands in his pockets. "Does Tom know I'm alive?"

"No."

"But you did." He looked up at her.

"Yes, when I saw you on TV." She glanced out at the ocean. "I knew when you used the phrase 'not in a million years' in that interview."

Chris nodded. That was precisely why he'd used that phrase. He wanted her to know. "I changed my name."

"Yeah, I know. You stole your brother's identity."

He nodded, feeling heat bloom in his cheeks. "But after all the crap went down, I got the inheritance and changed my name again. I legally changed it to my father's name."

Jessica hitched her breath in. "Chris Ryan?"

"Yeah." Biting his lip, he lowered his eyes to the sand and inhaled before bringing them back to her. He reached out and wiped a stray hair out of her face. As his finger grazed her cheek, she closed her eyes. "If you knew I was alive, why didn't you say anything to the police?"

Her eyes opened to his question, and she shook her head slowly. "I killed Marian. I killed her to save you." A tear finally slipped out of the corner of her eye. "I kept quiet for you," she barely whispered, her breath shaky and full of emotion.

They stared at each other.

"I think I have something you're going to need." He stepped closer, putting his hand on her cheek.

Leaning her face against the weight of it, she closed her eyes. His lips grazed hers, and she shot back a few steps.

"No." She put her hands up in front of her and bolted toward her home.

Chris did not follow. He watched her run, listening to the waves gently slosh on the beach. The hollowness in his chest filled with a devastation he had no words for. The fear in her eyes just before she ran cut him deeper than Frank's knife had, and he took a seat on the sand.

"What the hell do I do now?" He closed his eyes. He wanted to go grab her and force her into the car, disappear with her, wipe the fear from her eyes. He wanted her in his arms again, to feel her skin, her mouth, like in the dream.

He eventually climbed the steps to the road and slipped into his car.

He leaned back, looking in the rearview mirror, and stopped breathing.

The image of his dead stepbrother, Frank, returned his stare. "I'm going to cut her to pieces, and there is nothing you can do to stop me this time." Frank laughed and disappeared.

Chris's heart hit triple-time, and he jammed the car into gear. The little Corvette all but flew over the barren mid-day streets of York. He pulled into her driveway, and without hesitation, ran toward the door, burst into the house, and sprinted toward the screams.

He slid to a stop in the bedroom doorway, and his mind stalled. Tom struggled against invisible bonds holding him in the chair, his eyes wild and locked on his wife.

Chris followed his gaze to Jessica suspended against the opposite wall, her arms raised above her head, her wrists crossed like they were bound and her toes dangling inches from the floor. A knife, dripping with her blood, hung in the air in front of her, slowly waving back and forth. It slashed out again and tore through her flesh.

Her cry was laced with pain and her gaze was glued to the mirror next to her. Fear drained all color from her face, leaving her calico eyes wide and stark against the paleness of her skin.

Chris narrowed his eyes at the image.

Frank held the knife and looked in his direction. "Well, isn't this just the perfect trio? My little whore, pretty boy, and Ty." The ghost laughed and slashed out at Jessica again.

Another slice ripped through her abdomen, and Jessica screamed.

Chris picked up a paperweight from the nearest bureau. "The name's Chris, you son of a bitch!" He pitched it and shattered the mirror.

The knife fell to the ground. The invisible bonds holding Jessica to the wall released. He moved swiftly from the doorway and caught her before she hit the floor.

"Who the hell are you?" Tom bellowed.

Chris laid Jessica on the bed and looked up. Recognition flashed in Tom's eyes.

"Jesus," he whispered, and his face turned beet red. "Get the hell away from my wife!"

"I can fix her." Chris looked down at the cuts on her arms and stomach and then back up at Tom. "I can fix her," he said again and stepped away. "Please let me."

"Tom, it hurts," Jessica said. Her breath hissed between her teeth, controlled but still filled with pain. Blood seeped out of the wounds, running down her sides and staining the sheets. She reached for her husband, and Tom stepped closer, taking her hand, his eyes bouncing between her and Chris.

"She doesn't have the power to fix herself anymore," Chris said, and even he heard the desperation in his voice. "Please."

Jessica nodded and squeezed Tom's hand. "Either call 9-1-1, or let him fix me."

Tom stared at her, and the red in his face dropped a shade. Jessica's plea seemed to break through the stubborn wall of anger enough for him to decide. "Okay, do it."

Chris sat on the side of the bed and took her other hand. He looked over at Tom for a second before focusing back on her. "This is going to hurt," he said. "At least it did for me." Putting one hand on her shoulder and the other on the opposite hip, Chris hung his head for a second, homing in on the power pulsing in his veins, gathering strength. Then he leaned over and kissed between the stab wounds on her stomach. He mentally pushed, feeling the healing power Eric had given him shift back into her where it belonged.

His breath hitched in his chest at the sudden drain of pure power, and the subsequent blast that left him cold to the core.

Jessica arched her back and screamed, her body healing under his touch, infusing her with healing power. She fell silent, and the tension in her face smoothed out as she slipped into unconsciousness. Light danced over her body.

"Sweet Jesus," Tom whispered and looked at Chris in disbelief.

Chris sat up, meeting his gaze. "I'm sorry." He wiped her blood from his lips and moved away, dropping his gaze to Jessica.

She opened her eyes, and the colors swirled in her irises again, like they had five years ago.

When the light dissipated, Tom shot a glare at Chris. "What the hell just happened?"

Chris ran his hands through his hair nervously, looking at the shattered bits of the mirror. He licked his lips. "I think it was Frank's ghost."

Jessica nodded.

"How did you find us?" Tom pulled his hand out of Jessica's grasp, and it curled into a fist.

"I've known where you were all along." Chris glared at Tom in a silent challenge.

Just go.

Her thought hit him like a sucker punch, and he dropped his eyes to hers, inhaling at the plea in her gaze. "I gotta get out of here." He backed out of the room, his gait hurried as he shot out the front door.

"Wait," Jessica called.

He stopped with the driver's side door open and swung his gaze to her. Blood covered her abdomen, but no trace of where it had come from was visible. His gaze kept jumping between the bloodstains and her eyes as she approached the car.

"You told me to leave," he said.

She closed her eyes and nodded. "Yes. But I needed to say thank you." She covered his hand with hers and gave it a little squeeze.

The magnetic jolt pulsed through him at the touch of her fingers, but he pulled his hand away. "It's my fault. I must have led him here." He glanced at the house, where Tom glared through the window. "I've gotta figure out how to kill a ghost," he whispered as disbelief raked its fine nails over his skin.

"One moment, everything was fine, and the moment I opened the closet..." She shook her head and glanced over her shoulder before bringing her calico gaze back to him.

Something clicked in his head. "Mirrors," he said. That was how Eric and Jessica communicated before, and how Eric found him—through mirrors. His eyes went wide. "Jesus, Frank got to you through the mirror. You need to stay away from mirrors."

HIS CONCLUSION CHILLED HER, and she shivered despite the warm glow of power inside her. It felt very different from what she had gotten accustomed to while in the dungeons of Frank's prison. This power felt purified. Clean.

"You gave it back to me, didn't you?" she asked.

He nodded. "Now you can fix Emily."

His words caught her by surprise, swinging the door on her dream wide open. The bits and pieces she never could remember came barreling through her consciousness.

"Oh, Ty," she whispered, and the tears came. "If I had waited…"

"I would have lost Emily."

"Yes. But now, I've brought something worse." He looked back at the house and slid into the car. "Just stay away from mirrors."

Mind Games Chapter 6

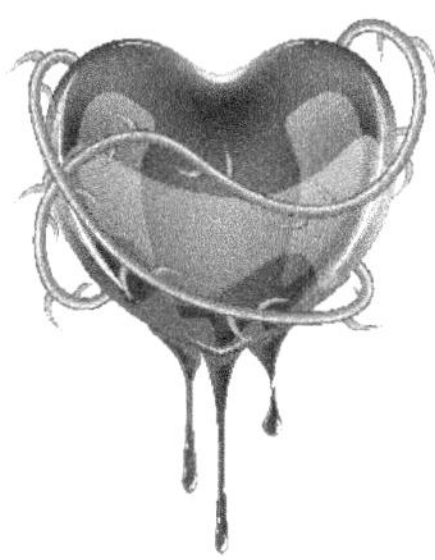

"WHEN WE SAW HIM on television, did you know? Did you know it was him?" Tom shot at her when she re-entered the house.

Jessica nodded, her heart thudding in her chest, and a fresh fear filled her mouth with a metallic, tinfoil taste.

He spun away from her and marched onto the balcony, then leaned against the railing with shoulders that sagged with anger and disappointment.

"I'm sorry," she said, stepping behind him.

Tom glared in her direction, still shaking from the rage filtering through his skin. "How many times have you seen him, Jessie?"

"Today was the first time since we left Albany."

Tom stared at the water.

"I love you, not him."

"Are you sure about that?"

She nodded, but she wasn't sure. She wasn't sure at all.

"Then come with me next week and bring the kids."

"I hate L.A. Besides, the kids love it here."

"And *he* is here."

"No." The first hint of anger reached the surface. "Damn it, Tom. This has nothing to do with him. I hate going west because I do nothing out there. You go off to work, and I wander around the house that you lived in with your previous wife, and I feel guilty. It's my fault that you're not with her today." She stormed into the house.

TOM GLANCED BETWEEN THE living room and the ocean, his anger diffusing. He'd never thought of it that way. She had given up claim to everything she had to be with him. She'd made a fresh start, away from her friends, her family, her kids, but he still had all the same contacts, along with the house he and his prior wife bought, along with everything they'd collected together. He hadn't made much of a fresh start because he'd never really let go.

"What if I sold that house?" he asked as he entered the bedroom.

"I would still hate L.A., but it would make it better." She flipped on the shower and peeled off the bloody exercise outfit. "I need to get ready for work."

"I'm coming to the studio with you." He didn't like the idea of her being alone with Ty Aris in the same town.

"Fine." She nodded and stepped under the spray.

Tom turned, his gaze landing on the bloody splotches on the carpet and the ruined sheets on the bed. A chill grabbed his tailbone and skittered up his spine. *I'll deal with that later.*

He paced in the living room, mulling over everything that had happened in the last hour.

Ty Aris, alive. How the fuck did that happen?

He had witnessed the gunshots, four bullet holes in the man's chest. How did someone walk away from that?

Jessica stepped out dressed in her leotard and dance skirt, her hair pulled back in a bun. Her eyes were wary, watching him trace his steps back and forth.

"You really had no idea he was here?"

She shook her head, keeping eye contact. "He caught me on the beach, and, basically, I freaked out. That's why I was out of breath when I got home. I ran at full speed. And then..." She waved toward the bedroom, drawing a shaky breath. Grabbing the keys off the hook in the hallway, she gave him a final sigh and headed toward the garage. "You coming?"

Inhaling, he nodded and followed her out of the house, then jumped into the passenger seat, still gnawing on the day's events.

Silence filled the car, and he didn't speak until they rolled down the road toward the dance studio. "I have a bad feeling about this."

Mind Games Chapter 7

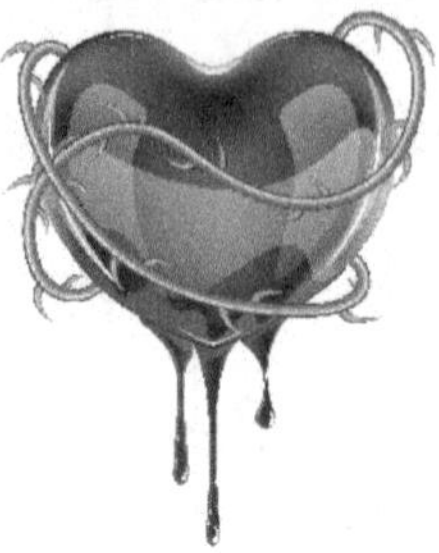

CHRIS WATCHED THE CAR back out of the driveway, and he followed them to the dance studio.

Mirrors. Jesus, doesn't she ever listen?

He pulled a U-turn and parked across the street, slamming the gear into neutral and yanked on the parking brake. Irritation threaded through him at her blatant disregard for his warning. He inhaled and settled in, his gaze planted on the front studio through the now-open mini blinds.

Distracted by her warm-up, his gaze kept drifting to her instead of the large mirrored wall. The old heat flared, filling him with bitter desire.

What am I doing here?

His answer came with a flash in the mirror, and he bolted from the car, his heart pounding as Frank's image wrapped his hands around her throat.

Again, he slid into the room, giving Tom a quick glance before growling his command, "Let her go!"

JESSICA'S GAZE FLICKED FROM the image of Frank to Chris. She clawed at the invisible hands crushing her windpipe. Tom sat frozen in the chair with the same wild-eyed look as before.

Help me! She screamed in her mind.

The rage in Chris's eyes aimed at the image in the mirror turned her heart into a frenzied drumbeat. Chris looked every bit the predator he had when she first saw him from her seat in the electric chair. He advanced closer to her, his eyes glued to the image of his dead stepbrother.

"The mirror, Jess," he said. "Break it!"

How?

CHRIS'S HEAD JERKED IN her direction, and her pleading eyes set him in motion. He stepped forward, throwing all his weight behind the punch. A great web spread into the glass, but the mirror didn't shatter.

It was enough to break the spell that held Tom in place, and he stood, swiveled, and pitched the chair toward the splintered image of Frank.

The mirror shattered under the violent impact. Shards of glass sprayed across the room.

The chokehold on Jessica released, and she crumpled to the floor, gasping for breath, looking up at the two men and the fragments of glass behind them.

"Damn." Chris shook his wrist, snapping red droplets across the floor. He raised his eyes from the bloody mess of his fist. "You are such a stubborn fool sometimes."

"You... you followed us?" Jessica asked.

"I told you to stay away from mirrors. A dance studio has mirrors, so yeah, I followed you." He glanced at the shattered glass. "You could have broken that." He crouched in front of her and pointed to where the mirror had been.

She blinked, and a crease formed between her eyes. "How?"

"Same way you blew those doors off their hinges," he replied.

She shook her head. "I had the energy from the electric chair. It was different."

Tom gawked. "I-I thought it turned off?"

"No, it was still live," Jessica said. "I burned the crap out of my hand, but the energy helped me blow your restraints. If you had still been strapped in when I was shot, the power surge would have killed you."

"I didn't know." He took her hands.

"You didn't need to," Jessica said. "A lot of things that happened down there you don't need to know about." She turned to Chris.

"You still can do those things. You just have to learn to do them to save your own ass, and not someone else's."

"I wasn't able to save Mike."

Chris dropped his gaze, feeling the flare of pain that accompanied the name within her. "That was my fault," he finally said. "I shouldn't have left you alone there." He took a deep breath. "But you still can do those things, Jess."

Jessica reached out to take his bleeding hand.

Chris pulled away even though he was pretty sure he had broken his hand. "No. You need that for someone else. Besides, it's not that bad."

"You're lying." Jessica glanced at his hand and then met his stare.

Chris smiled and stood up. "Take her to California with you, Tom." He walked out of the building, looking at his hand. "Shit," he whispered and picked a shard of glass out from between his knuckles.

Mind Games Chapter 8

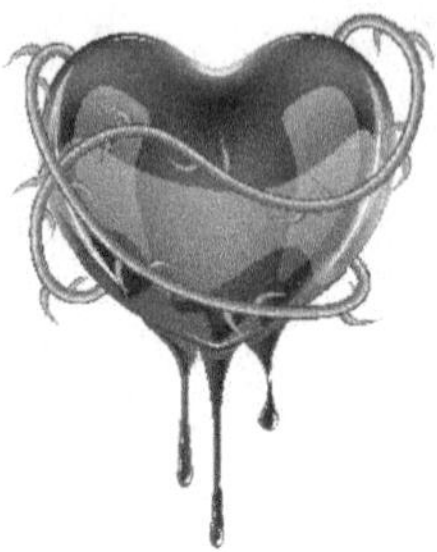

JESSICA AND TOM SWEPT up the glass in the studio in silence.

"How long has he been here, Jessie?" he asked her again.

"Today was the first time I saw him since we left that godforsaken place," Jessica snapped back.

"Then how the hell does he know about the dance studio, or that I want you to come to California?"

"I have no idea." She looked at him for a long time. "Tom, the dream I keep having," she began and stopped as the bell on the door rang. Her first student arrived.

Jessica walked into the lobby. "I'm sorry, we're closed today. There was a minor accident, and the mirror broke. I will be out of commission here for a few weeks until this gets fixed. I apologize for any inconvenience."

"What about the dream?" Tom asked when she came back into the studio.

"Emily died, and you left."

"I would never..."

"But you did," she whispered. "You will."

"It was just a dream."

"No, it was a glimpse of the future. He said he had the same dream. Over and over, like I have the past few years. It was a glimpse of the future that he changed by coming here today."

Tom pressed his lips together, unable to formulate any sort of comeback to her train of thought. Frustration pounded his muscles.

"In the dream, he asked me what I wanted, and I told him he couldn't give it to me."

"What did you want?" Tom asked, dreading the answer.

"I wanted Emily back," she said, surprising him. "He found a way to do that. He made sure the dream would never happen. Even if that meant losing me all over again." She blinked, and tears spilled down her cheeks.

"Jessie." He reached for her.

"I'm sorry, Tom, but it hurts. I never remembered the entire dream, but I used to wake up very sad. Now I know why. Today, I understood. You're going to end up really hurting me."

"I love you." He wrapped his arms protectively around her. "And I would never intentionally hurt you."

"I know." She looked out the window, shivering in his arms.

Mind Games Chapter 9

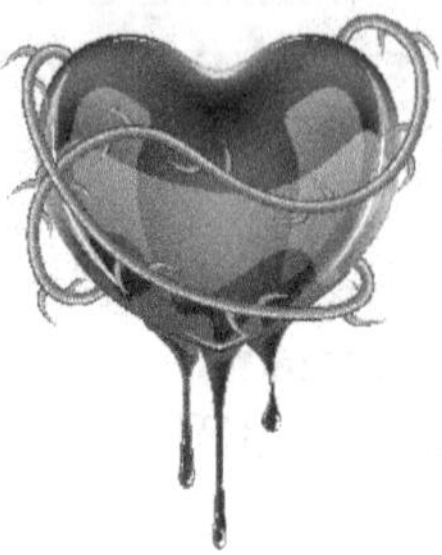

CHRIS WENT TO THE emergency room, and they patched up the cuts. Sure enough, the X-ray showed a few broken bones in his hand and wrist. They put it in a cast and sent him home with some pain pills.

He checked in at the hotel across from the beach and literally passed out from exhaustion.

The sun shone bright in his room when he woke. He rolled and glanced at the clock. His eyes went wide, and he shot into a sitting position. It was almost eleven.

After he went to the bathroom and brushed his teeth, he slipped his baseball cap on and headed out for a run. He trotted across the street and stopped at the top of the stairway. A very thin patch of sand greeted him, and high tide lapped the rest of the beach. He sighed, turning to the sidewalk to execute his exercise regimen. Hanging a right onto the road that passed Jessica's house, he barely gave it a glance, jogging past and stopping at the lighthouse a few blocks away. Chris climbed down the rocks and found a peaceful spot to sit for a while.

"You lied."

Her voice startled him, and he turned, looking up at her, too shocked to respond. She climbed down, took a seat next to him, and reached out to run her fingers over the blue cast.

"I like the color."

He stared at her and blinked, unable to believe she had followed him. Blinking again, he glanced down at the cast and shrugged. "I didn't realize how much of a pain in the ass a broken arm really is."

"How bad is it?"

"It's just a couple of broken bones," he said, shaking it off. "What really sucks is I'm right-handed, and my car's a five speed, and I hope I don't get any shit about my signature on the paperwork at the end of the week."

"Stop whining." She laughed and leaned into him, bumping him with her shoulder. "And don't you have a league of lawyers to sign things for you?"

He grinned and shrugged at the not-so-subtle jab. "Normally, but I didn't consult with legal counsel this time." He bumped her back and winked. "I bought some property all on my own."

"Getting tired of the city?"

"I kind of like it up here," he said, looking around and then returning his gaze to her.

"Why?"

"You have to ask?"

She hopped to her feet and stepped away, putting distance between them.

"Jess?" He looked up at her, squinting.

She waited.

"Did you love me?" he asked her sunlight-framed form.

She squatted so he could see her eyes. "You have to ask?" She stood and walked away.

Chris jumped to his feet. "Yes, I have to ask," he called after her. She turned in surprise, and he crossed the distance. "Did you love me?" He saw the turmoil in her eyes as she debated whether or not to answer him.

"Yes."

The sigh that came with the words tempered his impulse to take her in his arms. Doubt and underlying fear reflected in her eyes, and struck him like a dagger in the abdomen.

"But?"

"But I chose to marry Tom, even though I knew you were out there. I don't want to hurt him. So, you moving close by may not be the best of ideas."

"I disagree."

"How long before you do something you'll regret?" she asked, striking him silent.

The sharp pang in his stomach twisted. "I don't know." The plea in her eyes belied her words, and he stepped closer, the electricity between them increasing as he towered over her, trembling against the urge to touch her, to reach out and run his hands into her hair, to feel her lips under his, to taste her again. "How long until you give in to your feelings?"

She was quiet as she glanced out at the vast ocean. When she met his gaze, she said, "A million years." Then she walked away.

Mind Games Chapter 10

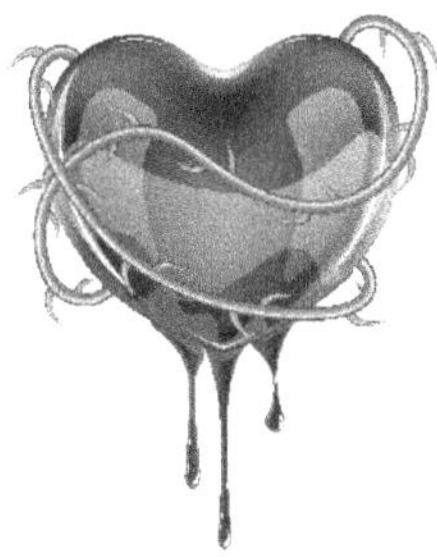

CHRIS SAT IN THE library combing through ghost folklore, but her words kept coming back to him. Each time their signature phrase echoed in his mind, the rock on his chest pressed down. Being near her again just increased the pain, and the knowledge of the futility of his actions.

This isn't a game I'm destined to win.

He huffed and stared at the open book in front of him, not seeing the text, only a jumble of letters that didn't compute. "I never lose," he mumbled under his breath, and glanced out the window at the bank of woods surrounding the town library.

With a deep inhale, he closed his eyes, wiping his face. "Focus, asshole."

This time, he saw the words on the page clearly, and he scanned the passages, trying to find a hint of a way to send the ghost of his stepbrother back to hell. There was nothing useful to address their particular situation in any of the dozen books he had stacked on the table, and he left in frustration.

The quaint center of town was lined with little ocean-side gift shops, and the delicious scent of boiling lobsters reached his senses. His stomach growled, and he followed the smell into a roadside market, then ordered a lobster roll for lunch. After taking a window seat, he ate while scanning the street until his eyes landed on a small sign advertising a fortuneteller. He raised his eyebrows and exhaled.

That's an avenue to consider.

He inhaled the rest of his sandwich, left the money for lunch on the table, including a hefty tip, exited, and crossed to the shop, debating for a fraction of a second before he wandered inside.

The foul stench of incense and sweat accosted him. He breathed through his mouth to quell the sudden lurch in his stomach. After removing his sunglasses, he scanned the scant room once his eyes adjusted to the dim light. A small table covered in a black fabric with glow-in-the-dark stars flanked by two rickety chairs graced the room, and in the center of the table stood a hazy crystal ball. Fog permeated the crystal, swirling, creating patterns that coincided with periodic infusions of smoke. A stack of tarot cards sat on the table, almost hidden from view behind the glass sphere. This room had all the cheesy trappings of a hoax, with one exception.

The fortuneteller herself.

A shiver tried to take hold of him, but he dismissed it.

The fortuneteller's beady black eyes narrowed, wrinkling her skin further. Her white hair provided a stark contrast to her dark skin and brightly colored sari. She stood, circled him, sizing him up, and returned to her seat. Once her robes were settled, she leaned on the table, waving her hand at the opposite chair.

"What ails you, boy?" Her voice was scratchy, as if she had just smoked a case of cigarettes.

He peeled five twenties off the stack of bills on his money clip and laid them on the table. "I need to know how to get rid of a ghost."

Her head cocked, and she closed her eyes. She slowly caressed the crystal ball between them and then her hands jerked away from the glass. A gasp slid from her lips, and her eyes flew wide like a broken shade. "Boy, you've got yourself one evil sidekick, and he's out for revenge."

Chris nodded, looking frankly at her. "So, how do I send him back to hell?"

Some of the luster faded from her cheeks, and her hand gripped the glass sphere like she was holding on for dear life. "He reached into the physical world."

"Yes, through mirrors."

Her hand relaxed, and she turned her wide-eyed stare toward the crystal ball, staring at the swirl patterns. He could almost hear the whisper of the air moving around in the sphere. "You must kill his spirit in the physical world."

He shivered. "How?"

"Take away his power, and he will fall."

Irritation crawled over his skin. He needed an answer, something he could work with, not this cryptic mumbo jumbo. "How?"

"You must lure him into the physical world and take his path away."

"How?" he asked again, and the slithering sensation on his skin made him shift in the chair. Uneasy didn't describe the feeling; it was more of a gripping dread itching at his balls, but he ignored it, focusing instead on obtaining information he could act on.

"She is the key, but you need to take the stand without her," she said. "You must make him think he has won. That is when he will be most vulnerable."

The picture she painted in his mind formed clearly in the crystal ball, and Chris's eyes strained in their sockets. Dread turned into icy terror, layering deep into his core, and he trembled, understanding exactly what was expected of him. He shook his head, slowly at first, and then much more adamantly.

"No," he whispered. "I'm not gambling with her life."

The fortuneteller stared into his eyes. "You must, or all will be lost."

Mind Games Chapter 11

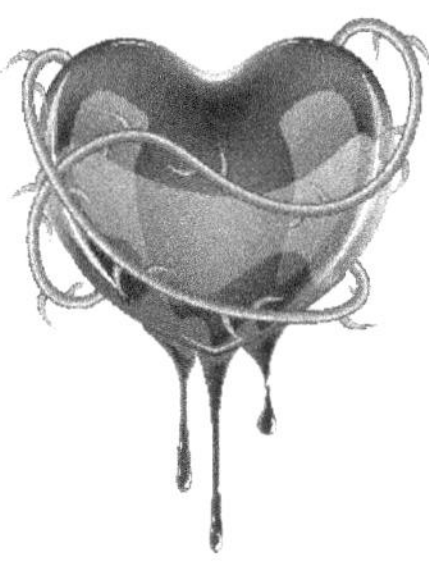

JESSICA HUNG UP THE phone, her blood thickening to pea soup quality, draining all the heat from her face, causing her breath to catch in her throat. She turned toward Tom.

He raised his eyebrows. "What is it?"

"Em," she answered. "Em is sick." She flew into the bedroom and began frantically throwing clothes in a bag while her heart clanged in her chest. "I need to go to Connecticut now."

"I'll drive." He tossed a few items into the bag.

Jessica stopped and ran a hand down her face. "All the headaches, all the complaints..." *All the dreams...* On some level, she'd known this was coming, but hearing Daniel utter the words "brain cancer" on the phone had been like a kick in the gut. She blinked back the mist covering her eyes and stared at Tom as the dream reared up in her mind again. "I really need you on this one. You can't go AWOL on me."

He crossed to her and gave her a hug. "I'm here for you, babe."

"I'm serious."

"I am, too." He picked up the bags and headed to his truck with her in tow, and they pulled out of the driveway as the sun dipped below the horizon.

Please God, please let the power he gave back to me be enough to save my baby girl.

Jessica prayed quietly, making empty promises in exchange for the miracle she already possessed. Tears slowly cut heated paths down her cheeks, and she reached for Tom's hand and clasped it tightly as the power wound into a tense ball in her stomach, centering, focusing, growing inside her, taking a life of its own.

Quiet permeated the car, laced with the soft echo of music coming from the speakers. The CD looped over and over, just loud enough to be heard over her silent tears.

"She'll be okay, Jessie." Tom pulled off the highway, navigating the roads to her ex-husband's house.

They hurried out of the car and rang the doorbell. LeAnn Connor opened the door with red and puffy eyes, then doled out hugs to Jessica and Tom as they entered.

"Where's Emily?" Jessica asked, wiping her own wet cheeks.

"Upstairs, sleeping," Daniel said, walking around the corner into view.

"I want to see her." Jessica climbed the familiar stairs, stairs she'd navigated every night for close to twenty years before Ty kidnapped her. Eric's door swung open when she reached the landing. She stopped, meeting his troubled gaze.

"I can't fix her." His eyes were as red and puffy as LeAnn's and Daniel's.

Jessica smiled and put her hand on his cheek. "It's okay, baby. I can."

Doubt etched his features, and he shook his head.

"Yes, honey. He gave it back to me."

Eric's mouth dropped slowly. "Ty?"

His reverently hushed whisper brought gooseflesh to her arms and sent a chill up her spine. She nodded.

Hope flared in her son's eyes.

Jessica turned and walked into Emily's room. She closed the door behind her and then took a seat on the side of the bed, studying Emily's face. Dark circles surrounded her eyes, even in sleep, the telltale sign that all was not well with her daughter.

"Emily?" Jessica ran her hand through Emily's hair.

Emily opened her eyes, and a sob escaped at the sight of her mother. She threw herself into Jessica's outstretched arms.

"I love you. I promise everything will be just fine." Jessica kissed her forehead, wishing the cancer eating her daughter's brain gone. She held her as the white light cascaded over her daughter's skin, letting her magic do its thing.

"Mom, it hurts."

"Only for a minute."

The sparks dancing over Emily's skin died down, and Jessica pulled away, scanning her face for the dark circles that had been there when she'd walked in the room. They were gone. Emily's eyes were clear of the haze of illness. Jessica took a deep breath, the power infused into her cells, growing stronger.

"Better?" she asked.

Emily nodded, her chin trembled before tears leaped to her eyes.

She held Emily, closing her eyes. She silently sent a simple prayer of thanks. Chris gave her everything she'd said she wanted, and more. The light behind the door in her subconscious burned brighter than ever.

"I need to talk to your father and LeAnn." Jessica stood up.

"I love you, Mom."

"I love you, too, honey." Jessica closed the door behind her and walked downstairs. She exchanged a glance with Tom before focusing on Daniel and LeAnn. "Danny, I want a second opinion."

"Jessie, we've had second opinions!"

"I want another opinion, or at least another scan of her brain. I want to see it with my own eyes. Please," she insisted. "We could bring her to Los Angeles with us and get one out there, if you can't get one here."

"No. If you insist on this, I'll bring her back to Yale New Haven Hospital, to the doctor we're comfortable with."

"I'm insisting. Call them and see if you can set something up for tomorrow or the next day, and I'll go with you."

Daniel nodded and exchanged a glance with his wife. "I'll try."

"Do you have a place to stay?" LeAnn asked.

Jessica shook her head. "I was going to call my folks, but it's a little late now."

"Why don't you stay here tonight?" Daniel offered.

Jessica looked at Tom and received a shrug in response. "That would be nice."

JESSICA COULDN'T SLEEP EVEN with Tom's arms protectively wrapped around her. She listened to his even breathing and then slipped out of bed when he started to snore. Throwing on her bathrobe, she slipped downstairs to the game room and slid behind the bar. She grabbed a wine cooler from the stocked refrigerator and cracked it open. Her gaze landed on the pool table, and she took a swig of her drink. It had been a while since the last time she held a cue stick. She racked the balls and broke, raising her eyebrows as three balls found their way into the pockets.

"Not bad," she said to herself.

"Everything all right?" Daniel rounded the corner into the room.

"I couldn't sleep. I hope you don't mind." She waved at the table.

"Not at all." He pulled out his cue stick. "Mind if I join you?"

"It's your table." Jessica took another shot and missed. "I'm a little rusty."

He cleared the table, and she shook her head as she re-racked for another game.

"You still can shoot rings around me," she said.

"What really happened to you, Jessie?"

"Danny," she sighed, studying him. They hadn't had any real time alone since she came back. Someone was always around, so he never asked beyond their original conversation when she first arrived back in their lives. "You saw enough on television. You really don't need to know."

He walked over to her and touched her face. "I'm sorry if I hurt you," he said. "I thought you were dead, and LeAnn..."

"I know. You fell in love with her, and I can see why. She really is a sweetheart. Besides, I'm not sure I could have come back anyway, even if LeAnn wasn't in your life."

Daniel took a step back; his eyebrows rose, and his lips slightly parted. After a moment, he snapped his mouth closed, the muscles in his jaw tightened. He turned away from Jessica, studying the pool table.

"Danny, what I went through... It was horrifying, and you don't just leave that behind. It follows you for the rest of your life. Tom and I have a connection. He was there; he saw what I went through, what it did to me. I didn't think I'd ever feel safe again, but he gave that to me down there, and it meant the world to me. He protected me when he could, and the times he couldn't still haunt him." She paused, and Daniel looked over his shoulder at her. "As much as I loved you and the life we had together, I never would have been able to go back. I would have never felt safe here."

She caught the raw hurt in his eyes and diverted her gaze to the pool table, lining up her next shot. The red-three-ball plunked into the pocket.

"Emily will be all right," she added, changing the subject.

"Jessie, she has cancer."

"We'll see." She looked at the table, assessing her next move, then crossed to the bar and took another swig of her wine cooler before returning her attention to the game.

Daniel grabbed her arm as she walked past him. "Cancer," he emphasized.

Jessica stopped and looked into his eyes. "Not anymore."

He let go of her, his mouth slowly dropping.

"I fixed her," Jessica replied, and took her next shot.

The ball went into the pocket where she expected it to. She continued to clear the table, and he stared at her, blinking every few seconds.

Jessica finished her cooler after the last ball plunked into the pocket. "I think I'm gonna call it a night." With that, she left her ex-husband staring at her, dumbfounded.

Tom stirred a little as she crawled back into bed. He wrapped his arms around her again, and yes, she still felt safe in his firm grasp.

Mind Games Chapter 12

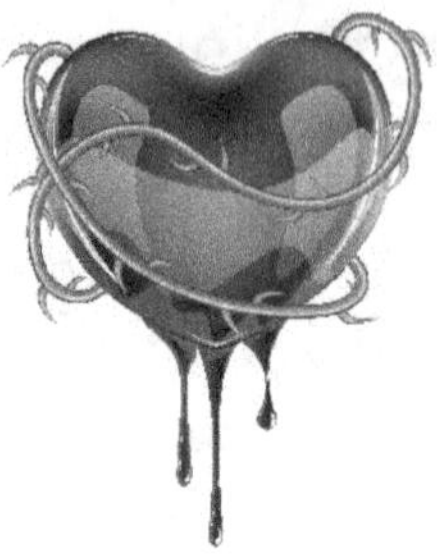

THE NEXT MORNING, JESSICA woke early, slipped into her jogging clothes, and shook Tom. "You coming?"

Confusion lit up his face for a moment, and he glanced around the room, wiping the sleep from his eyes. He blinked and brought his gaze back to her with a nod. "In a sec." He headed to the bathroom.

Jessica brushed her hair in the mirror and wrapped a hair band around her ponytail. When the temperature in the room plummeted, goose pimples peppered her flesh. She rubbed her arms, glancing up at the air conditioning duct, the most logical source of the sudden cold draft. She returned her gaze to the mirror and gasped.

Frank stood behind her in the reflection. He smiled a sadistic smile that promised violence and pain. The same one she remembered from the complex. Fear balled in her stomach.

A frigid hand wrapped around her throat, and he chuckled in her ear.

"No." She struggled in vain as the ghost shoved her shorts to her knees.

"Oh, yes." He spun her toward the bed and pushed her over the side.

Her teeth chattered, and she squeezed her eyes closed, filling her mind with the one name that she knew would hear her anywhere, blasting the silent siren with the force of an F-18 hitting Mach one.

Enduring the violent ice-cold thrusts, she glanced toward the mirror and whispered, "Ty, help me!"

Frank laughed. "If you think my little brother can help you here, you are mistaken. When I'm done with you, I think I'll go visit your daughter," he whispered in her ear.

The mirrors in both the guest room and Emily's room shattered to pieces, but not before Jessica saw the reflection of her savior's angry blue eyes.

THE SOUND OF SHATTERING glass set him in motion. Tom flew into the room, his eyes darting from the shattered glass to her crumpled on the floor, then landing on the dark bruises around her throat.

Crippling fear squeezed his heart, and it took him a second to draw a shaky breath. He closed the door behind him and shimmied past the shards to kneel next to her, silently searching her eyes. What he saw turned his blood thick, forcing his heart to pound harder. He gulped the last of the spit in his mouth.

"Frank was here," she whispered, and a tear rolled down her cheek.

He pulled her to his chest, praying he wasn't trembling like she was. Picking her up, he set her on the bed and shifted, tracing his finger along the fading marks on her neck. A thousand questions clouded his mind, and he returned his gaze to the shards on the floor.

"You broke the mirror?" he asked.

"No." She shook her head. "He did."

Tom wrapped his arms around her again and stared at the shattered glass. No explanation was needed. He knew whom Jessica was referring to. Both fear and a bizarre sense of relief accosted him.

Ty Aris.

Jesus, it's like he's been appointed as her guardian angel.

How the hell do I deal with that?

He didn't know how long the guardian angel routine would last before Chris crossed the line and hurt her again.

Mind Games Chapter 13

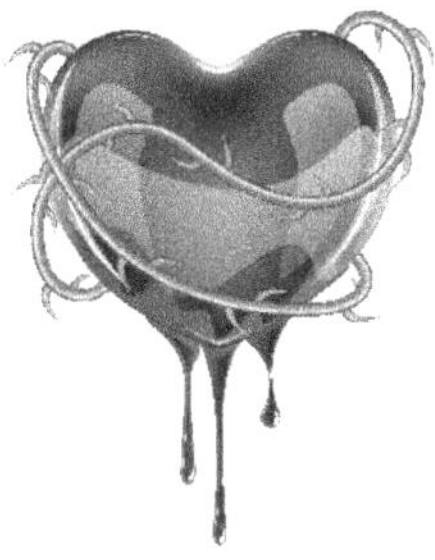

JESSICA'S SCREAM FILLED CHRIS'S head just like it had down in the complex. He bolted out of sleep, jumped out of bed, and flew into the bathroom where the only mirror available in the hotel room was.

Like a magic looking glass, the mirror shimmered into an image of Jessica being accosted by Frank's ghost. When her gaze met his, she whispered, "Ty, help me."

Frank's hips slammed into her, igniting an anger so hot Chris's skin burned. But when Frank's threat of paying a visit to Emily was uttered, Chris's rage turned into something unmanageable.

Fury overwhelmed him, and it escaped his control, along with the command hissing from his lips, "Shatter!"

The image crumbled and was gone.

Instantaneously, fear replaced the fury, and his legs gave way, collapsing beneath him as sure as the glass in the image. He caught himself on the sink.

"Jess!"

He couldn't see her anymore. Hot panic raced through his blood. The echo of the fortuneteller's words pinged in his brain.

This is what Eric must have felt like when he couldn't see Jess in the complex.

"Eric," he said.

Eric had once found him psychically, and Chris stared at the mirror, concentrating on getting a message to the boy who'd saved his life.

The reflection in the mirror altered, and with a blink, he stood in a room he didn't recognize. There was a commotion in the hallway on the other side of the door. A boy was sleeping in the bed, and Chris reached out to shake the child.

Eric looked up groggily at first, and then his eyes went wide.

"Please tell me your mom is all right," Chris said, his voice urgent.

Eric glanced toward the commotion. He stood up and opened his door. The tightness in his shoulders relaxed. He closed the door and looked back at Chris.

"She's okay." Eric nodded.

The image of the bedroom faded, and Chris kneeled down over the toilet. Vomit shot out of his mouth, shaking him as violently as his anger had.

"Holy shit." He gasped, leaning back against the wall as the last few minutes rolled through his mind.

He broke those mirrors. Not Jessica.

Mind Games Chapter 14

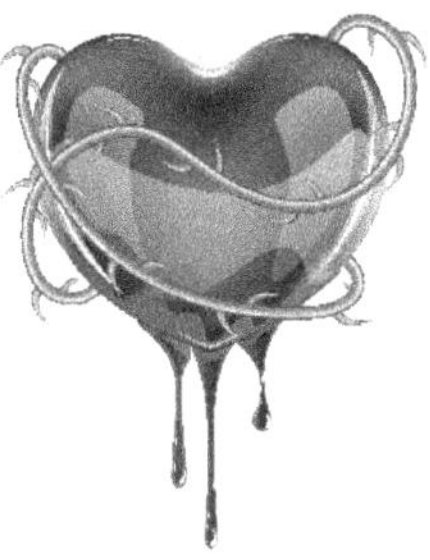

JESSICA GRABBED A GLASS of orange juice and curled into the overstuffed family room chair while Tom poured himself a cup of coffee in the kitchen. Still shaken from the encounter, she shivered and closed her eyes.

"He was here."

Eric's voice cut through the haze, and her eyes flew open to her thirteen-year-old kneeling on the floor before her.

"You saw him?"

Eric nodded. "He was worried about you." He glanced toward Tom. "What's happening, Mom?"

Relief swept through her. Eric was talking about Chris, not Frank. Her heart returned to normal, and she sighed. "Nothing for you to worry about."

"Then why would he come to me?"

Jessica thought for a moment. Her mind went back to all the times she could contact Eric through the mirrors at the complex. The connection she had with her son during those dark days was eerily similar to what she now had with Chris.

"Because my mirror was broken, and he couldn't see me."

"I still don't understand."

"He broke the mirrors to protect us," Jessica said.

"From what?" Eric shot a glare in Tom's direction.

Jessica saw the glare, and her heart broke. "Eric, Tom isn't hurting me."

"Then what was he protecting you from?"

"A ghost," Tom answered.

"The bad man." Eric gasped, his eyes going wide, causing Jessica to break out in goose bumps.

Jessica shot Tom a look that told him to keep his mouth shut. Eric didn't need to know about this, even though he figured things out pretty quickly, especially since he could read others' thoughts with little to no effort. She glanced back at Eric. "Yes, but I'll be just fine."

"He can't protect you." He pointed his thumb at Tom.

"Of course he can." She tried to smile, but it likely didn't convince either of them. "I'm going out for a run. You still coming?"

Tom nodded, and they headed outside.

While they jogged side by side down the quiet suburban street, the silence thickened.

"I'm sorry I wasn't there."

"It wasn't your fault. You can't be with me twenty-four seven."

"It's Ty's fault."

"No. It's not."

"He shows up, and this shit happens. It's his fault."

"If he hadn't shown up, Emily would be dying of cancer," Jessica snapped and sped up a little, pulling away from him. The contents of her recurring dream slammed into her chest like Frank's fist.

Tom caught up with her, but said nothing for a while.

With her feet rhythmically hitting the pavement, her mind drifted to Chris. The fury in his eyes this morning reminded her of the way he'd looked in the complex when Frank brought her bruised and battered body in the room for the first time. The look was murderous.

A gentle yank on her ponytail brought her back to the present.

"Stop it, Tom." She batted his hand away.

"Lighten up."

"Fuck you."

He grabbed her arm and stopped running. "Jessie, what's wrong?"

She was taking her frustration out on him, and it wasn't fair. This wasn't his fault. She knew he would do anything to stop it if he could.

"He threatened Emily." She began to run again.

Tom caught up to her. "He what?"

"Frank threatened to go after Emily." The anger burst through the surface, and she ran faster. "Ty heard what that bastard said, and then both our mirrors shattered."

Silence filtered between them again, their pace in harmony, each step echoing the other's.

"Do you think he's making this happen to screw with you?"

Jessica sent enough of a warning glare to make him take a sidestep away. "Ty isn't doing this. He wouldn't hurt me, and he would never threaten my kids."

"How the hell do you know?"

She stopped and glared at him. "I know."

"He hurt you plenty," Tom said, stopping a few steps ahead of her. "Or did you forget?"

"I haven't forgotten. But we both know why he did that."

"He's a kidnapper and a killer, Jessie. He should be in jail for everything he's done."

"I killed, too. I killed Marion."

Tom closed his eyes and put his hands on his hips. "That's different."

"How is that different?"

"You had no choice. She tried to kill you. What you did was self-defense. And don't you dare stand there and tell me Ty wouldn't grab you in a second and... and..." The muscles in his jaw worked, and he clenched his teeth together. "He brought this on us."

Jessica remembered the words she'd said to Chris at the lighthouse.

"Okay, I'll admit he may have led Frank to us, but I don't believe for a second he knew. Frank wants to kill all of us. He wants Ty to watch *me* die." She looked back toward the house. "He came to give me exactly what I said I wanted in the dream. He came back to save Emily." She started to jog again, and Tom followed. "I'd trade my life in a heartbeat for my kids." She met his gaze and pressed her lips together.

Tom kept pace with her. "What do we do now?"

"I have no idea."

They slowed as they approached the driveway, then walked the rest of the way. "I love you, Jessie."

"I know, and I love you, too." She slung her arm around his waist despite his sweaty shirt, and they walked up the front steps. "Did I thank you for coming with me?" She looked up into his blue eyes, thankful he hadn't backed away from family events like he had in the past.

"Not in so many words."

"Thank you." She got on her tiptoes, kissed him gently, and pushed the doorbell.

Eric opened the door and let them inside.

Daniel poked his head around the corner, the phone plastered to his ear, and he waved them into the kitchen.

"They can see her today," he said, covering the phone. "I just need to find someone to be here when Eric gets home from school."

"I'll stay," Tom offered.

She glanced at him sideways, suddenly irritated that he didn't want to come to the doctor's office with them.

"You sure?" Daniel asked, his gaze bouncing from her to Tom and back.

"Yep, I'm sure," Tom said, and he looked at Jessica. "You don't mind, do you?"

She narrowed her eyes and inhaled, putting on a smile that felt foreign and fake. "No. No problem."

"That settles it." Tom leaned down and planted a kiss on Jessica's forehead before heading upstairs to clean up.

Daniel confirmed the appointment and hung up the phone. "I can find someone if you want me to."

"No. Tom said he'd stay."

"But you want him with you," Daniel said with a cocked eyebrow.

Jessica chuckled. "I keep forgetting how well you know me."

Daniel smiled. "You gave him the look."

"Yeah, I did. Mind if I get some juice?" She didn't want to discuss her irritation at his pulling back again.

"Go ahead." He sipped his coffee.

"Is LeAnn coming?" Jessica poured herself a glass of orange juice.

"Yes, she always goes with me. She loves them like they're her own."

Jessica took a deep breath and nodded. Tom never really understood what it was like to be a parent; he wasn't around the kids enough. He certainly didn't understand the sacrifice she'd made when she gave Daniel primary custody and moved to Maine.

"Sorry, Jessie. I didn't mean to rub it in."

"You're lucky."

He nodded. "I know I am. I don't know anyone who is divorced and actually still gets along with their ex, either."

"It was a unique situation, Danny."

"Still, you didn't fight the divorce, and were more than generous with everything."

"I didn't want the money." Aris Industries had sent her a very large check for her pain and suffering. She'd given it all to Daniel and the children. She wanted to start over with Tom, and she couldn't accept the money knowing it came from Chris.

"I know. But I still appreciate it. It's made our life a hell of a lot easier." He smiled at his ex-wife. "Does Tom know how lucky he is?"

"Yes, I do," Tom said, walking into the room and wrapping his arms around Jessica. He leaned over and kissed her neck. "Mmm. Salty."

"I need to clean up." She wiggled out of his grasp and excused herself, leaving Tom and Daniel staring at each other.

"YOU SURE YOU DON'T want to be there for Jessie?" Daniel asked.

Tom's smile faded, his brain not registering Daniel's question. Instead, it focused on the bathroom upstairs.

"Shit, the mirror." He sprinted for the stairs, leaving Daniel in the kitchen. He burst into the bathroom just as she stepped into the tub.

"What is it?"

He looked at the wall, and her gaze followed. Her reflection stared back.

"Shit," she said.

Tom stepped into the room and closed the door behind him. "I'll just stay here while you shower. Okay?" He leaned against the closed door, watching the mirror with dread.

Don't know what I'll do if he shows up, but at least I'm here.

JESSICA QUICKLY WASHED AND rinsed her body and hair, her heart pounding in her chest the entire time, leaving her mouth dry and her throat throbbing. She turned off the water and reached around the curtain to grab a towel. The rush of cold air on her wrist made her hesitate. Dread wrapped its frigid hand around her heart, and she took a deep breath, reaching farther until the soft terry grazed her fingertips. She yanked the towel behind the curtain, her heart fluttering like a hummingbird's wings, her airway closing, restricting the flow as the panic attack gripped her. She wrapped the towel around her body and willed herself to calm down, forcing deep breaths. Slowly, she moved the curtain aside.

Tom's blue eyes met hers, his face pale with dread, etching lines in his forehead and around his tightly clamped lips. A layer of steam clouded the mirror, and relief washed through her, springing tears from her eyes. The lines in his face smoothed, and he crossed to wrap his arms around her and kiss her wet hair.

She nodded and clung to him. The mirror was clearing, and she didn't want to be in the room when it did. "Bedroom." She gathered her things.

They went into the bedroom so she could dress. He helped her with her hair by brushing it while she put moisturizer on her face. She put a dash of lipstick on and turned so he could see.

"Do I look okay?" she asked, twirling her wet hair and clipping it into an easy updo.

"You always look fantastic."

"Thank you." Her eyes welled with tears, but she blinked them back, clearing the sudden burning from the back of her throat. "I don't like being scared."

He laughed. "I know. You want to be in control of everything."

Surprised laughter burst from her lips. "I guess," she said just before his lips found hers, shutting off the laughter.

He pulled away, smiling and wrapping his arms around her tight, holding onto her for longer than he normally would. "Do you have any idea how much I love you?" he asked and released his hold on her.

"Yes, I do." Jessica turned and headed downstairs.

Daniel and LeAnn sat at the kitchen table with Emily, eating breakfast. Eric had already caught the bus to school.

"Hi, angel." Jessica kissed Emily on the cheek.

She turned to her mother with eyes that were bright and alert and pointed to the pile of pancakes on her plate. "I'm hungry."

Jessica smiled at her and then up at Tom. "Tom's going to stay here while we go to the doctor for more tests."

"Will you stay for dinner?" Emily asked.

"Yes." Both Jessica and Tom answered at the same time and smiled at each other.

"SO, DID YOU SETTLE on which college you want to go to?" Jessica asked Emily on the drive to the hospital.

"No." Emily picked at a hangnail, avoiding her mother's eyes.

"Why not?" She glanced into the rearview mirror and caught Daniel's warning glance.

Emily shrugged. "Just never got around to it."

"Well, where were you accepted?"

"UConn, University of Hartford, Boston University, and NYU."

"No Yale or Harvard?"

Emily chuckled. "No, no Yale or Harvard."

"So, which one do you want to go to?"

"I kind of like the idea of going to school in New York City."

Jessica raised her eyebrow. "Really?"

Emily nodded. "It's also one of the top ten schools for teaching in the country."

"You still want to be a teacher?"

"Yes."

"Then NYU it is."

Daniel cleared his throat and traded a glance with LeAnn as he turned off the highway, navigating the roads to the large parking garage attached to the hospital.

They didn't have to wait long before Emily was carted off for tests, including an MRI, along with routine blood work.

"Jessica, can I have a word with you?" LeAnn asked.

"Sure, what's up?" Jessica replied.

"Well, I don't want to tell you how to behave with your daughter, but..." She hesitated. "Is talking to her about a future that will never exist really a good thing?"

Jessica stepped back and looked her up and down. "Yes. It is." She put her hands on her hips as irritation bloomed. "Regardless of the diagnosis, people need hope. No matter how remote your chances, having something to cling to makes them possible. Imagine what would have happened had *I* not had a thread of hope." She looked over at Daniel, and he winced and kept staring at the floor.

"But it will make it harder for her to accept it," LeAnn said.

"Accept what? Dying? No way!" Jessica snapped. "You've been a grief counselor for way too long. Emily shouldn't accept it. She should fight it every step of the way. You shouldn't accept it, either." She glared at Daniel. "Enroll her in NYU. Let her live and enjoy and dream and laugh. Let her see that *you* haven't given up on her." She stabbed her index finger in the middle of his chest and turned back to LeAnn. "Don't bury her before she's dead."

LeAnn stepped back, her expression falling as quickly as her jaw. "I-I-I didn't mean to do that." She glanced at Daniel for support, but he was studying Jessica.

"If they come out here and give us the same prognosis, I expect you two to do that. To let her live and have her dreams, and show her you have hope. Otherwise, I swear I will take her with me," Jessica fumed.

Daniel swallowed and nodded, breaking Jessica's intense stare.

"Good!" She stormed off to find a bathroom.

Mind Games Chapter 15

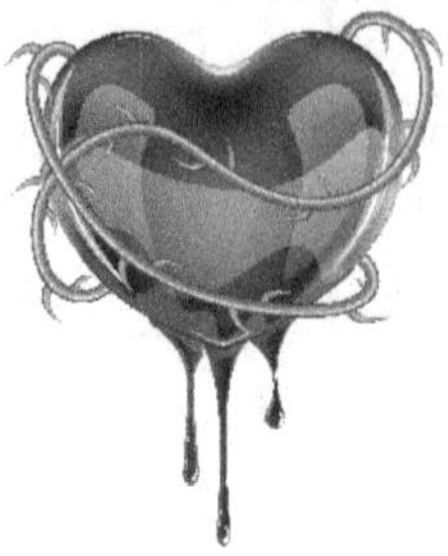

JESSICA GLANCED IN THE bathroom mirror and whispered his name softly. The image shifted, and Chris looked back at her in surprise, holding a razor inches away from his skin.

"Sorry, I didn't mean to..." She shrugged.

He smiled at her. "Call me?" He lifted his eyebrows.

She nodded.

"At least I didn't slip." He waved the razor and set it down out of sight. "This really is bizarre, Jess."

Smiling, she nodded again. "Yeah, it is." She knew just how off balance this peculiar manifestation of her power must be leaving him, especially considering how weird it was for her five years ago when Eric's little face appeared in her mirror.

"Is Emily okay?"

"She looked so much better last night after..."

"After you did your magic?"

She nodded. "They're doing more tests today, but I think she'll be fine."

"I'm glad." He smiled.

His smile could melt armor. Her heart skipped a beat.

"Thank you."

He inhaled, tilting his head to the side and studying her. His smile faded. "It's the least I could do, considering."

She paused, searching his eyes for any indication of insincerity, and found none. She gave a quick nod and turned to leave.

"Jess?"

She turned back to his intense gaze.

"Be safe," he said, and the image faded.

Jessica took a deep breath and walked out of the bathroom lost in thought. The seductive power of his smile seeped under her skin, and she wondered how long she could fight the undeniable connection.

Mind Games Chapter 16

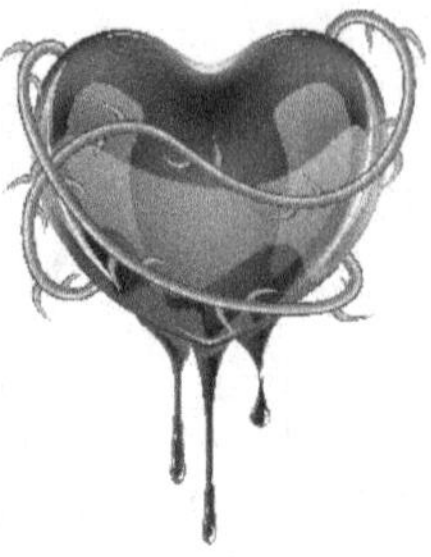

"JESSIE!" DANIEL WAVED HER over. "The doctor wants to talk to us." He escorted both LeAnn and Jessica into the office.

The doctor studied the MRI results side by side and scratched his head. He turned and looked at the three of them. "I've never seen anything like this." He looked back at the pictures. "This was the MRI that we took last week. You can see the tumor in her brain." He pointed to it, a black death sentence permeating Emily's brain. "And this is today." He shook his head. "There is no trace of a tumor. This is a healthy brain. If I hadn't been in the room when the MRI was done last week, I would have sworn there had to have been a mix-up with the images. But I saw that tumor with my own eyes..." He shook his head again, staring at the films before he turned to the three of them. "This is a miracle."

Daniel stared at Jessica. His mouth hung open in disbelief. "Jesus."

"What are you saying?" LeAnn asked.

"There is no trace of cancer." The doctor sat down. He removed his glasses and pressed on his eyelids. "I'd like to do some more tests." He opened his eyes.

"That's not necessary." Jessica stood. She looked over at Daniel and smiled. "I'd like to take my daughter home now."

"I think…" LeAnn began, but Daniel put a hand on her arm and shook his head.

"I think we *will* pass on the tests. She's been through enough," Daniel said.

"I'd strongly suggest some more tests to be sure," the doctor restated.

"I agree with my ex-husband. She has been through enough," Jessica said. "Thank you very much for taking the time to do this today." She stood to leave.

The doctor nodded and looked back at the film hanging in his office. "Miracle," he said as they closed the door behind them.

Mind Games Chapter 17

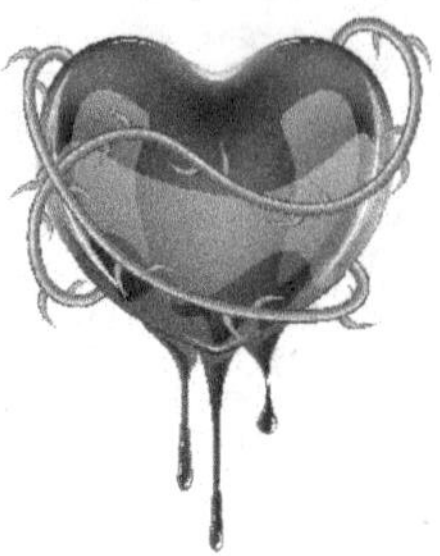

CHRIS REACHED OUT AND touched the mirror after her image disappeared.

"Damn." *It's been a weird day, and it isn't even noon.*

He walked out of the bathroom, picked up his keys and wallet, and headed out of the hotel, making his way to the lighthouse, where he took a seat on the ledge. The pungent aroma of seaweed and salt cascaded over the rocks, riding on the gentle breeze that filtered through his hair. Chris watched wave after wave crash against the rock barrier as high tide rolled in, hypnotized as much by the sound as the sun dancing along the ridge of each wave.

She couldn't really love me. Not knowing everything I've done.

Could she?

He closed his eyes and let the midday sun warm his face.

"How long till I do something I regret?"

He huffed at the spoken question. Her question. He opened his eyes, scanning the vast Atlantic. A part of him already regretted coming to see her, but if he hadn't, she would have lost Emily.

There were precious few times in his life where he'd made the right decision, and this certainly qualified. It felt good to know he'd made a difference, but he wasn't sure how long he could keep this masquerade going.

He wanted to be with her.

He wanted the dream.

But now he had a fucking ghost to deal with.

Mind Games Chapter 18

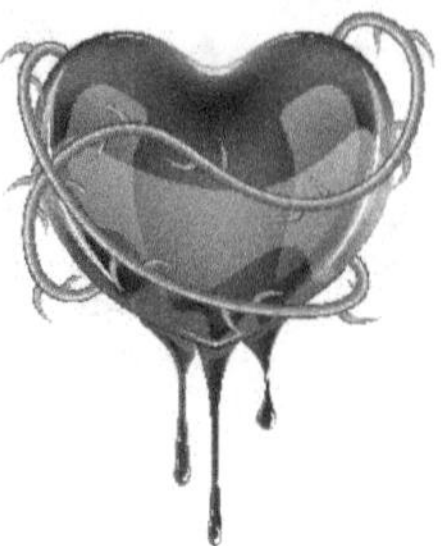

ERIC WALKED INTO THE house to find Tom in the family room, flipping through a photo album. "What are you doing?"

"Looking at pictures of your mom." Tom closed the album, sliding it back in place on the shelf.

Eric smiled. "She takes a lot of pictures."

"Yes, she does."

Tom scanned the shelves of albums.

Eric waited until Tom turned and met his gaze. "The bad man wants to hurt her again, doesn't he?"

Tom crossed to the couch and sat down, nodding. "I'm not sure what to do."

Eric opened his mouth and then closed it. He was old enough to know when saying something to someone would hurt them, and what almost passed through his lips would have hurt Tom very much. Tom couldn't do anything to help his mom. Only Ty could.

"I'm not sure either," Eric finally said.

"Ty actually..." Tom started and pointed at the ceiling.

"Yes, he actually appeared in my room."

"Why?"

"He was worried about Mom."

"Why do you and your mom care so much about him?"

Eric thought about this for a while. He had never spoken about what had happened to anyone. "Ty did a lot of bad things. When he took my mom, she was just another prisoner to him, but then things changed." Eric paused. "He fell in love with her, and I think she provided him with the redemption he was looking for." He glanced in Tom's direction. "He had every intention of getting her out of there when he returned with you."

Eric shifted on the couch and flicked his nail a couple of times. "When Ty left, that son of a bitch hurt her really bad." He looked up at Tom, waiting for some admonishment for swearing. When there wasn't any, he continued. "I don't know exactly what happened. All I know is she shut me out. I couldn't reach her at all, and I panicked. Kind of like Ty did today. So, I did the next best thing. I found him and made him promise to protect her. He saved both our lives. That's why I care. I think when I fixed him, I changed him more than Mom did." Eric looked down at his hands.

"He put her in harm's way, Eric."

Eric nodded. "I know. I understand more now than I did then." He took a deep breath. "But he still saved her. He saved you both." He looked up at Tom, studying him. "What he did in that room when the bad man returned nearly killed him. But the game he played, being... indifferent. That saved you." He pointed at Tom. "If he hadn't played it the way he did, you wouldn't have made it out of that room alive."

Tom's eyebrows went up. "How the hell do you know that?"

Eric stared at him. "I know a lot of things." He smiled and shrugged. "I can see all the different outcomes based on any given choice, and what he did was the only one that saved both of you."

Tom's eyebrows remained arched.

The flurry of questions in Tom's mind filtered through Eric's head, but he didn't want to answer any of them. He didn't want to divulge the glimpses of the future he had seen.

Since Ty had returned, his ability to see what was coming had been boosted, just like it had five years ago.

"Is this the first time you've talked about this?" Tom asked.

Eric nodded, relieved that Tom hadn't put one of the more pressing questions to him. He didn't like to lie, and he certainly didn't want to hurt Tom.

Tom put his arm around him and gave him a little squeeze. "Your mom loves you and your sister very much."

"I know," Eric said. "We miss her."

Tom leaned back and rubbed his face. "I'm sorry."

Eric shrugged. "It's okay. You made her feel safe."

Mind Games Chapter 19

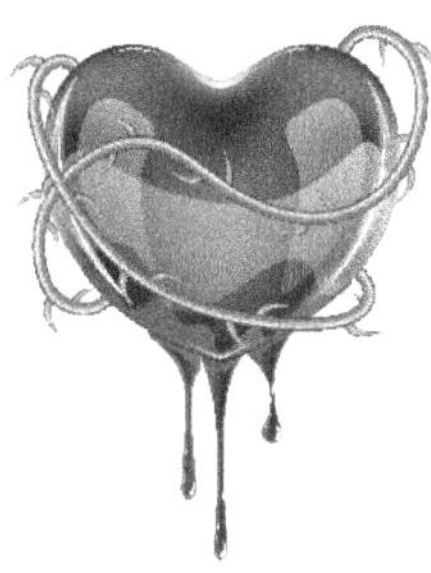

TOM PULLED OUT OF the driveway and Jessica leaned over to plant a kiss on his cheek.

"Thank you," she said.

"You can thank me when we get home."

She smiled and curled up in the seat, putting her head on his lap. He gently ran his fingers through her silky hair, thinking of the conversation with Eric.

Safe. Eric said I made her feel safe.

I'm not doing so hot in that department these days.

He glanced down at her, her chest rising and falling in the pattern of sleep, and he sighed, concentrating on the highway in front of him.

TOM CARRIED HER INTO the house, laid her on the bed, gently took off her clothes, and tucked her under the sheets. After undressing himself, he dumped his clothes into the hamper and headed to the bathroom without swinging the closet door closed.

When he stepped out of the bathroom, he froze in his tracks. The sheet lay crumpled at the foot of the bed. Jessica's wrists were crossed, her arms stretched over her head. Tom's gaze shot to the closet. More specifically, the mirror on the back of the door that now faced the bed.

Frank grinned back at him.

"Jessica!" he yelled, and tried to run toward the mirror but was slammed into the seat waiting for him. His arms were bound with invisible rope, tightening painfully against his skin.

"I'm going to have a little fun with your wife. Hope you don't mind." The ghost in the mirror laughed.

Tom turned toward the bed, seeing Jessica's wide, wild eyes.

"No," she whimpered, and her skin broke out in bumps, her breath frosting the air in quick bursts of fear.

Red handprints appeared on her skin, and fury filled every pore as Tom watched the downward progression. Burning rage shook through him, setting his heart on overdrive, and he struggled against the invisible bonds holding him to the chair. Flashbacks of the brutal rape he'd witnessed in the complex gripped him and panic settled in his bones.

"Leave her alone!" he shouted.

Tears blurred his vision, and frustration joined the already dangerous cocktail mix in his blood. He threw his head back, letting a guttural roar leap from his throat.

"You're not going to call Ty like you did this morning?" Frank sneered and pushed her legs wide.

She struggled, crying against the invisible tape now covering her mouth, and turned her head in Tom's direction.

He saw the plea in her eyes and almost heard the words *Call him!* from under the binds holding her voice in her throat. Tears slid down the sides of her cheeks, and she arched, her muffled scream of pain snapping his eyes from hers and turning them to the mirror.

There in full view, the son of a bitch was hurting her again, but this time, he knew how to stop it.

Tom screamed, summoning her guardian angel, a name he never thought he would ever rely on for help.

Mind Games Chapter 20

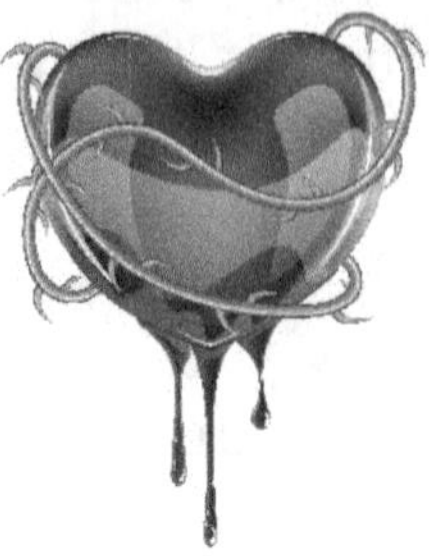

CHRIS SAT UP IN bed, blinking in the dark hotel room. His gaze landed on the clock. A little after midnight. An awful feeling scratched at the pit of his stomach. Distant laughter floated on the air. He stretched back in the bed, annoyed at the interruption.

He closed his eyes again, and that bad feeling bloomed into nightmare quality terror. Jessica's fear bowed him over, knocking the breath from his chest. Before he could throw the covers off, Tom's voice barreled his name.

Chris skidded into the bathroom, but all he saw was his own face looking back at him. "Shit!"

Closing his eyes, he grabbed onto her fright and rode the psychic connection right to her. When he opened his eyes, the mirror rippled, and the image of her bedroom came into sharp focus. The look on Tom's face told him enough; he didn't need to hear what Tom kept repeating to understand.

"Break it. Please, break it," Tom repeated. "Please, break it."

A snarl rose in his throat. "Shatter."

The mirror in the hotel room flew to pieces. Crystal shards tinkled on the tile all around him, and he prayed the same thing happened to their bedroom mirror. He spun and ran out of the bathroom, ignoring the tiny jabs of glass skewering the soles of his feet. After hopping into his jeans, he grabbed the room key and a shirt and bolted to his car.

Minutes later, he pulled into her driveway and yanked the emergency brake. At the door, he repeatedly jammed the doorbell, shifting his weight from foot to foot, debating on knocking the door down again when Tom swung it open.

"Is she okay?" Chris asked.

Tom just stared at him, grinding his teeth together.

"Is she okay?" He stepped into the house.

Tom put his hand on Chris's chest, stopping him from going any farther. "You brought that son of a bitch with you," he said, his chest rising and falling with the rage resounding in his voice.

"Is she okay?" Chris exploded and pushed Tom away, stepping farther into the hallway.

"Yes," Jessica answered from the entryway. She hugged the bathrobe wrapped tightly around her.

Tom's fist slammed into his jaw. Chris lost his balance, landing on his ass in the hallway, and before he could get to his feet, Tom had a fistful of his shirt. He yanked Chris off the ground and threw him toward the living room with a growl that reminded Chris of his uncle's attack dogs.

Chris rolled and scrambled off the floor. Tom threw another punch, and Chris parried, blocking it, along with the next several swings. He didn't fight back, and he didn't say a word. He just fended off the blows and let Tom get the rage out of his system.

Eventually, Tom sat down on the couch and put his face in his hands. "Son of a bitch raped my wife, and there wasn't a damn thing I could do about it," he said through his fingers.

Chris exhaled and took a seat on the couch next to Tom. "I'm sorry."

Tom turned his bloodshot glare in his direction. "I don't want to hear your fucking apologies. Just figure out a way to get rid of him."

"I'm working on it." Chris swung his gaze to Jessica. *Are you really okay?*

She nodded. "Thanks for stopping him. Again."

"Don't thank me," Chris answered. "Frank knew I wouldn't be able to stay away forever. He just waited. Watched and waited until I was stupid enough to..." He clenched his teeth against the rest of the sentence.

Jessica's chin trembled, and tears welled and rolled over the edges in slow motion. "If you hadn't come, I would have lost Emily."

Chris stood and started across the room. He stopped halfway, realizing it wasn't his place to comfort her, to wipe away her tears. His heart ached.

Tom passed by him and wrapped his arms around his wife, turning and displaying a warning glare Chris was accustomed to. He had seen it enough times in his stepbrother's prison to understand he was not welcomed.

Turning, he walked out of the house, leaving his heart in her hands. He paused at the side of his car, debating with the darkness that threatened to overtake him, the desire to grab her and run, to hold her, to love her, to own her like he once had, but he kept it at bay, fighting against his true nature.

Mind Games Chapter 21

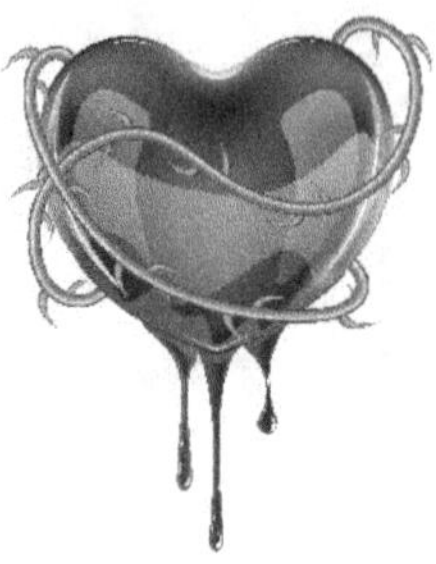

JESSICA GRABBED THE GREY Goose, a bottle of cranberry juice from the refrigerator, plucked a glass from the cabinet, and crossed to the porch. Her hands shook as she poured herself a mix of half vodka and half cranberry juice and then downed it. She poured a second glass, walked over to the banister, and leaned on it, looking at the image of the full moon dancing on the waves.

Tom wrapped his arms around her. "I cleaned up the glass." He kissed her cheek. "You okay?"

Jessica nodded, but wished everyone would stop asking that damned question. "Do you mind grabbing me a pair of jeans? It's a little chilly out here."

"Sure." He headed back in the house. He came back a few minutes later with her jeans, and she slid them on under the bathrobe.

Jessica finished the second drink and went to pour herself a third.

"You might want to slow down."

Jessica shook her head. "Not tonight." She stirred the drink with her finger.

"Jessie," Tom sighed, and she swiveled her gaze to him.

"Go to bed, Tom."

"Come with me."

Jessica shook her head again and looked away. She didn't want to go back to their bedroom right now. Not with the memory of her violation so fresh in her mind. She wanted to numb the pain, and more than that, she wanted to numb the drive to run straight to Ty. He was able to erase the horrors that bastard rained on her before, and all she wanted was the vile feel of Frank's hands gone.

Tom stepped toward her.

"Not right now," she said. "I want to be alone for a while."

He reached out to touch her face.

She caught his hand before his fingers reached her. "Not now, Tom." The warning in her voice was clear, and he recoiled. "Please," she added softly.

The set of his lips didn't change, but he sighed and nodded. "I love you, Jessie."

"I know, but I need some space right now. I promise I'll come inside in a little while."

He bit the side of his lip, tilting his head, his eyes carrying concern.

"I just need a few minutes alone after what happened. Okay?"

Nodding, he turned, leaving her on the balcony.

Jessica finished the third glass and poured herself another, the effects of the alcohol overriding her system. She polished off the fourth glass, reaching the numbness she craved.

She finished what remained in the bottle without the cranberry juice chaser. When she came up for air, her throat burned, and the heat spread all the way to her toes.

She needed to move, to run. To get away from the thoughts still present despite the inebriation making her feel more like rubber than skin and bone. She stumbled through the house, grabbing her iPod from her bureau, glancing at Tom snoring on their bed before heading out the front door.

Jessica weaved her way to the beach. The cool sand scraped at the bottom of her bare feet, and the breeze swept the tie of her bathrobe into the air. She stumbled, catching herself before she went down. She stopped and flipped through the songs until the one she wanted displayed. She pressed the button and "Calling All Angels" blared, assaulting her ears and making her wince. She turned the volume down and slid the iPod into her pocket.

Jessica danced down the beach, singing along with the music.

CHRIS DIDN'T WANT TO lie in the hotel room staring at the ceiling and harping on his situation, so he parked the car and crossed to the beach, finding a nice flat rock to stretch out on. The breeze was cool enough to keep him clear, but not enough to be uncomfortable. He studied the star filled sky, amazed at the clarity and vastness of the constellations.

I certainly don't get this kind of view in New York City.

He sighed and closed his eyes. As always, Jessica's graceful form danced across his eyelids, her voice traveling over the years as clear and sweet as the day she danced in his concrete prison.

A sharp note shattered the memory, and he opened his eyes. He sat up and scanned the darkness. The song continued, not from memory, but drifting on the wind from the direction of her house.

He hopped off the rock. His gaze locked on a weaving form and another off-key note marred her sweet voice. She stumbled and caught herself, laughing before resuming what she thought was dancing, but he only saw the flailing of a drunken woman. There was a grace to it that made him smile. Even inebriated, she still stirred need in him, and he moved toward her.

She spread her arms wide, spinning in a circle, and then lost her footing, but he was there, catching her before she fell over on the wet sand. With his arms wrapped around her waist, her voice trailed off, and they stared at each other.

His heart knocked on the walls of his chest. Burning desire overloaded his senses to the point that when she ran her hand into his hair and pulled him to her lips, he gave in. The passion transitioned into an exquisite tongue dance that left him breathless.

With a groan, he pushed her away and took a step back, his chest boiling with unfulfilled need. "You're drunk."

"Ayup." She stepped closer.

"Jess," he warned, his resolve waning. The rock wall behind him blocked any further retreat.

"Don't you want me anymore?" Her wide calico eyes filled with tears, and the sash on her bathrobe inadvertently unlaced and the fabric fell open, revealing her bare chest. She took another step toward him.

He laughed. "God knows how much I want you. But this isn't what *you* want."

"I need you, Ty." She slid her hands up his chest, and he closed his eyes. "I need you to erase what he did to me, to make it go away. You're the only one who can."

Her lips pressed through the shirt, creating heat that spread through him like liquid fire. "Jess." He tilted her chin, finding her lips. He pulled her against him. His hand caressed her bare breast, lingering on her nipple, which hardened under his touch.

Jessica fumbled with the buttons on his shirt, finally tearing it open. Her hands grazed his bare skin, her touch igniting him, and he was helpless to stop her exploration of his body. The cool spring air did nothing to quench the heat between them. She broke the kiss, trailing her lips along the line of his neck.

A low rumble formed in his throat. She ran her tongue down his chest, her hands already sliding over the fabric of his jeans, accelerating the throbbing in his member. She unclasped the button on his jeans, unzipped, and had his hard cock in her hands before her lips reached his belly button.

Her mouth slid over his tip, hot and moist, teasing him. He knew he should stop her, but this was like stepping into heaven. He laced his hand in her hair, guiding her movement. Blood pumped through his veins, pounding in concert with his heart, building with each stroke of her lips and each flick of her tongue. His hand tightened in her hair, and he groaned. His release rocked him to the core, and she swallowed every bit of him, sucking until his aftershocks subsided.

She sat back on her heels and smiled up at him, wiping her lips with the back of her hand.

Sinking to his knees in front of her, he ran his fingers across her cheekbone. "Jesus, Jess." The hammering in his chest continued as he scanned her half-naked form.

"Make love to me, Ty."

He hesitated, searching her eyes, searching for any seeds of doubt, for a reason to deny her what she'd asked, for a way to avoid this landmine, but there was no way out from under her spell.

In a rush of fabric, their jeans were shed, and he was on top of her, inside her, moving in concert with her like lifetime lovers. Her soft moans rolled down the beach with the fog. He moved slowly, running his hand through her tangled hair as it fanned out on the sand beneath her, savoring every sensation.

The colors in her irises swirled, reminding him of an approaching storm, equaling the torrent of emotions welling inside him. His lips found hers. The tongue dance began, mimicking his slow, lazy rhythm, building with passion, and cresting to frantic whirls, flicking, teasing, tasting as they climaxed together, their mouths muffling each other's cries.

He collapsed on her, his body trembling and satiated.

When his heart settled into a regular pattern, he lifted his head, glanced into her inebriated eyes, and wondered if she'd remember any of this. With a sigh, he rolled and retrieved his pants, then slid them on. He brushed the sand off her legs as best he could before he helped her dress.

"What am I going to do with you?"

Her face beamed with a drunken smile, and he helped her up, doing his best to wipe the sand off the back of her robe while she giggled and swayed.

Now what do I do?

Indecision froze him in place. He glanced between his hotel and the bluff where she lived, biting his lower lip, debating.

She slumped in his grasp, and his eyes fell on her slack face.

"You are going to be one hurting puppy in the morning." He chuckled, shifting her dead weight in his arms. "How pissed would you be if you woke up in my hotel room?"

He knew the answer, and that clinched the decision.

Chris hauled her over his shoulder and headed up the beach toward the bluff, carrying her home. After sneaking soundlessly around the back of the house, he navigated the steps of the deck, then set her in the lounge chair. He leaned against the railing to catch his breath, his eyes drifting to the table and the empty bottle of vodka, then back to her. With a great draw of air, he stepped closer and placed a kiss on her forehead before slipping away.

He took his time walking back to the hotel by way of the beach, still feeling her body beneath him and her mouth on his lips. Metal shimmered on the sand near where they had been, and he bent over, picked up the discarded iPod, slid the speaker bud in his ear, and smiled at the familiar song looping over and over.

Slipping it in his pocket, he headed back to the hotel. Tomorrow was a big day. He had papers to sign, and then he'd think about what the future might hold.

Mind Games Chapter 22

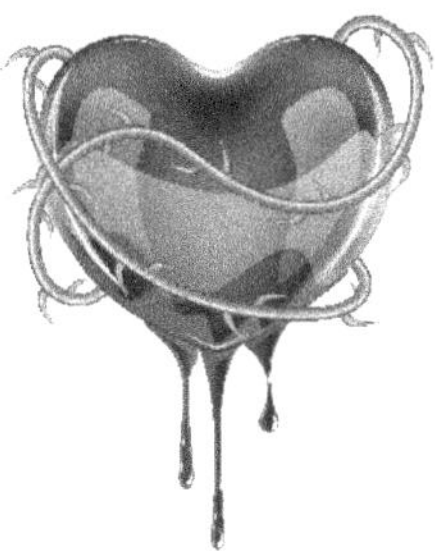

BETTY STOOD AS HE entered the realty office. She wore a nice white suit with an extra-lowcut shirt, just for his benefit. She fawned over him, even commenting on his cast and how awful that must be. Chris ignored her and read the contract the seller's lawyer handed him. He picked up the pen and signed the paperwork.

"Maybe you'd like some company to celebrate?" Betty batted her eyes and offered him a bottle of champagne.

"I'm all set," he said, taking the bottle from her and watching her deflate before his eyes.

He held out his left hand to thank her, and she shook it, flustered by his indifference.

Chris headed to his new home, pulled up to the gate, and rifled through the paperwork until he found the instructions. The gate opened with the old code, and he reprogrammed a new password before continuing to the house, pulling the Corvette into the oversized three-car garage.

Wandering around the yard, he grinned, stopping to scope out the lighthouse at the far bluff across the expanse of ocean. He calculated the distance, close to a five- or six-mile shot from where he stood to the lighthouse. Jessica's house was less than a half mile from there.

He turned and entered the house, tossing the keys into the air and catching them as he roamed from room to room. He dropped the pamphlets on the kitchen counter and the bottle of champagne, then opened cabinets and smiled at all the contents. The only thing absent was food. He needed to go shopping, but that was such a small thing. He ran his hands over the back of the couch in the entertainment room and picked up the remote control to the television. The television came on with the click of a button, and his smile widened as he walked over to the entertainment center, pleased at the caliber of equipment they'd left behind.

Chris carried his luggage upstairs into his new master bedroom and paused at the door.

She would love this bed, he thought and shook his head clear before emptying his suitcases.

He pulled the comforter back to make sure the sheets were still there. They had left everything as he'd specified—linens, kitchen utensils, and furniture.

The phone rang.

"Hello?"

"I'm calling to make sure everything is as you expected," Betty chirped into the phone.

"Yes, please don't call this number again," he replied and hung up on her.

He went back to the kitchen and made the half-dozen calls to put his affairs in order, including extending the grounds maintenance contract, maid services, contacting the security company to change passwords internally, give contact instructions, and call the phone company. He requested an unlisted number.

It was early afternoon when he finished. His stomach growled, and he needed to get food. He headed to the supermarket on Route 1.

Aimlessly walking down each aisle in the store, he filled his cart with whatever struck his fancy. When he rounded a corner, he collided with another cart, and before he could issue an apology, his gaze locked with Jessica's bloodshot eyes.

An instant rush of heat encompassed him, and he smiled. "Hi."

She glanced at his overflowing cart and raised her eyebrows. "Think you have enough there or what?"

"You look like shit."

She blinked, and her eyes widened.

"I mean, are you okay?" he asked, feeling like an idiot for blurting out the obvious.

"I'm okay, just a bit hung over. I went on a drinking binge last night and passed out on the deck."

Chris squashed the urge to say, *I know*. He smiled instead.

"Looks like you're shopping for the next year."

"I closed on a house today."

"That quickly?"

He nodded. "Want to see it?"

"Um." She looked at his cart, then back up at him.

"Never mind, bad idea." He walked away.

"No, really, I'd like to see it. It's just..."

Chris looked at her. "I promise I won't bite," he said. "Besides, I might need a hand getting this stuff to the house. I don't know if I have enough room in the vette."

Jessica laughed. "Well, if you don't have enough room..."

"You'll give me a hand?"

She sighed and nodded, and he turned back to the cart, wiping the smirk off his lips before he glanced back in her direction.

"Thanks," he said, and they headed toward the checkout, where he paid for both of their groceries despite her protests.

"What would you have done if you didn't bump into me?" Jessica asked as they stood by his overloaded car and the four more bags sitting in the cart.

He shrugged. "Probably would've given these to the nearest person." He put the rest of his bags along with hers in the trunk of her car. "I appreciate the help." He closed the trunk. "Think you can keep up?" He smiled and climbed into his Corvette.

Her laugh chased him out of the parking spot, and it took her a few seconds to catch up, handling her car like a racecar driver, keeping on his tail through the twist and turns, enough to make him nervous. He checked his rearview mirror every few seconds and chuckled as she waved at him.

JESSICA TOOK IN THE modest home and the manicured lawn as she passed through the gate and parked behind the garage he pulled into, impressed by the stately beauty of the property. She popped the trunk and grabbed his bags, then followed him inside.

"How'd you get furniture so quickly?"

"I bought the house with all the contents." He dropped the bags on the kitchen table. "Feel free to look around," he said, heading outside to get the rest of the groceries.

Jessica wandered through the house with her mouth gaping. It was beautiful, homey, regal, all the things she would have never pegged him for. She paused in the doorway of the master bedroom, taking in the finely crafted king-size bed. Drawing a deep breath, she fanned herself with her hand.

Oh my, what he could do to me in that bed.

What the hell are you thinking?

Admonishing herself, she shook her head and turned, jumping back a step. Chris stood behind her at the top of the stairs, his eyes the crystal blue of her dreams, intense, hungry, scanning her.

A tingle crawled up her spine, along with a fiery glow in the pit of her stomach. She forced a breath and side-stepped around him. Instead of investigating the rest of the house, she descended the stairs in a rush.

"I-I should go," she stammered.

"Come see the back first," he said, following behind her.

"Chris, I really should be going."

"Please."

"Okay, but I really need to leave after." She followed him into the backyard.

"Holy..." The pool was gorgeous, but it was the bay view that captivated her. She walked over to the rock wall surrounding the backyard and looked over the small marina and the ocean beyond. "This is amazing." *And familiar.* Her brow creased, and she glanced around, trying to place her surroundings.

"Not the view you have, but it's pretty good." He stood next to her, surveying the ocean.

"Pfft, this is a much better view than mine, and you know it."

The crooked, shy smile that appeared catapulted her heart into overdrive. Sexy was one way to describe it, more so than the cocky, all-knowing grin he usually flashed her.

He opened his mouth to speak but snapped it closed, and the smile vanished. He turned, heading back into the house.

The oddness of his behavior piqued her curiosity, so she followed him into the kitchen, watching him unpack the groceries and put the items away with no rhyme or reason.

"This place is lovely."

"Thanks." His eyes flashed in her direction and away, like he had something to say but couldn't quite formulate the words.

"What is it?"

Chris looked at her and crossed to the corner drawer, pulled it open, and plucked something from the contents. He approached her and placed it in her hand. "You dropped this on the beach last night."

She stared at her iPod.

"I carried you home."

Jessica stared at the music player, her mind reeling, searching the blank canvas that represented last night. A fragment of memory surfaced, and she blinked. "You kissed me?"

Chris laughed a little. *More than that.*

"How much more?"

He blushed. "I keep forgetting you can hear what I'm thinking," he said, avoiding the question and blocking her from getting any information from his mind.

"How much more?" she said again, her vision warping through fresh tears. *Oh God, what the hell did I do last night?*

"Jess."

His eyes said more than enough, and her hands flew to her mouth, covering the gasp. "We didn't!" Tears spilled over. "Tell me we didn't."

"We didn't," he lied, and she knew it immediately.

"How could you?" She took a step back.

"Me?" Chris pointed at himself, the first sign of anger flaring in his eyes. "You're the one who..." He closed his mouth and turned away from her, putting his hands on the counter.

"I was drunk."

Chris turned, and in two strides, had her in his arms. She saw the frustration in his eyes just before his mouth crushed down on her lips. Jessica struggled in his grasp, trying to ignore the sweep of raw lust, but this close to him, in his arms with his lips on hers, was too much. She opened her mouth, allowing his tongue to dip in and tangle with hers. His kiss weakened her knees, and she wrapped her arms around his neck, kissing him with the same fervor.

He pulled away from her and stepped back. "You want me just as badly as I want you." He took another step away from her. "So, don't stand there and blame it on being drunk."

"I'm..."

"You're what?" he snapped. "You're married?" He laughed. "Then why the hell did you seduce me last night on the beach?"

Her eyebrows rose, and she stepped back.

"That's right, you kissed me first. You undid my pants first."

"You should have stopped me."

"I'm in love with you, Jess!" He completely lost his composure. "Why the hell would I say no when every fiber of my being wants to take you in my arms every single time I see you?" He took a deep breath. "You're lucky... if you hadn't passed out..." He ran his hand through his hair. "I carried you back to your house, to him. Do you know how much it took to do that?"

"I... I..." She didn't know what to say to the pain and anger visible in his eyes.

"You what?" he growled, advancing on her, looking like the predator in the complex five years ago.

The kitchen door closed with a bang, making her jump.

He glanced at her shirt, and the buttons unhooked in quick succession.

She gasped and grabbed at her shirt, buttoning it up as fast as he undid them with his mind. "What are you doing?"

He looked back into her eyes. "Using what you gave me," he said, and her pants began to unzip.

"Ty, don't." She zipped them back up.

He pushed her against the wall, and his hands slid up her shirt. It was like walking into an inferno, hot, sensual, consuming. She trembled under his touch, running her hands into his hair and taking a handful before this got any further out of hand.

She yanked his head back. "Don't!"

His hands went up in the air, and he backed away. "I'm sorry."

"God help me," she whispered.

"Go home."

"Ty?"

"Don't call me that," he snapped. "I left everything dark and evil back in that room. I let him die that day." He turned away from her. "At least I thought I had. Until now."

She stepped toward him.

"Go home, Jessica," he warned, glaring over his shoulder at her. "You can't stay."

"Chris." She took another step toward him.

"If you stay, I won't be able to let you go."

He held her gaze this time, and what she saw scared the daylights out of her. She backed out of the kitchen and into the garage, turning to head to her car.

"Jess?"

"What?" She stopped at her car door without looking at him; she didn't want him to see the tears tracking down her cheeks.

"I'll still do what I can to protect you if he comes back."

"I know." She got into the car.

The wheels spun on the gravel, and she tore out of the driveway without looking back.

Mind Games Chapter 23

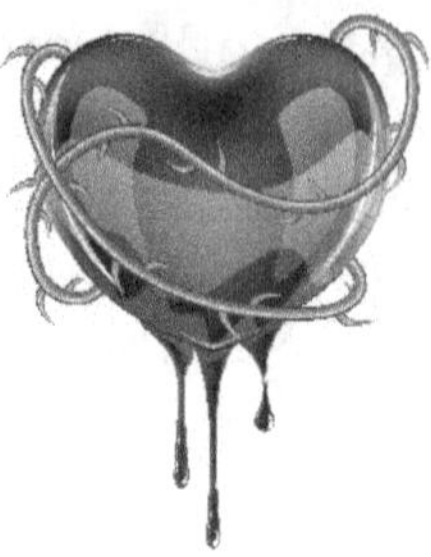

JESSICA PARKED THE CAR by the beach and got out, looking at the sand like she had never seen it before. The events of last night remained sketchy and broken. A kiss here, the caress of his hands there, his blue eyes glimmering down at her, and the dimples etched in his cheeks from the sexy smile she loved so much.

Each fragment dragged the breath out of her, not because of her betrayal—betrayal would have been manageable—but because of the purity of the emotions wrapped around his raw power.

Consuming.

Overwhelming.

Irresistible.

God help me, I still love him.

She looked toward the bluff as guilt bit at her, paling compared to the magnetic pull from the opposite side of the beach where his new home stood.

Slowly, she slipped back into her car and headed home.

"What took you so long?" Tom asked, crossing to grab the last of the grocery bags from the trunk.

"I went for a drive."

"Where?"

"Down by the marinas. I needed to think." The lie came too easily, and she wanted to scream, and tear her hair out, and erase the silky feel of his hands against her skin. She concentrated on putting the food away, avoiding eye contact.

"Jessie?"

His worried tone pulled her gaze to him, but she still couldn't meet his wide-eyed stare.

"Look at me." He crossed the room.

She forced herself to meet his gaze, and the torrent locked inside broke through. Tears blurred her vision and burned her throat.

"I'm so sorry," he apologized.

Oh God, he thinks I'm upset with him?

The thought knocked a hole in the center of her stomach, devastated her, and almost knocked her to her knees.

The tears that brimmed were accompanied by a shallow sob.

He wrapped his arms around her, pulling her to his chest and saying "I'm sorry" over and over, stroking her hair.

She pushed him away. "Stop saying you're sorry." She wiped her face. "Please stop apologizing to me. It's not your fault."

"I left the closet door open, and I couldn't stop him."

Jessica looked up into his baby-blue eyes and sighed. "Neither could I."

"But he can." Tom stepped away from her. His lips tightened into a thin line as the muscles in his jaw worked.

Jessica studied her hands. "Yes, he can stop him, but that doesn't matter because I'm with you, and there's nothing on earth that can change that." She tried to smile, but it felt foreign on her lips.

"Yeah, right."

"Cut the shit. You weren't raped by a ghost. You're not the one he wants to kill."

"And there's nothing I can do about it! Do you know how useless I felt?"

"Well, join the club!"

They stared at each other as their words sank in.

Jessica closed her eyes, feeling the weight of the last few days heavy on her shoulders. "I'm sorry. It's been a hell of a week."

Tom nodded. "I'm actually glad the kids are coming this weekend."

"Me too."

And I need to get the hell away from this town.

She hugged him, and when she pulled back, she said, "Can you book three more tickets for us next week?"

The smile that spread over his face made Jessica want to cry. She couldn't imagine the hurt he would feel if he ever found out.

"Really?"

"Yes, I need to get away just as much as you do. Even though L.A. isn't my favorite place to visit, I think we've all earned a vacation. And I'll come with the kids to the set if you still want that."

"I would love that." He swept her off her feet and kissed her.

"Stop."

"Why? They aren't due until later tonight, right?" He kissed her neck.

"Really, Tom, stop." She pushed him away. "Not now. I need to make dinner."

His grin widened, and his hands wandered over her. "I'm only hungry for one thing." He nibbled on her ear.

"Raincheck." She skittered out of his grip, unable to stand being touched after all that had happened. The only one she didn't seem to have an aversion to was Chris, and that burned right through her.

"All right." He sulked away and settled on the living room couch.

He will never forgive me.

Mind Games Chapter 24

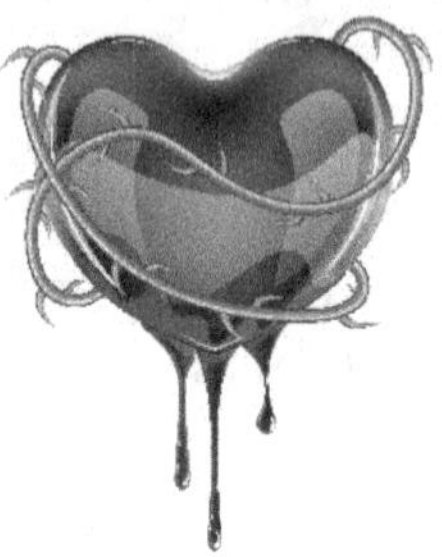

CHRIS STEPPED BACK INTO the kitchen and squashed the urge to smash everything in sight. He closed his eyes, willing the feral beast inside to calm the fuck down. This wasn't a situation within his control, and as much as he wanted her, she was not his for the taking.

Still, he replayed the last few minutes over in his mind, relishing her every move, the feel of her lips, the frantic flush in her face as she buttoned up her shirt.

His eyes snapped open. "What the..."

Her shirt had *unbuttoned* on its own accord. The second they started unlacing, he had wanted her shirt off, to feel her skin again, but he was across the kitchen when that happened.

"Jesus."

His gaze shot to the remaining groceries on the counter, zeroing in on the six-pack of beer. He put his hand out and willed a can to come to him. The entire six-pack flew to his hand.

"Holy fucking shit!"

He looked at the cupboards and thought *Open.* Every one of them opened. "Close," he said, and they all closed.

"What the hell did she do to me?" He stared at the six-pack and, with a trembling hand, peeled one off and cracked it open, then drained it in one long chug.

Power surged inside him, raging through his blood, getting stronger with each use. He suddenly understood the fear in her eyes five years ago when he'd told her that Eric wanted to help her unlock the door that contained this. That this ungodly power was the only way for her to get out of that hellhole.

"Jesus," he said as he walked out into his backyard.

She really couldn't break the mirrors anymore. When he healed her, she transferred this dark shit to him.

Chris inhaled. If Jessica had had an inkling of how to use this power back when he had kidnapped her, he wouldn't be alive today. He sat down in the lounge chairs facing the harbor, willing one of the hurricane lamps to light. Flame leaped from the wick and then settled into a slow burn.

Underneath the shock and fear racking his brain, possibilities began churning in his stomach. A slow smile formed, and he glanced toward the lighthouse.

Mind Games Chapter 25

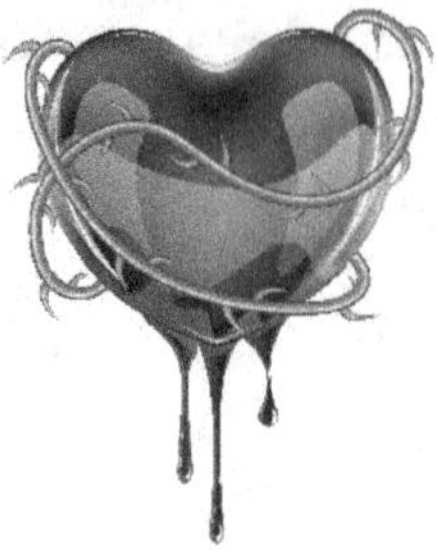

CHAOS DESCENDED ON THE house when Daniel and LeAnn dropped the kids off.

"Guys, take your things to your rooms," Jessica said.

Eric and Emily grabbed their bags from Daniel and LeAnn and ran down the hall to their rooms.

Tom chuckled. "It always looks like they're moving in every time they come."

"I told them to pack light," Daniel said.

"Speaking of packing," Jessica began. "We would like to take them out west for the week."

"I think the kids would love that," LeAnn said.

Tom smiled and put his arms around Jessica. "I'm planning on taking them on the set with me."

Daniel and LeAnn exchanged a glance.

"That ought to be fun," he said.

Jessica nodded and looked up at Tom. "Pretty plastic people."

"Don't laugh. I can make you one of them." He kissed her cheek.

"We'll be heading out on Sunday night, and we'll be back in town next Saturday. We can drop them at the cottage on the way through town," Jessica said, breaking free from Tom's arms. She brought Daniel and LeAnn to the door and hugged them goodbye.

"Have fun, Jessie," Daniel said.

"I intend to." Jessica closed the door and walked back into the living room.

The kids were crowding around Tom and firing questions at him about who they would see and what they would get to do in Los Angeles. He smiled over at her.

"Okay, guys, stop badgering him." Jessica shooed them away from him.

"Mom, can I use the phone?" Emily asked.

"Who are you calling at this hour?" Jessica asked, looking at the clock. It was after ten.

"Sara. She's going to flip when I tell her I'm going to L.A."

"Sure," Jessica said, remembering when she was a senior in high school. She looked around for Eric and saw him leaning on the banister out on the deck. She went out and put her arm around him.

Eric looked at her. "Thanks, Mom."

She squeezed him. "I just thought it was time we went out there as a family."

"That's not what I'm talking about," he said. "I'm talking about Emily."

She looked south out at the water. *Thank Ty.*

"You miss him?"

Jessica turned to Eric, the smile on her face fading. She nodded a little and then glanced inside at Tom.

"Tom can't protect you, Mom." Eric looked back at the water.

"I know. But that doesn't make me love him any less."

Eric nodded and headed inside. He plopped himself next to Tom on the couch.

Jessica looked back toward the south. She closed her eyes for a minute and felt his lips on hers again. Yes, she missed him. She turned, heading back inside.

"I'm turning in early," she announced, then kissed Tom and messed up Eric's hair.

"Night, babe."

Jessica popped her head into Emily's room. "Don't stay on too long, okay, Em?"

Emily smiled and nodded.

She changed into a nightshirt and headed into the bathroom to brush her teeth. His name floated to the forefront of her mind.

The mirror rippled, and Chris stared back at her with his toothbrush in his mouth. He spit in his sink.

"Your timing is impeccable, as always," he said, wiping his mouth with the back of his hand.

"I'm sorry about today."

Chris nodded. "Me too." He paused. "By the way, you gave me a hell of a gift."

Jessica's mood grew dark, and she narrowed her eyes.

"I'm not talking about the beach, Jess. Although that was quite... memorable." He didn't do a good job of suppressing his smile.

Before she could turn away, he blurted, "I'm talking about the power you gave to me."

She turned back to the mirror. "What are you talking about?"

Chris lifted his hand where she could see it, and his toothbrush levitated up into his palm. His eyes never left hers. "It's not just mirrors anymore. In case you hadn't noticed, I undid the buttons on your shirt without touching you today." He blushed and shrugged. "It's gotten stronger. Each time I break a mirror or move something, it gets stronger."

That's why the power felt different inside her. What she had left was pure light, not tainted with the darker, more dangerous power she'd harbored all her life. That power she'd locked away for a reason, and now he had it. Fear laced her blood, bringing a metallic tinge to her mouth.

"Last night, did you make me…" she began.

Chris's warm expression cooled, and he shook his head. "No, Jess. That was all you. Besides, I haven't figured out how to manipulate people with this yet."

"Yet?" she asked, raising her eyebrows.

"I figure if I can control a person, I can control a ghost."

Jessica tilted her head. "I'm not sure it would work the same."

"Why not?"

"A person is physically here. A ghost isn't." She looked at him. "Even though Frank can physically hurt me, I'm not sure we can hurt him unless we can get him physically in the room with us."

Chris took a deep breath and shook his head like he was chasing a thought away. He sighed and put his hand on the mirror. "I can try."

Jessica put her hand against the reflection, expecting to feel the cool glass, but instead she felt his skin. The jolt of touching him flared heat in her soul. He laced his fingers through hers.

"You can try," she agreed, and slowly pulled her hand away.

"Good night, Jess."

"Night," she whispered.

The image faded, and she looked back into her own haunted eyes.

Mind Games Chapter 26

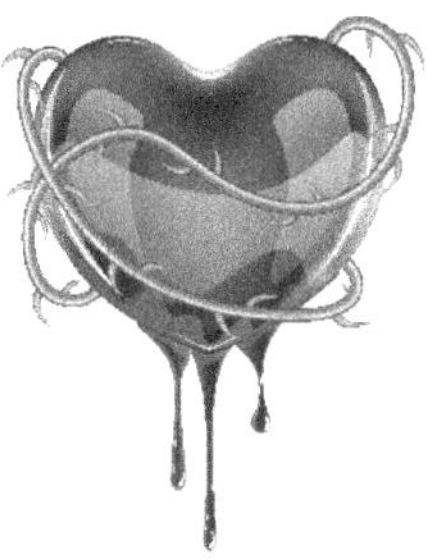

EMILY GLANCED AT THE clock on the nightstand; it was after one in the morning. "Oh shit, I need to get going," she said to Sara. "If my mom comes in, she's going to kill me. I'll talk to you tomorrow."

She hung up the phone and plucked her hairbrush out of her bag. When she turned toward the mirror, her breath caught in her throat.

Someone stood behind her.

She whirled around to nothing but a pocket of frigid air. She snapped back toward the mirror, and a cold hand grasped her throat.

Black eyes looked at her with a wicked smile. The ghost yanked her bra off, and she stared at his reflection with wide, frightened eyes.

"If you scream, I'll kill everyone in this house." His ice-cold hands ran over her skin.

Terror beyond anything she'd ever experienced gripped her. She shook at the ghost's arctic touch.

"You're hotter than your mother."

He tossed her onto the bed, but she rolled, trying to get away. But the form materialized above her, slamming her on her back, and tied an invisible rope around her wrists, binding her to the headboard.

She struggled, but she didn't cry out even when he peeled her pants off. "Please don't."

The rope tightened around each ankle, anchoring her legs wide. She tried to struggle, but it was no use. Whatever was in the room wasn't letting her go. Frigid hands began exploring.

A small sob escaped. "I'm a virgin. Please don't."

"Not anymore." He laughed in her ear and shattered her innocence.

When he finished, he gave her cheek a pat. "I will definitely be back for more of this. And if you tell anyone, I will kill your mother and your brother, as slowly and painfully as I can. And you will watch. Understand?" he hissed in her ear, and then the frigid pocket of air dissipated.

The bindings around her wrists and ankles were released. Emily rolled onto her side, curling into a tight ball as silent sobs racked her, and blood trickled down her legs. Slowly, the tears dried, and she got up and headed to the shower to erase the vile feel of him. She stripped and stepped in before the spray warmed, more concerned with feeling clean than the water temperature. She ran the bar of soap over her skin, but no matter how hard she scrubbed, she knew she'd never feel clean again. When her skin was red and her fingers shriveled, she shut off the water and stepped into the steam-filled bathroom. Rifling through the cabinets, she finally found what she was looking for—a package of panty liners. She ripped open the box, affixed one to the crotch of her underwear, and slipped the garment on.

She hesitated in front of her bedroom door and turned away. Too frightened to go back in, she opened Eric's door and crawled into the bed next to him.

Eric woke up and looked at Emily. "What's wrong?"

"Nightmare." Emily rolled so her back was to him.

Eric looked at her for a few minutes. "You sure?"

"Yes." Emily closed her eyes.

Eric put his hand on her back. "Night, Emmy," he whispered.

"Night, squirt," Emily answered, and tears trickled down her cheek, dampening the edges of the pillowcase.

Mind Games Chapter 27

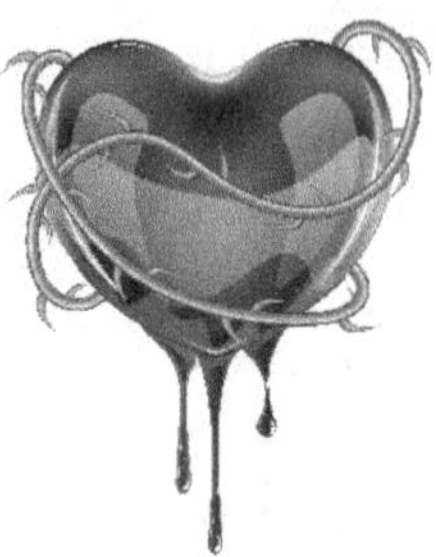

JESSICA STRETCHED THE SLEEP from her body and then leaned over to plant a kiss on Tom's cheek. He didn't stir. She hopped out of bed, threw on her jogging clothes, and walked down the hall to check on the kids.

When she pushed Emily's door open, her eyes went wide. She wasn't in her room, and there was blood on the bed. Jessica bolted to Eric's room with her heart in her throat. A sigh of relief escaped her at the sight of both Emily and Eric, back to back, their light snores alternating.

She went back to Emily's room and stripped the bed. Her period sometimes surprised her as well. She nervously looked at the mirror as she passed by, then deposited the dirty sheets in the laundry room before heading out for her run.

The sun was low on the horizon as she stepped onto the beach. It wasn't long before she got lost in the music and the rhythm of her feet on the sand. Her eyes half open under the sunglasses, she didn't notice at first when he moved next to her and kept pace. A shadow crossed hers, and Jessica glanced over in surprise.

"You snuck out on me." Tom smiled, and his blue eyes sparkled. He had a baseball hat on backwards, and morning stubble still graced his face.

Jessica smiled. He always looked so sexy in the morning, and today was no different. "I didn't want to wake you at the crack of dawn." She pulled the speaker farthest away from Tom out of her ear and handed it to him.

Tom put the speaker in his ear. "I didn't get my snack last night." He smiled over at her.

Heat filled her cheeks, and somehow a good night's sleep had erased her unease. "Play your cards right and you just might get one tonight."

Tom grinned and grabbed her around the waist, interrupting her morning jog by pulling her to him and planting a kiss on her lips. "Morning, babe."

"Morning. Now get your ass moving."

They trotted to the house after running the length of the beach twice. Both kids sat curled up on the couch watching television when they walked in.

"Mind if I go down to the beach?" Eric stood and stretched.

"Sure, go ahead," Jessica answered with a smile, but the smile faded when she glanced at Emily's pale face. "Em, are you feeling all right?"

Emily looked up at her and nodded. "I was on the phone really late with Sara and then had a nightmare."

Something about her answer seemed off. "You sure?"

"Yes, Mom." She rolled her eyes.

"Just making sure." Jessica ducked around the corner into her bedroom and closed the door behind her.

The shower was already running, so she peeled off her clothing and crossed into the bathroom, quietly stepping into the shower behind Tom. Wrapping her arms around him, she kissed his back, closing her eyes against the fine mist.

Tom rotated in her grasp, ran his hand into her hair, and leaned down to kiss her. "Snack time," he purred and lifted her into his arms.

Jessica wrapped her legs around her husband, and he kissed her, sliding inside. She closed her eyes and moved with him as the hot water beat down. He turned and pressed her back against the wall, kissing her neck and then her lips again, quickening his pace. She moaned softly under his lips and arched into him as her first orgasm ripped through her.

"Yes," she whispered and quickened her pace, feeling the release building again.

Tom arched into her and came, causing her next orgasm.

She arched back, trembling as she whispered, "Ty." She opened her eyes to Tom's wide-eyed stare, his mouth agape.

"You just said his name." Tom blinked and set her down, stepping away.

"Don't be ridiculous." Jessica reached for him.

"Jessie, you said his name."

"I didn't mean to."

"Bullshit." He stepped out of the shower and slammed the door behind him.

"Tom." She turned the water off and opened the door.

He glared at her. "You said his name," he growled. "While I was making love to you, you said *HIS* name." He wrapped the towel around his waist and shook his head. "I can't do this. Not with him."

Jessica grabbed a towel off the rack and wrapped it around her. "I'm sorry."

"Look, I've heard you call out his name in your sleep for years." He ignored the surprise on her face. "It was hard enough to deal with knowing you still had feelings for that monster when I thought he was dead." He shook his head and turned his back to her. "Finding out he's alive, and now this? I can't do it." He leaned on the sink, his head down.

"Tom, I'm with you."

"Are you?" He looked over his shoulder. "Are you really with me?"

Jessica walked to him and put her hand on his back. "Yes. I'm really with you. I am your wife, and I love you."

"But you still have feelings for him."

"He saved Emily." Her eyes pleaded for him not to push.

"But you still have feelings for him." He turned toward her.

Jessica went to say something and then closed her mouth. She looked into his angry blue eyes and nodded a little.

Tom closed his eyes and blew his breath out. He inhaled and opened them, the anger now mixing with heartache. "If he touches you, I'll kill him." He clenched his teeth. "So help me God, Jessie, I will kill him."

Jessica nodded again and stepped toward him, putting her hand on his cheek. "Tom, you have my heart." She wrapped her arms around his neck.

Reluctantly, he put his arms around her.

Neither one of them saw the flicker in the mirror.

Mind Games Chapter 28

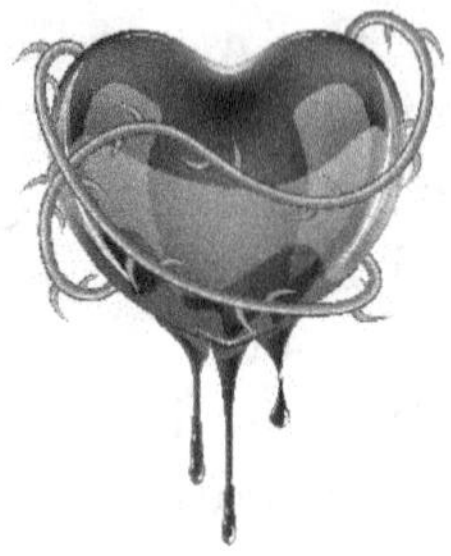

CHRIS STEPPED AWAY FROM the mirror and strolled out of his bathroom, lost in thought. She said his name. *His name.*

With a steaming cup of coffee, he drove to the beach and climbed down the stairs onto the sand. A fair amount of people gathered on the beach, walking, jogging, playing Frisbee with their dogs. There were even a few yoga freaks stretching and contorting for their morning exercise.

Sighing, he focused on a group of teenagers playing soccer. The ball bounced beyond the goal, and one of the kids ran after it.

Chris concentrated on the boy. "Trip," he whispered.

Nothing happened.

Disgusted, he shook his head and picked up a couple of stones, walking to the water. He skipped the first stone and willed it to continue to skip. The inanimate object obeyed his silent command, bouncing off the waves over and over until he could no longer see it.

He skipped a second stone and then put his hand in his pocket, watching the surfers on the waves. The overwhelming sensation of being watched tickled his skin, and he glanced to his left, toward the bluff, his eyes falling on a familiar face a few feet away.

"Ty."

Chris tilted his head and raised an eyebrow at the awe in the boy's tone. "Please call me Chris." He extended his left hand.

Eric's eyes dropped to his hand, and he reached out and shook it. "I didn't know if you were real or not."

Chris laughed and looked back at the ocean. "I'm just flesh and blood, Eric, so stop looking at me like I'm the second coming of Christ."

"Sorry," Eric mumbled. His hands slid into his pockets, and he stood silently at Chris's side. "How'd you know I'd be here?"

"I know a lot of things."

Chris inhaled and turned his gaze back to the boy. "Like what?"

"Like you've got to be the one to save my mom this time, and you know how."

Chris broke out in goose bumps. "Eric, I don't know how..."

Eric rolled his eyes. "Yeah, you do."

Chris shook his head.

"Yes, Ty, you know." Eric stood square in front of him. His eyes bore into Chris's.

"No," Chris said. The thought of using Jessica as bait raked a fresh wave of fear over his skin.

"I don't like it any more than you do," Eric said. "And you're gonna have to help her open the door in her mind so she doesn't die." He pulled an old skeleton key out of his pocket and extended it to Chris.

"No. I'll find another way." He didn't want to accept that key. The last time Eric gave it to him, he'd nearly died. They'd all nearly died.

Eric sighed, taking Chris's hand and dropping the key in his palm. "There isn't any other way. If you don't, he'll kill all of us. That includes me and Emily." The colors in his eyes swirled, just like Jessica's.

Chris slid the key into his pocket and stared at the ocean for a while in silence. Eric's words, along with the fortuneteller's directive, created a storm in his mind. A storm clouded by the memories of Frank carving her tender skin while he watched.

A crippling dread made his knees weak, and he had to take a step back to steady himself. "I don't know if I can do this, Eric. Besides, Tom will never let me use her like that."

"Tom doesn't control my mom."

"But she loves him. He has her heart," he said, repeating the words she'd said to Tom this morning.

"He may have her heart, but you own her soul."

Chris shivered and closed his eyes. If he owned her soul, she was just as damned as he was.

"You love her?"

"Yes, more than life itself," Chris whispered, looking back at him.

"I'm betting on that." Eric's eyes slowly cleared. "I gotta go." He walked away.

"Eric?"

"What?"

"You know how to call me if there's trouble, right?"

"Yes. The same way I reached you before," he answered.

"That's right. If you think he's in your house, call. Understand?"

Eric nodded. "Thanks." He paused. "For everything."

"I'm the one who should thank you. You gave me my life back." He put his hand out, and Eric shook it.

Chris watched Eric until he was out of sight and then looked back at the ocean.

"Sweet Jesus." The thought of using Jessica, putting her in harm's way, was not one he wanted to entertain ever again.

He ambled back to his car and headed home. Once there, he slumped on the couch and leaned his head back.

"I can't do this," he whispered and looked around. His gaze landed on the bar in the corner, and he got up, crossing the room. It was fully stocked, and he reached for an unopened bottle of Grey Goose.

Jessica's poison. Well, if it's good enough for her, it's good enough for me.

He slipped a DVD into the player and poured himself a drink before pressing play.

The screen filled with the first time he'd made Jessica regret the phrase 'Never in a million years.' The seduction unfolded, and he watched, aroused and bitter. He poured another glass and sat back with the bottle in one hand and the glass in the other, watching the only flick he'd put together that never made it to the street.

The scene changed, and he drained his drink. On-screen, she swayed to the music in the concrete cell, and he poured another glass and downed the fiery liquid, trying to drown the need thrumming in his veins. The need to be with her, to hold her, to make love to her again and again for the rest of his life.

Mind Games Chapter 29

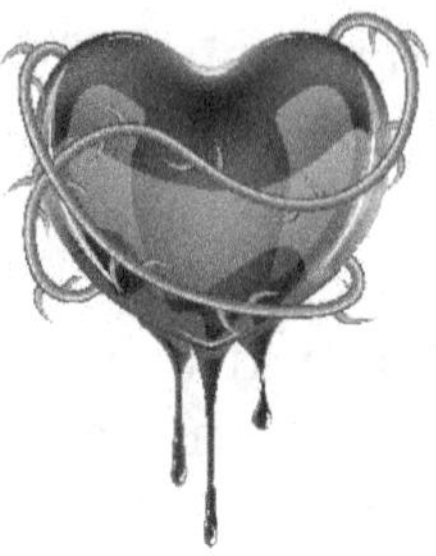

JESSICA STOOD WITH A glass of orange juice in her hand, staring out the slider when Eric walked in the front door. "Where've you been?"

"I took a walk on the beach," he answered.

She turned and gave him a smile. "See any girls?"

Eric blushed and shrugged, his gaze moving from hers to Tom's and back. Worry lines creased his forehead, and Jessica gave a slight shake of her head, silently relaying not to ask. With a nod, he disappeared into the kitchen.

Tom sat in the lounge chair, his gaze pasted to the script in his hand, attempting to work, but Jessica knew better. The tense set of his jaw, along with the stress ball he squeezed in his right hand, told her he was still angry.

Jessica made up her mind. She had to tell Chris goodbye.

"I need to run to the store." Jessica headed out to her car.

Ten minutes later, Jessica pulled up to the gate, staring at the control pad. She hesitated with her finger a millimeter from the bell, then she punched the first four letters of her name and pressed send. She inhaled when the gate opened.

Figures he'd use my name as his password.

She closed her eyes for a moment and drove in.

At the front door, she reached for the doorbell and stopped. Instinctively, she knew it was unlocked. She opened the door and stepped inside. She heard the television and walked into the family room.

An empty bottle of vodka sat on the coffee table, and Chris continued to stare intently at the screen. She followed his gaze and gasped when she saw what was playing. It was her and Ty a lifetime ago.

She instantly regretted not ringing the doorbell.

Chris turned and shot to his feet. "Jess." He pushed the stop button on the video, and the screen went dark. He scanned her from her head to her beige flip-flops with glossy eyes and then took a couple of unsteady steps in her direction.

"You're drunk."

"Yup." He grinned and continued his zig-zag path across the room, approaching her.

His eyes hungered for her, turning them deep blue like a clear late afternoon sky.

"You look hot today," he added.

She found herself pinned to the wall by an invisible force, and her heart thundered in her chest with his every step.

"Ty, please."

He smiled. "Please what?" he purred and leaned in to kiss her.

The moment his hands landed on the curve of her waist and his lips pressed against hers, her purpose for coming was lost, and only need consumed her.

He broke the kiss and stepped back, scanning her again, and with a slight cock of his head, her shirt tore open, the buttons pinging on the floor as they rolled away. He closed the distance, his lips drinking in her neck, his tongue tickling her skin.

"Please. Let me go."

A sound so unlike him welled up from his chest and he giggled, his hands sliding under the hem of her skirt until his fingers found her underwear. In a grand flourish, he tore them off and tossed them over his shoulder.

Her shirt peeled off and flew to another corner of the room, along with her bra. She stood half naked and trembling against the invisible hold, his hands traveling over her skin, his lips finding the curves of her breasts and feeding the frenzy gripping her.

"Let me go."

He smiled and released her from his mental hold, but his exploration of her body continued. The seduction of his lips, his tongue sliding down her stomach, kept her in place. His silken hands left trails of heat behind their caresses, almost burning her skin with desire.

He dropped to his knees and yanked the skirt around her ankles, and when she stepped out of it, he tossed it over his shoulder, his eyes sparkling with mischief.

One lick was enough to drive her over the edge. She tilted her head back into the wall, letting a soft moan escape. Her hands laced into his thick hair, pulling him closer, spreading her legs wider for him.

He rolled his tongue around the spot that drove her wild, toying with her, bringing her to the brink and slowing down enough to sustain the plateau. His fingers teased with their slow penetration, and she wrapped around them, each stroke producing a delicious tingle. Her body burned for him, and each touch, each flick of his tongue, each press of his lips fanned her passion.

He broke his mesmerizing hold, working his way up her abdomen, his lips trailing over her breasts and up her neck until they covered her mouth in an exquisite tongue dance that left her breathless. He set her body on fire, rendering her helpless. The kiss broke, and he met her gaze with a smile that seared her soul.

"Tell me you want me," Chris whispered in that smooth, sexy voice she couldn't deny.

"God help me, I do want you, but I can't do this."

A SINGLE TEAR SLIPPED from her eye. The flurry of her thoughts accosted him, seizing his muscles in place.

"Don't go," he whispered and traced her lips with his fingertips. "Don't go to California."

"Ty. I came to say goodbye."

Chris's breath hitched in his chest, the words sharper than a knife cutting his flesh. Tears sprang, blurring his vision, and he buried his head into her neck.

"No." He shook his head like a five-year-old refusing punishment. "No."

"Yes," Jessica said. "You have to let me go."

"Eric told me I had to save you," Chris said. "So, you can't say goodbye just yet."

Jessica put her hands on his face. "I'm not coming back from L.A."

"Just twist the knife in my chest a little more, why don't you?" Chris snatched up her clothes from the corners of the room and then shoved them at her.

She took them and crossed to the couch, putting the garments back on. She sat down, and a sob escaped. "The buttons are gone."

Chris inhaled and hung his head. The anger decreased a notch, replaced by a bleak despair that blanketed him, leaving his skin cold and his heart guarded.

He raised his gaze back to hers. The panic he saw grilled his nerves. "How can you leave after everything that has happened?"

"Because I'm married." She sighed.

"I can take care of that."

"Don't you dare," she growled and shot to her feet.

Chris willed her to sit down, and she did.

Jessica dropped her gaze to her shirt. "How the hell am I going to explain this?" She lifted the empty edge, showing only little tendrils of thread where the buttons had once been. Tears tracked down her cheeks again.

God damn it!

He hated when she cried; it always tugged at his heartstrings, and this time was no different. He kneeled in front of her, taking her hands in his. He bent over, closed his eyes, and rested his forehead on her knees, concentrating, willing the buttons back to their original origin. The exertion and the reason behind it dragged hot tears from his eyes, burning his throat and dampening a spot on her skirt. The power inside increased a notch, and he trembled while trying to contain it.

Her sob yanked his head up, and he stared at the perfectly buttoned shirt before bringing his bleary gaze to hers.

"You have to let me go."

"I did that once. I can't do it a second time," he replied, wiping his face with his sleeve.

"You have to." Jessica put her hand on his cheek.

"Why? Why am I always the one that has to give up what I want?"

"Stop that." She tried to get up, but he wasn't letting her.

Chris stood and took a step away from her. "So, this really was goodbye?" He waved at the room, the anger ebbing back, sobering him up. "What if I don't want to say goodbye?"

She closed her eyes. "I don't want to be angry with you."

"You're angry?"

"I don't want to be, but if you keep acting like a child…"

He raised his eyebrows and then turned away, biting down his own furious retaliation. He crossed to the slider and stood with his arms crossed, debating, reflecting on what he had done today, on how many times she'd asked him to let her go.

"I'm sorry," he whispered after a few minutes of silence.

"For what?"

"For not stopping."

"I never asked you to stop. I asked you to let me go."

Chris slowly turned, not understanding the difference.

"Chris, you didn't do anything here today that I didn't want, but I need you to let go."

"I can't let go. Not until I know you're safe." He paused. "Not until you, Eric, and Emily are safe."

"I think we'll be fine in California." Jessica stood.

"He found you in Connecticut. Why do you think he won't find you in California?"

She shrugged and smiled a little. "One can hope?"

"Eric said that if I didn't take care of this, Frank would kill all four of us."

A crease appeared between her eyebrows.

"You, me, Emily, and Eric."

Her eyes narrowed. "When did you talk to Eric?"

"This morning on the beach. That's what prompted this." He picked up the empty bottle and set it back on the table. "He said I knew how to get rid of Frank, but Jess, it scares the shit out of me."

"You know how?"

"I think I do, but I'm not sure I can do it." He took a deep breath. "Maybe California isn't such a bad thing. Maybe he won't find you there."

She crossed and gave him a hug.

He smelled her hair, clean with a hint of coconut. Closing his eyes, he catalogued the scent so it would always bring back the feel of her in his arms.

"Thank you," she said against his neck.

"For what?"

"For letting me go." Jessica pulled away and walked out of his house.

Mind Games Chapter 30

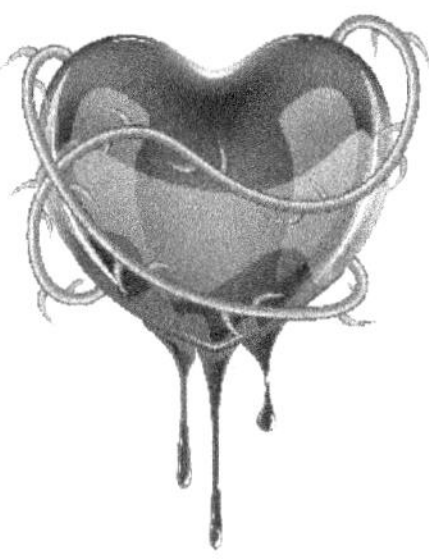

JESSICA BLINKED BACK THE tears, wiping her eyes with the hem of her sleeve as she drove to the store to grab a couple of items she forgot yesterday. After tossing the items in her cart, she checked out. Moments later, she turned on the ignition of her car, and her cell phone rang.

"Hello?" she answered, pulling out of the parking space.

"Where are you?" Tom asked.

"At the store," she answered and heard him suck in his breath. "I took a drive into Kittery and looked for a couple of outfits before I stopped at the grocery store."

"Find anything?"

"Nothing I wanted," she replied. *Liar!* The guilt encompassed her. This time, she didn't have any excuse. She had given in to her feelings today without the aid of alcohol.

"Uh-huh," Tom grunted. "Sure about that, Jessie?"

Jessica glanced in her rearview mirror, and her eyes went wide. His truck was on her tail, following her out of the parking lot. He flipped his phone closed, glaring at her frazzled gaze in the rearview mirror.

"Shit." Her mouth went dry, and her blood hammered in her chest. Excuses whirled in her mind, all of them tossed out as callously as she had tossed the phone into the passenger seat.

After she pulled into the garage, she grabbed the bags, trying to get into the house as quickly as possible, to the safety of the kids and the opportunity to avoid this fight until her heart settled down and she could think clearly.

"Hello," she yelled.

No answer.

Tom came in and slammed the door behind him. "I called Dan and asked him to come get the kids because we had some things to discuss, and it would be better if the kids weren't here to witness it," he growled and threw his keys on the table.

Jessica had never seen him this angry. She shrank against the wall.

"I assume that house is his?"

"You followed me?"

"You bet your ass I did." He pushed her against the wall. "What were you doing, Jess?" Anger seethed from him.

"Telling him he needed to let go. I was saying goodbye." She met his fury-filled baby blues.

"You sure took your sweet time."

"He didn't like it when I told him I was staying in Los Angeles with you."

Tom's jaw tightened, and his eyes narrowed.

"So help me, if he laid a hand on you..."

Swallowing, she shook her head. "He's worried about Frank's ghost."

Tom inhaled and blinked, taking a step back. "You told him you were staying in L.A.?"

She nodded and the anger in his eyes diffused.

"You seriously want to stay in L.A.?"

No. The thought leaped into her brain, but she had the presence of mind not to let it escape. "Yes. It's your home."

"Wherever you are is my home. Why did you lie to me?"

"Would you have let me go see him alone?"

Tom laughed. "Not on your life."

She raised her eyebrows and shrugged. "That's why, and it was something I had to do. I already hurt you enough this morning, and I didn't want to make you angry."

"I'm still pissed, Jessie." He walked into the living room.

She didn't enjoy lying to Tom. She didn't like it at all. "I'm sorry." She sat next to him on the couch.

Tom took her hand in his. "Sometimes loving you is hard."

"What do you mean?"

"I knew when I married you. I knew you loved him, and I never really understood why. Not with what he did." Tom shifted. "I completely understood why Ty fell in love with you, because it happened to me as well." He took a deep breath. "But until last week, I believed he was dead. That's the only way I could deal with knowing you loved him. And now that I know he's not... It's just hard."

"Does it change the way you feel about me?"

"No. But I'm afraid I'm going to lose this time."

"It's not a competition."

He cocked his head and pressed his lips together. "Look, he'd kill for you in an instant, and he was willing to lay his life on the line for you five years ago. I have no doubt that he'd do the same today if that's what it took to keep you safe."

Jessica picked at her nail, trying to read between the words. "You think I'd choose him over you?"

He shrugged and looked away.

"I married you." She poked his chest. "And I love you."

"I know you do. But you love him, too." He uttered a slight laugh. "Hell, you protected him for five years."

Tears brimmed and she wiped her face. She couldn't deny what he said. "I'm not as gentle and sweet as you think I am. I killed Marian." Her gaze wandered out the window. "And I helped kill Frank."

"Ty killed Frank. He just used you as the vessel."

"I'm not so sure."

Tom pulled her chin so she was looking at him. "I was there, remember?"

Jessica nodded. "But I wanted him dead," she whispered. "I set Ty free. I made sure you didn't die in that electric chair. I blew the doors off the hinges, every one of them in that place, and I killed Marian. I could have gotten out of that chair if I really wanted to, but I wanted him to suffer and die just as much as Ty did."

"We all wanted him dead, Jessie. I saw what he did to you." He shuddered. "He got what he deserved."

"But now he's back and looking for revenge, and neither of us can stop him this time."

Tom sat back and looked at her. "You can't?"

She shook her head. "I no longer have *that* power. Ty has it now."

Tom raised his eyebrows. "What?"

"I guess when he transferred the healing power to me the other day, I transferred the other side to him." She paused. "So I can heal every time Frank stabs me, but I can't stop him."

"So, until Frank is gone, Ty is in our lives?" Tom leaned back in the chair and looked at the ceiling.

"I'm hoping that moving to Los Angeles does the trick." Jessica leaned into the nook of his shoulder.

He put his arm around her and kissed her hair. "I hope you're right."

Mind Games Chapter 31

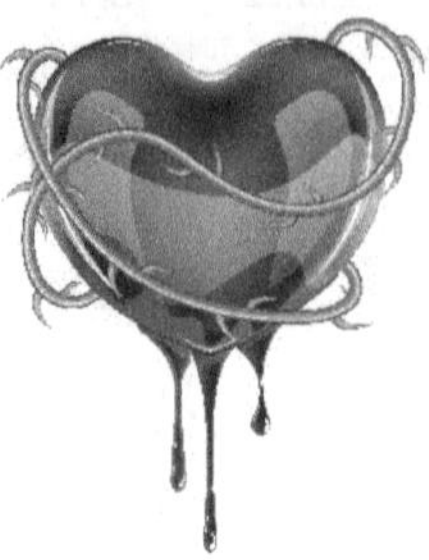

CHRIS SAT ON THE couch with his head in his hands for a while after Jessica left, feeling empty and hollow without her. His mood darkened, and a flash of power escaped. The empty bottle shattered.

Frustrated, he walked to the rock wall, scanning the marina.

"I can't believe I let her go again. I can't fucking believe it!"

He turned back and looked at the house he had bought to be near her, his pathetic attempt to woo her, to capture the dream, and his fury stepped up a notch. Chris slammed his cast on the rock wall, pain reverberating all the way up his arm, and he glanced toward her house.

"God damn it!" He headed back inside, grabbed his car keys, and left the house, locking it up behind him.

Chris drove to the lighthouse and then walked down the street. He stood on the corner, watching her house, just waiting.

Tom has to leave the house sometime, he thought, and as if on cue, Tom walked out the front door and got into his truck. The truck pulled out of sight and he trotted to the front door.

"Open," he commanded, and the door swung open. He walked in and saw her on the back porch, leaning on the railing with her back to him.

"Did you forget something?" The smile on her face froze when her eyes landed on him. "What are you doing here?"

Without answering her, he took her in his arms and pressed his lips to hers.

She pushed him away. "No."

"Yes." He went to kiss her a second time.

"You can't just come in here and do this."

"I can't let you go."

"You have no choice. We aren't in that cell anymore. This is the real world, and I made my choice a long time ago."

"You love me."

"Doesn't matter. I chose Tom. I married him, knowing you were out there somewhere."

"Jess, I can't do this without you."

"Bullshit. You've been fine for five years without me. You have to leave. Now. Before he gets back."

"No."

"He followed me today, and if he finds you here, he will kill you. He doesn't know anything happened, but if he sees you here, sees the way you are looking at me, he will. Please go."

"He can't touch me." *Not with what you gave me.* "Besides, my car isn't here," he added to calm the panic he felt radiating off her.

"Do you want to hurt me more than you already have?"

Chris felt the mental slap and stepped away from her. "I want the dream."

"You can't have it. You changed everything when you came, and I'm so thankful. You gave me Emily back," Jessica said. "But I don't want to leave Tom. I love him, too. He's the one who has my heart."

"But I have your soul," Chris whispered.

Jessica nodded. "Yes, you do, and you know what it would do to me if I lost Tom."

Chris took a deep breath. It would destroy everything he loved about her. "So, I lose again."

Jessica closed her eyes and dropped her head. "Yes."

He hated losing. It just wasn't natural, and losing her was worse than losing his life. Pain gripped him, spreading from the center of his heart outward until it throbbed in his fingertips. He turned, quickly descending the staircase to the back lawn, then taking one last look over his shoulder before he disappeared around the corner.

Regardless of her words, what he saw in her eyes was the same pain rushing through him, like a piece of their souls were melded together, and one without the other left an incomplete person. An imbalance that fate did not take kindly to.

Mind Games Chapter 32

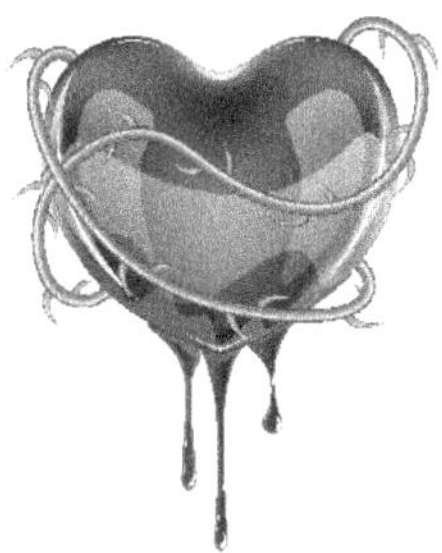

"EMMY, DON'T BE TOO long. We have to leave in a little while," her mother called through the closed door.

Emily stared at the door from the center of her room, fear keeping her still and trembling in his vile grasp. An ice-cold hand clamped over her mouth, and she felt his breath on her neck. His other hand was already buried in the front of her pants.

"Going on a little trip?" Frank licked the side of her face. "Remember, you scream, they all die." He chuckled, and his hand moved from over her mouth to her chest.

She shook, her gaze glued to the mirror, glued to his sadistic, laughing eyes. "Not again," she whimpered.

"There is nothing like virgin pussy," he whispered in her ear, moving her toward the bed. He pushed her over onto her stomach and parted her cheeks. "Except maybe for a virgin ass."

His laughter echoed in her ears. Pain rippled through her, paralyzing her in place until his vile assault concluded and he leaned close to her ear. "I'll be waiting for you in California."

Emily lay on her stomach, sobbing into the bed. She reached down and pulled her jeans up slowly, wondering what she had done to deserve this. She finally got a hold of herself and dragged her suitcase out, then threw all her things in without thought.

He knew where they were going. He was going to be there, too.

Both thoughts brought another wave of tears, and she snatched the phone off the floor.

"Hey, Sara," she said, her voice shaking.

"What's up?"

"Do you believe in ghosts?" Emily zipped up the suitcase.

Her question was met with silence.

"You okay, Emily?" Sara asked.

Emily cried quietly. "Do you believe in ghosts?"

"I don't know," Sara said. "Why?"

"I think I've got one."

"How do you know?" Sara asked.

Emily let out a hysterical laugh.

"What is it, Em?" Sara asked, her voice nervous.

"He..." She let out a little sob. "He raped me."

"What? Who?"

"The ghost." Emily wiped the tears off her face. "I have to go. We're flying to California tonight." Another sob escaped her. "He said he'd be there waiting."

"Shit, Em. What are you going to do?"

"I don't know. But he threatened to kill my family if I told them."

"You sure he can?"

Emily thought about his violation of her, how painful it had been, and how his hand around her throat the other day felt.

"Yes," she finally whispered. "I'll call you tomorrow." She hung up the phone and rushed to the bathroom, then closed the door behind her. She splashed cold water on her face and wiped it with a towel just as Eric knocked on the door.

"Em, I gotta go."

"Use the one near the kitchen," she snapped and heard him shuffle away.

This was going to be a long trip. Maybe he wouldn't find her there, she hoped, but deep down, she knew he would show up and do more unspeakable things to her.

Mind Games Chapter 33

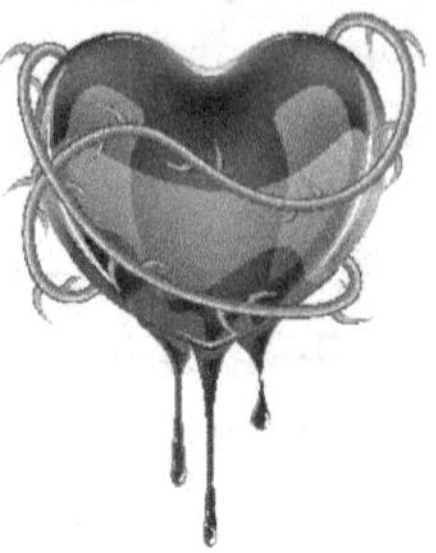

THE PLANE LANDED WITH a bump at LAX in the wee hours of the morning, jerking Jessica awake. Tom had his arm protectively around her and he snored softly.

Thank God for first-class seats. She glanced at the kids across the aisle.

Emily shook Eric awake. "Wake up, squirt. We're here." She yawned.

Jessica kissed Tom on the cheek. "Wake up, honey."

His grip tightened around her, and his eyes blinked open. He stretched and smiled at her. "Did you get any sleep?"

"A little." She had been awake for most of the trip thinking about Chris. She missed him already and felt a pang of guilt.

"Good." He looked over at the kids. "You ready?"

Eric grinned. "You bet."

Emily was more subdued, but she nodded and stood when the seat belt signs went off.

Tom stood and grabbed their carry-on bags from the overhead compartment as they headed off the plane. The luggage area was sparsely crowded, with half-awake passengers waiting for their bags. A driver stood to the side with a sign stating 'Whitman family' by the luggage turnstile. Tom signaled to him and handed over their carry-on luggage. The driver waited until they collected the checked bags and put them on the cart, then led them out the doors to a stretch limousine parked out front.

Eric's eyes went wide. "Cool."

Emily grinned. "Way cool." She climbed inside.

Jessica and Tom smiled at each other. Being famous had benefits and while Jessica had gotten used to this treatment out in L.A., it was brand new for the children. Emily and Eric bounced around the inside of the limousine, opening all the cabinets and drawers, playing with the windows and the privacy curtain. The kids reveled in the perks of the limousine, standing up through the sunroof, waving at the people on the streets as they passed by. Tom paid the driver to go the long route through Hollywood and Beverly Hills before they headed to his house in Malibu.

"Do you have anything going on today?" Jessica asked as the driver pulled into the familiar driveway on Malibu Road.

The beautiful, white Mediterranean-style home loomed in front of her. It never ceased to amaze her at how beautiful his home was with its neat, clean lines and breathtaking views from the outside, and yet cool, sterile, and unfriendly on the inside. Each room was decorated in a postmodern style that accented the clean lines of the house; there were a lot of white walls, mirrors, and chrome throughout the layout, which was nothing like their house in Maine. It definitely didn't feel like home.

As she stepped out of the car, she thought about Chris's home, with its warm Victorian décor and soft accents, which were much more in tune with her tastes than this stale museum.

"My agent has a script he wants to talk to me about. I'm meeting with him in about an hour." Tom got out of the car, unlocked the front door, and waved the kids inside.

"Doesn't he usually send you the scripts before you meet?"

"Yes, he's being very cryptic about this one, though." Tom shrugged. "He said that it was being filmed on the East Coast and could be one of the hottest movies of the season, but he wanted to talk to me in person before he gave me the script."

"Will it interfere with the show?"

Tom took a deep breath. "This is the last season for the show. I've only got half a dozen more episodes to tape."

Jessica turned in surprise; he hadn't told her about this. "You're kidding?"

He shook his head. "It's been a great run, but it's time to call it a day. I'm tired of being Superman." He shrugged and grabbed their suitcases, heading to the master suite.

Jessica picked up the kids' suitcases and headed to the bedroom wing behind Tom. She put Emily's suitcase on the bed in one of the guest rooms and looked around. It was just too white for her tastes. When she looked into the mirror over the bureau, a small chill went down her spine. She headed out of the room into the second guest room, setting Eric's suitcase on the bed and shaking her head. The rooms were almost identical.

She walked into the master suite, and Tom grabbed her around the waist, planting a kiss on her lips.

"I'm so glad you came."

"Me too." She hugged him. She looked at the sliding closet doors. They covered the far wall of the room, and they were mirrored. She shivered and prayed that they were far enough from Frank's grasp.

Eric ran into the bedroom. "Mom, have you seen the pool?"

"Yes, honey, I have."

"Can we go swimming?" He bounced.

"Sure, when I get back," Tom said.

"Emily, we can go swimming!" he yelled and ran out of the room.

"Maybe I'll take him surfing later today." Tom led Jessica back into the main living area of the house.

"I'm sure he'd love that," Jessica replied.

"I'd love what?" Eric asked and opened the refrigerator. There was very little inside. A gallon of juice and a six-pack of beer graced the shelves. He grabbed the orange juice and put it on the table.

"Tom wants to take you surfing." Jessica opened the pantry. It was as empty as the refrigerator.

"I didn't know you were coming out," he said in defense of the empty kitchen.

She raised her eyebrows. "But still?" She waved her hand at the pantry.

"I don't eat here. They have food on the set, and then I hop on a plane to see you." He shrugged. "Want to go out for breakfast? I can drop you off at a great place to grab a bite and join you after my meeting?"

Mind Games Chapter 34

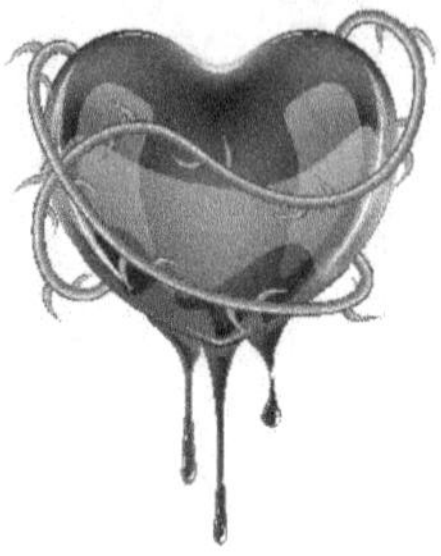

TOM WALKED INTO HARRY Cartwright's office and extended his hand with a smile. "It's good to see you, Harry."

Harry stood and shook Tom's hand. "You, too." He reached to the side of his desk, producing a script, and moved around the formidable desk to sit on the more informal overstuffed couch and chairs on the opposite side of the office. He motioned for Tom to take the seat across from him and set the script on the table. "I wanted to discuss this with you in person," he said pointing at the bound script. The words Survival Games graced the front cover.

"Okay. What's it about?" Tom asked, reaching for the copy.

"Your wife," Harry said, making Tom freeze halfway to the table.

"What did you say?" Tom sat in the chair.

"It's her story, Tom." Harry took a deep breath. "And it's very good."

"You've got to be kidding me." Tom stood up. He looked down at the script as if it were an alien being.

"They got permission to film in the complex in Albany."

Tom tore his eyes away from the cover, meeting Harry's gaze, and the heat drained from his face and fingers, leaving him cold, on the verge of shivering. He leaned back in the chair, speechless.

"They want you to play the part of Ty Aris. The two of you are the only ones who met him, and lived to tell about it, so you have the inside track on the part."

Tom looked at the script. Hesitantly, he leaned over and picked it up. "I've got to be out of my fucking mind."

"It's written based on the tapes. There was so much footage of what went on down there."

"Who wrote it?"

"Sharon Young."

She was the reporter who he'd called in favors with to leave Jessica alone.

"Jesus," Tom said. "I honestly don't know if I could ever set foot down there again. Much less play *him*."

"Tom, this is an opportunity of a lifetime. We are talking Oscar material here."

"Bullshit."

"Seriously. It is along the same lines as *Silence of the Lambs*," Harry replied, leaning forward in his seat. "And it comes with a huge ticket."

Tom took a deep breath. "How much?"

"Thirty million."

Tom raised his eyebrows. "Really?" He flipped open the script and read a page. He shook his head. "I don't know if I can do this."

"Tom, you would get to play a seriously deranged man. This would blow the mold that you have built with this Superman gig right out of the water and open up so many doors for you.”

“Jessie will not be happy.”

“So, you'll do it?”

“I didn't say that.” Tom looked up at him. “I'll read the script and then decide. If I can actually get through it.” He closed his eyes for a moment. “Harry, that was such a fucked-up situation. It was hell, and I'm not sure I want to relive it.”

“You wouldn't be reliving it as yourself. You'd be recreating it as Ty Aris.”

Tom let out a short laugh. “Somehow, that seems worse. You weren't there. You didn't see his eyes when he cut his stepbrother's balls off.”

Harry's mouth dropped open. “I thought Sharon used creative embellishment in the script.”

“No. That was real. Ty's a sick motherfucker,” Tom said. “Let me read it, and I'll give you an answer next week.” He stood. “Who do they have in mind to play me?”

“They're talking with Colin Farrell.”

“And Jessie?” Tom asked.

“They don't have anyone for her part yet,” Harry replied. “Any thoughts?”

Tom shook his head and laughed. “I'll have to think about that. Let me read the script, and I'll get back to you.” He looked at the script, chewing on his lower lip. “Does Sharon have the tapes?”

“Yes.”

“I'll let you know.” Tom walked out of the office with the script in his hand.

Mind Games Chapter 35

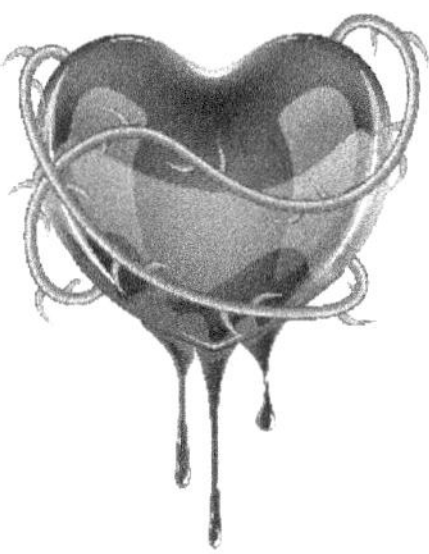

TOM GOT OUT OF the car and gave the keys to the valet. He tried to smile as he approached the table, but didn't do a very good job of it.

"What's up?" Jessica asked.

"Not much," he said after he ordered a coffee.

"Well?" Jessica pried.

"We can talk about it later." Tom opened the menu. "Have you eaten?" he asked, looking at the absence of a plate in front of her. The kids were already eating.

"I waited for you." She smiled, and the waitress came over and took their order. "You're not even going to give me a clue?"

Tom gave her a warning glance and a shake of his head. "I need to read the script."

"Is it the show?" Eric asked around a mouthful of pancakes.

Tom smiled at him and messed up his hair. "No, sport, it's a movie."

"What's it about?" Emily asked.

"Not sure," Tom lied. "I still need to read it."

They continued to shoot questions at him, and he fended them off until agitation bubbled over and he blew up. "Stop! I don't know if I'm going to do the movie, so just stop and let me eat."

They all looked at him, completely stunned.

Tom took a deep breath, closing his eyes. "Sorry, guys, I'm just a little tired," he said, looking around the table.

"No problem. Can we still go swimming when we get back?" Eric asked.

"Sure, you can," Jessica said.

Tom avoided Jessica's questioning stare, focusing on the food in front of him instead.

They finished their meal in subdued silence and then headed home.

"Can we stop at the grocery store on the way?" Jessica asked.

"Sure," Tom said. He pulled into the local grocer in Malibu and waited in the car while they went shopping. The moment they disappeared in the store, he flipped open the script and began reading, flipping through the pages with rapt attention.

The passenger door unlatched, and he jumped, slamming the script shut.

"That good?" Jessica asked.

He blinked a couple of times, staring at her. His questions about her capacity for forgiveness flared up again by what he'd read. Ty Aris was portrayed as an arrogant bastard who thought he could take what he wanted whenever he wanted. The worst kind of sexual predator.

"Tom?"

"Um, uh, yeah, I guess," he stumbled, still perplexed. He slid the script in the door pocket and then helped her load the groceries into the back of the truck.

They drove the rest of the way in silence. Tom wondered how much of what he'd read was true and how much of it was Hollywood. He realized he didn't know as much as he thought about what she went through down there, which made it more difficult for him to understand how she could ever forgive Ty. He needed to see those tapes; he needed to know.

He pulled into the garage and helped them carry the groceries to the kitchen. "I need to make a phone call." He disappeared into the study with the script.

He flipped through the rolodex and found the number he was looking for. He hesitated for a moment and then dialed.

"Morning, Sharon," he said when she picked up the phone.

"Tom, it's been a long time."

"You have the actual tapes?"

"Have you read the script?"

"I started it," he admitted. "Do you have the tapes?"

"Yes. Why?"

"I need to see them," Tom replied. "I need to know."

"Are you going to take the part?"

Tom was quiet, struggling with the answer. "I'm not sure."

"You know, he wasn't the one who actually killed the victims. Until that girl who cut him, he didn't actually pull the trigger, so to speak."

Tom laughed. "He orchestrated every kidnapping. He just did his killing at a distance. Whether or not you believe it, he is a cold-blooded killer. You just don't have it on tape."

"So, why do you want to see the tapes?"

"I want to know what happened to my wife." He looked out the window at Jessica and the kids in the pool.

"I thought you knew everything?"

"I only saw what Frank showed us in that room," he said. "It wasn't everything."

"Read the script, Tom."

"I need to see it."

There was silence on the other line.

"Sharon?"

"Read the script, and then we can talk." She hung up on him.

Mind Games Chapter 36

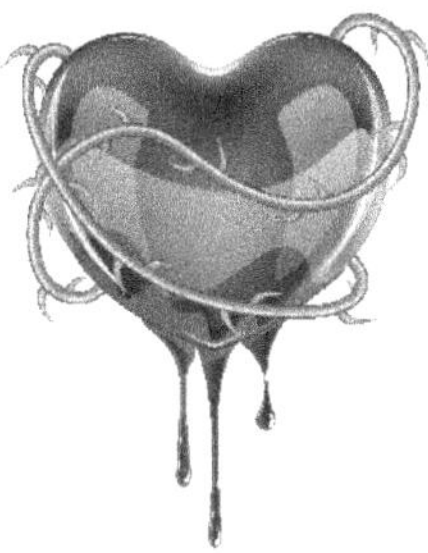

CHRIS PULLED INTO THE garage of his apartment building in New York and handed his keys to the valet, taking the ticket as he walked away. He took the elevator up to the penthouse and walked into the familiar setting, peeling off his coat and throwing it onto the chair.

The sun setting over New York filled his windows as he crossed to the balcony and leaned on the railing. He hoped the city, his city, with the constant assault of noise and activity, would be enough to lessen the hurt pounding in his veins. Wandering around the estate in Maine had been pointless, and he needed to get away before he did something he would eventually regret.

She was out there now, probably just getting ready for dinner with him.

"Damn," he said, and his heart sank another notch. He walked in and turned on the television, flopped on the couch, and channel surfed until something caught his eye on E!. He flipped back.

The banner headline shot him bolt upright. "Jesus."

He recognized the drab concrete and the chilling chairs planted in each of the rooms. The film crew went from room to room in the complex he and his brothers ran for close to ten years before he'd grabbed Jessica. Hollywood had the audacity to make a film of what had happened. His jaw slackened. A sick feeling in the pit of his stomach grew when they walked into the room where Frank had died. He turned the volume up to hear what the reporter was saying.

"And my sources tell me that the producers are talking with Tom Whitman, one of the only survivors of this dark and evil place, about taking the lead role."

Chris laughed. "Jessica's going to flip," he said to the television, but his laughter died in his throat.

His eyes focused on the mirror in the background behind the reporter. Frank smiled directly at him, and then the image was gone.

He shivered and wondered if anyone else watching had seen that. He looked toward the bathroom, suppressing the urge to run in and call Jessica.

Mind Games Chapter 37

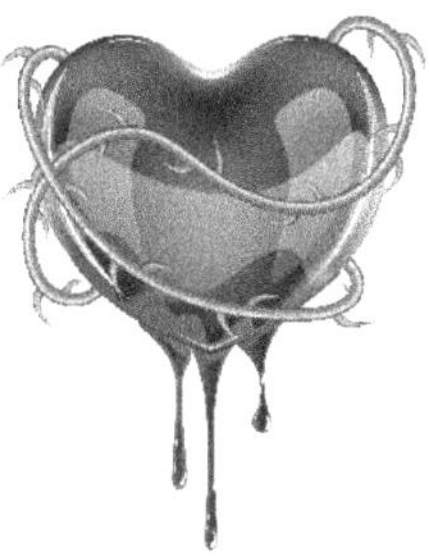

JESSICA LOOKED UP AT the office window as the kids played. She had seen Tom on the phone a few hours before looking down at them, and then he'd disappeared from view and hadn't left the office since.

"I'll be right back." She headed into the house. She pushed open the door and stepped into the office. "Are you okay?"

He slowly looked up at her and shook his head. "No, I'm not."

"What's wrong?" She closed the door behind her.

He held up the script and tossed it at her. "They want me to play him."

She caught the document and flipped it open. Ty's name stared back at her from the pages of the script, in screaming bold print, and a little squeak escaped her as she read.

"My sentiments exactly," he said. "They're filming in the fucking complex." Tom stood up, running his hand through his hair. He walked over to the window and looked out at the kids in the pool.

Jessica couldn't speak, and her legs gave out under her. She crumpled to the floor. "They can't." She finally gasped, closing the script.

"They are," he said, not turning, but looking at her in the glass's reflection.

"You're not thinking of doing it?"

"They're offering thirty million," he said.

"So what?" she snapped, finding her strength and getting to her feet. "You can't do this."

The glare he shot in her direction made her take an involuntary step backwards, and a thread of fear weaved its way into her skin.

"What he did to you..." The fury radiated off of him. "How can you..." He clenched his fists in frustration. "How could you love that psychopath?" he snarled and stepped toward her.

The thread bloomed into a whole blanket of fear spreading over her, suffocating her. She took another step away, but he reached out and wrapped his firm hands around her upper arms, yanking her to him.

"How could you kill for that son of a bitch?"

"Tom, you're scaring me." Jessica tried to pull away from his grip, but he held fast, smiling bitterly.

"That bastard is alive, and right now, I want him dead. I swear to God, Jessie, if he ever comes near you again, I will kill him." He scanned her and leaned over, kissing her roughly to make his point.

She believed every word and kissed back, wrapping her arms around his neck when his hands slid from her upper arms to her waist. The kiss deepened, and his hands wandered.

"Stop." She pushed him away.

"I'm going to take the part."

Jessica's mouth dropped open. "You can't."

"The hell I can."

She threw the script at him and stormed out of the room, running across their house into their bedroom, slamming the door, and throwing herself face-first on the bed.

The door opened and closed, and his footfalls crossed the room. "Jessie."

She ignored him.

He walked over to the bed and put his hand on her bare calf. "Jessie," he said, running his fingers over the back of her leg and the lower curve of her back.

"Go away."

He sat next to her and rubbed her back.

She finally turned and looked at him. "Why?"

"Because it's a good story, and it's an opportunity for me to break the good guy roles."

"But it's my story."

"No, it's his story. You and I just happen to be a part of it. I'm not thrilled about going down there again."

"You want to portray him as a monster," she said, looking up at his face.

"He is a monster."

"Not anymore." She turned away. "He has pieces of me and Eric in him now."

"But he was one. Until he met you. That's the way I want to play it. He still did some nasty shit after he met you."

"Like what?"

"Like killing my wife and what he did to you at the end there."

"I don't want you to do it."

"I know. But I need to." Tom reached out and touched her face.

"Why?"

"I need to understand, because right now I absolutely don't. After reading that script, if it's anything close to the truth, I can't fathom how you could forgive him for what he did," Tom whispered. "Never mind how you fell in love with him."

Jessica was quiet for a while. "Ty only did two horrible things to me while we were down there. He electrocuted me in that chair and raped me after he knocked you out. That's it."

Tom scoffed.

"You don't have all the facts. It was psychological warfare down there, and yes, he played serious mind games with me, but I also played him. I never gave him what he wanted."

Tom blinked. "You willingly slept with him."

She tilted her head a little. "Yes, but that's not what he wanted. The whole point of what he did down there was for him to feel power. He even told us as much, remember?"

Tom nodded.

"In every video they made me watch, in every scene he took part in, he wanted someone to beg or tell him they wanted him. Ty wanted confirmation that he was in control." She paused to let this sink in.

"He wanted me to tell him I wanted him, that I loved him. He wanted the words, not the physical act." She paused. "I never said the words he wanted. I never told him I wanted him or loved him until he was lying on the floor, dying. So, I played the game too."

Tom laughed. "Damn, girl, you still surprise the hell out of me sometimes."

"Good." She looked over at the clock. "Are you going to take Eric surfing?"

Tom ran his hand down her side and smiled, looking back into her eyes. "In a few." He leaned down to kiss her.

"Not now." Jessica rolled away.

"Yes, now." He pulled her back, kissing her.

"Tom," she said under his lips and tried to push him away.

He ignored her rebuff and continued to kiss her, stretching on top of her, running his hands up her sides. He pulled away and smiled. "You are too sexy in this bikini, and the kids are having fun in the pool." He leaned up and peeled his shirt off, then tossed it on the floor.

"The kids…"

He reached around her back and unclasped the bikini top. "Will be fine in the pool," he finished and undressed her. Hunger laced his eyes as he crushed her lips under his.

His bare chest rubbed against hers, and a delicate heat spread between her thighs. His tongue twirled with hers, sexy, sensuous, and when he broke the kiss, she squealed in protest.

The smile that spread over his lips made her shiver with anticipation. He lowered his head, his lips trickling down the line of her neck while his hand wandered between her legs, massaging her.

"Tell me you want me," he said softly, his breath tickling her.

She leaned her head back and closed her eyes, letting her body respond to his touch. "Tom."

His mouth suckled each breast, running his tongue over each of her hard nipples. Then he kissed every inch of her stomach. "Tell me," he whispered in an all-too-familiar smooth and sexy voice.

Jessica broke out in goose bumps as she looked into his eyes. This wasn't Tom. No, he was playing the part of Ty to a tee.

"Stop it." She tried to pull away, but he pinned her down under him, smiling. "Tom STOP!"

He shook his head. "I don't want to." He kissed her breasts, teasing her with his tongue. "Neither do you." He slid his body between her legs and slowly let go of her arms to run his hands into her hair, then hold her face as he kissed her hard. His tongue explored her mouth, and she made a small noise of protest, yet she wrapped her arms around him, anyway. "Tell me," he demanded and kicked his pants off.

"No." Defiance and heat stirred inside her. The little game was arousing in a way she hadn't ever felt with anyone but Ty.

He moved down her body, running his tongue as he went, smiling. And she let out an audible sigh. He paused at her belly button, where he rolled his tongue gently and ended with a kiss. He continued moving downward, and she trembled.

He laughed softly and kissed the inside of her thigh, running his tongue from the inside of her knee all the way to her hip joint. He repeated with her other leg and then licked her.

Jessica hitched her breath, arching her back. "Oh, God," she whispered.

His finger entered her, his tongue still rolling, sucking, provoking. Heat filled every crevice, and she moaned, covering her mouth with one hand and running her other into his hair.

A rush of wetness accompanied her orgasm. She tilted her hips into his mouth, letting him lap her until the tremors subsided.

He kissed his way to her lips, kissing her and sliding his hardness into her sweet slickness. He pulled away, staring down at her with bright, passion-filled eyes. "Say it."

Jessica wrapped her legs around him and moaned under his hard thrusts. "I love you," she whispered. "God, how I love you." She moved her hips in rhythm with him.

"Not as much as I love you." He kissed her again, and they both climaxed together, holding each other tight.

Tom leaned on his elbows and looked down at her, shaking his head. "Damn," he said breathlessly.

"What?"

"That kind of power is intoxicating," he said. "*You* are intoxicating."

"I don't like the fact that you were acting."

"I'd much rather audition with you than anyone else on earth." He smiled down at her. "How'd I do?"

Jessica said nothing, but heat filled her cheeks. "Go take Eric surfing."

Tom smiled and pulled out of her, then climbed off the bed and slipped into a pair of swim trunks.

"You really do have a nice ass."

"Thanks." He crossed the room and gave her a peck on the lips. "You, too." He reached around and squeezed hers as she stood.

"Go on. I'll be down in a second." She smiled and grabbed her bathing suit, heading for the bathroom to clean up.

Mind Games Chapter 38

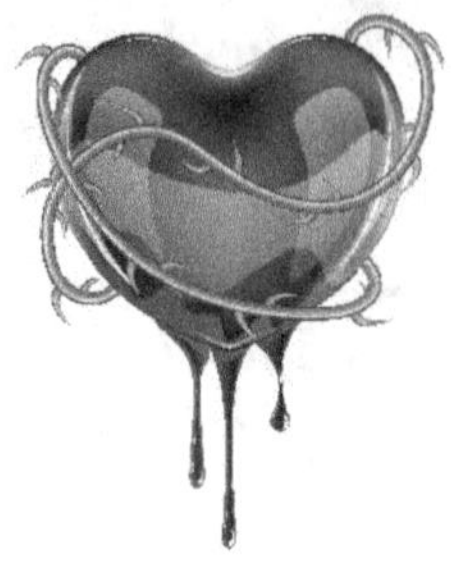

EMILY RUBBED HER EYES as she walked into the bedroom and flopped on the bed in her bathing suit. After closing her eyes, she drifted to sleep.

The temperature plummeted, and she stirred, feeling herself being propped higher on the pillows. She opened her eyes to see him kneeling over her, his crotch in line with her mouth.

"No," she whispered.

"Oh, yes." He looked over his shoulder toward the open door and the noise of people in the house. He clamped his hand around her throat and leaned close. "I'll be back tonight, and you'd better be here, or else." He vanished.

Emily shivered and stared at the ceiling, sobs escaping in quiet intervals. Once she recovered enough to not make a scene, she headed to the bathroom and splashed water on her face. She stared at her reflection in the mirror.

Maybe it would have been better if I still had cancer.

A stubborn anger welled up inside her. "Don't even think that," she said to her reflection. She stormed back into her room, grabbed her suitcase, and pilfered through it until she found the things she wanted to wear. She headed back to the bathroom to take a shower.

As she stood under the hot water, anger boiled inside with every minute that passed. She decided. She would not be in her room tonight, period, end of story. She turned off the water, got dressed, and headed out onto the deck in time to see Tom and Eric riding a wave.

Mind Games Chapter 39

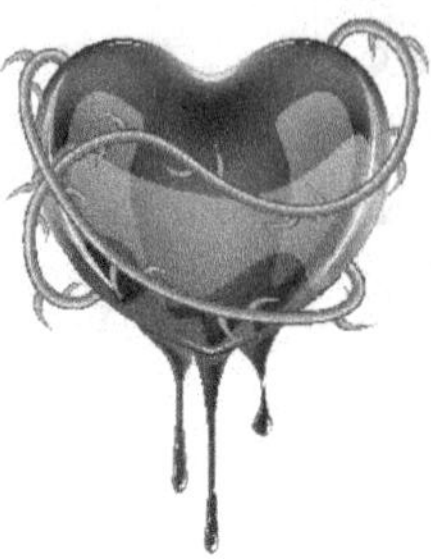

CHRIS LOOKED AT THE ceiling as the sunset streaked the room. He listened to the sounds of the city filtering up the building to the penthouse and again wondered what she was doing. He glanced over at his bathroom. Slowly, he got up and walked in, but he hesitated before he looked in the mirror.

He closed his eyes and concentrated. "Jess?"

JESSICA STEPPED OUT OF the shower and wrapped the towel around her. Chris's voice permeated the room, and she glanced toward the bedroom in time to see Tom slide his shirt on.

Tom smiled at her. "Don't take too long. We have reservations for seven, and I want to swing by the studio."

She smiled back and nodded, waiting to hear the bedroom door close. When it did, she looked at the mirror into Chris's eyes. "Bad timing."

"Sorry, just needed to see you and make sure everyone is okay."

She looked at the image and didn't recognize the room. "Where are you?"

"My place in New York."

"You left York?"

"It got cold in Maine without you." His gaze dropped.

"Why did you really call?"

Chris brought his gaze back to hers and shrugged. "I saw a news story."

Jessica looked at him expectantly. "And?"

He shuffled uncomfortably, realizing he didn't know how to tell her. "They're making a film."

Jessica tilted her head, watching his discomfort. "About?"

Chris lowered his eyes. "About what happened," he said. "They're filming on site." He looked back at her.

Jessica nodded. "I heard."

Chris's eyes went a little wider. *She already knows.*

"Yes, I already know. I'm not happy, but..."

"Is he going to take the part?"

"Yes." She glanced towards the bedroom and sighed.

"He's going to play me?" Chris laughed at the irony.

Jessica nodded.

"How are you with that?"

Jessica let out a laugh. "I'm not sure." She thought of earlier today and shivered. "I certainly won't be visiting the set."

Chris offered her a sad smile. "I'm sorry," he said, his eyes reflecting the pain he carried with him for all his less-than human acts.

"I would have never met Tom." She shrugged. "I have to go. We're heading out soon."

"Any signs of psycho?"

She smiled and shook her head. "Knock on wood."

"Call me if he shows up," Chris replied.

"I will."

He hesitated. "Bye." The image faded.

Mind Games Chapter 40

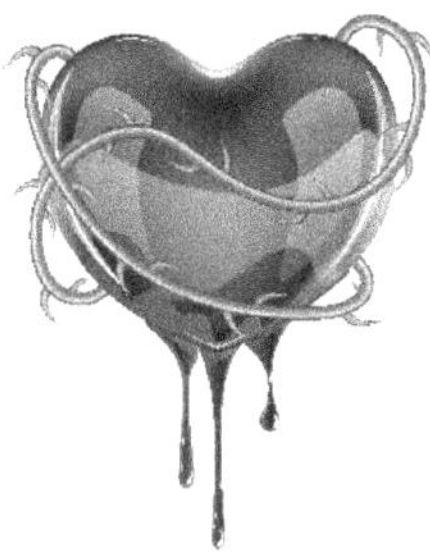

TOM STOOD WHEN JESSICA came into the living room. She wore a white dress that flared at the hem with delicate white sandals. It reminded him of the dress Marilyn Monroe wore in the famous picture of her standing on an air grate.

Jessica's hair flowed over her shoulders, creating a dark backdrop for the dress. She was a vision. A slow smile graced his lips, accompanied by the realization of how lucky he was that she was his wife.

"Ready?" Jessica walked up to Tom and gave him a peck on the cheek.

"You look great," he said, giving her the once over with a grin.

They corralled the kids into the car, and Tom swung into the security office at the studio with Jessica and the kids to get passes for the following day. Once they were all signed in and passes handed out, Tom showed them the various *Metropolis* sets, including the inside of the Daily Planet.

Eric walked around in awe, looking up at the lights and the large cameras that the viewers never saw. Emily, a little less intrigued, was still impressed with the set. Her eyes lit up when they walked into the wardrobe, and she saw the racks of dresses fit for Lois Lane. She pulled out a red-hot number and held it up, smiling at her image in the mirror.

Tom leaned over and whispered in Jessica's ear, "I want one of my own."

Jessica's eyebrows creased.

"A child, with you."

She went to say something, but closed her mouth and looked away.

"You don't?"

"I didn't say that," she said. "I just..."

He shrugged. "Just what?"

Eric stopped his exploration and stared at them.

"We never talked about that," she said. "And now isn't really the time." She smiled and tilted her head toward Eric.

Tom glanced in Eric's direction, offering a smile to put him at ease. "We'll talk later," he said to her. "Kids, we need to get going."

LATER THAT EVENING, TOM closed the door of their bedroom.

"Why not?" he asked.

She stopped and turned, turmoil dragging the edges of her lips into a frown. "My tubes are tied."

Shock filtered through him, followed by an odd sense of loss.

"We never talked about it before. Didn't you think it was strange that we never used any type of birth control?"

"I never thought about it."

"Besides, I'm getting a little old."

"No, you're not."

"I'll be forty-seven this year."

"You still look like you're thirty. You look younger than I do." He glanced in the mirror.

"Thanks, but that's neither here nor there. I can't get pregnant."

Tom peeled his clothes off. "Can it be reversed?"

Jessica shook her head. "They removed a section of each tube, so it's irreversible. I never planned on having any more." She looked down at her hands. "I never imagined I'd be with anyone else."

Tom slid into bed and leaned on his elbow, looking down at her. "Could we try something else?"

Jessica hesitated. "These days, anything is possible. But you have to know, I had two very difficult pregnancies. That's the reason Danny and I decided not to have any more."

"How difficult?"

"Neither one was life threatening. I was very sick for the first half with Emily and for the entire nine months with Eric." She shrugged. "I was in the hospital a lot for dehydration with both, but I developed gestational diabetes with Eric."

Tom closed his eyes. He had heard of gestational diabetes, but didn't know enough to know what that meant.

"I only had gestational with Eric, but they said that if I had more children, I'd be at risk for type 1." She paused. "You know how afraid of needles I am, so the choice at the time was easy."

Tom slowly rolled onto his back, staring at the ceiling. Disappointment ebbed into every fiber of his being. "If we go forward with this, is there a chance I could lose you?"

"There is always that chance, even if I didn't have the history of complications. Age alone is a deterrent. But we can talk to a doctor if you'd like and see what could be done." She rolled on her stomach and propped herself on her elbows, looking down at him. "We can see?"

He looked into her eyes and put his hand on her cheek. "You would do that for me?"

She nodded. "Yes."

Tom pulled her toward him and kissed her, wrapping his arms around her. "I love you."

Jessica smiled and laid her head on his chest, closing her eyes. "I love you, too," she whispered and drifted off in his arms.

Tom watched her sleep, gently combing his fingers through her hair. She had no clue how much she meant to him, or how afraid of losing her he was. He kissed her forehead and closed his eyes, drifting into a restless sleep.

He woke with a start several hours later and couldn't breathe. Invisible hands were wrapped around his windpipe, and the room was cold enough so he could see fragments of what little exhale he could produce.

The blankets were thrown off the bed, and Jessica was nowhere in sight. Panic bit at his nerves. Invisible hands yanked him from the bed and threw him into a chair where he had a full view of the mirrored closet. Frank let go of his throat in the image, and Tom sucked in a gasping breath before the tape covered his mouth.

Jessica lay on the floor. She wasn't moving.

Tom struggled, and the imaginary tape wrapped around his wrists, tying him to the chair. He kicked out.

Frank hit him in the temple, temporarily knocking him into darkness.

Mind Games Chapter 41

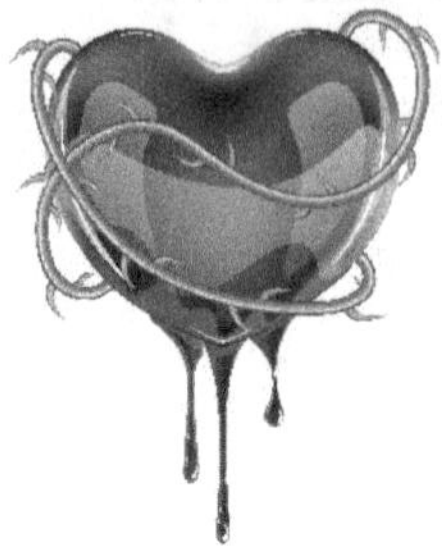

EMILY DRIFTED OFF ON the couch, but woke up to a ruckus. Her heart leaped into her throat. She ran down the hall to her mother's bedroom and threw the door open.

Tom was unconscious in the chair, and her mother was unconscious on the floor by the bed. Frank was standing over her, smiling. The blade of a knife shimmered in the light of the hallway.

"Don't," Emily whispered.

"Then you'd better get your ass in your room."

"Okay, just don't hurt them," she pleaded, backing out of the room.

Frank looked at her as a slow, evil smile spread across his face. "You'd better make it worth my while."

Emily nodded.

Frank put them both back in their bed and pulled the covers over them. "I will be waiting." He disappeared.

Emily looked at her mother and stepfather. Her hand flew to her mouth to stifle a sob. She closed the door behind her and walked to her room in dread.

"Next time you don't do as I say, I will kill your mother." His black eyes bore into her. He was stretched out on the bed with his hands behind his head, waiting for her. "Now close the door and show me what you can do."

Emily closed the door and bit back the tears as she walked toward the bed.

"Take off your clothes."

Despair wrapped around her heart, shaking her hands and running waves of gooseflesh over her skin. She hesitated.

"I can gut your little brother like a fish. Would you like to see that?" Frank produced a knife out of thin air and started to get up.

"No," Emily said.

The knife disappeared, and Frank settled back down, putting his hands behind his head again.

Emily obeyed his every command, her skin crawling and her stomach clenching in burning knots for the duration of his assault. She silently sobbed and shivered while he tormented her in every way possible for what seemed like hours.

When he finished with her, he smiled at her pain. "I'll be back again tomorrow night. If you're not here, I'll do this with your brother, and then I'll carve him up while you watch."

He disappeared, leaving her broken and sobbing on the bed.

Mind Games Chapter 42

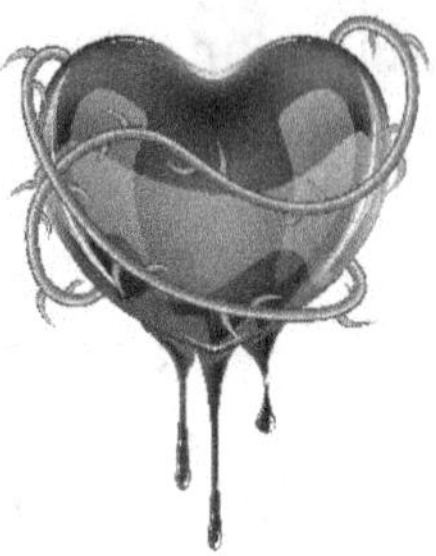

JESSICA ROLLED OVER AND groaned, hearing her name in the distance. Her head felt like someone had planted an axe in it, much worse than any migraine she could remember. "Tom?"

Tom didn't respond.

Jessica opened her eyes and gasped. A bruised handprint stood out on his throat, and the skin surrounding his temple was discolored, even in the bedroom's darkness.

"No," she whispered and put her head on his chest, closing her eyes in relief as the steady beat of his heart resounded in her ear.

She leaned over and kissed his temple, sending a little healing power into him. The bruises faded, and his eyes fluttered open.

They stared at each other for a moment and then swiveled their gazes to the mirror.

"What happened?"

Jessica shook her head. "I don't know. I just woke up, and you were unconscious, with bruises on your throat and face."

Tom sat up and looked at his reflection.

"I fixed them. They're gone now."

His eyebrows fused together. "My mind is foggy as hell, but I think Frank was here." He looked at the bed and around the room. "We weren't in the bed."

"I went to sleep in your arms, and I woke up next to you. What do you mean, we weren't in bed?"

"You were unconscious on the floor, and he put me in that chair..." He looked at his reflection again. "Maybe it wasn't real. Maybe it was just a nightmare."

"My head certainly feels like I was hit. Wish I could make this headache go away." She glanced at the clock, and it blinked 4:17 before she closed her eyes, succumbing to the darkness again.

Mind Games Chapter 43

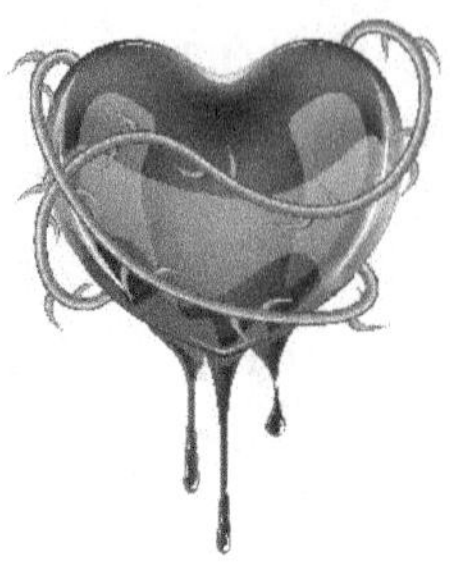

CHRIS WOKE UP WITH a horrible headache. He looked over at the clock. Seven o'clock.

"Jesus." He held his head and stumbled into the bathroom. He threw open the medicine cabinet and fumbled through until he found the Excedrin. He popped open the top and then downed three, following it with a handful of water. He looked at the reflection as he closed the cabinet and his eyes widened.

Frank smiled back at him. "I wonder what Tom would do if he knew she slept with you, little brother?"

Chris stepped back. "You're not my brother. You never were."

Frank chuckled. "We share the blood of so many innocent lives. That makes us brothers."

"I will send you straight back to hell if you so much as touch her. Understand?" Chris snarled, his hands clenching into fists.

"You're a fool if you think you can stop me. Hell is waiting for you, little brother, and so am I." He faded away.

Chris panicked. "Jess!" he yelled and concentrated. He saw their dark bathroom, but nothing else.

"Shit." He tried again. Nothing but the bathroom appeared. He couldn't home in on her whereabouts like he usually could.

Three possibilities flashed through his mind. She's in a deep sleep, she's unconscious, and the third possibility sent renewed waves of panic through him. *She can't be dead*, he thought frantically.

"Eric," he said, feeling his heart pounding too hard in his chest. He closed his eyes and sent out the signal, searching until he felt the connection. "Eric," he said louder and opened his eyes to Eric's bed. He glanced around the room a moment, taking it in. It was a little cold and sterile, with chrome and white furnishings, which was not like Jessica at all. "Eric," he said again and reached down, touching the sleeping boy's shoulder.

Eric's eyes flew open, and he jumped away from Chris until recognition set in. "What is it?"

Chris shook his head. "I don't know. I just have a bad feeling." He looked around again. "Can you check on your mom for me?"

Eric nodded and slipped out of bed, looking at Chris curiously as he walked out of his room. A few minutes later, he returned. "They're sleeping."

"You sure?" The feeling that things were not right escalated.

"Tom is snoring," Eric said. "And Mom rolled over when I opened the door."

Chris sat down on the edge of the bed as a small dose of relief slowed his heart rate to normal. He still had the nagging feeling that something wasn't right.

"Check on your sister." His internal alarms grew louder.

Eric raised his eyebrows. "Okay." He snuck out of the room again. Then he came barreling back into the room, out of breath, like he'd run up a flight of stairs. "Ty, she's not answering." He looked frantically at Chris.

"I don't know how to get to her."

Eric grabbed his hand and pulled him down the hallway, much to Chris's surprise. Again, he was struck by the lack of Jessica's touch in the house as he got a glimpse of the living space. Eric pointed to her door as they stopped in front of it.

Chris closed his eyes. "Unlock." He opened his eyes, and he was back in his bathroom.

"Shit," he barked in frustration and tried to get back, but couldn't. He would just have to wait until Eric called him or he could reach Jessica.

Mind Games Chapter 44

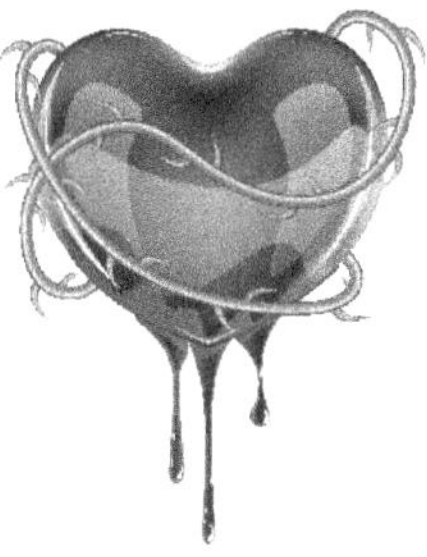

ERIC HEARD CHRIS SAY unlock just before he disappeared. Emily's bedroom door popped open in front of him, and Eric stepped inside. She was under the sheets, sleeping.

"Emmy?"

Her eyes flew open at the noise, and she jumped back in the bed and gasped.

"Emmy?"

She closed her eyes and let out a long breath. "Squirt."

"Your door was locked."

Emily looked at the door and back at him. "Then how did you get in?"

"Ty."

Emily shivered, and her face went pale.

"Ty isn't the bad guy," Eric said, reading her face. "He's the one that protects us." He thought he sounded much like he did five years ago when they thought their mother was dead.

"How?"

Eric turned and looked at the mirror. "Ty?"

Chris stared at the two of them and then closed his eyes in relief. "Thank God." He looked back up. He glanced from Eric to Emily and offered an awkward smile to her slack jaw and raised eyebrows.

EMILY LOOKED INTO THE eyes of the man who had changed her life, recognizing his face. "I've seen you before, on television." She tilted her head in thought. "But your name isn't Ty."

"It's Chris."

She gasped. "Ty was your brother."

Chris glanced at Eric and then back at her and nodded.

"So why did you answer to Ty?" Her eyes narrowed.

"I don't know. It just seems to work that way."

Emily crossed her arms, raising a skeptical eyebrow.

He took a deep breath. "Ty always protected me. He was my brother, and I loved him, even though he did those awful things." He paused. "And he loved your mother, so I think he would want me to protect your family."

"How do you know he loved her?" Emily asked, her voice softening.

Chris glanced at Eric again and then back at her. "I saw the videos, Emily. He died for her."

Emily dropped her gaze and bit her lip before she glanced at Eric for confirmation.

"He loved her," Eric confirmed, looking directly at Chris as if the two were communicating silently.

"Okay, so what are you protecting us from?" Emily asked. Hope filled her chest, and she continued chewing on her lower lip.

Chris glanced at Eric and then back at her. "Someone who wants to hurt your mother. But I'm not about to let that happen."

"What about us?"

"I'll protect you, too," Chris said. "If you are ever in danger, just call out my name and I'll do my best to get to you. Unfortunately, I'm kind of stuck getting to you through a mirror." He shrugged.

"Actually, you need to call out the name Ty, not Chris," Eric said.

"All I have to do is say 'Ty' and you show up?" Chris nodded.

"What if someone is hurting us? How do you stop them?" she pressed. She needed to know. She needed something to cling to, and the man in the mirror just may be her only hope.

CHRIS WAS SILENT AS he studied her. There were more questions swirling around her head, but he couldn't read her beyond the desperation in her eyes.

"It depends," he finally said.

She looked at Eric and then back at Chris. "What if it isn't a person?"

His mouth went dry, and the heat drained from his face. A cold certainty bit at his backbone as he turned his gaze to Eric. "Can I talk to your sister alone?"

Eric and Emily exchanged a glance, and she gave a nod. The moment Eric stepped out of the room, Emily's teary gaze met his.

"He's been there," Chris said. Anger flashed, and his jaw tightened.

"Who?" Emily asked as the tears brimmed and rolled slowly down her cheeks.

"Frank's ghost," Chris said. The reaction in Emily's eyes was enough of an answer. But her nod solidified it. "Sweet Jesus, you're still in high school." He closed his eyes. "This is going to kill your mother."

"You can't tell her. He said he'd kill all of us."

Chris looked at her, understanding the mind game Frank was playing. Chris had played the same one on his victims not so long ago when his name actually was Ty. He gripped the sink and hung his head. When he looked back up at her, she took a step back in fear.

"I am going to kill that son of a bitch," he seethed.

"Thank you."

"Just call."

EMILY NODDED AND SAT back on the bed as he disappeared. It took her a few minutes to recover from the shock, but the swirl of questions continued, and she needed answers. She wiped her eyes and headed into Eric's room. He was sitting in bed waiting for her and gave her a big hug when she sat next to him.

"Are you okay?"

She nodded. "I will be. Thank you."

"Don't thank me, thank him," Eric said. "He came to me tonight because he didn't feel like things were okay."

She narrowed her eyes at him. "His real name isn't Chris, is it?"

Eric looked away.

She turned his face back to her. "His real name is Ty, isn't it?"

Eric said nothing as he looked into his sister's eyes. "Ty had a scar on his face."

She considered what her mother had done to her. If she could make cancer go away, she could make a scar disappear. "Maybe he didn't even have a brother," she said.

"He had a brother," Eric whispered. "I saw him die."

Emily stared at him, waiting for some sort of explanation, and when he offered none, she asked, "How?"

Eric shrugged. "The same way he can see us. I saw more of what happened to Mom than I wanted to."

Emily threaded her hand in his and squeezed.

Eric shook his head like he was shaking away a nightmare. "His name is Chris."

"Level with me."

"Promise me you won't tell Mom."

"He hurt her, Eric," Emily said, remembering some stories she had heard.

"He saved her. And he saved you."

Emily's mouth dropped open. "What are you talking about?"

"I fixed Ty. I wasn't sure I could. He was so much worse than Mom had been, but I had all of Mom's power, too." Eric took a deep breath. "He was lucky because if it had taken any longer to convince Dad I was fine, Ty would have died. I gave him everything I had, and it not only fixed the bullet holes, it got rid of all his scars. That's why I couldn't fix you when I tried. I gave it all to him."

"You still haven't told me how he saved me," Emily replied.

"He knew you were sick. He found Mom and gave her the power back."

Silence filtered between them.

"What did he want to talk to you about?" Eric asked.

"The ghost."

Eric stared at her, and she avoided his eyes. "He hurt you?"

Emily nodded and the wall holding the tears back crumbled. Eric's arms encircled her, squeezing her to him, and the words he whispered pulled a sob from her chest.

"Ty will make sure he doesn't hurt you again."

For the first time since that ghostly devil assaulted her, she felt a genuine spark of hope.

"You mind if I sleep in here for the rest of the night?" she asked when her tears dried.

"Not at all," Eric said.

They curled up on the bed, their backs touching, giving her a small sense of security, but it was a long time before she drifted back to sleep.

Mind Games Chapter 45

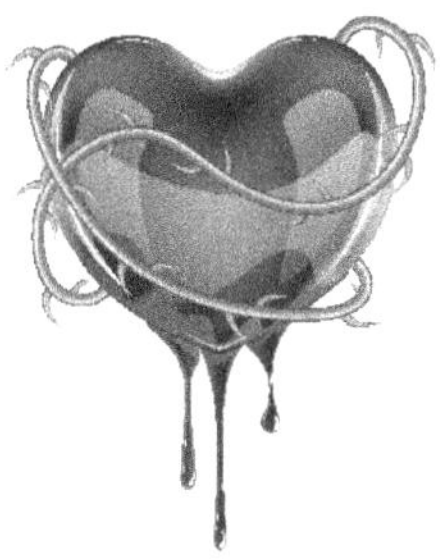

THE MORNING ROLLED AROUND faster than any of them wanted. While Tom woke the kids, Jessica stepped into the bathroom toward the shower.

She turned at the sound of a throat clearing.

Chris's eyes scanned her naked form and quickly shot away. "We need to talk, Jess."

Jessica grabbed the towel and covered herself. "Not now, Ty," she said, annoyed at his timing.

"Yes, now," he insisted. "Frank has been there."

"How do you know?" None of the mirrors in the bedroom were broken.

"Let's just say I know." Chris masked his thoughts, so she couldn't read them. "You need to come home."

"I am home."

"Then I need to come there."

"No. Let it go. Let me go."

"Jess, I can't."

"You have no choice. Goodbye." Jessica turned and let the towel drop. She stepped into the shower without looking back.

Mind Games Chapter 46

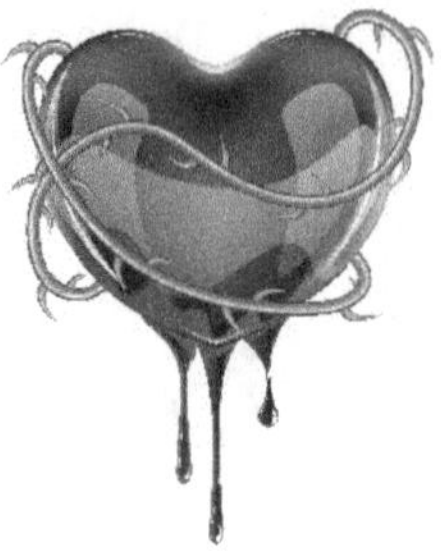

CHRIS WATCHED IN FRUSTRATION and then walked out of his bathroom three thousand miles away from her. He looked at the mid-morning Manhattan skyline.

"What do I do now?" he asked the skyscrapers. "What the hell do I do?"

He paced back and forth restlessly. He couldn't let Frank touch Emily again. He was certain of that, but he didn't know how he was going to stop this madness if Jessica didn't come home. He knew what had to be done, whether or not he wanted to, but the standoff with Frank needed to be in Maine and not California.

Chris pulled on his coat, grabbed his camera, and headed out. He walked across the street into Central Park and meandered through the walking paths, his mind preoccupied with Jessica and how to get her back on the East Coast.

The click of a gun hammer caught his attention. He stopped. Slowly turning, he looked down the barrel of a mugger's .38 Special.

"Give me your wallet," a strung-out junkie demanded.

Chris let out a stifled laugh. "I don't think so."

The mugger stepped back and lowered the gun a little, taken aback by the response. He recovered quickly, pointing the gun back at him. "I'll shoot."

Chris tilted his head a little to the right and narrowed his eyes. "Really?"

"Give me the goddamn money!"

"No. Give me yours." He smoothly transitioned into Ty's fearless persona.

The mugger took another step back. "You're fucking crazy!"

Chris smiled. "You have no idea." He took a step toward the mugger and then lifted his hand to his head, his index finger pointing like the barrel of a gun.

The mugger followed suit, his eyes popping in their sockets, and perspiration broke out across his forehead. A stain slowly spread on the kid's pants, and the distinct stench of urine filled the air.

"Bang." Chris laughed, but he didn't squeeze the imaginary trigger. Instead, he willed the mugger to slowly release the hammer and flip the safety on. When he relinquished physical control over the mugger, the kid bolted away as fast as a cartoon exit.

That was fun.

Chris chuckled and continued his amble through the park. He walked across the bridge by the pond and looked over at the Plaza Hotel, stopping to lean on the wall. He lifted his Nikon to take a shot of the hotel and froze with the camera midway to his face.

Blinking, he turned back the way he came. What he had just done with that kid dawned on him.

"Damn."

He could've just as easily made that kid pull the trigger as Jessica had. The sudden realization that he now could control people left his muscles tight with anticipation, and he wondered if it was just the danger in the situation that let that release.

He continued his meandering south through the city, taking pictures in the Village, Little Italy, and Chinatown of whatever struck his fancy before hopping on a subway back to the Upper West Side and his apartment.

Chris walked into his darkroom and set developing the pictures in motion.

After hanging the negatives to dry, he left the darkroom and flopped on the couch, restlessly flipping through the channels until he finally threw the remote on the table in disgust.

His mind wandered back to the junkie.

"Imagine what kind of trouble I could find after dark."

The idea thrilled him, and a slow smile spread over his face. He needed to exercise this newfound benefit.

"What the hell."

Mind Games Chapter 47

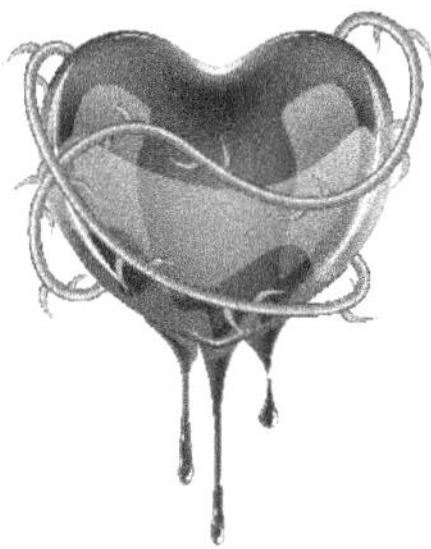

CHRIS DOZED OFF ON the couch, waiting for darkness to fall on the city. Another dream took hold, but this was different and disturbing. Crossing through her bedroom, he carried her limp and bloody body in his arms. Tears blurred his vision, and harsh gasps tore from his lungs.

He sat up straight when he heard his name, blinking and looking around in confusion. The nightmare remained clear in his head.

"Jesus." He wiped his face and headed into the bathroom, then looked curiously at the mirror. "Jess?"

She appeared in the mirror, clearly upset.

"What's wrong?" Chris asked, his gaze darting from corner to corner.

"It's not Frank."

"Then what is it?" He was more than a little confused, especially since her hair partially hid her eyes.

"I needed a friend."

Chris stepped back in surprise, raising his eyebrows and pointing to his chest. "Me?"

Jessica nodded, meeting his gaze with teary eyes.

"Okay. What happened?"

"Tom and I got into a fight."

Chris glanced down at his sink. "I'm sorry."

"It had nothing to do with you. It's not always about you," she snapped.

"Oh," he said sheepishly. "Then what was the fight about?"

"He was pushing me to let the kids audition for some show that the director is producing."

"That's insane." Chris had as much distaste for the Hollywood scene as she did, especially since he moonlighted as a special effects artist a lifetime ago.

"I told him it wasn't the life that I wanted for the kids, and he asked if it was the life *I* wanted. Before I could stop it from coming out, I said no."

"That had to hurt."

Jessica nodded. "He didn't want me to watch the next scene." Her eyes filled with tears. "I was just so angry, it slipped out."

"Ah, Jess, what is it that you do want?"

"I hate L.A.," she whispered. "I hate his house."

"It certainly isn't you."

Jessica's brow creased. "How do you know?" She wiped the tears from her face.

"I had a little talk with Eric last night." He masked his thoughts; she was in no condition to hear the rest of what happened.

"Why?"

"I thought something was wrong. I told you this morning I thought Frank was there, but I couldn't locate you, so I did the next best thing. I woke Eric up to check on you." He shrugged. "Guess it was a false alarm. You could have just been having a nightmare."

Jessica looked at him thoughtfully. "I want to go back to my house in Maine. At least I have friends and family there," she said. "Coming out here every once in a while is okay, but I've only been here two days and I am already homesick."

"I can't give you any advice, Jess," Chris said. "I'm an East Coast guy myself. Besides, you already know how I feel. I can't exactly be neutral on this one."

Jessica nodded. "At least the kids are with us this time."

"You've got a couple of great kids there."

"They are, aren't they?" She laughed a little. "Tom taught Eric to surf yesterday, and he did so well, and you also should have seen them today—they were great on camera."

Chris tilted his head. "Pardon?"

"Tom got them walk-on parts on the show. And they were better than some of the professionals."

"Surprised you let them do that."

"I thought it was a onetime thing, but I'm not so sure after the conversation I had with Tom. I think he planned it with the director. I should have seen it coming."

"You can't see everything coming," Chris replied. "Don't beat yourself up. He'll come around, and if not—" he shrugged "—I'm always here for you."

"Thanks, Chris," she said. "I'm going to venture out."

"One more thing," Chris said before she left.

"Yes?"

"Be careful. I think Frank knows where you are."

"I'll be careful. If not, you'll hear me screaming,"

Chris shivered, and goose bumps appeared on his arms. The bumps under his cast chaffed.

Her final words echoed in his ears. He hoped like hell he wouldn't hear her scream any time soon.

He regarded his reflection and closed his eyes for a moment. "She needed me," he said, and slowly grinned.

Mind Games Chapter 48

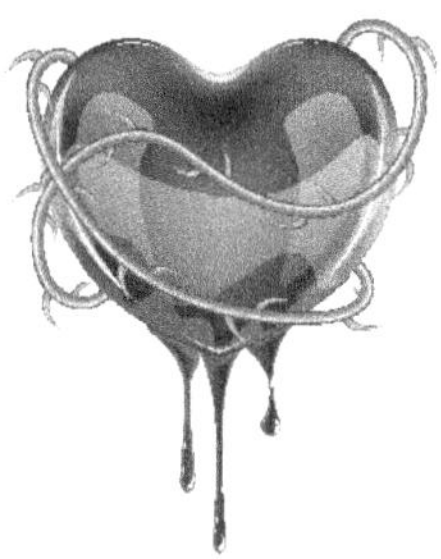

JESSICA VENTURED OUT OF the dressing room, and quietly joined her kids in the shadows as they watched the next scene.

"Cut!" The director walked over and pulled Tom aside.

"He's having a hard time with this scene," Emily whispered to her mother. "This is the tenth take."

Jessica closed her eyes and took a deep breath. This was her fault. When she opened her eyes, he was striding toward her, leaving the director looking after him in disgust in the middle of the set.

Tom grabbed Jessica by the arm and pulled her back to the dressing room, his face a mask of aggravation, leaving the entire cast and crew in stunned silence. He slammed the door behind him.

"I don't want you watching," he snapped. "I don't want you here!"

"You don't mean that." Jessica tried to diffuse his anger.

Tom grabbed her by the shoulders. "You don't want to be here," he said through clenched teeth. "Then I don't want you here either."

"Tom, I never said I didn't want to be with you."

"You said you didn't want this kind of life."

She hesitated for a moment. "I never wanted to be in the spotlight, and I don't want my kids there either," she replied, feeling the bite of anger again. "You, of all people, should know that." She yanked herself from his grip and walked to the back of the room, where she leaned on the counter and looked at him in the mirror.

"God damn it." He took a step toward her. "Jessie, the spotlight hasn't changed who I am."

"There's no privacy here. I don't want people poking around in our past, or our present, for that matter."

"What do you want me to do?"

"When this show is over, I want to go back east, permanently. With you. I don't want to raise a child out here. I know I said I wanted to stay out here with you, but I can't stay here. It's too…" She struggled for the words. "Plastic."

Tom laughed.

"Don't laugh at me," Jessica warned. "It's too fake out here. There is no sincerity. Everything seems shiny and clean, like your house, but it's really just empty and cold."

His eyebrows arched. "You think my house is empty and cold?"

"Yes."

"It's classy."

"No, Tom, it's beautiful, but it's cold. There's no character in that house."

"So, you're saying my dead wife had no character?"

"She may have had character, but she didn't decorate the house with it."

He clenched his fists and glared at her. When she turned to face him, he stormed to her and towered over her. "You are not the best judge of character, Jessie."

She went to push him away from her, but he grabbed her wrists and pinned them to the mirror, leaning her back painfully against the counter as he came within inches of her face.

"Tom, you're hurting me."

"Maybe you like that."

Jessica's eyes narrowed. "Let me go."

"Or what?"

"Let go," she repeated and clenched her teeth.

"No."

Jessica brought her knee up into his groin, hard enough to shock him, but not hard enough to do real damage.

He let her hands go and stumbled back a step, leaning over in pain. He looked up at her in shock. "What the hell did you do that for?"

"You didn't let go."

"But…" He took a step toward her.

"Do you want me to dropkick you?"

He stepped back, grabbing the chair and sliding it under him. "Jessie," he said as he leaned his forehead on his hand, shaking his head slowly back and forth.

"What."

"I'm sorry."

"You'd better never do that to me again, or I'm gone."

He closed his eyes and leaned his head back. "What's happening to us?"

Tears blurred her vision, and she trembled, his question lighting doubt—doubt that they'd be able to get through anything, doubt that their marriage was strong enough to endure.

He stood slowly and limped over to her, then took her in his arms. "I'm sorry." He held her and stroked her hair. "I love you, Jessie."

She nodded into his chest, swallowing the sobs.

He pulled her away from his chest. "Are we okay?"

"Yes." She looked up into his blue eyes. "You're going to need them to fix your makeup." She pointed to the smeared face paint on his forehead.

He glanced at his reflection and uttered a laugh. "You want to watch the scene we were trying to do?"

She nodded.

They walked out together, feeling all the eyes in the studio looking in their direction. Jessica blushed at the unwanted attention. He kissed her on the cheek and headed off to get his makeup fixed for the scene.

"THANKS FOR COMING TODAY," Tom said as they slid into the car.

"You guys were great." Jessica looked back at the kids.

"I never knew so much went into making a show," Eric marveled.

Tom's phone rang, and he dug it out of his pocket while driving. He flipped it open. "Hi, Harry."

"Did you have time to read the script?"

"I'm going to do it." Tom glanced over at Jessica.

"That's terrific! They want to meet you in New York next week. They plan on flying to the complex for a walk-through on Monday and then they want you running lines for auditions to fill the spot of Jessica on Tuesday back in the city."

"But I still have obligations with the show."

"I'll take care of that. You can take the red eye on Tuesday. They can shoot your scenes later in the week. I already made the arrangements."

Tom glanced at Jessica, knowing that it meant really long days, and he wouldn't be able to spend any time with her at the end of next week. "Tell them I want a room at the Plaza starting Sunday night."

"Will do. I'll arrange for a flight out of Boston on Sunday," Harry said.

"Make it two tickets."

"Consider it done."

Tom closed the phone. "How does a couple of days in New York City sound to you?"

"When?"

"Sunday, Monday, and Tuesday," he answered. "I'll be gone most of Monday, but I'll be back for a late dinner. Same with Tuesday."

"Sounds good," she said, grinning at the prospect.

Tom shut off the car as the garage closed, the kids ran into the house, and he waited until the door closed behind them before he looked at Jessica. "About earlier… I'm sorry."

"You scared me today. You've scared me more than once since we arrived." Jessica opened her car door and cast a glance his way. "And I don't like that at all."

"Jessie." He stepped out of the car.

She paused at the door with her back to him, the tension written in her stance.

He walked around the car and took her hand. "I'm sorry."

"I know." She looked up at him. "Please don't do it again."

Tom nodded, biting back the urge to ask her why not. After all, she had forgiven Ty for far worse.

"What do you want to do about dinner?" he asked, looking at his watch and driving those thoughts away.

"Let's order in. I don't feel like cooking."

Mind Games Chapter 49

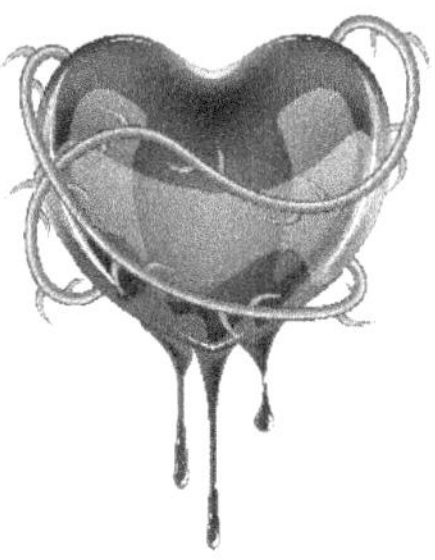

CHRIS STOOD ON HIS balcony, watching as the moon rose above the city. He looked at his watch and smiled. He still had at least four hours to kill before Emily might need him. It was time to have some fun. He grabbed his leather jacket and headed out the door.

He loved the city this time of year when the air cooled off faster than the ground, making the fog roll up from the pavement in the streets, creating a nice, cool blanket of white for him to float through. He trolled the streets, walking without purpose, his head inclined and both hands shoved in his jacket pockets, hiding the cast from view. He glared through his bangs, listening to the sounds around him and entering a neighborhood that was not safe for anyone alone after dark.

He heard footsteps behind him, and he tensed. There was more than one person following him. A smile slowly spread across his face.

He slipped into an alley and slowed his pace, staring at the walls surrounding the dead end. Laughter sounded behind him.

He took his hands out of his pockets, turning to face his attackers. "You don't want to fuck with me," he growled low in his throat.

Kids wearing black and red gang colors surrounded him. They were young, maybe late teens or early twenties, all black, and all held a holier-than-thou attitude.

The first gang member pulled out a switchblade, and the rest of the posse followed suit.

"You lost, shithead?" the oldest of the group asked as they surrounded him. "There ain't no whitey in my hood."

Chris looked around the circle, counting seven of them, all with knives drawn. He smiled and looked back at the one he assumed to be the leader. He was as tall as Chris, equally broad-shouldered and looked downright mean.

"Got money, shithead?"

"I will say this one more time," Chris warned and stared down the leader. "You *do not* want to fuck with me."

"We gonna cut you up." The leader of the gang stepped forward, pushing the button on the switchblade. A long, sharp blade shot out.

Chris shook his head slowly and stretched his smile further. "Then you're all going to die."

They laughed at him and all of them lunged with their knives at the same moment.

"Stop!" Chris whispered.

Every one of them stopped short, within inches from Chris's body.

Chris laughed as shock registered on the leader's face. "I told you not to fuck with me," he snarled, and he silently commanded each of his attackers to bury their knives in their own hearts.

In unison, seven blades pierced seven hearts. He stood in the center as each fell to their knees and then over on their backs. He stepped over the leader's dead body and walked out of the alley, shrouded in fog.

He continued his leisurely pace through the city with a smile, feeling the power grow with each unfortunate encounter. By one in the morning, he had rid the city of over a dozen thugs, none of which was smart enough to heed his warnings.

As he approached the village, he heard a scream in an alley to his left. He hesitated, then ran toward the noise. There in the alley was a young teenage girl, probably no older than sixteen, being raped by three men. She was crying with one man in her mouth, and the other two argued as to who was going to fuck her this time.

Chris stormed into the alley, anger welling up inside him. "Get away from her," he snarled.

When the man getting a blow job pointed a gun toward him and pulled the trigger, Chris felt the power surge out of him. The bullet never reached him; it disintegrated under the stream of heat that blasted from Chris, along with the man holding the gun. Chris turned his gaze to the other men, who were now backing away in fear. He walked over to the girl and held his hand out to help her up.

"Do you want me to let them go?" he asked her, keeping his gaze on the men.

She took his hand and said no very softly as he helped her up.

"What do you want me to do with them?" he asked, and the two men froze in place, the fear on their faces visible.

Despite still shaking and crying, she glared at her attackers, her face transforming into a mask of vengeance. "The same thing you did to the other one."

Chris looked back at them and let the power go again, vaporizing the other two men. "What else do you need?" he asked, turning back to her.

She wrapped her torn clothing around herself and looked at him. "Who are you?" she asked in awe, still shaking.

"Just think of me as your guardian angel." He took off his coat and wrapped it around her shoulders, leading her out of the alley. "Hospital or home?"

"Home." She sniffled and pointed him in the direction where she lived.

"What were you doing walking alone at this hour?"

"I was at work. My mom usually picks me up, but she got tied up at the hospital and I didn't want to wait." She let out a small sob.

"If you were my daughter, I would have told you to wait."

"She did. I told her I'd get a ride from someone at work."

"You lied to your mother?"

The girl nodded. "I've walked before. It's not that far. I just didn't think..." She let out another small sob and pointed to the apartment building they were approaching.

"Sweetie, it's not safe for a girl your age to be alone on the streets at this hour. Wait next time," he said.

They stopped at the corner, and he took his coat back. He watched her cross the street and open the door to the building, and then he took off in the dark, back toward his apartment building.

Chris looked at his watch. It was close to two in the morning. He glanced over his shoulder at the apartment building in the distance and smiled. Helping that girl was far more satisfying than everything else he had done tonight. It felt right, like giving Jessica the power back to save Emily.

He walked into his apartment and dropped his keys on the counter, then stripped the jacket off and tossed it on the chair in his living room. He grabbed a Corona and settled on the couch, flipping the television to the local Fox News station and waited, periodically taking swigs from the bottle.

God, I want to talk to Jess. He closed his eyes, smiling at the power raging inside of him.

He opened his eyes as a breaking story unfolded on the news about a gang of youths and an apparent suicide pact.

"Wrong." He grinned at the television.

How many people did he save by ridding the earth of those maggots?

His smile dissolved when he heard Emily call his name.

Chris dropped the beer and bolted into his bathroom, sliding on the tiles and grabbing the sink to stop his momentum. He looked into Emily's room and saw Frank kneeling over her with one hand around Emily's neck and the other between her legs.

"Let her go," Chris growled, and Frank looked at him in surprise.

Mind Games Chapter 50

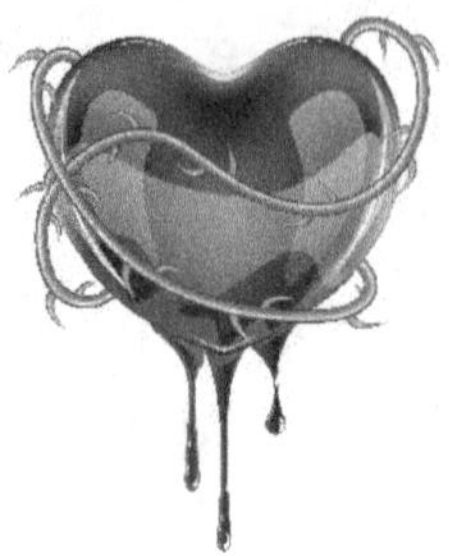

TOM RETREATED TO HIS office to review the script again. The doorknob rattled, and he looked up to see Jessica step into the room and close the door gently behind her. "Hey, babe."

Jessica walked behind the desk, then turned his chair toward her. "Don't make him into a complete monster."

He closed his eyes and leaned his head back in the chair. His hatred for Ty Aris contradicted with the disgruntled respect the script formed in him, and he sighed.

"Jessie." He reached out and pulled her onto his lap before opening his eyes. "He told me he needed to push you away when we were in that room together. I didn't agree with how he went about it, but I knew. I watched what hearing you cry did to him. Ty may very well be the bravest son of a bitch I've ever met. He stood in those chains knowing what was going to happen to him, and wasn't one bit afraid of dying. I, on the other hand, was scared shitless." Tom stared at the shifting colors in her eyes.

"He had such faith that you would make a miracle occur. He just didn't think he would be the one to be saved by it." He reached over and picked up the script. "It's all in here, so I can't really portray him the way I want the world to see him." He dropped the script. "The way I want *you* to see him."

Jessica wrapped her arms around Tom and nuzzled her head in the crook of his neck. "This is going to be hard on us, isn't it?"

"Yes." Tom squeezed her tight. He wondered if thirty million was worth it or not. "Think you can stick it out with me?"

"I can if you can," Jessica replied and pulled away. She traced his face with her fingertips and then kissed him. "I love you, Tom. I can't imagine my life without you."

Her words brought a smile to his face, and he hugged her tight. "I need to rehearse my lines for tomorrow. Want to run lines with me?" he asked and pulled away.

"Sure, can we do it in the hot tub?"

His eyes sparkled at the prospect. Usually, the hot tub led to sex. "I need to run the lines, Jessie."

"I know. But we will have bathing suits on this time. Can't go buff with the kids here."

Tom nodded and made copies of the pages he needed to review while she went to change. He dropped the copies on the desk by the slider to the deck and glanced at his watch. It was only nine, and both kids were sacked out on the couch.

He stopped Jessica in the hall on the way to the bedroom. "Let the kids sleep."

"You want wine?"

"I'll pass. I need to get up early tomorrow."

"Do you mind if I have some?"

"Not at all."

They rehearsed the lines together in the hot, swirling water. Jessica finished her wine, and tipsiness edged in. She grinned at Tom and licked her lips.

Tom plucked the copies from her hand and tossed them on the concrete. Moving between her legs, he pulled her to him in the steamy water. "I know what that smile means." He ran his lips along her neck.

Jessica leaned her head back. "The kids," she whispered.

Tom glanced back in the living room. "Still sleeping." He grinned back at her and reached into the water, peeling her bikini bottoms off. His swim trunks found a similar resting place on the concrete.

Tom smiled at her after they finished and reached behind her, grabbing both their swimsuits. They slipped them on in the water and settled back in the hot tub, letting the euphoria linger a while longer.

"I need to get some sleep." Tom climbed out of the hot tub. "I'll get the kids after I change."

AFTER BRINGING HER WINE glass into the kitchen and folding the blankets on the living room couch where the kids had been, Jessica stopped in each of the kid's rooms to straighten up. She grabbed their dirty clothing and dropped them in the laundry baskets. She folded up the beach towels draped over the mirrors and put them on the corner of the dressers, then kissed each of them goodnight and closed their doors behind her.

A COLD DRAFT DRIFTED over Emily's skin. She shivered, reaching for covers that weren't there.

Her eyes flew open at the frigid caress between her thighs, and she stared right into Frank's black eyes.

"Hello, sweetheart." He yanked her underwear off.

"Ty!" The name came out in a shaking cry.

Frank's sly grin faltered, his eyes hardened, his hand flashed out and clamped around her throat. The other hand mercilessly slammed inside her, his entire fist burying into her. Pain raked through her.

"How do you know that name?"

She caught a flash in the mirror out of the corner of her eye.

Chris slid into view and his growling voice overrode Frank's. "Let her go!"

Within a blink, the mirror blew to bits, and Frank disappeared, leaving her gasping for breath and staring at the empty frame where the mirror had stood seconds before.

THE SOUND OF SHATTERING glass echoed through the house.

Tom shot to his feet, his gaze darting around the dark room and falling on the shards glinting on the carpet.

Jessica slid on tile and skittered to a stop on the bedroom carpet, her gaze fixed on Tom before taking in the open closets, the mirrors gone, smashed to bits all over the white rug. "What the hell happened?"

Tom's face went ashen, and he bolted down the hall and threw open Emily's door.

Wide, shocked eyes met his, then Emily's gaze returned to where her mirror had been moments before.

"You okay?" he asked. When she nodded, he tore into Eric's room.

Relief settled into him at the sight of Eric untouched and still asleep. He navigated carefully through the shards of mirror to the side of the bed and shook Eric.

Eric blinked sleepy eyes at Tom and then his gaze traveled to the empty mirror. "I thought I saw you put a towel over the mirror. Who folded it up?"

Tom turned to the bureau, and on the corner, folded neatly, was the towel that he had draped over the mirror after he had carried each of them to bed.

"I did," Jessica answered from the doorway. "All the mirrors in the house except the one in our bathroom broke, but nothing else did. I don't think it was an earthquake."

Tom nodded, and their eyes met. "Which means..." he 'trailed off and looked beyond Jessica at Emily.

"Ty," Eric said aloud, and they all looked at him.

"We need to clean up the glass." Tom scooped Eric up, carrying him down the hall. "So, you and your sister should go into the living room and wait till I give the all clear signal." He put Eric on his feet in the hallway and turned back toward the mess.

"Where's the vacuum?" Jessica asked.

"I'll get it." He headed through the house to the utility closet.

ERIC AND EMILY WATCHED from the couch as he came back through with the vacuum hose.

When he disappeared back down the hallway, Eric turned to Emily.

"What happened?"

"Frank came, and I called him." Her eyes were still wide with awe. "He blew the mirror up and Frank disappeared." She flipped on the television. "He blew all the mirrors in the house up." She looked over at Eric. "Did you know he could do that?"

Eric smiled at her. "He can do a lot of things now that he couldn't before."

"What do you mean?"

"When he gave Mom back the healing power, she transferred her other power to him," Eric said. "I felt it when I met him on the beach."

"What other power?"

"The one Mom used to release Ty and kill Marian."

Emily just looked at him. "Why didn't I get any powers?"

Eric shrugged. "I don't know. Maybe you're more like Dad, and I'm more like Mom. Besides, I don't have any powers now."

"Yes, you do. You can read people's minds," Emily replied. "Just like Mom."

"That's not a power, though."

"Yes, it is."

Eric shrugged. He didn't think it was a power, more like a side-show trick that he wished he didn't have sometimes. He picked up the remote and flipped on the television as the first siren flew by outside.

JESSICA WALKED INTO THE living room and saw the red and blue lights pass by the house. "What the..." She looked down at the kids as the second pair of black and whites flew by the house. She walked over and flipped the television channel to a local news station, taking a seat as the breaking story banner appeared.

"Police and scientists are investigating a seismic anomaly in the Malibu Beach area. Several residents have called the emergency response number reporting shattered glass. Scientists at this time cannot confirm whether or not a small earthquake occurred, but the anomaly seems to be localized. We will keep you apprised of the situation as more information comes in. In the meantime, please make sure that items are secured properly in case of subsequent activity."

Jessica stood up and walked down the hall and into her bathroom, to the only mirror left in the area. "Ty?"

He was leaning on the sink in his bathroom in New York with his head hung low. "Everything okay?" he asked without looking up and blocked her from getting into his mind.

"You shattered all the mirrors in the area. Not just the ones in this house."

He looked up, and she stepped back.

"He was there."

Jessica blinked. She had been in the bathroom, and Tom was asleep in the bed. "I didn't call you, though."

"I've been keeping watch," he said, fury still burned in his eyes. "We need to send him back to hell, Jess."

"Where was he?"

Chris looked at her without saying a word.

"Where?" Jessica demanded.

"He went after Emily."

Jessica felt the room spin. Her eyes rolled up in her head, and she fell in a dead faint.

Chris caught her. Jessica's eyes blinked open to his arms around her. She looked into his eyes, registering the look of surprise he had on his face.

"Jessie?" Tom called.

Chris gently set her on the floor. "Bye." He disappeared.

Mind Games Chapter 51

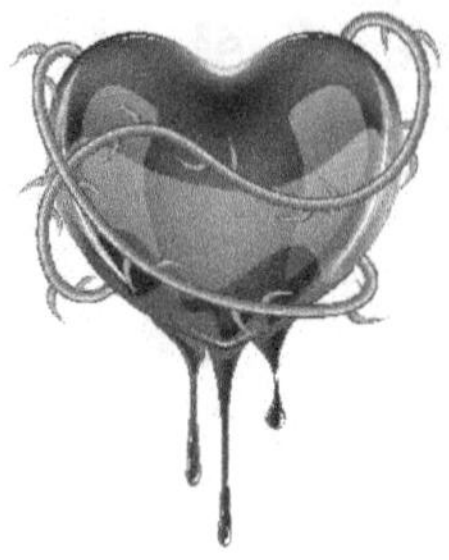

CHRIS STOOD BACK IN his bathroom, blinking and looking around. His reflection stared back at him, his mouth still open. When she fainted, on instinct, he'd stepped to catch her, and he did—in California.

He thought about what Eric had done the other night as well, and his eyes went wide. Eric physically pulled him through their house.

He slowly sat down on the bathroom floor and ran his hand through his hair. The ramifications of this were huge.

"What the hell did they do to me?" He gazed up at the mirror. He closed his eyes and leaned back against the wall.

"Ty?" Jessica called again.

He stood up slowly with his back to the far wall. "What did you do to me?" He stared at the mirror as if it were the portal to hell. It rippled her into view.

"I don't know, but you caught me when I fainted."

Chris nodded, and he stepped toward her, consciously willing himself there. He felt the transition, and within a blink, he stood in front of her in her bathroom on the other side of the country. Shock and confusion clouded his brain as he looked around and then back at her. He wrapped his arms around her and kissed her.

"This is real." He gasped. "Oh, God, this is real." The tremors started racking his body. "What did you do to me?"

Jessica shook her head and touched his face. "How?"

His heart raced, pounding on the inside of his rib cage, tempered by the soft flesh of her hand placed on his chest. "I have no idea." He pulled away. Eric's words on the beach resounded in his head. "Maybe I really do have your soul," he said, closing his eyes.

The transition took hold. When he opened his lids, he was back in his bathroom in New York, staring at her through the mirror. Neither of them said a word.

"What did you do to me?" Chris asked after he found his voice.

Jessica shrugged. "I, uh… I'm not sure."

Chris leaned against the wall and dragged a shaky hand through his hair. He thought the ability to vaporize those bastards was unsettling, but astral projection across the country was in a whole other league of weird.

"I'm sorry."

He laughed a pitch higher than normal because of his jumbled nerves. "I guess I owe you a huge debt of thanks for not knowing what to do with this power when I had you down in the complex. If you had an inkling of what kind of damage you could do, I would be dead."

Jessica offered a hint of a smile. "Thank you for protecting my little girl."

He gave a nod and walked away from the mirror, still reeling from the experience.

Mind Games Chapter 52

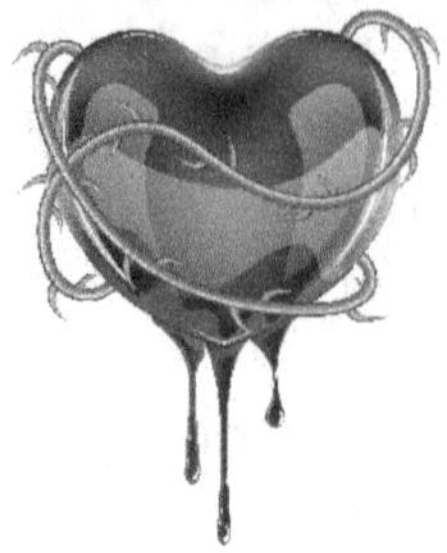

TOM STOPPED JESSICA IN the hall as he headed to their bedroom with the vacuum.

He grabbed her arm. "He blew mirrors out for an entire mile. How can I compete with that?"

"It's not a competition, Tom."

"You know what I meant."

"I'm not a fucking prize."

"Jessie," he said in exasperation, and put the vacuum down. "You're my wife, and that's my family sitting in the other room. I can't protect any of you. I have to rely on a psycho from our past for that." He took a deep breath. "A psycho that is still in love with you, and he is more of a threat to me out here than he ever was down there."

"Your family?" Her eyes filled with tears.

"Yes, my family," he said, and his eyes softened. "Jessie, I'm the one who put the towels over the mirrors in their rooms."

"And I took them down." She gasped. "I let him in."

Tom shook his head. "You don't know that. You didn't know who he was going after."

Jessica nodded. "He went after Emily."

"Did she tell you that?"

Jessica looked at him, opening her mouth and closing it again before she finally spoke. "No. Emily didn't tell me."

He looked at her in confusion, and when she avoided his eyes, shock and anger came raging back. "He told you? How the hell could he tell you?"

"Let it go."

"Do you have the same connection with him that Eric has?" When she wouldn't look at him, he knew.

He picked up the vacuum and stormed into the bedroom, muttering under his breath. He vacuumed up the remainder of the glass, turned out the lights and slid under the covers without saying goodnight to her.

HE STORMED OFF. JESSICA would deal with him later. She walked down into the living room and looked at her children sitting on the couch. Her eyes bore into Emily until she finally looked up.

"Why didn't you tell me?" Her gaze swiveled to Eric. "Either of you, why didn't you tell me?"

"Why don't you ask Tom that same question?" Emily snapped.

"What are you talking about?"

"Tom saw the ghost feeling me up on the set today," she said. "That's why he screwed up the party scene."

She would definitely deal with him later. "That's neither here nor there, missy," she snapped. "You should have told me about the ghost."

Emily cried. "He threatened to kill us all. And I didn't know about Ty."

Jessica closed her eyes. "I'm sorry for yelling." She sat down on the couch, shutting the television off. "Eric, it's time for you to go to bed. I need to talk with your sister." She leaned over and kissed his cheek. "I assume you're the one who introduced Emily to Ty?"

He nodded.

"Thank you. Now go to bed."

They watched Eric until he was out of sight.

"You didn't tell me Ty could do things," Emily said.

"He still doesn't know how to get rid of Frank's ghost, though."

"Do you?" Emily asked.

"No. All I know is to stay away from mirrors. The only one that doesn't seem to channel Frank is the one in my bathroom. That channels Ty." She shook her head and laughed. "God, this sounds like a bad horror movie."

Emily smiled a little.

"Why didn't you tell me?"

"He said he would kill you."

"What did he do to you?" she asked and when more tears slipped down Emily's face, Jessica's heart broke. "He raped you?"

Emily nodded.

Jessica wrapped her arms around her daughter. "He won't ever touch you again," she said as fury encompassed her. "That I promise you. We will find a way."

"You and Tom?" Emily whispered.

"No. Me and Ty." She knew he was the only one who could get rid of Frank. Jessica looked toward her bedroom and wasn't sure she and Tom would make it through this. "Do you need me to stay up with you?"

"I'm okay, Mom. Ty made sure of that." She smiled. "I want to meet him. To say thank you."

Jessica pulled away. "Em, I don't know about that." She took a deep breath. "If Tom and I make it through this, you will never meet Ty. I plan on getting as far away from him as I can." Her eyes filled with tears. "I can't say no to him, so I can't be near him."

"And if you and Tom don't make it?"

"I don't even want to think about that," she said. "I need to have a little chat with Tom, so if you don't need me to stay with you…"

"I'll be okay." She grabbed the remote and flipped the television on.

Jessica kissed Emily on the forehead and headed back to their room.

Tom glanced at her but didn't say a word. When she got into bed, he rolled so his back faced her.

"No way." Jessica flipped the light on. "You don't have the right to be pissed at me."

Tom rolled and looked at her. "What's your problem?"

"You didn't tell me about Frank." She watched his expression change. "That was a mistake."

"But Jessie…" He sat up.

"Uh-uh. She is my daughter. I had a right to know."

"I wasn't even sure if what I saw was real."

"Bullshit," she snapped. "You had the presence of mind to hang those towels. You should have told me."

"What would you have done?"

"I don't know. But you still should have told me."

"Who's bullshitting who? You would have run right to him. That's why I didn't say anything." He lay back down, turning onto his stomach with his face away from her, hugging his pillow.

"Tom, if you can't get past the fact that we need his help to get rid of Frank, we will never make it."

Tom turned his head toward her.

"I'll do whatever it takes so that bastard doesn't get another chance to rape Emily. Even if it means losing you."

Tom closed his eyes and sighed. "I'll do my best." He turned his head away again. "But if he touches you, I'll kill him."

Jessica rolled on her side and ran her hand gently over his back. She leaned over and kissed his shoulder, afraid of what he would do if he ever found out about what happened in Maine. "I love you."

Tom looked back at her. "I know you do." He leaned over and kissed her. "I love you, too." He rolled over and wrapped his arms around her, and she shifted within his grasp, so they were spooning each other. "Very much," he whispered and kissed the back of her head. "Good night."

Jessica lay in his arms with her eyes closed and listened to his breathing turn to light snoring, her mind rolling around what she may have to do to get rid of Frank. Her last thought before she slid into a restless sleep was of Ty's haunted gaze.

Mind Games Chapter 53

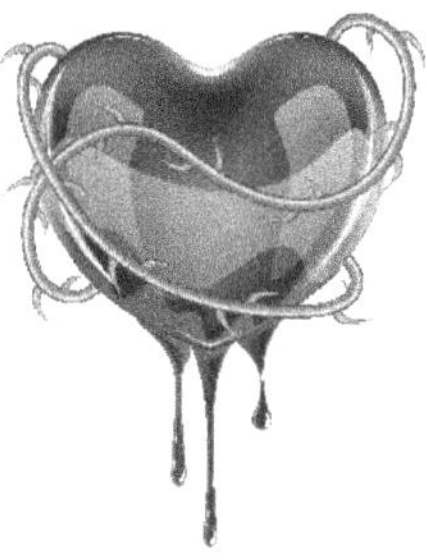

TOM SLIPPED OUT OF bed and turned the alarm off so Jessica wouldn't wake up, then got ready for work. Before he left, he sat on the side of the bed and looked down at her sleeping. He brushed the hair away from her face and leaned down to gently kiss her. "I love you."

She didn't stir, but a small smile appeared on her face. She rolled away from him and whispered, "Ty."

Tom closed his eyes and suppressed the urge to scream. He got up and left without another word. Anger alternated with a hollow despair pulsing in his chest. He tore out of the garage in his BMW Roadster, blaring the radio and squealing the tires. He drove fast, trying to outrun the feelings assaulting him. Above all, the turmoil was the certainty that his time with Jessica was coming to an end and, like the situation with Frank, there wasn't a damn thing he could do about it.

He peeled into the lot and slammed the brakes, sliding into his parking spot.

Stacy gasped. "Jesus, Tom!"

He got out and slammed his car door, then sent a glare her way. "Bad morning."

"I've never seen you like this."

"I've never felt like this," he grumbled as they walked in.

"Trouble at home?"

Tom nodded. "You could say that." He walked away.

"Tom?"

He turned to look at her.

"You know if you need to talk, I'm here."

"Thanks. But I've got to figure this one out on my own."

"It was nice to finally meet Jessica's kids," Stacey said with a smile.

"They are great, aren't they?"

"They both have potential. Eric is the cutest kid, and Emily is as beautiful as your wife."

"Jessica will never let them actually go into acting. She wants them to go to college, and I can't say I disagree."

"Mark wants her daughter in the show he's producing."

"It won't happen," Tom said, stepping into his dressing room and closing the door on the conversation. He glanced into the mirror and shook his head. "Jessie, what are you doing to me?" He went about pushing her out of his mind and getting himself into character for the show.

It was another long and grueling day on the set. Afterward, Tom slipped into his car, closed his eyes, and turned the key in the ignition. The radio blared, making him jump a mile and then laugh at himself. He turned the music down and headed home, expecting an equally grueling evening.

Mind Games Chapter 54

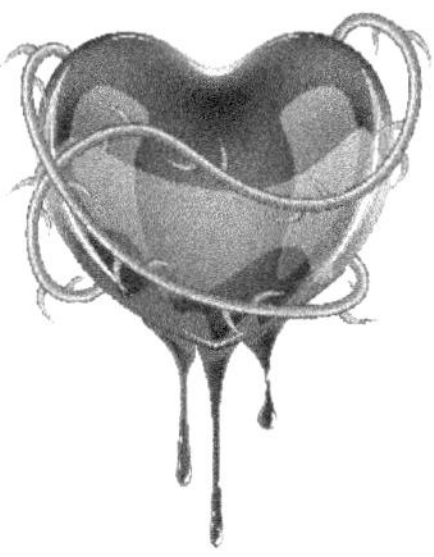

JESSICA WOKE TO THE noise of the television in the living room and Emily chattering on the phone in her room. She stretched and slid out of bed, then put on her workout clothes and headed into the bathroom to brush her teeth and hair.

In the mirror, her reflection stared back, and she let out a huff, half expecting him to appear. She leaned over and spit. When she stood, his blue eyes returned her gaze.

"I was wondering when you'd get your lazy ass out of bed," he said.

"It's only a little after nine here."

"Don't you usually get up early?"

"Have you been waiting in your bathroom all morning for me?"

Chris laughed. "No. I knew when you woke up."

"You knew when I woke up?"

He shrugged. "Yep."

"Okay, if you say so." She ran the brush through her hair and put it up in a ponytail.

"I know, it's strange. But then again, everything about this relationship is strange."

"It's a relationship now?" The next thing she knew, he had her in his arms again. "Ty, let go of me."

"Not until you start calling me Chris."

"You will always be Ty to me."

"Ty was a mean son of a bitch," Chris said. His smile faded. "I'm not anymore." A small smile spread across his lips again. "Well, not really."

"You still need to let go." She squirmed in his arms.

"Do you really want me to? Because I'm not getting that vibe from you."

Jessica stopped squirming and looked up at him. "Yes, that's what I want."

"You sure?" He leaned forward and kissed her.

She closed her eyes as his lips touched hers, the kiss as intoxicating as a fifth of vodka. She had to blink her eyes open when he pulled away. "I need you. I need you to help me kill Frank again."

Chris slowly let her go. "I'm not sure I can do that."

"He raped my little girl. I can't let that happen again."

Chris shook his head slowly. "I'm not sure, Jess," he said, his eyes filling with fear and doubt. "I don't know if I'm strong enough."

"Strong enough?"

Chris nodded. "Yeah. I don't know if I can."

"We need to try." She debated on telling him she would be in New York at the beginning of the week.

His eyes widened. "You're coming to the city?"

"Stop doing that."

"Sorry."

"Yes, I'll be in New York from Sunday through Tuesday."

"Will you have any free time?"

Jessica smiled a little. She had two days of free time. "Yes. Tom's busy during the day, and I have no desire to go with him on this one. He'll be back for dinner, so that leaves me some time."

"Shopping?"

"No, I'm not that big on shopping. I thought I'd go to the Met."

His eyebrows rose. "Museum?"

"Yes. Don't look so surprised."

"I just thought, a woman in New York with free time. Shopping was the obvious answer."

"I'm not an obvious woman."

His dimples made a brief appearance. "Can we meet for lunch on Monday?" he asked, blushing and transitioning back to his apartment in New York.

"Are you asking me on a date?"

He cocked his head and shrugged. "I can explain what I think we have to do, then."

"Okay. Where?"

"Where are you staying?"

"Uh-uh. I'm not meeting you at a hotel."

The smile that graced his face made her weak in the knees.

"Why not?" he asked.

Jessica blushed. "Public place."

Chris laughed. "How about the Four Seasons?"

Jessica nodded. She had only been there once with Daniel, but the food was superb.

"I'll meet you at the bar at noon?"

"You know they have a dress code?" She had never seen him in anything other than jeans.

"Don't worry, Jess. I clean up real nice," he said with a slight southern accent to bring his point home. "Go for your morning run." He faded away.

Jessica chuckled and turned to leave her bathroom, stopping abruptly.

Emily stood in the doorway, her eyes wide and her jaw slack.

"How long have you been there?"

"Long enough to know you're meeting him for lunch."

"Emily, you shouldn't eavesdrop."

"I want to talk to him now."

Jessica's mouth dropped open. "Don't you use that tone with me."

"Please," Emily pleaded.

With a heavy sigh, Jessica nodded. Against her better judgment, she glanced at the mirror. "Ty?"

"Forget something?" Chris's amused expression turned sour when he saw Emily in the room with Jessica. "Oh. Hi."

Emily looked at her mom and then back at Chris. "I wanted to say thank you." She looked down at the floor.

Within a blink, Chris appeared in the bathroom next to Jessica.

Emily stepped back, her eyes wide and frightened.

"Don't be scared," Jessica said.

"But, but…" She reached out and poked his chest. "He's in the room with us."

Chris laughed. "I'm sorry, but the look on your face is priceless."

Jessica smacked his arm with the back of her hand.

"It's funny," he said, shrugging.

"You have a broken arm?" Emily asked.

Chris smiled and held the cast up. "Yep, smashed the mirror in your mother's dance studio with it. That was before I knew I could do things with just a thought." He tapped his temple with his index finger.

"Can I sign it?" she asked, surprising both Chris and Jessica.

"I guess so."

Emily went running out of the room.

"WHAT THE HELL ARE you doing?" Chris whispered, sending a sideways glare at Jessica.

"She wanted to meet you."

Before he could respond, Emily was back with a black pen.

She took his arm, holding it out so she could write on the inside surface of the cast. She etched, *'Thank you for saving my life, twice. I will never forget you. Em'* into the fiberglass and stepped back.

Chris looked at the autograph on the cast in silence, blinking back the sudden swell of emotion making his vision blur. "Anytime." He looked over at Jessica.

I'll find a way.

He willed himself out of that room and stood in his bathroom, looking down at the message that Emily had written on his cast. The print was actually there on the fiberglass wrapping. He crossed to the living room and sat down on the couch, staring at the scrawled message. It was his fault Frank was haunting them. He didn't deserve this kind of thanks.

He looked out the window and thought about the girl he'd saved last night. She'd had the same look of awe and gratitude on her face as Emily had this morning.

Chris shook his head. "I don't deserve anyone looking at me like that."

He stood and headed out the door of his apartment. He needed some fresh air, and the sun was out, so a walk in the park seemed like just the therapy he needed.

His mind wandered back to Jessica. Lunch, he thought and grunted, crossing into Central Park. As he passed the Metropolitan Museum of Art, he stopped and stared at the entrance before glancing at his watch. He didn't have time to explore the museum today, so he continued his walk.

Maybe he'd show up on Tuesday and surprise her. The more Chris thought about her, the more he realized he knew very little about Jessica. Sure, he knew her birth date, her medical, dental, and marital history, even where she had worked before he kidnapped her. And in the time he had with her in the complex, he discovered her favorite color, that she hated to lose, and she hated sappy romance novels. Outside of that handful of items, though, he didn't know her, but he wanted to spend the rest of his life finding out the little things.

The small smile that had formed with his reminiscing faded, replaced by a melancholy, hollow feeling in his chest. He wasn't sure he would ever get the chance to have what he wanted.

Mind Games Chapter 55

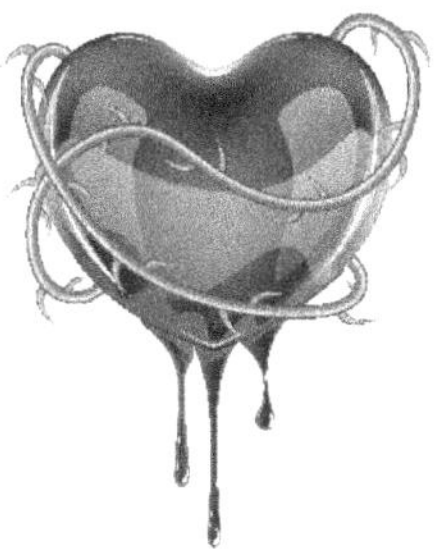

JESSICA QUIETLY READ A book while she soaked up the sun, but after every line in the book, Chris's blue eyes interrupted her progress. Her thoughts drifted to the feel of his hands on her skin, his lips on hers, and she had to take a deep breath and sweep the thoughts away. After reading the same line a dozen times, she snapped the book closed.

"I'm going for a walk," she said to the kids and tied a sheer wrap around her waist, wandering down to the water's edge.

She walked slowly, watching the waves roll up onto the sand as the gentle breeze swirled her hair around her face. The Pacific didn't have the same strong seaweed smell at low tide as the Atlantic, and the beach was more granular than the fine sand in York.

Jessica stopped and sighed, wishing she were on the other side of the country on her beach instead of this sandy white stretch in California. She missed her home.

"You're a difficult woman to track down." A female voice startled Jessica. Sharon Young stood a few feet away, and she had a pad and paper in her hand.

Jessica recognized her instantly; she had been relentless five years ago.

Jessica let out a little laugh. "What are you doing here?" she snapped and started toward the house.

"I wrote the script," Sharon said, making Jessica pause and glare over her shoulder. "I saw the videos."

"And?" Jessica turned halfway toward Sharon.

"There were things that couldn't be explained. Do you care to comment?"

Jessica fully turned, stepping toward her. Her head inclined as she glared up over her sunglasses. "No, I don't care to comment."

Sharon laughed. "I wouldn't think so."

Jessica didn't like her tone, but turned back toward the house.

"You did something, didn't you?"

Jessica felt her anger turn up a notch, and she turned back toward Sharon in disbelief. "Excuse me?" She slowly took off her glasses.

"I saw the videos," she repeated.

Jessica stared her down. "I don't know what you're talking about."

"Something happened in that room, and I think you did it," Sharon said. "He told Tom that you would make a miracle happen. I heard him."

Jessica shook her head. "I have no idea what you are talking about. And I am livid that you would try to make a quick buck off what happened down there. I bet you even insisted that Tom play the part. Didn't you?"

Sharon smiled. "You bet I did."

Jessica tilted her head and slid her glasses back on. "It will take a hell of a lot more than this to break up our marriage. And isn't that what you're really after?"

Sharon's expression dropped a little. "I could show him the videos."

"Tom knows more than you think."

"Then why did he call me asking to see them?" She smiled sweetly back at Jessica.

She didn't show it, but the statement rattled her. "He took the part. He'll want to study what he can to get more of the flavor of exactly who Ty Aris was."

"He called before he accepted the part."

"What's your point?" Jessica took another step toward her and saw fear flash in Sharon's eyes. "Oh, that's right, you want Tom to yourself." She laughed and then gave her a deadly glare. "You won't get Tom just because you have videos of those animals raping and beating me. If anything, he will better understand what I did to survive."

"It's such a tragic love story," Sharon stated, feigning pity.

"Love had nothing to do with it. Now, if you will excuse me, this interview is over." She turned and walked back toward the house.

"Just one more thing I thought you should know."

Jessica kept walking.

"I slept with Tom five years ago, in return for leaving you alone."

Jessica stopped short. She took a deep breath, put her game face on, and slowly turned. Sharon stood with her hands on her hips, smirking.

"I don't really care what happened five years ago," Jessica said, her voice coming out as a low growl in her throat. "But if you think you're going to get a second chance with my husband, you've got another think coming." She stalked over to where Sharon stood. "I really wouldn't mess with me if I were you," she threatened with a smile and removed her glasses completely, sending Sharon back a couple of steps. "Now I suggest you get the hell away from me before I do something *you* will regret."

Sharon backed off, her walk turning into more of a run. She shot wary glances over her shoulder like she half expected Jessica to be right behind her with an axe.

Jessica watched until she was out of sight and then headed back to the house. She passed by the kids and went inside to take a shower without saying a word.

So that's why they all miraculously backed off my case five years ago.

Tom said he pulled some strings, but Jessica never suspected he had crossed the line. She wondered what other favors he did to get the wolves to back off. She closed her eyes, feeling the anger simmer just below the surface, telling herself that she had no right to be upset with him after what she had done recently.

From inside the shower, she heard Chris call her softly, and she shut off the water. She stepped out and looked in the mirror, not bothering with a towel. "What do you want?"

Chris stared at her. "I... I can see you're okay. I'll talk to you later." He turned to go.

"Don't." Jessica reached for a towel.

"Don't what?"

"Don't go yet."

"What's wrong?"

Jessica looked at the ceiling. "I just ran into a reporter on the beach." She glanced at him. "She wrote the screenplay and has the videos of what went on."

"You know, I can shut the entire thing down if you want me to," he said. "At least the use of the actual complex."

"How?"

"When I sold Aris Industries, I put a stipulation in the contract stating that they couldn't use that space for anything. They were actually supposed to destroy it. I have a right to sue for breach of contract. All you have to do is say the word."

"It would bring way too much attention. Neither of us needs that right now."

"It would also bring me a hell of a lot of money."

"Don't you already have enough money?"

Chris shrugged. "But it would be fun."

"You're such an ass sometimes."

"And here I thought I was an ass all the time," he shot back, making her smile a bit.

But her smile disappeared again. "Tom slept with the reporter."

"You slept with me."

Heat flushed her cheeks. "You don't need to point that out to me." She paced in the small space in front of the mirror. "He slept with her five years ago to get her to back off the story."

"You slept with me five years ago, too."

Jessica glared at him. He wasn't helping. "I had little choice in the matter then."

"Jess, you can't be upset with something that Tom did five years ago. And he had the right intention. He was protecting you."

Chris was right. Tom had the right intentions, but he still went about it the wrong way. "Having the right intention doesn't always make it right. Besides, she's a real bitch."

Chris smiled. "Ah, that's why this is bothering you."

"Fuck you," Jessica snapped.

Chris stepped into the room. "Gladly."

"Go back to New York."

"If you say so." He disappeared from the room and reappeared in the mirror. "Jess, you know I'd like to see your marriage end for the obvious reasons, but this isn't something you should get upset about. Were you even married to him at the time?"

Jessica thought about it. The reporters had backed off about a month before they were married. "I don't think so, but it had to be within a month of the wedding."

"Give the guy some slack."

"I don't know if I can."

"It was five years ago, Jess. If you can't let it go, then you can't expect him to forgive you if he ever finds out about what happened on the beach."

"He will kill you if he finds out about us, and my marriage would be over instantly. Tom hates you, truly hates you."

"With good reason. I killed his first wife, and I'm in love with his second wife. If the tables were turned, I'd feel the same way."

"How many people *did* you kill?"

"Too many," he mumbled. "I'll be paying for those sins for eternity, but for now, while I'm still alive, I'm just trying to do a little good to make up for all the bad." He offered a half-hearted smile. "Still, I'm no angel."

Jessica nodded.

"Your daughter threw me for a loop yesterday. The way she looked at me, as if I was some sort of hero." He laughed. "Me, a fucking hero. That's laughable. The girl in the alley looked at me the same way, and I don't deserve that kind of treatment."

Jessica cocked her head to the side. "The girl in the alley?"

"I saved a girl who was being attacked by three guys."

"What'd you do?"

"I killed them. Vaporized. Nothing was left but dust."

She gasped. "Ty?" she said, disappointment lacing her tone.

"They deserved it." He crossed his arms.

"You can't do that."

"It was self-defense. They raped that girl, and one guy shot at me. I just let loose."

"He shot you?"

"The bullet never made it to me. I'm amazed I didn't hurt the girl when I lost control, but I vaporized the bullet, the gun, and the guy. I told you, if you had a clue of how to use this power five years ago, you would have killed me."

"You don't control it. It controls you."

He smiled at her. "You're wrong, Jess. It's all just a matter of degree. The degree in which you control your temper is directly related to the degree in which you have control over the power. It's a lot like the healing power. You can control the level that you release into someone to heal them. It's not all or nothing. And exercising the ability also increases the level of power and makes it more precise."

"You've been exercising the power?"

"You bet. If I'm going to be in a position to send Frank back to hell, I better damn well know how to control and use what you gave me to get it done. Otherwise, we are both dead."

Jessica shivered.

"You should get some clothes on," Chris said. "And cut Tom some slack. He's a good guy. If you can forgive me after everything I've done, it should be a cakewalk for you to let this go."

"Thanks. It's nice to have a friend to talk to about this stuff."

Chris smiled. "Friend, huh?"

"Yes. Friend," she said. "I don't have many."

"That's a surprise. I would have thought you'd be surrounded by friends."

"I know a lot of people. But I don't have any who I confide in. I certainly don't have anyone who I can talk to like I can with you."

"Outside of Tom, you mean?"

She shook her head. "We don't talk like this. Until recently, we didn't talk about what happened to us. Don't get me wrong, we do talk, but it has never come easy when it's about that period."

Chris looked down at his hands.

"You hurt me, physically and emotionally. He saw that, and it's hard for him to understand how I could forgive you, much less love you. So, we don't really talk about it," she said, watching as he avoided her eyes.

"I don't even understand it." He looked up at her.

"You don't?"

"I never understood how you could remain so..." He struggled for the right word, "Kind." He shook his head in frustration. "That's not the right word." He thought for a moment and his eyes lit up when the word came to him. "Grace. You have grace, and I don't mean just in the way you move. It was in the way you spoke to me, and looked at me, even when I hurt you. There was definitely anger and defiance, but underneath, there was always faith and grace. Which, to be honest, in the beginning, I just wanted to beat out of you." He looked away from her. "But in the end, that's what got me. So, I know why I love you. I just don't understand how someone with such faith and grace and goodness could ever love me."

"I saw beneath the anger and indifference. I saw your soul, and it wasn't the same as the monster you were in there. It was the man standing before me today."

Chris's eyes filled with tears. "You really are my angel."

"Ty, I'm not an angel. I've done things. I've killed, I've lied, and I've cheated, so don't put me up on a pedestal."

"You did those things because of me."

"Killing, yes, but I lied and cheated long before you came along." She laughed at the shock on his face. "I loved Mike for years. Granted, we never acted on it beyond a kiss, but I still technically cheated on my husband."

"Jess, without you, I would still be that monster."

"You don't know that."

"Yes, I do. We would have continued until we either got caught or were killed." He took a deep breath. "So, even though you may think you've fallen, you are still my angel. I'm trying like hell to be Chris Ryan, but there are some things that just won't die. You need to get dressed. Because if I have to look at you standing there in a towel any longer, I'm coming through this mirror and will do something we both will regret."

"One more question."

"What's that?"

"Have you been with anyone else?"

Chris looked at her for a long time and then shook his head. "I'm not answering that question."

"Why not?"

"Because, frankly, it's none of your business."

Her mouth dropped open. "I'll see you in a few days." She walked out of the room in a huff.

CHRIS WATCHED HER GO, smiling. She hadn't expected him to respond like that. He didn't want to tell her he hadn't slept with anyone else since he left the complex five years ago. He certainly had women throwing themselves at him, especially when they found out he was rich, so he could have his pick of several beautiful women, but he didn't want anyone else.

If Jessica knew, he would give her all the control. He couldn't do that, no matter how much he loved her. He needed to protect his heart from getting crushed because he knew how this game would end.

Mind Games Chapter 56

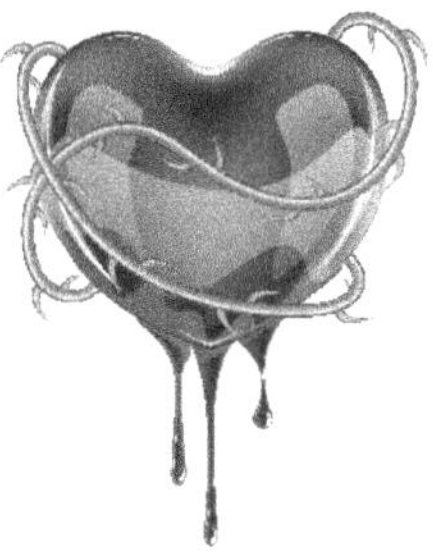

TOM CAME HOME TO find Jessica sitting on the deck with a drink in her hand, looking out over the Southern California sunset, the children happily playing video games inside.

"Did you have a good day?" he asked and went to kiss her hello.

Jessica turned, so he kissed her cheek instead of her lips like he'd intended. "It was good until Sharon Young ambushed me on the beach."

He recoiled in shock.

"You slept with her, Tom?" Jessica stood and walked down to the sand.

Tom followed. "It was the only way to get her to back off." His heart pounded in his chest. He knew how much Jessica disliked Sharon. "Besides, we weren't married yet."

Jessica turned and looked at him with a healthy dose of anger in her eyes. "But we were planning on getting married, weren't we?"

Tom nodded and looked at his feet. "I'm sorry. I didn't know what else to do."

"How many times over the last five years has she come calling for favors?"

"Many, but that was the only time I gave in." He let the silence fall between them.

Jessica turned her back on him. "She has the videos?"

"Yes."

"And you asked to see them?"

"Yes."

"Why?"

"Because I need to know how much of the script is true." He put his hands on her shoulders. "If it is, I can't fathom why you don't hate him like I do."

"Some of the videos are missing. You wouldn't get the complete picture, even if you saw each and every tape she has."

"What are you talking about?"

"Chris was involved with the operation."

"But they cleared him of all wrongdoing."

Jessica laughed. "Ty erased everything that would incriminate him." She turned toward him. "You won't see the first time Ty put me in the room with Chris and Frank. I didn't know they were his brothers at the time, and I was drugged, so I put on a good show to piss him off. That's why the phrase 'never in a million years' was so paramount to our relationship. I didn't just say it to him in the electric chair. I said it in that room to Ty after I screwed his brothers, and he wanted some action." She took a deep breath. "That was the last time he allowed anyone else to touch me. I told you I played some serious games with his head, too. Ty was pissed when he found out that Frank raped me. You won't see the video of him beating the crap out of him because Chris was also in the room."

Tom stared at her.

"Ty started protecting me long before he realized he was in love with me. So, you can go see those tapes, but you will never have the full picture." She walked back toward the house.

Tom followed her and grabbed her arm. "He raped you, Jess."

Jessica nodded. "Yes."

"How do you get past that?"

"You know as well as I do why he did that."

"I'm not talking about when the three of us were in that room. I'm talking about you tied to a mattress and saying no, and him not listening."

She rolled her eyes. "He stopped, Tom. He never... completed the act. Besides, that wasn't rape."

"Yes, Jess, it was. No means no."

"Except when you're tied to a bed and the man seducing you just wants to hear the word yes. He just wants you to admit what he already sees in your eyes. That's not rape. That's a survival game."

Tom closed his eyes. He would never understand. "All right. I guess I'll never get it." He studied the harsh tilt of her eyebrows, the tight set of her lips, and the anger in her eyes, making the swirl of colors darker, more ominous. "But I expect the same thing from you where I'm concerned."

Jessica raised her eyebrows.

"I expect you to let it go, and forgive me where Sharon is concerned."

Jessica closed her mouth. "I will, eventually." She headed back inside.

Tom followed her in, feeling like a scolded puppy. He half smiled at the kids. "What's for dinner?"

Jessica glared at him over her shoulder.

"Okay, you guys want to go out?" he addressed the kids, ignoring Jessica.

"Sure. Where?" Eric switched the video game off.

"We could go to Planet Hollywood if you'd like?"

Jessica rolled her eyes, and Tom smiled. He knew she wouldn't want to go to such a touristy place, but it would be fun for the kids.

"That would be so great! Do you think we will see any movie stars?" Eric asked in awe.

"What am I, chopped liver?"

Eric smiled. "You know what I mean."

Tom laughed and nodded, crossing and wrapping his arms around Jessica's waist from behind. "You game, babe?"

"Sure," she said.

Usually, Tom hesitated before using the kids to his advantage, but this time he didn't. They needed the diversion.

He caught Jessica's reluctant smile. "I figured it's the last night here with the kids, so we might as well do something fun with them."

"Classic avoidance." She glanced over her shoulder at his grin. "Okay, I'll let it go. But if she comes near us again, I'm going to slug her."

"Fair enough," Tom said. "Can I have my kiss hello now?" He leaned over and kissed her before she could answer.

THEIR DINNER WAS FILLED with colorful conversation and the laughter of the children as they ate at the restaurant. They saw a couple of movie stars, and both Tom and Jessica rolled their eyes at the kids' excitement. After all, they were just people. Eric giggled each time someone came to the table to get Tom's autograph.

Jessica stopped laughing when Sharon Young walked in. Tom put his hand on her knee when she approached the table, shooting Jessica a look that said to keep her cool.

"Well, well, well. If it isn't the happy family." Sharon smiled smugly and stood behind the children's chairs.

Jessica's hands balled into fists under the table.

"Back off, Sharon," Tom said, his voice clearly sending the warning out.

Eric looked from his mother to Tom and then to the woman standing behind him, and his eyes narrowed. "You're the reporter bitch that wouldn't leave my family alone."

Emily's mouth dropped open.

"Eric, you don't speak like that to a stranger," Jessica scolded.

Eric looked back up at the woman. "But she wants to ruin your marriage, Mom."

Sharon took a step back, looking at Eric like he was a large, deadly bug.

Tom smiled. "Sharon, this is not the time or the place for this discussion. And I don't appreciate you ambushing my wife on the beach. We had a deal."

Sharon smiled. "That was five years ago and now, with the movie, she's fair game again. Perhaps another favor is in order?" She raised her eyebrow at him.

Tom shook his head. "Not happening, Sharon." He gripped Jessica's knee tighter as she started to get up.

Jessica knocked his hand away and got up, heading toward the restrooms in a silent rage.

That bitch has the audacity to ambush me here? She stopped in the middle of the restaurant and turned back to the table. *Bullshit!*

Sharon had her back to her, and Jessica tapped her on the shoulder. When Sharon turned, she punched her in the face and then stormed off to the restroom with a small smile of satisfaction playing on her lips.

Sharon's nose had broken under the force of her fist.

TOM LOOKED AFTER JESSICA and grinned. Sharon stood there holding her bloody nose, screaming, while the staff ran back and forth in confusion.

He got up, threw some cash on the table, and looked at the kids. "Time to go," he said, then crossed and stopped next to Sharon. "I told you to back off." He headed toward the restrooms to collect his wife.

Jessica came out of the bathroom and Tom stood a few feet away, a smile plastered on his lips.

"Hell of a right hook," he said.

Jessica shrugged and looked at the commotion at their table. "Where are the kids?"

"I sent them to the car." He put his arm around her waist, escorting her out of the restaurant with a big grin on his face. "I kind of like seeing you jealous."

Jessica elbowed him in the side hard enough for him to sidestep away from her. "I told you I'd slug her if she came near us. I think I broke her nose."

Tom looked back over his shoulder as they got into the car. "Hope she doesn't have you arrested."

Jessica burst out laughing. "She wouldn't dare."

"You punched her, Jessie." Tom's smile disappeared.

"She was propositioning you," Emily said from the back seat. "Mom had every right to smack her."

Tom looked in the rearview mirror at Emily.

Jessica turned in the seat and looked at her children. "I'm sorry. I shouldn't have done that. Not in front of you."

Emily smiled at her mother. "It's okay, Mom."

"No, it's not. I didn't handle that very well." She looked over at Tom. "That reporter was relentless five years ago, and Tom got her to back off."

"By sleeping with her," Eric said.

Tom nearly swerved off the road in surprise.

Jessica looked at her son. "We've all made mistakes," she said, her eyes penetrating and intense.

Eric nodded slowly, giving in to her will. "Sorry."

Tom drove in silence. He hated they knew what he had done, even though it was to protect their mother. It wasn't something he was proud of by any means. He looked over at Jessica, his eyes conveying the regret he felt. She reached over and took his hand.

"We've all made mistakes," she said again, squeezing his hand.

Mind Games Chapter 57

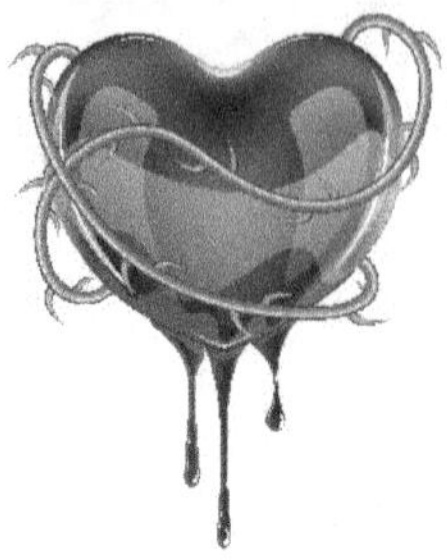

THE NEXT MORNING JESSICA woke before Tom did and lay watching him sleep. She traced his lips lightly with her fingers and then combed his hair back with her hand, leaning in and kissing him gently.

He stirred and smiled sleepily at her.

"I love you, Tom," she said, feeling the weight of her own mistakes. "I'm sorry I got so mad yesterday."

"It's okay, babe." He yawned and stretched, glancing toward the clock. Then he reached over, pulled her close, and snuggled with her.

"I still feel safe in your arms," she whispered.

Tom kissed her neck, nuzzling as his hands wandered. He gently pulled at her underwear, and when he looked up, she saw the lust in his eyes. He rolled, pulling her on top of him.

Slow, sweet, morning sex, riding him somewhere between asleep and awake, sensual and surreal. She arched into him, purring and stretching through three rounds of hitting the snooze button. Surfing the wave until they came together, moaning and collapsing on each other.

The alarm went off again.

"I have to go to work," Tom said.

"I know." Jessica smiled down at him, but made no attempt to move.

He rolled her off and got up, stretching as he stood.

She pulled the covers back around her and curled up in the warm sheets, closing her eyes again and slipping into sleep.

JESSICA OPENED HER EYES to the bedroom in Maine, her arms tied to the bed. Chris was strapped to a chair. Fear jolted her as Frank's knife carved the crooked scars back into his cheeks.

"That's the Ty I know." He looked over at Jessica. "I'm going to fuck the life out of her while you watch."

She shivered, her heart driving terror to every pore and her gaze traveling between the knife and Chris's frantic eyes.

"But before I do..." Frank slammed the knife into Chris's leg, and he cried out in pain. "I promise you'll see her die before you do." Frank yanked the knife from Chris's thigh.

"No!" Jessica screamed, watching the blood pump out of his leg, spurting with every beat of his heart.

Both his panic and her own gripped her when Frank turned his sights on her, advancing with malicious intent.

SHE SAT STRAIGHT UP on the bed, the scream escaping from her. Her eyes darted around the unfamiliar room and landed on Tom as he skidded from the bathroom, a towel around his waist and his face half covered in shaving cream. The momentary tightness in his stressed features smoothed out.

"Nightmare?"

Jessica nodded, and he came and sat on the edge of the bed, running the back of his fingers gently across her cheek.

"Jesus," she said through short bursts of breath, shaking.

"You okay?"

"No." She glanced at her husband. "I think we die. Oh God, I think we die."

"We aren't going to die, Jess." He pulled her to him.

"Not you, Tom. You weren't there."

He went rigid against her and pulled away, his jaw clenched with frustration, and then he turned and crossed to the bathroom without another word.

Jessica walked into the bathroom a few minutes later and reached for her toothbrush with a trembling hand.

"That bastard ruined a perfect morning," Tom said.

Jessica's gaze flicked from him to her reflection, and she nodded, thinking he was referring to Frank. Her skin had a pale pallor, dulling her calico eyes in a haze of fear.

Tom rinsed his face and met her gaze in the mirror. He blinked and stood straight. "What did you see?"

"Frank. Frank tied him to a chair and stabbed his leg. I think he hit an artery. There was so much blood. He said Ty would see me die before he did. And then Frank came for me." Tears blurred her vision, and a pained sobbed escaped. "That's when I woke up." She buried her face in Tom's chest.

Tom slowly wrapped his arms around her. "I won't let that happen, Jess. You aren't going to die," he said, but his voice belied his words. He kissed the top of her head and squeezed her. "So much for the perfect morning, huh?"

Jessica nodded against his chest and pulled away, wiping her eyes. "If something happens to me, promise you'll protect Emily."

"Nothing is going to happen to you."

"Promise me, Tom."

Tom met her gaze. "I promise," he answered and hugged her. "But nothing is going to happen to you."

"Thank you."

"I have to go. I'm already late." Tom glanced at his watch. "I'll have a car here when I get home. The flight takes off at eight." He kissed her and left.

Jessica splashed water on her face and reached for a towel to wipe it off.

"You had the nightmare, too," Chris said, making her jump when he appeared in her bathroom.

Jessica nodded, and hot tears painted her face again.

Chris wrapped his trembling arms around her. "That means when it happens, I have less than five minutes to kill Frank, and get to you, before I bleed to death," he whispered into her hair. "I'm not sure I can do this." He disappeared.

"Ty?" She sobbed. He didn't answer her. "Chris?" she corrected. "Please."

He looked back at her in the mirror, silent, but his eyes still carried the horror of the dream. "I have to go, Jess. I'll talk to you later."

"I need you to be okay."

He smiled a little. "I will be," he said, and his smile faded. He looked at his watch. "I have to go."

Jessica nodded and watched him disappear.

She slipped into her running gear and left the house. It was still very early, not yet six on the West Coast. She became lost in the sound of the breaking waves as she ran alone on the quiet beach. His words kept resounding in her ears *Less than five minutes before I bleed to death.* She let out a little sob.

She walked slowly back up the stairs after running for what seemed an eternity and grabbed one of the beach towels to wipe her face. The kids were up and flipping through the television channels as she walked in.

"Hi guys." She smiled and blocked her mind. She didn't want to worry Eric.

Jessica stepped under the warm water with her thoughts three thousand miles away. "God, Chris," she whispered with her eyes closed. And could almost feel his arms wrap around her. She kept her eyes closed as she felt his lips on her neck and heard him whisperer her name.

Her eyes flew open, and she turned to an empty shower stall, gasping.

CHRIS STOOD IN HIS shower stall with his eyes closed and a smile on his face. He had heard her and felt her and kissed her and whispered her name. He looked up as he turned the water off, still holding the shower rod with his broken wrist.

Mind Games Chapter 58

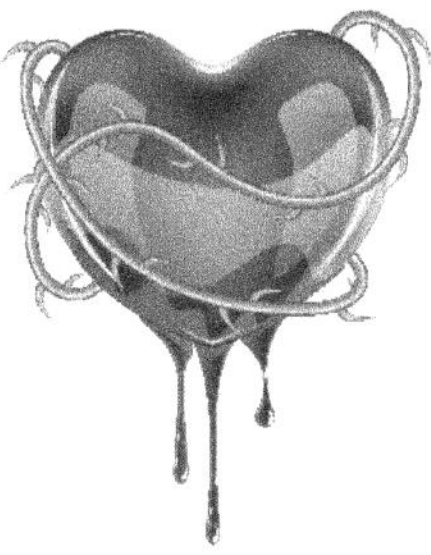

THE TRIP BACK EAST was uneventful. They all slept soundly on the plane and landed in Boston as the sun came over the horizon.

"Oh man, I hate losing that time." Tom groaned and stretched the sleep out of his limbs.

Jessica stirred and looked at him with sleepy eyes. "We're already there?"

He nodded. "And we have another hour or so on the road." He stood and grabbed their carry-on luggage, then shook Emily and Eric awake. "Time to get moving." He yawned.

They departed the plane and headed down to the luggage turnstiles; then collected their own bags this time and carried them out to the truck in the parking garage themselves.

Tom laughed as the kids groaned. "You can't always be spoiled like we were in L.A. Sometimes you just have to do things by yourselves."

Both Emily and Eric rolled their eyes at him.

"And this coming from the pretty, plastic person," Jessica teased.

He mouthed the words *bite me* at her and smiled.

The kids were sound asleep again by the time they hit the 93N interchange from the airport, and Jessica was asleep as he turned north on Route 95.

Tom turned the radio up, singing softly as he drove. Jessica mumbled in her sleep as he rolled through the tolls in New Hampshire, and he turned the radio down to see if he could make out what she was saying.

"Enlighten me," Jessica purred in her sleep.

Tom looked over at her and saw her smile, and he had the feeling that he wasn't the one starring in her dream. "Jess," he said loud enough to startle her out of sleep.

Her eyes fluttered open, and she looked around and then back at him. "What's wrong?"

He glanced over at her. "You were talking in your sleep again."

"Oh."

"What were you dreaming about?" he asked, trying to sound nonchalant.

"I have no idea."

He snorted in the driver's seat.

"Did you just snort at me?"

He glanced at her.

"Why'd you snort at me?"

"You know damn well."

"Are you upset with me?"

"You were dreaming about him," Tom said. "Again."

Jessica looked back out the window and sighed. "I can't help what I dream about, Tom."

"I thought after five years you would have let him go."

JESSICA WATCHED THE WATER as they drove over the bridge into Maine. The sign for York Harbor brought a wave of feelings she didn't expect and every single one of them revolved around Chris Ryan.

She looked back at Tom. "I'm sorry." She looked back out the window.

"Stop apologizing, Jess, and start letting go." He flipped on the blinker for their exit and then stopped at the light at the end of the exit ramp.

The kids stirred in the backseat.

"Are we going to Dan's first?"

Jessica looked at the clock. "Sure," she answered and looked back at her children, who were stretching and looking around.

"Are we going to tell him?" Tom asked.

Jessica looked back at Emily. "I wouldn't know what to tell him."

Tom seemed at a loss as well. "What about the mirror in her room?"

"There isn't one in my room," Emily said, overhearing the conversation.

Jessica nodded; there weren't any in the kids' rooms when she lived there, either, just in the master bedroom and bathroom. "I think she'll be safe there." She smiled. "Did they replace the mirror in your bedroom at home?"

"Not that I know of."

"Don't let them until you hear from me," Jessica said as they pulled into Daniel and LeAnn's driveway.

"Don't worry, Mom. We'll be all right," Eric said.

They got out of the car as Daniel and LeAnn stepped out of the house. Hugs and kisses were exchanged, and Tom grabbed their bags from the car and carried them into the house.

"We had a great time," Emily said to LeAnn.

"Will you stay for breakfast?" Daniel asked.

"Thanks, but I think we'll pass," Tom said.

Daniel laughed. "Did the kids drive you nuts?"

Tom shook his head. "No, the kids were great. I just have a long week coming, and I'd like to get a little rest before it begins. By the way, you may want to tape the show this week." He smiled at Eric and Emily. "They both have cameo appearances."

Daniel looked over at Jessica. "Really?"

"They were superb, Danny," Jessica said. "So much so that the director wants them in his next project."

Emily and Eric's heads swiveled toward their mother.

"I said no," she said. "You can make that choice after college if you still want to go that route." She walked over and gave each of them a hug. "I'll see you next weekend."

Daniel and LeAnn exchanged a look.

"We made other plans next weekend," Daniel said. "I hope that's not a problem?"

"What plans?" Jessica asked.

"We're going to see my parents and wanted to bring the children," LeAnn said.

"That's not a problem," Jessica answered after a moment. It would give her some much-needed time alone with Tom.

"'Bout ready, hon?" Tom asked.

"We'll see you in a few weeks." Jessica smiled and kissed Emily and Eric goodbye. "I love you."

"Love you, too," both children said in unison.

EMILY YAWNED AS SHE watched them drive away. "Mind if I go take a nap?" she asked her father and stepmother.

"Go ahead," Daniel said.

Emily picked up her bag, went to her room, and closed the door behind her. She crossed to her closet and put her suitcase away. The mirror on the inside of her closet door caught her eye a little too late. She felt the ice-cold hand cover her mouth before she could utter Ty's name.

"I've missed you," Frank's ghost whispered in her ear, and she shivered. "You were very bad the last time I saw you, calling on my brother for help." He reached around with his other hand and unzipped her pants, then pushed them down.

She tried ramming her elbow into him, but while she felt him holding her, her elbow seemed to pass through the air behind her. She tried to call Ty's name, but his hand muffled her cries.

He laughed. "Your attempts to escape me are pathetic." The blade of a knife dug into the skin on her neck. "And I wouldn't even try to call his name if I were you, unless you have a death wish."

Fear struck her silent. The futile cry died in her throat, replaced by a dull throb as her heart pumped faster in her chest. Even with a knife to her throat and a hand over her mouth, he still was able to drop her pants.

"Now, if you call him when I take my hand off your mouth, I will slit your throat before he can help you. Understand?"

She nodded and only let out a small whine of protest, but she didn't call out, not with the cold blade pressing on her skin. She cried silently, and in her mind, she screamed for her brother to help her.

The doorknob to her room moved.

"Emily?" Eric asked from the other side of the closed door.

"Make him go away," Frank said, pulling her up against him, keeping the knife in place at her throat.

"Trying to get some sleep," she called out, willing her voice not to shake.

Eric, call Ty, NOW.

ERIC HEARD HER SILENT plea, closed his eyes, and screamed the name in his mind.

"All right, I'll see you when you wake up." He made shuffling noises with his feet, as if he were walking away.

He looked toward the living room where his folks were happily watching the morning news. Inhaling, he focused back at Emily's room and charged, throwing all his weight through his shoulder and into the door.

Mind Games Chapter 59

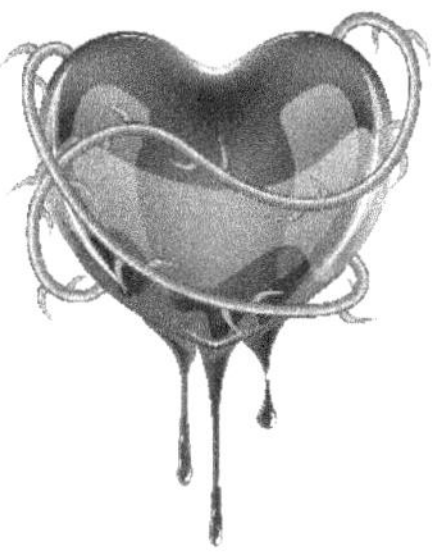

CHRIS SAT ON HIS couch, watching the morning news when the volume and power of Eric's scream barreled through his head, making him wince. He flew into his bathroom and focused on the mirror, and Emily's bedroom at the cottage came into sharp focus.

Frank had her laid over the side of the dresser, pumping his hips into her relentlessly. Before he could say a word, the bedroom door came crashing in, and with it came Eric.

"Let her go, you son of a bitch," Eric growled, and the bedroom door slammed shut behind him as he caught his balance. Eric's fierceness took all three of them by surprise.

Frank pointed the knife in his direction. "You're next."

"I don't think so," Chris said from the reflection in the mirror.

Frank turned, dragging Emily with him. The knife dug into the soft flesh of her throat.

"You can explain to her mother," Frank said.

The knife slowly moved away from her skin despite the muscles in Frank's arm straining against the invisible hand. Chris wasn't the one controlling the knife, and his gaze swiveled to Eric.

Eric had his hand close to his throat and was pushing his palm away. Sweat beaded on his forehead, and blood dripped from the cut in his hand.

"Jesus," Chris whispered and looked back at Frank, sending his own signal to break the mirror.

THE MIRROR SHATTERED AND Frank disappeared. Emily quickly pulled on her pants and ran to Eric before her parent's footsteps reached her bedroom.

"You stopped him from hurting me." Emily stared at the deep gash in his hand.

Eric's eyes rolled back in his head, and he fainted. Emily caught his limp body just as her folks barged in.

"Dad, Eric cut his hand pretty bad," Emily said as Eric blinked back into consciousness.

"How the hell did that happen?" Daniel snapped, his gaze traveling to the broken mirror and back.

"We were roughhousing," Eric said. "And I lost my balance and broke the mirror."

Daniel looked from Eric to Emily and back. "You're going to need stitches for that, and then you two will spend the rest of the day in your rooms."

Emily and Eric exchanged a glance.

Daniel hauled Eric to the hospital, leaving LeAnn and Emily at the house to clean up the glass.

"We should let Mom know," Emily said.

"She doesn't need to be bothered with this," LeAnn said.

"She needs to know."

"Your father and I will make that call. You need to stay in this room and think about what happened." She walked away, then closed her bedroom door behind her, leaving Emily frustrated.

"The hell with that." Emily walked out of her bedroom and picked up the phone, then dialed as she looked defiantly at LeAnn.

LeAnn took a step in her direction.

"Don't even think about it," Emily warned. The endless rings of the house phone sparked panic in her, and she slammed the phone down in the cradle, staring at it like it was a king cobra ready to strike.

Oh, shit—he's there!

Her frightened thought pushed her muscles into action. She spun toward the door, taking off and running at full tilt toward the beach and her mother's house.

Mind Games Chapter 60

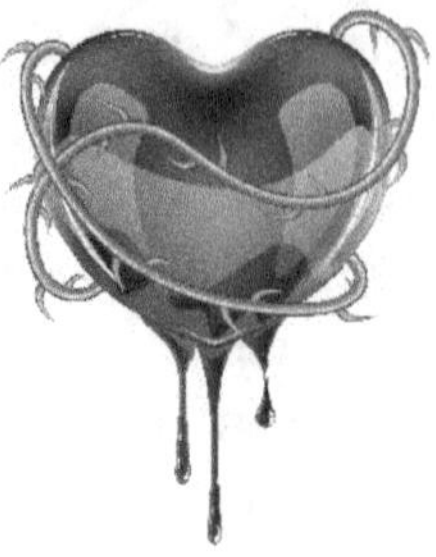

JESSICA AND TOM DROVE to their house in silence.

"I think I'm gonna go for a run." Jessica walked inside and held the door open for Tom.

"Want company?" He carried their bags to the bedroom.

"I'd love some." She went into the bathroom to put her hair up.

"I'm looking forward to a quiet weekend." Tom sighed as he pulled on his running apparel and watched her do the same.

"Me too." She grabbed her iPod out of her carry-on bag.

They headed out. She handed him the speaker, and they jogged side by side down the street and onto the beach as the music played.

"I'm sorry if I upset you on the drive," she said.

"I really shouldn't let it bother me as much as it does."

Jessica looked over at him with a small smile. *God help me if he ever finds out.* She looked toward the road. Emily was running at top speed down the sidewalk, dodging the people walking in her path. Even from this distance, Jessica could see the panicked expression on her face.

She stopped in her tracks, making the earbud yank out of Tom's ear as he passed by.

"Now what?"

"Em!" she called at the top of her lungs.

Emily's head whipped around, and the panicked wild-eyed expression smoothed some. She slowed, climbing down the next set of stairs onto the beach. Tears streaked her cheeks.

Jessica jogged to her. "What's wrong, honey?"

Emily fought to catch her breath. "Eric, cut." She gasped. "Frank." That was all she could get out before she sat down hard on the sand.

Jessica's heart went cold as she kneeled in front of Emily. She tried not to let her daughter see the fear those words had caused. "Does he need me?" she asked, looking toward the cottage.

"No, he's okay. Just his hand is cut." She got her breath back. "Dad took him to the hospital to get stitches." She put her hands on her knees and her head on her arms for a second. "I forgot about the mirror in my closet, and he stopped Frank from killing me."

"Ty?" Tom asked from behind them.

Emily shook her head. "Eric." She looked at her mother. "Ty made Frank disappear by breaking the mirror, but Eric stopped Frank from slitting my throat." She shook her head. "I'm not sure how, but the knife cut his hand instead of my neck."

Jessica remembered another time that Eric had put himself behind the tip of Frank's knife and shivered. "Did Frank..." She couldn't bring herself to ask the question.

Emily nodded, and the tears picked up.

Jessica wrapped her arms around Emily and looked up at Tom. His gaze hardened, and he turned away.

LeAnn pulled up to the curb and got out of the car. "Young lady, you get in the car right now."

Jessica stood, putting herself between Emily and LeAnn as Tom turned back around.

"Go home, LeAnn," Jessica warned, causing LeAnn's mouth to drop.

"I don't know what she's told you, but she's grounded for the rest of the weekend because of what she and Eric did."

Tom took Jessica's arm as she went to step toward LeAnn.

Jessica snapped her head around and looked at him. "Let go," she said, her teeth grinding together.

He shook his head a little and gave her a warning glare. *She doesn't know,* he thought.

Jessica heard him, and her eyes softened. "Thanks." She turned back to LeAnn. "LeAnn, why doesn't Emily stay with us for the night?"

"I don't think that would be appropriate, considering. Danny said she wasn't to leave her room. Did she tell you he's at the hospital with your son?"

"Yes. She also told me what happened," Jessica said. "And believe me, LeAnn, you don't know what's really going on. I will not let Danny punish the kids for this. It wasn't their fault."

LeAnn looked at Jessica in shock. "How can you say that? They were roughhousing, and Eric broke her mirror and cut his hand pretty badly. I'd say that's cause for punishment."

"That isn't what happened," Jessica said.

"Then what did?"

"All you need to know is that I'm going to take care of it," she said. "And keep my kids away from mirrors," she added. "I'll talk with Danny."

"Mirrors?" She looked at Jessica and then Emily. "Does this have to do with the mirrors breaking at the house when you were there?"

"Yes."

Jessica turned to Emily. "You go home with LeAnn. I promise I'll make this go away." She raised her gaze to LeAnn. "Take her home and take care of her," she said, relinquishing her daughter into the care of her stepmother. Jessica turned and headed back to their house with Tom in tow.

"What are you going to do?" he asked when they entered their bedroom.

"Stay here," she commanded and walked out of the bedroom and into the guest room where Emily had slept before they left for California. After locking the door behind her, she walked into the center of the room, glaring at the mirror.

"I'm right here, you son of a bitch. Come and get me!" she roared, and he didn't disappoint her.

This time, Frank physically appeared in front of her and grabbed her by the throat, then threw her into the wall.

"I've waited a long time for this," Frank snarled, and he barreled down on her, yanking her from where she landed.

Tom started banging on the door and yelling her name.

Jessica spun out of Frank's grasp. "You raped my little girl. I'm going to send you back down that hole you crawled out of." She drop-kicked him in the crotch, and he actually lifted off the ground when her foot connected.

Frank's ghost recovered quickly from the blow and grabbed her by the hair, dragging her to the bed. "You are going to pay dearly for that," he hissed, tossing her down and ripping her shirt in the process. He produced a knife out of thin air and started toward her. "I'm going to cut you to pieces."

TOM THREW HIS SHOULDER against the door, but it wasn't opening against his repeated attempts. The sounds inside the room turned his blood to ice. He leaned his back against the door and bellowed Ty's name at the top of his lungs.

Mind Games Chapter 61

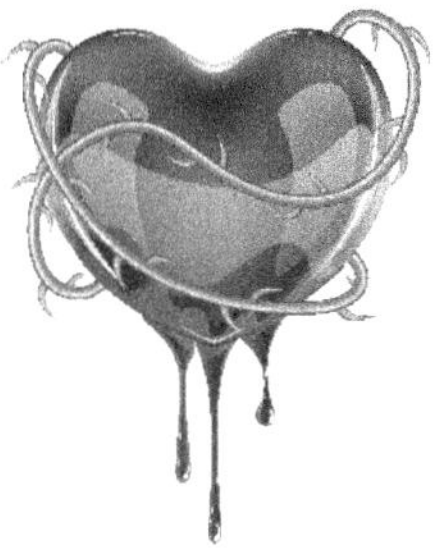

CHRIS PACED IN HIS bedroom, trying to figure out what had happened. Eric had nearly blown his brains out when he screamed his name, a lot like Jessica had done in the complex. The pounding in his temples left a dull ache, remnants of Eric's siren.

Chris continued the restless path back and forth between his bedroom window and the bathroom, turning over what had happened in his head.

He needed to talk with Jessica, but Monday seemed like an eternity.

He walked over to his bedroom window, looked out at the Manhattan skyline, and sighed. They had to do something about Frank, regardless of the stakes; he had to send that son of a bitch back down the hole he crawled out of. Chris shook his head as the end of that phrase passed through his mind in Jessica's voice.

He looked curiously toward the bathroom until he heard Tom cry out his name, then he bolted.

JESSICA ROLLED AWAY FROM the arc of the knife and onto the floor, her face a mask of fury that Chris didn't recognize. She grabbed the lamp and pitched it at Frank. The lamp broke on impact.

Frank yelled with the same level of fury and launched at her. She spun out of the way again, but the knife caught her in the side, drawing blood. Countering his move, she slammed her elbow into Frank's face and twisted away. Frank went down.

She backed up against the far wall. Her gaze locked on Chris's and that connection knocked his senses into high gear. Silently, he sent the command that burst the mirror into a thousand tiny shards.

Mind Games Chapter 62

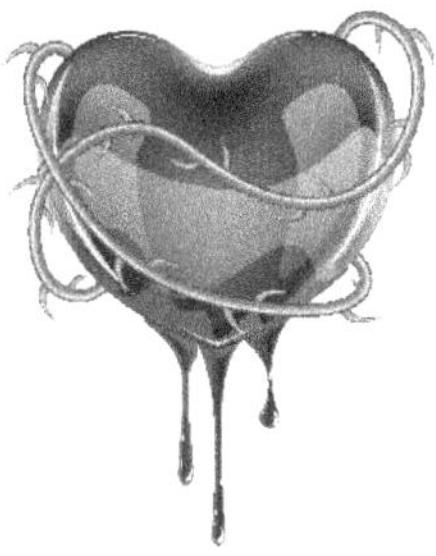

THIS TIME WHEN TOM threw himself at the door, it gave and flew open. Jessica stood on the opposite side of the room, hair in her face, shirt ripped, blood dripping from her side, and her chest rising and falling. She roared in fury, tossing her head back with the force of it, and stormed past Tom. He followed her into their bathroom.

"Why the hell did you do that?" she screamed at the mirror.

Tom's blood ran cold when the image in the mirror changed. Instead of the furious reflection of his wife, Ty's hard blue eyes stared at her.

"He would have killed you, Jess," Chris said.

"Then I would have dragged him to hell with me," she shot back, her entire frame shaking with the flurry of anger raging inside her.

Jesus, this is fucked up, Tom thought.

Chris met Tom's stare. "Yes, this truly *is* fucked up."

"I want him dead!" Jessica bellowed, her entire form leaning forward with the force of it.

Tom heard the mirror in the other guest room shatter, and his mouth dropped.

"Just so you don't do something stupid like that again," Chris snapped at her.

Jessica screamed and then spun, throwing a punch at the wall. She buried her fist in the drywall. After pulling her hand out, she cradled it against her chest, leaning against the wall with her forehead. "I want to kill him. He cannot EVER touch her again, even if it means I have to die to get it done."

Chris clenched his jaw.

Her words sent alarm racing through Tom's blood, and he glared at the image in the mirror. *You'd better goddamn well fix this mess, understand?*

"I'll figure out a way." Chris's image faded.

Tom pulled her to him, feeling her resist at first, and then give in, allowing him to wrap his arms securely around her. "Don't ever do that again. Ever."

She shook in his arms and the terror that had gripped him when he couldn't get into the guest room faded.

"I don't know what I'd do if anything had happened to you, Jessie," he said into her hair.

She broke his grasp, crossed to the bathroom, and turned on the shower, stepping in with a warning glance. It was not a look of invitation.

He turned and sat in the chair in the bedroom, waiting for his turn in the shower.

The last few weeks flowed through his mind while he looked toward the bathroom. Things clicked in his head. He slowly got up and walked in, then opened the shower door.

"How many times have you talked to him like that?" He pointed over his shoulder at the mirror.

Jessica just looked at him, anger still radiating off her, but it had been tempered by the hot shower.

"How many times?" he yelled at her, his anger brewing for different reasons.

"Back off," she shot back, glaring.

He blinked. "What?"

"Back off."

He stepped into the shower with his clothes on and cornered her. "I will not back off. You are still my wife." He leaned his arms on the wall next to her, fire flaring. "I don't like this at all, Jessie. You'd better damn well remember who you're married to, or otherwise you'll be out on your ass so fast it will make your head spin," he growled low, and stormed out of the shower, leaving her shaking against the wall.

Tom sat in the chair in his dripping clothes, fury churning in his belly. He glared at her when she stepped into the bedroom wrapped in a towel. "You never answered my question."

She took a deep breath. "Let it go."

He shook his head. "Not in a million years," he said, using her words against her.

Jessica winced and took a step backwards.

He stood up and started toward her, peeling off his wet shirt. He threw it on the floor and grazed her from head to toe with his eyes. "You're my wife. Mine, not his. Understand?"

She nodded and put her hands on his chest to keep him at bay, but he wasn't in the mood to be denied. He yanked her closer. "If you ever cross that line with him, you can kiss this goodbye."

Crushing her lips with his, he kissed her passionately, stripping the towel off her and guiding her to the bed, hell-bent on making sure she knew what she'd be losing. He threw the covers back and swept her onto the mattress. Every stroke of his hands, every swipe of his tongue, every whisper from his lips, a deliberate act to bring her to a level she hadn't been before with him.

Teasing her, he ran his tongue slowly down the side of her neck from her ear to the nape, listening to her suck in air as goose bumps appeared and she shivered. He smiled wickedly and met her gaze, taking her breast in his mouth and rolling his tongue around her hard nipple, suckling, nibbling until she moaned his name.

His fingers caressed her, slow enough for her to add her own hip circles to his touch. Anger and desire fueled him, creating a sensation of heat that he didn't think possible. He trailed his lips down her stomach, lingering at her belly button, discovering its depth and breadth with his tongue.

He kissed her inner thigh, sucking, creating a small hickey before sliding his lips over her, blowing a small stream of air. She whispered his name again. When he moved to her other thigh, he made a matching hickey, making his claim known in the marks on her skin.

Slowly, he licked the length of her vulva, parting her with his tongue, exploring, tasting until she arched into his mouth, the air sucking into her lungs each time he passed over her sensitive bud.

He rolled his tongue over her again. "Is that what you want?"

She gasped. "Yes, oh my God, yes."

He flicked his tongue over her bud and slowly penetrated her with his fingers. She moaned and her muscles wrapping around his fingers with a rush of slickness, but he wanted her dripping and begging. He met her intense gaze.

"Oh God. Please Tom, I want you."

He smiled and continued his quest to make her want him more than anyone on earth.

With her hand laced in his hair, she writhed under him, her hips matching the movement of his hand, and she arched with each orgasm. A healthy sheen of sweat covered her skin, mingling with the salty taste of her.

She gasped after the fourth orgasm. "Please, Tom, oh God, please make love to me."

He moved his mouth from between her legs to her breasts and then her lips, covering her moans and plunging deep inside her.

They moved together, the kiss blending with their frantic heartbeats, and he pulled away, slowing down, gaining control again as the reason for this ecstasy surfaced. He ground his hips into hers, pulling his length out and then just as slowly sliding in balls deep.

"Jesus, Tom!"

He smiled and raised his eyebrow. The next round, he slammed his hips into her and stopped, grinning as she arched and called his name. She wanted him to move faster, but he slowed down, relishing her pleas and her half-closed eyes glazed with rapture.

The fire inside him flashed into an all-consuming inferno. He could no longer control his passion. He sped up, the volcano churning in his belly, and finally exploding inside her. Every muscle seized at the strength of his orgasm, and he groaned her name, pressing the length of his throbbing member inside her. After shocks gorged him, setting his arms into trembling risers. He rolled, pulling her on top and collapsing beneath her, his arms lying out by his sides like lead weights.

Air rushed in and out of his lungs, fueling the exertion and sending oxygen to the far reaches of his trembling flesh. He couldn't think of another time that even came close to matching this sweet satiation.

He met her gaze. "I love you, Jessie."

She smiled. "Thomas William Whitman, you sure know how to make the earth move."

Tom laughed. "We both need a shower now."

"Mm-hm." She rotated her hips in a slow circle, grinding into his groin. "Not yet." She kissed his sweaty chest.

"Do you want to kill me?"

"No, I want to fuck you," she whispered slyly.

He responded to her crude purr, hardening again under her hip gyration.

"You have the energy?"

She nodded. "I'm the Energizer Bunny, remember."

God, how could he ever forget *that?*

She'd run them ragged day after day in the complex, better than any personal trainer he'd ever had. He ran his hands up her thighs and hips to her waist, sliding along her sweat-slicked skin, fueling his need for her.

His anger became lost in the lust in her eyes. She ran her fingers gently over his chest, causing a shiver to ripple through him. His gaze traveled from her face down the front of her, landing on the hint of a scar on her side. He traced it with his fingertips before looking back into her eyes. The magnitude of the stunt she'd pulled today crashed down.

"You scared me today."

"I'm sorry," she whispered, and the playful glint in her eyes turned serious.

He sat up, kissing her, his tongue exploring the depths of her mouth. A content groan rumbled in his chest under the sweetness of it. He broke the kiss, lying back and letting her set the pace.

Rolling her hips, she slowly made love to him, alternating between kissing his lips and sucking his earlobes. He studied her, memorizing the intensity of the moment. When he couldn't stand her slow seduction any longer, he sat up, wrapping her legs around him, and slammed his length in her over and over, watching her eyes roll back in her head with each thrust.

They came together, fingers digging into flesh and cries of released passion mingling on the air.

Tom fell back on the bed, drained of all energy. She laughed, seemingly energized by the activity.

"Jeesh, doesn't anything tire you out?" he asked.

Jessica laughed. "Nope. Want to go again?"

Tom laughed. "I don't think I can."

"Awwww, are you tired?" She rolled on her side.

"Very." He smiled and pulled her closer, kissing her forehead. "Nap time, then I'll think about it." He closed his eyes again. Sleep dragged him into darkness within seconds.

HIS LIGHT SNORE SIGNALED to Jessica that he was asleep, and she slipped out of his grasp, then covered him with the sheet before she headed to clean up. Her eyes lingered on the mirror, and she chastised herself. After the amazing sex she'd just had with her husband, Chris should be the farthest thing from her mind. But he wasn't. He was there, lurking in the shadows, tainting the pleasure.

Tom was right—she had never let go. With the warm water cascading down her skin, she wondered if that was possible, or if their fates were entwined to the point of no return. The connection certainly was undeniable.

"Damn it!" She shook her head angrily. There he was again. Why couldn't she just erase the history, the need, the love? Her nails dug into her scalp as she lathered her hair, scratching relentlessly, trying to wash him from her thoughts.

Tom might forgive her for the beach because she had been drunk, but there was no excuse for what happened at Chris's house. If he ever found out, she would lose him. She wouldn't make that mistake again. The warm water did nothing to wash away the guilt in her soul. That was something she would have to carry around forever, whether or not she liked it.

Finally, she turned the water off and stepped out, reaching for the towel with fingers that looked like prunes. Thick steam filled the bathroom, and she wiped a swatch from the mirror. It took a second for her to realize the eyes looking back weren't hers.

"Are you okay now?" Chris asked.

Jessica nodded. "You have to go. We'll talk at the restaurant."

Chris sighed. "I've never seen you like that. You really lost it there."

"He hurt my babies."

Chris nodded. "But you put yourself in a position where Frank could have killed you. Then who would keep your kids safe?"

"You," Jessica said without hesitation. "You would keep them safe."

Mind Games Chapter 63

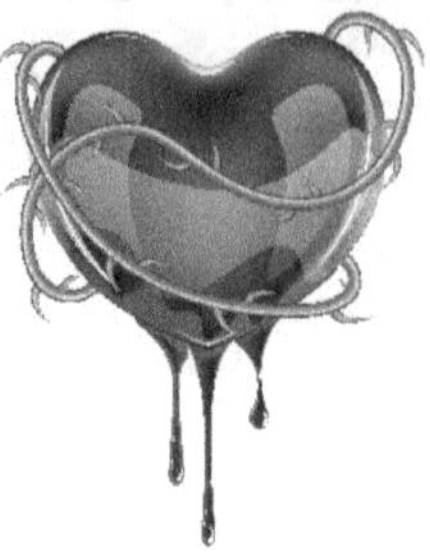

THE PHONE RANG, AND Tom reached over and grabbed it off the hook. "Hello?"

"Is Jessie there?"

Tom held the phone out, his sleepy eyes meeting hers as she crossed from the bathroom. "It's Dan."

She took the phone. "How's Eric?"

"He's in his room right now. What the hell is going on?"

"You shouldn't punish them," Jessica said.

"So LeAnn tells me, but I still don't understand what the hell she was babbling about."

"Danny, I can't really explain..."

"Did you know the hospital gave me the third degree?"

Jessica closed her eyes. She could imagine the questioning he'd had to endure if they thought foul play had occurred.

"They said it was a clean slice, not something that would happen with the explanation he gave. I've been through the wringer today, Jessica, and this 'I can't really explain' shit isn't going to fly."

"It wasn't their fault. It was mine."

He laughed. "Yours? How, Jessie?"

"I can't explain, but they aren't safe if there are mirrors in their rooms," Jessica replied, knowing she sounded crazy.

"What the fuck are you talking about?"

Tom sat up and held out his hand for the phone.

Jessica relinquished the phone to Tom, a rarity for her, but she was tapped out. She couldn't listen to Daniel reaming her after the day they'd had.

"Dan," Tom said. "Just hold your horses." He listened, keeping eye contact with Jessica. "I know you're upset, and you have every right to be... But you need to understand. I know, but..." Tom closed his eyes and his teeth clacked together in frustration. "Dan, just shut up a second," he finally snapped. "Your kids are great kids, so cut them some slack. What happened today was not remotely their fault, and I understand the need to have boundaries, but in this case, it doesn't apply." He took a breath. "And what Jess told LeAnn about mirrors is extremely important." He waited. "I know. It doesn't make sense, but it still is important." He laughed a little. "We'll fill you in someday when this is all over." He nodded and handed the phone back to Jessica.

She took it. "We'll be by in a little while to see him, okay?" She hung up, focusing on Tom. "I can't believe you did that."

"I'm not completely useless." He smiled and rolled out of bed, heading for the bathroom.

Jessica waited on the deck for him, scanning the ocean and concentrating on not swinging her gaze to the south. Toward *him.* But her thoughts went there anyway, falling back on the nightmare she'd had the other day. She shivered and rubbed her arms.

"You ready?" Tom asked from the doorway.

Jessica turned, watching while he folded up the sleeves to his neatly pressed gray oxford. "I should have called earlier."

"You were a little preoccupied."

Heat filled her cheeks, and she smiled, then approached him and wrapped her arms around his waist, rising on her toes to catch a kiss. "Let's go."

"Do you mind walking?"

"Not at all."

It was only a couple miles from their place down to Daniel and LeAnn's cottage. Jessica and Tom held hands, listening to the sounds of the ocean, walking along the ridge of sand just shy of the high tide line.

"I need to say something," Tom said, interrupting the comfortable silence. He looked out at the water and stopped, letting go of her hand.

"What is it?"

Tom took a deep breath and locked his gaze with hers. "I was serious earlier."

"I know you were."

"I just wanted to make sure you understood the consequences."

"I do."

He held her gaze. "Just so we are perfectly clear. If you ever give in to him, I *will* file for divorce."

The pounding of her heart in her throat made it difficult to swallow. She nodded. "I understand."

They walked the rest of the way in silence.

ERIC SAT ON THE front stoop waiting for them.

Jessica looked at his bandaged hand and wrapped her arms around him. "I'm sorry, baby." She took his hand and went to kiss it, but Eric pulled it away.

"No, Mom, you're going to need everything you have to save you and Chris." He looked at his mother and then up at Tom and smiled awkwardly.

"It's all right," Tom replied, although it was anything but all right.

Eric held his gaze. "It really isn't good to hold on to that kind of hatred."

Tom looked away.

"He only wants to help us," Eric added.

Tom's gaze snapped back to Eric, and his jaw tightened. *That's not all he wants.*

Eric didn't respond to Tom's last thought because he was right. "Really, Mom, I'll be just fine."

Jessica looked up at Tom. "Can you check on Emily?"

He nodded and stepped into the house.

"Chris said you stopped Frank from killing Emily." Jessica sat down next to Eric and put her arm around his shoulders.

"I did," Eric replied.

"You surprised the hell out of him."

"I know."

"How do you know?"

Eric smiled and looked at her. "Mom, I know a lot more about you and Ty than either of you knows." His eyes bore into her. "I can get into your heads anytime I feel like it."

Jessica's mouth dropped open.

"You really shouldn't have done what you did. That was dumb. You can't fight Frank without him, Mom. He has to actually be there, not just a reflection in the mirror." He inhaled. "You can't stop Frank alone. He *will* kill you."

"You know how we can stop him?"

Eric nodded. "Ty does too. He has for a while."

Anger welled up inside her, and her hands balled into fists. *Chris knows how to stop Frank, and he hasn't yet?*

"Don't be angry with him. It's dangerous, and he doesn't want to put you in the position he needs to," Eric said. "I don't want to see you hurt, either, but it's the only way."

Jessica closed her eyes and took a deep breath.

"You were meant to be with him."

"No, Eric. I was never meant to be with a killer."

Eric laughed. He looked at her long and hard, the colors in his eyes swirling slowly. "You are the only one who can save him from himself, and he is the only one who can save you from Frank."

Jessica glanced at her hands and then off toward the south where his house was.

"Besides, you love each other."

"Eric, I love Tom," she clarified, but deep down, he'd struck a chord.

"You think you do, but it's not the same, and you know it."

"I'm not discussing this with you." She gently touched the bandages on his hand.

"Don't worry, it'll heal just fine."

"How did you get to be so grown up?"

He leaned over and kissed his mother's cheek. "I'm not grown up, Mom." He looked away. "I just happened to have the curse of seeing bits of the future along with the other things I can do." He glanced at her. "I suppose that's part of what I inherited from you."

Jessica smiled a little. "I suppose."

Mind Games Chapter 64

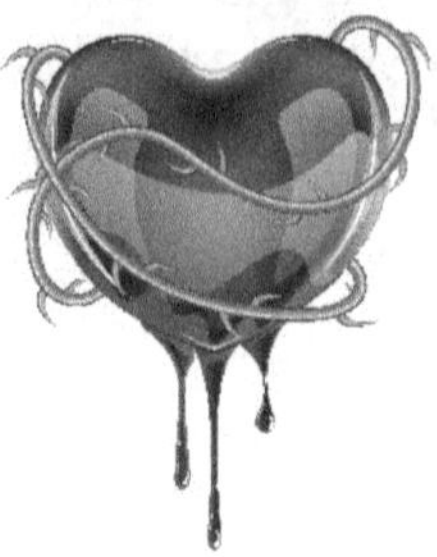

CHRIS LOOKED OUT AT the moon rising over the city and smiled. He wasn't going to pass up a Saturday night on the prowl, especially after the morning he'd had. He threw on his leather jacket, pocketed his keys, and headed out to rid the city of some trash.

He wandered slowly through the park, and when he heard the hammer click on the gun pointed in his direction, he laughed softly. He slowly turned to see the strung-out kid who he'd run into earlier in the week. The kid's eyes went wide.

"You still trying to score?" Chris knew this kid wasn't a killer, just a petty thief.

He nodded, and the gun shook.

"Put the gun away." He decided to see what would happen without using his power.

The kid lowered the gun and put the hammer back in its resting place.

"What's your name?" Chris asked.

The kid looked around and then back at Chris. "Matt."

Chris put his hand out. "Give me the gun, Matt." When Matt handed him the gun, Chris smiled. He flipped the safety on and slid the gun into the waistline of his pants at the small of his back, and pulled his jacket down to hide it from view. "You need to get yourself into rehab. You're too young to waste your life like this."

The kid shuffled back and forth, his eyes darting around. "I just need a fix."

Chris shook his head. "I'm not going to help you get that. But I will bring you to a place where you can dry out."

"I don't want to dry out." He backed away.

Chris tilted his head. "Yes, you do." He sent a little push.

Matt blinked a few times. "Okay." He allowed Chris to lead him to a local drug and alcohol rehabilitation facility, where he checked himself in.

Chris peeled off enough cash for Matt to complete his rehab and handed it to the receptionist.

"Who are you?" Matt asked in awe.

Chris smiled. "Just think of me as your guardian angel." He turned to leave.

"Thanks, man."

Chris looked over his shoulder and nodded. "Any time, kid."

He left the facility and headed back toward the park. He didn't think his next encounter would end as pleasantly as the one with Matt. He thirsted for the thrill, and just like Matt's addiction, Chris was compelled by the high of ultimate control. Before the night was over, he would feel that power again, and the thrill wouldn't be disappointing.

Chris swung by his apartment and dropped the gun on the counter. He ventured out again and jumped onto the train, heading into a crime-laden section of the Bronx. He was met with hostile glares as he got off the subway and headed up to the street.

"You lost, boy?" an old bum asked as Chris passed by him on the stairs.

"Nope," Chris answered and continued on his journey without a second look.

It didn't take long for trouble to find him. When he felt the tip of a knife touch his side, he pushed the power outward, sending the knife and his assailant flying. He turned and looked at the man who'd tried to stab him.

He scrambled away from Chris, his eyes wide with fear, and he grabbed for the discarded knife on the pavement.

"I wouldn't try that again if I were you."

"What the hell are you, man?" He stood, holding the knife in front of him, pointed at Chris.

"Your worst fucking nightmare." Chris probed inside the man's mind, finding the justification that he was looking for.

The power shot out like an invisible hand and wrapped around the thug's neck, cutting his air off. The man turned blue, and his body shook with oxygen-starved spasms. Chris sent out another jolt, and the man's neck snapped, instantly killing him.

Chris walked away leisurely with a smile on his face. He continued his stroll down the streets until he heard something in the alley ahead. Fearlessly, he entered the dark path between the buildings, dodging the trash bins and garbage strewn on the ground. The alley's dead end held five men beating the crap out of a younger man.

Leaning against the corner of the building, he crossed his arms. "You might want to ease up there," he said, startling them.

The younger man looked up through swollen eyes at Chris as his legs gave out from underneath him. He fell to the ground, drawing their attention back to him. One man went to kick him, but the snap of his knee filled the sudden silence. He burst out screaming, crumbling to the ground and holding his useless leg. The rest of the men looked at him, stunned into inaction.

Chris walked up to the younger man and helped him up while the rest of the crew stepped to help their fallen comrade. He gave them a warning glare and started out of the alley with the beaten man. Chris heard a sound he was becoming familiar with and turned his head toward the thugs.

"You really don't want to do that," he growled low in his throat as he looked down the barrel of a 9-millimeter.

"We don't have a beef with you, but that boy there, we aren't finished with him."

"Yes, you are." Chris turned his back to them.

The report of the gun was lost in the rush of scorching air he let loose. The bullet never reached him, and the man holding the gun never knew what ended his life so abruptly. Neither did the other four standing behind him.

The beaten man looked back at the swirl of dust in the alley. "What happened to him?" he mumbled through his swollen, bleeding lips.

"Dust." Chris offered no more explanation. "What did you do?" He asked as he helped the man to the far corner.

"Wrong place, wrong time," the man said, causing Chris to study him closer.

"Bullshit." The man had tried to pick pocket one of those men, and he was trying to do the same to Chris. "And I wouldn't touch my wallet if you know what's good for you."

The man pulled away and looked at Chris closely. "Who are you?"

"I've been referred to as the Angel of Death a time or two." He smiled, amused by the analogy given his recent adventures. "But tonight, you can consider me your own personal guardian angel." He checked his pocket. His wallet was still there. "Just stay out of trouble," he warned and walked off into the night shrouded in fog.

Chris wandered down into a more residential area of the Bronx. A child's scream caught his attention, and he turned toward a house with open windows.

The child kept repeating, "Daddy, please don't hit me."

Chris could see enough in the front window, and when the man belted the boy, sending him across the room, Chris flashed back to his own childhood.

It was rare for Ty and his stepfather, Jacob Aris, to be alone together at the house, never mind bonding in any fashion. However, on this particular Sunday, they were watching an intense match- up between the Buffalo Bills and the Denver Broncos. Both cheered for the Bills and added colorful commentary to the game. It was the fourth quarter, and the Bills were trailing by a field goal with less than two minutes on the clock.

Buffalo was making a run down the field when Jacob decided he wanted another beer. "Get me a beer," he ordered from his recliner.

Ty hesitated, his eyes still glued to the television.

"Go get me a beer!"

The fun of the day ended abruptly when Ty glanced at his stepfather. The mean-spirited glare told him that this wasn't a request that could wait. Ty got up, moving as fast as he could to grab the last beer from the refrigerator so he could see the rest of the game. As he approached the chair, the beer slipped from his hand and smashed on the hardwood floor.

"You stupid son of a bitch!" Jacob shot out of the chair, swept the bottle neck off the floor, and approached Ty. His hand curled into a fist as fury took hold.

When Jacob swung, Ty ducked.

Jacob stumbled forward, and his fist caught nothing but air. His second attempt was more focused and caught Ty in the chest, sending him onto the floor.

His head bounced with a thump on the hard wood, and stars filled Ty's vision. When his eyes focused again, they widened in terror. The sharp edge of the bottle was an inch away from his eye. Jacob's knee pressed against his chest, pinning him to the floor.

"You little shit! You broke my last beer!" The sharp point of the bottle moved closer to Ty's eye with every angry word.

When Jacob raked the glass down his face, ripping the skin from under his eye to just below his jawbone, the pain was worse than anything Ty had experienced in his young life. A wail of a scream barreled out of his chest.

"Shut the fuck up!" Jacob bellowed and stood, towering over Ty, pointing his finger. "Next time you'd better not drop my drink."

He pressed his hand to his burning cheek, tasting the coppery slick blood as it oozed into his mouth from his severed skin. His vision tripled as he pulled his hand away. Blood dripped off his palm, making his stomach lurch.

His hand returned to his cheek, to where the scar had been, that vivid feature that had disappeared five years ago with Eric's magic. His stomach rolled.

The man in the house swung at the child again. Chris let the power loose as the fury came back full force. The man inside the house exploded into a million tiny bloody pieces.

Chris turned and walked away, shaken by both the memory and the strength of the power he'd let loose. He could still hear the child screaming from a block away.

He slipped down to a subway station and headed back to his Manhattan apartment. The gun still sat on the countertop in his entryway. He stared at it and, for the first time in his life, the thought of ending it all entered his mind. He picked up the gun and looked into the barrel thoughtfully.

How many people have I killed in my lifetime? What's one more?

He looked at the shroud of night over the city and back at the gun with a measure of indecision. The autograph from Emily inscribed on his cast caught his eye, and Chris slowly put the gun back down.

He walked out onto the balcony and leaned on the railing. "What the hell am I doing?"

Mind Games Chapter 65

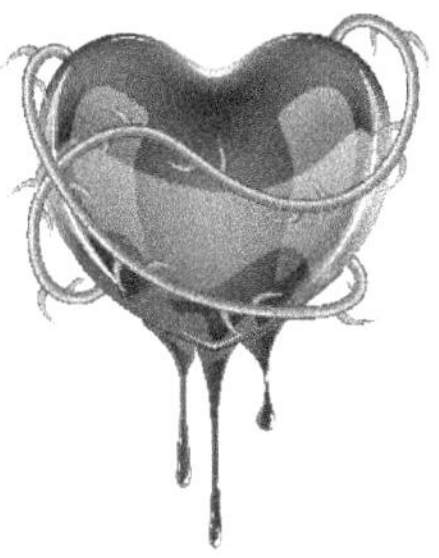

"CHRIS?"

Chris rolled over in his bed. He didn't want to talk with her with the events from last night too fresh in his mind. She would know the moment she saw him. He closed his eyes again and turned onto his stomach, ignoring her.

"Come on, I know you're awake."

He looked back toward the bathroom and sighed. "I'm coming," he mumbled and climbed out of bed. "What?" He looked sleepily at her reflection.

She blinked and stepped back, her eyes scanning his bare chest and then jumping back to meet his face. "Are you okay?"

"Not really." He looked away from her swirling calico eyes.

"What's wrong?"

"Just had a rough night," he replied without looking at her, his mind going back to the gun.

Her eyes widened. "Please don't!"

"Don't what?" He met her gaze, not knowing whether she was referring to the thoughts of suicide that had gone through his mind or the fact that he had killed again.

She stepped forward and transcended into his bathroom, taking his hands. "Don't even think about it. I would miss you."

He pulled her close. "I don't know if I can live without you in my life," he whispered, letting her into his mind, into his tortured soul. He wrapped his arms around her and put his head down on her shoulder in submission.

Jessica held onto him and closed her eyes, broadcasting thoughts of her own. *I'm not sure I can, either, but that's what has to happen when this is done.* When she opened her eyes, she was back in her own bathroom.

Chris stared at her in the mirror and clenched his jaw. Her thoughts resounded in his head, and it hurt more than he ever thought it would, like someone had reached inside and ripped his beating heart from his chest. He turned back toward his bedroom.

"Don't go."

Chris stopped, but didn't look at her. He took a deep breath. *What did you expect?* The answer was simple. He expected the original dream; he expected to be with her.

"CHRIS," SHE WHISPERED, AND when he looked at her this time, she saw Ty. The intense need she remembered was in his eyes, and her heart skipped a beat.

"I'll see you tomorrow." He walked out of range.

The image faded, but not before she heard the music turned up loud to tune her out. The look on his face rattled her. The entire encounter rattled her, and she looked back at Tom sleeping peacefully in their bed. Guilt ravaged her, and she nearly let the sob locked in her chest free. Instead, she took a deep breath, gaining control over her roller-coaster emotions.

She decided a run was in order and changed into her jogging outfit. Running always cleared her mind ever since the days in the complex; it was her escape, her salvation. With her iPod buds in her ears and the music blaring loud enough to drown reasonable thought, she jogged down to the beach and let loose, running hard and fast, attempting to outrun the swirl of emotions building in her stomach. But when she passed the spot on the beach where they had screwed around, she slowed down, staring at the sand.

The way he made her feel was unparalleled to anything else she had ever encountered. It even left the sensuous heat that Tom created yesterday in the dust. When Chris touched her, her entire body ignited. Physically, he ruled her, and she couldn't resist him, couldn't say no to him. Even a lifetime ago, when he was Ty Aris, holding her captive and she hadn't wanted to, he still melted her resolve with one touch. Chris owned her body and soul, and until today, she believed Tom had her heart. But seeing the depth of hurt in Chris's eyes had torn the fabric of her beliefs, and shot straight through her, leaving her feeling hollow and wondering if it was indeed Chris who owned her heart.

A fragment of a vision she had in the complex crossed her mind, and she stumbled and caught herself before resuming her stride. That dream of him kneeling on the snow with an engagement ring proposing was in the backyard of his house in York.

Jesus, no wonder it looked so familiar.

Mind Games Chapter 66

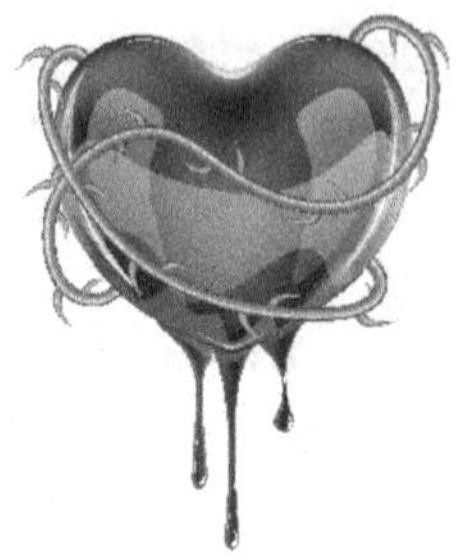

JESSICA STOOD AT THE entrance to her closet, scanning the dresses. "What should I bring?"

Tom stepped away from his suitcase and crossed to the closet. "You brought those dresses back with you, right?"

"Yeah, but which ones do you want me to bring?"

He glanced at the rack and pulled the little red number out, then handed it to her. The next dress he picked was an elegant black evening gown. He bit his lip, scanning the rest, and picked a pretty white floral gown as well. His eyes lit up, and he replaced the white dress and chose a midnight blue number, smiling. "You always knock me out when you wear this, and I have a feeling I'm going to need it tomorrow night."

Jessica took the dresses and laid them out in the garment bag. He avoided her eyes and picked out three suits, shirts, and ties. He finally turned and looked at her. What she saw made her heart leap into her throat. A dread bordering on fear laced his blue eyes. She couldn't help but wonder why he was going through with this. Going back to the hellhole they'd endured, the place they should have died. She couldn't do that. Not for love or money.

"I'm so going to need you tomorrow night." He passed by her.

"Why are you doing this if it's going to be that hard?"

He inhaled and turned toward her. "Come here." He put his hand out.

Jessica took it and walked in front of him.

He took her other hand and kissed her. "I'm doing this because I have to. I need to face my demons," he said. "I've never put that time behind me. I've tried, but it's always been there, and we never talked about it much until he came back." He took a deep breath. "I knew when I married you that you loved him. I just didn't know he was alive, and I'm not sure we would be together if I had." He looked into her eyes. "So, I have to do this, because if I don't, we aren't going to make it."

Sadness descended, and Jessica's eyes welled with tears, blurring her vision until she blinked them back. She couldn't envision life without Tom, either, but the thought didn't bring on the crushing sensation in her chest that never seeing Ty again did.

"Okay," she said.

THEY LANDED IN NEW York at three o'clock. By the time they got their bags and were driven to the hotel, it was close to four in the afternoon. They checked in and dropped their bags off in the hotel room.

"Dinner reservations aren't until seven." Tom stretched. "Feel like taking a walk?"

"Sure. Where to?"

"Central Park is just across the street."

They strolled leisurely through the park and stopped at a concession stand near the carousel for ice cream. She let Tom take control of the conversation, listening to him drone on about the show and what he wanted to do past this movie, but the electricity in the air distracted her. Chris was somewhere in the city, and she knew it.

As she walked by the fountain, the uncanny feeling of being watched scratched at the skin at the base of her neck. She paused, scanning the crowd.

"Pretty fountain," she said, and her gaze met Chris's.

He peered over the lens of a camera on the opposite side of the fountain. Her eyes widened before she turned her head in the direction they were walking, pretending she had seen nothing unusual, and adding another nod to what Tom was saying.

Jessica's breath caught in her throat, and heat prickled over her skin, making her shiver. The effect of being within a hundred feet of him was like an electric jolt, intense and unexpected. Before she walked around the bend and out of sight, she cast another glance in his direction, but she couldn't locate him in the crowd. Disappointment snuck under her skin.

She ate her ice cream cone, her mind drifting.

Tom stopped short, causing her to come back to the here and now with him. "Are you even listening to me?"

Jessica blushed. "I'm sorry. I guess I've got more of a case of jet lag from our trip back east than I thought."

He shook his head and looked at her sideways, inhaling deeply, and he continued walking. "I'm going to need to run my lines for the show. Think you can get your head here long enough to help me out?"

"No need to get pissy with me," she snapped back and plopped the last piece of the ice cream cone in her mouth.

He snorted and let go of her hand. "You haven't been with me all day."

She took a deep breath and pushed the aggravation back because he was right. "Okay, you will have my attention from now on. I'm just wiped from yesterday."

Tom laughed. "I thought you were the Energizer Bunny."

She shrugged. "Yeah, well…" She smiled at him. "I've never had that many in a single day, sweetheart."

"That's not entirely true."

His mind painted a vivid picture of Frank's sadistic orgasm machine, and the smile on her face disappeared. Anger singed, and she turned and walked away without another word.

He caught up to her. "I'm sorry."

She said nothing until they were in the hotel room, and then she turned on him. "I can't believe you said that." She flopped on the bed and buried her face in the pillow. "That was just so wrong." She turned her head and looked at him.

"I'm sorry." He stood with his hands deep in his pockets.

She saw the sincerity in his eyes, but it did nothing to diffuse her anger. "I can't believe you would even put *that* remotely in the same space as yesterday. You compared a killing machine to... to... to us making love." She turned her head before he could see the tears spill out.

He sat on the edge of the bed and ran his fingers through her hair.

"Don't." She didn't want him touching her, not after that comment.

He ignored her, continuing. "I'm sorry," he said again, softly.

Jessica cried silently in the pillow. That memory haunted her, and she kept it locked up inside as best she could, because whenever it got loose, she broke down. She closed her eyes and drifted to sleep under the soft combing of her hair.

Mind Games Chapter 67

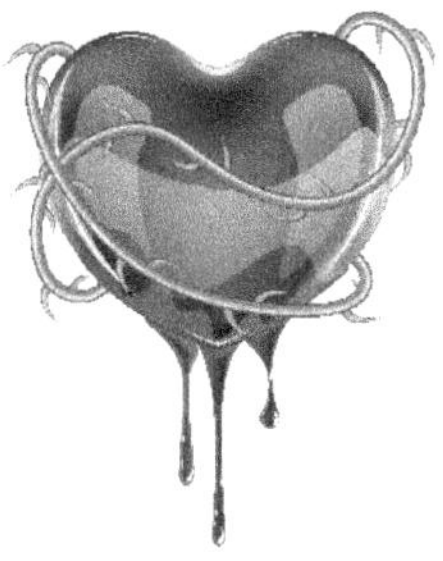

CHRIS LOOKED THROUGH HIS camera lens again in surprise and snapped her picture. She was here, now, less than a football-field length away from him. He smiled as he zoomed in on her, licking the ice cream cone and snapped another picture. He lowered the camera, noting that they were holding hands and heading his way. He moved to the opposite side of the fountain so their paths wouldn't cross. He sighed. When she paused and looked over her shoulder at the fountain, he held his breath.

He lifted the camera up to his eye again, and he caught her expression on film as she looked back. He slowly lowered the camera, feeling the same intensity of emotions raging through her blood.

"Christ," he whispered.

It took every ounce of strength he had not to go after her and sweep her away. He was on his home turf now and wondered if he could persuade her to stay with him this time. Instead of following her, he headed back to his apartment.

Mind Games Chapter 68

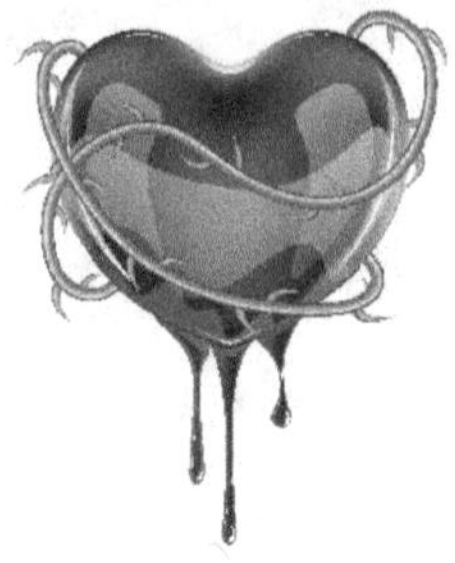

*S*HE WALKED IN THE *front door of his house and then crossed through the kitchen, glancing at the discarded cast on the floor before heading out the back door. A trail of clothes led to the side of the pool and his powerful strokes drove him through the water.*

He pulled himself out of the water and went into the cabana to grab a towel.

God, I want him, she thought, and he turned, their eyes meeting.

"You shouldn't be here, Jess." He stormed past her into the house, shaking from the cold.

She followed him up to his bedroom, and he turned, his eyes pleading with her. "You don't understand," he said, and his eyes shimmered with tears.

"Enlighten me."

Hands shook her awake. Jessica blinked, staring at Tom in confusion.

"We need to get ready for dinner."

She nodded, still in the dream's fog and wandered into the bathroom, then started the shower and stripped off her clothing.

Tom slipped into the shower behind her, wrapping his arms around her waist, startling her. "I'm sorry," he said again as he kissed her wet neck. "I didn't mean to make the comparison. It's just that I'm going to be there tomorrow and…"

"I know. I forgive you," she said.

He ran the soap gently over her body. She let him wash her, closing her eyes and enjoying the sensual way his fingers ran through her hair, combing the strands with conditioner and then rinsing. Showering with him was always on par with having a day at the spa, relaxing and rejuvenating.

He turned off the water and grabbed two towels, then handed one to her and wrapped the other around his waist. "I reserve the right to a rain check."

"We'll see." Jessica smiled smugly and slipped past him.

He reached out and grabbed her around the waist. "We'll see?" He laughed and looked at their reflection. "We are going to have a beautiful child."

She looked at the reflection and laughed. "That's quite vain."

"Seriously. Look at us."

Jessica did. "Pretty plastic people." She smiled and looked up at him. His hair was a dripping mess, like he'd shaken it as he stepped out of the shower. His well-defined chest glistened with moisture, and his eyes were the blue that made women swoon. He really was beautiful to look at, and yes, they would have exceptionally good-looking children if that was what the fates had in mind.

She slid out of his grip, walked into the room, and put on a black lacy bra with matching panties before slipping the black dress over her head.

Tom whistled. "How did I get so lucky?"

Jessica shrugged and looked up at him. "You're not the lucky one. I am." She ran her hands down his chest. "Now get dressed or we'll be late."

He pulled on his black suit with a mauve-colored shirt and a gray, black, and mauve tie to complete the ensemble.

"You should have gotten the top spot last year in the Sexiest Man Alive poll," she said.

He blushed and gave her his shy smile. "Let's go." He put his hand out for her.

She took his hand, and they left for an evening of dinner and dancing at the Rainbow Room. The dinner was fantastic and afterward, Tom led her onto the dance floor.

He held her close, slowly twirling her around the floor expertly. "I love you, Jessie."

"I love you, too." She looked up, and he planted a kiss on her lips.

They left around eleven, but instead of taking a taxi, Tom suggested they walk. It was only a few blocks between Rockefeller Center and the Plaza Hotel. He took off his jacket and put it around her shoulders when she shivered from the chill in the air.

With his hand around her waist, smiling, he sighed. "Thank you."

"For what?" she asked, looking over at him.

"For a wonderful night that will help me get through the day tomorrow." He didn't look at her right away. "I wish you were going to be there with me."

"I can't."

"I know," he answered and held the door to the hotel open for her. "But I can still wish," he said as they stepped into the elevator.

HE FLIPPED THE LOCK to the hotel room, then approached her and pulled the clip from her hair. Soft curls cascaded over her shoulders, and he had to stifle the plea that wanted to be heard. Desperation gripped him, and he crushed her lips under his, exploring her mouth with his tongue, teasing, tasting, relishing the skillful dance. Despite what he'd told her on the beach, if it came down to it, he couldn't leave her, not for long anyway. In that moment, he understood Ty, understood the need she drove in him because he couldn't fathom life without her.

He reached behind her and unzipped her dress, then pulled away to watch it drift down her body and crumple elegantly around her ankles. "I need you tonight."

Tom made love to his wife, taking her every move, every touch into his memory as if this were the last time they would be together. He held her tightly in his arms afterwards while she drifted to sleep with a small smile of satisfaction on her lips. He smelled her hair and squeezed her a little tighter, thinking about the day ahead of him. Closing his eyes, he hoped sleep would come, and eventually it did, but so did the nightmares.

Mind Games Chapter 69

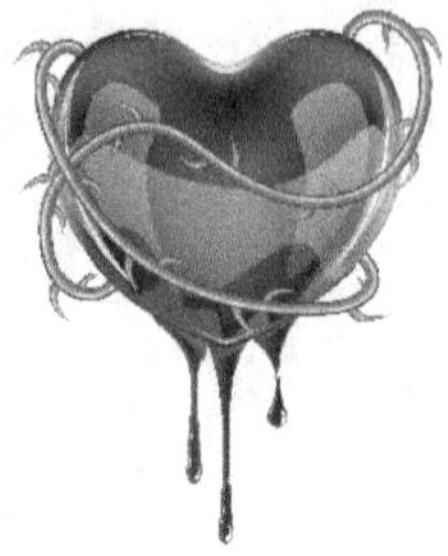

THE ALARM WENT OFF, shocking him awake. Tom sat up, looking down at Jessica. He took a deep breath and rubbed his face.

"Shit," he whispered and got out of bed. After a shower and a shave, he dressed in a suit and tie and sat on the side of the bed to put his socks and shoes on.

Jessica rolled over and opened her sleepy eyes. "What time is it?"

"Almost seven."

"What time's your flight?"

"I've got to be at the West 30th Street heliport in a half hour."

"You'd better get moving."

Tom smiled. "Don't worry, they won't leave without me. I should be back around five, and we have dinner reservations at seven." He kissed her and stood. "What do you have going on today?"

"I was going to go down to the South Street Seaport and see that human body exhibit, but I'll make sure I'm here when you get back."

"I would appreciate that." He leaned down and kissed her again. "I love you."

"Love you, too." She stretched.

Tom took the elevator down and walked out to the front entrance to the waiting town car. The driver opened the door.

Tom scowled. "What are you doing here?"

Sharon Young smiled. "I wouldn't miss this for the world."

"This isn't a trip to Disneyland."

"John is meeting us at the helipad," Craig Humphrey, the producer of the movie, said, glancing between Tom and Sharon.

Tom nodded and took a seat. "Sorry for snapping."

Sharon put her hand on his thigh. "It's okay."

Tom stared at her hand, her audacity bringing frustration in full force. He brushed her hand away. "Please don't do that again." He was in no mood to be toyed with, especially today.

Quiet and reserved on both the trip to the heliport and the helicopter ride, he did the best he could to prepare himself to enter that hellhole again.

The helicopter landed behind the warehouse near the private garage, and everyone stepped out, ducking under the whoosh of the helicopter blades. Tom hesitated at the chopper door, staring at the open garage, remembering the sweet taste of freedom that it had instilled in him when he had first seen the garage and the open night beyond five years ago.

He took a deep breath and stepped onto solid ground.

Sharon took his arm. "It's okay."

He jerked his arm away from her. "It's anything but okay." He walked into the garage.

"Are you ready for this?" John asked.

Tom nodded as the CEO of Empire Technologies walked up and introduced himself, shaking hands with all of them. He escorted them to the elevator.

"I guess they had a hell of a time reprogramming the elevator in the beginning, but at least now it operates with only a key instead of requiring a retinal scan." He handed over the keys to Craig.

Tom stared as the closed elevator doors behind them. The shakes took hold with each millisecond the elevator plummeted, taking them into the bowels of the complex, to the source of his nightmares. He pressed against the back wall, trying to melt into it and his breath locked in his chest. A thin high wheeze slipped out as he pulled air into his lungs. The momentary panic attack made even the act of breathing a difficult task.

When the elevator slid open, Tom's gaze fell to the floor, and he half expected Frank's discarded eye to be where Jessica dropped it. A measure of relief swept through him, allowing him to draw air into his lungs without the burning sensation in his chest, but that was short-lived.

The expedition party stepped off and turned expectantly, but he clung to the back of the elevator, unable to take the steps needed. He closed his eyes, uttering a laugh that bordered on hysterical.

God, I wish Jessie was here. The thought alone gave him the strength to open his eyes and take shaky steps into the hallway, but the whoosh of the doors closing behind him struck terror in his heart. He spun around, ready to leap between the closing doors. The click of the doors drawing together registered in his panicked brain, and he drew in a deep breath, settling his shot nerves.

"Are you okay?" Sharon asked.

"I don't know if I can do this." The wheeze in his chest returned, and sweat trickled down the small of his back, an unpleasant sensation that exacerbated the panic attack. He crouched down, put his hand on his forehead, and forced deep breaths, willing himself to get control. To get his shit together, as Ty had once told him.

Tom raised his eyes to John. "Shit, John, I don't know if I can do this." He gasped through his restricted airway. His breath came in harsh pulls. He fell to his knees, desperately trying to catch his breath as he hyperventilated.

"You and I have known each other for a long time, Tom. I knew you long before this happened. You can do this." He crouched next to Tom, putting his hand on his shoulder. "If you have to get into character to do it, then go for it."

Tom understood what his friend was saying, and he was able to catch his breath, but he still wasn't sure he could do this. "You don't get it. I was supposed to die down here," he whispered and hung his head.

"But you didn't." John stood up. "Now get your shit together."

Tom whipped his head up, glaring at John. "That's what he told me before Frank brought her into the room."

John smiled. "Better?"

Tom stood and nodded, taking a deep breath. "Game on," he said, stealing the phrase from the character he had signed up to take on. He waltzed past them, his face a mask of concentration as he led them to the control room. He flipped on all the camera controls, reversing what he and Jessica had done five years ago. All the monitors came to life. He stepped back, scanning them.

"Jesus," Sharon whispered.

"He won't help you now," Tom growled and glared at her.

Sharon stepped back.

"You wanted to see what things were like down here. How about a ride in one of those chairs?" He pointed at the monitors but never took his eyes off her. "Come on, Shar, what do you say?" He stepped toward her, making her take another step back. "It's such a rush."

"You're scaring me," she said.

John and Craig looked on.

The fury riding in his blood got the best of Tom and he laughed. He grabbed her by the arm and dragged her down the hall into the last room he had been in. The chairs were still there, and so was the table with all the tools except the ones that had been used. He swung her around and into the chair that he had been strapped in.

"You want to know what it felt like to think this was the last thing you'd ever feel?" He tightened the strap around her chest. "The last thing you'd ever see?" He pointed over his shoulder at the chair behind him. "He sliced her. I watched while Frank sliced her up with the knife." He leaned on the arms of the chair, gripping the wood to temper the shakes flowing through him.

He wasn't just talking about five years ago; he was talking about just a couple of weeks ago. He could almost hear Frank laughing.

He stepped back and looked at the mirror. "Ty was being pulled apart, and she was being cut up, and neither of them made a noise." He took a deep breath. "Not one fucking noise." He turned and looked at the chair and the chains, and something inside him clicked. "They just stared at each other. It was like they weren't even here."

What the hell kind of connection did they have?

He stared at the mirror, thinking about the other morning. *Jesus.*

"I can't play this part." He returned his focus to John.

"You just did," John said.

Tom laughed. "That wasn't Ty," he said. "Ty didn't lose control."

John and Sharon exchanged a look.

"He did with her," Sharon said.

Tom turned and looked at them. He shook his head. "I don't think so. I think he calculated everything and ended up getting away with murder."

"He died for her, Tom," Sharon said. "That wasn't calculated."

Tom laughed. "You bet your ass it was." He continued to laugh. *If they only knew.* As his laughter died down, he looked at John. "I can't do this. I can't make him into a hero."

"Tom..." John started.

"He killed so many people, John. I can't make him into a hero." He turned away. "He isn't a hero. He isn't afraid to die, either, not for my wife. He would jump off the Brooklyn Bridge for her if he had to, but that still doesn't make him a hero." He looked around the room and then back at the chains. "No matter how much he tried to redeem himself, he still is evil at the core." He looked back at the three of them. "We can't let the world see him as a hero. That's irresponsible, no matter how brave and self-sacrificing he was at the end. It doesn't matter. He's still a killer at heart."

Sharon looked down at the floor as Tom walked over to the chains and touched them.

"I want to see the other rooms." Tom looked over his shoulder. "The one we were in and the one she was in."

They nodded, leading the way. They brought him to the room that the three of them had shared for six weeks. Tom walked in and looked at the chair in the center of the room. He flashed back to the day Frank had come back, the way he manipulated her, cut her, raped her, and Ty sat watching it all with that godforsaken smile on his lips, like he was entertained by the show.

To this day, he never understood how he could remain so calm, so in control, especially since Tom knew better. He walked over to the chains in the wall and crouched down. He took the one he had put on Ty's ankle, holding it thoughtfully.

"I hate him," he said. "I hate that my wife loves him." He tossed the shackle as he stood up and faced them. "After everything he did to her, she forgave him. I still don't get that." He shook his head.

"Maybe it's time you see some of those tapes," John said.

Tom looked at him and tilted his head. "You've seen them?"

John nodded. "She showed me them, and I asked her to write the script." He pointed in the general direction of Sharon. "Tom, he loved her."

Tom nodded. "I know that." *He still does.*

"He treated her differently than any other prisoner over the years," Sharon said.

"Lucky me," Tom said sarcastically, and walked into the adjoining bathroom.

He looked at the shower and leaned his head against the wall. He glanced over at the mirror and remembered the day she'd healed the bruise on his face with a kiss. These were things they didn't know about, things they couldn't see in the videos. The script called for a malfunction in the chain shackles because they couldn't fathom any other reason how Ty got loose and saved them. Even with the miracle speech.

Tom walked out of the bathroom and out the door into the hallway. Jessica had done nothing until Eric was in danger, and then all hell had broken loose. He put his back against the wall in the hallway and closed his eyes.

They came out of the room.

"Where is her room?"

"Just a couple of rooms down." John started walking toward the elevator. He opened the door and let Tom walk in.

Tom looked at the set-up. There was a chair and a mattress, which was a recurring theme in all the rooms, and to his left was the treadmill that she had spoken about. He walked over to it and picked up the shackle on the handrail.

What looked like rust graced the metal, but he knew better. It was her blood.

"Jesus," he whispered.

"That's just the beginning," a voice said with a laugh from behind him.

Tom whirled around. There was no one in the room with him, but the temperature dropped, and he shivered. Tom turned toward the mirror, and Frank grinned back at him.

The door slammed shut. Tom's mouth went dry, and he backed into the concrete wall, feeling the cold, rough surface with his fingers.

"I'm going to finish what I started here. Starting with you." He pointed a knife at Tom. "I want her to watch *you* die."

The banging on the door snapped his attention away from Frank, and the spell broke. The temperature returned to normal just as the door flew open.

Tom glanced back at the mirror, and all that was looking back were his wide, scared eyes and pale, blotchy face.

"You look like you just saw a ghost," Sharon said.

Tom tore out of the room and into the hallway. He fell to his knees for a second as fear tore through him. Trembling, he caught his breath, kneeling with his hands on his thighs. A hand touched the back of his neck, and Sharon crouched next to him.

"Please don't," he said. "Just leave me alone right now."

John leaned down next to Tom. "What happened in there?"

"I think this place is haunted," he whispered and looked over at John.

"Don't be ridiculous," John said. "We've been down here at least a dozen times."

Tom swallowed and nodded.

"Maybe it's just your mind playing tricks on you," John said.

Tom nodded again. John would have him put away if he told him what had been happening in their lives for the past two weeks. He slowly stood up, breathing through his nostrils, slow deep breaths that reined in the fear. He prayed that Jessica and Chris could get rid of Frank before he started filming. Otherwise, who knows what would happen to the cast and crew down here?

John walked him through the rest of the complex, including the kitchen areas, and then back into the control room. Tom flopped down into the chair and put his head in his hands. He slowly looked up at the monitors and rested his chin on his fists, taking a deep breath. This trip did nothing to put his demons at rest; it only stirred up more.

He turned in the chair. "Are the tapes here?"

"I only brought a couple with me," Sharon said.

Tom put his hand out. Sharon stared at it and looked over at John. He nodded, and she reached into her purse, pulled out two discs, and handed them over.

"I'm going to call up to have lunch sent down," Craig said from the doorway.

When they nodded, he picked up the phone on the console and pressed 0. The CEO's secretary answered and took the order for them, then told them the food would be delivered in about an hour.

Tom slipped the disc into the DVD player and pressed play. The main monitor filled with a scene of Jessica tied to a mattress in a red dress and Ty sitting on the side feeding her grapes, strawberries, and whipped cream.

His fists kept clenching and unclenching under the table as he watched Ty seduce her. He asked for the words, even though it was evident in her eyes. She wanted him, and that burned Tom to the core. She never looked at him the way she looked at Ty. Not back then, and not now. A small spark brightened in his soul, the fires of anger burning low, stoked by each gentle scene they showed him.

Shock encompassed him when Ty left the room instead of finishing what he'd started. The next several scenes dug under his skin, and he shifted in the seat, the burning in his soul scorching with new kindling. The poker game where Jessica bet her freedom on one hand of a five-card stud struck a chord.

"*I never lose,*" Ty commented after he won the poker hand.

Tom shivered. Could Ty win this battle, too? Could he really yank Jessica out of his life?

In the next scene, Ty asked Jessica if she believed in redemption. A cold sweat broke out on Tom's neck.

"Jesus," he said. Jessica had actually granted his wish of redemption, or more specifically, Eric had.

The dinner, followed by Jessica willingly giving herself to him, was torture. Tom closed his eyes. His chest felt like someone dropped a fifty-pound weight on it, and he hung his head, knowing he was going to lose and lose big.

Fear and despair laced through his bones. He blinked back the sudden onslaught of tears. How could he be so stupid, so blind? Could Jessie really refuse him?

None of them knew just how much these tapes scared him. Ty was alive and embedded in their lives, and this just made him much more of a threat than Tom had imagined.

"What's on the other disc?" he asked when the scene flashed to the room with the three of them in it.

Sharon switched the discs and pressed play. Tom hardly recognized the face on the screen—the scar, sure, but the eyes... The eyes were devoid of humanity, of caring. He pushed the chair back.

Ty looked bored, except when they begged for him, and every woman did, their eyes drinking him in like he was some sort of god. When they begged, his eyes altered, turning into a vision of self-loathing, reminding Tom of the day he broke Jessica.

The rush he spoke of when they were in captivity only manifested itself when he flaunted his first seduction of Jessica to Mike. A devilish gleam glimmered in his eyes. Other than taunting Mike, Tom couldn't find any hint of pleasure in the videos he took part in.

He came to life when Jessica appeared, and that scared the shit out of Tom.

The only footage of Ty killing someone was the girl who'd cut his arm and that could have been construed as self-defense.

"He never pulled the trigger," Sharon said softly as she ejected the disc.

Tom laughed and looked at his watch. It was almost four in the afternoon. They had been down there for close to seven hours.

"Don't let these videos fool you. Ty is a killer. He pushed the button, setting off the explosive that killed my wife." He looked over at Sharon. "You have no idea what that man is capable of." He looked at the three of them. "Do you have the video of us in the room that last day?"

They nodded.

"So, you have it on film. He castrated his stepbrother and pulled his eye out of the socket without a thought. He let that machine tear him apart, and he smiled when he watched it," Tom said. "Jessica didn't see the smile; I did. He is a sick son of a bitch."

"Many people will see what he did to Frank as just," Sharon said.

Tom nodded. "True, he got what he deserved," he said. "I admit he was crazier than Ty." He took a deep breath. "But Ty is not a hero, and we have to do a little rewriting to remind the world of what he did before he met Jessie." He looked at them. "Otherwise, I'm not doing this."

He stood up and headed toward the elevator. They followed him silently, and no one spoke until they were back in the helicopter.

"So, you will do the movie?" Craig asked.

"Only with some rewriting," Tom answered.

Sharon nodded. "But only if you work on it with me."

Tom took a deep breath and looked out the window. Jessica would not like that at all. He looked back at her and nodded. "But no funny stuff," he warned.

Sharon touched the bandage plastered over the bridge of her nose. The hollow of her eyes still held an ugly black-and-blue tone. "Okay."

Tom looked out the window as the helicopter made its way back to the city. The day had been grueling, and a new terror, one worse than Frank, gripped him. Losing Jessica—to death, to Ty; it wouldn't matter—losing her would destroy him.

Mind Games Chapter 70

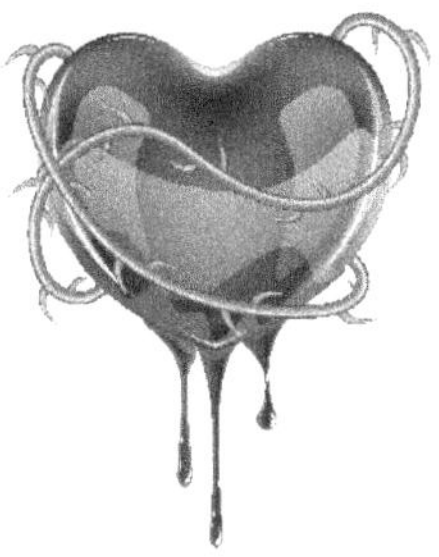

JESSICA STIRRED, OPENING ONE eye toward the clock. "Holy shit." She shot up. It was already ten thirty. She jumped out of bed and high-tailed it into the bathroom to get ready for her lunch with Chris.

She walked into the Four Seasons at a little after noon and climbed the steps while scanning the restaurant. There he stood in a gray pinstripe suit with a blue shirt that was open at the collar. His hair was just as perfect as the fit of the suit, looking like he'd just stepped out of the pages of *GQ*. Chris turned, and the smile that lit up his face made her tremble.

CHRIS NEARLY FELL OVER as the smile spread across his lips. The red dress she wore looked so much like the one he made her wear that day in the complex. She was more stunning today than she had been five years ago. Taking a deep breath to quench the heat that layered his skin, he walked up to her and took her hand, then kissed it in gentleman's fashion.

"Little red dress. Are you trying to kill me?"

"You look amazing," she said, still studying the finely tailored suit.

"I told you I clean up well." Chris signaled for the hostess, and they were seated in the pool room next to the window. Chris held her chair for her as she sat and pushed it in gently, laughing lightly at her wide-eyed gaze.

"I had no idea." She glanced around the restaurant.

"Can I start you off with something to drink?" the waitress asked.

"Just as long as it isn't Grey Goose, right?" Chris winked at Jessica.

Jessica blushed. "Can I have a glass of zinfandel?"

"I'll take a scotch on the rocks." He watched the waitress walk away before leaning back in his seat. He cocked his head to the side, studying Jessica, wondering how much they had in common, like if she was a Yankee's fan or even if she liked sports.

"What?"

He smiled and shook his head. "Not important."

"What?" she asked again, smiling.

He rolled his eyes. "Red Sox or Yankees?"

"Red Sox, of course."

"Figures." He glanced at the waitress, nodding as the drinks were set on the table.

"Don't tell me you're a Yankees fan?"

"Avid." He nodded and shrugged. "What about football?"

She smiled. "Guess."

"Pats?"

"It would be a sin to live in New England if I didn't like them. Jets?"

Ty laughed. "No, Buffalo. You actually watch football?"

Jessica smiled. "Hell yeah, I love football. I never miss a game."

"Baseball?" he asked hopefully.

Jessica held her hand up and shook it back and forth. "Not so much. It's kind of boring, but I will watch the Red Sox if nothing else is on and they're playing the Yankees." She smiled at him. "I like to see your boys lose."

"They don't lose very often."

"They have lately."

"Touché." He grinned and picked up his drink. The waiter arrived, and he ordered for the both of them. "Hope you don't mind."

"Not at all."

Chris looked at her for a long time and his smile faded. "If you could have anything in the world, what would it be?"

Jessica watched him as she thought about the question. "World peace." She laughed.

Another child. Her thought echoed in his head, and he focused on her calico eyes. "Seriously, just for you. What would it be?" he asked.

"Seriously?"

He nodded.

"Okay, I'd like my grandfather's property in New Hampshire back. We used to go there every summer as kids, and he had the best spot on Lake Wentworth. It's called Sunset Point. The sunset streaked across the lake from Mount Ossopie directly to our dock. My best childhood memories are there." She took a sip of wine. "What about you? What is it that you want if you could have anything?"

"You."

"Besides me."

He sat back in the chair, biting his lower lip. "Anything in the world?"

She nodded.

He took a deep breath, focusing in on the exact moment his life went to shit. "I'd go back in time to the morning my dad died and make sure he had his bulletproof vest on." He took a sip of his drink and held eye contact with her. "My dad was a cop. He died in the line of duty."

Jessica's eyes softened.

"If he had lived, my mother, Anna, and Chris would all be alive today and I never would have done the things I have." He snorted. "Hell, my brother and I would probably be cops hunting down psychos like me."

"How old were you?"

"Seven. Sorry, but that was the beginning of the end."

"Chris. What are we doing?"

He smiled a little and shrugged. "Being friends."

"Okay, I'll buy that for now." She smirked at him and leaned back. "So, what do you do?"

He raised his eyebrows. "Do?"

"Yes, what do you do?"

"Anything I want," he answered as the waitress came by with their food.

"Seriously?" Jessica asked and cut into her steak.

Chris shrugged. "I take a lot of pictures. I take karate classes. I watch the ball games down at a bar on 7th Street." He shrugged again. "Basically, go where I want, when I want."

"With whom you want?"

Chris shook his head. "There isn't anyone else I want to be with, Jess."

Jessica went to say something but decided against it; instead, she took another bite of steak.

He watched her in silence for a while. "We can't talk here."

"What do you mean?"

"Frank," he said. "We'll talk at my place after."

"Oh, no." Jessica shook her head.

"I promise I will not make you do anything that you'll regret. Besides, I can show you my portfolio while we talk."

Jessica looked at him warily. "I don't know."

"We both had the nightmare. This isn't the place to discuss that," he said, trying to sound perfectly reasonable.

"If I agree, you have to promise me you won't let anything happen."

Chris nodded. "I'll do my best." The knot in his stomach tightened. He wasn't sure if he could keep that promise.

They finished their meal, and he peeled off a couple hundred-dollar bills and handed them to the waiter with the check. Jessica gave him a tilt of her head as they stood up to leave.

"What?" he said as they started down the stairs. "I tip for good service?"

"You tipped a hundred percent of the meal."

"So," he said. "It's not like I'll ever run out of money."

"You do that to see their reactions."

"No." He smiled. *Maybe she does really know what makes me tick.*

"Ya-huh." She smacked him lightly.

Chris laughed and opened the door for her.

Jessica glanced at him. "You have such a nice laugh."

Their eyes met, taking the chill right out of the air. She took a deep breath, looking away.

CHRIS HAILED A CAB and rattled off the address. They pulled up in front of the apartment building that flanked the north side of Central Park. Jessica scanned the scenery and stepped out of the cab. He escorted her inside, and they took the elevator to the penthouse.

Jessica actually sighed as she looked around at the deep-brown leather furniture and rich walnut tables and bookcases. He had a couple of colorful throws on the back of the couch and chairs. The walls on either side of the entertainment center were filled with books, and she recognized most of the authors. His apartment had warmth and character that she didn't expect, much like the house in Maine.

"It's lovely," she said.

He opened up the French doors to the balcony and showed her out. The panoramic view of the city brought a smile to her lips.

Chris ducked out of view for a moment and came back with a black portfolio that he unzipped and placed on the table in the living room.

Jessica stepped away from the beautiful cityscape and took a seat on the couch, opening the portfolio. It was filled with eighteen by twenty photographs he had taken, and she shuffled through them.

"These are phenomenal." Jessica picked up a picture of a little Chinese girl playing with popsicle sticks on the sidewalk. "I love this one." She held it up. "You've got a lot of talent. I mean a lot of talent." She sifted through the pictures again.

Chris beamed. "Thanks."

He sat down and took her hands in his. "Jess?"

His touch set her on fire. She pulled her hands away and stood up, heading out onto the balcony.

He followed her out. "We have to talk about what we need to do to get rid of Frank."

"I know," she said, but didn't turn. "How's this going to work?"

"I need to use you as bait."

She spun around.

"And apparently I will need to do things quick, or we both die." He walked up to her and touched her face. "This is not something I want to do. I will have to let him hurt you, Jess." His voice shook. "I need to make him think he won." His eyes filled with tears. "Then I'll have to use everything you gave me to kill the bastard and help you fix both of us." He kissed her. "I just hope like hell that I'm strong enough," he whispered against her lips.

Jessica stepped back into the balcony wall. "Ty, you promised."

"I know, but I'm in love with you and you're here." He leaned his arms against the balcony on either side of her. "If you can look me in the eye and tell me you don't want me the way I want you, I'll let you walk out of here with no questions asked."

"I'm married," she said, her breath hitching in her chest as he stared into her eyes. Tom's words screamed in her head as loud as her body screamed to be with Chris.

"That's not what I asked you to tell me." He waited without breaking eye contact. "You can't, can you?"

She shook her head, and he leaned in to kiss her. She gave in to the heat between them as his strong arms wrapped around her.

He picked her up, carried her to his bedroom, and set her down on the floor next to the bed. He unclasped her dress and watched it drift to the floor. Lowering to one knee, he slid her heels off one at a time, then stripped her panties and slid his hands up her body, removing her bra in the process. He took a step back, taking her in while his breath came in quick bursts. His eyes met hers.

Jessica stepped closer and unbuttoned his shirt as she stared into his eyes. She peeled it off and ran her hands down his smooth, chiseled chest. Her fingers found the button to his pants, undoing the fine Armani trousers and letting them slip down his legs.

Need flared inside her.

Need to be one with him, as if her soul couldn't survive otherwise.

CHRIS SLID HIS SHOES off and kicked both shoes and pants away.

He studied her, memorizing every curve. His heart pounded with the fire burning inside him, and within a blink they were in each other's arms, kissing, hands wandering, not able to get enough. He picked her up and moved her onto the bed, sliding into her instantaneously.

"Oh, God!" Jessica arched into him.

He kissed her neck, slowly moving his hips, trying to control himself. He wanted this to last, and he closed his eyes, willing her body to do as he wished. Her moan had his name on it, and he smiled. He felt the power shift. He kissed her, and she arched, climaxing, her body responding to his every touch, his every movement. He pulled away from her lips, taking a shaky breath.

"Tell me." He searched her eyes.

"I want you." She arched into him, meeting the sinuous motion of his hips.

He smiled down at her and continued his slow, methodical movement, watching as she built up to another orgasm.

"You're driving me crazy."

His smile broadened.

"Faster." She gasped and pulled him down to her mouth. Kissing him hard as he moved his hips faster, she kept pace, gently moaning under his lips.

He deepened the kiss and felt her orgasm. He released, sending his seed deep within her, willing a miracle to occur. He lay on top of her in bliss for a while until her breath slowed down to normal. He propped himself up on his elbows again and looked into her eyes.

Jessica met his gaze, and he smiled, kissed her, and rolled onto his back.

"Jesus, Jess." He sighed, the connection still a living, breathing force between them.

Jessica rolled away and sat up on the side of the bed.

He reached for her, feeling the shift of her thoughts. "Don't go."

"I have to." She stood up and gathered her clothes. "Tom will be back soon."

Pain sharper than any knife pierced his abdomen.

She turned toward him. "I never said I'd leave him."

Chris closed his eyes and pressure as great as a metric-fuck-ton of rocks pressed down on his chest. "I know, but Jess..." Tears brimmed and slid down her cheeks, locking the rest of the words in his throat.

"I can't do this." She threw her clothing on. "I can't love you like this," she whispered.

"But you do." He reached for the pair of jeans that were hanging over the end of the bed and slid them on.

Jessica hung her head and nodded, giving him a small seed of hope.

He went to her and wrapped his arms around her, and against every instinct raging inside him, he said, "I'll walk you back to your hotel. But Jess, this is the last time." He pulled away. "I know I started it, and I probably will try again if given the chance, so unless you intend to leave him, you have to be the one to say no." He ran his thumb over her lips. "If we do this again, I won't let you go." He stared into her eyes, silently conveying what he meant.

If she slept with him again, he'd move heaven and earth to keep her by his side, no matter the consequences.

Mind Games Chapter 71

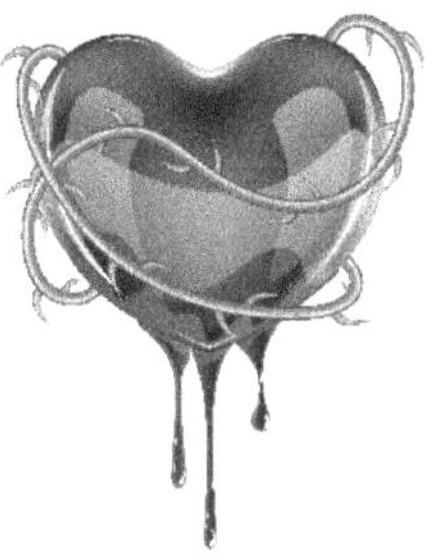

ONCE IN THE HOTEL room, Jessica stripped, jumped into a hot shower to wash the smell of him off her body, and tried to keep the guilt at bay.

Outside the bathroom, Tom called, "Hello?"

She returned the salutation, shutting off the shower. She wrapped herself in one of the hotel's plush towels and squeezed the water out of her hair, then ran a comb through the wet tangles before doing a quick touch-up on her makeup. She stepped into the hotel room.

Tom sat in the chair with his eyes wide and a cloth stuffed in his mouth. A knife hovered in front of him.

Her clean body broke out in a cold sweat. Her heart hammered in her chest. Terror gripped it and squeezed.

Tom's tie slowly pulled from around his neck.

Jessica stepped closer. "Leave him alone!"

"Pretty boy and I have been having a little chat, haven't we?" Frank materialized in the room.

Jessica took a step towards them, but Frank put the point of the knife to Tom's neck, piercing the skin. Blood trickled down the line of his throat.

She froze. "Please don't hurt him," she whispered. "I'll do anything you want, please." Tears blurred her vision, and she blinked, forcing them out of her eyes.

Frank laughed and pulled the knife away. "You're going to show your husband exactly what you did to my little brother on the beach."

Jessica's mouth fell open, and her gaze shot to Tom. His jaw tightened, and a crease appeared between his eyes, the depth of his pain visible in his blue irises. She lunged at Frank. He backhanded her, sending her sprawling onto the floor. Pain plumed in her cheek, and she pressed her palm to the spot and grabbed the slipping towel.

The fabric yanked from her fingers and was tossed into the corner. "I prefer my sluts to be naked."

She looked up through her wet hair. "You son of a bitch."

Frank walked behind Tom and put the blade to his neck. "Come on. He deserves the same thing Ty got on the beach." He looked down at Tom. "Has she ever given you a blow job?"

Tom shook his head. That was one thing Jessica never attempted, and he'd never pushed the issue.

"She's got a mouth that just won't quit. You're in for a real treat." Frank walked to Jessica, grabbed her by the hair, and dragged her to him. "Let's just say I'm granting you a final wish before you die." He looked at Jessica. "Do it, or he dies right now."

Jessica reached up with trembling hands and unzipped Tom's pants, then pulled his limp dick from the fabric. Hot tears choked her, sliding down her face as she coaxed him with her hands.

"You didn't have a problem sucking the juice out of Ty."

Jessica glared up at Frank and then moved her gaze to Tom. His eyes hardened, and his jaw tightened, fury and fear mixing in his blood and all of it tainted by the want she saw in his irises. He hardened in her grasp. She turned her attention to him, slid the tip of him into her mouth, and closed her tear-filled eyes.

A low rumble escaped through the gag in his mouth, and she stole a glance. His eyes were clamped tight, and his head was tilted back. His chest rose and fell in quick bursts, groaning each time she rolled her tongue around the sensitive flesh before continuing to run her lips up and down his throbbing shaft.

"That's it, suck him dry," Frank whispered in her ear.

Jessica sent a silent cry out to Chris with her room number and prayed he would be here in time.

Tom's hands gripped the armrests, his body stiffened, and a muffled groan accompanied the explosion of semen into her mouth. Jessica swallowed, then gasped and sucked until Frank yanked her away, launching his own brutal assault.

TOM'S TEAR-STAINED LASHES PARTED, and he struggled against the bonds holding him in the chair. The image before him drew fury to the forefront of his emotional baggage. Frank raped his wife with the same violent bravado he'd had five years ago in the complex. *Fucking bastard!*

The thought barreled from his gagged mouth, muffled by the fabric, but pronounced enough to make Frank laugh.

He pulled out of Jessica and tossed her on the bed; the knife appearing in his hands again. "Interesting choice of words." He pointed the knife in Tom's direction before turning his gaze to her. "That wasn't all that happened on the beach, was it?" He turned back to Tom. "She fucked him too," he whispered in his ear.

The words seared through him, and he shot a glance in her direction.

"You bastard," Jessica sobbed.

Frank chuckled. "Oh yes, she fucked him, all right. Right there on the beach."

Tears burned his throat as he inhaled through his nose, meeting her pained gaze, seeing the truth in her eyes. *How could you?*

A sob escaped her lips.

"But my favorite was this afternoon."

Tom screamed under the gag, biting down on the fabric and glaring at Jessica. She didn't deny it. She didn't call Frank a liar. She just sobbed on the bed, her eyes filling with tears, tears that tracked down her cheeks, and told him everything this bastard said was the truth.

"So, what do I do with you today?" Frank asked.

Jessica's arms and legs stretched wide on the bed.

"Reenact what you did with Ty?" He ran the knife over her stomach. "Or maybe I'll just go around the world with you like I did with your daughter." He stuffed the tie into Jessica's mouth before her lungs filled with a scream, muffling any shrill cry that she might have built up.

Frank advanced on Tom as Jessica struggled against invisible bonds holding her to the bed.

He smiled at Tom and tilted his head. "How about a little murder-suicide today?"

Tom's fear was muted by his anguish. Jessica had slept with Ty of her own accord after he had given her that ultimatum. He could forgive her for anything that occurred before that, but today... She'd slept with him today of all days. Pain tore him from his silent rant, and he gazed down at his arm, the knife tearing flesh, tendons, and veins from his elbow to wrist. He screamed into the muffled rag. Frank sliced his other arm, and another hot flare of pain accosted him, burning his arms and making his stomach roil. The smell of blood filled the room.

Jessica spit the tie out of her mouth. "No, please no, not him," she sobbed.

Frank dropped the knife on the floor and climbed up on the bed. He wrapped Tom's tie around her neck and pulled both ends, restricting her airway. "I've always dreamed of fucking the life out of you."

The hotel door banged open. Chris entered, slamming the door behind him. Out of breath, words hissed out of his chest, "Get away from her!"

He pulled a gun out of the waistline of his pants, pointed it at Frank, and pulled the trigger.

Frank dissolved before the mirrors burst. The bullet slid through the fading image of Frank and slammed into Tom's shoulder beyond the image. Dull pain flared in his shoulder, but it didn't compare to the cocktail of betrayal brewing in his heart.

"Shit." Chris put the gun on the bed, reaching for the tie around Jessica's neck.

THE MOMENT THE INVISIBLE bonds holding her disappeared, Jessica jumped off the bed and fell to her knees in front of Tom. Sobs ripped from her chest as she pressed her lips to his arms, sending her magic into his flesh, healing the knife wounds. He let out a muffled cry, clenching his teeth on the rag.

She traced the bullet hole in his shoulder and turned to Chris. "Can you get the bullet out?"

Chris closed his eyes and tilted his chin to his chest, a line appearing between his eyebrows in concentration.

Tom screamed as the bullet backed its way out from being wedged in his shoulder. Jessica caught it and then leaned over, kissing the wound, mending it with her healing power.

Tom squeezed his eyes shut, and when he opened them, they fell on Jessica.

A mixture of feelings swirled in his eyes, but the moment Chris handed her one of the hotel robes, his gaze hardened. He pulled the gag from his mouth.

"You son of a bitch!" He launched at Chris, slammed him into the wall, and wrapped both his hands around his neck.

"Tom, don't!"

"I told you I'd kill him if he ever touched you," he growled and glared back at her.

An invisible force tore him from Chris and flung him across the room.

Jessica shot her gaze at Chris, catching the flash of anger in his eyes.

"Don't," Jessica said, walking into his line of sight.

The hammer click caught their attention. Jessica spun. Tom leveled the gun at Chris, his glare screaming murder.

"YOU DO NOT WANT to do that, Tom," Chris said.

"How many times?" Tom growled low. "How many times did you fuck my wife since you've been back?"

Jessica hung her head, and a sob escaped.

Chris met his angry glare and held up two fingers. "She was drunk the first time." He shrugged, trying to soften the blow.

"And you let him?" Tom yelled. His teeth clenched in rage. The gun shook in his hands. "After what I said the other day, you still let him?"

Jessica nodded.

"She chose you, Tom," Chris said, but the rage in Tom's gaze gave him pause. He exercised the power she gave him. "Put the gun down."

Tom slowly released the hammer and put the gun on the bed.

"Step away," Chris said.

Tom obediently stepped back with wide eyes and a slack jaw.

Chris leaned across the bed, picked up the gun, flipped the safety on, and put it in his belt at the small of his back. He released the mental hold on Tom and stepped away. "Just calm down."

Tom's eyebrows shot up. "Calm down?" He looked down at himself. "I'm covered in my own blood, and my wife was nearly strangled to death by a ghost! As if that's not bad enough, I find out from *that* son of a bitch that she's been sleeping with *you*. I think it's a little late to calm down," he raved. "I don't want to see you near her ever again. Ever!"

"Tom, I need him." Jessica turned toward him.

Tom moved his steady glare to her. "What did you just say?"

"I need him. He is the only one who can get rid of Frank," she said, tears still running down her bruised cheek.

His mouth dropped open. "I don't give a damn. I don't want you near him."

"Frank raped my little girl," she screamed. "I told you I would do anything so that doesn't happen again."

"Then you do it without me," he snarled.

"If I have to, I will," she whispered and put her face in her hands. Sobs tore through her, and she slowly crumpled to her knees.

Chris took a step toward her.

"Get out!" Tom demanded.

"I'm not leaving her with you." Chris laughed. "Not like this."

"She's my wife. Now get the hell out of my hotel room." Tom took a step toward him.

"Chris, just go," Jessica said from behind her hands.

Chris looked from Jessica back to Tom. "I swear to God, if you hurt her..."

"I'm not like you, Ty. I would never intentionally hurt her," Tom snarled.

Chris inhaled deeply at the dig.

"Please, just go," Jessica said.

He nodded as their eyes met.

Thank you for saving our lives. "Go," she whispered.

AS SOON AS THE door shut, Tom stormed past her and into the bathroom. The door locked, and the shower turned on.

She glanced at the god-awful mess before her. Grabbing the towel from the corner, she kneeled on the floor and wiped up the blood surrounding the chair.

Tom's blood.

A sob escaped, then another and another until it turned into one continuous moan, shaking her entire frame. Tears mixed with the blood that the towel couldn't absorb.

He finally came out of the bathroom, with eyes red from crying. "Jessie, how could you?" He sat on the edge of the bed.

"It was inevitable," she whispered, staring at her crimson hands.

He got up and walked over to her, then kneeled behind her and rested his forehead between her shoulders. "I can't believe you slept with him, Jessie," he whispered, and a raspy sob escaped.

"I didn't intend to."

"I can't do this."

"If he hadn't come, you would have died. I can't do this without you."

"You have to," he whispered into her back. "I can't get past this."

"I need to wash this off," she sobbed and felt him move away.

She stumbled into the shower, blinded by the torrent of tears, her chest heaving sobs in harsh pulls. *I never should have married him, no matter how much I loved him.* She scrubbed the blood from her skin until the water ran clear, then wrapped a towel around her and stepped into the bedroom.

He sat stoically on the edge of the bed with his head hung low enough so she couldn't see his eyes, then pointed toward the bag sitting by the door. "You have to go."

She couldn't leave him like this. She didn't want to leave him at all. A fresh set of tears sprung in her eyes. She stepped closer.

"Don't," he said.

"I never meant to hurt you." She took another step toward him.

He raised his head, glaring at her. "If you come near me, I will hurt you, and I mean it."

She froze at the hateful look on his face. "I don't want to lose you."

"You should have thought of that before you slept with him."

She took another step toward him. "Tom, please."

HE STARED AT HER. He still wanted her. He still needed her. And he still loved her. Despite all she had done. Losing her to Ty burned, fanning the fury inside him. He grabbed her arms and pulled her to him, so they were eye to eye.

"I don't need you anymore," he hissed and stripped off the towel. "I don't want you anymore," he said, wishing it were so.

He kissed her roughly, threw her on the bed, and climbed on top of her. "And I don't love you anymore." The last sentence came out as a low growl from his throat.

He ripped his pants off and plunged inside her, letting his desire get the best of him.

"I don't want you, Jessie," he growled, pinning her wrists to the bed.

She cried underneath his thrusts until he finally climaxed and then fell on top of her.

"I don't want you," he whispered, lying through his teeth. Tears blurred his vision. "God damn you, Jessie." He wrapped his arms around her and held her until he stopped shaking, clinging to the last moment of having her in his arms. Then he pulled away and wiped his eyes. "I called a car for you. They're taking you to the house in Maine."

"Tom."

"I can't, Jessie." He looked at her, and the fury was gone. Pain of losing her replaced it. "No matter how much I love you, I can't get past this," he said. "It's over."

Tears continued to track down her cheeks. "Promise me you will protect Emily if anything happens to me," she said, her voice shaking.

He closed his eyes and nodded. The bed moved as she got up to get dressed. He finally opened his eyes when the sounds in the room stilled.

"I'm sorry," she said from the bedside. Her regret registered in her eyes, but her apology couldn't wipe the betrayal out of his mind.

"Goodbye, Jessie."

"You know I love you," she whispered and picked up her bag.

He shook his head and smiled sadly. "No, you don't love me, Jessie. You love him and always have. I just happened to be the one who made you feel safe for a while."

Mind Games Chapter 72

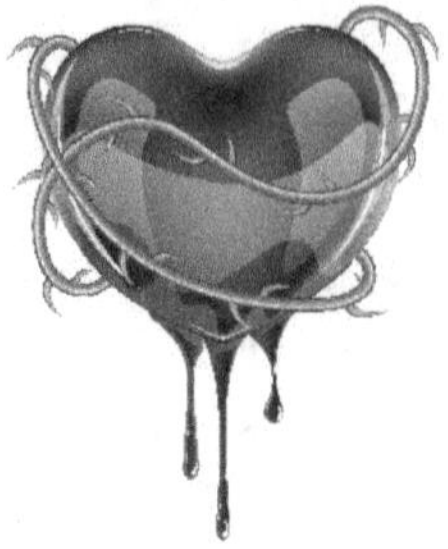

CHRIS PACED BACK AND forth in his apartment. Her pain came through in waves, but she was blocking the mental connection, not letting him get to her mind.

"Damn it," he muttered and walked out onto the balcony, looking over at the Plaza Hotel. "I should have never let her leave here."

He looked at the package that was delivered today and opened it, then pulled the script out. Laughing at the title, Chris poured himself a drink and then sat in the early evening sunset, flipping open to the first page. He read what would eventually become his legacy.

As the moon shone over Manhattan, Chris closed the script and looked out at the night sky. He could barely see the stars over the city's glare, and he sighed, missing the crystal-clear view he had in Maine. He looked back at the script.

"Chris, I guess I did a good job of erasing you from that place," he whispered. "But I also erased any redeeming quality whatsoever in me." He closed his eyes and struggled with his ego. He thought about what Jessica had said the other day when he told her he could shut down the production.

He picked up the phone and called his lawyer.

"Sam, can you get an injunction against them so they don't use the underground complex?" he asked after he explained the situation, and he smiled at the answer. "Can I pick it up and deliver it personally in the morning? They're doing a casting call here in New York," he explained. "Thanks, Sam. I'll meet you at the courthouse at ten."

Chris debated whether to go out for a walk and decided against it. With his level of exhaustion, who knew what trouble he'd find. Instead, he crawled into bed and drifted to sleep at the same time Jessica did.

Mind Game Chapter 73

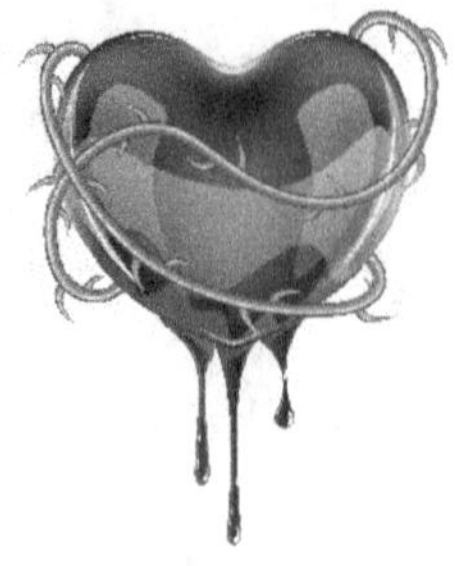

THE MORNING CAME FAST, and Chris begrudgingly hit the buzzer, clinging to the dream of making love to her again. He climbed out of bed and slipped into the shower.

Picking out his best power suit, he donned a black Armani with a white shirt, opting to pass on a tie. He didn't need a tie to make his point. His black Forzieri wing tips still sat where he'd tossed them yesterday, and he slid them on. Diamond-studded cufflinks completed the ensemble, and he stood back, appraising his reflection. Money and power—that was exactly what he wanted to project.

He picked up his wallet and headed out the door for the courthouse.

Sam Trueman represented the Aris family for as long as Chris could remember, and he had been appalled by what happened five years ago. Sam never once doubted that he was Christopher Aris and took him at his word when he said he had no clue of what went on in the complex. He felt a twinge of guilt. Sam was a good man, and Chris had completely snowed him.

He smiled as Sam trotted down the steps and handed him the papers. "Thanks, Sam."

"I understand why you're so upset, but you have to understand the buzz the movie is already causing. Even though we buried your identity, it could be dredged up again if someone were a gifted detective," Sam pointed out. "You may end up in the crossfire again, along with the survivors."

"Tom Whitman has agreed to play Ty, so they're already in the crosshairs," he said.

Sam's jaw dropped for a fraction of a second. "Do you want me to come with you?"

Chris took a deep breath. "I think I can handle this one. But thank you." He folded up the papers and slipped them into his jacket pocket.

He hailed a cab and gave the address of the studio on Avenue of Americas where the casting call was. He walked past the security guards with a friendly nod and bypassed the line of actors and actresses waiting to read for the parts, then marched right into the rehearsal room.

He approached the table where the producer and director sat with Tom and the writer, Sharon Young, keeping his expression neutral, unreadable.

Wide eyes and slack jaws followed him across the room.

He reached into his pocket and slammed the injunction on the table in front of the producer. "You can't use the complex." He leaned on the table, projecting anger he didn't feel.

"Son of a bitch," Tom growled.

Chris turned his attention to Tom. "I'm sorry. Who are you?" He straightened, scanning Tom as if he had never seen him before.

Tom sat speechless, staring at Chris.

"Who the hell are you?" the director asked.

"Christopher Aris," he barked.

Sharon gasped, staring from behind a nose bandage and two black eyes courtesy of Jessica and her amazing right hook. "You look just like him."

Chris turned his attention to her. "Who?"

"Ty," she whispered reverently.

He narrowed his eyes, inspecting her like a lab experiment gone wrong. "He was my brother. It would be safe to assume we look alike." He swung his attention back to the producer, who was looking over the paperwork and going paler by the minute. "I'm not pleased that this movie is being made. What my brothers did was deplorable, and I will not allow you to film in the complex." He turned to leave.

"I know who you are," Tom snapped and stood, his hands balled into fists.

Chris turned around in surprise. "I'm sorry. I still don't know who you are."

Tom shoved the table aside and advanced on Chris.

Chris moved into a karate-ready stance. "I have to warn you, I am a second-degree black belt."

Tom hesitated. "Son of a bitch." He glared and stepped back.

"Very well, then." Chris put his arms back down with a nod. He looked back at the producer. "If you fight the injunction, I'll tie you up in court for years."

With that, Chris walked out of the room.

Mind Games Chapter 74

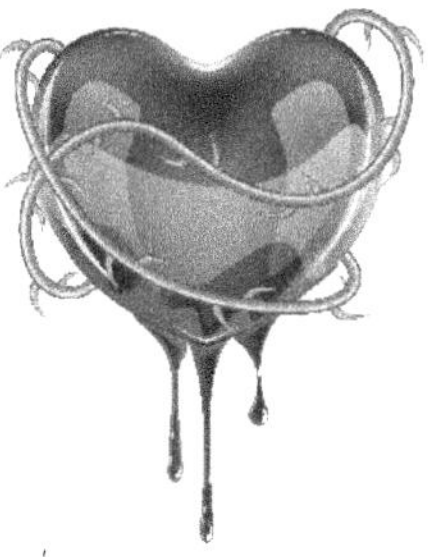

SHARON FANNED HERSELF WITH the script. "Wow."

"Wow?" Tom glared at her. "All you can say is, wow?"

"What the hell crawled up your ass today?" she snapped. "That man is smooth, sexy, and one of the richest men on earth." She looked back at the door. "He went underground after he sold Aris Industries. *I* couldn't even find him."

Tom laughed and turned back toward the door. He shook his head because he couldn't say a word without them thinking he had truly lost it. "God damn it." He took a seat at the table.

"What's wrong?" John asked. "You've been nasty all morning."

"It's personal."

"Trouble in paradise?" Sharon smiled.

Tom glared at her. "Jessica and I broke up." He ignored the shock on all three faces sitting next to him. "So, anything having to do with the Aris's and this movie is on my shit list right now." He took a deep breath. "Keep going," he demanded.

John called the next actress in to read, handing copies of the head shot to the three of them.

Mind Games Chapter 75

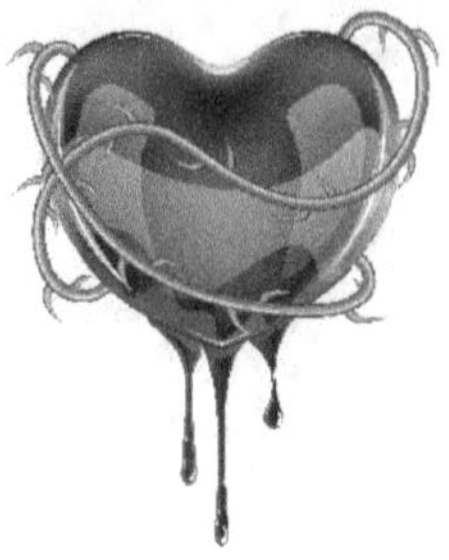

CHRIS KEPT IN CHARACTER until his apartment door latched behind him, and then he started laughing. He went to the mirror in the bathroom. "Jess?"

His laughter died in his throat when she appeared. Her rumpled hair complemented the ripped sweatshirt she wore, and the skin surrounding her eyes was red and puffy.

"What?"

"Are you okay?" He glanced at the bathroom décor. She was back in Maine.

She shook her head.

"You need me?"

She hesitated and then looked up at him. "I don't know."

"You throw a hell of a punch." He smiled, and her brow crinkled. "I ran into that reporter today."

"Where?" she asked, and he opened his mind to her inspection.

"I served an injunction at the casting call."

Jessica started to cry. "She was there?"

Chris nodded. "Yeah, Jess, she wrote the script."

"He didn't tell me."

"Why would he need to? It's legit."

"Stop defending him." She shook. "He kicked me out last night. He said it's over."

"*That's* why he lost his cool."

"Wouldn't you?"

"No, not in front of a reporter." He had expected some level of anger, but it wasn't like Tom to make a scene and draw that kind of attention, especially in full view of a reporter like Sharon Young.

Tears brimmed, cascading down her cheeks.

"I'll be there as soon as I can."

"No. I need some time."

"Well, I'm coming to Maine, anyway. You have a pen?" He smiled a little as her eyebrows rose. "I'm giving you my cell phone number, Jess. I haven't given that out to anyone for something like twenty years, so it's a big deal."

She reached into the drawer and grabbed a lipstick. She wrote the numbers on the bottom of the mirror as he read them off.

"Call if you need to talk."

She scanned him for a moment. "What are you wearing?"

"Armani." He smiled. "Call if you need me."

"Thanks."

"Anytime." He turned away from the mirror.

"Tom's a fool." He wondered if Tom could stay away from her for very long once his anger subsided. "I give it a month at best," he muttered under his breath. He would forgive her anything just to be with her, and couldn't imagine anyone else not being able to do the same.

He threw open the closet and grabbed both suitcases, then threw the contents of his drawers in them. He wasn't planning on coming back anytime soon, not if he got everything he wanted. He flipped open his laptop and sent an inquiry to a realty firm in the general area that he remembered Jessica talking about yesterday. If he played his cards right, he might just be able to give her the one other thing in the world that she'd said she wanted. He already gave her Emily and another incredible miracle that she wouldn't know about for at least a month.

He smiled, thinking of the one thing she wished for silently that he'd made happen. He no longer had any remnants of healing power. He had used the last of that to turn that trick as he made love to her yesterday, completely reversing the surgery she'd had thirteen years ago. Too bad it wouldn't be Tom's. His grin widened.

After folding up the portfolio, he dropped the script inside and zipped it closed. With his suitcases, camera gear, and the portfolio in hand, he headed off to Maine. As he drove onto the highway, he checked his voice mail. The weekly report from his investment banker indicated his investments were doing well. Little did Jessica know, she was the heir to his entire fortune, and had been since the day he sold the company. If anything happened to him, she would be a multibillionaire.

He pulled into his home in York Harbor a little before five and brought his suitcases inside. Then he slid back into the car and ten minutes later, he pulled into her driveway, still in his Armani suit. He rang the doorbell and slowly took off his sunglasses when she opened the door.

Jessica's mouth fell open. "Oh man, Sharon must have been drooling over you," she said before she could catch herself.

He grinned. "Just a wee bit." He stepped inside. "I know you said you didn't want to see me yet, but I needed to make sure you were really okay."

She closed the door behind him and walked into the living room with him following. "I'm afraid I'm a bit underdressed compared to you." She looked down at her sweatpants and torn sweatshirt.

"You're still beautiful to me."

She let out a little laugh and glanced back at him. "Tom called me this afternoon on his way to the airport. He was a little ballistic, and said that if I saw you, to tell you that you are a fucking asshole. The best goddamn actor he ever saw, but a fucking asshole just the same." She looked him up and down. "What the hell did you do?"

He grinned. "I waltzed into the casting room and served the injunction in person. I pretended I didn't know who Tom was. I told them that if they tried to fight it, I would tie them up in court for years." He laughed. "I wish I had it on video. It was priceless, especially the reporter. She was looking at me like I was her next meal." He sighed and wiped a stray hair out of her face, his laughter winding down as their eyes locked. "If you let me into your life, I'll never leave you."

Tears filled her eyes.

"I haven't been with anyone since I fell in love with you, even when I was down there."

"Five years?"

He nodded. "Tom is an idiot to let you go."

"He hates you, and I slept with you. Imagine how you'd feel if I slept with Frank after all he put us through."

Her question struck him silent. He blinked and took a step back, tilting his head as he dug deep for the answer. "It wouldn't matter. Nothing you could do would stop me from loving you."

"But would you ever trust me again? Would you be able to get past it?" she challenged.

That was more difficult for him to answer. "I don't know," he said honestly and looked out the window at the open water. "But eventually I would, because the alternative of not having you in my life isn't a choice I'd be able to live with."

"He can't," she said. "He will never get over it."

"Then he doesn't love you like I do."

Jessica gaped at him and then turned, walking out onto the balcony.

Chris followed her outside. "You have no clue how hard it was to stay away for the last five years." He closed his eyes and listened to the ocean, letting the quiet settle between them. "Did you ever think we were meant to be, Jess?" He opened his eyes.

She turned on him. "You're playing the fate card?" She laughed. "You think it was fate that made our paths cross? It was God's plan? Come on, Ty. You kidnapped me. I just happened to be in the wrong place at the wrong time, and here we are. There is no such thing as fate." She shook her head. "How do I know you're not just acting with me?"

"You don't," he said. "Just like I don't know if you're playing me or not." He put his hands on her shoulders. "We're both very good at games, but you wouldn't risk your marriage, and I wouldn't risk my freedom just for a roll in the hay." He leaned in and kissed her. "Besides, you can't fake what that does to both of us." He smiled, pulling away.

HER LEGS FELT LIKE rubber and her heart kicked into high gear. All from his kiss.

"I can't do this right now," she said breathlessly and slid past him back inside. "You said I had to say no. I'm saying no right now, because if Tom walked through that door." she hesitated and looked at him, "I don't know what I'd do. So, until I can give you an answer…"

Chris nodded. "Okay. I'll go." He turned to leave.

"Thank you," she said.

"For leaving?" He looked back at her.

"No, for coming."

He smiled and walked out of the house, leaving her with his words and the feel of his lips on hers.

Mind Games Chapter 76

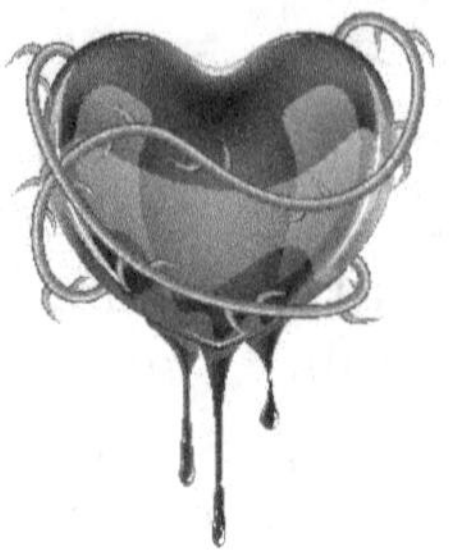

JESSICA WOKE THE NEXT morning and went for a jog on the beach. She kept going over everything that had happened in the last few weeks, how her life had unraveled so quickly and completely. She missed Tom. For the last five years he had been her rock, the one who made her feel safe and secure, and now he was gone, all because she couldn't say no to Chris.

Chris was a completely different story. He made her feel alive; his intensity alone was enough to make her swoon any time he was in the same room, let alone when he touched her. Even the slightest of grazes set her skin on fire. They had a connection that was undeniable, and she wondered if Eric and Chris were right about fate.

Thoughts suffocated her mind as she stopped in the middle of the beach and walked to the water with her hands on her hips. Jessica fought back tears and watched the sun dance on the water.

Finally, she headed back to her house to clean up.

After she took a shower, she threw on a comfortable pair of jeans and headed out the door. She drove to his house and punched the code into the security box, then waited as the gate opened. Her heart beat faster as she pulled up the drive. Music drifted out the cracked windows, and she smiled at his choice of artists. Instead of ringing the doorbell, she tried the latch. It opened effortlessly. Uttering a quiet laugh, she stepped inside.

Nickelback's "Savin' Me" filled the house. The clanging of pots led her to the kitchen, and she leaned against the doorjamb, watching him cook. The raw power of the voice belting out of his chest was as sexy as everything else about him, perfectly on key, and perfectly seductive. She had never heard him sing before, and she smiled.

Is there nothing this man can't do?

As if on cue, he flipped an omelet in the frying pan and caught it easily in the air. The music transitioned to "Here Without You" by Three Doors Down. He slid the omelet onto the plate next to the stove and turned off the burner.

Chris almost dropped his plate when he turned. The note he was singing faded as he stared at her. He picked up the remote and pointed it at the entertainment system in the living room, dialing the music down to a respectable level. He had a pair of sweatpants on and nothing else. His hair was a mess, and he had morning stubble on his face.

He smiled at her. "I've got to remember to lock the front door, now don't I?"

Jessica nodded.

"You want some breakfast?" he asked, offering her his plate.

Jessica hesitated. She didn't remember ever seeing him look as sexy as he did right now, and wasn't sure she really wanted to stay considering the heat prickling across her skin.

"I can make more for myself." He put the plate down on the other side of the table for her. "Really." He smiled, completely disarming her.

"Okay." She sat down.

"Would you like some orange juice?"

"That sounds good."

He poured her a glass and handed it across the table to her. Then he went to the refrigerator, pulled out the eggs, chopped vegetables, shredded cheese for his omelet, and brought them to the counter next to the stove.

She took a bite of the omelet as he mixed the eggs for his. "So, you actually can cook."

"I hold my own." He smiled over his shoulder. "It's kind of necessary up here, but in the city, I ate out a lot because I don't have a kitchen like this one. Besides, it's a bitch cooking for one." He poured the eggs and a handful of the chopped vegetables in the pan and glanced at her. "Want to see something cool?"

Jessica shrugged and continued to devour the omelet.

Chris looked at the refrigerator, the door opened, and then the egg carton and the container with the cut vegetables drifted through the air, back to where he had taken them from. The refrigerator door closed, and then he looked over at her with a smile.

Jessica had her next bite halfway to her mouth and froze at the display.

"Comes in real handy sometimes." Chris chuckled and flipped his omelet, then sprinkled cheese on it and folded it over so it would melt. He waited a few moments and then slid it onto his plate and turned the burner off.

Sitting down, he looked over at her, then at the refrigerator, and it opened. Two containers drifted to the table. He grinned, grabbing the salsa out of the air, and then opened it and poured some on his omelet before meeting her stark gaze.

She still hadn't taken the bite that was halfway to her mouth.

"You want some?" He offered her the salsa.

Jessica blinked, looked at the container and then back to him, and shook her head. She finally took the bite.

Chris shrugged, put the salsa back on the table, and ate his breakfast. He still had a smile on his face, and amusement danced in his eyes as he looked at her.

"Holy shit," Jessica finally said after she swallowed.

"You're telling me." He laughed and took another bite. "I just concluded that I don't need to struggle with the shampoo in the shower anymore. It was actually comical when I figured that out. I had been moving things around and controlling the power for at least a week before that revelation came. I felt like such an idiot."

Jessica laughed as well. "I'll bet." She went back to eating.

"So, what are you doing here?"

"I'm not sure," she said.

He stood, taking their plates and placed them in the sink. "Why aren't you sure?" He turned, leaning on the counter with his left hand.

Jessica sat at the table and looked at him. She didn't dare move for fear she would end up in his arms. She shrugged. "I had nowhere else to go, and I wasn't in the mood to hang out at the house all day wallowing in self-pity."

"That's a step. So, what do we do now?"

Jessica looked around and then back at him. "Got any cards?"

Chris smiled. "A little strip poker?" He waggled his eyebrows.

Jessica laughed and shook her head. Both of them flashed back to the same conversation five years ago.

Chris inhaled. "I'm sorry, Jess."

"For what?"

"For fucking up your life."

Jessica sighed and stood up. She walked over to him and wrapped her arms around his neck. He slowly wrapped his arms around her.

"You didn't completely fuck it up," she whispered and laid her head against his bare chest.

He tilted her chin up. "Yes, I did. Twice now."

She put her head back against his chest and listened to his heartbeat.

Chris kissed the top of her head and then pushed her away for the first time since he'd met her. "I can't have you this close to me." He stepped around her and walked into the living room, taking a deep breath. "I'll be down in a few." He headed up the stairs.

The shower went on upstairs, and Jessica walked outside to the stone wall, looking out at the bay. She sat on the stones and waited for him to come out. Several sailboats came and went before he strolled out.

"Let's take a ride." He looked at his watch.

"Where to?"

"I want to see your grandfather's place."

She raised her eyebrows. "Why?"

Chris shrugged. "Something to do that will keep us out of trouble?" He offered her a crooked smile.

"Okay. Can I drive the 'vette'?" she asked as they stepped into the garage.

He handed her the keys without a second thought and went to climb into the passenger seat. "Just a sec." He ran into the house, then trotted back a few seconds later with a CD and popped it into the player as he settled into the seat next to her.

Jessica grinned as she threw the Corvette into reverse, peeled out of the garage, spun the car around, and barely missed her parked car. Chris paled in the seat beside her, and she laughed.

"Ready for the ride of your life?" She threw the car into gear and had shifted into third by the time they flew through the gate.

"Jesus Christ!"

She laughed and looked over at him. "This car moves."

"Next time, I'll drive." He gripped the seat.

"Am I making you nervous?" She barreled onto the highway going about seventy, which seemed slow compared to her breakneck speed through the suburban roads leading to his house. She quickly sped up to ninety, weaving between the traffic and laughing aloud.

"Um, yes," he said.

"Don't worry, I promise I won't kill you." She sent him a playful grin. She handled the car expertly and whooped with joy as they topped one hundred. Her hair whipped around her face in the wind.

"Do you have a death wish?" he asked as they flew off the highway exit ramp.

She shook her head, slowed to seventy, and turned up the music. "There are a lot of things you don't know about me. First, I drive fast. I never owned a sports car, but I can make an economy car perform like one." She smiled as she glanced over at him. "I never thought there was much difference, but damn, this thing is awesome."

"You are crazier than I am."

"Neither Tom nor Danny would let me drive if they could help it. Mike had an aversion to being in the car with me as well."

"Smart men," he replied.

She gave him a sideways look. "Bite me."

"With pleasure." Chris took her hand and brought her palm to his lips, and then he gently bit her thumb. He smiled, with her thumb still between his teeth.

The heat index in the car went through the roof and she pulled her hand away, taking a deep breath.

"Sorry."

"Stop apologizing. It's irritating me."

"Okay." He grinned and looked out the window.

She took his hand and bit his thumb, then put her lips around it and sucked as she slowly pulled it out of her mouth. "There. We're even."

"Not even close. Girl, you are killing me," he said as he leaned back in the seat, running his hands through his hair. "*Killing* me."

"Oh, and you don't try to do the same to me?" She raised her eyebrows, glancing in his direction.

"I don't have to try."

She tilted her head and nodded. "Touché." Just being this close to him did it to her. Her smile faded. "Do you think it will last?"

"Yes. I love you, Jess. That will last until the day I die." He looked out at the road. "As far as the chemistry between us, I don't see that fading, either. It's gotten stronger over the last five years." He looked at her. "At least for me it has."

Jessica nodded in agreement and slowed the car down, searching for the sharp right that was coming up. "It has for me, too."

The car swerved, executing the near 180-degree turn onto Pleasant Valley Road in Wolfeboro.

"I'm not sure anyone will be there yet. It's still early in the season," she said.

"That's all right." He glanced at his watch.

She slowed to a crawl, swinging onto the dirt road leading to the lake. When she got to the fork in the road, she stopped.

"I believe you want to go this way." He pointed toward the right side of the fork.

Jessica nodded and pulled the car down to the right side of the fork. The current owner of the property, Mr. Franklin, was sitting on the patio, and he stood as the car approached. Chris hopped out before Jessica cut the engine and walked up to him, extending his hand. As she got out of the car, the owner handed Chris a pair of keys.

Jessica looked at Chris, and her jaw went slack. Mr. Franklin climbed into his car and drove away with a friendly wave.

Chris smiled at her and held out the keys. "After the paperwork goes through, this place is yours."

She was dumbfounded. "Two days? You pulled this off in two days?"

He grinned. "Everyone has their price."

"You were already planning on coming here today?"

He nodded. "But I didn't expect to get here so fast. We're a little early. The realtor isn't bringing the papers for me to sign for another twenty minutes. Mr. Franklin already signed them earlier this morning." He laughed. "I made him an offer he couldn't refuse." He said it with the Godfather accent and winked at her. "Show me." He waved at the property.

"I can't accept this."

"This was one of the things you said you wanted most. I gave you both." His lips spread into a knowing smile.

"Oh, Ty. Emily was enough. You didn't have to do this."

"Do me a favor. Please start calling me Chris. He was always the best part of me, anyway."

Jessica crossed the lawn to the edge of the wooden dock. Sun glinted off the water as she scanned the expanse of the lake and Mount Ossipee in the distance. She stepped onto the faded boards, and the wood creaked with each step as she crossed to the edge and looked down into the crystal-clear water.

She glanced back at him. "I learned to swim off this dock. My dad made us swim from the dock to the beach before we could swim out to the rocks." She pointed to the center of the cove. "You can't drive a boat through; you have to go around the buoys because this area has a chain of rocks just under the surface."

Chris looked down at the water at the end of the dock. "How deep is this?"

Jessica tilted her head and gave Chris the once-over. Going from memory, she said, "Probably over your head."

He raised his eyebrows. "It's so clear."

"It's clear out at the buoy, too."

Chris scanned the property from the end of the dock. His gaze moved from the houses in front of the dock, down the crescent-shaped beach to the rocky point housing a gazebo. His smile captured the excitement filling her core.

"I can understand why you love this place," he said.

She led him to the small house and used the key to open it.

"Oh my God!" Jessica glanced around the little pine living room. "They didn't change a thing." She opened the bedroom doors and looked in. Both still had pairs of double beds. She closed her eyes and inhaled, the sweet smell of pine drifting all around her. She led him through the tiny galley kitchen and out the back door, where the double plank boardwalk started, leading to the beach and the gazebo beyond.

She slipped off her flip-flops and stepped onto the sand, the tiny grains filtering through her toes as she walked to the shoreline. The water was cold on her feet, not as bad as the ocean in Maine, but cold just the same.

She laughed aloud as she spread her arms out, twirling with her face tilted toward the clear blue sky.

CHRIS'S SMILE FADED.

Letting Jessica go seemed like an impossible feat. The beauty of the surroundings was nothing compared to the image of her twirling on the beach. He closed his eyes and looked away, pushing his feelings back into the well of his soul.

She would never choose him, even with this.

Chris inhaled and shoved his hands into his pockets, returning his gaze back to her.

"Sunset Point," she said as they walked up to the gazebo. She climbed over the railing and stood in the small tidal pool surrounded by a cluster of rocks, including those that the gazebo was built on. She looked up, grinning just like a child.

She crouched, picked up a rock, and grabbed a small crawfish. Holding her prize up for him to see, she laughed. "We used to spend hours in here terrorizing these things when we were little." She put the crawfish back in the water and climbed onto the far rocks.

Chris climbed down and took a seat next to her.

"I can't accept this."

"It's already done, Jess," he said. "The deed is in your name."

"I never asked you to do this for me." She stood and headed up the path without him.

Chris caught up with her. "I know you didn't. I wanted to do this."

She stopped on the front lawn. "Just so we get this straight, you can't buy me."

"I never presumed I could. Besides, you wanted me long before I had money." He leaned in and planted a gentle kiss on her lips. "You wanted me even with the things I did." He kissed her again, deeper and more insistent. Suddenly, he pulled away, stepping back before he did something he couldn't recover from.

He turned and walked to the dock, then sat down on the steps to get his composure back.

Jessica followed and sat next to him. She took his hand in hers and kissed it. "Yes, I wanted you long before the money, so you don't need to throw it around to impress me."

The realtor pulled up then.

Chris stood. "Wait here."

Jessica turned, watching as he scribbled his name on the papers where the realtor pointed. Soon, he trotted back and took the seat next to her again.

"You chose Tom over me on Monday." He took a deep breath. "Is that what you really want?"

"Is that what this is all about?"

"No. I did this because I wanted to. Now answer my question."

Jessica looked out over the lake and back at him. "Right now, I don't know what I want."

"Then why did you come by this morning?"

"I needed a friend. And you're it," she said without looking at him.

He took her hand. "I can't just be your friend, Jess," he said. "I'm not sure I can let you go if he comes back. I don't know if I can walk away again."

Jessica nodded and inhaled deeply, unclasping her hand from his. "I love you both," she said. "He made me feel safe when I didn't think I would ever feel that way again."

Chris studied his hands.

"Then there's you." She sighed. "You're like an electrical current, a living, breathing danger zone that I can't stay away from, no matter how hard I try. I always figured we'd run into each other again someday, and the dreams... well, they just kept reinforcing it."

"The last five years were just as hard for me as they were for you." She let that settle in the air between them. "I've never been able to let go, and Tom knew it." She took a deep breath. "He's not coming back, Chris."

"You don't know that."

"You didn't see his face."

"What if he comes back? What will you do then?"

Jessica shrugged and glanced in his direction. "I don't know. But I'm still his wife."

End of conversation.

Chris stood up. "You ready?"

She nodded. "Sure you don't want me to drive?"

He broke out in a smile. "Yeah, I'm sure." He opened the car door for her. "I want to get home in one piece."

"Wuss."

He pulled out onto Route 4 toward Maine as "Calling All Angels" piped from the radio. They exchanged a glance.

"Did you ever get the significance of why I picked this song?" she asked.

"It gave you hope." He smiled a little and started singing to the music.

HE'D NAILED IT. SHE twitched in the passenger seat.

"Don't look so shocked," he said between lyrics.

His voice melted her just as much as his touch did, and she sighed, closing her eyes. Eric's words echoed in her head. *You're the only one who can save him from himself.*

"You are."

"Hmmm?" she replied, opening her eyes.

"Nothing." He continued singing softly to the songs on the radio.

The only sound for miles was the soft lull of his voice singing to the radio. She drifted into a state somewhere between awake and sleep, totally relaxed with the sun beating down on her face.

"You have no idea how much I need you," he whispered.

"Yes, I do," she whispered back without opening her eyes.

"Shit, I thought you were sleeping."

She opened her eyes, glancing in his direction, and sat up at the sight of his crimson cheeks.

"My God, you're blushing." She laughed.

"You weren't actually supposed to hear that."

"Why not?"

He looked over and sighed. "Because."

She waited, looking at him expectantly.

"Jesus, Jess!"

"I'm waiting."

"Because I'm trying like hell to keep some distance."

"Why?"

"Because if I let you in all the way, you could completely destroy me." His voice rose above the music, and he glared at her. "And I have absolutely no control over this."

"Welcome to my world."

HE PULLED THE CAR over on the side of the road and threw it in neutral, then ripped the emergency brake in place. He stormed out of the car and leaned on the trunk, fighting for internal control. Her car door opened.

"Don't, Jess." he warned over his shoulder.

Jessica walked to the back of the car and leaned against it next to him.

"When Tom comes back, I lose," he said. "I never lose." He looked down at her. "Ever." He pulled her close, crushing her lips under his. He let her go just as quickly and stormed around the car and into the driver's seat before he gave in to the need pummeling his muscles.

She tentatively slipped back into the passenger seat.

He waited until she buckled her seat belt and then floored the car, sending gravel a hundred feet behind them. He shifted quickly and pressed the gas pedal down, achieving zero to sixty in a few seconds, trying to outrun what he was feeling.

"Chris."

He just drove, paralleling her speed earlier. He slid into a restaurant that he had seen on the way up, threw the car in first gear, and shut the engine.

"I'm hungry," he announced and got out of the car. He walked around and opened her door. "You coming?"

"Only if you cut the attitude."

He looked down at her. "I can't," he said through clenched teeth.

"Huh?"

"If I do, I'll end up ripping your clothes off and taking you right here."

SHE TOOK A CLOSER look, recognizing the insane need in his eyes. She got out of the car slowly and started walking toward the entrance of the restaurant, then turned to him quickly, making him bump into her.

"Cut the attitude," she demanded, and then turned back.

His hands descended onto her shoulders. "You don't want that," he whispered in her ear. "Because if you let me sleep with you again, I'll make sure Tom can never come back."

Jessica's eyes went wide, and she stopped in her tracks, turning slowly. "Oh, no you didn't."

Chris held her gaze but said nothing.

"Uh-uh." She shook her head. "You do not get to threaten him." She held her hand out. "Keys."

"If you sleep with me again, there's no going back," he growled low in his throat. "I won't let it happen and if that means taking him out, so be it."

"Give me the keys! Now!"

"No. I'm hungry. I'm eating."

They stood in the middle of the parking lot, glaring at each other, oblivious to the cars driving in and out around them.

"Then I'll walk." She stormed out to the road in the direction they were originally headed.

CHRIS WATCHED JESSICA STOMP off. He put his hands on his hips, looked down at the pavement, then back at her, taking a deep breath.

"Shit." He trotted after her. When he caught up to her, he put his hand on her shoulder. "Stop."

"Why should I?" She tore her shoulder out of his grasp.

"Because I'm an idiot, and it's too far for you to walk."

Jessica slowed down and stopped, but didn't turn around.

"I'm sorry. It's just hard, okay?"

"It's not okay," she said, the bite of anger no longer reflecting in her voice. "It's not okay at all." Tears made tracks down her cheeks.

"Damn it," he whispered. He turned away to get his composure back. "I know it's not okay." He turned back to her. "I just don't know what else to do." He reached out and brushed a hair from her face. "You already have me wrapped around your little finger." He smiled a little and looked sheepishly down at the ground. "But as I said in New York, if we do that again, I won't let you go, and I'm not sure you really understand what that means."

"Enlighten me," she said, wiping the tears away.

"He's going to come back, Jess." He looked at her. "Eventually, he is going to want you back, and you're going to go." He sighed, intently staring her down. "We both know I don't fight fair, not where you're concerned, so do you really want me fighting for you?" He drew a long breath at the look on her face. "I still have some restraint where you're concerned, but if we end up in bed again, that will fly right out the window. It's bad enough now..." He glanced up the road. "Maybe I will be okay when Tom comes back and you go with him, but I'm not even sure of that."

"He's not coming back, and even if he did, you don't know what I'll do," Jessica said. "I don't even know what I want right now."

"But as you said earlier, you're his wife."

"Yes, I am. But I'm not sure that's where I belong. If I was truly happy with Tom, I would never have allowed myself to be with you." She looked away. "Even though it was inevitable, it still hurts like hell that he left." She started walking back to the restaurant.

"Do you want to grab lunch or head home?" he asked as they walked through the parking lot.

"I'm hungry, too, so lunch sounds good. What time is it, anyway?"

Chris looked at his watch. "Almost two."

"The only thing I've got going today is the show tonight. It's the one with the kids in it, and I want to tape it."

"You really want to spend all that time with me?" he asked as he held the door open for her.

"Not particularly, but what else am I going to do?"

His expression fell.

"I'm kidding," she said, poking him in the stomach when she passed him.

"That was just mean."

She held up two fingers when the hostess asked how many in their party. "You really don't know me very well," she said after the hostess sat them and walked away.

"What do you mean?"

"I couldn't pass up an opportunity like that. Are you kidding?" A smile played on her lips.

"I forgot. You like to play games, don't you?" he said, reaching out and taking her hand. He turned it palm up and slowly traced the lines with his finger.

Her cheeks flushed, and his smile widened.

She went to pull her hand away, and his grip around her wrist tightened.

"I told you a long time ago that I didn't want to play games with you. I lied." He continued tracing the lines on her palm and wrist.

"Stop." She inhaled deeply.

Intimately familiar with all the erogenous zones on a woman's body, Chris knew how to exploit every one of them, and he was pleased that he hadn't lost his touch. He stopped and released her wrist, closing his own eyes, then blew a slow stream of air from his lips to gain control.

"Can I get you two something to drink?" the waitress asked.

"Ice water," both of them said at the same time without taking their eyes off each other.

"Do you know what you would like?"

"Not yet," Jessica said, breaking eye contact. "But if you wouldn't mind bringing the water now, that would be great."

"I know what I'd like," he said in his smooth, sexy voice, and scanned her up and down after the waitress left.

Jessica blushed. "What is your favorite song?" she asked, opening the menu.

The waitress arrived with the water and took their order. She left a moment later.

"I'm not sure whether to drink this or dump it over my head," Chris said.

"Same here." She took a sip. "Now, what's your favorite song?"

Chris thought about her question for a while. "I don't know. Right now, one doesn't stick out. There are so many that I'd categorize in my list of favorites."

"Okay, favorite artist?" she asked.

"All time or current?"

"All time."

"Pink Floyd," he said without hesitation.

"Current?"

"Nickelback," he replied. "You?"

"Add to your list Aerosmith and Bon Jovi, and we pretty much match up."

He smiled. "A rocker. I would have never guessed."

"Babe, I'll always be a rocker at heart." She laughed. "Loud music and fast cars. That's me."

"Aren't you getting a little old for that?"

She shook her head. "No, I'm only twenty-nine."

"If I didn't know exactly how old you were, I might actually believe that."

"How old are you?" she asked.

"I'm twelve years younger than you are, almost to the day."

"When's your birthday?"

"July seventh."

"Sevens." She looked at him and laughed.

"What's so funny?"

"Seven is my lucky number." She broke out in goose bumps. "You turn thirty-five this year."

"You definitely don't look your age, Jess."

The waitress came with their food.

"How old do you think she is?" Chris asked the waitress.

"Chris," Jessica scolded.

"I don't know, early thirties?" she guessed.

Jessica smiled. "How about him?" She pointed to Chris.

"Mid-thirties." She smiled at Chris.

"Bingo," Jessica replied, laughing. "And don't you dare tell her how old I am," she warned Chris, and he snapped his mouth shut.

The waitress looked between the two of them.

"I'm a little older than he is," Jessica replied.

The waitress smiled and wandered away.

"A little?" He picked up the burger and took a bite.

She smiled and took a bite of her salad.

"This is nice." He leaned back in the seat.

"Yeah, it is."

"I can't remember the last time I had a date." Then he laughed. "Yes, I can." He looked at her as the dinner he'd brought her flashed through his mind. With her in the white floor-length dress, she had looked like a goddess.

"The steak dinner? Seriously, that was your last date?"

"Yes."

"What about before that?"

"High school," he said. "Senior Prom. I think my date's name was Cheryl." He took a deep breath. "I screwed around in college a little, but the scar made it tough, and by the time I got out, Frank had drafted me to set up the complex. That took a few years, and by the time it was finished, we already had our first prisoners. He said I was brilliant, and the fool that I was believed him." He glanced out the window.

"You were brilliant at editing," she said, causing him to look at her. "What I saw you do with that video? It was amazing."

"Really?"

"Yes, just like the pictures you showed me in your apartment. They were brilliant." She blushed. "You seem to have a natural brilliance that comes through in everything you do."

He raised his eyebrows.

She laughed nervously. "Even the way you seduce me..." She met his gaze. "You were just as brilliant being evil. Now, you just have to channel that the right way." She studied her hands. "So, Frank was right. You are brilliant."

He blinked. "Evil?"

"Yes, Ty, you were the embodiment of evil when we first met." She met his gaze. "And you were brilliant enough at it to scare the hell out of me."

"You were scared of me?"

"Yes."

"The only time I saw fear was the first time in the chair," he said. "Then all I saw in your eyes was defiance."

She laughed. "I played the game well, didn't I?"

Chris recoiled in his seat.

"You started protecting me long before you realized it."

His jaw dropped.

"I was trying to survive, and the videos you played for me that first day on the treadmill... They gave me exactly what I needed to do just that."

"What was that?"

"Your weakness," she said.

"Which was?" He shifted uncomfortably in the seat.

"You needed to hear them beg, and you needed to win." She finished her water. "I never gave you either of those things." She paused. "I never gave you the power you so desperately wanted over me. If I had, we wouldn't be sitting here today." She sat back in the chair. "The only thing I didn't plan on was falling for you."

He laughed and ran his hand through his hair, frazzled by her admission. "You have got to be kidding me."

She shook her head. "I am almost as good as you at playing games, and Mike could have told you that. You were absolutely right, though. I did want you, but I wasn't ever going to tell you that down there."

"You continue to surprise me." He waved for the check.

"I'm far from an angel, Chris. Not quite as far as you, but..." She shrugged. "I know how to drive someone crazy, and I know how to make a man fall in love with me."

"You mean you know how to manipulate people," he said, and the waitress headed over. Chris peeled two hundred-dollar bills and handed them to her. "Keep the change."

The waitress became completely flustered at the massive tip, thanking them repeatedly.

Chris glanced sideways at Jessica.

"I guess," Jessica said, answering his earlier statement as they headed outside. "But I'm not really a manipulator. I'm a motivator."

Chris laughed, thinking about the junkie he'd put in rehab. "So, you knew how to use the power."

"No, I didn't know how to use it," she said seriously.

He looked down at her as he held the car door open. "You may not have realized it, but that's probably what you were doing." He kissed her on the lips. "Either way, I'm glad, because in some way, you granted me this freedom that I have now." He walked around the car and slipped into the driver's seat.

"Ty, what do you really want?"

"The dream," he said without hesitation. "To be with you," he added for clarification as he glanced over at her. "For the rest of my life." He put the car in gear and slid smoothly onto the road, heading back toward Maine.

"We have to deal with Frank's ghost before I can think about a future anywhere," Jessica said as she watched the scenery pass by.

If we live through that, then I'll worry about what I'm going to do about you.

Chris cast a sideways glance at Jessica as her thought broadcasted in his head. "All I know is when I'm with you, I'm the person I want to be." He paused. "And when I'm not, I'm more likely to revert into old habits."

"You don't have a split personality, Chris. You can control that if you want to."

"But without you, I don't want to control it." He let the silence fill the car. When he pulled into the garage and cut the engine, he sat still, mulling over what he wanted to say. "I used to think you ruined me. But actually, what you did was save me." He slowly got out of the car and stretched. "Are you coming in?"

JESSICA HESITATED, STUDYING THE hopeful glint in his eyes. He had done an amazing thing for her this morning, and she was grateful, but she wasn't sure she wanted to tempt fate.

"I promise I'll be a gentleman," he said in all sincerity.

"Yeah, I've heard that before," she spouted before she could stop it. Heat filled her cheeks.

"I'll teach you how to play chess. Then I can dazzle you with my culinary expertise." He grinned, his eyes sparkling. "And if you're game, we can watch the show here, and I'll burn it on a DVD for you."

"I don't know." She hesitated and closed her car door. It would be refreshing to have a man cook for her. With the exception of pancakes, Tom was a disaster in the kitchen.

"I promise." His eyes pleaded with her.

"Can you really keep your hands off me for that long?" She raised her eyebrow.

"Can you?"

Jessica shrugged.

"You just have to understand the ramifications if we can't," he said.

"Do you want me to stay, or don't you?"

"Yes. I want you to stay."

"All right, I'll stay." She followed him into the house, amazed that it was already four in the afternoon. "You know where I was supposed to go today?"

"No. Where?"

Her breath hitched. "I was supposed to go to the doctor's today." She turned to Chris. "Tom wanted us to have a baby." She blinked back the tears, gritting her teeth against them.

Chris took her in his arms, holding her as she cried. "Shhhh," he cooed.

She finally pulled away from him and wiped her eyes. "I can't have children anymore." She sniffled.

"I know."

"How?"

"Medical records."

Her eyebrows knitted together in confusion as she studied Chris.

"I pulled medical and dental records for everyone I kidnapped," he said. "That way, I'd know what issues we might deal with medically." He shrugged. "We altered the dental records, so they matched back to the person we wanted the world to think was dead."

She looked at him in disbelief. "How'd you do that?"

"I'm a whiz at computers and can hack into any system. There isn't a firewall built I can't hack through."

Jessica laughed. "What, are you a member of Mensa or something?"

"Ty was. He's a fucking genius."

She raised her eyebrow. "Wow. Is there anything that you can't do?"

He thought for a moment. "I can't get pregnant," he replied with a silly smile.

Jessica couldn't help but laugh. "No, you can't."

Chris grinned.

"Are you really considered a genius?"

"Yes."

"Wow, you've got the whole package going on, haven't you?" She sat on the couch.

"I don't know about that." He walked out of the room and returned a few minutes later with a beautiful marble chess set. He set it down on the coffee table and took a seat in the chair. "Chess is a game of logic and strategy forcing you to think at least a move ahead."

"You sound like a textbook."

Dimples appeared briefly in his cheeks, and then he took a deep breath. "Just listen, okay?"

She nodded.

Chris explained the functions of each piece, holding them up for her to see as well as the goal of the game, making sure the board was set up properly before they began. "You ready?" He reached over and grabbed the remote to put some music on low.

"You really would have played this with me when we were down there?"

Chris nodded. "I was interested in seeing how you do. Still am," he said. "Do you want something to drink before we start?" He stood and walked into the kitchen.

"What do you have?" she asked as he opened the refrigerator.

"I've got beer and a couple of bottles of wine. I've also got Grey Goose." He glanced in her direction.

The humor in his eyes made her laugh. "You're never going to let me live that down, are you?"

He shook his head. "You were so funny stumbling down the beach and singing completely off-key at the top of your lungs." He laughed. "If I hadn't caught you, you would have face planted in the sand." He looked over at her. "And the next day, you looked like death warmed over. It's just too good to let you live down."

"Do you have a white zinfandel?"

"Yes." He pulled the bottle out of the refrigerator.

"Thanks." She took the wineglass he offered.

He raised his glass. "To better days ahead of us." He clinked her glass and took a sip.

She stared at him. "Us?"

He shrugged. "Humor me, okay?" And then he looked at the wineglass she held in her hand and back at her as his smile faded. She went to take a sip, but he reached over and took the glass from her. "That's probably not a good idea."

"Why not?"

He looked at her and raised his eyebrows. "I don't know what I was thinking. We don't really mix well with alcohol."

"One glass isn't going to kill us," Jessica said, reaching for her glass.

"Okay." He slowly handed her the glass. "Ready?" he said, pointing at the board, and she nodded.

The game took a couple of hours, and when Chris grinned and uttered checkmate, Jessica stared at the board trying to figure out what went wrong.

"Shit," she said.

He sat back in the seat.

Jessica glanced at the clock and raised her eyebrows. No wonder she was hungry.

"What would you like?" he asked, reading her thoughts.

She shrugged and reached for the bottle. He picked it up as he walked into the kitchen.

"Hello?" she said as she followed him into the kitchen. "I'd like some more wine."

"No," he said, putting the cork into the bottle and taking her glass to put it into the sink.

"Why not?"

"I already told you why."

"There's something that you're not telling me." She stepped closer. "You're blocking me from your thoughts."

"I don't want you to get drunk." He opened the cabinets and surveyed what he had for food. "What would you like for dinner?"

"Chinese," she said.

He looked over his shoulder at her. "Okay."

"You know how to cook Chinese food?"

"How hard can it be?" He crossed to the phone and flipped open the phone book. "What do you want?"

"Spicy chicken and rice," she said through a sudden case of giggles possessing her. "You are too funny."

Chris walked up to her. "I love your laugh," he said as he pulled her close. He leaned down and kissed her, running his good hand into her hair. Slowly, he pulled away with his eyes bright blue and full of lust. He took a few steps back and stared at her. "I promised."

"Yes, you did," she said. She turned and walked outside to the rock wall and leaned on it, looking at the boats coming into the bay. When he laid his hands on her shoulders, she leaned her head back into his chest.

"Did you ever think it would be like this?" he asked as she watched the boats.

"Like what?"

"So strong it actually hurts?"

She shook her head.

"Me neither." He turned and went inside.

Jessica thought she heard a doorbell but didn't move to go inside. She wasn't sure what to do about her life. If Tom came back, would she go with him? She looked over her shoulder at the house and then back at the water. She didn't know.

If Ty hadn't killed...

She shook her head, clearing that thought right out of her mind. The question was which one could she live without? She thought she knew the answer, and she sighed.

"Hey Jess, food's here," Chris called from the door.

She wandered back inside. He had set the table for them and pointed to her place as he got them each a glass of ice water. She ate quietly, lost in her own thoughts.

"Do you know what you're going to do yet?" He finished the food on his plate.

She met his gaze. "No," she said simply, lying to him. "I can't think past getting rid of Frank right now."

He stood up, brought his plate to the sink, and threw it in. He took her empty plate as well. "Why are you lying to me?" he asked and leaned on the counter, his back to her.

The glasses in the sink shattered.

She jumped. "I'm not."

The radio shut off, and he slowly turned. "You can't fool me anymore, Jess."

"I don't know what I'm going to do!" she yelled. "It changes from one moment to the next, and you can't expect me to make a decision like that." She snapped her fingers. "My marriage is in the shitter right now. I've got a ghost that wants to hurt me and my family. I've got you, and I don't know what the hell to do with you. I want to run right now, but I can't." She looked at him and swore under her breath. "I'm a fucking mess." She walked into the family room and flopped down on the couch.

He took the seat next to her, putting his arm around her shoulders. "I've never been good at being patient."

She looked up at the clock over his television. "The show's going to be on in a few minutes. You said you would record it for me?"

"Will do." He stood, setting up a blank disc in the DVR. "What channel?"

"Sixteen."

He set the DVR to record and turned the television on. Chris sat down and put his arm around her. "You okay now?"

She shrugged.

He leaned over and kissed her cheek. "Now?"

She shrugged again as the screen filled with the image of her husband. She looked down at the rings on her hand and back to the screen as the teaser faded and the beginning credits came up.

I shouldn't be here.

HE WATCHED HER INSTEAD of the show, making a mental note that she looked at her wedding ring. The thought that ran through her mind was like a knife in his heart. He moved his arm from around her shoulders and crossed them in front of him as he watched the commercials.

The next scene that came up made her brighten up. It was the newsroom scene, and when Eric walked into the camera shot, she smiled. Her focus was now on her son, not Tom, and Chris was relieved.

He watched the short walk-on role, impressed with the kid's natural talent. "Eric did great."

They watched the show unfold, and when they got to the party scene, Jessica was excited again, until she saw the camera pan by her daughter.

Frank was in the room with his arms around Emily's waist, whispering in her ear. The frozen smile on Emily's face screamed with fear.

"TOM SAW HIM. GOD damn it! He saw him and didn't tell me until after that son of a bitch attacked Emily." Anger ignited in her. What she saw plainly on that video was not just a quick flash, as Tom had led her to believe.

Jessica's cell phone rang, and she reached for her purse and ripped the phone out, looking at the number. She flipped the phone open. "I don't want to talk to you right now."

"I didn't see the cut, Jessie. Otherwise, I would have had that scene taken out," Tom said.

"You knew!" she hissed into the phone and turned her back to Chris.

"I didn't know that was in the show."

"That's not what I was talking about. You knew he was after Emily."

TOM WAS QUIET ON the other side of the country. He glanced at Sharon and the script laid out in front of them, openly eavesdropping on his conversation.

"Come on, Tom. We need to finish the rewrites for the movie," she said loud enough for her voice to be heard by his wife.

Tom glared at her.

"Who the hell is that?" Jessica asked.

"Don't even go there. You stepped over that line first," he whispered, turning his back so Sharon wouldn't hear.

JESSICA HUNG UP THE phone. It rang again almost immediately. She looked at the number and opened it. She didn't speak, and neither did he.

"Where the hell are you anyway?" he finally asked.

Jessica turned and looked at Chris. "It doesn't matter anymore. Bye, Tom."

She closed the phone. On the television screen, Tom's character kissed Lois Lane.

Jessica's eyes blurred with tears, and she glanced at her wedding ring. The voice in the background had been Sharon's, and she hitched her breath as her gaze rose to the television screen. The camera panned, and she saw the image of Emily flash on the screen again. This time she was really smiling, and Frank wasn't anywhere to be seen.

"We need to do something about Frank. Now. Tonight," she seethed, her hurt turning to fury.

"Jess, it will keep till the morning. We have to get some things anyway, and there aren't any stores open right now."

Jessica looked at the clock and then back at him. "Home Depot has mirrors, and they're still open."

"No, we'll do it tomorrow," he insisted.

Jessica glared at him and then up at the ceiling as a new thought dawned on her. *There are mirrors in his bedroom.* She headed toward the stairs and halted in her tracks against her will.

"Let me go." She glared at him.

He held his head low, looking at her through his bangs. "No, Jess, not here. Besides, I'm not ready to die tonight," he said, shocking her into reason.

Jessica blinked at him and looked away. "Let me go."

He shook his head and walked over to her. "Not until you promise me you will not do something stupid."

She sighed and looked up at him. "Let go!"

"Promise me!"

Jessica rolled her eyes and nodded. "I promise." The invisible hands that gripped her disappeared. "You've gotten pretty good with that."

"I need to know where that door is, Jess," he said.

She looked at him, not understanding what he was saying at first, and then it clicked. Her eyes went wide. "Why?"

"Because Eric said I had to be the one to open it, and he gave me the key." He reached into his pocket and pulled out the key ring. "I'm surprised you didn't notice it." He held it up.

Jessica remembered Chris had said something about seeing Eric on the beach the day she came to say goodbye and found him drunk. "I still don't understand."

"Eric said it had to be me that opened the door, or otherwise..." He shrugged. "You had the dream. You can guess what happens to both of us if we don't get that door open."

Jessica nodded.

"Can you show me where it is?"

"I'm not sure."

"What do you need?"

"I need you." She looked up at him.

He smiled sadly and looked over at the television, then back at her. "You're still his wife," he said, nodding toward the screen.

"I don't care."

"Yes, you do," Chris said. "That's why you're feeling angry and reckless right now."

Her face scrunched up as tears fell. "Damn it, Ty." She turned away from him. She yanked her wedding ring off, pitched it across the room, then sat down on the floor and cried into her hands.

Chris kneeled down and put his arms around her. "I'm sorry, but until you can honestly say that you want to be with me for the rest of your life, we can't," he whispered in her ear. "Now, how do I get to that door?"

"You have to get in my head like Eric," she said. "I've got to let you." She sniffled and turned toward him, kissing him before he could pull away. She wrapped her arms around his neck tightly and pushed him back on the floor, moving on top of him.

HER KISS DEEPENED, AND he groaned under her mouth, drawing into her much like the transition through the mirrors. He tightened his grip, and the room disappeared and was replaced by a long hallway where he stood alone, staring at the white light spilling around the edge of the door at the far end of the hall. He'd seen this once before, in the mirror's reflection five years ago, right before the chains that were tearing him apart released.

"Holy shit." The strength of the power behind that door made what was flowing through him feel like a match flickering in the wind. He blinked and pushed her away from him onto the floor of his house, his breath wheezing in his chest. His gaze caught on her swirling, storm-laden eyes.

"Sweet Jesus," he whispered and sat up.

She stared at him, her chest rising and falling as hard as his. "Gives a whole new meaning to being inside me, doesn't it?"

He let out a little bark of a laugh and nodded. He ran his hand through his hair and stood. The show credits rolled, and he blinked. That little journey took twenty minutes out of the day.

He brought his gaze back to her. "I have to get there faster, or otherwise, we're dead."

Jessica raised her eyebrows and Chris pointed at the television.

"Twenty minutes. Not good enough." He helped her off the floor and planted another kiss on her, this time launching into the hallway instead of being pulled by her. He broke the kiss, his breath locked in his chest, and he stepped back into his family room, glancing at the clock. A good ten minutes had passed, and he shook his head, meeting her gaze again.

"Still not good enough." He turned his back to her and glanced out the sliders at the darkness that took over his backyard. His mind rolled over the process, trying to find the key.

The key! How can I be so stupid? After pulling the key ring out, he slid the old-fashioned skeleton key off and twirled it in his fingers. Palming it, he turned and crossed, taking her in his arms once again, crushing her lips. When they parted, and his tongue tickled hers, the transition occurred. The familiar hallway surrounded him, and his heart leaped into his throat. The reverse happened when he broke the kiss, and this time when he looked at the clock, not even a minute had passed.

"I need this in my hand." He held up the key.

Jessica stared at the oddly shaped metal and nodded, returning her gaze to his. "I should be going."

He glanced over at the television. "Do you want me to edit the part of Frank out?"

"You can do that?"

He raised an eyebrow, and she chuckled.

"Yeah, all right, that was a stupid question. I know. I've seen what you can do."

"I'll bring it over in the morning after I get the things we need."

She hesitated. "I'm not sure I want to be alone tonight."

"You can't stay here." Chris put his hands out at the reaction on her face. "Not because I don't want you to, Jess. There are mirrors in the bedrooms here."

"If we die tomorrow..." Her eyes went wide and sincere. "I want a chance to say goodbye."

"Consider today just that." He approached her. "I don't really know if we'll both make it through this." He touched her face. "But today... today was worth dying for." He kissed her on the cheek. "I'll see you in the morning, Jess," he whispered and took her by the arm, escorting her out to her car.

Mind Games Chapter 77

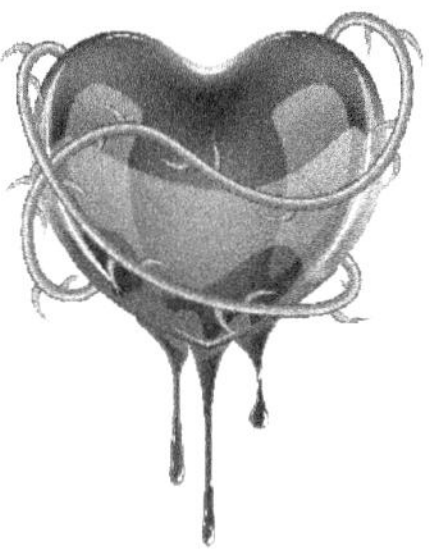

CHRIS WALKED BACK INTO the house after watching her leave and took a deep breath. He wanted to go with her and hold her all night in his arms, but he knew that would be nailing the lid on his coffin. He needed a little distance to prepare himself for what the morning would bring.

The discarded wedding ring caught his eye, and he picked it up, putting it on the coffee table, then went to work editing the show like he'd promised. It took less than an hour for him to string the video together without the commercials or Frank, and he put the new disc in a case and set it down next to her wedding band.

Instead of going to bed, he went to switch on the television and froze. Frank's faded image stared back from the dark screen.

"You think you can win?" He laughed. "I'm going to make sure you see her die before you do," Frank growled and then was gone.

Chris shivered and almost gave in to his need to run to her, but he knew that would just prolong the saga with Frank. If he went to her now, he wasn't sure he could do what he needed to kill Frank. He had to prepare himself and be completely ready for this, or otherwise he might be apt to back out because it no longer was just two lives at stake. There was that third miracle he had yet to tell her about.

Chris got up and took his shirt off. He moved the table aside and did karate forms to center his energy and focus. After a couple of hours, he stretched and headed to bed, feeling revived and focused and ready to take on the world.

Mind Games Chapter 78

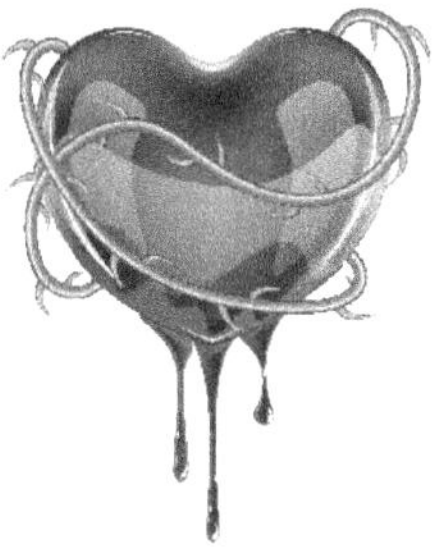

JESSICA DROVE HOME, DISAPPOINTED that he hadn't come with her. She really didn't want to be alone, and she was still angry with Tom.

In the garage, she opened her phone and hit the redial button, waiting for him to answer.

"What?" he snapped.

"What if I told you I had gone to the doctor?" She needed to know if there was any glimmer of hope.

Silence, and then the shuffle of a chair answered her.

TOM GOT UP FROM the table that he was sitting at with Sharon, walked to the other side of the room, and leaned against the wall with the phone to his ear. "Did you?"

"Does it really matter to you?" Jessica started to cry.

Tom closed his eyes three thousand miles away and put his forehead against the wall. "You slept with him," he whispered, pain in his voice.

"Do you still love me?" Her voice shook.

Tom was quiet again for a moment. "I'll always love you." He took a deep breath. "I just can't be with you after what you did. Not right now."

"You should have told me about Emily right away, Tom."

"I know." He glanced over his shoulder at Sharon; she stared back, impatiently tapping the pen on the table. "Did you go to the doctor?"

"No," Jessica replied. "You told me not to bother." She stifled a sob.

"Then where were you all day?"

"Out," Jessica whispered. "I took a drive."

"Were you alone?"

A sigh followed by silence came through the phone line.

"Are you alone now?"

"Yes."

"Did you..." He stopped himself from asking the question.

"No. No, I didn't." She paused. "Did you sleep with her again?"

He had gotten fall-down drunk last night, and Sharon had been there with him. "I was drunk," he answered.

"You slept with her?" she repeated.

"Yes."

"Oh," she whispered, not knowing what else to say.

"You screwed up first," he said, trying to ease his own guilt.

"It's really over. Isn't it?"

Tom stood with his head hung as tears blurred his vision. He blinked them back. "I don't know, Jess. I just don't know."

Silence followed.

"I have to go." He didn't say goodbye, he just ended the call.

JESSICA KNEW THAT TOM didn't drink very much when he was filming, so the magnitude of his actions shocked her. She also knew the hurt she felt was unjustified compared to what she had done to him. Jessica closed her phone and climbed out of the car. She looked at her ring-less hand as the tears flowed.

There was still hope with Tom, which made the choice so much more difficult.

TOM HUNG UP THE phone and leaned his forehead against the wall for a moment. He missed her, even though he was still bitter and angry over what she had done. He missed the way she felt in his arms. He had been so sure in the hotel that it was over. And yesterday when Chris had waltzed into the auditions as well, but drunken sex and three thousand miles put distance and doubt in him.

Tom loved her and wondered if he let her back in his life, would he ever be able to forgive and forget? Looking over at the table where Sharon sat poring over the script, he wondered if Jessica could do the same. Slowly, he walked back and sat down.

Sharon looked over at him and commented, "She really has you wrapped around her little finger, doesn't she?"

"Leave it alone."

"Why? You're with me now."

He laughed. "Just because I fucked you doesn't mean I'm with you."

"It does if you don't want her to get hurt. Besides,"—she smiled sweetly—"I've got some really wild pictures from last night. How would you like to see these go to print?" She shuffled through some of the more lewd pictures on her phone for him to see.

He looked at her with disgust. "I'm not doing this." He stood to go.

"You told me some pretty interesting things last night."

"Like what?" He didn't remember what had happened. He just knew he woke with her naked in bed, and there was definite evidence of screwing around.

"Oh, let's see, like Jessica slept with Christopher Aris, and he pretended not to know you in the audition room. You ranted about that for quite a while. And then you said something that could land you in the nuthouse. You told me that there was a ghost after you." She shook her head. "So, if you don't want her to get hurt and all the things I have on you published for the world to see, you *are* with me." She smiled and batted her eyes.

Her lack of subtlety wasn't lost on him as anger raged inside and he sat down.

"I've got an appointment with a lawyer for you tomorrow. You're going to divorce that bitch and marry me."

His jaw dropped. "You're out of your mind."

"No, I just know what I want. Now, let's get back to work." She looked at her watch. "We have dinner reservations in an hour."

"You would want to be with someone who hates you? That is so fucking pathetic."

"You want to be with that lying, cheating bitch, knowing she would rather be with someone else?" She smiled back. "*That* is pathetic."

"She never said she would rather be with him." Tom stood up. "We're done here, and I'm not hungry." He left the room.

"My car is still at your house. I'm coming home with you."

"You are not coming in."

"Yes, I am, and you're going to show me the time of my life." She walked over to him and ran her hand down his arm. "You don't seem to understand what I'm saying to you. I'll go after her, and I don't mean as a reporter. I've got a reason to pay her back personally now." She laughed lightly. "I'll have her killed. All I have to do is make one brief phone call and it will look like you did it because of the affair. Got it?" She smiled and tilted her head. "Although it would be fun to kill the bitch myself."

He turned on her. "God help you if you go after Jessica." His fists clenched in rage.

"Oh, but I will leave her alone if you keep me busy."

He grabbed her by the throat, calling her bluff as fury got the better of him.

Sharon pulled out her cell phone. "All I need to do is press send and she's dead." She whispered hoarsely as he continued to squeeze. She held up the phone so he could see the text message. It was a confirmation for a hit on his wife. "And if I happen to have an accident, or God forbid, die, that's also confirmation."

Tom stared into her eyes and slowly let go. What he saw reminded him of Frank, and he shivered. Tom thought about Jessica's powers, afraid it still wasn't enough to stop the crazy bitch standing in front of him.

He closed his eyes and nodded, saying, "I swear, if you ever hurt her, I will kill you." He opened his eyes and glared at her, resigned to sacrificing his marriage to keep Jessica safe.

She smiled. "As long as you do what I want, she'll be safe." She gathered up her papers and headed out the door with him.

She chattered endlessly in the seat beside him on the ride to Malibu, silently driving him out of his mind. For the first time since he'd met Jessica in that hellhole, Tom prayed she would choose Ty instead of him, and he wouldn't have to break her heart.

His heart, on the other hand, had already turned to stone.

Mind Games Chapter 79

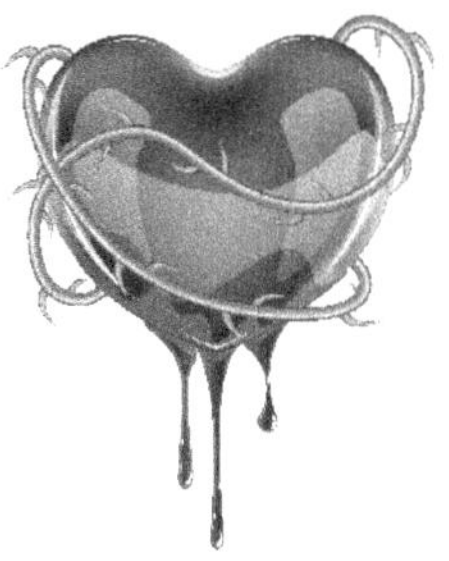

CHRIS WOKE UP EARLY, deciding a run was in order. He threw on his shorts and a sleeveless shirt, then headed off to the stretch of beach in York. He parked his car and put the baseball cap on backwards over his sleep-tousled hair, then stretched as he looked over the ocean, shivering a little from the cool breeze that billowed off the water. Trotting down the steps, he thought he recognized her heading in his direction. He jogged toward her.

Jessica smiled, and her eyes sparked with interest. She wasn't the only one on the beach that reacted that way to him either. But for all the lusty looks he received, he only cared about one.

Chris turned and joined her instead of passing by. They approached the end of the beach, and Jessica headed toward the stairs to head home.

"My car is back that way." He pointed over his shoulder.

"My house is this way." She looked sideways at him.

"I can drive you." He swung her around, heading in the general direction of his car. He smiled down at her as she kept pace. "A little longer won't kill you."

"But Frank might," she replied.

Her badly attempted humor made his smile fade. "Yeah, I know." He slowed down. "Jess, are you really ready for this?"

She stopped in the sand a couple of paces ahead of him and turned. "No, but I'm going to do it anyway, so don't back out on me now."

He looked out over the water and up at the blue sky. "Well, if we're going to die, we picked a beautiful day to do it." He glanced back at her.

She looked at him strangely, narrowing her eyes. "I talked to Eric last night, and he told me to ask you about a miracle."

He blinked and looked away. "I'll tell you about it sometime when we can look back on this day and laugh."

"Reverse?" She looked quizzically at him. "What did you reverse?"

"Nothing." He clamped down on all thoughts regarding that miracle, shoving them into a box at the back of his mind.

She put her hands on her hips and tilted her head. "You're lying."

"Yes, I am." He started walking toward his car.

"Why?" she asked as she caught up to him.

He gazed over at her. "Because now is not the time to discuss this. Ask me after today." *Providing we make it through.*

She sighed. "I'll ask again tomorrow."

She went to get into the car and picked up the clothes on the seat, raising an eyebrow.

"I figured I could clean up at your place." He took the clothes from her and put them over the emergency brake, shifting uncomfortably in the driver's seat.

She smiled at him. "I love it when you get all shy like this." She laughed. "It's so unlike you."

Heat filled his cheeks. "It's the effect you have on me," he said as he reached into the glove compartment. He handed her the disc along with the wedding ring he'd taped to the case so it wouldn't get lost, then put the car in gear, driving the short distance to her house.

JESSICA SHOWED HIM TO the guest bathroom, gave him a couple of towels, and headed off to the master bathroom to clean up.

She took a long shower, letting the water revive and relax her. She jumped when she opened the shower door to get a towel. Chris casually leaned against the doorjamb with his arms folded, just smiling.

His black dress shirt hung open over the faded pair of Levi's he wore, and his hair looked as if he'd towel dried and shook it. His blue eyes sparkled like the afternoon sky on a clear, crisp winter day.

"Sorry," he said, but didn't move. "I figured you wouldn't mind, considering."

She wrapped the towel around her self-consciously. "Are you just going to stand there?"

The way he was looking at her took her breath away. His choice of attire was not lost on her either. It looked very much like what he had worn in the complex when he took her to dinner.

He nodded, surprising her yet again. "You still haven't decided."

"I talked to my kids last night." She squeezed the water out of her hair and then combed it away from her face.

"I gathered from the question Eric told you to ask me."

"Eric still thinks we're meant to be."

"And Emily?"

"Emily doesn't really understand, but she'll back me with any decision I make."

"So, she's in Tom's court."

"Not necessarily. She just thinks that all you've done is hurt me versus the fact she has seen me happy with Tom in the past."

Chris nodded. "She's right. All I have done is hurt you." He straightened up and looked away, his arms dropping to his side.

"That isn't even remotely true," Jessica said, causing him to look back at her. She walked over to him and put her hands on his bare chest, looking up at him. "Not at all."

"I've hurt you plenty." He looked down at her, and his jaw tightened.

"But you also gave me my daughter's life, and yesterday, you made me smile and actually laugh when I really needed it." She ran her hands slowly up and around his neck and pulled him down to meet her kiss.

He reached up as she kissed him and removed her arms from around his neck, then pushed her gently away. "We don't have time for this right now," he said shakily as his eyes slowly took her in from head to toe. "I brought something for you to wear as well."

When he smiled, it didn't reach his eyes, and she knew exactly what he'd brought.

"It is in the living room and once we get the mirrors in here, you have to put that dress on and walk in here without me."

Jessica saw the mixed emotions in his eyes. "It'll be fine, Chris."

"We don't know that. What we know is that we're going to get very hurt." He blinked back the tears glossing his eyes.

"You can't back out on me," she said, feeling his hesitation. "I can't do this alone, and you know that."

"DON'T WORRY. I'M NOT going to back out on you, and I hope to God I don't fail." He knew if he did, he would lose her for eternity. She was going to heaven, and he was hell-bound. "Now, get dressed." He backed away from her and walked out of the bedroom. "We've got some mirrors to buy."

When she came out, he offered her a smile. "I guess you're driving because your car is bigger than my Corvette," he said. "That's even scarier than what we have to do today."

Jessica chuckled and walked into the kitchen to grab her keys.

"We're not going to somewhere like Home Depot?" he asked when she pulled into the public parking lot downtown.

"No. I figure if I'm going to die in front of a mirror, it's going to be a classy one, not just a sheet of mirrors like I have at the dance studio. And there's a quaint little furniture store here that I love."

"You know I'm going to blow them to smithereens, right?"

"Uh-huh. But you can afford it."

He laughed. "You're definitely a piece of work."

"After spending an actual day with me, you sure you still want to be with me?" She grinned at him.

He shook his head, and his smile faded. "I'm not sure at all anymore," he said. The smile on her face fell and her eyes flashed with surprised hurt. "Just kidding." He walked past her, chuckling under his breath.

"Jackass," she said, and he turned in surprise.

"Such language."

"Oh, bite me," she said, laughing.

He held the door to the store open for her with a grin. "Don't tempt me."

THERE WERE A LOT of mirrors in the store. Fear laced through her, creating a metallic taste in her mouth. Her laughter died in her throat.

Chris put his arm around her shoulders. "It's going to be okay," he said, leading her into the store. "Which ones do you want?"

"How many do we need?"

He laughed. "We only need one, but maybe we should rely on your lucky number."

"Seven?"

He nodded.

She looked around and then back at him. It felt right.

"It feels right," he said, mirroring her thoughts.

Jessica walked into a room that had several old-fashioned Cheval mirrors. She crossed to one that was beautifully crafted in cherry. She looked at her reflection and Chris's beyond her. He was smiling.

"That's the one I would have picked," he said to her reflection.

A salesman walked toward them. "Can I help you?"

"How many of this style do you have in stock?" Chris asked.

"We have three," the salesman answered.

Chris nodded. "We'll take them."

He looked for confirmation from Jessica. She nodded her approval.

"We also need four wall mirrors that would complement these."

The salesman lit up.

BACK AT THE HOUSE, Chris made Jessica wait as he set up the mirrors in a semi-circle at the foot of the bed. Each one was still covered with a sheet, creating a solid wall of covered mirrors. He grabbed the chair and set it where he remembered in the dream, then looked around the room.

"Here goes nothing." He stepped behind the mirrors and grabbed sheet after sheet, hurrying out of the room that now had a wall of uncovered mirrors. He closed the door behind him and walked into the living room, glancing at his watch. It was almost ten.

Jessica stood on the deck, her dress billowing gently around her in the wind. Chris dumped the sheets unceremoniously on the floor and went out to her. Fear, raw and raging, boiled in his blood, shaking his entire frame.

He slipped his arms around her waist and kissed her neck. "I love you, Jess," he whispered and took in the scenery for what could be the last time.

Mind Games Chapter 80

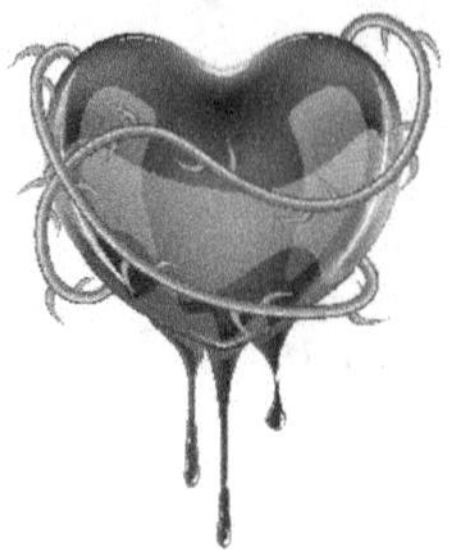

TOM WOKE FROM A nightmare and looked around him. The clock blinked seven o'clock. He shot out from under the blankets. He was going to be late.

"Shit," he said, glancing at his unwanted companion, and squashed the urge to smash in her face. Instead, he went into the bathroom and brushed his teeth. He spit and looked into the mirror, and the mental grip took hold.

Frank stared back at him. "I think I'll forgo the pleasure of killing you for now." He stepped aside, waving to the bedroom set-up. "But I figured I'd give you a front-row seat to watch your slut die today."

Tom couldn't move. Terror raged through him as his gaze shot from one side of the room to the bank of mirrors.

Oh God, she bought mirrors.

Frank sat on the edge of the bed and looked at the bedroom door expectantly.

"No. Please, no," he begged the image.

Frank looked at him. "Oh, yes."

Tom heard the door to their bedroom in Maine open. Jessica walked into the room and into Tom's line of sight. She was in a white dress, looking more beautiful than he ever remembered.

"Oh God," he whispered.

She didn't react. She couldn't see him or hear him. His heart thundered in his ears, and he struggled to break the mental hold Frank had on him.

Frank grabbed her and threw her across the room. She hit the wall hard and turned to face the mirrors, but Frank was on her before she could turn all the way. He ripped the dress off, then grabbed her by the hair and tossed her on the bed. She struggled but didn't make a noise. Frank punched her when she tried to sit up, and she fell back, dazed.

"NO," Tom screamed, still trying to break the spell that held him in place.

Frank handcuffed her to the bed and stripped the rest of her clothing off before producing a knife out of thin air. "Call him."

Jessica clenched her teeth.

Frank ran the dull edge of the blade over her body. "Call him," he insisted. "Or die alone."

Jessica let a tear slip out of her eye. She leaned her head back and her scream filled the room. "TY!"

Mind Games Chapter 81

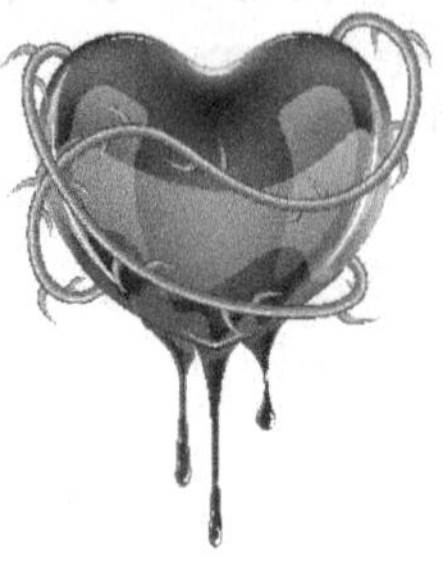

CHRIS FLEW INTO THE bedroom. Jessica was already tied to the bed, naked. His breath locked in his throat, and he stared at the stainless-steel handcuffs on her wrists. It wasn't an imaginary bond like the first time he'd careened into this bedroom less than two weeks ago.

Frank's laughter hung in the air. Chris stepped closer, within the arch of the mirrors, meeting her terrified gaze. Her fear cut him deep, and doubt crept into his heart.

Before he could spin around to the mirrors, hands were on him, slamming him into the chair hard enough to knock the wind out of him. He caught the image of Tom watching in horror in the far mirror.

His good hand was yanked in place on the chair arm, and a thick rope appeared, winding around the chair, binding his wrist in place. He swung his cast in the general direction where he thought Frank would be. Searing pain flashed in his abdomen. His gaze dropped to the butcher knife sticking out of his stomach. Blood spread over his shirt and down the front of his jeans.

He had no time to react before that invisible hand slammed the cast down on the chair and tied it in place. Frank's ghost was much stronger than Frank had been in life. The next blow hit Chris square in the nose, knocking his head back into the wood and causing him to see stars.

Jessica's screams brought him out of the daze. He shook his head, focusing on the room again. The tip of the blade tore through the skin just below his eye. He winced, sucking the air through his clenched teeth as the ghost raked the blade down his face, resurrecting the jagged scar he'd had for most of his life. He let his rage build with the pain.

The knife drifted to the opposite cheek and carved the same ugly scar, and then Frank materialized before him.

"That's the Ty I know." He turned toward Jessica. "I am going to fuck the life out of you while he watches." He smiled. "But before I do…"

He slammed the knife down into Chris's thigh, severing the femoral artery and forcing a cry of pain from his lungs.

"I promise you'll see her die before you do." He laughed, yanking the knife out, and headed to the bed, then mounted Jessica and plunged the knife in her side.

Jessica screamed.

"NO!" Chris bellowed.

Frank yanked the knife out of her flesh and switched hands. With a second slam of his hips, he buried the knife into her other side, smiling at Chris.

Chris struggled against the bonds, tears blurring his vision and his voice barreling from his chest in a ream of curses and promises he wasn't sure he'd be able to keep. Blood pumped out of his leg with every beat of his heart, making him dizzy and lightheaded. If he didn't get to her soon, they both would die. Panic threatened, and Frank laughed, turning his concentration back on Jessica.

The moment Frank took his eyes off him, Chris seized the opportunity and looked down at the rope around his wrists.

"Snap," he whispered, his voice drowned by Jessica's scream as Frank's knife sliced across her stomach. The ropes burst open at the same time Frank buried the knife in her chest, missing her heart by inches.

Chris moved like lightning, despite his wounds, grabbed Frank by the hair, and yanked the knife out of Jessica. Every mirror in the room burst into a million tiny shards, vaporizing before they hit the ground. Chris ripped him off her, spun him around, and planted the knife in his back. Frank screamed and fell to his knees, trying to reach the handle.

There was no escape; Chris had stripped him of all power when he'd trapped him here.

Chris jumped on top of Jessica and looked at the handcuffs, willing them to release her. His gaze snapped to hers the moment the metal clanked against the headboard.

"It hurts." Her labored breath wheezed.

He slipped the key that Eric had given him out of his cast where he'd hid it, gripping it with grim determination.

"God, please," Chris whispered and leaned down to kiss her, closing his eyes, praying that both she and the gift he gave her would make it through this ordeal. The transition was quick, fueled by his mounting panic and dissolving consciousness.

Blinking open his eyes, he saw the door at the far end of the hall. There was no way he'd get there in time. He twitched, sending a blast of power toward the locked door. It blew off the hinges and white light barreled down the corridor toward him. Chris braced himself for the pain he knew was coming.

Jessica cried out under his lips, bringing him back into the room with her. He clenched his teeth as pain exploded in his thigh, the healing pain infinitely worse than the knife had been. He turned away from her to see Frank slowly standing up with the knife still embedded in his back.

"Burn in hell, you son of a bitch," he snarled, letting his rage strike out.

Frank's ghost burst into flames. Screams of agony filled the room, and the floor opened, letting the death demons loose to drag his burning essence back to the bowels of hell.

Somewhere in an Albany graveyard, the inside of Frank's casket flashed into flames until there was nothing left but ashes.

The brightness faded, leaving Chris stretched out over Jessica on the bed. The power raged inside him, churning, coiling, begging to be released and he closed his eyes, laying his head on her shoulder, concentrating on restraining the beast within. His arms wrapped tightly around her, and he kissed her neck, feeling for a pulse with his mouth. The steady thrum of her blood throbbed against his lips and relief flooded through him, springing tears to his eyes.

He pulled back. She hadn't regained consciousness yet. He picked her up, carrying her to the bathroom as harsh sobs ripped from his chest. The warm shower soaked through his clothes, and tendrils of red-stained water seeped down the drain.

She stirred in his arms, and when her eyes opened and met his, he tried to smile, but couldn't quite accomplish it. Blood still stained her perfect, unmarked skin, and the vision of Frank repeatedly stabbing her wouldn't let go. He set her on her feet, bringing his shaking hand to her cheek, and kissed her.

The kiss was slow at first, and she pressed against him, her fingers nimbly unbuttoning his shirt as the tongue dance ramped up. Steam rose from the shower stall, not just a product of the hot water, but a manifestation of the heat between them. When Jessica reached to unbutton his wet jeans, Chris grabbed her hands.

Every fiber of his body wanted her, but he knew if he did this, he would never let her go. She was still married to Tom. Without a word, he stepped out of the shower and backed out of the room, his entire frame trembling.

"I can't stay." He gasped. Tears stained his unscarred face. He turned and bolted from the house, hopped into his car, and tore out of her driveway.

Mind Games Chapter 82

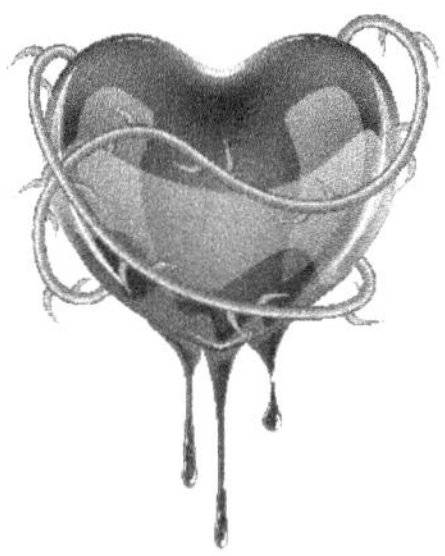

TOM PANICKED, SCREAMING AT the mirror, tears burning his eyes and throat. His intense gaze didn't even divert when Sharon flew into the room.

"What the hell is—" Her voice stopped.

Air. He needed air. His lungs couldn't get enough air. The panic attack was much more debilitating than Frank's invisible spell.

"Where the hell is he?" The words squeezed out of his constricted chest.

Jessica answered by calling Ty's name at the top of her lungs.

Chris flew into the bedroom, and Tom chanted the same words over and over and over like an omen that could save his wife. "Break the mirrors, break the mirrors, break the mirrors."

The knife plunged into Chris's thigh.

"Oh, Jesus!" Tom yelled in horror. "How long does it take to bleed to death? Jesus, do something!"

Frank plunged the knife into Jessica.

The strength bled out of his legs.

"Break the fucking mirrors!"

Rope snapped over Jessica's scream. Chris blurred across the minimal distance. The second he grabbed Frank, the mirror in the bathroom shattered, spraying glass across the room and releasing the mental hold.

Tom collapsed onto the floor, kneeling and holding his stomach tight. The cool tile against his forehead gave him some reference to where he was. His breath wheezed, and he drew in a gasp.

"Jessie," he screamed, and then the sobs started.

How could she live through that? How?

He crawled to the toilet and threw up. "Jessie," he sobbed. "Please be okay. Please, God. Please."

The hand on the back of his neck made him stiffen. He wiped his mouth and looked up at Sharon through tear-stained lashes.

"Get out," he hissed.

Her gaze traveled between him and the space that the mirror once occupied, her features stark against the paleness of her skin.

"Get the fuck out of my house," Tom bellowed at her.

She looked down at him and then back up at the wall. "What a story."

He could see the wheels turning in her head. He shot to his feet and grabbed her by the throat, slamming her into the wall. "If you so much as breathe a word of what you saw, I'll let him loose on you," he growled.

Her eyes went wide. She gulped and nodded.

Tom let her go and turned to the toilet again as another round of vomiting gripped him. Then he brushed his teeth and walked on shaky legs into the bedroom.

After picking up the phone, he called the studio. "I'm running late. I'll be there in an hour."

Sharon walked into the bedroom, and he glared at her as he hung up.

"Was that real?" she asked, pointing to the room.

Tom laughed. "Yes. That was as real as you and I are standing here. That was Frank's ghost, the ghost I told you about in my drunken stupor."

Sharon's eyebrows rose, and she glanced toward the bathroom. "She called out the name Ty. Is he alive?"

"No, Sharon, Ty is as dead as a doornail. That was Christopher Aris, and he and Jessica needed to do that in order to get rid of Frank's ghost." The partial truth came easy because she was the last person on earth he wanted to explain his duplicity to. If she knew, he would never be free of her. "Now, if you don't mind, I'd like to call my wife to see if she's alive, and I do not want you anywhere near me right now."

"If she is alive, remember, that could be a temporary thing."

"Get out of my bedroom," he warned.

After she left, he locked the door behind her. The cell shook in his hands, and he hit the familiar speed dial.

"Please, God. Please, God. Please, God," he whispered, each ring drilling a hole further into his core.

"Hello."

Her voice set off another round of tears, and he sat heavily on the corner of the bed. "Jessie, thank God, you're okay."

"Tom?"

"Yes. I saw. He made me watch," he said through gasps, his emotions squeezing the air out of his lungs.

"Tom, breathe. Deep breath in. That's right. Now slowly exhale. That's right," she said, calming him down. "I'm okay. Well, as okay as one can be after something like that. Now breathe." She took a deep breath and exhaled.

"Did you get him?" Tom asked when he felt some semblance of control.

"Chris did."

"Is he still there?"

"No, he kind of freaked out and took off," she said. "I need to go after him, Tom."

Tom closed his eyes. "Is that what you really want?"

Quiet permeated the phone line, and she sighed. "I'm so sorry."

"Is he what you really want?"

"Yes, he is. I love him, and this is where I belong."

He took a deep breath as both relief and loss accosted him. "Just know I will always love you, no matter what you read about me. It will always be you who has my heart."

"I know, and you still have a piece of mine as well. Thank you for keeping me safe for all these years." Her voice cracked, and he could tell she was crying.

"Always." Tom hung up the phone. "I'll always keep you safe."

He headed to take the shower he'd started over an hour ago.

Mind Games Chapter 83

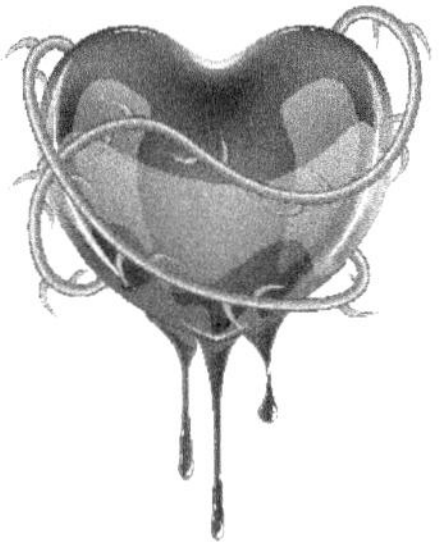

CHRIS SHOOK ALL THE way to his estate. It took him three tries to type in the password on the keypad that opened the gate. When it finally rolled open, he slammed the gas, tearing up the gravel driveway as he went. He stumbled into the kitchen and rummaged through the drawers until he found the shears he was looking for. Then he cut the soaking wet cast off his arm. The shakes made the task difficult, but he finally got most of the way through and then dropped the scissors so he could rip the fiberglass from his arm.

Stripping the wet, blood-soaked clothing off, he headed outside to the pool and dived into the water, cooling the heat inside him down to a low simmer. He swam lap after lap, trying to escape his feelings until exhaustion overwhelmed him. Then he grabbed the edge and put his forehead on the cool concrete. He closed his eyes, letting his breath slow to a normal pace.

He climbed out of the frigid water and walked into the cabana house, then grabbed a towel and wrapped it around his shivering body.

Jessica stood at the far side of the pool.

He stopped in his tracks. "You shouldn't be here, Jess." He breezed past her into the house.

She followed him, and he vaulted up the stairs and into his bedroom. He turned as she walked in behind him.

"You don't understand," he began, tears blurring his vision.

"Enlighten me." She stepped closer.

"I almost got both of us killed." Tears spilled over, slowly rolling down his cheeks. "I almost got you killed," he whispered. "I almost got..." She didn't know she was pregnant yet.

Jessica nodded. "We knew that would happen."

"Talking about it and seeing it are two very different things." Chris ran his hand through his wet hair.

"You saved me." She took another step toward him.

He took a step backwards. "You need to go." The need to take her in his arms became unbearable.

Jessica took another step toward him and pulled the straps of her sundress, untying them and letting the fabric fall to the floor. She smiled.

"Jess," he whispered, staring at her perfect body. A burst of pent-up energy escaped. The bedroom door slammed closed, making her jump. He stepped back into his nightstand. "You don't understand."

"Enlighten me," she said again, taking another step closer.

"If...if..." Chris stuttered as she stopped in front of him.

"If what?" she said, touching his hand that held the towel.

"Jess, if..." He closed his eyes, and she kissed his chest. "Jess, I won't be able to let you go. Not again." He opened his eyes and looked down at her. "If we do this…"

She pulled the towel away. "I am here," she whispered, looking up into his eyes.

His resolve melted away.

She knelt in front of him, slipping his hard member into her mouth.

He sat back on the nightstand and gripped the edges with his hands, his breath coming in short bursts. "Jess," he whispered as she sucked him gently. "Jess."

He closed his eyes and ran his hands into her hair, pulling her away from him and up onto her feet. Trembling, he leaned over and kissed her. He broke the kiss and looked into her eyes, searching as the passion threatened to sweep him away.

"I would give my life to be with you." He ran his fingers over her lips. "But you need to know, if we do this, I will never let you go." He paused for his words to sink in. "Tom can't have you back, even if he wants you. There is no going back after this." He looked at her intensely. "Do you understand?"

"Yes, I understand. Do you?" She ran her hands up his chest.

He smiled a little. "Enlighten me," he whispered, giving in to her completely.

"I'm here. I made my choice. Now make love to me." She took his face in her hands and kissed him.

"Say it," he whispered, pulling away from her lips.

"I love you…Chris."

His heart soared, and he smiled. "About that miracle…" He placed his hand on her lower abdomen. "You are carrying my child."

Her hand fluttered to her mouth and then she flew into his arms, squeezing him in a hug that expressed her outpouring of joy.

He picked her up in his arms and lay her down on the bed, then made love to her slowly with his hands and mouth, savoring every inch of her as she whispered his name over and over and over again.

"I love you," he whispered, and finally slid his aching shaft inside her.

Mind Games Epilogue

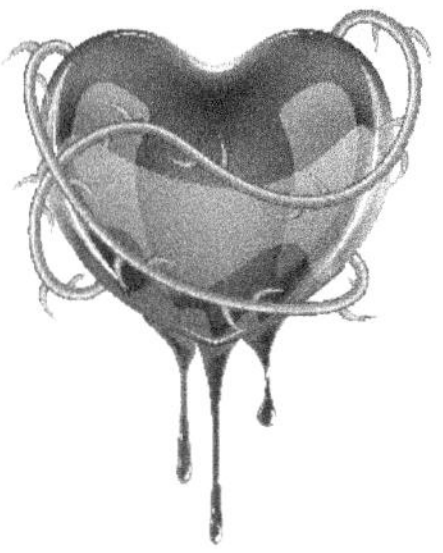

CHRIS PULLED UP TO the studio and glanced at Jessica. She covered her mouth for a second, willing back the nausea.

He smiled. "CJ causing trouble today?"

"CJ?" she said from behind her hand.

"I'd like to name my child after Chris." He looked down at his hands and then over at her. "I figure if it's a boy, we can name him Christopher James, and if it's a girl, Christina Jo. Either way, we can call the baby CJ. What do you think?"

She smiled. "I like that." She had said little since he'd picked her up at the doctor's office. "I'm carrying twins, Chris. I wish you had been there to see them with me."

"Oh, babe." He slowly smiled and put his hand on her stomach. No wonder she'd popped early. "I thought it was just a routine visit this time."

She nodded. "It was supposed to be, but when he saw the size of my belly, he did a quick ultrasound to make sure things were okay. The babies aren't identical twins. Each one is in their own little amniotic sac. It was amazing to see their heartbeats on the monitor." She smiled again, like she knew what they were having.

He lifted his eyebrows. "Are you going to tell me?"

"Boys. We're going to have two boys."

He leaned over and kissed her. "Did you have another name in mind?"

"What about calling him Ty?"

Chris shook his head. "No. I want that name behind us."

"Okay, then, how about Thomas Patrick?"

Chris tried not to wince, but said nothing. "We could always name him John Patrick," he joked, knowing she was a big Tom Clancy fan. He got out, grabbing the umbrella, and walked over to help her out of the car.

"Very funny." She smiled as the late August wind blew their jackets around them.

They ran into the studio together to get out of the rain.

"CJ and Tommy... I like those names," she said, and the door closed behind them.

TOM WATCHED FROM ACROSS the street in the rental car. He looked down at the divorce papers and took a deep breath. This was going to be more difficult than he'd thought. He hadn't seen her since that evening in New York when he asked her to leave. With a sigh, he put the papers in his jacket and pulled his car into the lot, then stepped out into the cool August rain.

When he entered, Chris froze with a hanger halfway to the rack. Tom felt the blood drain from his face as he looked at Jessica's protruding belly, his jaw going slack and the papers in his hand momentarily forgotten.

"What are you doing here, Tom?" Jessica asked, causing both Tom and Chris to snap out of their momentary paralysis.

Chris finished hanging up the jackets and walked up behind Jessica.

"Divorce papers," he said as he held them up. "How...?" He nodded toward her and licked his lips. "How far along are you?"

"I'm in my fifteenth week," she said. "Twins. Go figure." She smiled and shrugged as Chris put his hands on her shoulders.

Tom did the math in his head and stared at her. She was pale but radiant at the same time, and he still felt that overwhelming pull of wanting her. He looked at the papers and back at her as the timeline clicked.

He gasped. "New York?"

"I assume you want me to sign those." She pointed at the papers, ignoring his question.

Tom looked at the papers again, went to hand them to her, and hesitated. "Was it New York?" He pulled his hand back. "You mean to tell me they could be mine?"

"No, they aren't," Chris said.

"Chris." Jessica turned. "Do you mind? I'd like to talk to Tom alone."

A measure of uncertainty flashed in his eyes, but he nodded and walked away.

"Tom." She sighed and turned back to him.

"Could they be mine?"

"I made my choice, Tom, so this conversation is irrelevant." She put her hand out for the papers.

He slowly handed them to her. "If..."

Jessica took the papers out of his hand and walked over to the counter, then reached for a pen. She signed all the entries on each designated page. She turned, handing him their signed divorce decree. "I understand you're getting married."

He detected a hint of bitterness in her voice, and he closed his eyes. He took a deep breath and nodded. It was splashed all over the tabloids and had been since Sharon began blackmailing him.

"Are you carrying my child?" he asked again.

"No, they aren't yours, Tom," she replied.

Tom looked at the signed papers and then back at her. "I still love you," he whispered and leaned over to kiss her cheek. "Be safe, Jessie," he said, looking beyond her at Chris, who was watching them from the doorway to the office.

Keep her safe, Chris, he thought.

Chris nodded.

He turned to leave. "Goodbye."

"Goodbye, Tom," she said. The sadness in her voice caused him to glance back.

The last view he had of her before the door closed was a tear slowly sliding down her cheek, and then she turned away, forever.

The End

Continue with Ty and Jessica's story on the next page with END GAME

End Game Chapter 1

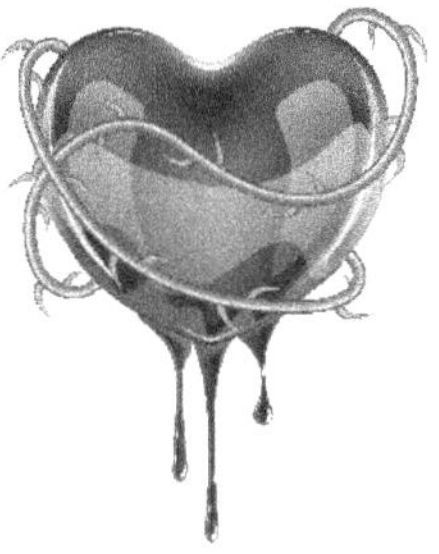

THE DREAM GRIPPED TOM Whitman, and he moaned in his sleep.

He ran his hands up her thighs, then hesitated on her waist. She moved her hips in slow circles, her arms reaching into the air and her body bending gracefully with each arch. Tilting his head back, he closed his eyes, breathing the air in slowly and reclaiming control.

He opened his eyes, staring into hers as she playfully rode him, both on the edge of a smile and her fingers running over his chest, causing him to shiver. His hands slid seductively over her body, her skin smooth and slick. He lingered on her nipples, running his thumbs over the hard nubs. Her body glistened with sweat, and her eyes sparkled when she whispered his name.

"Jessie," he whispered, sitting up in his bed three thousand miles away from the bedroom in the dream. The same dream he'd had night after night after night for the last five years.

He looked over at the clock on the nightstand. It was four in the morning. He wiped his face, glancing at the sleeping woman who had ruined his life. Closing his eyes, he suppressed the urge to strangle her to death. He slipped out of bed and threw jeans and his bathrobe on. After picking up his cell phone, he snuck outside onto the beach.

Tom sat in the dark and listened to the ocean, scrolling down his phone list until her number was highlighted. He stared at the phone and then closed it.

It had been almost five years since he'd delivered the divorce papers to her, but he went through this routine every night. He put his head on his knees, and the emotions he held at bay for so long came rushing back.

To hell with it. He opened the phone again, pressed the send button, and put the phone to his ear. When she answered, he closed his eyes and was silent.

THE SHRILL RING OF her cell phone woke Jessica Whitman from a sound sleep, and she glanced at the caller ID before she answered the phone. "Tom?"

"Jessie." His voice shook, and she could tell something wasn't right.

"Is everything okay?" She glanced around her empty bedroom. The covers on the other side of the bed were thrown back. Chris was nowhere to be seen.

"I miss you."

She sat up and looked at the clock, calculating the time difference between east and west coasts. "Tom, it's four in the morning in California. What the hell are you doing?"

"Going crazy without you."

Jessica blinked, stunned. Not a word from him since he'd delivered the divorce papers. Nothing for five years and now this?

Before she could formulate a response, her two boys bounded into the bedroom, followed by Chris saying, "Happy Valentine's Day, Mommy!"

"Tom, go back to bed. I have to go," she said into the phone, smiling at her family.

"Wait!"

Jessica took a deep breath. "Hold on."

She put the phone on her shoulder and looked down at the tray Chris had put in her lap. A perfect heart-shaped pancake covered with strawberries and whipped cream sat on the plate.

"Thank you very much," she said to CJ, Tommy, and Chris. "Happy Valentine's Day." She kissed each of the boys. "Mommy has a phone call she needs to finish, okay?"

"Okay," her boys said, and then they ran out of the room.

Jessica glanced at Chris and put the phone back to her ear. She mouthed one minute and held up her index finger to Chris. "What is it, Tom?"

Chris's eyebrows rose.

"We finally finished the movie."

"I know," Jessica replied. The studio had fought the injunction, and after close to four years tied up in court, they finally got the ruling they'd hoped for and began filming last year.

"The premiere is in a couple of weeks in New York City."

"And?"

"I'd like you to be there."

She said nothing, debating on how to let him down easy.

"I'd like you and Chris to be there," he clarified. "Please."

"Why?"

"I need you there."

"It's been five years, Tom. Besides, Sharon will be there with you. You don't need me."

The click of his teeth and his sharp inhale traveled over the phone line, and she actually felt the rage welling up in him from across the country.

"Tom, is everything all right?" she asked, glancing up at Chris and knitting her brow.

Tom laughed at the question, and then the distinct sound of a harsh sob filled the line. "It hasn't been all right since..." He let silence fill the space. "How old are they now?" he asked, changing the subject. "Your kids, how old are they?"

"They just turned four last month."

"What'd you name them?"

Jessica hesitated, and Chris nodded. *Tell him.* Both his eyes and his voice in her head prompted.

"Christopher James Ryan. We call him CJ."

"And?"

"And Thomas Patrick Ryan," she whispered, her eyes never leaving Chris's.

THE NAME SANK IN, and Tom was silent. He closed his eyes and put his head back on his knees, not asking the question that shot into his head. He didn't want to know, not now, especially since he'd made damn sure he'd never have a child with his bitch of a wife. He took care of that when Sharon demanded he get her pregnant, telling her he was sterile and then making an appointment the very next day. Snip, snip and his lie became fact.

"Please come to the premiere."

"Hang on."

She covered the phone with her hand, but he could still hear her muffled explanation to the man she'd chosen to be with over him. "They finally finished the movie, and Tom wants us to go to the premiere in New York."

Chris let out a surprised laugh. "Why?"

"Why do you want us there?" she asked.

Her kids came back into the room, arguing until Chris sent them out.

Tom sighed. Hearing the boys in the background numbed his heart again, and he gazed out at the dark ocean. "Because I need you to see the movie."

"I don't think that's such a good idea."

"I need you there," he pleaded, his voice barely a whisper. "I need you at the premiere. Please."

"Why do you need me there? Is this a publicity stunt?"

"God, no." Tom recoiled. "I need you to see the movie. I *need* you to," he whispered, his voice shaking. "Please."

"I'll see what we can do."

"Jessie, you don't understand. You have to be there."

"Tom, I said we'll see." Irritation crept into her voice.

He took a deep breath. "'We'll see' means no." He knew her well enough to know that was her favorite stall tactic. "Please." He needed to see her again, even if it was from a distance, even if she was with *him.*

Silence and then a sigh. "All right, we'll be there."

"Tell him to put Christopher Aris on the guest list, not Chris Ryan. I don't want people finding out where we are," Chris snapped from the background.

"Tell him I will." Tom paused, tossing around the next question, debating on whether or not to ask. "Did you two ever get married?"

"No," Jessica answered.

Tom closed his eyes and lay back on the sand. He mulled this over and tilted his head back, opening his eyes so he could see his house. He looked back at the stars above him and entertained an evil thought.

He sat up and shook his head, erasing the idea. It would put Jessica at risk, and he wasn't willing to do that.

"Thank you for saying you'll come. Bye, Jessie." Tom lay back down in the sand and closed the phone, then put his hands behind his head, staring at the constellations and wondering what his wife would do when she saw Jessica walking down the red carpet.

End Game Chapter 2

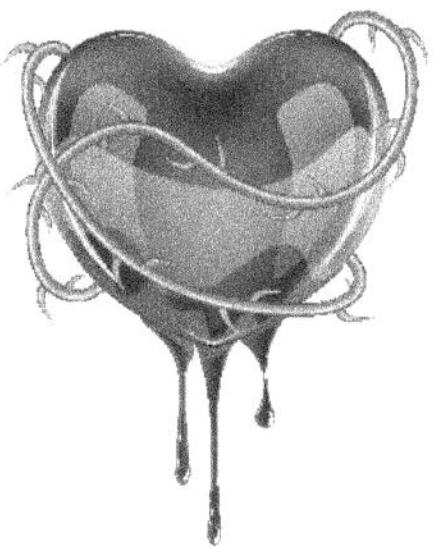

CHRIS SAT ON THE edge of the bed next to Jessica. "I can't believe you said yes."

Jessica shrugged. "Aren't you the least bit curious?"

He shook his head. "I read the script."

"When?"

"I had a copy delivered to me in New York the day the boys were conceived. That's when I pushed the injunction."

The first bite of the pancakes diverted her attention from the morbid conversation to the delectable treat on her plate. "Did you make this?"

"No. CJ and Tommy insisted on doing it themselves, and they wanted the heart to be just perfect, so we have a garbage can full of less-than-perfect tries. The kitchen is a disaster." The grin she'd fallen in love with surfaced, accented by dimples in his cheeks.

"You are so good with them, you know." She laughed. "If you asked me ten years ago, I never would have guessed how wonderful a father you would turn out to be."

"Being a father is one of the best things that ever happened to me." He leaned over and planted a kiss on her lips. When he pulled back, his smile faded. "Are you going to tell him?"

"Tell him what?"

"That he has a son." CJ was definitely Chris's child with light brown hair and bright blue eyes, but as both Jessica and he suspected, and a paternity test confirmed, little Tommy wasn't.

Jessica shook her head. "No."

"He has a right to know."

"I know, but he's going to want to see him."

Chris nodded.

"I wouldn't allow that bitch to set foot in our home, never mind anywhere near our son."

"I wouldn't either. I'd make her stand outside in the snow whether or not she wanted to." He grinned. "Maybe she would even freeze to death," he said enthusiastically, his eyes wide and sparkling with humor, making Jessica burst out in laughter.

"Thanks." Jessica held up a fork full of pancake for him to taste. "I'll give Em a call later and see if she'll come to the city and watch the boys while we go to the premiere."

"Why don't you ask both of them to come to the city with us?" he asked after he swallowed the bite he had taken from her.

"If Eric wins the game this weekend, he may be in the finals next weekend in New York, anyway." She plopped the last bite in her mouth.

"I'm going to go clean up the disaster area." Chris took the tray from her.

Jessica slipped out of bed and headed into the bathroom to freshen up. She took her time, enjoying the hot water of the shower on the chilly February morning. She stepped out of the bathroom to an unusually quiet house. She crossed to the hallway and stopped in her tracks.

A trail of red, pink, and yellow rose petals flowed down the stairs, and at the bottom, a beautiful fur coat and a matching pair of fur slippers waited for her. She slipped them on and continued to follow the petal trail through the family room and out into the backyard.

Her heart skipped a beat at the sight of him leaning against the rock wall in his tailored Armani suit, his crisp white shirt open at the collar the way she liked it. His cheeks and hands reddened from Maine's frigid February air.

The scene was so familiar to her that her hand fluttered to her mouth, and her eyes welled up with tears. The dream she'd had long before she met him, the one she believed impossible when she was imprisoned, and the one she fought against while married to Tom, finally materialized before her eyes.

He dropped to one knee in the snow, pulled a small jewelry box from his pocket, and opened it, revealing the most beautiful one-carat diamond ring. Taking her left hand in his, he whispered, "Happy Valentine's Day, babe." His lips curved into the smile that melted her heart. "Will you marry me?"

Jessica swallowed the lump in her throat and nodded. "Yes. Yes, I'll marry you."

He slid the ring on her finger and stood, then wrapped his trembling arms around her and planted a cold kiss on her lips. "You just made me the happiest man on earth." He led her back toward the house.

The boys danced around the door, crowding them when they walked in.

"We helped Daddy with the flowers," CJ bragged.

"Did you like them?" Tommy asked.

"Yes, I loved them." Jessica smiled and gave each one a big hug.

"Hey, boys, why don't you head into the playroom and give your mom and me a few minutes, okay?" He watched as they obeyed his request, tearing off together to the playroom.

She wiped the tears from her face and stripped the coat off before studying the ring on her hand. "This is absolutely beautiful."

"I almost got you a ten-carat rock, but I didn't think you would like something that flashy." He buried his hands in his pockets, shivering.

"This is just perfect." She looked up at him and smiled, throwing her arms around his neck. "You're shaking."

"It's fricken' cold out there, and you took longer than I expected." He wrapped his arms around her, nuzzling his frigid nose into her neck, nibbling on the tender skin over her clavicle.

She laughed. "You took longer than I expected, too," she said, referring to the proposal. "And you didn't have to do that outside."

"It wouldn't have the same effect."

"What wouldn't have the same effect? Waiting this long or the exceptionally romantic way that you asked me?"

He shrugged as he pulled away. "Both." He planted a kiss on her lips. "Jessica Lynn Ryan, my wife. Who would have ever thought?"

"I knew long before we ever met."

His brows knit together in a crease.

"I had a couple of dreams about you when I was with Danny."

"Really? What kind of dreams?"

She shrugged and lowered her gaze to the sparkling diamond. "Like the first time we actually met. Face-to-face in the chair." She looked up at him, any trace of a smile disappearing. "I know, kind of freaky. I can still remember the day I had the dream."

Chris cocked his head. "Really?"

"Yes. I actually thought it was triggered by something I saw." She let out a little laugh. "We were coming back from Danny's brother's place in Vermont and stopped in Burlington to have lunch on the pier overlooking Lake Champlain. It was really ironic. As we were leaving, we ran into an old friend of mine whom I hadn't seen for a couple of years and ended up hanging out on the pier for a lot longer than we'd planned."

Jessica chewed on her lip for a second, her gaze traveling to the window and the snowy backyard. "The pier had one of those little gas stations at the end that serviced the boaters, and we watched several boats come and go."

She stopped, tilting her head, losing herself in the memory. "I remember an exceptionally sweet speedboat, the sleek, fast type, and I think it was midnight blue, but I don't remember the name on the back—just that it was written in bright yellow script. To be honest, I was a little envious. God, how I would have loved a machine like that when I was a teenager!" She smiled and flicked her gaze back to his for a second.

He inhaled.

"Anyway, one of the boys on board was just staring at me with his soda halfway to his mouth, looking like he just saw a ghost. Normally, I would have just ignored him and walked away, but those wide blue eyes... My

Lord, those were the most amazing eyes I had ever seen." Jessica chuckled and sighed.

"The boat's name was *Anna*," Chris said, interrupting her train of thought.

Jessica blinked, the memory barreling back as clear as if she were standing on that pier. "I think you're right." She narrowed her eyes and scanned the memory, specifically the boys on the boat, and she broke out of his arms, her gaze snapping to his eyes. His amazing wide blue eyes.

"Jesus Christ, that was you." Her arms erupted in goose bumps. "You and your brother looked so much alike. The only difference was the scar, and that's what I thought triggered the dream."

"What were you wearing?" he asked, his voice cracking, and he stepped backwards into the kitchen counter.

"A white sundress."

Chris burst out laughing, but it was his nervous, high-pitched laugh. "You." He pointed at her. "You were the angel I saw?"

"What are you talking about?"

"I remember glancing up and it looked like you had a halo of light all around you. Chris razzed me for years because I actually said the word 'angel'; out loud." He looked down at her. "Jesus, Jess. You were my angel, even back then." He took a deep breath and shivered. "That still doesn't explain how you knew we would end up together, though."

"A few years later, I had a dream of what just happened in the snow." She pointed toward the backyard. "I think it was after Emily was born. So, I knew. I knew somehow we'd end up here, together."

Chris just stared at her, his rosy cheeks going pale.

"When you had me strapped in that chair and we first looked at each other, I had a sense of déjà vu, but I couldn't place where I had seen your face before, and later when you tried to seduce me with the strawberries, the look in your eyes made something click, and the dreams caught up with me. When I kissed you back, that's when I knew for sure." Jessica sighed and took a deep breath.

"So, you've been playing me ever since we met?"

Jessica raised her eyebrows a little. "No, I haven't been playing you."

He looked down at the ring on her finger and back to her eyes, pressing his lips together, his doubt visible in the tightness of his jaw. "Then why did you marry Tom?"

Jessica shifted and looked down at the engagement ring, avoiding his gaze. "I loved him and thought I could change my future."

A BARK OF A laugh left him, and he turned away from her, frustrated. "He almost derailed my morning, and now this. This is just priceless."

"It took a while for me to realize I belonged with you. I never felt like he was a part of me, like I do with you."

He turned toward her.

"Chris, there's no place I'd rather be." She pulled away and went into the kitchen, then returned with two envelopes in her hand. "Maybe this will help you understand." She kissed him and handed him the cards.

He opened the first card. It was a Valentine's Day card from the boys, and he smiled as he read it. Her card was sweet, but the sentiment wasn't what made his throat clench with unshed tears. It was what she'd written that touched him far more.

Dear Chris,

I love the life we have made together. You have given me such beautiful gifts in the boys, and your love and quiet strength have brought me more joy and happiness than I thought possible. I love you.

You are my soul mate, and I would be lost without you.

Forever yours,

Jess.

"Soul mate?" He blinked back the mist covering his eyes and crossed to her, then took her in his arms.

"Yes. You are my soul mate." She leaned up and kissed him. "You make me feel like no other man ever made me feel."

"And how is that, Jess?" He ignored the urge to pull the thoughts from her mind. He wanted to hear her say the words.

"You make me feel loved. It's in the way you look at me and the way you touch me..." She blushed. "I had never felt that kind of passion, that kind of electricity in my life until I met you, and it has only grown stronger since we've been together."

Chris smiled down at her. "Good."

"When do you want to get married?"

Chris looked at his watch. "How about right now?"

Jessica laughed. "You're serious."

He nodded.

Jessica hesitated. "I want Emily and Eric there with us."

"Okay. What about this weekend?"

Jessica shook her head. "Eric has a game."

Chris thought for a moment. "Then how about when we're in the city? We could go to City Hall with the kids and get married, catch an early dinner and then go to the premiere after?"

"You really want to do that?"

"I want to marry you," he replied. "I admit it's not the most ideal situation, but it's the next weekend Eric's supposed to be with us."

"You can set it up that quickly?" she asked, then smirked, realizing how dumb a question that was. He could move mountains in record time when he set his mind to it.

"The question is, do you want me to?"

"Yes. I'll call Emily to make sure she's available." She grinned, and he kissed her neck.

The distant arguing of the twins interrupted them.

"Hold that thought." She pulled away and headed up the stairs, looking at the ring on her hand with a smile.

End Game Chapter 3

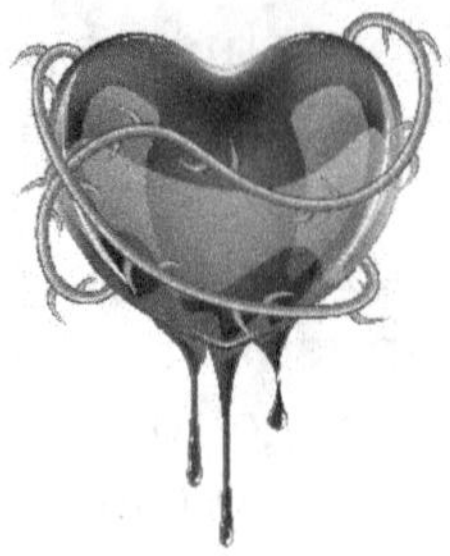

TOM LAY ON THE beach watching the sky turn from the black of night to the various colors of dawn.

She named one after me.

The thought kept repeating over and over and over, sobering him faster than usual, more effective than a jug of coffee or a slap in the face. This, coupled with the fact Jessica and Chris had never married, gave his restless brain a ray of hope.

He closed his eyes and drifted to sleep on the sand. Ice-cold water smacked his face, and he sat up, gasping.

Sharon stood over him, her face a mask of disgust and the bucket still in her hand, drops sliding down the side and dripping on the sand. "I'm getting sick of finding you passed out on the beach. When this premiere is over, I'm checking you into rehab," she announced and stormed back toward the house.

"Bullshit," he called after her. He stood up and darted past her, blocking her path.

Sharon stopped on the steps. "If you don't do what I want, I'll order the hit," she reminded him, like she had numerous times over the last five years whenever he pushed the envelope.

Tom narrowed his eyes and ground his teeth together. "I'm not a fucking alcoholic," he snapped, although even he had doubts about that. It was the only way to escape this hell called his life. His acting abilities only got him so far for so long, and then he relied on the bottle to make the world believe this lie, this masquerade she insisted upon. Hatred burned in him, turning his natural boy-scout nature into a dark, brooding, and volatile man he didn't recognize. He turned and entered the house.

"You will do as I say," she ordered and slammed the door closed.

Tom stopped in his tracks, his hands balling into fists, fists that wanted to pummel every bone in her body until nothing was left but a bloody pulp. He took a deep breath, gaining control over his murderous thoughts with the help of the dull pain of his fingernails creating welts on his palms.

She stalked in front of him. "Understand?"

He willed his hands to relax, afraid they might take on a mind of their own and strike out at the blonde bitch blocking his path. "I'm not going to rehab."

"Then you are going to stop drinking on your own."

"Drinking is the only way I can get through the day being married to you."

Her expression fell, her eyes widening and tears springing to the corners, and he reveled in the pain he saw there.

"If you take that away from me, I may end up killing you." He skirted around her and crossed to the master bathroom, then shut and locked the door behind him. He turned on the shower and looked at himself in the mirror.

"What the hell have I become?" he asked his reflection. Eyes devoid of compassion looked back. He dropped his chin to his chest, closing his eyes and praying for the strength to get through another day without killing the woman who called herself his wife.

End Game Chapter 4

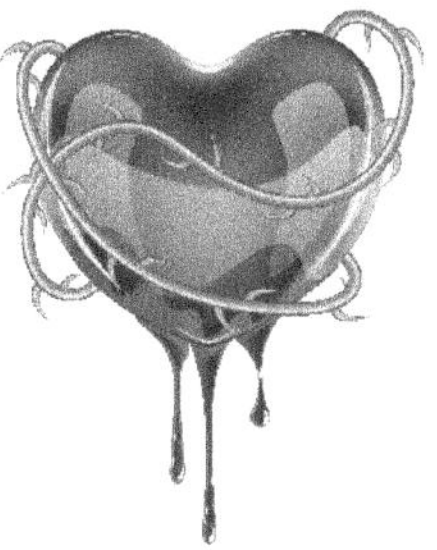

"HE ASKED ME TO marry him," Jessica announced into the phone.

"It's about time," Eric replied.

Jessica laughed. "He just wasn't ready, Eric."

"He was ready the day he walked back into your life five years ago, Mom. He was just afraid of the answer."

Jessica looked out the back door at Chris playing in the snow with the boys. "I know, but he shouldn't have been." She smiled when he let the boys tackle him. "Anyway, think you can get away next Thursday night?"

"To babysit?"

"Stop being such a smart ass. You already know why I'm asking."

"I know and yes, I wouldn't miss your wedding for the world," Eric replied. "Want me to tell Dad?"

"No, I think it would be better coming from me. Is he there?"

"He's at work. You want to talk to LeAnn?"

"No, I'll call him later. How's Sandy doing?" Daniel and LeAnn had a daughter a couple of months before Jessica had the boys.

"She's a little terror. She's into everything and Dad is going nuts. It's really fun to see him get riled up."

Jessica chuckled. "The boys try to get into things, but it's impossible for them to get away with anything."

"Yeah, I know," Eric said. "It'll be the same when I have kids."

Outside, Chris got pelted by the snowballs the boys rocketed at him. "Mmmm."

"Anyway, I need to get going. I've got practice."

"We'll pick you up next Thursday after school."

"Happy Valentine's Day, Mom. Give my brothers a hug from me. Same with Chris."

"I will. Happy Valentine's Day, and good luck at the game this weekend."

"Mom?"

"Yes, sweetie?"

"Think you and Chris can make the game?"

"Where is it?"

"Worcester."

"We'll be there," she said. "I'll get the particulars from your dad."

"Thanks, Mom. See you on Saturday."

She dialed the familiar number to the house on the other side of town that Tom had given her in the divorce settlement. When Emily took a teaching job at York High School, Jessica gave her the keys to the house. She planned to sign over the deed to her as a wedding gift when the time came.

"Hi, Mom," Emily answered.

"Emily, can you take next Friday off?"

"Why?"

"Chris and I are getting married."

Emily let out a little laugh. "It's about time."

"That's exactly what Eric said. So, can you take the day off?"

"Sure, where's the wedding?"

"We're getting married in New York, so we'd pick you up next Thursday and have you with us for the weekend in the city." She took a breath. "And I'd need you to sit for the boys Friday night if you wouldn't mind?"

"I'd be delighted to. Do you want me to watch the kids for the entire weekend?"

"Thanks, but if Eric's team wins this weekend, the finals will be in the city on Saturday."

"Ah, okay. Where's he taking you Friday night?"

Jessica paused and took a deep breath. "We're going to a movie premiere."

Silence blanketed the line. "What premiere?"

"*Survival Games*. Tom called and asked us to come."

"Really?" Emily said with a quick burst of shocked laughter.

"Yes. We were a little surprised as well."

"And you chose the same day to get married?"

"Chris wanted to get married today, but I wanted you and Eric there, and next Friday is the first opportunity for all of us to be together."

"Did Chris ask you to marry him before the phone call from Tom or after?"

Jessica knew where Emily was going. "He didn't ask me to marry him because of Tom's call. It wasn't a spur-of-the-moment thing. He and the kids planned it, beginning with a pancake breakfast in bed and a rose petal trail leading me out to the rock wall," she said. "Chris froze out there waiting for me, and he had a ring, so it wasn't because Tom called."

"I'm sorry, but..."

"Em, he had to have the flowers here before this morning and the ring. He planned this with the boys," she repeated. "The call from Tom was just terrible timing."

"It's just ironic, that's all."

Jessica chuckled. "I know, but despite the phone call, it turned out to be the perfect morning, and the proposal was so completely romantic. I'm not talking a petal here and a petal there. It was a solid path of yellow, pink, and red rose petals from the upstairs hallway, down the stairs, through the family room, and the entire length of the backyard. And Chris must have stood out in the cold for close to a half hour in just his Armani suit waiting for me to get my lazy butt out of the shower. The poor guy's teeth were chattering, but I didn't have the heart to point that out when he dropped to his knee."

"Oh, Mom, how perfect! You said he had a ring?"

"I'll swing by on our way to the studio and show it to you," Jessica replied, studying the bright diamond in the sunlight. "I need to give your father a call to tell him and see if I can pull Eric from school next Friday."

"Dad doesn't like Chris."

"I know, but that's his problem, not mine."

"Good luck," Emily said. "I'll see you later."

Jessica hung up, dreading the next call. Daniel, her first ex-husband, had never accepted Chris and probably never would. He reminded Daniel of the man who kidnapped her and changed the course of their lives. If he ever found out the truth, that Chris was that man, all hell would break loose. Accessory to murder was a pretty serious charge, and Ty Aris had committed several in his lifetime.

She took a deep breath and punched in the numbers. "Hi Danny," she said when he picked up his phone.

"Hi, Jess. Is everything all right?"

"Yes, everything's fine. I'm calling to see if I can pick up Eric on Thursday night next week. I know he would miss school on Friday, but it's for a really good reason."

"What reason is that?"

"I'm getting married." She listened to the silence on the other end of the line, biting her lower lip and turning away from the escalating snowball fight outside.

"Are you sure you want to do that?"

"Yes, I am." *More sure than the day I married you.* "Danny, he's a very special man, and he makes me happy. I know you're worried because he grew up with the Aris family—but he isn't one of them."

A sigh came over the line. "Okay. I'll let Eric skip school next Friday. But Chris has to come in with you this time when you pick the kids up."

"I'll make sure he does, but don't give him any shit. Okay?"

"I'll try not to," he said, and she knew he'd slip some derogatory comment in anyway. He always did whenever they ran into each other in York. "You coming to Eric's game this weekend?"

"Yes, we are. Eric said it's in Worcester?"

"At the Worcester Centrum. Tipoff is at three."

"We'll be there. See you then." She hung up the phone and walked back into the family room.

Chris and the kids rolled in with a flurry of snow flying off their pelted coats, leaving mini puddles on the tiled entry.

"We're on for next Friday." She smiled.

Chris crossed the room and nuzzled his chilly face into her neck. He chuckled and held her tighter when she tried to get away from his frigid nose and hands.

"Your hands are freezing," she complained with a laugh.

"I think it's time we get Mommy." He laughed and picked her up, then dropped her on the couch as fair game for the boys.

They pounced, tickling her with their chilly fingers, and Chris joined in the fun.

"Stop." She gasped through her laughter, their tiny hands burrowing in her armpits, wiggling and tickling relentlessly while Chris held her arms in the air. When Chris let go, she wrapped her arms around each of the boys, pulling them to her sides and stopping their playful attack.

"Come on. We need to get into dry clothes." Chris started for the stairs. CJ and Tommy ran past their father and out of sight. He glanced at Jessica and smiled. "I still can't believe how lucky I am." He climbed the stairs, disappearing from view.

The boys came bounding down a few minutes later in dry clothing. Jessica set them up with their favorite video and wandered upstairs. She closed their bedroom door behind her and walked to the bathroom, then leaned against the doorjamb, watching him step out of the shower. He wrapped a towel around his waist and sent a sly smile in her direction.

"I wouldn't bother with clothes," she said.

"Is that so?" He approached her, beads of water glistening on his skin. His eyes sparkled like the surface of the lake when the sun hit it. After pulling her to him, he kissed her, running his hands under her shirt and peeling it over her head.

As always, his touch set her on fire. Every fiber ached, longing for his hands, his mouth, craving him like an addict craves heroin.

"Where are the boys?" he asked, his hands preoccupied with the button on her jeans.

"Watching that video they like," Jessica said, pulling him to her lips. "Make love to me."

"Every day of my life," he purred and stripped her clothing, then maneuvered her onto the bed, his towel discarded along the way.

Each stroke of his hands, each flick of his tongue, each graze of his lips created a wake of ecstasy that rippled through her body, eliciting moans she muffled with the back of her hand.

He worked his way back to her mouth, sliding into her, satiating her, and she met his thrust, pulling his hardness farther into her, filling her. Tendrils of pleasure spread through her, making her gasp for breath. She ran her fingers through his wet hair, pushing it away from his face as he stared down at her. His hips moved leisurely, relishing the slow burn.

"I love you...Mrs. Ryan," he said, his grin surfacing again.

"Back at you, Mr. Ryan." Cresting, she arched, her eyes rolling back at the power of the orgasm. Every muscle tightened, heightening the pleasure with each stroke. "Oh God, Chris!"

THE SHEER BLISS OF being inside Jessica overwhelmed Chris, and he lost control, speeding up the motion of his hips, thrusting deeper with each pass until his muscles seized and an eruption shot inside her, triggering another of her sweet orgasms. Aftershocks gripped him, and he collapsed on top of her, relishing the curve of her neck, the warmth of her body, and the tickle of her breath.

He sighed and propped himself up on his elbows, studying the swirl pattern of her eyes before glancing at the bedroom door, sending out his sixth sense to see what the boys were up to. He offered Jessica a half smile. "We left them to their own devices a little too long. They're getting into trouble."

He closed his eyes and sent out the command for CJ and Tommy to sit back down on the couch, and then opened his eyes back up. "That will hold them for a few minutes." He slipped off her and went to find some clean clothes.

JESSICA STRETCHED AND THEN climbed out of the bed, following the path of discarded clothing, putting each garment back on. "Chris?"

"Hmmm?" He stepped out from the closet, zipping up his jeans.

"Why did you take so long to ask?"

He pulled his sweater over his head, then met her gaze. "You never mentioned marriage, so I thought maybe it wasn't really what you wanted." He walked over to her and took her hands. "I got the rings after the boys were born, but it took me this long to get up the nerve."

Jessica put her hand on his cheek. "I would have said yes the day I made the decision to be with you. I thought you knew that."

He shifted and dropped his gaze to the floor. "I never believed you really wanted to be with me."

"Are you honestly that insecure?"

He nodded, meeting her eyes. "I've always been where you're concerned. I keep thinking I'm going to wake up, and this will all be a dream." He touched her face and kissed her gently. "We have to get downstairs before they destroy the family room." He pulled away from her lips and led her out of the room.

Halfway down the stairs, his words sank in. "Rings?"

He smiled back at her. "I bought matching wedding bands."

"Can I see them?"

"As soon as we get lunch for the kids." He headed down the stairs.

The pillows, throw blankets, and cushions from the couch were strewn over the living room floor, and the boys were sitting on the cushion-less couch, looking up at them with guilty expressions.

Chris looked at the mess and then back at the kids.

"He started it." Tommy pointed at CJ.

"Liar, you started it." CJ glared at Tommy.

"It doesn't matter who started it," Chris said, looking squarely at CJ. "What matters is that you clean it up. And Christopher James, you shouldn't lie. That makes me angry." His eyes bore into his son.

"Ha-ha," Tommy whispered.

"Thomas Patrick," Chris said, his eyes switching targets. "That was not right, either."

Both Tommy and CJ hung their heads and picked up the pillow cushions, and put them back on the couch.

Jessica stood on the stairs, watching him handle the boys. Chris's look of disapproval always put them in line. It was as powerful as his smile.

He glanced over at her and winked, causing her to turn her head so the children wouldn't see her smile. She hurried into the kitchen and made them sandwiches and chocolate milk, then put it on the table while Chris supervised the cleanup effort.

When CJ and Tommy sat down at the table, Chris disappeared and returned a moment later with two small ring boxes. He opened them both and set them on the counter. Matching platinum wedding bands adorned with diamonds glittered out at her.

She smiled. "I love them."

"Yours is engraved."

Jessica picked up the ring and read the inscription.

All my love always & forever, Ty.

A tidal wave of emotions slammed into her at seeing his real name, and her eyes welled up with tears. "Ty," she whispered, blinking the mist away. Pressing her lips together, she swallowed the lump in her throat. She hadn't called him by that name since the day they'd sent Frank's ghost back to hell.

"I was tempted to put something with the phrase 'a million years' on it, but I thought that would be in poor taste," he said, cracking a smile.

She nodded and put the ring back in the box. "They're beautiful." She sniffled and wiped her eyes.

"I couldn't bring myself to put Chris in the engraving. I hope you don't mind."

"I don't mind at all. It's who I fell in love with." She kissed him. "And I miss calling you by that name," she said, too softly for the boys to hear.

Chris wrapped his arms around her. "I miss hearing it."

End Game Chapter 5

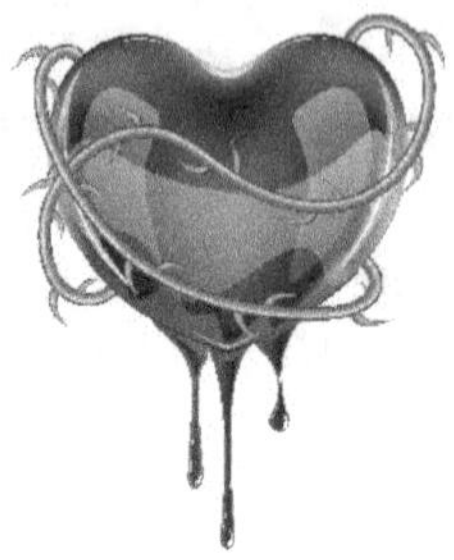

"I'M GOING OUT FOR a while. Is there anything you need me to pick up?" Chris said, grabbing his coat off the rack.

"I don't think so." Jessica checked the refrigerator. "We're all set."

Chris grabbed his cell phone. "You two be good for your mother," he said to the kids.

"We will," they said in unison, and he headed out the door.

Chris drove to the local mall and sat in the parking lot, dialing his lawyer's direct line. "Hi, Sam, it's been a while," he said into the cell phone.

"It's been too long, Chris. How are you?" Sam Trueman replied.

"I'm doing very well, but I need a huge favor."

"What can I do for you?"

"I need you to set up a wedding ceremony at City Hall next Friday."

"Who's getting married?"

"I am. She said yes." He leaned his head back against the seat.

"You're finally going to make an honest woman of her. I'm glad to hear that. Do you want me to draw up a pre-nup?"

"Not necessary, Sam," he said.

"Look, I know she's the mother of your children, but…"

"Sam, she doesn't have a clue what I'm worth. She's never asked. Besides, she's been listed as my sole beneficiary from the time I sold Aris Industries, and I don't think marriage is going to change that." He took a deep breath. "It's not like she sought me out. I went after her."

"I never understood why you went after her."

Chris took a deep breath. He spun the same story over and over through the years, so it came easily this time. "She loved him, and I needed to find out why, especially after everything he did to her. When we met, the connection was immediate and overwhelming. I never experienced that before, and let's face it, I had been with a lot of women before I met Jessica. None of them affected me the way she did." He smiled; this part of the storyline was the easiest to explain because it was the truth. "The way she still does."

"Are you sure about her? You sure she isn't trying to trap you and get your money?"

"She never once mentioned marriage in all these years, and that's one of the reasons it took me so damn long to ask. We have two children, Sam, and she's been more than patient." He thought about their conversation this morning. "She's the one I've been searching for all my life. She's my soul mate."

"Okay, I'll set everything up on one condition."

"What's that?" Chris sat up straight in the car. He didn't like ultimatums.

"That I can be there to see you get married," Sam said.

Chris smiled and nodded. "Absolutely. You're the closest thing to family that I have, Sam, so it would mean a lot to me if you were there."

"What time do you want me to set it up for?"

"How about two or three in the afternoon?"

"Consider it done. I'll shoot for three unless you hear otherwise, and I'll see you on the steps of City Hall a little before three."

"Thanks. And one other thing..." Chris said, explaining the remainder of the arrangements he wanted Sam to execute. He folded the phone and stepped out of the car, heading into the mall looking for a jewelry store.

He already had a wedding gift in mind and strolled up and down the displays looking for the exact match. He stopped in front of a cabinet with a platinum diamond eternity necklace and matching bracelet.

"I'll take these." He tapped the glass, looking up at the jeweler. "And I'd like to see your selection of diamond earrings."

The jeweler looked at his worn jeans and scuffed leather jacket and raised his eyebrows. "Sir, this necklace alone is ninety-five thousand dollars."

Chris nodded and glanced at the nametag gracing the man's lapel. "I can read, Hal."

After a couple of blinks and an apologetic smile, the jeweler placed a choice of platinum diamond earrings out for him to look at.

A quick glance and he settled on a set of 3/4 carat studs, and then Hal rang up the purchase and took his credit card to swipe it in the machine. After he signed the receipt, Hal wrapped each box in ornate silver paper adorned with a white bow.

He smiled, walking to the car with the three pristine packages. He wanted her to sparkle when they walked down the red carpet at the premiere, and he wanted everyone to know she belonged to him.

End Game Chapter 6

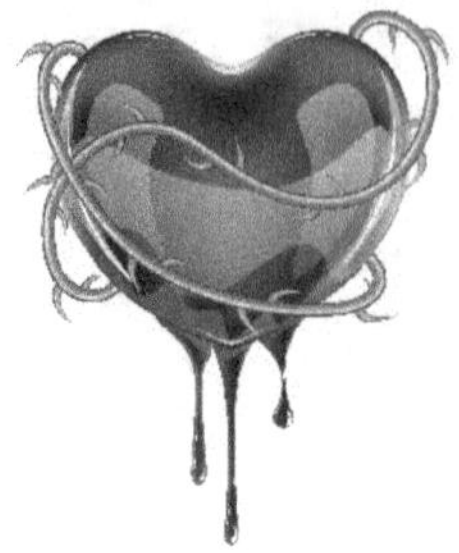

QUIET MET CHRIS AT the door. He slipped inside to the bedroom and hid the bag in his bureau before searching the rest of the house for his family.

Computer clicks and animated sounds filtered out of the den, and he swung the door open, smiling as the boys played on their computers. The pre-kindergarten software walked them through the letters of the alphabet and simple word recognition. CJ was much further along in the program than Tommy.

"Hi, hon," Jessica said over her shoulder when he came up behind them.

Leaning over, he kissed her gently on the top of the head. "Everything is taken care of, even your dress."

"What did you do?" she asked.

He grinned.

"You didn't."

Chris nodded. He'd ordered an exact replica of the white dress she wore on their first date. "Yes, I did. Was that too presumptuous of me?"

"No, not presumptuous at all. It's a beautiful dress. Did you make sure all the kids were taken care of too?"

"No, should I?"

"Um, yes. The boys will need suits, same with Eric. I'm not sure if he has one at home or not. And I'm sure Emily would love something new. You can ask her on the way to the studio. And what about you?"

"Armani." He smiled down at her. "I figured the black pinstripe with a white shirt. Do you want me to wear a tie?"

Jessica thought about it. "No, I like it better when you have the open collar. Makes me hotter looking at your bare neck," she whispered.

"Damn, girl, if I had known that, I would have burned all my ties a long time ago." He laughed.

"Daddy said a bad word," Tommy announced.

Jessica stifled a laugh.

"Yes, Daddy said a bad word, so don't you be repeating it," Chris said.

Jessica looked at the clock. "Okay, kids, time to wrap up. Karate class starts in an hour, and I promised Emily we'd swing in."

THEY SWUNG IN TO Emily's house fifteen minutes later, and everyone barged in creating chaos in their wake. Emily came out of the kitchen and doled out hugs to everyone before studying the rock on her mother's left hand.

"It's about time." Emily looked up at Chris. "I was beginning to think you would never marry my mother."

Chris felt heat plume in his cheeks and shoved his hands in his pockets, shifting his weight from foot to foot as he studied the pattern of the carpet. He finally met her gaze. "Do you want me to pick up a dress for you for the wedding?"

Emily raised her eyebrows and pointed at him, switching her gaze to her mother. "Is he serious?"

"My idea, and trust me, he has great taste," Jessica said.

"Well, okay."

Chris sized her up. "You're what, a size six?" He looked down at her feet. "With a size six and a half or seven shoes?"

Emily's eyes widened. "Yes, size seven, and that's just creepy."

"Sorry." Chris had always been exceptional at sizing people up. He could have guessed her height and weight within an inch and a couple of pounds as well, but decided not to subject her to that sideshow trick of his. "What's your favorite color?"

"Blue."

Jessica and Chris exchanged a smile as the same conversation they'd had ten years before flashed through each of their minds.

"What color blue?" he asked, holding eye contact with Jessica.

"Caribbean blue."

"Hmm." Chris looked back at Emily. "I'll figure something out for you. We have to get moving, or we're going to be late, Jess."

"Do you want to come to Eric's game with us this weekend?" Jessica asked.

Emily smiled. "Sorry, I have plans."

"What's his name?" Chris asked.

"Bill. He's a new teacher at the high school."

"When do I get to meet him?" Chris paused at the door, turning toward his soon-to-be stepdaughter.

Emily laughed until she realized he was serious. "You're kidding, right?"

Chris grinned. "Yes, and no. Someone has to keep an eye on you up here."

Jessica grabbed his arm and yanked him out of the house, rolling her eyes at her daughter. "Sorry, Em. We will see you next week."

Emily laughed and closed the door.

"I guess I freaked her out a bit." Chris smiled over at Jessica, got in the car, and pulled out of the driveway.

"Ya' think?" She laughed. "What would you do if she brought him to meet you?"

He chuckled. "I'd ask him what his intentions are." He looked sideways at her and grinned. "I'd make sure I made him real nervous. Anyone who hurts her will have to answer to me."

"She's not your daughter, Chris."

Chris shrugged. "It doesn't matter. Emily and Eric are your kids, and that's close enough for me. Besides, I'll be their stepfather soon enough."

"You would love every second of terrorizing her boyfriends, wouldn't you?" She smacked his leg lightly as they pulled up to the studio.

He grinned over at her. "I have to get my kicks somehow."

"You really are twisted."

He laughed and got out of the car, then held the back door for the kids. They followed Jessica in, and he grabbed the bags. He met the kids in the office and dressed them in their karate gis, then changed in to his as well before he sent them into the karate studio to warm up.

Chris glanced at his watch. Ten minutes before the first students would arrive. He crossed to the front studio and leaned on the doorjamb to watch Jessica warm up.

"My wife." He sighed. He still couldn't believe this was actually happening. Not with his past, and he wondered how long this paradise would last before his bubble burst.

He wandered back to the rear studio and found the boys wrestling on the floor. Chris cleared his throat, and both boys shot to their feet.

"He started it." CJ pointed at Tommy.

Tommy looked at his feet and stood in a ready position with his hands behind his back. "Sorry, Daddy."

Chris looked between Tommy and CJ. "You both know better."

"I know," they said in unison.

"Well then, you know what's coming next, don't you?" He stood with his arms crossed, looking down at them.

"Awe, Dad, do we have to?" CJ whined.

Chris nodded. "Twenty pushups."

Both children mumbled and dropped, executing the pushups while Chris counted. Students began filtering in during the punishment, and he nodded acknowledgement to each one. The boys completed their pushups just in time for the start of class.

Twice a week they held four hour-long classes in the studio, two before their dinner break and two after. The boys attended the karate classes before dinner, and then they were sequestered in the office, amused by educational videos until they dozed on the plush couches and their parents gathered them up for home.

Chris walked into the office and smiled at the boys sprawled out and snoring on the furniture, the television droning on with one of their animated favorites. He took a second to just stare at his kids, and the same dreamlike veil covered his eyes, creating a mist he blinked away. Valentine's Day always brought back his insecurities, and this morning's call from Tom didn't help. With a sigh, he reached for the remote and clicked Nemo off, then switched to the local college basketball game and kicked back in the chair, waiting for Jessica's last dance class to end.

AFTER THE LAST STUDENT left, Jessica straightened up the dance studio, closed the blinds, and shut off the lights. She pushed open the office door and sighed at the sight of him. Chris gave her a sideways glance, the dimple briefly appearing in his cheek before he returned his attention to the last thirty seconds of the game. He turned her on something fierce, sitting in his black gi with his feet still bare, the edges of his hair damp with sweat and the evidence of a good workout found in the color of his cheeks. Jessica inhaled to keep her overactive libido in check until they got home.

"You ready?" He flipped the television off and turned, smiling.

He knew what made her crazy, and he played it up, sliding over and wrapping his arms around her. His lips grazed hers, salty and sweet, and the trail of his tongue along the line of her neck sent shivers through her. His hands glided from her waist down her back until they cupped her ass, gripping and caressing.

"Stop," she whispered without conviction.

Chris laughed softly, his breath tickling the nape of her neck. "I'll never stop." He kissed her again, pulling her closer.

"We have to get the boys home." She begrudgingly pushed him away.

Chris grabbed her arm as she went to walk away. "I'm serious."

She looked at him with a confused expression.

"I'll never stop loving you. Even a million years couldn't make the way I feel fade away." He let go of her and turned to gather up their children.

"Ty?" She said his name for the second time in five years.

Chris stopped and turned back to her. "As much as I like hearing you say that name, you can't. Not here, not until we're home and alone in our bedroom. Otherwise, I'm going to lose control." He took a deep breath. "Because baby, you have no idea what hearing you say my name really does to me."

"I bet I have an inkling." Oh, she knew. She knew because saying his real name created an electrical current that filled the space between them, driving her into his arms and magnifying the heat to the point of flashover.

After letting her go, he gathered the boys in his arms and offered her a knowing smile before he headed to the car.

"I NEED TO GET up early tomorrow. I have some things I have to do, but I'll be back in time to get you and the kids for class." Chris pulled out of the parking lot, heading home.

"Where're you going?" She tried to pry into his mind but came up empty. Chris could shut her off from reading his thoughts ever since he inherited the power raging in his veins.

He smiled. "For starters, I have to get three suits and a dress."

"And that's going to take you all day?"

Chris shook his head and looked at her sideways, his eyes twinkling in the darkness. "It's a surprise."

Jessica took a deep breath and let it go. She knew she'd never get it out of him, no matter how hard she tried. The last five years reinforced his secret-keeping abilities. Any time he hinted at a surprise, it never slipped, and his mind put the information under lock and key so even his son couldn't reach into his thoughts and pluck it out. They all learned when Daddy had a surprise, it was well worth the wait.

Jessica waited in the bedroom while Chris tucked the boys in their beds. Her heart sped up in anticipation and when he stepped into the room and closed the door behind him, she smiled and whispered, "Ty."

Half a second later, he had her in his arms, and clothing dropped at random intervals as he led her toward the bathroom and the shower beyond. His hands slid over her skin, followed by his lips, creating ripples of heat centered low in her abdomen. Making love to him on a normal day was breathtaking, but tonight, he was ravenous, fueled by the use of his given name. She gasped at the sensations he elicited with his hands and mouth. The steam coming from the shower paled compared to the steam they produced.

"Oh God." Jessica gasped, her back planted against the cool tile and his hands exploring the hot cavern between her legs. His mouth teased her nipples, nibbling, licking, sucking until his name rolled off her tongue. "Ty."

"Tell me what you want," he said, looking up at her.

"You. I want you," she said, giving him the power he craved.

Chris smiled and dropped to his knees, kissing her stomach. "Is this what you want?" he asked in his smooth, sexy voice, slipping his finger inside her.

She shook her head and ran her hands through his wet hair.

Chris trailed lower and rolled his tongue around her sensitive nub. "Is that what you want?"

"God, yes." She wrapped her leg over his shoulder, giving him free rein to lick her to his heart's content.

The way he played her body reminded her of a concert pianist, smooth and slow at first, striking each chord with gentle bravado until passion overtook him and his motions reached a crescendo. Wetness rushed from her, and she moaned, digging her fingers into his hair.

He didn't stop with her first orgasm. He continued, wreaking havoc with her body until she panted "yes" over and over and over, her form trembling from ecstasy. Only then did he make his way back up to her mouth, kissing her with the same insane passion thrumming through her veins.

She wrapped her legs around his waist and sighed under his kiss, his hardness sliding in and out of her with controlled passion. His hands gripped her ass, pulling her to him with each slow thrust. Another rush of fire burst from her, and she bit his lip, stifling a high-pitched, satiated whimper.

"Say it." He stared intensely at her through his wet hair.

"Ty." She gasped. "I love you."

Chris lost control, wrapping his arms tightly around her, kissing her deeply, his hips arching into her over and over again, increasing the speed and power of each thrust until he finally exploded inside her, creating another delicious orgasm of her own.

Her body felt like a wavy noodle that had boiled too long, and she was glad his arms were wrapped around her because if he let go, she was sure she'd collapse on the shower floor.

"God, Jess." He leaned into her against the wall, his voice laden with exhaustion. "You're going to end up killing me." He lifted his head from her shoulder and smiled. "I think my heart stopped on that one." He slowly uncoupled and set her on her feet, steadying her when she wobbled before stepping back under the warm spray.

Jessica leaned against the tile, glad for the solid wall behind her because her legs still hadn't fully recovered. She watched him tilt his head back and let the water stream onto his forehead, raining down his body with a small smile of contentment on his lips.

After a few moments, his blue eyes opened and met her gaze. Reaching for her, he pulled her into his arms and pressed his lips to the top of her head. "I am so in love with you."

"I know." She looked up. "So, where are you going tomorrow?" She smiled, and for a brief instant almost glimpsed his thoughts before the door slammed closed with a mental bang.

Dimples appeared briefly, and he snatched a quick kiss before grabbing the soap and lathering up. "That was sneaky."

She returned his grin. "I try."

End Game Chapter 7

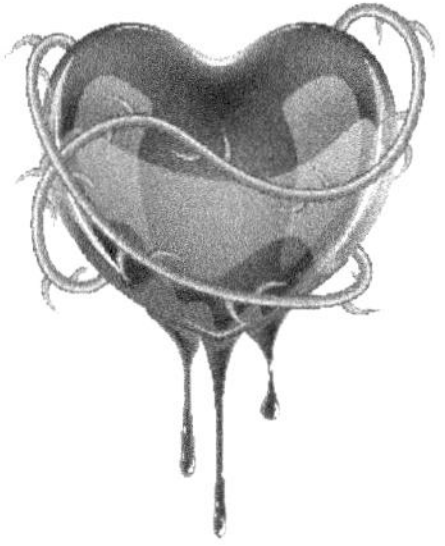

CHRIS GOT UP VERY early for his road trip. Darkness still blanketed the room when he sat on the edge of the bed and wiped a stray strand of hair out of Jessica's face, kissing her slack lips. Still in the clutches of sleep, she mumbled his name, and his heart soared at the smile that formed on her face.

God, he loved her, and that was what he clung to on the drive to Connecticut. Two hours later, he pulled into the driveway of his destination and rubbed his palms on his thighs, wiping the thin sheen of sweat away.

He swallowed and stepped out of the car, staring at the average colonial and crossing to the door. Each step twisted the knot in his stomach. He hesitated at the doorbell, taking a deep breath and then chuckling at his jumbled nerves. *This is worse than waiting in the cold for her yesterday.*

Shaking the jitters out of his head, he licked his lips and pressed the doorbell.

Joanna Campbell answered the door, and her eyebrows rose. She looked around Chris, expecting to see her daughter and grandchildren in tow. When they landed on the little red Corvette in the driveway, concern flashed over her features. She shot her brown eyes to his, adjusting her spectacles and opening the storm door. "Is everything okay?"

Chris stepped inside. "Everything's fine. I wanted to talk to Russ. Is he around?" Chris smiled, trying to disarm Jessica's mother. He took his coat off and hung it on the stair railing.

Joanna led him into the family room where Russ was reading in his favorite recliner. He had aged well. Jessica had inherited her high cheekbones and graceful body from her mother, but she had a lot of her father in her, too, most notably the intensity of his stare and the same shocked expression he sported when he was surprised.

"Everything is fine," Chris repeated, seeing the surprise turn to concern almost immediately. "I just needed to talk with you." He sat down in one of the chairs, looking at his hands before he met Russ's questioning stare. Chris drew in a deep breath. "I came to get your blessing. I want to marry your daughter."

Russ took a deep breath. He closed the book he was reading as he seemed to formulate his thoughts. "I have never been very fond of you. Your family history bothers me, and I don't know why you sought out my daughter to begin with."

Chris felt the bite of his words and went to speak.

Russ stopped him with a shake of his head and a raised hand. "I know you told me, but I'm still not buying it."

Chris looked down at his hands and then back up at Russ. "I've loved your daughter since I first met her, Russ."

"I know that, Chris. But there's still something about you I can't quite put my finger on, and it bothers me as much, if not more, than your family history.”

“Russ, my father was a cop, so my family history isn't what you think it is,” Chris said, leaning back in the chair.

Russ raised his eyebrows. “Oh.”

“He died in the line of duty. My mom was so messed up by my father's death that she married the first man to come along. Unfortunately for us, that was Jacob Aris, and yes, he was a mean son of a bitch,” Chris said. “I learned a lot of things from being in the Aris household: I learned to hate everything that they stood for and vowed to never treat people the way they did. Unfortunately, my brother was not as diligent as I was in keeping them from getting into my head.”

Russ narrowed his eyes, studying Chris and the outpouring of information, which was by far the longest conversation the two of them had had in the five years he had been with Jessica. “All right, I'll give you a break on the family history.” He tilted his head a little, as if hearing something in the distance. “But I still have a feeling that there's more than meets the eye where you're concerned.”

Chris laughed. *Oh yeah.* “Not much, Russ. What do you want to know?”

“I want to know if you had anything to do with what happened to my daughter ten years ago.”

Chris's smile disappeared, and he shook his head, blocking all thoughts. “No.” He maintained eye contact with Jessica's father while his heart clamored in his chest.

Russ nodded, seeming to believe the lie. “I still don't understand why, but my daughter loves you, and you seem to make her very happy." He chewed on his bottom lip and inhaled through his nose. "So yes, you have my blessing to marry her, but if you ever hurt her, you will have to answer to me," he finished, staring him down.

Chris nodded. "I couldn't hurt her," he said, suppressing the word 'again' from his response. "Ever." He held his future father-in-law's stare. "I love her too much," he added, and then couldn't help the grin that spread over his face. "What are you two doing next Friday?"

"We have nothing on the calendar. Why?" Joanna asked.

"I think it would mean a lot to Jess if you were at our wedding. We're getting married in New York City next Friday."

Russ sat back in his chair. "So, what was all of this?" He waved his hand in irritation.

"Your blessing means a lot to me."

"And if you hadn't gotten it?"

Chris shrugged. "I would have married her, anyway."

Russ sighed and nodded, turning his gaze toward his wife.

"We would love to be there." Joanne beamed.

Chris stood and smiled. "I'll have a car pick you up on Thursday night, and I'll get you a room at the Plaza, but you have to do me a favor." He looked from one to the other.

"What kind of favor?" Russ asked.

"I want to surprise Jess. I don't want her to know I arranged this."

Joanna and Russ both nodded, agreeing to keep the arrangements on the QT.

"I'll arrange for transportation from the hotel to City Hall on Friday as well." He stood.

"One more question," Russ said.

"Sure," Chris replied.

"Does Jessica know what you're worth?"

Chris shook his head. "Why, do you?"

Russ smiled. "I did my research."

Chris returned his smile. He would have done the same thing if he had a daughter, regardless of her age. "She will never want for anything," he assured Russ. "Neither will our kids, or our kids' kids." He held out his hand, and his father-in-law-to-be shook it.

"Welcome to the family," Russ said.

End Game Chapter 8

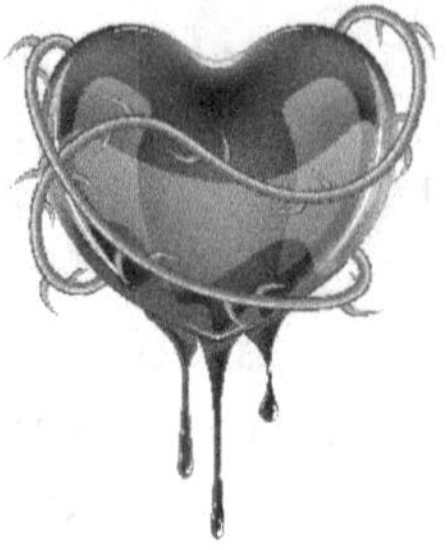

JESSICA WOKE UP TO the boys climbing into her bed.

"Where's Daddy?" CJ asked and snuggled next to her.

Tommy climbed in on the opposite side of Jessica and promptly fell back asleep.

"Daddy had some things to do today." Jessica yawned. "He'll be back a little later." She pulled both boys close to her and glanced at the clock. "Get a little more sleep. It's still very early." She closed her eyes and sleep threatened.

"Mommy?" CJ whispered.

Jessica's eyes fluttered back open. "Hmmm?"

"Is Daddy's name Ty?"

The question woke Jessica as effectively as a slap would have. "Why do you ask?" she asked, stalling enough to cloak her thoughts. She turned and took in her four-year-old son, the spitting image of his father in so many ways, but his gifts exceeded both hers and Chris's combined. He could reach into their minds and extract information at will, which annoyed the hell out of her at times. A four-year-old should not know what is going on in the adult realm, even though his intellectual level bordered on genius.

"You called him Ty yesterday, and that was the name he put on the inside of your ring," CJ said.

"Ty was Daddy's brother, and he died saving my life." It killed her to lie to her son, but he was just too young to understand or have the burden of the truth laid on him.

CJ's eyebrows scrunched together in a skeptical mask that did not belong on the face of a four-year-old. He closed his eyes, and Jessica felt the force of his mind-scan crumbling the mental block she'd put in place when he asked the question.

"He had a scar?" He gasped, and his eyes flew open.

"Christopher James, do not do that! You can't just force your way into people's minds. It's not right."

"Sorry, Mommy, but you weren't telling the truth, and you and Daddy both told me lying is wrong."

"CJ, there are just some things that you are too young to understand." *Drop it,* she commanded with her thoughts.

His expression hardened. "You can't control me, Mommy. Only Daddy can."

Jessica shivered. "Let it go, CJ. We will tell you about Ty when the time is right."

"When will that be?"

When you're over eighteen. "When the time is right."

CJ sulked. "I don't want to wait that long."

"CJ, you are four years old. I am your mother, and I am telling you to drop it now." She closed her eyes and pretended to go back to sleep, but she didn't fool her son.

"I'm sorry, Mommy," he said after a few minutes of silence.

"I know. Now go back to sleep like your brother."

"I can't. I'm awake now."

Jessica smiled. There would be hell to pay later when he was overtired, but she nodded. They slowly slid out of bed, quietly slipping out of the room without waking Tommy.

"Want to help me pick out a wedding gift for your father?" Jessica ruffled his hair.

"Sure. We could get him the new Play Station."

Jessica laughed. "I'm sure Daddy would love that, but I was thinking of something a little more personal, just for him."

CJ bit his lip. "How about a new car?"

Jessica smiled at her son. Games and cars—that's exactly what she expected him to come out with. It made her happy to know he was just like every other four-year-old in that respect.

"Sweetheart, I think I want to get your father a gold chain," she said. She loved looking at his neckline and always thought that a nice, simple chain of gold would accentuate it. "Or a watch," she added. His watch was getting old. "Or both. Anyway, we can go over to the mall as soon as I exercise, and your brother is up and moving. Don't wake him," she scolded when CJ looked up at the ceiling. "It's way too early. None of the stores are open yet, so let him sleep."

CJ gave his mother the 'Aww, Come On!' look that Chris gave her any time he wanted to do something, but she wouldn't allow it.

"You certainly are your father's son." She laughed. "What do you want for breakfast?"

"Pancakes. We didn't get any yesterday."

"Okay, pancakes it is."

End Game Chapter 9

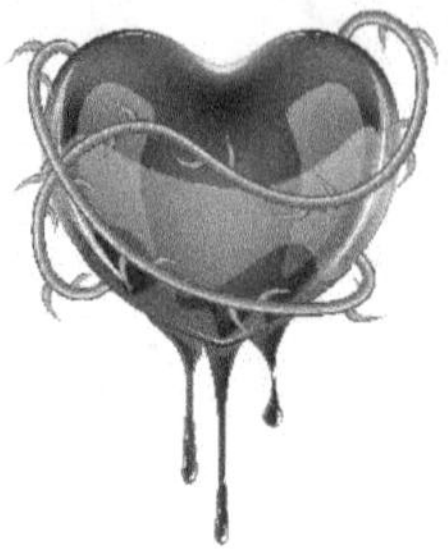

TOM STUMBLED OUT TO the beach again and looked at his watch—four thirty in the morning. He closed his eyes and took a deep breath, cracking open the new bottle of scotch and taking a swig directly from it. He pulled out the cell phone from his pocket, stroking it with his fingers before he tipped the bottle to his lips again, letting the smooth liquid fire deaden his shot nerves.

Sharon had made him fuck her again tonight—while he was sober—dangling the threat of killing Jessica over his head in order to get him to perform. He hated the feel of her, and every time he fucked her, he lost a piece of his mind. At least when he was drunk, he didn't care as much. But sober, she made his skin crawl, so the only way he could give in to her demands was to become the character he had played in the movie she wrote. He momentarily became Ty Aris and fucked his wife without passion or conviction, just silent rage.

He drained the remainder of the bottle in one long pull, sending the cool liquid down his throat, where it instantly spread warmth and heavenly numbness through his body.

"Fuck it," he mumbled and tossed the bottle in the sand. He blinked a couple of times, his eyes slowly focusing on the names on his phone as he scrolled through the list until her number came into view. Without over-thinking it, he pressed the call button and dropped on his back in the sand. The stars blurred in and out of focus.

Tom didn't care if he woke her up. Hearing her voice yesterday had been a small beacon of light in his otherwise dark life.

End Game Chapter 10

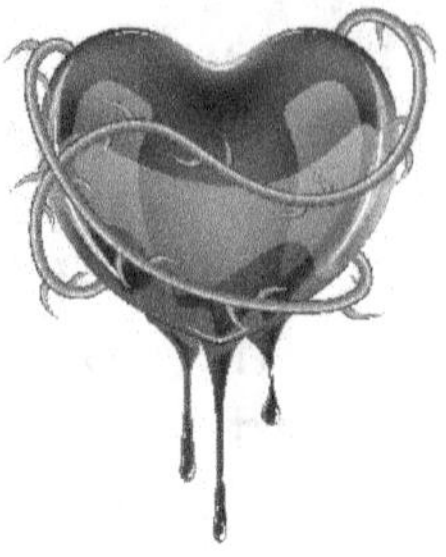

JESSICA FLIPPED A PANCAKE. The ring of the phone pulled her attention away from the hotcakes. She glanced at the clock and then over at the phone, and her heart raced. There were only a few reasons she could think of for her phone to ring at this hour, and none of them were good. She answered without looking at the caller ID.

"Hi, Jessie."

"Tom?"

"Hope I din't wake you," he slurred.

"No, I was up. Why, in God's name, are you calling me?" She placed the plate of pancakes in front of CJ and poured syrup on them, listening to Tom breathe on the other end of the phone line. She smiled at CJ and then left the kitchen. "Tom, is everything all right?" She closed the living room door behind her and crossed to the window, staring out at the snow-covered front lawn.

"No, Jessie. Everythin's not aw-right."

"Have you been drinking?"

"I been drinkin since you left. Is da only way I can get through da day."

Jessica closed her eyes. She felt the sadness in him from three thousand miles away. "You need to stop drinking."

He laughed at her. "You have no idea." He stopped and was silent. "I can't."

"I won't come next Friday unless you promise me you'll be sober," she said, not really knowing whether or not it would have any weight with him.

Quiet permeated the line, followed by a sigh. "I promise I'll be sober. Can I ask you sommin?"

Jessica hesitated, afraid of the question. "Sure."

"Did you ever love me?"

The question shot through Jessica, and she stifled a gasp. "Yes, I loved you."

"I still love you. You're the love of my life, always were, always will be."

"Tom, don't."

"What woulda happened if I hung in there instead of sending you away in New York?" he pushed. The words were a little clearer, but the slow speech gave away just how drunk he was.

Jessica thought about the question. She didn't want to answer it, not in the state he was in. "I don't know."

"Was that an 'I don't know,' meanin you don't want to hurt me, or an I don't know what woulda happened had we stayed together?"

"Tom, you know as well as I do I would have never made it for the long term with you. Not in California. And if I were on the East Coast anywhere near Chris..."

"You would be with him, anyway." Tom closed his eyes. "So, I was doomed from the beginning."

"I'm sorry." Jessica didn't know what else to say. "But honestly, I couldn't leave him, not again, not after everything that happened." She closed her eyes. "I just couldn't."

"But you never married him either."

Jessica balked at the slyness of the comment. "I am going to marry him."

"When?"

"Next Friday."

"God damn mother fucking son of a bitch," Tom muttered. "Don't marry him."

The venom in his voice hardened her heart, bringing back the memory of the night he'd told her to get the hell out of his life. That raw rage with which he forced himself on her, telling her he didn't want her, didn't need her, and didn't love her.

"Tom, go back to bed." She went to hang up.

"Don't hang up!" Tom yelled.

"I'm marrying Chris next Friday, whether you like it or not."

"But the premiere?"

"We will be there."

"You're getting married and then coming to the premiere?"

"Yes."

"Why?"

"Because you asked me to be there," Jessica said, *and because I didn't know that Friday would be my wedding day.*

Only Tom's ragged breathing came over the line.

"Mommy?" CJ stood at the door to the living room.

"CJ, Mommy is on the phone," Jessica said without turning around. "Go check on Tommy for me, okay?"

"Okay." The click of the door followed.

TOM HEARD HER UTTER the name, and it was like a knife going through his heart. "Is Tommy my son?" He waited and when she didn't answer, he asked, "Is CJ?"

"No, CJ isn't your son," Jessica answered immediately.

"But Tommy?"

Jessica was silent again.

"Jess, are you still there?" Tom asked, her lack of an answer immediately sobering him up.

"I'm here."

"Do I have a son?" he asked, sitting up straight.

"Yes, Tom, you have a son," Jessica admitted. "But the only reason that it happened was because of Chris."

Tom couldn't breathe; the emotions gripping him were sudden and overwhelming, and the most pronounced was fear. "Oh, my fucking god." He shot a glance back at the house, tremors flowing through his entire six-foot-three frame. "She can't ever find out."

"Who? Sharon?"

"Yes, Sharon." *You don't understand.* "I have to go." He flipped the phone shut before he revealed too much to his ex-wife. Sharon would kill both Jessica and his son out of spite because Sharon thought he couldn't have children.

The phone rang in his hand, shattering the silence of the early morning in Malibu.

Tom open the phone but didn't say a word.

"What don't I understand?" Jessica had caught his thoughts and the panic flowing through him before he'd hung up the phone.

"You don't understand." He closed his eyes. "If she finds out..." He slowly opened his eyes. "If she finds out, she will kill him. And she will kill you."

JESSICA LAUGHED AT FIRST. His silent fear gripped her, killing the laughter in her throat. His absolute panic was greater than just the normal 'oh crap, my wife's going to kill me' kind of thing. His words took on the character of truth, enough so that she closed her eyes and sent herself three thousand miles away, the transition pulling her essence through the phone line until she felt the sandy grains under her bare feet.

Tom's eyes widened, and his jaw dropped. He stared at her solid form on the beach before him.

"I've only done this with mirrors in the past." She blinked, taking in his disheveled appearance, and the discarded bottle on the sand next to him.

The phone slipped out of his hand and landed in his lap, but his hand remained next to his ear. She kneeled on the sand in front of him.

He blinked a couple of times before speaking. "Are you really here?" He reached out and touched her cheek.

"Yes, and no." Jessica pulled away from his touch. He looked like hell, and her heart broke. "Why would your wife kill your child?"

Tom closed his mouth and looked at her. "Please don't refer to that bitch as my wife." Hatred radiated from him.

"Tom, why did you marry her if you hate her so much?"

He shook his head. He didn't want to say the words, not aloud, so he framed them in thought, knowing Jessica would hear him. *Blackmail, Jessie. She has an open-ended contract on your life, and if I do anything she doesn't like, she'll put it into effect just to spite me.*

Being hit by a car would have been more pleasant than the shock and pain accompanying his thoughts. Her eyes misted. A mini-movie of his life, highlighting the worst of the past five years, rolled through her mind, a silent recounting just for her, including the fact that he'd had a vasectomy and lied to cover it up.

Jessica covered her mouth and looked up at the house. "You gave up your life for me?"

Tom nodded.

"And you gave up the option of having children because of me?"

"No, that was my choice. I would never bring a child into this world with that bitch."

"I'm so sorry." Fury and sorrow alternated for dominance, and she couldn't blink the tears away fast enough.

"Jessie." He closed his eyes and clenched his teeth, his hands balling into tight fists for an instant before he relaxed them and opened his eyes. "At least you're safe. That's all that really matters to me."

Jessica hung her head, and the tears brimmed, creating hot, wet paths down her cheeks.

Tom moved toward her and tilted her face up to him. "Please don't cry," he said, and his own tears fell from his bright blue eyes. "Please," he whispered and leaned in to kiss her.

The soft warmness of his lips on hers sent a pulse through her frame, and she pulled back. The transition yanked her breath from her lungs, and she opened her eyes back in her living room. His sobs filtered through the phone line.

He gasped. "Jessie."

"Tom, I will make it right."

"You can't. Not without placing yourself in danger, and I won't allow that." He sniffled, his voice raspy but under control. "And now that I know I have a child, there is nothing I wouldn't do to keep him safe. I'm sure Ty feels the same."

"He does, and he loves both of them equally." Jessica looked over her shoulder. "The same way he loves Eric and Emily. They are all pieces of me, and he places them on the same pedestal."

"I'M COUNTING ON THAT," Tom said. "I'm counting on him to keep you all safe." He drew a long breath. "Because I'm not sure how much longer I'll last before I kill her."

"Don't. You will never be able to live with yourself."

"You would be surprised what I can live with, Jessie." He looked back at the house. The bedroom light switched on. "Very surprised. I have to go. I'll see you next Friday."

He stood and erased the history of the call before he closed the phone. He walked to the waterline. Sharon's footsteps and disgusted mumbling behind him reached his ears, and he took a deep breath, controlling the onslaught of rage.

"Come back inside, Tom," Sharon ordered.

"Go to hell."

When her hand touched his arm, he brushed it away. "Don't touch me," he growled, his tone as ferocious and deadly as the glare he sent her way.

She stepped back, her chin dangling in shock.

"Never again, Sharon."

"What the hell are you talking about?"

"I am never touching you again, do you understand?" He turned and took a step toward her, looking like the predator he played in the film that was coming out next Friday. "Ever."

"Then she dies." Sharon turned toward the house.

Tom grabbed her and swung her toward him, placing his hand in a death grip around her neck. "You don't seem to understand at all." He pulled her so she was close to his face. "If I touch you again, it will be to squeeze the life out of you." He threw her away from him and stormed into the house, picking up the empty bottle on the way.

He dropped the bottle onto the family room table and headed into the farthest guest room, the only room in his house that didn't hold bad memories, and he crawled into bed wondering if he had truly lost it or not.

Did that really happen, or was it just a hallucination brought on by downing a whole bottle of scotch?

"Dear God," he whispered.

He had a son.

End Game Chapter 11

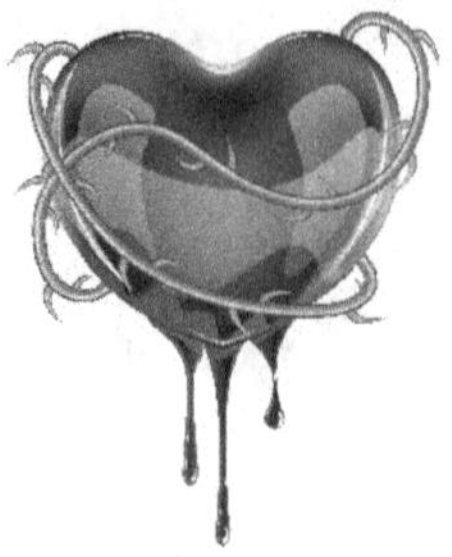

JESSICA HUNG UP THE phone and closed her eyes. "Sweet Jesus."

Was Sharon really that insane?

"I did break the bitch's nose." She chuckled at the memory of bones crushing under the power of her fist. But even that wasn't something that warranted a death sentence.

She opened the doors to the living room, then crossed to the stairs and stopped. The conversation slammed into her again, as did the truth in his fear, the look in his inebriated eyes when she'd materialized in front of him. Tom wouldn't lie, not to her. Her legs lost strength, and she grabbed for the banister with a gasp. He gave up his freedom to keep her safe, and if he didn't do what Sharon demanded of him, a dead body would be delivered to his door. Her dead body, to be exact. If Sharon found out Tom had a son, *her* son would be in danger.

Delicate strands of fear wrapped through her, and she shuddered.

CJ stepped into view at the top of the stairs. "Mommy, I won't let anything happen to my brother," he assured her and turned to walk away.

"CJ," Jessica said, sharper than she'd meant to.

He turned back. The look on his face reminded her of his father's expression, fierce and determined.

"Come here," she whispered.

CJ obediently came down the stairs and stood in front of her.

Jessica kneeled down, so she was face-to-face with him and took his little hands in hers. "Baby, how much of that conversation did you hear?"

His brow knitted, and he cocked his head. "Everything, Mommy, even when you weren't here anymore."

Jessica closed her eyes.

"That man called Daddy Ty."

Jessica opened her eyes, locking her gaze with her four-year-old son. She didn't know what to say.

"That man is Tommy's daddy?"

"No, your father is Tommy's daddy and always will be. That man just helped me make Tommy. But it was your father that made you and Tommy possible."

"Did that man help make me?"

"No, honey, your father helped me make you. You are definitely your father's son."

"That man is very angry, but not at you. He loves you like daddy loves you."

Jessica exhaled. "I suppose he does. His name is Tom, and he's a movie star. I was married to him before I met your father."

"You were married before?"

Jessica nodded. "Twice."

CJ raised his eyebrows. "Twice?"

"To Uncle Danny and to Tom. Emily and Eric are the children I had when Uncle Danny and I were married a long time ago."

CJ nodded. He had seen some pictures that Eric brought once when he explained how they were brothers. "I knew about Uncle Danny," he started, "but I didn't know about the other man."

Jessica thought about how to explain Tom to her son. "He was there when I was hurt and helped keep me safe. He knew Ty, too."

"He knew Daddy?"

"No, not really," Jessica said, because it was true. Tom didn't know Chris. He only knew what he saw down in the complex and the limited exposure to him five years ago. He didn't know what a really wonderful, compassionate, and loving man Chris really was.

"Oh," CJ said, the crease deepening between his eyes. He looked at his feet, chewing on his lower lip like Chris did when he was mulling something over. "But I thought Daddy *was* Ty."

"No, honey, I told you. Ty died," Jessica said.

CJ WAS TEMPTED TO just barrel in her mind and pull out the truth, but the frankness in her gaze made him partially believe her. Although, there was something underneath, deep inside her, when she said the name, something powerfully strong and pure in her, and very dark and cold when his father had said the name the other day. Together, they balanced.

His eyes widened. "You balance each other."

"What?" Jessica recoiled.

"You and Dad balance each other."

Jessica smiled. "Yes. Daddy and I balance each other."

"Eric told me you and Daddy were meant to be together." CJ smiled. "He said it was written in the stars."

JESSICA LAUGHED. IT WOULD be like her oldest son to say that. "I don't know about it being written in the stars, but I believe we were meant to be together."

"Mommy?" Tommy interrupted. "I'm hungry."

"Mommy made me pancakes," CJ bragged.

"Can I have some?" Tommy's big blue eyes looked so much like his father's had minutes before on a beach in California.

End Game Chapter 12

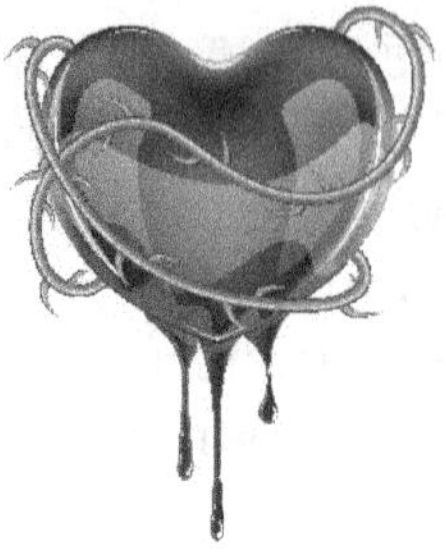

JESSICA WRAPPED UP HER workout and showered while the boys played in their room, and then she corralled them for a trip to the mall. Usually, they were a handful at the stores, but today they were on their best behavior, and that thrilled her.

At the jeweler's, they pointed out all sorts of gaudy bling for Daddy, but she ended up deciding on a simple eighteen-inch gold chain and a gold and platinum Rolex watch with diamond chips as wedding gifts. She let the boys choose one of the less conservative pieces—a sterling silver Celtic cross on a thick, braided chain that would be at home around Rick Ross's neck. The jeweler wrapped them at her request and handed them over with a smile.

"How long would it take to have a ring engraved?" Jessica inquired.

"That wouldn't take long, just a couple of hours."

Jessica produced the wedding band that Chris had bought and wrote what she wanted engraved, then handed both to the jeweler.

"No problem. I'll have it for you by noon."

"Thank you." She smiled and walked out of the store. "Okay, boys, we have a couple of hours to kill here. What do you want to do?" she asked, knowing full well they were going to insist on going to the Discovery Zone.

"Discovery Zone!" they both yelled out at the same time.

"Let's go." She led them to the giant playscape within the mall with huge, oversized tunnels, ladders, slides, ball pits, and trampolines galore. The children were in their element, jumping, sliding, crawling, and running through three stories of the plastic wonderland while Jessica watched from the sidelines.

After close to an hour and a half, she called the boys, and they headed to the food court for a bite to eat before heading back to the jewelers.

Jessica took the ring and read the inscription that covered most of the space inside.

Ty, a million years isn't long enough. Yours forever, Jessica.

Chris would love it. She smiled and handed over the money to the jeweler, then replaced the ring in the box. It would have been in poor taste for him to put that phrase in her ring, but she thought it was absolutely appropriate for her to put it on his.

"Thank you." She grinned and left the store.

Jessica put the packages in her shoulder bag, took the hand of each boy in hers, and headed out of the mall. While walking through Nordstrom's, she ran smack into Chris.

"Daddy!" both boys exclaimed and tore their hands out of their mother's grip.

"What are you doing here?" He smiled and raked the boys to him in a big bear hug.

"Picking up some things," she replied.

Chris tilted his head a little. "You got the ring inscribed?"

"Among other things. Will I ever be able to surprise you?"

Chris let out a laugh. "Afraid not, babe."

Jessica's mind drifted to the phone call, and her smile faltered.

Chris set the boys down on the ground and straightened his back, the amusement disappearing from his eyes. Trepidation seeped into his gaze. "He called again?"

"Yes," she said, taking out the box that contained the ring and then handed it to him. "But you have nothing to worry about. Read the inscription."

He took the ring out and read what she had etched in the metal. Reading the words slowly, he took a deep breath and glanced over the shining metal into her calico eyes. The hesitation evaporated, replaced by that raw energy that made her tingle all over.

He slid the ring back in the box and stepped closer, grazing her cheek with his lips and placing the box in her hand. "Did I tell you 'I love you' today?"

The sheer proximity of his mouth to hers caused her to salivate, her heart pinging a mating call despite their surroundings.

"That's not all Mommy got!" Tommy grinned and CJ hit him in the arm.

"Be quiet!" CJ said, staring at Tommy.

Chris smiled down at his two boys and then back at Jessica. "Really?"

"Don't you dare snoop," Jessica warned, but she could tell it was too late from the smirk on his face.

"I promise I'll act surprised," he whispered in her ear. "I've got to find a dress for Emily." He stepped back. "Want to help?"

Jessica looked down at the boys and then back up at Chris. "I think these guys need to get home and take a nap before we have to go to the studio tonight." *They've been so good, but I can't see that lasting in women's apparel shops.*

"Point well taken. I shouldn't be much longer. Her dress is the last thing I need to get. Everyone else is taken care of." He smiled and ruffled the boys' hair. "Be good for your mom."

"We will!" they said, in sync as always.

He glanced back at Jessica. "We can talk about that call when I get home." He leaned over and planted a gentle kiss on her lips before heading off toward the formal dresses.

CHRIS PULLED INTO THE driveway, brought the bags inside, and hung them in the front closet. He settled into the couch, waiting for her to come downstairs. He smiled at her when she stepped into view.

"Get everything you needed to?"

"Yep. And I arranged for a car to pick us up next Thursday at three. We'll swing by and get Emily and then head down to Connecticut for Eric."

"About that. Danny wants you to come into the house when we pick Eric up," Jessica said. "I'm sure he'll mention it at the game on Saturday."

Chris laughed. He had never set foot in Jessica's old house for many reasons. The biggest being he really didn't want to see what her life was like before he snatched her out of it.

"There is no reason to continue avoiding seeing where I used to live before you met me."

"Before I kidnapped you," he clarified. His eyes bore into her.

"Chris," she sighed. "I forgave you a long time ago for what you did to me. I'm marrying you, for God's sake."

"Still doesn't wipe out the fact I disrupted your life."

Jessica walked over to him. "Yes, I will admit, you turned my life upside down. But Jesus, Chris, the gifts you have given me, nothing could replace them." She pointed to the ceiling, referring to the boys.

"I've brought you more pain than a person has a right to bear."

Jessica put her hands on his chest. "That's the thing. You haven't. Your stepbrother was the one who hurt me."

"I left you with him."

"But you didn't know, babe."

The smile that spread on his lips chilled her. "I should have known better."

She raised her eyebrows. "How?"

"I knew he was a sadist. I watched him kill dozens of people—hell, I filmed it. And you were the only woman there at the time. Even if he hadn't heard me tell you about Jacob, he still would have hurt you."

"When are you going to forgive yourself?"

He shrugged, tracing her cheek with his fingers. That was a question he didn't have an answer to. Not when his nightmares reminded him of all the death and destruction he'd had a hand in. "What about Tom? I screwed up your life with him, too."

She nodded slowly and looked down at her hands. "He's the only one who was even in the same vicinity as you, as far as feelings are concerned." She took a deep breath and met his gaze. "But I chose you."

"He left you."

"He was angry with me, but he hadn't slammed the door on our marriage. I was the one who did that."

"I thought…"

"You thought wrong. *I* chose you." She poked him in the chest. "And it had nothing to do with the fact that my marriage was on the rocks. It had everything to do with the fact that I can't live without you." She spread her hand out on his chest, feeling the strong, steady beat of his heart under her palm. "I chose you," she repeated. "So, all this insecurity needs to stop right now. I will *always* choose you."

He looked down at her in disbelief and then a smile spread slowly across his lips as what she'd said sunk in. "Always?"

"Yes, Ty. Always."

He closed his eyes for a moment and pulled her close. "The kids are asleep?"

"Yes." The spark between them ignited her, the silent rain check from the mall being redeemed.

"In here or upstairs?"

"Here, now," she replied and pushed his shirt over his head. She kissed his chest and unbuckled his pants, trailing kisses down his abdomen as she pulled his clothing off. Pushing him back on the couch, she stripped and straddled him, the urgency to have him fill her taking over. Rocking her hips, grinding into him with each slow circle, she grinned.

He peeled her shirt off and tossed it aside. Then he took her breast in his mouth as she purred his name.

"Ty." The word came out in a sigh of content.

His striking blue eyes rose to hers. "Jess, you have got to stop calling me that." He kissed her hard, his hands sliding to her waist, his thrusts deep and strong. The tongue dance stripped them of breath until he pulled away from her lips. "You're bringing out the animal in me."

She arched into him with the same bravado. "Maybe I like the animal in you."

He laughed and took her breast in his mouth again, his tongue flicking her hard nipples. She moaned, closing her eyes and grinding her hips in time with his languid motion.

Her eyes blinked open, and her gaze dropped to his. She gasped. "That's the look that drives me insane."

"What look is that?" He smiled and pulled her closer, running his tongue up her neck to her ear.

"When you're horny, your eyes smolder." Her eyes rolled back in her head, her body seizing, and wetness rushed, creating sweet friction with each stroke of him. Tremors gripped her, and she laughed, meeting his intense gaze again. "You look at me like you want to eat me alive." She kissed him, wrapping her arms around his neck.

"That's because I do," he mumbled from under her lips. She smiled as they quickened their pace with both the kiss and their hips.

He arched into her, lifting her off the couch for a moment with the power of his explosion. A high-pitched squeal of delight slipped from her lips, drowning the groan that flowed from his mouth. Their tongues tangled, still exploring and hesitant to pull away. Trembling, he settled back on the couch and laughed under her kiss.

She pulled away and stared at his satiated eyes.

"Smolder, huh?"

"Yes." She blushed and uncoupled, then stood and stretched before she gathered their clothing. She tossed his pants to him and slipped hers back on. "That look got me even when I didn't want it to."

He raised his eyebrow. "Does that mean I can have you any time I want, just with a look?"

"Pretty much." She paused with her shirt in her hands, just staring at him.

"What?" he asked self-consciously.

"You are just so damn hot to look at. I can't believe you turn forty this year."

"I feel like I'm seventeen when I'm with you." He smiled and pulled the shirt back on, waltzing across to where she stood topless and moved her into his arms. "I just can't seem to get enough." He kissed her and fondled her bare breasts.

"You're going to have to because the boys have just woken up," she said, pushing him away and quickly slipped her bra and shirt on.

He grinned as his eyes grazed her.

"Stop smoldering." She fanned herself.

He inhaled and looked at the ceiling, listening to the shuffling of little feet. "We never talked about that phone call."

Jessica turned toward him. "We need to. I was worried enough about the way he sounded on the phone to project myself out there."

His gaze snapped to hers. The confession rocked him to the core. She hadn't done that since she showed up in his shower in New York City five years ago. "Why?"

"Because he said Sharon would kill Tommy."

The bizarre statement made him step backward. No one, but no one, could threaten his kids. Both irritation and disbelief crawled over his skin. "What?"

"I told Tom he had a son, and he freaked. He apparently had a vasectomy when Sharon demanded they get pregnant."

Chris blinked; he still didn't grasp how that equated to a death threat against his kid. Things were firing off in his brain. Her thoughts, memories of what was said and not said, forming a cloud of anger. "What?"

"Sharon has been blackmailing him for the last five years."

"How?" He wanted the words; he wanted her to confirm what he saw in her mind.

"Me. She has an open-ended contract on my life. All she has to do is activate it."

The world swam in front of his eyes. That fear about his bubble bursting crashed down on him and he sat on the couch.

"And Tom said if she found out about Tommy, she would kill him out of spite."

"Over my dead body," Chris said, the anger now a flurry buzzing around his head. "He's my son, not Tom's, and God help her if she comes after this family." He looked at her and snapped his teeth together. "I can stop her dead in her tracks right now if you say the word."

"If she dies, the contract is automatically put into effect."

"Doesn't matter. I can stop anyone dead in their tracks."

"I know, but not unless we have to, okay?"

Chris took a deep breath, calming the frenzied beast running amok inside. "Next Friday night ought to be interesting."

"I'm tempted to give her another right hook."

"You are much kinder than I am, Jess. I was thinking more along the lines of seeing her explode into a million pieces."

"Daddy?" CJ said from the stairwell.

Chris turned and wiped the grin off his face. "What's up?" he asked, as if he hadn't just been thinking about killing someone.

The fear in his son's eyes prompted him to stand and cross the room.

He smiled up at Tommy. "Why don't you go see your mom? I need to have a chat with CJ."

Tommy's eyes widened as he turned to his brother, and they exchanged a glance as he skirted around his dad and ran across the family room to his mother.

Chris focused on CJ again. "I didn't mean to scare you." He led him into the living room, reminding himself that this was a four-year-old, even though he had the intellect of someone much older. He kneeled in front of his son.

"Daddy, you want to kill someone. I felt it," CJ said with wide, scared eyes.

Chris hung his head for a moment. "Sometimes adults get mad and want to hurt people," he said, bringing his gaze back to CJ's. "Especially if that person puts people you love in harm's way."

"Hurting someone and killing them are different, and they're both wrong."

Chris nodded. "Yes, they are, but protecting someone you love isn't wrong."

CJ chewed his lip. *I would protect my brother.*

Chris smiled at the simple thought. "Yes, you would protect Tommy, just like I would protect every one of you. Sometimes your daddy takes that a little too far, though."

"Is that when Ty comes out?"

"I told you, Ty was my brother, and he died," Chris lied, easily this time.

"Daddy, lying is wrong, too."

Chris sat back on his ankles and measured what he was going to say next. "Christopher James, you are four years old. You aren't ready to know about Ty yet," he said, mimicking the words that Jessica had said earlier.

"But your name is Ty," CJ replied. "Ty Aris."

Darkness crept over Chris's vision like a sheet of ice blanketing his soul and his jaw tightened, especially when CJ recoiled into the cushions of the couch away from him. "Where did you hear that name?"

"Inside of you," CJ answered, his eyes welling up with tears.

Chris stood and walked out of the room, shaken to the core. If CJ could pull that name out of his subconscious, what else could he see about his dark past? The years he spent collecting people for his stepbrother's black-market porn business, and every death he'd witnessed, haunted his nightmares. He felt unworthy of happiness because of all the horror he had been an accessory to, and he was terrified that his children would find out what a monster their father really was. He walked out the back door to the rock wall overlooking the bay. The cold bit at him, but he didn't feel it.

The snow crunched under her approaching footsteps, and the warmth of her hand on his back did nothing to quell his turmoil.

"He knows."

"No, he doesn't," Jessica replied.

"He pulled my name out of my head. What else can he see?" Chris turned to her.

"He can't see anything, Chris."

"He pulled my name out of my head, Jess." He grabbed her arms. "I had that locked up so deep…" He shook his head and released the tight grasp he had on her. "How can I teach them right from wrong if they know where I've been?"

"It's not where you've been, honey. It's how you live your life now that matters. Showing that you know the difference goes a long way. Living up to the morals and values that you are teaching them matters."

A bark of a laugh escaped. "I should be in jail, or dead, for that matter."

"Don't you dare say that!"

He rolled his eyes at her. "You know it's true."

Jessica clamped her mouth shut and looked out at the ocean, shivering.

The cold settled into his bones as well, and he knew he had to talk to his son before the boy pirated more critical information locked away in his memory.

"Let's go in where it's warm." He led her back to the house.

He walked to CJ, picked up his son, and carried him into the kitchen. "My name once was Ty Aris. But I had it legally changed to Chris Ryan, so that's my name now."

"Why did you change your name?" CJ asked.

"That's a really complicated story I'll tell you about one day, but in the meantime, you shouldn't repeat to anyone that your father's real name is Ty Aris."

"Why?"

He inhaled through his nose, trading a glance with Jessica before going on. "Because Ty Aris did some terrible things, things that if they catch up to me, they could take me away from you and your brother for a very long time."

CJ's jaw tightened and his eyes darkened. "I wouldn't let that happen."

Chris allowed a strained smile to surface. "If the police ever come looking for me, you are not to interfere. Understand?"

CJ pressed his lips together for a moment, then he nodded.

"Do you know where the name Chris or Christopher James comes from?"

CJ shook his head.

"Chris was my brother." Chris smiled at CJ. "You're named after my brother."

CJ's eyebrows rose. "You really have a brother?"

"Yes, I did, and I loved him very much, but I couldn't protect him, and he died." Chris blinked back the sudden mist covering his eyes.

CJ glanced toward his mother and back. "Why'd you and Mommy say Ty died?"

"Because the really bad part of me died when I met your mother." He cleared his throat. "I think that's about enough of my past right now, okay, buddy?"

"Okay, Daddy." He smiled and gave his father a peck on the cheek.

Chris put him down and watched him tear into the family room and hop on the couch next to Tommy. Sweet, oblivious Tommy—God, how he wished his son could have been normal like Tommy. But no such luck. CJ carried that magical gene from Jessica, and with it, the power to control the world.

End Game Chapter 13

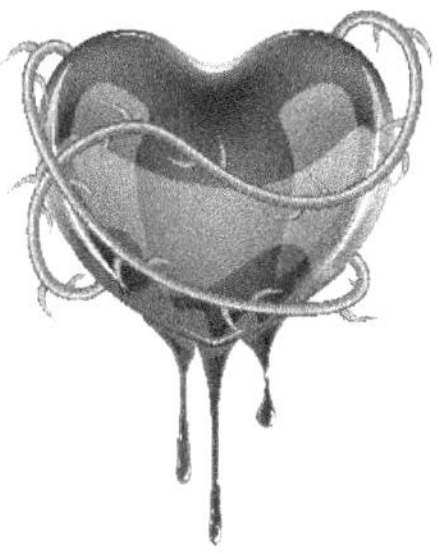

TOM WOKE TO BRIGHT sunshine filtering in the window. He turned to the clock. The numbers blinked, and so did he. It was almost noon. He rolled out of the guest room bed and then strode into the master bathroom shower. His head felt like someone had hit him with a two-by-four. He undressed and stepped under the warm spray. Water cascaded over his body, and he leaned his head back under the stream, running his hands over his hair and then down his face as the late-night events replayed in his alcohol-soaked brain.

His eyes shot open, and his heart palpitated in his chest, constricting his lungs.

She had been there.

On the beach with him.

"Christ," he said. He had a son. *I need a drink.*

"Shit," he said under his breath. He promised her he'd be sober for the premiere. He didn't know if he could go three hours without a drink, never mind three days. A week and a half seemed like an impossible feat.

He turned, facing the water, and tilted his head low, letting the water pulse on the top of his head and run down his back, drumming all thoughts from his pounding head. Closing his eyes, he drifted into a standing stupor until the shower door swung open.

Tom opened his sore eyes and glared at her without moving. "Don't even think about it," he warned. "I told you last night that the only way I'm touching you again is to kill you. Now get the fuck out of my bathroom."

"It's my bathroom, too!"

"If you get in this shower stall with me, it will be the last thing you ever do." Death couldn't have been a more persuasive argument. The twinge of fear that displayed in her eyes gave him a heady buzz of adrenaline, of triumph over the crazy bitch.

She closed the shower stall and exited the bathroom in a hurry.

He finished cleaning up and walked into the bedroom with a towel wrapped around his waist. Sharon sulked in the bed with her arms around her knees.

"Why do you hate me so much?"

Tom laughed. "You've got to be kidding me." He pulled on his clothes, glaring at her. "You constantly threaten the life of the woman I'm in love with."

"You can't still love her."

"I always will. That's something your threats will never change."

"She left you."

"That's because I was a jackass."

"She cheated on you."

Tom considered that and nodded. "But you're the one who ruined my life." He turned to leave the room.

"How so? After this movie, you're going to be one of the most wanted actors in Hollywood," Sharon barked at him.

"I'm trapped in a marriage I don't want to be in with a woman whom I hate more than anyone else on this earth, and I couldn't give a rat's ass about my career right now. That's how you ruined my life." He closed the door behind him, crossed the expansive living room to the kitchen, and looked in the refrigerator.

His gaze kept going to the bottle of Grey Goose on the shelf. He smiled at the memory of Jessica with the hellish hangover and reached for the bottle. His fingers grazed the smooth surface, but he stopped.

"Damn it." He slammed the refrigerator door.

Instead of plying his body with alcohol, he did something he hadn't done in months. He changed into his running gear and grabbed his iPod, then headed onto the beach and slipped the buds into his ears, picking the playlist he and Jessica used to run to regularly when they were married.

He ran, lost in the music and the memory of his ex-wife until he dropped in the sand. Glancing at his watch, he let out a shaky laugh. The hangover exaggerated his exhaustion, and the meager forty-five-minute run only proved just how out of shape he was. With Jessica, forty-five minutes was just the warm-up.

What the hell happened to me?

He looked out at the cool Pacific and received no words of wisdom.

Getting to his feet, he shuffled back to the house, then stumbled in and ignored Sharon's raised eyebrow. He breezed past her to the master bathroom and just made it to the toilet before the evening's indulgence came up. The stench of alcohol seeped from his pores, and he gagged again, vomiting the remaining acid churning in his stomach.

The second shower of the day renewed his energy, and for the first time in years, he felt a ray of hope as the water washed the sweat from his body.

End Game Chapter 14

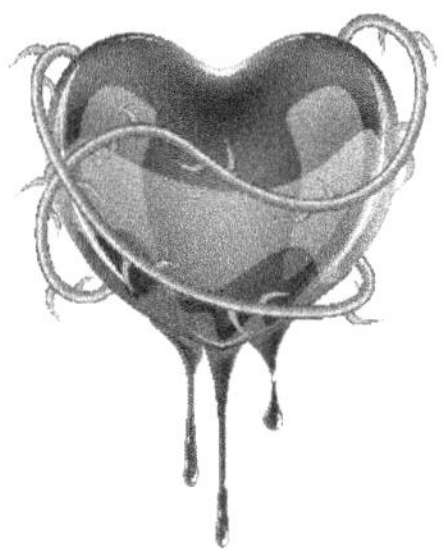

THE REST OF THE week flew by. Saturday morning, Jessica got out of bed early, kissed Chris on the cheek as he slept, grabbed her MP3 player, and on a whim, grabbed the cell phone before heading out of the house. She hopped into the car and drove the few miles to Long Sands Beach for an early-morning run.

She pulled up to the curb and looked at the empty stretch of beach with a smile. Arctic wind rattled off the ocean, enough to drive off most of the morning joggers, but she looked forward to the tingling cold ripping at her cheeks and the hard-packed sand under her feet. She deposited her keys into the pocket of her sweats and opened the car door.

The phone rang before she got her feet on the pavement and she switched up her iPod for the cell phone, slipping the earpiece in and turning it on.

"Hello?" She slammed the car door and crossed the sidewalk to the staircase leading to the sand.

"Hi."

"Hi," Jessica replied, her voice muffled by the wind.

"Where are you?" he asked, his voice slurring a little.

"Just started my run."

"And you brought your phone?"

Jessica laughed. It was unusual for her to carry her cell phone on runs; she much preferred getting lost in the music on her iPod. "I had a feeling."

It was Tom's turn to laugh.

"You're drunk again, aren't you?"

"Yes," he admitted. "I made it most of the week, but I just couldn't stand being with her another second without killing her or blowing my fucking brains out."

"Jesus, Tom." Jessica stopped running. She looked out over the Atlantic as the cold February breeze whipped off the water and into her face. The other line buzzed. "Hang on." She clicked over to the other line.

"Tell him to stop calling you," Chris whispered into the phone.

"I will, babe. Go back to sleep."

"Okay."

Jessica flipped back to Tom and started running again. "Are you still there?"

"Yes, I am."

"Chris wants you to stop calling me."

"What do *you* want, Jessie?"

"I want you to stop protecting me."

Tom laughed. "I can't do that. It ain't in my nature to put you in harm's way."

"You need to let go."

"Why?"

"Because I'm not available, Tom."

"That didn't stop *him* five years ago."

Jessica let the silence fill the space as she ran. "There is a difference," she finally said.

"And what is that difference, Jessie?"

"Chris and I were meant to be together."

Tom snorted into the phone. "Yeah, right. You're meant to be with him about as much as I'm meant to be with Sharon."

"I'm going to hang up now," she said, her tone as cold as the wind whipping through her hair.

"I'm sorry. Just talk with me for a while, okay?"

Jessica took a deep breath. "Tom, this isn't a good idea."

"Please. It'll keep me sane for a little longer."

"What do you want to talk about?" Jessica sighed, giving in to him.

"Tell me about my son."

Jessica smiled. "Tommy is the sweetest boy." She turned on the beach and headed back toward her car. "He looks a lot like you, with black hair and your eyes."

"Is there any of you in him?"

"Chris tells me he has my face. He says Tommy and Eric look a lot alike." She laughed softly. "But all I can see in him is you."

"Does he have any special abilities like Eric?"

"No. He doesn't. But CJ is a completely different story. He's the spitting image of Chris, and my God, he has powers that put ours in the dust already. I can't control him at all, but Chris... Chris keeps him in line." She smiled. "He is amazing with them, Tom."

Tom snorted again.

"Will you please stop that? You don't know him at all, so keep your comments to yourself."

"Jessie, he killed people for fun."

Jessica took a deep breath. "Tom, don't go there."

"You are going to marry a murderer. How does it feel?"

"Why don't you tell me?"

"It sucks."

"I'm in love with Chris. He's the one I've been searching for my whole life."

"Bullshit. That's just crap, Jessie, and you know it."

Jessica climbed the stairs to her car, anger seeping into her. "I am hanging up."

"Don't!" Tom yelled as she cut off the call.

Her phone rang almost instantly, and she answered.

"I'm sorry."

Jessica said nothing while she unlocked her car. She slid inside, listening to him breathe.

"Maybe I would be better off dead."

"Now that's a load of crap."

"At least you'd be safe. I hear drowning isn't a bad way to go."

Jessica transitioned and put her hand on his chest to stop him from getting any closer to the Pacific Ocean. The anger radiated like a living, breathing being.

He took a step back.

"You don't call me after five years and talk to me about suicide," she growled and took a step toward him. "You don't fucking do that!" Her hand balled into a fist, and she threw a punch at him. It caught his jaw, and he fell back on his ass in the sand.

Tom looked up at his ex-wife with his mouth hanging open.

Jessica squatted in front of him. "I can forgive a lot of things, but suicide isn't one of them. Capice?"

Tom nodded. He reached out, grabbed her by the shoulders, and pulled her to his lips, and then she was gone. "Shit," he said. "Come back."

"No." Jessica started her car. "I'm going home, and you are not to call me again."

"Will you still be at the premiere?" he asked before she hung up the phone.

"I told you I'd be there. Bye, Tom." She disconnected the call. She dialed her house and Chris answered. "I told him, but I don't know if it'll keep him from trying, though."

"Are *you* all right?" Chris asked.

"He mentioned suicide."

"Jesus. What did you do?"

"I punched him." She turned down the familiar road.

Chris started to laugh.

"It's not funny." Jessica pulled up to the gate and pressed the code in.

Chris stopped laughing. "Sorry, babe."

He opened the garage door just as she cut the engine.

Jessica took a deep breath and stepped out of the car, meeting his gaze. "We have to do something."

"All you have to do is say the word, and she's gone." He snapped his fingers.

"No, that isn't the way to do this. Killing isn't the answer."

"Sometimes it's the only answer."

"Not in my world." Jessica walked past him.

"Do you still love him?"

Jessica stopped in her tracks.

She turned toward him, seeing that hesitation again, that insecurity that burned her. "Yes, and I always will, just like I still love Danny." She walked back to him. "Just like I loved Mike. They all played a big role in my life. But here's the thing you need to remember…" She paused, searching his eyes. "I'm yours,

Chris, heart and soul, and there is nothing on this earth that could take me away from you. This time, 'till death do us part' is for real. I'm not leaving, and neither are you."

Chris wrapped his arms around her and kissed her. "We'll figure something out. I promise."

"Thank you. Are the kids up?"

"Not yet." His eyes sparkled as they scanned her, and then he slowly smiled.

"Come on, I'm all sweaty."

"I don't really care." He pulled her close again, his hands wandering. "Do you?"

Her resolve went out the window with the trail of his lips on her neck. "I guess not."

He swept her off her feet, carrying her up the stairs to their bedroom. He set her down and locked the door behind him in case the kids woke up before they had a chance to make love. He stripped his robe and discarded it on the floor, licking his lips.

Jessica undressed and chuckled. "Smoldering."

Chris smiled and pulled her naked body to him. He ran his tongue up her neck. "Mmmm, salty." He bit her earlobe.

She gasped at the sharp pain, and then it was forgotten as his lips covered hers.

"And so sweet." He pushed her down on the bed. "Heart, soul, and body."

"Yes," she whispered, getting lost in the graze of his touch, in the taste of his mouth, in the musky scent of his skin, and in the rhythm of his body. Pure ecstasy enveloped her, and she cried out his name, panting with each glorious thrust of his hips until he finally collapsed on her, spent.

"There is nothing like morning sex with you." He slid off her, pulling her to him, nuzzling in her hair, spooning her.

"I need to clean up," Jessica whispered after a few minutes of cuddling.

"Not yet," he said, his voice laced with sleep.

"The boys are going to be up any minute," Jessica insisted and tried to pull away.

Chris grinned as he yanked her back. "You're so nice and warm," he purred and buried his face in her hair, wrapping his arms tight around her waist.

Jessica laughed. "Just think of how good a hot shower would feel." She broke his grip and headed into the bathroom.

"That was just mean." Chris rolled on his back, looking after her.

"Get your lazy ass out of bed." Jessica grinned over her shoulder.

Chris smiled and stretched. "This lazy ass is going back to sleep." He pulled the covers around him and rolled onto his side.

Jessica came out a little while later to find Chris snoring softly in bed. After picking up the trail of clothing and throwing it into the hamper, she sat on the edge of the bed, sighing at the small smile on his lips and the peaceful rhythm of his breathing.

"I would be lost without you." She leaned over and kissed his cheek gently. "Completely lost." She walked out of the room and closed the bedroom door behind her.

CHRIS OPENED HIS EYES and looked at the bedroom door. "You and me both," he whispered and rolled onto his side, closing his eyes again.

Less than a week. He told himself. *Less than a week.*

Darkness descended.

He opened his eyes to her chained to a wall wearing the white dress; the gunshot resounding so loud that he jumped, but Jessica didn't flinch. The bullet passed through her body, leaving only a small circle of red on the immaculate white dress.

"Fuck you," Jessica spit in anger.

Sharon pulled the trigger again. This time, the bullet ripped through her bare shoulder, leaving an oozing bullet hole.

Jessica still didn't flinch.

Sharon stormed across the room and put the gun to her forehead.

"Jess!" Chris screamed, shooting up in their bed, his entire body drenched in sweat and his breath coming in short bursts.

Jessica flew into the room, her eyes snapping to the mirror like Pavlov's dog, half-expecting to see the sadistic ghost of his stepbrother again.

"I'm okay. It was just a nightmare," he said, and the panic on her face eased. He tried to smile, but the vividness of the dream gnawed at him, reminding him of the dreams leading up to the horror that happened with Frank's ghost. "Jesus." He ran his hands over his face and swung his legs over the edge of the bed. He headed into the bathroom without looking back at her.

Jessica followed him. "What was the nightmare about?"

Chris looked over his shoulder at her with the shower stall open. "Losing you."

He slipped into the shower. He closed his eyes as the water cascaded over his body, wiping any traces of tension from his muscles. He lathered his hair with shampoo, rinsed, and then just stood under the stream of water. Chris let his mind wander back to the dream, analyzing it.

The room she had been in looked like a mechanical room; the walls were brick with exposed metal studs. Plumbing and electrical wires were visible on the walls. The chains that Jessica had been tied with were looped on the plumbing pipes and secured together with what looked like padlocks, not actually built in the wall like at the complex. Handcuffs held her wrists to the end of the chains. The flooring looked like double plywood planking.

Chris furrowed his brow, forcing the details to the forefront of his mind. If he could identify the place, he could prevent the dream from coming true. After all, he had altered the future once before.

He slowly opened his eyes. She hadn't been alone in that room either. "Jesus." He turned, put his hands on the wall, letting the water hit the back of his neck, and closed his eyes again. "What else?"

In his mind, he scanned the room, and his eyes landed on four children. Chris's lungs seized, and he couldn't breathe, his eyes flying open like broken shutters. What he saw crushed his heart. He hitched in his breath and exhaled slowly, hell-bent on changing their future so that vision never saw the light of day.

Chris turned the water off and wrapped a towel around his waist. He wiped the steam off the mirror and looked at his reflection. "Over my dead body," he whispered and shivered, pushing the dream into the depths of his mind, closing the door and locking it so no one could get to those images but him.

End Game Chapter 15

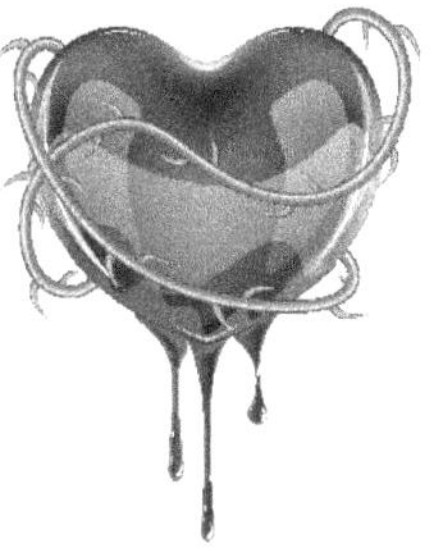

"WHO ELSE IS GOING to the game?" Chris pulled out of the garage in their car, the boys seat belted in the back and playing their handheld games.

"I think only Danny and LeAnn. I'm not sure if they're bringing Sandy or if they have a sitter."

"Sandy's coming?" Tommy asked from the back seat.

"I'm not sure, honey," Jessica replied. "But this isn't playtime. We are there to watch Eric's game, not horse around. Understand?"

"Yeah." Tommy sulked and went back to his game.

CJ had drifted off to sleep.

Chris looked at her sideways, sending her a grin full of mischief.

"That goes for you as well," Jessica said, pointing at him.

"Can't I mess with Dan just a little?"

"No." Jessica looked back at the kids. "Tommy, why don't you put the game down and take a little nap like your brother?"

"Okay, Mommy." He closed the game, putting it on the seat next to him. Within a few minutes, he was sleeping too.

"Now, why would you want to mess with Danny?"

Chris smiled. "He doesn't like me very much."

"No shit, Sherlock."

"Why not? I'm a likable guy."

"You are such an ass sometimes."

"I guess, but he's planning on giving me a hard time about you again." He glanced over at her as they took the 495 South exit. "I swear he is worse than your father."

Jessica looked out the window. "You remind them of what happened to me. God, if they ever knew."

"They would kill me," he replied, thinking of what he would do in their shoes.

"Probably."

Chris got quiet as his past swooped in around them. "I'm sorry."

"I know you are," Jessica replied and took his hand. "Maybe if I had said something to you on that pier…"

He kissed her hand. "The world is full of shoulda, coulda, woulda, babe. We can't turn back the clock any more than we can stop what fate has in store for us."

They drove the rest of the way to the sports complex in silence, listening to the soft music flowing out of the radio, each lost in their own thoughts.

"I'm not so sure if you had said something back then that it would have changed the way things turned out, Jess," Chris said as he parked the car. "I'm surprised you even remember that day. Besides, you didn't even give me a second look."

Jessica laughed. "You are so wrong. I gave you a second look that day, babe. You were just so cute." She blushed. "Jailbait, but cute as hell."

He glanced at her and let out a huff.

"You really don't know, do you?"

He looked back at her and shrugged. "No idea of what?"

"Of how you affect women—the scar did not make a hoot of a difference. At sixteen, you had those big blue eyes that would make any girl swoon. And at thirty, you were by far the sexiest man I had ever laid eyes on."

Chris blushed and glanced over at her. "It took a long time to get to that point, Jess. There is no way I would have had the nerve to approach you at sixteen or even twenty. I was so inexperienced. I didn't have it in me then." He slowly smiled. "As much as I would like to think things would have been different, I'm not so sure. I think timing was everything where we are concerned."

Jessica sighed. "What you have isn't something that is learned with time. It's all natural and inherent in the way you are. You had those smoldering bedroom eyes at sixteen. If I had run into you again when you were eighteen or twenty, I would have fallen in love with you in a second."

Chris laughed. "Oh, baby, you are so sweet." He leaned over and kissed her as he pulled the keys out of the ignition. He stepped out of the car and opened the back door, then gently shook CJ and Tommy awake. "We're here, boys." He glanced at Jessica as she opened the back passenger-side door to unhook Tommy.

"Although I think it would be highly unlikely that at that age you would fall in love with someone twelve years older than you were," Jessica said as she closed the door behind Tommy.

Chris smiled. "You didn't look a day over eighteen when I saw you standing on that pier."

It was Jessica's turn to laugh.

"I'm serious. It's like you found the fountain of youth. You haven't aged a day since I yanked you out of your life. You're going to be fifty-two, and I'd be surprised if anyone thinks you're any older than thirty-two."

She smiled. "I think *you* are my fountain of youth."

"What's a fountain of youth?" CJ asked as they walked to the sports complex.

Both Jessica and Chris laughed.

"You know, if we had actually met earlier in our lives, you wouldn't have Emily or Eric." He opened the door for her. "Or Tommy," he added as the door closed behind them.

"I guess timing was everything," she said. "You realize I wasn't able to do anything except catch glimpses of the future and read people's minds until we met?"

Chris stopped and slowly turned toward her. "You never healed anyone before me?"

Jessica shook her head. "No, and to my knowledge, neither did Eric."

They stared at each other for a moment.

"So, it was *you*. You made it possible, not Eric."

Chris blinked. "Huh?"

"We never could use our powers until we met you."

CJ and Tommy looked back and forth between their parents.

"Eric said you were meant to be together," CJ replied. "You balance each other," he added with a smile.

They strolled into the stadium, looking at each other in awe.

"Really?"

"I think so."

"Holy…" He didn't finish the thought as they walked into the basketball arena.

"I guess soul mate was an understatement." Jessica smiled as she waved at Daniel and headed down to where he was sitting.

Chris glanced in her direction, letting out a small laugh. "Understatement of the millennium." He trotted down the stairs. "Hi, Dan, LeAnn."

They took the seats in the row behind them.

Daniel turned. His eyes betrayed the mistrust he felt toward Chris. "You finally got the nerve."

Chris smiled. "Yes. I understand you're less than thrilled about it."

"Chris." Jessica shot him a warning glance.

"Jessie, he's right. I'm not thrilled."

"Danny!" LeAnn hit Daniel in the arm with the back of her hand.

Jessica traded glances with Chris. "This isn't the time or place."

"Let's take a walk, Dan. Then you can say what's on your mind." Chris stood. "You want anything at the concession stand?" he asked Jessica.

CJ went to say something, and Chris held up his hand. "I know. I've got you and Tommy covered."

"Just water," Jessica replied.

Chris headed up the stairs with Daniel in tow and said nothing until they were in line at the concession stand. "Go ahead." He turned toward Daniel.

"You screwed up her life." Daniel glared at him.

You don't know the half of it. "How do you figure that?"

"She and Tom were happy before you came along."

"Jess is happy with me," Chris countered. "That's not really what's eating you, is it?"

Daniel took a deep breath. "I don't think you are who you say you are."

Chris looked at him and then back at the concession list. He knew what was coming, and while it probably wasn't a good idea to go down this road, he did anyway. "Who do you think I am?"

"I think you're actually Ty Aris."

Chris glanced back at him with a smile. "And if I were, what exactly would you do?"

Daniel's jaw dropped, but he closed his mouth quickly. "I would make sure Jessica knew."

"Just for giggles, what would you do if she already knew?" He turned toward Daniel, the smile still playing on his lips.

Daniel took a step back.

"What if she loved me, anyway?" Chris raised an eyebrow, his eyes intently locked on Daniel's. He laughed at Daniel's expression. "I'm not Ty Aris," Chris said after a few moments of enjoyment at Daniel's expense.

"But you are an Aris."

"Hell no. I was never an Aris." He glanced back. "Despite my mother's ill-conceived idea that we take on the Aris name."

"Your brother was."

Chris shook his head, turning toward the concession stand. "No, he wasn't either."

"But you are Ty Ryan."

Chris stiffened, and he slowly turned toward Daniel. "Let's play this game for a moment, because I am curious as to what exactly you would do if that was a true statement."

The anger that flashed in Daniel's eyes made Chris smile.

"You sadistic bastard."

"Hold that thought." Chris turned back toward the counter as the couple ahead of them left the line. He ordered two sodas, a beer, a water, and a large popcorn and then turned toward Daniel. "What do you want?"

Daniel just stared at him, his gaze like sharp daggers intent on slicing him in half.

"Beer, soda, what?" Chris pushed.

"Beer and Diet Coke."

"Anything else?"

"No."

Chris paid for the items and handed Daniel the drinks. He balanced the tray of beverages and popcorn and stepped away from the counter. "Now, where were we? Oh yeah, you just called me a sadistic bastard. But you never told me what you would do if it was true?"

Daniel looked at him and then at the door. "She can't."

A slow smile spread over Chris's face and he felt a moment of sheer glee when Daniel visibly shivered. "Oh, she can, and she does. And your kids adore me as well. Why don't you ask Eric who I am?" he teased, pushing Daniel's buttons.

When Jessica walked into the hall, Daniel's face transitioned to beet red. Chris dropped his gaze, swallowing a lump of guilt that formed in his throat at her sudden appearance.

"You are the bastard that yanked her out of my life," Daniel growled

Jessica stepped in front of Chris. "Danny," she said, capturing his attention. "Stop."

Daniel glanced back up at him. "Son of a bitch. How can you be with him? How can you marry him?"

"Danny. He is not who you think he is."

"Does Tom know?" he asked, glancing between Chris and Jessica.

"Does Tom know what?"

"That you're with the man who kidnapped and terrorized you."

"He didn't terrorize me, Danny. Besides, the man who kidnapped me had a scar."

"I saw firsthand what you did with Emily. If you can cure cancer, removing a scar should be a cakewalk." Daniel walked away, shaking his head.

Jessica and Chris followed and almost ran into him as he turned back.

"I could kill you." He glared at Chris.

Chris smiled and shrugged. "Get in line."

Daniel stared at him and laughed. "Jesus. You really are that son of a bitch, aren't you?"

Chris didn't say a word, and neither did Jessica.

"You have no proof of that." Chris exchanged glances with Jessica. He headed back into the coliseum and trotted down to the seats, then plopped himself next to the boys.

DANIEL STARED AFTER HIM and then looked at his ex-wife in disbelief.

"He saved me, Danny. And he saved Tom as well."

"Does Tom know who you're with?"

"Chris saved Emily, too," she replied, ignoring his question. They stepped back into the coliseum.

"How did he save Emily?"

"He was the one who gave me the power to heal," she said, and Daniel shot a glance back at his ex-wife. "If he hadn't come to see me five years ago, Emily would be dead today."

"I still don't understand why you're with him."

"I love him. I have since we were in that godforsaken place."

Daniel's eyes narrowed. "Didn't he hurt you down there?"

She glanced down at the ring on her hand and then over at Daniel. "No." She looked back down at Chris. "Not in the way that you are thinking. His brother Frank did, both physically and mentally." She pointed her thumb at Chris. "He tried to protect me and almost died more than once in the process."

Daniel stared out at the floor as the teams came out.

"Danny," Jessica said, capturing his attention again, "you can't say anything to anyone." Her eyes pleaded. "Promise me."

"Jessie. I can't promise that."

"Then promise me you will talk to Eric first before you do anything." Jessica headed down the stairs, replacing the worried frown with a smile as her son came bounding onto the basketball floor with the rest of his team.

Eric caught her eyes as they began their warm-ups and then looked up at his father. His smile faltered, and Jessica muttered under her breath. He shouldn't have to worry about this right now. She slid into her seat, giving Chris a warning glare before refocusing on the warm-ups.

Eric passed the ball to a teammate and walked over to the sidelines to say hello to his family, his eyes never leaving Daniel's.

"Dad, I'll explain later, I promise," Eric whispered, giving his father a quick hug.

"Hey." Eric smiled over at Chris and stepped away from Daniel.

"Give 'em hell." Chris smiled back.

CJ and Tommy jumped up and yelled, "Hi, Eric!"

"I'll see you after the game." Eric pointed at the boys and headed back onto the basketball floor.

Daniel sat and handed LeAnn her diet soda. He turned and looked at Jessica, his eyes questioning her silently.

"Let it go," Jessica said softly and then looked over at Chris. *I could just wring your neck.*

CJ laughed. "Mommy's mad at you, Daddy."

"I KNOW," CHRIS WHISPERED to his son and looked sideways at Jessica, sending his awkward smile that always disarmed her.

Daniel turned, and Chris shrugged, taking in the glares aimed in his direction from both his wife and her ex-husband. He ignored the silent daggers and focused on the floor, feeling the brunt of the guilt eating away at his stomach.

After the first quarter, Chris leaned over. "I'm sorry for fucking up your life," he whispered so only Daniel could hear.

Daniel stiffened in the seat and Chris sat back and watched the game.

At halftime, Daniel turned around and looked at Chris. "You didn't."

Chris glanced over at Jessica; she was busy talking with LeAnn about the kids. The boys were playing their handheld games quietly while they waited for Eric to come back out. This left Chris and Daniel just staring out at the cheerleaders in silence.

"Want another beer?" Chris asked after a few minutes.

Daniel nodded, and the two men headed up the stairs to get another beer.

"I'm supposed to be watching my son in the regional semi-finals, and you lay this on me?"

"You asked."

"You could have just lied like you have been for the past five years."

"You already knew." Chris looked back at him. "No matter what I said, you had your mind made up. You're right about one thing, though."

"What's that?"

"My life is nothing without her." He stepped to the counter. "Two beers." He peeled off a twenty and handed it to the concession stand attendant. "Keep the change." He handed Daniel one of the beers.

"Who else knows who you are?"

"Besides Eric and Jess?" Chris looked over at him.

"Does Tom know?" Daniel remarked as they stood in the hallway.

Chris nodded. "Emily knows as well."

"Emily knows?"

Chris nodded and took a sip of his beer.

Daniel turned away, his free hand curled into a fist and his jaw tightened. "Why do my kids care about you so much?" he asked and turned back.

Chris shrugged. "You'll have to ask them."

"I'm asking you."

Chris took a deep breath. "Eric seems to think I'm some kind of hero that was put on this earth to look after his mother." He laughed. "That's funny, if you really think about it." He took a sip of his beer.

Daniel glanced down at his beer. "I remember how angry Eric was when he saw you on the television. He kept saying you were supposed to protect Jessie."

"Yeah, I was supposed to, but I didn't know what Frank had in store for us and was stupid enough to leave her there with him," Chris replied.

"What about Emily?"

His jaw clenched, and he looked away from Daniel. "Let's just leave it at that, Dan. You don't want to know what happened to your daughter. All you need to know is that I stopped it."

Daniel stepped back when Chris looked at him again. "What happened to Emily?" he asked, this time reaching out and grabbing Chris's forearm.

"Do you believe in ghosts?" Chris asked, gauging Dan's reaction.

"What?" Daniel let go of his arm, looking at him like he was insane.

"Okay. Did you ever wonder how all those mirrors broke?" Chris looked at him sideways, shifting gears.

"Yes," Daniel said. "Tom said he would tell me someday."

Chris laughed. "Sorry. I just find it funny that Tom would even entertain the idea of telling you what was really going on." He looked at Daniel. "Frank's ghost came after us." He chuckled at the look on Daniel's face. "All of us." He raised his eyebrows to convey his meaning. "And his ghost was just as twisted as he was in real life."

"What happened to Emily?" Daniel whispered, his face going red.

Chris didn't say a word, but the look on his face must have said it all. "I sent him back to hell," he finally said, and walked back into the coliseum.

Daniel's thoughts swarmed, and Chris walked away until the word rape crossed Daniel's mind. Chris stopped and slowly looked back, meeting his gaze and sending a slight nod in his direction. All the color drained from Dan's face.

"Sweet Jesus." Dan made his way down to where Chris stood.

"You might want to block those thoughts," Chris said as CJ turned and looked at them. "Both CJ and Eric can hear your thoughts without trying. It's a little tougher for Jessica, since she has to concentrate."

"And you... what do you have to do to hear what others are thinking?"

Chris laughed, ignoring the question. "You haven't figured out how to block your thoughts? I'd have thought years with Eric would have made you an expert by now."

"How do you block someone from reading your mind?"

"Random thoughts. You think of inconsequential random images. It comes across like static, and nothing is clear."

"But how do you *think* if you're concentrating on random things?"

"You learn to do both at the same time. Multitasking for your brain." He smiled.

"Can I ask you another question?" Daniel said as they stood at the top of the steps, looking down at the basketball court.

"Shoot."

"How did you live after being shot four times in the chest?"

Chris pointed to the basketball court. "Your son. Ironically, he's the reason we're both standing here today." He trotted down the steps and joined Jessica as the second half began, leaving Daniel standing on the landing above.

Eric had better have a good reason for doing what he did, Daniel thought. *Because we're all now accomplices to mass murder.*

Jessica's gaze snapped to Chris.

"Uncle Danny?" CJ asked.

"What's up, little man?" He smiled back at CJ.

"What's an accomplice?"

"It's a helper," Daniel answered, and his thought transmission cut off.

"Oh, okay."

The basketball game ended up in double overtime, and Eric's team squeaked the win in the final seconds of the game, putting them in the regional finals. The finals would take place the following Sunday afternoon at Madison Square Garden.

Jessica and Chris exchanged a smile. They were going to be in the city anyway, so that would work out pretty well.

"Eric will already be in the city with us next weekend. Perfect timing," Jessica said.

"Are you coming down Saturday night?" Chris asked Daniel and LeAnn as he stood.

"We hadn't thought about it," Daniel replied. "Odds were against them winning this game."

"Would you like me to make arrangements for you?" Chris asked, surprising both Daniel and LeAnn.

Daniel glanced at LeAnn and shrugged. "Arrangements?"

"Do you want to come to the city next Saturday and stay overnight somewhere?" Chris clarified. "Or were you just planning a day trip on Sunday?"

"As I said, we hadn't thought about it," Daniel said, glaring at Chris.

Chris put his hands up. "Okay, I get it. But the offer stands. If you want to stay, it's on me."

"You can't buy me off," Daniel said under his breath as they walked up the stairs.

"I'm not trying to." Chris glanced over his shoulder at Daniel.

"Bullshit."

Chris laughed as they walked out to the parking lot. He turned to say something and saw Daniel's fist coming toward him. He blocked the punch easily and took a defensive posture. "I'm a third-degree black belt, Dan. You don't really want to try that again."

LeeAnn balked. "Danny, what the hell are you doing?"

Jessica had both boys in front of her. "Danny, don't do this."

Daniel's eyes burned with fury as he swung again, and this time he found himself against the nearest pole with his arm twisted behind his back.

Chris held him there. "Dan, I understand you're angry, and you have every right to be. But you have to know, if you try to take me down, you take everyone who knows with me, too. That's the way it works. As I told Tom, you have absolutely no proof whatsoever. For all intents and purposes, I am Christopher Ryan, and I had no clue what my brothers were doing." He spoke softly so only Daniel could hear, and then he let Daniel's arm go.

Daniel glared at Chris and stepped toward LeAnn.

"What are you doing?" LeAnn snapped at him as he approached her.

Daniel shook his head. He looked at Jessica and the boys. "I can't believe you love him."

"I do. And I'm marrying him on Friday."

"Eric's not going," Daniel snapped.

"Yes, I am." Eric walked out into the garage. He smiled and winked at CJ and Tommy, then he turned and looked at his father and LeAnn. "I think this conversation is better suited for a private dining room in one of the local restaurants. Don't you?" He looked over at Chris.

"I think we'll pass. We'll pick Eric up on Thursday."

"No." Daniel glared at Chris.

"Danny, what has gotten into you?" LeAnn yanked his arm.

"Dad," Eric said, walking into his father's line of sight. "I'm going to Mom's wedding."

"The hell you are." Daniel swiveled his angry gaze toward his son.

"Daniel Spenser Connor," Jessica said loud enough to get everyone's attention. She stood with her hands on each of the boy's shoulders, her eyes swirling with anger. Moving the boys aside, she walked until she was standing toe to toe with Daniel. "I would like my son at my wedding."

"Not if you're marrying him." He pointed at Chris.

"You don't have a say in who I marry."

"But I have a say in whether or not my son attends the wedding. And I don't want him to have anything to do with that man ever again."

"*That man* is the best thing that ever happened to me," Jessica shot back. "And because of him, you were able to find the best thing that ever happened to you." She pointed at LeAnn. "So don't stand there and act all sanctimonious on me."

"Sanctimonious?" Daniel gawked at her. "What is sanctimonious about not allowing my son to associate with a killer?"

"Danny?" LeAnn looked at her husband and then over at Chris.

Chris had picked up both of the boys. "I'm out of here." He walked away with the boys in his arms.

"Daddy, what was Uncle Danny talking about?" CJ asked.

"My past," Chris said as he looked at his son and then glanced over his shoulder. Jessica was still having it out with Daniel.

"Uncle Danny is really mad at you," Tommy said as he looked back at his mother, arguing with Daniel.

"He'll get over it."

"I'm not so sure," CJ replied.

Chris laughed softly. "You're probably right."

"DANNY, WHAT'S GOING ON?" LeAnn asked again.

Eric and Jessica exchanged a look.

"Chris is the man who kidnapped her." Daniel glared at Jessica.

LeAnn looked at Jessica and then at Chris, walking away with the two boys. "I thought Ty Aris kidnapped her."

"Chris *IS* Ty Aris."

LeAnn looked at Jessica and Eric and then back at her husband. "What in God's name are you talking about?"

"Dad, he isn't who you think he is. We changed him." Eric pointed between Jessica and himself. "He has saved a lot of people since we changed him."

"But that doesn't wipe out the fact that he killed a lot of people, too."

"Dad, he and Mom belong together. They need each other. And he loves her more than you or Tom ever did."

"You don't know that."

"Yes, I do. I know more than you give me credit for," Eric replied.

"Why did you ever save his life?" Daniel snapped at Eric.

"Because he saved Mom and let her go. He wasn't supposed to die down there, Dad. And he didn't have to come back five years ago, either, but he did to save Emily."

LeAnn's jaw dropped, and her gaze bounced between her husband and her stepson. "Are you telling me that Daniel is right?"

"Yes," all three of them replied at once.

Chris pulled up alongside them and rolled the passenger side window down. "You coming, Jess?"

Eric turned to Chris. "Stay for dinner," he said, prompting both Chris and Daniel to laugh. "Please, Chris."

Chris looked down and then over at his soon-to-be stepson. "I don't think your father would appreciate that. Besides, we've already ruined the festive mood. You should celebrate with your family."

"You *are* family," Eric replied and glanced over at his parents.

Jessica turned back to Daniel. "I'll see you Thursday." She stepped toward the car.

"God damn it," Eric said, and everyone looked at him. "I want to go to dinner with all of you."

"You don't always get what you want, Eric," Chris replied as Jessica opened the door.

"I want to go to dinner with Eric," CJ said, and the car stalled.

Eric smiled at CJ. "Thanks."

Chris threw the car into park and tried to restart it. An empty click filled the garage, and he turned in the driver's seat. "CJ, stop that."

"No, Daddy. Not until you and Uncle Danny make up."

Chris laughed and glanced out at Eric and Daniel. "I don't think Uncle Danny wants to make up with me."

Daniel moved toward the side of the car, but his shocked expression announced he wasn't moving of his own accord.

"Uncle Danny, you and Daddy need to make up," CJ said from the back seat.

"CJ, let Uncle Danny go," Chris yelled, anger lacing his voice as he turned, staring down his son.

"Uh-uh," CJ said.

Chris stared him down. He pressed his lips together and turned toward the side window. "Sorry, Dan. I guess we're all going to dinner together."

"Daddy's mad at you," Tommy whispered to his brother.

CJ smiled a little. "Uncle Danny?"

"I guess it's dinner," Daniel said through clenched teeth, glaring at Chris.

"Cool!" Eric hopped into the car with Chris and Jessica.

"Eric, you're coming with us," Daniel insisted.

Eric smiled. "Uh-uh, this way we'll all end up at the restaurant together."

LeAnn put her hand on her husband's shoulder. "There's a great steak place up the road. We could go there."

"I'll let you lead the way." Chris started the truck and pulled over to the side, waiting for Daniel to get his vehicle.

"What the hell were you thinking?" Jessica hit Chris's arm. "You shouldn't have told him who you were."

"Dad already had the idea in his head, Mom. There were just too many things that didn't add up." Eric looked at Chris. "Your story really sucked, dude."

Chris glanced in the rearview mirror at Eric and took a deep breath. "How else was I supposed to explain my sudden appearance? It would have been easier if your mom had stayed married to Tom." He immediately regretted it.

"Excuse me?" Jessica said.

Daniel pulled up next to the car and glared over at Chris. He peeled away, and Chris followed behind him.

"Then we wouldn't have had to come up with a story." He glanced over at her. "It was either that or the truth, and as you can see, the truth went over so well today." His voice was laced with sarcasm.

"Daddy?" CJ said, and the concern in his voice made Chris glance in the rearview mirror.

"Yes?"

"You killed somebody?"

Chris stared at his son in the mirror and took a deep breath. "Yes."

"Oh." CJ and Tommy exchanged a look.

"What I did wasn't right," Chris said.

"Were you protecting someone?" Tommy asked.

Chris took another deep breath and glanced at Jessica. Pain shot through his chest.

"No. I had no good reason to do what I did."

"You protected me, Chris," Jessica said after a moment.

Chris nodded and glanced at her and then back at Eric.

"It's all right," Eric replied. "We all still love you."

"Yeah, Daddy, I still love you," CJ said.

"Me too."

Chris shook his head. *I can't do this.*

Jessica reached over and took his hand. *You don't have to do it alone, babe.*

He glanced over at her. "I'm the one who has to live with it, Jess, so yes, I have to do this one alone." He followed Daniel off the highway and pulled into the restaurant, then parked next to them. He turned to his boys. "Daddy did some horrible things before I met your mother, and that's why Uncle Danny is angry." He turned off the ignition and looked at Eric. "Let your father be angry, Eric."

"No," Eric replied.

"Yes, he has that right." Chris got out of the car and opened the back door without looking at Daniel and LeAnn, who were now standing at the front of their car, waiting. He unhooked CJ, picked him up, and moved aside so Eric could get out. Eric already had Tommy in his arms.

"Are you all right?" Jessica asked, coming up beside Chris and CJ.

"Not particularly, but we can talk about it later." He smiled sadly over at Jessica.

Chris walked into the restaurant first and cornered the hostess, asking for a private room or a very secluded table for the seven of them. He flashed cash and was rewarded with a private room.

When they were seated, he looked at Daniel. "I regret most of the things I did, but I don't for one moment regret kidnapping your wife," he said. "Or letting you live," he added after a moment's pause. "Both things were my choice, and believe me, letting you live was a pretty hard sell for my brother. He didn't like anyone left behind, but because you had kids, I would not leave them orphaned, and hurting children was not a line I was ever willing to cross." Chris kept eye contact with Daniel. "And yes, at first Jessica was just another toy to be played with, but there was something about her that got me, and that's why we are sitting here today."

Daniel went to say something, but LeAnn put her hand on his leg, shaking her head. He glanced over at her and took a deep breath. "What really happened with Emily?" He looked back at Chris and Jessica.

"Frank hurt her," Eric said, "and he hurt Mom, too." He took a sip of ice water. "He tried to kill them," he said, pointing to Jessica and Chris as he set his glass on the table. "And almost succeeded."

"He tried to kill Tom and Emily too," Jessica whispered. "He got to us through the mirrors when Chris showed up."

Daniel shot a glance at Chris.

"Yeah, I guess the bastard waited until I went to her. He knew I couldn't stay away forever." Chris took a deep breath. "Your son was the one to save Emily's life, though." He looked at Eric. "I just broke the mirrors."

"But Chris, if you hadn't come when you did, we would have lost Emily to cancer," Jessica reminded him.

LeAnn's jaw dropped. She looked at Daniel and then back at Jessica. "Can someone please explain this to me?"

"Jessica has the power to heal," Daniel replied. "And I think Eric does, too."

Eric shook his head. "I don't anymore. Only Mom does. I used all that magic on Chris." He glanced at Chris. "I can only read minds now."

"Not exactly," Chris countered. "You seem to be able to put yourself in between a knife and those you love. I've seen you do it twice now."

Daniel blinked. "Holy…" He looked at Chris as memories of Eric with blood all over him flooded his mind.

Chris nodded. "And his hand five years ago, but better his hand than her throat." He shrugged.

LeAnn went completely pale.

"Better catch your wife," Chris said, and LeAnn tilted limply to the side.

Daniel caught LeAnn. He splashed a little water on her face and wiped it with a napkin when she came to.

"Imagine how I felt when I somehow ended up with this." Chris smiled at her. He held his hand up, and they all watched his glass levitate into it. "Cheers," he said, and wrapped his fingers around his glass and put it to his lips.

Daniel and LeAnn looked stunned.

"My sentiments exactly." He smiled at them. "All courtesy of Jess." He leaned over and kissed her cheek. "It seems we make a powerful combination when we're together." He laughed as he looked over at CJ and then back at the rest of the table.

"They were meant to be together, Dad," Eric said again. "And I am going to the wedding."

Daniel didn't say a word.

Chris turned and summoned the waitress. "She and I will have the petite filet mignon with béarnaise sauce and roasted vegetables. Medium rare on both." He glanced at the menu and then ordered chicken strips and French fries for the boys.

"I'll have the same as him." Eric pointed at Chris.

"Us too," Daniel said.

"Can I have a couple of bottles of Chateau Bordeaux Red as well?" Chris smiled at the waitress and handed her the menu. He looked back at Daniel and LeAnn as the waitress left the room and took a deep breath. "What else do you want to know?"

"Why?" Daniel asked. "Why did you do it?"

Chris looked at his children and then back at Daniel and shrugged. "Power," he finally said. "It was intoxicating, especially for someone who had been powerless most of their life."

"Why her?" Daniel pointed at his ex-wife.

Chris exchanged a look with Jessica, and he shrugged. He wasn't about to tell Daniel about his ex-wife's indiscretion. "I saw her and had to have her. Little did I know what I was in for."

The boys watched the exchange with curiosity.

"I'm the only one in my family that's left," Chris began. "My father was a cop who died in the line of duty. There were four of us, including my mother, and three of us died at the hands of the Aris family."

"You're not the only one left. We're here," CJ said.

"Yes, you are." Chris smiled and messed up his hair, glancing at Jessica and then back at Daniel. "I watched my brother die, and there was nothing I could do to stop it." His eyes glossed over with tears at the memory of Chris being blown to bits. "So, I've gotten some of what I dished out slammed back in my face already."

"Jesus," Daniel whispered.

"He had nothing to do with it." Chris smiled.

Daniel laughed. "You really are a piece of work."

Chris shrugged and grinned. "I try."

"That wasn't a compliment," Daniel snapped. "I'm surprised Tom didn't kill you."

"Believe me, he wanted to," Chris replied. He glanced over at Jessica. "I couldn't exactly stay away from Jess." He blushed and looked at the boys and then sideways over at Daniel and LeAnn with a small grin. "The rest is history."

Their meals arrived with the bottles of wine, and everyone ate in silence.

Chris poured a glass of wine for himself and offered the bottle to Daniel. Daniel nodded and held up his glass. LeAnn and Jessica both declined and exchanged the same look. They were now the designated drivers as Daniel and Chris finished the two bottles themselves.

Chris got the check, and they got up to leave the restaurant.

"I still don't like you," Daniel said as they walked outside.

"I'm so hurt." Chris put his hand over his heart dramatically. He was a little tipsy, so he pulled the keys out of his pocket and handed them to Jessica.

Daniel laughed at the gesture and even more at him handing Jessica the keys. "Do you have a death wish?"

Chris laughed. "Better to have her drive right now. Besides, it'll sober me up quick."

Eric picked up CJ and gave him a big hug, then handed him over to Chris to hook him in his car seat. He did the same with Tommy and turned to Chris. "I'll see you Thursday." He smiled and gave Chris a hug, then he turned to Jessica. "Bye, Mom. I love you."

"I love you, too, honey." Jessica hugged her oldest son and watched him slide into the back seat of Daniel's car. "Congratulations on getting into the finals." She smiled.

Chris turned toward Daniel and LeAnn. "D'ya want me to make those reservations for you?"

Daniel took a deep breath, looked over at LeAnn, and then nodded back at Chris. "Sure, but I still don't like you."

"What? I'm a likeable guy!" Chris smiled his crooked, tipsy smile and put his hands out in a shrug.

"No, you're not." Daniel laughed and slid into their car.

End Game Chapter 16

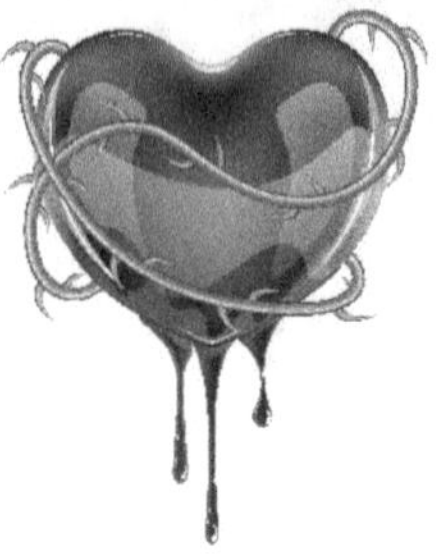

DANIEL WOKE THE NEXT morning and got the Sunday paper as the prior day's events kept replaying in his mind. He still couldn't fathom why Jessica was with that man. As he flipped through the entertainment section, he saw an advertisement for Tom's movie stating that it was being released this weekend.

He glanced at the clock on the wall. It was almost eleven, which meant it was eight in the morning on the west coast. He picked up the phone and flipped through the address book that LeAnn had on the desk. He found the number he wanted and dialed it.

"Hello," a groggy female voice answered.

"Hi, is Tom available?" Daniel asked.

"Hold on," she stated, and then put the phone down.

A few minutes later, a male voice, equally groggy, answered. "This is Tom."

"Tom, it's Dan. Dan Connor."

There was silence on the other end. "Is everything all right?" he asked after a moment, sounding wide awake now.

"Yes, everyone's fine." He took a deep breath. "How could you let her leave you for him?"

"Let me call you back in a sec. I assume the number is still the same?"

"It is." Daniel listened to the dial tone. He hung up the phone and waited.

TOM PULLED ON SWEATPANTS and a sweatshirt and grabbed his cell phone without a word.

"Who was that?" Sharon asked.

"An old friend." Tom left the room, heading onto the beach. He scrolled down the numbers until he found Dan Connor and pressed the send button, taking a seat on the cool sand.

Daniel answered the phone in less than one ring. "Tom?"

"Yep." He squinted out at the morning surf.

"How could you let her go, especially knowing she was with him?"

"With whom?"

"You know damn well who I'm talking about," Daniel snapped.

Tom scanned the beach and then glanced over his shoulder. Sharon was nowhere to be seen.

"I couldn't compete with what he offered her, Dan."

"Bullshit."

Tom laughed. "She slept with him while we were still married. She couldn't say no to him."

"So, you just let her go? I thought you loved her."

"I do. More than you know." He glanced over his shoulder again. Still no sign of Sharon, so she must have gone back to sleep.

"She's marrying him."

"I know. On Friday," he said.

"And you aren't going to stop it?"

"Dan, I'm married," he said, almost gagging at the words coming from his mouth. "Besides, he'll take good care of her. Trust me."

"But he's the son of a bitch who kidnapped her."

"Yeah, but he's also the son of a bitch who saved her life. How did you find out about him, anyway?" Tom asked, thinking one of the kids must have slipped up.

A pause came over the line, and then Daniel said, "He told me."

"No shit. That was pretty ballsy."

"I actually asked him, and at first he played like it was a game just to see what my reaction would be, but then he finally admitted who he was." He let out a small laugh. "He can be a scary son of a bitch."

Tom laughed. "Dan, you have no idea just how scary he can be. You weren't there. You never saw him in action."

"Then why didn't you fight for her?"

He sat quietly, looking at the waves.

"Tom?"

"He never loses," Tom finally replied. "Ever." *Which is what I'm betting on.*

Daniel was quiet for a moment. "Jesus."

"He has nothing to do with it."

Daniel laughed. "That's what he said last night."

Tom smiled. "I guess playing him in the movie kind of rubbed off on me a little."

"I read the movie is being released this weekend?"

"The premiere is in New York on Friday," Tom said. "They're coming."

"Jessie and Chris?"

"Yep."

"No shit."

Tom chuckled at the shock in Daniel's voice. "I called and asked her to come."

"And she said yes?"

"She did." He grinned. "Blew my mind when I found out it was their wedding day."

He scanned the landscape again. Sharon was now on the porch, looking at him on the beach. She was too far away to hear any of the conversation, but he stood and walked down to the water's edge, anyway.

Daniel took a deep breath. "I still can't believe you let her go."

"Well, Dan, we are even there. I couldn't fathom how you let her go, either."

Daniel laughed. "I found LeAnn."

Tom shook his head. "LeAnn isn't Jessica."

"No, she isn't, but she is the love of my life."

Tom hung his head. "Jessie was mine. I've got to go." He glanced back at the house and took note that Sharon was now walking down the steps to the beach. "Bye, Dan." He hung up the phone and erased the history, then slid the phone back into his pocket. He stood and looked out at the water, pondering whether he should do something to stop the wedding or not.

"Who was that?" Sharon stopped next to him.

"An old friend. He saw the movie was finally being released and wanted to say congratulations," Tom said without looking at her.

"You'd better not be lying to me," Sharon snapped.

Tom slowly looked over at her, glaring. "What would you do if I killed myself?"

Sharon smiled. "I'd make sure that bitch died, too."

The flash of anger that encompassed him took control, and he grabbed her by the throat. "She is not a bitch, and if you call her that one more time, I'll snap your fucking neck." He let her go and stormed back to the house.

He closed and locked the bedroom door and took a shower. While the hot water pelted down on his skin, he made a decision, one that he hoped would not come back to haunt him. He dressed, packed, and made a phone call.

Sharon sulked on the couch in the living room, and when she saw him, she sat up straight, staring at the suitcase in his hand. "Where do you think you're going?"

"Getting as far away from you as I can," he said, looking squarely at her.

She balked. "We have a premiere in New York in less than a week."

"Don't worry, I'll be there," he snarled at her. "But not with you."

He went to leave and saw her open her phone out of the corner of his eye. He hesitated and looked over at her. "Do you really want to die?" He turned back toward her and dropped the suitcase. "Because you will if you press that button." He stepped toward her as his hands curled into fists.

She slowly closed the phone. "Who's to say I won't as soon as you leave?" she snapped at him.

"*I* say so, because I know how to unleash hell, and I'll send him straight to you if you put her in danger," Tom growled. "And when he comes to collect, you will wish to God I had been the one to kill you." He turned on his heels, picked up his bag, and walked out of the house.

The town car was waiting for him, and he hopped in.

"L-A-X." He leaned back.

His flight was leaving in less than two hours, and he couldn't wait to be on the other side of the country, away from her for the first time in five years. He slid his phone out of his pocket and dialed the familiar number.

Chris picked up. "Hello, Ryan residence."

Tom was quiet for a moment. "You'd better damn well protect her." He knew as soon as he left, Sharon would make that call.

Silence filled the line.

"You there?"

"I'm here."

"I gather from the tone in your voice Jessica has already told you about our little conversation."

"Yep," Chris replied.

"I left Sharon today." He closed his eyes. "I hope the threat that I put on the table before I left was enough," he said without believing it. "But if it isn't, I'm calling to give you fair warning."

"Fair warning of what?" Chris did the same thing that Jessica had done twice over the past week. He transported himself into the car with Tom.

Surprise rattled through Tom. "Shit." He put up the divider between himself and the driver while still holding the phone in his hand.

"Does she know about Tommy?"

"No. But if she finds out…" He looked into the eyes of the man he'd once hated, realizing just how much Chris cared about the boy Tom sired.

Chris clenched his teeth. "I'll kill anyone who comes near my family."

"Don't," Tom said, knowing that he could kill Sharon with just a thought. "I promise, if she puts out the contract on Jessie, I will be the first to hand her over to you. We don't know for sure if she made the call, but I know that if she ends up dead, it's automatically put into effect."

"I should kill you for putting her in danger," he seethed. "For putting my son in danger." He leaned forward. "Just so we get one thing straight, you may have contributed the sperm where Tommy is concerned, but he is MY son." The words spit out from his clenched teeth.

Tom hadn't considered how Chris would react. The fact he wasn't already dead was a good indicator of his chance of survival.

"The next time you see her, she will be my wife," Chris said.

"I know." Tom smiled. "But the fact that she was married to me before didn't stop you. Why should it stop me?"

"Because you will lose. She chose me, and that hasn't changed."

Tom smiled. "Want to bet?"

"I would bet my life on it," Chris said without hesitation and smiled as Tom's faltered. "I have to run, but thanks for the warning. Believe me, no one will get to her. I'll see to that. Besides, no one really knows where she is, now do they?"

"No, but they know where the rest of her family is, and she kept both the house and the studio in her name," Tom replied.

Chris's expression changed. "Emily." He disappeared.

"What about Emily?" Tom said into the phone as he stared at the spot where Chris had been.

"Emily is living in the house. If the call is made, how fast do you think they'll move on it?"

Tom didn't know, but based on Sharon's face, he would venture to guess pretty damn fast. "Fast," he said after a moment.

"We'll see you Friday evening. Make sure Sharon is there. I will want to have a word with her."

"Oh, she'll be there." Tom smiled, realizing he had just unleashed hell. "She wouldn't miss the premiere for anything, and I can't wait to see the look on her face when the two of you show up."

CHRIS SMILED. SHARON DIDN'T know. That was a very good thing. Surprise was in his court.

"Same here." For once, the two men shared something other than Jessica in common. The sweet taste of revenge coursed through his veins.

He hung up the phone and stood looking out the window of his house for a second as he contemplated what he needed to do to keep them safe. The property here was vulnerable to attack from both the road access, even though it was gated because it could be penetrated easily, and from the water, the cliff he lived on was not that big and easily scalable for even a novice climber. He trudged back into the family room.

"Who was on the phone?" Jessica looked up as she put on her coat.

Chris handed her the phone and went up to their room. She walked into the room a moment later.

"Who was on the phone?" she asked.

"Tom." Chris went to walk past her.

She grabbed his arm.

"He left Sharon," Chris said, and her eyes widened. "Yes, there probably is a contract out on your life now. And no, she has no clue about Tommy. No one is going to hurt you," he promised and led her back downstairs, where the boys couldn't eavesdrop.

End Game Chapter 17

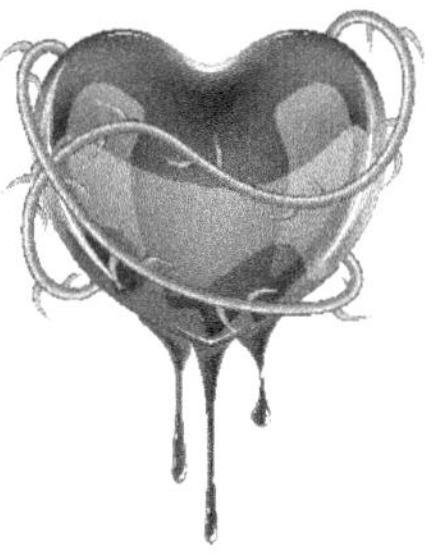

SHARON STARED BETWEEN HER phone and the front door, anger simmering to a boil in her blood. *Bastard doesn't think I'll do it? Fuck him!*

She found the text in her draft folder and pressed send. That was the text that would make it all fall on Tom's shoulders. Then she made the first of several calls.

"I want her dead," she said into the phone.

She listened for a second. "Yes, if anyone's with her, take them out, too," she said. "Yes, including him."

She'd make them all pay, and Tom would take the fall.

She called several contractors she had on retainer and repeated the same conversation. Every one of them understood what she wanted, and the word on the street spread like wildfire. Within a couple of hours, every hired assassin on the East Coast had Jessica's picture and the instructions.

End Game Chapter 18

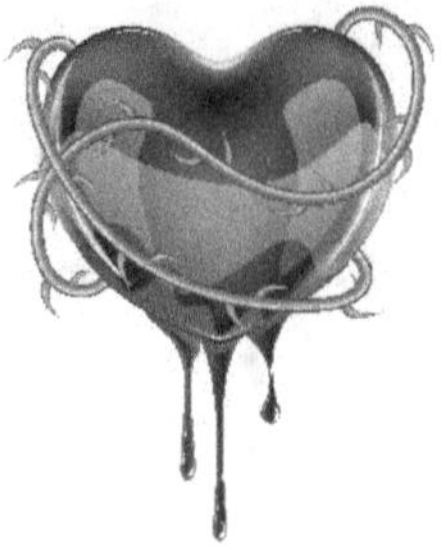

CHRIS SAT ON THE couch and ran his hands through his hair. "I can kill her right now, Jess."

"No."

"Why not?"

"Because we don't know if she actually put a contract out on me. And even if she does, you can't just kill her."

"Sure I can."

"Not if you ever want to teach them right from wrong." She pointed to the ceiling, her eyes sparkling with anger.

Chris sighed and looked down at his hands. She was right, and that irked him. He looked up and opened his mouth to speak.

"No buts, Chris. The *only* reason to kill is in self-defense," she said. "If they come after us and we have no other alternative... That's the only way I will stay with you."

Chris took a deep breath, fighting between the urge to destroy the vicious bitch on the West Coast and the need to keep his family safe. In his mind, one would take care of the other, but he didn't want to lose Jessica. "So, what do you suggest we do?"

"Nothing."

He raised his eyebrows. "Nothing?"

"Yes, nothing. We continue doing what we usually do until something happens."

Chris just stared at her. "You have got to be kidding."

"No, I'm not." She put her hands on her hips defiantly.

"You are so fucking stubborn."

Jessica smiled.

"That, my dear, was not a compliment." He stood and pulled her into his arms. "I'm not letting you out of my sight until after the premiere."

"Don't be ridiculous."

"Do you remember the last time you ignored my warnings?"

Jessica's eyebrows scrunched, and she shook her head.

"I broke my wrist on the mirror in the studio. You are not leaving my sight, understand?"

Jessica took a deep breath and nodded.

He hugged her and kissed the top of her head. *Five more days*, he thought.

"For what?" she asked, reading his mind.

"Till you're my wife and you're safe," he whispered into her hair. He pulled away from her. "Call Emily and ask her to keep her eyes open for anything weird."

"Why?"

"Because I have a feeling the first contact will either be at her house or the studio. They're both still in your name."

Jessica went pale. "Oh God."

"Don't worry. She'll be all right. Just tell her to call if there's a problem, and I don't mean by using the phone."

Jessica nodded and picked up the phone. "But what do I tell her?"

"The truth."

She looked at the phone and then over at Chris. "I can't scare her like this."

Chris walked over and plucked the phone out of her hand. "The alternative is worse." He dialed the phone and waited.

A male voice answered.

Chris looked down at the number he'd dialed. It was the right one. He put the phone back to his ear. "Is Emily there?" he asked, trading a glance with Jessica. "Hi, Em. Who was that?"

"Just a friend. How was Eric's game?" Emily said.

"Ah. Yeah, the game was great and Eric's in the finals next weekend."

"That's great. I'll finally be able to see a championship game."

"The timing certainly worked out." He inhaled. "I'm calling because we need you to do us a favor."

"What did you do?" she asked.

He hadn't realized his tone captured some of his trepidation and he cleared his throat. "Nothing. We just need you to let us know if you see anyone you don't know hanging around the house." He kept eye contact with Jessica. "And call if there's any trouble."

"Like pick up the phone and call?"

He remained quiet.

"Oh, god..."

He caught the faint fear as thoughts of Frank's ghost passed through her mind. "Not that kind of trouble." The terror radiating through the line eased. "But it is serious, so if you see something, say something. And if you can't pick up the phone, you remember how to call me, right?"

"Maybe I should have Bill stay with me here," she said.

"I'm not sure that's such a good idea. How well do you know him?"

"He's a teacher at the school." Emily said.

Chris pinched the bridge of his nose. "Just be careful, and call if anything weird happens, okay?"

She sighed, the heaviness of it hanging in the air. "Way to be all cryptic and vague."

Chris chuckled. "Yeah, well, it's better than telling you there are hoards of assassins coming after your mother, and the last known address of hers on record is where you are living."

"Ha-ha. Fine. If I see anything weird, I call by phone or if it's crazy weird, I'll call you the same way I did five years ago."

"Thanks, Emily. We'll see you Thursday. Bye." Chris hung up the phone and looked at Jessica. "She has company, and he might stay with her for a few days." He took a deep breath. "Perhaps I should pay them a visit."

"Don't you dare. She's a big girl."

Chris looked at her. "I am so glad we didn't have a girl."

Jessica laughed. "Truthfully, so am I. That would have been an absolute nightmare."

Chris pouted. "It wouldn't have been that bad."

"Yes, babe, it would have." Jessica walked over and gave him a peck on the lips, running her fingers over his chest.

Heat tingled through his sweater where her fingertips trailed. He looked down at her hand and then drifted his gaze up to hers, a smile playing on his lips.

"Perhaps," he conceded and pulled her against him, his lips finding hers and his libido kicking into high gear.

"No, perhaps about it. You know I'm right," she said when the kiss broke.

Hunger ravaged him, and his hands wandered in opposite directions, one digging into her hair and the other grazing down her back until he cupped her ass. The sweet taste of her strawberry lip gloss fed his appetite, and he swept her off her feet, vaulting up the stairs into their bedroom.

He set her down and stepped back with a playful smile. He tilted his head, and her clothes shredded, flying off her body in different directions.

Jessica let out a surprised laugh, looking at the ruined clothes spread out like the aftermath of a bomb.

Chris's grin grew wider as he scanned her naked body. "You are one fine-looking woman." He pulled off his sweater and threw it aside.

"Not fair." Jessica was rewarded with the sound of ripping cloth as his clothing succumbed to the same fate.

He stepped out of the pile toward her. "Better?"

She nodded, and he took her in his arms, dropping to the floor where they stood. The need to slide his throbbing member inside her overpowered everything else. Urgency overrode comfort. They made frantic, urgent love on the floor.

"There's nothing like a death threat to get the blood flowing, now is there?" he said as they lay spent and staring at the ceiling next to each other.

"Shut up." Jessica laughed.

"Why don't you make me?" He looked over at her.

She reached over and covered his mouth with her hand.

He laughed and pushed her arm away. "That's not what I had in mind."

"I know. But it's going to have to do for now."

"Party pooper." He sat up, surveying the mess he made.

Jessica sat up and did the same. "You couldn't have waited a couple seconds longer for me to take off my clothes?"

He grinned at her and offered a shrug.

"That was one of my favorite shirts." She pointed at the clothing carnage.

"You can buy another one."

"I've had that for years. I won't be able to find another one like it."

"Then I'll have one made for you."

She sighed. "It's going to be a really long week, isn't it?"

"Yes." He stood, helping her up as well.

New clothes came out of the drawers, and they dressed in silence, each lost in what the week might bring.

"I'll clean this up." Chris zipped his jeans.

"Good, because I wasn't planning on it." She left him to clean up the shredded fabric.

End Game Chapter 19

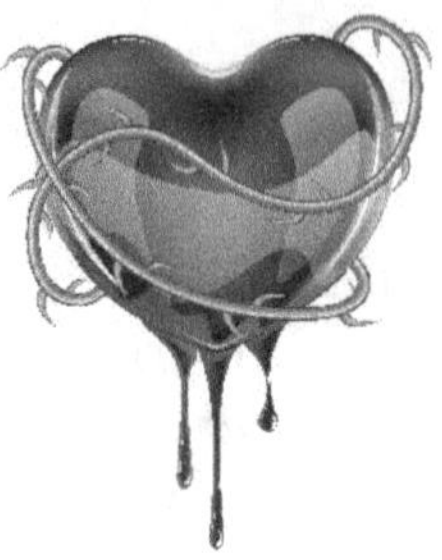

TWO DAYS HAD COME and gone since Tom's call. Just like their last days in the complex, Chris could hear the ticking in the back of his head, the sands of time running out. Tense didn't describe his mood over the next two days. Every ring of the doorbell, every strange car, every ring of the studio buzzer grated on his nerves to the point he wouldn't let Jessica out of his sight except when he conducted his karate classes. Even then, every second he couldn't see her put him on edge.

Chris stood in the office, waiting for Jessica to switch into her sweats. The Closed sign now hung on the front door. He inhaled, his eyes passing over the sleeping boys and back to the bathroom door.

Tomorrow night, we'll be in New York.

"Chris, you need to relax," Jessica said as she stepped out of the bathroom.

He sent her a strained smile and leaned over to pick up the boys. Before he could gather them in his arms, the door buzzer rang. Adrenaline rushed through his veins, and he exchanged a glance with Jessica.

"Stay here," he whispered, scanning the thoughts of the intruder in their lobby.

It wasn't a student.

He turned, putting a disarming smile on his face, and stepped in full view of the stranger. "I'm sorry, but we're closed."

The first in a long line of assassins stood with a gun pointing at him, expecting his demeanor to change, expecting him to crumble under the threat of bodily injury. It was laughable, especially given the hell he'd endured at the hands of his stepbrother.

Chris chuckled. "You don't want to even think about that, dude."

"Black belt versus a gun. I'll take my chances." The intruder smiled, his finger tightening on the trigger.

Chris tilted his head. "It has nothing to do with being a black belt." He willed the man to move the gun to his own temple.

His eyes widened as they dropped to the gun in his hand, watching the progression until it pressed against the skin of his forehead. Shakes wobbled the barrel, and the intruder snapped his terrified gaze from the gun to Chris. "Who are you?"

"Your worst fucking nightmare," Chris answered. "Now, tell me everything, and I may let you walk out of here alive." He crossed his arms, waiting.

The clasp of the office door reached his ears.

"Jess, get your ass back in that room," Chris commanded.

"Don't kill him."

"Get back there with the boys," he said without breaking eye contact with the man who was sent to kill her. "Now," he growled.

The office door closed behind him.

"What's your name?" he asked the intruder.

"Fuck you."

Chris raised his eyebrow, and the man's finger tightened on the trigger. "Let's try that again. What is your name?"

"John." Sweat drizzled down the sides of his face and his gaze bounced between his trigger finger and Chris.

"Who sent you?"

"Her ex."

"Wrong answer. Her ex called to give me a heads-up." He pursed his lips and crossed his arms. "Now, John, unless you want that gun to go off, I suggest you tell me who sent you?"

"I got a text from Tom Whitman," John said.

"Show me." Chris allowed John to pull the phone out of his pocket with his spare hand, the gun still pressed firmly to his forehead. He snatched it out of his hand and then scrolled down the list of texts until he got to the one ordering Jessica's hit. He recognized the number. He raised his eyes to the assassin. "Was that all the instruction you got?"

"Ye—"

"Be very careful how you answer that, because I can tell if you're lying to me."

John gulped and opened his mouth a few times before his gaze landed on the gun. "No. I got a phone call too."

"And the phone call wasn't from Tom, was it?"

He shook his head.

"Who was on the phone?"

"Sharon Whitman."

"That a boy. Think you can handle another question?" Chris toyed with the hit man.

A shaky nod answered him.

"What exactly did she tell you to do?"

"I can't tell you that."

"Sure, you can. Or you'll die just like that." Chris snapped his fingers. "What's she worth?" He changed the subject, pointing his thumb over his shoulder.

"A million dollars."

Chris laughed. "What's your life worth?"

"Fuck you," John said, but with less conviction than the first time.

"You know, my patience is wearing a bit thin right now." He waved at his surroundings and stared John down. "You come into my dojo intending to do harm to my family. What would you do in my shoes?"

John swallowed and shrugged.

"Tell me what your instructions are."

"You're out of your fucking mind."

Chris bit his lip and willed the gun from John's forehead down to his crotch. The barrel pointed at an angle that would blast both his dick and his balls clean off. "Tell me what I want to know, or I'll make sure you die a slow, painful death."

Tears filled John's eyes, and a small dark stain spread over the front of his jeans. Words tumbled out, blending together in a frantic tone as if the imparting of information would somehow save his life. "Sharon wants her dead, along with anyone I found with her."

"You would have killed my children?"

John flinched, and his gaze shot between the gun and Chris, his eyes betraying him.

A rumbling growl formed in Chris's chest. The power coiled inside, building, seething, and ready to strike. But it was her voice in his head that erased the red aura of fury from his vision.

Calm down, babe.

He drew a deep breath and took a step forward, pointing at John. "You are a lucky son of a bitch," he said with clenched teeth. "Because I'm going to let you go. But if you so much as step foot in the state of Maine again, I'll know, and I won't hesitate to kill you."

He willed John to put the gun on the ground in front of him and step back. John did as Chris silently commanded.

"And you are going to do me a little favor. On Friday night at seven o'clock on the dot, you will call Sharon, and you tell her she just unleashed Ty Aris, and he's coming after her. Understand?"

John nodded and shivered, his gaze darting between his escape route and Chris.

"Now repeat what you're going to do."

With a shaky voice, John reiterated Chris's demand.

"Good boy. Now get the hell out of here." Chris pointed at the door, and it swung open at the precise moment he let up on the mental hold.

John bolted in an exit worthy of a cartoon. Gravel and smoke filled the parking lot as his car careened onto the road at break-neck speed.

Chris smirked. *That kid won't ever set foot in Maine again.*

He turned to see Jessica peering out of the office door. "That ought to slide through the grapevine pretty quickly."

"What do you mean?"

"A million dollars is not enough for most professional assassins to walk into the lion's den with a useless weapon." Which meant only someone seriously deranged would try to kill Jessica once word got out.

He picked up the gun and walked back to the office, then dropped it into the duffel bag. His heart thundered in his chest, and he clamped his teeth together as both anger and fear threaded his veins. "I guess she made that call."

Why can't I take the bitch out?

"Because. It's still wrong."

Chris laughed and glared at her. "And giving the order to kill my entire family isn't wrong?" Without waiting for an answer, he zipped the duffel bag and tossed it to her before grabbing a sleeping child in each arm.

She followed close behind him and slipped into the passenger seat while he strapped the kids into their car seats.

With a glance over his shoulder, the lights in the studio shut off and the locks on the doors flipped closed. He sat in the driver's seat and took a deep breath, turning the ignition key and then shifted the car into reverse. He pulled out without saying a word, glimpsing a tail in the rearview mirror.

"Where are you going?" Jessica gaped when he took a turn he normally wouldn't take.

"We've got company." He pulled to the side and stepped out of the car, then moved to the center of the road away from the driver's open door.

Bright lights blinded him, and the car stopped less than a hundred yards away. The rev of the engine turned the molten fury in Chris to a churning boil waiting to be unchained. The squeal of tires as the car lurched toward him set off the eruption.

Power honed over the last five years leaped out of Chris. The car blew to pieces, the explosion echoing on the glass surrounding them and the pieces evaporating to dust before they hit the ground. All down the street, lights flipped on. Chris jumped into the driver's seat, then peeled out before anyone could ID the car.

Jessica's wide, stark stare caught his glance, and he shook his head, returning his gaze back to the road. The boys mumbled and fell back into the stupor of sleep.

"Chris?"

"Don't you dare judge me right now."

"But…"

"But what? You heard what they were thinking just as clearly as I did." He sent a glare at her.

She nodded and turned her gaze to their surroundings. "Where are you going?"

"I'm going to get Emily."

Her head snapped back. "Oh God, you think…"

He glanced at her and nodded. "That's where I would have gone."

JESSICA SHIVERED AT CHRIS'S deadly gaze as much as his words. The horror of what he'd done to the car following them dissipated. He was right. She had heard their murderous thoughts, but killing still wasn't the answer. Yet he did so without qualms.

"Damn straight I did." He shut off the headlights. "And I'll do it again if I have to." He turned off the car, let it coast down the hill into the driveway, and set the emergency break.

"Chris."

He met her gaze. "What do you want me to do, Jess? Disarm them so they can come after us again? I'm not taking that chance with their lives." He hooked his thumb toward the backseat. "Sharon's instructions were to kill you and anyone with you. Anyone."

"They wouldn't…"

"Yes, they would." He turned to the back seat and stared into his son's wide eyes. "CJ, make sure no one gets in this car but me and Emily." When CJ nodded, he swiveled back to her. "Stay here with them, understand?"

Jessica nodded, and Chris hopped out and closed the door as quietly as he could. She tried to swallow, but fear left her mouth dry as a convection oven and her tongue stuck to the roof of her mouth. Scraping it off with sheer will, she glanced back at her four-year-old son. His expression matched his father's, and protective energy radiated off him in powerful waves. The only one getting near the car was his father; anyone else was toast, literally.

"Baby, you don't need to do that," she said to CJ.

"Yes, I do. Daddy said so." He looked at her. "Daddy said I had to protect you and Tommy while he went to get Emily." He looked at the house. "And she isn't alone."

Jessica's eyes went wide, and she turned toward the house, reaching for the door handle. It didn't budge, and she looked back at CJ. "Let me out."

"No, Mommy."

CHRIS CLOSED THE DOOR silently behind him. Emily's fear tickled his mind. He scanned the house from the shadows, zeroing in on her whereabouts in the living room, and he stepped to his right for a better view.

A man with a gun paced in front of the chair she was sitting in. Chris took another step right into her line of sight. Her eyes flashed recognition and then looked toward the kitchen.

More than one. Jesus, that bitch worked fast.

He cleared his throat, and the gun swung in his direction. The man never got all the way around before he turned to dust.

Chris took a step into the room and his gaze landed on a man lying in a tacky puddle of blood. He looked up at Emily as a tear rolled down her cheek.

Bill died trying to protect me.

Chris closed his eyes for a moment and then opened them, looking toward the kitchen and then back at Emily. She nodded. He hooked his thumb toward the bedroom, and she shook her head.

There's only one more.

"Yo!" he called.

The man poked his head into the room, and in a repeat performance, Chris vaporized him.

"Dust, baby." He turned to Emily, then untied her and ignored her wide, frightened eyes. "Get your things. You're coming with us."

Chris followed Emily to the bedroom and stood in the doorway, scanning the room and sighing. The last time he'd set foot in this room was the day he and Jessica sent Frank's ghost back to hell. He nearly lost everything that day. He shifted his weight, glancing away from the nightmare memories toward the door while Emily threw a bunch of clothing and accessories into a suitcase.

"I'm sorry I wasn't able to get here in time."

"I'm sure Bill is, too."

Her voice hitched in her throat enough for him to turn back to her. He realized it wasn't just her hands that were shaking, and he stepped into the bedroom, crossing to her and took over packing while she leaned on the end of the bed, letting sobs leak from her chest. He closed the suitcase and gently took her elbow, leading her out of the bedroom.

"Where are we going?"

"To my place in the city. You'll be safe there until after the wedding and premiere."

Emily gasped and stared at him, her jaw falling a few inches.

"Yes, I'm marrying your mother, and yes, we're going to the premiere. That's the only way to stop this madness."

"Why do they want my mother?"

Chris sighed. "It's a long story, but nothing is going to touch this family."

She nodded, and they headed to the car.

Chris threw the bag in the back and opened the door for Emily.

Dark rings of exhaustion circled CJ's eyes, and his tired gaze met Chris's.

"Good job, buddy. Now you need to get some sleep, okay, sport?" Chris smiled reassuringly at his son and closed the back door.

The smile disappeared the moment he slid into the driver's seat, and he glanced at Jessica. "Two more down." With an eye on the rearview mirror, Chris navigated the streets, zigzagging from road to road until he was sure they weren't being followed.

Forty-five minutes later, he pulled into their garage and leaned back in the seat, rubbing his face with his hands. "Well, that was interesting," he said, glancing at Jessica.

Jessica began to cry. "Why is this happening?"

Chris got out and went around to the passenger door, then took her in his arms.

"Why?"

"Bad karma," he whispered, and she laughed.

"That's not funny."

"Yes, it is." He smiled and looked at Emily in the back of the car, and then at the two sleeping boys. "We need to pack and get the hell out of Dodge." He wiped the tears from her face. "They won't know to look for us in the city."

He helped her out of the car and transferred the boys, car seats and all, to the rear seat in the Hummer, leaving the middle seat for Emily. Her suitcase went into the luggage hull. He turned, heading inside to pack their stuff.

While Jessica went upstairs to change and pack, he grabbed the garment bags out of the closet and hung them on the coat rack by the garage. He vaulted up the stairs and took over packing their bags while Jessica disappeared into the boys' room to grab clothing and toys for them, including their little handheld games.

Chris dropped the wedding gifts and rings into his carry-on, made sure they had their dress shoes for the wedding and hauled the suitcases downstairs, then piled them in the back before laying the garment bags over the neat stack.

He returned to grab the bags Jessica had packed for the boys. "We need to stop in Connecticut and pick up Eric."

She nodded and glanced at the dance leotard she wore. "I need to change," she said, handing him their suitcases and appraising his attire. He still had his karate gi on. "So do you."

"I'm good. I'll change when we get to the apartment. I can move much quieter in this, and I have a feeling that I may need to."

Fear flashed in her eyes.

"Yeah, my sentiments exactly. I don't know if they'll hit Dan for information, but..." He shrugged. "Hurry." He turned and climbed down the stairs, then packed the last of the bags in the back and slammed the trunk closed.

He walked into the family room and paced, waiting for her to come downstairs. The chirp of the phone interrupted his restless gait, and he snatched the handset off the cradle.

"Hello."

"Chris?" Daniel asked in an unsteady voice.

"Shit," he said. "They're there, aren't they?"

"Yes."

Daniel's fear skated through the phone line like an Olympic gold medalist, snapping at Chris's nerves. "Give the phone to them."

"Listen and listen good," the voice threatened into the phone.

Chris closed his eyes and then opened them to Daniel's family room and a scruffy thug with a gun planted on Daniel's head.

LeAnn fainted, and Daniel's jaw dropped.

"No, you listen, you son of a bitch," Chris growled and let loose.

The men with guns inside Jessica's original house turned to dust.

He swung his gaze at Eric and pointed at him. "We're coming to get you." He turned to a very pale Daniel. "Sorry, Dan."

He blinked and turned to find Jessica staring at him from the stairwell. After crossing to her, he grabbed her hand and hauled her out to the Hummer.

"Get in," he snapped and slid into the driver's side. He paused for a moment and looked between the keys and her crossing in front of the Hummer. "Wait, you drive."

She grabbed the keys out of the air, and they switched places.

"We need to get there fast, and you're the fastest driver I know." He looked back at Emily from the passenger seat. "Buckle up. Your mother drives like a bat out of hell."

Jessica spun the Hummer out of the garage and waited as the door closed behind them. "Lock up, please."

He closed his eyes, setting every outer door deadbolt in place. "Done."

She turned the car around and headed out at a pace that would be the envy of any Indianapolis 500 driver.

A little over an hour later, she pulled into her old house with Emily, CJ, and Tommy asleep in the backseat.

Christ, I can't leave them unprotected out here. "Damn it." Chris glanced into the back of the car and then back at the house. "CJ!" His voice barreled through the car, startling everyone.

CJ sat up, his eyes wide, locked with Chris's.

"Sorry, buddy, but I need you to do that thing again. Think you can?" he asked, hating himself for asking this of his four-year-old son.

CJ looked around the car and then at the house and nodded. "Okay, Daddy."

"I'll be right back," he whispered and leaned over, then gave Jessica a peck on the cheek. He got out of the car and walked to the door, scanning the house with his mind. He couldn't sense any danger. A ton of fear, but no malicious intent.

He looked around the property and did the same. All clear—for now. Chris rang the doorbell and held his breath.

Daniel opened the door, his face still pasty, and his hands had a slight tremble to them. "Jesus."

"Not exactly." Chris physically stepped into the house for the first time. He looked to his left into the living room. The first thing he saw was a curio cabinet full of crystal animals. He raised his eyebrows and briefly studied the house.

"What the hell happened?" Daniel asked, pulling Chris's attention back to him.

"Tom left his wife." Chris stepped down the hall to the back of the house, absorbing the details as he went, recognizing things here and there that had Jessica's distinct flavor, surprised to see that her touch hadn't been completely obliterated by Daniel and LeAnn's after all these years.

Daniel followed Chris, and he finally found his voice again as they entered the kitchen. "What does that have to do with what happened here today?"

Chris turned and looked at him. "Everything. She put a contract out on Jessica." He surveyed the kitchen and family room, catching a doorway out of the corner of his eye, and he headed in that direction.

"Where are you going?" Daniel answered, exasperated.

"Going downstairs to get Eric," Chris said, looking back at Daniel and opening the door to the finished basement.

"How the hell do you know where he is?"

Chris paused and turned. "Dan, I know everything."

"How did you appear here, and what did you do to those men?"

Chris shrugged. "I knew you were in danger, so I fixed it." He headed downstairs, then crossed to the pool table and turned toward a door at the far side of the room. "Eric."

Eric flew out of the furnace room and into Chris's arms, his frame shaking against Chris.

"It's okay now," Chris said in his ear. "Go get your things." He let him go and followed him up to the main floor, then waited by the door.

"What the hell are you?" Daniel said from behind him.

When Chris turned, Daniel stepped back. "Dan, I've been called a lot of things, from a natural born killer to the Angel of Death to a guardian angel, but really, I'm just the man who fell in love with your wife."

Daniel blinked.

"Look, CJ is protecting everyone in the car, and I don't have a hell of a lot of time, certainly not enough to explain what I am." He glanced up the stairs, uneasiness itching into his frame, and he shifted his weight from foot to foot. "Eric!"

"I'll be there in a minute."

Chris turned to Daniel. "I would suggest you, LeAnn, and Sandy hightail it out of here for a few days."

"I'm not leaving my home."

"Please. If you aren't here, they can't find out where we are, and you won't get hurt," he said. "Jess wouldn't be able to live with that."

Daniel traded a glance with LeAnn and returned his gaze to Chris. "What about the city?"

Chris nodded. "I'll make sure there's a room for you at The Carlyle. That's where I booked you for Saturday night. I'll see if I can extend it." Chris watched Eric bound down the stairs with a duffel bag. "I promise I'll keep him safe."

"All right," Daniel conceded and gave Eric a brief hug.

Uneasiness turned to all-out alarm, and Chris stiffened. "Shit." He bolted from the house just as a car pulled up on the side of the road, hidden by the thick tree line surrounding the property. The engine puttered and turned off.

The Hummer purred in the driveway, sending plumes of exhaust into the frosty night. Chris sent a warning glare toward Eric and Daniel and mentally pushed them to the side of the house, away from any chance of being hit by a stray bullet.

Chris walked toward the car, purposely acting clueless.

"Freeze," a man said, and stepped out of the shadows with the gun.

Chris had to stifle a laugh. *What hit man yells freeze? This guy sucks!* He turned and stared at the armed intruder, his hand halfway to the car door. Silently, he sent a message to CJ that he had this covered, and the electric shield around the car disintegrated.

"You'd better tell your friend not to touch the vehicle, or he will die," Chris warned, loud enough to be heard by both the man pointing the gun at him and the second one skulking toward the Hummer from the opposite side.

The man holding the gun laughed.

"I wouldn't laugh." Chris sent out the silent but deadly signal as the other man reached for the car door. The smell of singed hair bloomed, and his partner vanished. "You're next." He pointed at the gunman.

The assailant pulled the trigger. The gunshot echoed in the driveway, but the bullet didn't make it to its target. The bullet and everything in its wake vaporized under a stream of heat that actually peeled the paint on the bumper of the car, leaving a waft of burning flesh on the air and a pile of ash on the ground.

"Eric, hustle," Chris yelled and opened the back passenger door. He looked over at a stunned Daniel. "Get your family out of here NOW."

DANIEL DIDN'T NEED ANOTHER command from Chris. He bolted inside, and they were out of that house within fifteen minutes, fully packed for a long weekend in New York City.

End Game Chapter 20

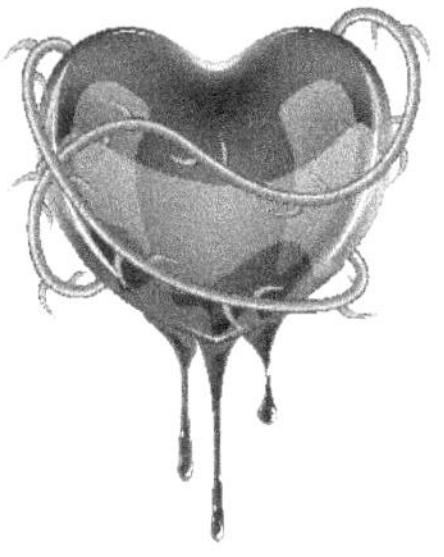

CHRIS KEPT HIS GAZE on the side mirror as Jessica drove down the dark highway. Once they switched onto 91S outside of Hartford, he let his tight muscles relax and vowed to make Sharon pay dearly for putting his family in jeopardy.

The uneven sounds of light snoring drifted from the back seat, and he glanced over his shoulder. All the kids were sacked out, the excitement draining every one of them.

He turned his attention to Jessica. "How are you holding up?"

"Not very well."

"Do you want me to drive?"

Jessica nodded and pulled into the rest station in Middletown. He stepped out, inhaling the clean, crisp air, missing the ocean tinge of their house in Maine. He caught her at the back of the truck, wrapping his arms around her in a tight bear hug. "I love you, you know."

Jessica nodded against his shoulder. "You killed tonight."

"Yes, and I'm sure I'll have to do it again."

"CJ would have killed, too." The words came out wrapped in a sob.

"I wouldn't let that happen, Jess. I just needed to know there was some protection around you. CJ's the only one that can do that in my absence." He pushed her hair away from her face. "I've already been working with him on control. Karate is part of that discipline. He had the car protected, and yes, if either of those scumbags had touched it, they would have died on contact. But I knew they were coming, and that's why I came out of the house when I did."

Jessica looked up at him with eyes filled with tears and doubt.

Chris swallowed hard at the look on her face. "I still want to marry you on Friday. Do you still feel the same?"

She nodded, wiping her face with her hands.

"Just so you understand, anyone who comes after us will die."

"Yes." Her hoarse whisper filled the night just loud enough to be heard over the idling engine. "You understand they'll keep coming as long as I'm alive."

"No, babe, that's not the case. As soon as that first one from Maine spreads the word, this will stop. The five that I vaporized will only add to the urban legend. Trust me. The smart ones will back off completely."

Chris hadn't told her exactly what he said to the first assassin, but it was enough to send John bolting out of the studio with thoughts of never setting foot in Maine again.

"It's freezing. We can continue this in the car," he said, and they both continued to the opposite sides. He slid into the driver's seat and buckled his seat belt. "You ready for this?"

"Game on." She wiped the tears from her face.

"Game on," he agreed. "Besides, Sharon doesn't know I changed my name to Chris

Ryan." He sent a sideways glance at Jessica. "At least not yet," he corrected. It wasn't buried so deep that it couldn't be found, but someone would have to do a hell of a lot of digging to get to it.

Another thought popped into his mind, and he chuckled.

"What?"

"I could change my name to my original name."

"I don't think that'd be such a good idea. No offense, but I wouldn't want Aris as a last name."

Chris glanced at her and let out a sharp bark of a laugh. "I was talking about the name on my birth certificate, honey. I never want to be associated with the name Aris again."

"Oh. What *was* your last name?"

"You're marrying into it."

She raised her eyebrows.

"You didn't know that?"

"No, I thought Ryan was your father's *first* name."

Chris's rich laughter filled the car. "No, babe. Ryan was our surname, not my father's first name. You're taking my original last name when we get married. Ty Alexander Ryan, nice to meet you." He grinned like a fool and put his hand out for her to shake.

Jessica took his hand in hers and brought it to her lips, chuckling a little at him. "I'm sorry. I just assumed it was your father's first name." She blushed. "So, what was his first name?"

He glanced over at her and grinned. "It's the only reason I allowed you to name our second son Thomas. My dad's name was Tom. Thomas Patrick, to be exact."

"And here I thought you were being so diplomatic with me, letting me name him after his father."

"I'm not that much of a pushover, Jess. Besides, you didn't choose the name Thomas William." He glanced at her. "That wouldn't have gone over well, but you just happened to lay my dad's name on the table. Who was I to say no?"

She laughed and looked out the window. "I can't believe you can still surprise me like that." Jessica laced her hand in his, and they drove in silence for a while. "Irish?"

"Aye, lassie," he said with an impeccable Irish accent.

"It's funny. We never talked about these things before."

"What else do you want to know about me?"

"Why did Marian hate you so much?"

Chris took a deep breath. "She said she loved me, but I wasn't interested in any sort of relationship with an Aris. Unfortunately, that didn't stop me from screwing around with her. She got pregnant." He glanced over at Jessica. "She wanted the baby, and I didn't. I made her get an abortion."

"Ah."

He sent another sideways glance her way. "Does that bother you?"

"No, but it certainly explains her hostility. Had you ever been in love before me?"

"No."

"Never?"

"Not ever. I never let anyone in." He glanced over at her. "I bet you fell in love weekly as a teenager." He smiled, turning the conversation away from him. He didn't want to dredge up more of his brutally repressed past.

Jessica blushed. "I think before I went to college, the longest time I dated someone was something like three months." She laughed. "In college, I dated someone for two years, but it was never really exclusive, at least not for me." She looked back at the kids and then over at him. "But to this day, I think he must have been gay. He only kissed me once. Hell, I kissed his roommate more times than I can count." She let out a little laugh. "My boyfriend's roommate was the male slut of the campus, and I was still a virgin, so I was fair game. He never got me into bed, but not for lack of trying. I think that's why we were such great friends. Any time I got frustrated at the lack of attention my boyfriend gave me, I'd go to see him, and he would do his best to make me feel sexy. He was a hell of a kisser."

Chris's mouth hung open. "You were a virgin in college?" He looked back at the road in time to see the Welcome to New York sign.

"Yes." She looked out the window.

"Was Dan your first?" he asked.

"No, he wasn't. I didn't say yes until I was twenty-two, and the only reason I did was he had the courtesy to ask instead of just assuming it was his right. I started dating Danny the day after he dumped me. So, Danny was sort of a rebound guy."

"So, you married on the rebound?" He raised his eyebrows at her.

"No, I loved Danny." She tilted her head a little. "But I married Tom on the rebound."

The car swerved a little.

He looked over at her. "From Dan?"

Jessica shook her head. "I was rebounding from you when I married Tom."

He pulled her hand to his lips and kissed it. "I can't wait for Friday."

"Neither can I."

They drove the rest of the way in silence, and eventually Jessica fell into a light sleep.

Chris rolled down the window as he pulled into the garage where his apartment was. The familiar valet walked over to the car, smiling.

"Hi, Mr. Ryan. It's been a while," Jason said, looking at the monster Hummer with envy. "I like your new wheels."

"Thanks, Jason. I still have the 'vette, but with the two kids, you know..." He shrugged. "I have a ton of stuff in the back and a carload of sleeping people, so I'll just bring her up, if you don't mind." He reached into his wallet, pulled out a hundred-dollar bill, and handed it to Jason.

"I can't take that, man. I haven't done anything," Jason said, putting his hands up in the air.

"By the way, has anyone been asking for me?" Chris asked.

"No, no one's ever come around asking about you. Why?"

"Good. If someone does, you haven't seen me in years. Okay?" He reached into his wallet and pulled out four more bills. "And you will let me know after they leave." He handed Jason $500.

"Are you in trouble?" Jason asked, eyeing the money.

Chris shook his head. "No, I'm not in trouble." He smiled and gently pushed his influence on Jason. "You haven't seen me in years, deal?" He put the money in Jason's hand.

Jason looked at the money and back up at Chris. "Yeah, man. Deal." He smiled and pocketed the money.

Chris drove up to the top floor of the garage and found his spot, the closest to the elevator, a perk of owning the penthouse. He slid out onto the concrete and stretched before he latched his door and crossed to the passenger side.

He opened Jessica's door and leaned in to kiss her on the lips. "Wake up, babe. We're here."

Her eyes fluttered open. "We're here already?"

"Yes." He helped her out of the car before opening the back door and shaking Eric awake. "Hey, sport. Time to wake up. You, too, Emily."

They rolled out of the car and stood with Jessica while he unhooked the boys. He handed CJ to Eric because he was closest, and then he picked up Tommy, ducking carefully as he pulled him out of the car. He closed the door behind him, and his gaze traveled over his shell-shocked family. He nodded toward the elevator, and they moved together, letting him lead the way. He reached into his pocket and pulled out his keys as they rode the elevator up to the top floor, fumbling for the right key and trying not to wake Tommy. He held open the door to his apartment as they filed in.

"This way," he whispered to Eric as they headed down the hall to one of the guest rooms.

He pulled the covers back and lay Tommy on the far side of the bed, then turned and took CJ from Eric to tuck him in next to his brother. He pulled the covers up and looked down at the two of them, taking a deep breath. He said a silent prayer to keep them safe and then headed out of the room, closing the door behind him.

"I need to get the things out of the car. Want to give me a hand?"

"Sure." Eric followed Chris out of the apartment.

As the elevator doors closed after them, Chris leaned against the back wall and closed his eyes. "You didn't call when they came." He opened his eyes.

"I was a little busy protecting my family. They wanted Mom's address up in Maine."

"Did your father give it to them?"

"No, he said he had no idea where she lived. They made him call the house. They put a gun to his head, and when that didn't work, they put the gun to LeAnn's head as well. I couldn't stop it either. Believe me, I tried, but I wouldn't have been able to stop a bullet. I hate feeling helpless like that," he said. "Then you appeared. What the hell did you do with them?"

Chris slowly grinned. "Vaporized the motherfuckers."

Eric's eyes went wide.

"Ashes and dust, just like the ones out by the car. They never knew what hit them." The elevator doors opened, and they stepped out.

Chris lifted the back door of the car. "Looks like we're moving in. It's funny what you'll throw in a bag when you don't have a hell of a lot of time, isn't it?" He handed Eric his sister's suitcase, the kids' suitcase, and his duffel bag, then he grabbed Jessica's and his bags and the garment bags containing the wedding clothes. He closed the hatchback with a thought and locked the car as well, smiling at Eric as he walked by. "Who needs keys?"

Eric was quiet on the ride up. "Do you regret it?" he asked as the elevator opened and they stepped out.

Chris stopped and looked at Eric. "Killing them?"

Eric nodded.

"No," Chris said without hesitation, keeping eye contact with his soon-to-be stepson. "Does that bother you?"

"Oddly enough, it doesn't," Eric answered. "But why are they after her?"

"Sharon Whitman put a contract out on your mother."

"Why?" Eric asked.

Chris opened the door to the apartment. "Tom left her." He headed into the master suite. He laid the suitcases on the bed and took the kids' bag from Eric. "I only have one other room. Do you mind sleeping on the couch tonight? I'll have the kids sleep on the floor for the rest of the stay, but I don't want to disturb them. They've had a rough night."

"Wasn't that a king size bed in the guest room?" Eric pointed over his shoulder.

Chris nodded.

"There's enough room for me with the boys in there," he said.

Chris laughed. "You obviously have never slept in a bed with them. They're small, but man, can they take up space."

Eric smiled and nodded. "I'll brave it with my little brothers." He dropped his bag in the room and brought Emily's into the room on the other side of the hall, then deposited it onto the bed.

They headed into the living room where Emily and Jessica were talking.

"I still don't get why she would do that." Eric said, resuming the conversation as he plopped himself in the chair and looked around the apartment. They had never been here before.

Chris exchanged a look with Jessica.

"She's been blackmailing him since we split," Jessica said.

Both Emily and Eric looked over at her.

"How?" they asked in unison.

"With your mother's life," Chris said as he walked behind where Jessica was sitting and put his hands on her shoulders.

Darkness crept into Eric's eyes. "You could kill her right now."

"All in good time." He smiled, and Jessica stiffened under his hands. Her thoughts flashed back to a place ten years ago when he had said those same words, and then all hell broke loose. He bent down and whispered in her ear, "Don't worry about that. Things have changed drastically since then." He kissed her cheek and looked back at Eric and Emily, straightening his back. "I'm marrying your mother. Then I'll deal with this situation. In my own way. Now, if you'll excuse me, it's been a long night." He kissed Jessica's cheek and headed to the master bathroom to wash the sweat and smell of death from his skin.

The warm water cascaded over his aching body, loosening the knots that had set ever since the warning call. A cold draft grazed his skin when Jessica opened the shower door and stepped in with him.

"Ty," she whispered, and ran her hands over his back.

Heat spread from her touch, encompassing him, and he turned his head, letting a playful smile surface. "Beg."

"No." She smiled and cocked her head. "You beg."

He chuckled, their game turning, morphing into more fiery foreplay. "You want me to beg?"

"Yes."

His lips trailed from her earlobe down the line of her neck. "Please, Jess. Please tell me you want me. Please tell me you love me. Please tell me what I need to hear." Each phrase was punctuated with a swipe of his tongue on her skin. He lingered on her breasts, whispering "please" between each suckle. His hands caressed her skin, making their way between her legs, blazing the trail for his lips.

He licked her, and her hand threaded into his hair.

"Oh God," she breathed and leaned against the tiled wall, wrapping a leg across his back.

"Please cum for me," he said. "I want to taste you tonight."

HIS WORDS, HIS TONE, the pleading in his voice, the sensuous revolutions of his tongue, all combined into the elixir she needed. She cried out with the power of the orgasm gripping her, his mouth slurping the slickness of her mixed with the warm water raining down her body. Tremors flowed through her, and she bit her lip, stifling a moan that welled in her chest.

"Oh, God!"

His gaze traveled up her body to hers, and he smiled, his demeanor taking the dominant role again as he stood, kissing her stomach, chest, and neck before his lips found hers.

"Beg for me," he commanded and covered her mouth with a powerful kiss.

She pushed him back against the far side of the shower, the need for him overriding every other emotion inside her. But the game still had to be played out. She panted against him, her tongue twirling with his, her heart pounding, fueled with desire. She stroked him with her hands, and he groaned, squeezing her ass, pulling her closer.

Breaking the kiss, she stared into his smoldering eyes and licked her lips. "Please, please, I need you. I want you to make love to me."

He crushed her mouth with his, squeezing her against him and turning the water off. His lips never once left hers as he picked her up, stepping out of the shower and laid her gently on the bathroom floor. Then he slid into her with a thrust of his hips.

He pulled away from her lips and shook his head, spraying water all across the room, smiling. "Smoldering yet?"

"Oh, yeah." She grinned up at him. "From the moment I said your name. I swear that's your instant aphrodisiac."

"You have absolutely no idea how powerful hearing you say that is." He slowly arched into her, grinding his hips into hers, and her body responded, shuddering with the strength of another orgasm. "And *you* are my aphrodisiac." He continued his slow pace and leaned down, grazing his lips over hers and laughed softly as he moved his lips to her neckline, running his tongue from her collarbone to her earlobe. "I love you," he whispered and gently bit her earlobe. "Do you love me?" he asked, grazing her lips and moving to her other earlobe.

She gasped. "Yes."

"Say it." He looked into her eyes, bringing the heat level between them to almost unbearable.

"I love you!" The words accompanied another wave, and she arched off the floor, her eyes rolling back in her head and her nails digging into his shoulders. "Oh God, I love you!"

HE SQUEEZED HIS EYES closed, coming with such force that Jessica came again on the heels of her dissipating orgasm. Collapsing on her, he whispered in her ear, "I'll love you for all eternity." He wrapped his arms around her and rolled so she wouldn't have to lie on the hard floor any longer.

Jessica propped her chin on her fist and looked at him.

He lay with his head back and eyes closed, one arm wrapped around her and the other out wide on the floor. "I am so tired."

"It's been a long day," she whispered and put her head on his chest.

"Bed. Hang on." He exercised a different kind of strength. His jaw tightened, and his eyebrows furrowed as he concentrated. After a moment, his body lifted off the ground with her on top. Her gasp brought a smile to his lips, but he didn't say a word until they safely set down on the bed. "I didn't want to get up."

He wrapped both arms around her and turned his head toward the bureau. The drawer opened, and a pair of boxers floated to the bed. Chris reached out and took them in his hand.

He winked at her, and her suitcase opened. A nightgown floated over to her.

She sat up on him, raising her arms, and laughed as the silk slipped over her skin. She rolled onto her back, and he pulled on the boxers without sitting up.

He blew her a kiss and passed out from exhaustion.

JESSICA CURLED UP IN the crook of his arm and did the same. Her last coherent thought was *show off,* and then she drifted into the dark void of exhausted sleep.

She woke up in the same position she had fallen asleep and glanced over at the clock. "Holy shit." She sat up straight. It was close to one thirty in the afternoon.

Chris didn't even stir; he was out cold.

The bedroom door remained closed, which meant the boys hadn't come in to wake them like usual. She slipped out of bed and opened the closet, looking for something in the way of a bathrobe. Finding nothing, she grabbed one of Chris's chambray shirts and slipped it on over her nightgown, then headed out of the bedroom.

Quiet blanketed the apartment, eerie and silent, and she opened the guest room where the boys slept. Empty, and so was Emily's room. She crossed through the undisturbed living room and pushed the door to the kitchen open, expecting to find the kids around the table eating lunch. Again, empty.

Fear snuck under her skin and her heart reacted, throbbing in her throat as she made her way back to the bedroom.

She stopped in the doorway. The neatly made bed and absence of luggage set her heart into overdrive. Chris wasn't there. No one was.

Panic bit at her heels. She turned, running at that sluggish speed that accompanies nightmares. The entry way elongated to an impossible distance, and she ran, barreling through the front door and stumbling to the elevator.

"Come on, come on, come on." She shifted from toe to toe impatiently, and when the doors whooshed open, she shot inside, stabbing the button for the top garage level.

The doors slid open, revealing an empty spot where the Hummer had been. Chris lay facedown on the pavement with a knife in his back and his legs crushed to a pulp.

"Ty!" Jessica screamed.

HANDS SHOOK HER. "JESSIE!" Chris's voice broke through the veil of sleep.

She blinked. Her eyes fluttered open to the dark room.

"You were having a nightmare," he whispered, and she threw her arms around him, still shaking from her dream. "Frank again?"

"No. I woke up, and everyone was gone, and you... you... you..." She couldn't say it.

"I was what?"

She clung to him like a frightened child. "You were dead."

"I don't plan on dying any time soon, babe." He stroked her hair, whispering, "shh" and rocking her until her tremors subsided.

Jessica glanced at the clock; it was two in the morning. She had only been asleep for two hours, and she closed her eyes, snuggling into him and sniffling, wiping the tears away.

"Love you," he whispered and drifted back to sleep.

The morning came sooner than Jessica wanted, and she woke as Tommy climbed into the bed next to her.

"Hi, Mommy," he whispered.

Chris snored lightly in her ear, and he still had his arms wrapped around her.

"Hi, baby." She smiled at Tommy, the nightmare a distant memory.

"CJ snores like Daddy." Tommy crawled under the covers. He immediately closed his eyes and drifted back to sleep in the protective grasp of his mother.

Jessica glanced over at the clock, and it read a little after eight. "Chris?"

"Hmmm?" he mumbled without opening his eyes.

"Do you mind if I go for a jog?"

Chris opened his eyes and glanced at Jessica and Tommy beyond her. "I think it's safe, especially if you're all bundled up," he whispered in a voice scratchy from sleep.

Jessica slid her arm from underneath her son and slipped out of Chris's grip, giving him a brief peck on the cheek. She rummaged through her suitcase, hoping she hadn't forgotten exercise clothes in the mayhem of packing last night, and was pleased to see that her brain had been functioning after all. She slid on a pair of silk long johns and a matching top, pulled on a pair of sweatpants and sweatshirt, and headed into the bathroom where she brushed her teeth and pulled her hair back in a ponytail.

As she went back into the bedroom, she debated on a winter hat and decided in the interest of security to put one on, as well as a pair of light gloves. She slid her jogging shoes on and walked over to the side of the bed, looking down at Chris and Tommy, who were now both sound asleep. She leaned over, kissed his lips anyway, and quietly left the apartment.

End Game Chapter 21

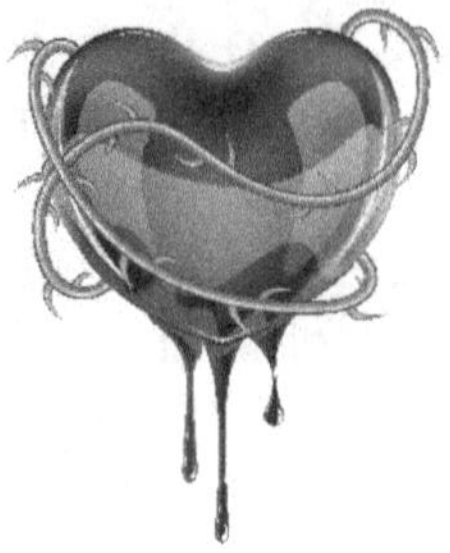

JESSICA SLID HER SUNGLASSES on and slipped her earphones in as she walked out of the lobby and crossed the road to enter Central Park. She switched her music player on and began running slowly through the jogging paths, thinking about everything that had happened last night.

She didn't notice the shadow jogging behind her until a hand landed on her shoulder. Jessica reacted quickly and violently, knocking him down with a spin kick that Chris had taught her.

"Jessie!"

His familiar voice stopped her in her tracks. Tom stood, holding his ribs and staring warily at her. He picked up his baseball cap and slid it on backward, like he always did when they were married. "Hell of a spin kick you got there."

"What are you doing here?"

He shrugged. "The premiere's Friday. I didn't have anywhere else to go. Besides, I figured he'd bring you here. I just assumed he still had a place in the city somewhere."

Jessica nodded and began jogging again. Tom caught up to her.

"And I figured you would go jogging."

Jessica glanced over at him. "You look a little better than the last time I saw you."

"I haven't had a drink since then. It's been tough, though."

"I'd kill for one right about now."

"Why, did something happen last night?"

Jessica let out a small laugh. "Oh, yeah." She kept jogging.

He reached out and stopped her. "What?"

"Sharon put a contract out all right." She yanked her arm away from him. Anger welled up in her for the first time since the assassin had walked into the studio. "Chris let one live."

She started running again. He kept pace with her.

"The rest, well, they didn't get the chance to hurt anyone," she said. "My kids saw what Chris did. And my four-year-old kept watch while Chris went to get Emily and Eric."

"I'm sorry."

Jessica looked over at him. "My *four-year-old*." She sped up.

"Which one?" Tom asked, speeding up too.

"CJ," she answered. "Chris's son. I told you, he has more power inside him than Chris, Eric, and me combined." She let out a little laugh. "And he is on pace to be a genius, just like his father."

Tom's eyebrows scrunched together, and he cocked his head to the side, looking more like an inquisitive puppy than a forty-year-old man.

She glanced over and caught his look. "Ty was a member of Mensa."

"And Tommy?"

She looked over at him again. "He's sweet." She smiled, refraining from saying 'like his father.

"Are you sure he doesn't have any abilities?"

Jessica shook her head. "He hasn't shown any signs at this point."

Tom quietly jogged with her for a moment. "Can I see him?"

Jessica kept running as she thought about it. "Someday."

"When?"

"When it's safe," she answered, shutting him down completely, and then a thought crossed her mind, making her tense up. She looked around them and over her shoulder. She couldn't see anyone following them, so she relaxed a fraction.

"What are you doing?" Tom asked, watching her.

"Making sure we haven't been followed. Being with you could be my death sentence."

Tom slowed to a stop. "Shit." He turned, tracing his jogging route back in the direction he had come.

Jessica breathed a sigh of relief. She had felt the turmoil in him when she said he could be her death sentence and was glad that he made the decision to leave her alone. Until this blew over, she couldn't associate with him. Otherwise, she'd put her entire family in danger. The only exception to that was the premiere, where she would confront Sharon in front of the world. She smiled at the thought and kept running.

She kept going until she passed in front of the Plaza Hotel and stopped. The blood drained from her face. She hadn't been back in this spot for just under five years, and she shivered, remembering the last time she was here.

"I had the same reaction," Tom said, making her jump. He was sitting on the bench behind her, trying to get his breath. "That was the last time I stayed at the Plaza until Sunday night."

Jessica put her foot on the bench next to where he sat and tightened her shoelaces. She switched feet and did the same with the other one while she glanced over at him. "What are you doing?"

"What do you mean?" He tried to sound innocent as her eyes bore into him.

"I'm getting married tomorrow, Tom."

"But you aren't married yet." He stood up and stretched.

"That doesn't matter," she shot back and stretched her legs on the bench without looking at him.

"Yes, it does, Jessie. You shouldn't be marrying a killer."

"Look..." She spun toward him. "I love him."

"You loved me, too," he pointed out. "That didn't seem to stop you from being with him when we were married."

Jessica glared at him and ran down the path that led straight through the park, back toward the apartment.

He took off after her, then bolted by her and stopped ahead of her, waiting for her to catch up. He started jogging a few paces ahead of her until they were in an extremely secluded spot in the park. He turned and took her in his arms, kissing her.

Jessica struggled against his tight grasp. "Tom, stop," she said from under his lips, inadvertently giving his tongue access to her mouth.

"Uh-uh," he replied without taking his mouth from hers, his tongue tasting the line of her lips.

"Let her go," Chris growled from behind them, his voice low and dangerous.

Tom's head whipped around, and his eyes locked with Chris's. His arms shot from Jessica, holding them out as he took a step away from her. She ran into Chris's arms.

"Don't hurt him," Jessica whispered, trying to diffuse the fury radiating from Chris.

"I should have known you would try something stupid. You led them right to her, you dumb son of a bitch."

"Who?"

"The fucking assassins your wife sicced on us." He glanced down at her. "I had a funny feeling and followed you. It's a good thing too." He raised his sharp glare in Tom's direction. "But don't worry, *those* assholes won't get a second chance." His teeth clenched, and he pointed at Tom. "And if you *ever* touch her again, you will find yourself in the hereafter, just like the bastards who keep trying to kill her. Now get the hell away from us." He turned and led her away.

TOM STARED UNTIL THEY disappeared from view, the frosty air chilling him to the bone as much as Chris's words had.

Assassins?

Here?

Shit.

He backtracked toward the Plaza again, trying to slough off the devastation encompassing his heart, but the pressure continued. She hadn't kissed back, and that leveled him, crushing any hope of ever holding her in his arms again. Chris was right, he had really lost this game. He craved the numbness that came from drinking. He shuffled back to the hotel, throwing himself face-first on the bed in despair.

"Did you think she would really pick you?"

Sharon's voice set off a volcanic eruption of fury. Tom's head shot up, his eyes narrowing at his quarry.

"Get out! Before I kill you." He pushed himself up and started toward her.

"I saw her tying her shoes while you sat on the bench next to her. What a pathetic loser. You ran after her just like the sick puppy you are, and based on how you look now, she shot you down," she taunted and pointed her index finger at him. "Because of you, she's dead."

Tom bit his tongue, knowing she was wrong because Jessica had the most extraordinary guardian angel this side of heaven. He went into gear, putting on the best acting job he had done in years, and let his eyes tear up.

"You bitch." He let the pain ring clear in his voice. "You fucking bitch," he screamed and took a step toward her, his hands balling into fists.

"I would hold that temper in check unless you want to go to jail."

He raised his eyebrow. "What the hell are you talking about?"

"If you leave me, I will release this letter to the police." She handed him a copy. "I have the original tucked away in a safe place."

He took it from her and scanned it. The frigid air outside was nothing compared to what slithered over his skin. He tightened his jaw against a shiver. His eyes rose from the confession letter penned in his own handwriting to her smug, smiling face and lost control. Fury struck in the form of a cracking backhand, and Sharon crumpled to the floor.

She laughed, her hand covering the bright red splotch on her cheek. "You being a drunk is a real benefit at times."

He clenched and unclenched his hand and looked back at the letter, slowly crumpling it and dropping it to the floor. "What makes you think that makes a difference now?" He reached down and took her by the throat, squeezing as he picked her up.

"If I die, her entire family dies."

He released her and stepped back. "You wouldn't."

"Oh yes I would, and I've got another lovely confession letter for that as well," she said, rubbing her neck.

Rage narrowed his field of vision, coloring the edges fiery red. He lashed out, striking her with his full weight behind the punch, connecting with the tender skin of her cheek, just below her right eye.

She sailed backward, tripping over the edge of the bed and falling to the floor. He followed, grabbed a handful of her shirt, and slammed her into the wall.

"There are far worse things than dying," he growled. "Far worse." He tossed her across the room and stormed out.

Tom walked into the hotel bar, still in his jogging outfit, and sat at the beautiful mahogany bar, then ordered a scotch straight up. "Keep 'em coming," he said to the bartender and put a couple hundred-dollar bills down on the surface.

"It's a little early," the bartender said.

Tom laughed. "I'd say it's about time." He downed the scotch and pushed the glass back to be refilled.

Two hours later, he stumbled to his room and passed out on the bed, oblivious to anything around him.

End Game Chapter 22

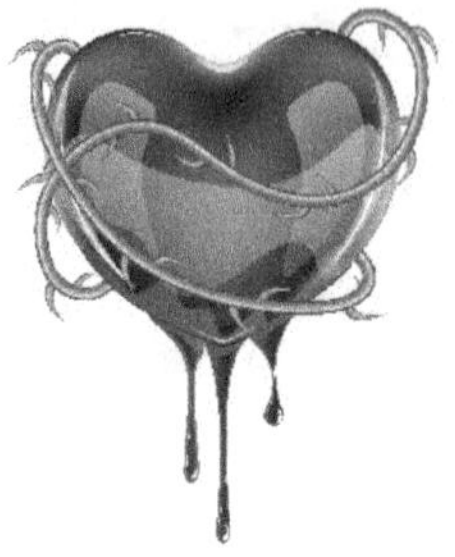

DESPITE THE ROCKY START to the day, the rest quietly flew by.

After dinner, Chris stood and gazed at Emily. "Do you mind watching the kids while your mother and I go out?"

"Not at all," she said.

Chris slipped down the hall to the bedroom, and Jessica followed.

"Where are we going?" she asked.

He reached into the closet and pulled out her fur coat. "You're going to need this." He handed her the coat and grabbed his long wool one. Turning, he rifled through his suitcase until he pulled out the two wrapped jewelry boxes and slid them into his pocket. "I'm giving you your wedding gifts a day early."

She smiled, getting the hint loud and clear, and pulled out the two gifts from her, leaving the necklace the kids picked out in her suitcase. "Where are we going?"

"It's a surprise." He took her by the elbow and escorted her into the living room. "Don't give your sister a hard time." He looked directly at CJ. "Understand?"

"Yeah, Daddy."

They gave hugs and kisses to the boys, and as Chris passed Eric, he ruffled his hair out of habit.

"Come on, man, I'm almost eighteen." Eric knocked his hand away.

"Yeah, but you'll always be the little boy who saved my sorry butt." Chris smiled at him. "That will never change."

"Whatever," Eric said to his soon-to-be stepfather.

"Eric saved you?" CJ looked up at his father.

Chris nodded and headed out with Jessica for the surprise date with his fiancée. They left the building all bundled up against the mid-February air, and he hailed a cab. He gave an address to the driver and leaned back, smiling. They pulled up next to the marina, and Chris paid the driver, holding the door and helping Jessica out of the car. A seventy-five-foot yacht sat on the dock with white Christmas lights wrapped around the deck.

A man in captain's garb approached them. "Mr. Ryan?"

"Yes."

"This way, please." He escorted them to the yacht and helped Jessica board.

"The cabin is all set for you, sir." He opened the door and waved them inside, but did not follow.

A gas fireplace burned in the corner, and rose petals covered the floor, giving the room a sweet rose tang with an underlying hint of vanilla, courtesy of dozens of candles. But the centerpiece drew her eyes: a lush round bed flanked by an extra-long nightstand holding strawberries, champagne glasses, and a chilled bottle of champagne. Alongside the strawberries sat a silver bowl full of whipped cream.

Chris took her coat and draped it on the chair, then peeled his off as well before crossing to the sound system. When he pressed the play button, soft music piped through the room. He walked to her and wrapped his arms around her, taking a steadying step when the boat pulled forward, beginning their evening cruise around Manhattan.

"Surprise."

She surveyed the room, her heart pounding with rejuvenated adoration. Her gaze lingered on the strawberries and whipped cream before turning toward the windows, the city lights trailing in every direction. "Wow. How long do we have?"

"As long as you want. When we go up on deck, that's when they'll head back."

"Ah." She smiled at him. "And what exactly did you have in mind?"

He grinned and tugged her shirt over her head, glancing toward the strawberries. "Ten years ago, I made a sorry attempt to seduce you. This time, I want to do it right. This time, I want to love you the way you deserve to be loved."

She melted in his arms. Overwhelming joy and underlying anticipation tingled through every skin cell, and she blinked back a thin film of tears. His eyes, his words, his hands owned her.

She whispered, "Oh, Ty."

He undressed her, leaving only her bra and underwear for the moment. "Just one more thing." He went over to his coat. He pulled out a box and brought it to her. "Your first wedding gift."

She slid her fingernail under the shimmering paper, daintily peeling it away from the blue velvet box. Before she opened it, she caught a quick glance at his face. He grinned like their four-year-olds on Christmas morning. She opened the lid, and her hand fluttered to her mouth. Brilliant diamonds sparkled from the crushed velvet, more diamonds than she had ever seen.

She raised her eyes to him. "My God, Chris, it's beautiful," she whispered.

He took the diamond eternity necklace out and clasped it around her neck. "Not nearly as beautiful as the neck it sits on." He smiled, swept her in his arms, and then placed her on the bed. After stripping off her bra and underwear, he took a seat on the edge of the bed and ran his fingers from her neckline to her belly button and sighed. When he looked back into her eyes, he smiled. "Smoldering yet?"

"Oh yeah," she said, her skin breaking out in goose pimples.

He picked up the first strawberry and put it to her mouth, and she wrapped her lips around the sweet fruit, biting the bulk of it and leaving only the stem in his hand.

A hint of a dimple appeared in his cheek, and his eyes positively sparkled, more so than the diamonds gracing her neck. She swallowed the treat and licked her lips, watching him toss the top onto the tray and dip the next one in the whipped cream.

He barely touched her lips with the strawberry, leaving a hint of cream on them, and then he ran the strawberry down the side of her neck, leaving a thin path of white. He bit into the strawberry, put the remainder of it back on the tray, and leaned over to kiss her. She turned her head, grinning and trembling, and he paused, letting a soft chuckle escape.

That chuckle thrilled her as much as the heat of his tongue riding the length of the whipped cream trail as he gently removed it from her skin. Heat that spread over her body and pooled between her legs.

"I don't know if I can hold out as long as I did the first time." He picked up the next strawberry with a shaky hand. "Hell, I still don't know how I walked away from you then."

Jessica smiled. She was the last person to answer that question; she herself had almost given in to her desire in the same situation a lifetime ago, chained to a mattress in that cold concrete room with a much different man running strawberries and whipped cream over her skin. She wondered if they would be here, now, and so in love if she had given in to his whims.

"I'd like to think so." He dipped another strawberry in the cream and ran it in between her breasts before offering it to her. Leaning over, he licked the cream off her skin, slowly, deliberately, creating an inferno in her, aided by the spread of his lips into his signature smile.

"Tell me you want me."

She laughed and shook her head. Not yet. Oh no, she wanted to draw this pleasure out. She wanted the seduction. She wanted his tongue buried between her legs, and she wanted to see him lose control first.

He raised an eyebrow and dipped his finger into the bowl, then brought a healthy dollop of whipped cream to her nipples. He traced the hard nubs before letting her suck the sweet confection from his finger. He leaned over, licking the cream from each breast, lingering on her nipples, flicking, nipping, and sucking.

Wisps of pleasure ran from each breast, sending her heart into the frantic mating beat that echoed between her legs.

He moved onto the bed, spreading her legs and kneeling between them. Anticipation of his touch sent tremors down her spine, and his blue eyes penetrated her. His grin widened, deepening the dimples in his cheek. His cream-dipped finger traced a line from her knee to inside her hip, cool compared to the lightning heat of his tongue. The slow progression produced a sweet wetness, an aching for him to finish this slow madness and just make love to her. He repeated the motion with her other leg, and she sighed, shivering, with her arms pinned above her.

He took a moment to explore her belly button with his tongue, the depths, the shape, the trembling skin surrounding it, ending with a wet kiss before he met her gaze. "God, I love you," he whispered, and the repeat seduction changed direction from the original. Instead of crawling up her body and gently kissing her like he did ten years ago, he kissed a line straight to the spot she craved.

What he did with his mouth, his tongue, his fingers, shot her into orbit. She arched into each wet rush he elicited. Orgasm after orgasm after orgasm, she yearned to feel him inside her, his body pressed to hers.

"Please, please, dear God, please fuck me," she whispered.

Chris continued his erotic feast and then peeled off his clothing. Moments later, he trailed kisses up her stomach, lingering for a moment on her chest, and then to her lips. Nothing compared to his hardness sliding inside her. She moaned under his mouth, their hips circling as lazily as their tongues. Chris controlled his passion and she reveled in hers.

He lost control for a moment, riding hard and fast, a line of sweat forming on his forehead, and then he stopped.

"Don't stop!"

Closing his eyes, he exhaled and chuckled. "Almost got me, but not quite." He opened his eyes and grinded with slow hip circles, smiling down at her pleading eyes. "Say it."

"I love you." She yanked him to her lips, kissing him with abandon. His familiar game set her into overdrive. She gasped when she came up for air. "Faster."

He laughed. "Beg." He continued his slow, seductive pace.

"You are driving me crazy. Please."

He pulled out and then slammed his full length into her, his grin widening. "Like that?"

"God, yes!"

Moving deliberately, he repeated the slow, hard strokes, and each time her body responded, shuddering, coming, causing her to cry out with the power he had over her. Before him, she couldn't imagine ever loving so completely, so deeply, like he was a part of her. Now he owned her, mind, body, and soul.

They matched motion for motion, movement for movement, hip thrust for hip thrust, creating a pleasure so surreal that for a moment she thought she was dreaming.

He chuckled, and she opened her eyes, staring into his bright blue irises, into his soul.

"This isn't a dream," he said, smiling down at her, gleaning her thoughts.

"If it is, I never want to wake up," she said, her voice hoarse from exertion. "Now roll."

Dimples appeared, and he rolled, adjusting so they lay in the center of the round bed. His hands grasped her waist. She smiled at the slightly wet edges of his hair and the sex-crazed gleam in his eyes and then sat up, circling her hips and stretching her arms in the air. His hands explored her torso, her breasts, her waistline. Sensual brushes against her damp skin, creating a masterpiece of heat.

She glanced around at the steamed windows, watching small droplets of water slice through the fog, and smiled before returning her attention to him. Grabbing his wrists, she pinned them by his head, taking control of the pace and riding him hard until the orgasm consumed her, ripping a cry of pleasure from her chest.

Shuddering with aftershocks, she kissed him, slowing her hip movement and catching her breath. "Tell me what you want," she whispered as she pulled away from him.

"You. All I've ever wanted is you." He wrapped his arms around her and took the reins, rolling and pulling her legs apart, and then frantically slammed his hips to hers. Arching, he cried, "Jess!"

The force of his load triggered another orgasm, and Jessica shook with it, repeating "oh, God, oh, God, oh God" until the trembling subsided. Out of all the times they made love over the past ten years, tonight was by far the ultimate in sensual satiation. She wrapped her legs around his trembling ones, the two intertwined like a human pretzel.

"Jesus, woman, that was amazing." Chris propped himself on his elbows and stared down at her. A silly smile was plastered on his lips and his eyelids were at half-mast. He rolled off her and stretched on the bed next to her, closing his eyes for the moment. "Give me a second, and I'll be good for another round."

"Okay. In the meantime..." She slid off the bed, crossed to her coat and pulled out the box containing his chain. She crawled over him, straddling his lap. "Your wedding gift."

He leaned on one elbow and opened the box, smiling at the chain glimmering in the candlelight. "I love it," he said.

Jessica plucked it from the box and clasped it around his neck, and the glint of gold resting on his collarbone did exactly what she thought it would. Her body clenched in response to the sudden swell of heat. She pressed her lips against the skin just below the chain, tasting the salty tinge of his sweat, his musky scent overpowering the rose petals. Passion ignited.

"I love you." She sat up, twirling her hips, grinding against his resting shaft.

He responded, stiffening under her weight.

This time, they moved hard and fast, entwined in a mass of arms and legs, his lips tracing the graceful curve of her neck, his teeth nibbling her earlobe, tickling the skin with his short bursts of breath.

"Jess," he whispered. "Oh God, Jess."

The sigh that followed accompanied his fall backwards, dragging her down on the bed with him.

His strong heartbeat echoed in her ear, her head nestled on his chest and their breath labored. Calming, she traced his chest and shoulder blade with her fingers, trailing the fine gold. He stroked her hair, running his fingers through the long locks, deepening her state of relaxation.

Finally, she lifted her head and met his peaceful gaze.

"I knew tomorrow would be a little hectic, and I wanted to have a special night with you," he admitted. "So, I guess this is our pseudo wedding night."

He kissed her cheek and rolled her off him, then sat up and grabbed the champagne bottle. He popped the cork, poured two glasses, and handed one to her.

"Here is to a million years of happiness." He clinked her glass and took a sip, his eyes sparkling as much as the bubbly. Nimbly, he plucked a couple of strawberries out of the bowl and handed one to her. "These are fantastic."

"They are." She smiled and put her lips around the strawberry, sucking it before biting down, severing the sweet fruit from the crown.

"I swear, girl, you are going to kill me."

She chuckled, running her fingers down his sweaty arm. "I think we need a shower."

"Mm-hm," he replied. "I like shower sex with you."

Jessica laughed. "You have energy for more?"

"Hell yeah." He smiled. "This is just the beginning. I can go all night with you."

"We can't leave the kids all night. They'll worry."

"True, but I'm not ready to go back." He kissed her neck. He leaned up and ran his finger around the outline of the diamond necklace. "This looks beautiful on you."

"It's a beautiful necklace."

"On an exquisite woman." His eyes smoldered.

She glanced at his lap, his cock hardening to attention. "Good God, Chris, you're going to end up killing *me*, not the other way around."

"I'm not Chris right now."

"Ty, you are insatiable."

"That I am," he agreed and kissed her. "Come on."

He pulled her off the bed and led her into the master bathroom. The shower was typical of any boat, a snug fit for two, but he pulled her in anyway. Their lips found each other, tongues rolling in lazy circles, exploring the depths of each other's mouths. Soapy hands wandered, washing, cleaning the sweat off their skin. Lather ran down the drain, forgotten in the wake of the kiss.

He pulled away and took the soap, cleaning himself before returning the soap to the shelf. He ran his clean hands through her hair, getting it soaked in the stream of warm water.

Jessica ran her hands down his chest, over his finely chiseled abs, and down to his hard member, wrapping her fingers around him. "Insatiable," she said, chuckling. She stood on her tiptoes and kissed him before dropping her kisses to his chest, trailing down over the path her fingers blazed. Dropping to her knees, she took him in her mouth, rolling her tongue over the sensitive tip. The sweet scent of Ivory soap drifted from him, and the trickle of warm water gave her lips a slick surface to glide on.

"Jess," he whispered and leaned against the wall with his hands buried in her hair.

She sucked him with long, slow strokes, alternating between sucking and licking the length of his hard shaft, flicking her tongue around his tip before sliding his length into her mouth. She smiled at the tremble in his hands while they stroked her soaking hair, at his throaty, sexy voice repeating her name with reverence.

She sped up her strokes and was rewarded with a torrent flooding her mouth, and she sucked through each subsequent tremor until he groaned. She sat back and wiped her lips with the back of her hand, squinting into the spray.

Chris's glossy eyes met hers as he reached down, helping her to her feet. He grabbed her face and kissed her hard, not caring where her mouth had just been.

"I can't wait until you're my wife." He turned off the water.

"I can't wait to be your wife." She wrapped the towel he offered around her. She crossed into the room and found the trail of clothing, then slipped her clothes on and glanced in his direction in time to see his boxers cover his sweet ass. She stood, scanning his bare torso, her eyes lingering on the gold against his skin. She licked her lips.

He laughed and raised his eyebrows. "You want to go again?"

Jessica blushed; she could go all night, just like Chris could. "We have to get home soon." She reached into the pocket of her coat, then pulled out the other gift she had bought him. She shyly handed it over.

He opened it, smiling. A slick two-tone Rolex with diamonds as the four points on the watch and chips for the rest lay inside the box. "Wow." He slid it on his wrist, and set the clasp, smiling up at her. "You definitely have great taste."

"I like to think so."

He turned, pulling two more boxes from the inside pocket of his coat, and then handed them to her.

"You got me more than this?" She touched the necklace.

She opened the boxes and gasped at the matching bracelet and earrings, then put the studs in her ears and held her wrist out so he could put the bracelet on. "You went overboard," she said, checking out the prisms of light reflecting off the bracelet.

"I want you to sparkle tomorrow."

"I love you." She wrapped her arms around his neck and planted a kiss. "But we have to get home." She moved his wrist so she could see the time. They had been gone for close to four hours.

"I would be lost without you." He stepped out of her arms and slipped his shoes back on. He shook his hair and ran his hands through it to get it in some semblance of order before grabbing their coats and helping Jessica with hers.

The boat passed the Statue of Liberty when they emerged on deck. Chris gave a nod to the captain. Jessica shivered in the cold air, her wet hair enhancing the chill, and Chris wrapped his arms around her.

"Do you want to wait inside?"

"No, the Manhattan skyline is so beautiful. I can deal with a little chill."

He chuckled. "It's freezing out here."

She turned and looked up at him. "Do you want to wait inside?"

"No." His dimple-enhanced grin flashed. "I like the view, too. I still can't believe we're getting married tomorrow."

"Yeah, well, if our wedding night is anything like tonight, we might be dead by the end of the weekend." She smiled up at him.

He burst out laughing, pulled her closer, and kissed her. "If we didn't have the boys, I would never leave the bedroom again."

Her laughter died in her throat as the nightmare came flooding back.

"What is it?" he asked.

"Nothing." She smiled uneasily at him.

He waited, raising his eyebrow.

"The nightmare I had last night."

"Honey, it was just a nightmare, and as I said last night, I don't plan on dying any time soon. I've got the rest of my life with you, and I want it to be long."

BECAUSE ONCE I DIE, that's it. I'm heading straight to hell, never to see you again.

And that was his worst nightmare.

End Game Chapter 23

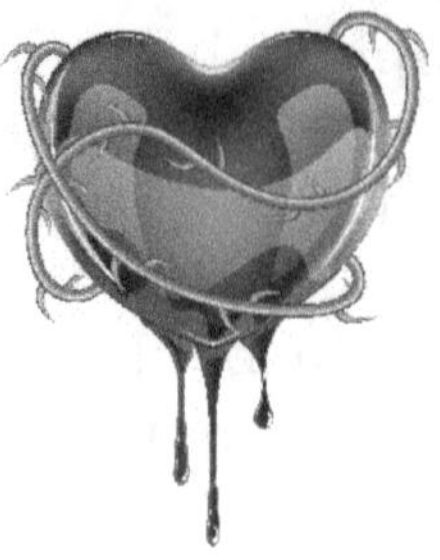

THE DARKNESS ENVELOPED CHRIS, and it was so cold. He shivered, looking for any signs of light. The complete blackness disoriented him, and he slowly circled, his arms in front of him, reaching for anything solid. He pushed the ebbing panic away.

"Jess?" The sound of his voice fell flat as if in a void. "Jess," he screamed, but as before, the sound went nowhere.

He kneeled down and put his hands on what he thought was the floor and pulled them away from a sticky slime in disgust.

Laughter filled the void.

Chris jumped.

"You will never see her again," the familiar voice boomed.

Chris covered his ears, wincing at the decibels pressing against his eardrums, flaring sharp pain. Deep darkness blinded him, and he couldn't see where the voice came from.

"You will never see anything again." The laughter continued. "Welcome to hell, little brother."

Chris sat up in bed, his eyes wide with terror as they darted around the dark room. The familiar setting coming into focus slowed his frantic heart. Jessica slept peacefully in the bed next to him and he sighed, glancing at the clock. It wasn't even four in the morning.

He rubbed his face, lying back on his pillow. He stared at the ceiling, trying to make heads or tails of the nightmare, and when no answers came, he rolled on his side and ran his fingers gently through her hair. He closed his eyes and felt the texture of each strand against his skin, memorizing the feel and smell of it. He ran his hand down her arm, and a slow smile crossed his lips as she stirred under his touch.

She rolled and looked at him. "Morning."

"Not quite. It's only a little before four."

"What are you doing awake?"

"Nightmare," he answered, continuing to graze her skin, his eyes still closed.

Jessica moved closer to him. "Was it Frank?"

"In a manner of speaking, yes," he said, continuing his exploration of her body with the tips of his fingers, memorizing her curves and the feel of her skin.

"What are you doing?" She laughed as he ran his hand up her side, tickling her unintentionally.

"Memorizing the way you feel."

"Why?"

"I may need to know."

"Chris?"

He opened his eyes and looked into hers, seeing the concern. "I'm not going anywhere," he assured her. "Go back to sleep. We have a long day today."

She did as he said, drifting back to sleep within minutes.

Chris closed his eyes and continued memorizing the feel of her skin, and he, too, drifted back asleep as his hand came to rest on her waist.

End Game Chapter 24

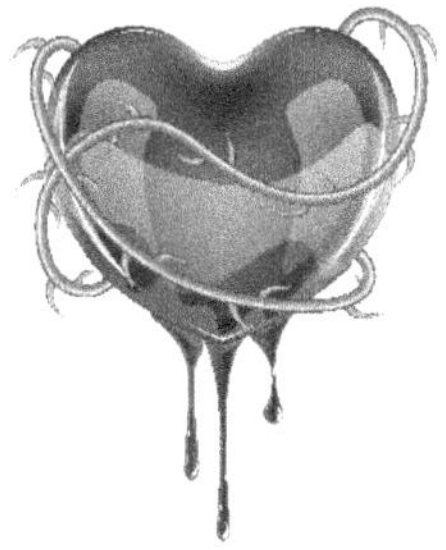

THE BED SHOOK, JERKING Chris awake.

CJ and Tommy jumped on top of them. "It's time to get up!"

"Hey, we told you to stay out of their room," Eric whispered from the hallway.

"It's okay." Chris rubbed his eyes. "What time is it, anyway?"

"A little after noon," Eric replied.

"You were able to keep them out of here this long?" Chris asked with a small laugh as Jessica wrapped her arms around CJ and Tommy, doling out kisses.

"It wasn't easy. But we figured you needed your rest."

"But that only gives us a couple of hours to get ready." Jessica released the boys and hopped off the bed, heading into the bathroom to start her wedding day preparations.

Chris watched her go and then turned his attention to the boys. "Thanks. We needed the rest." He stretched.

CJ and Tommy tackled him, and Eric gave a nod, turning away from the door.

"Eric, I have a suit for you," Chris called after him as the boys relentlessly tickled him.

"I know," Eric said. "I got it from your closet last night. Thanks." He disappeared from sight.

The boys continued wrestling with Chris, tickling and jumping back and forth like little lemurs.

"Have you two eaten?" He grabbed their little hands.

"Yes, we had breakfast and lunch," CJ answered.

"Then I guess it's time for a bath."

"Aww, do we have to?" they both whined.

Chris nodded and threw back the covers. "You need to be nice and clean and be the perfect little gentlemen today, understand?"

They nodded.

"Can I carry the rings?" CJ asked.

"You each can carry one."

"I want to carry Mommy's," Tommy said.

"That's okay. I want to carry Daddy's." CJ pushed his little brother.

"Let's go." Chris pulled on a pair of sweatpants.

Bathing two four-year-old boys was a little like herding cats. Chris had to stifle laughter a few times and mop up stray puddles from the constant splashing. He managed to get their hair washed and their bodies squeaky clean before pulling them out of the tub, then towel drying and dressing them in their little suits.

"Now this means you can't get into anything until after the wedding, you hear?"

CJ nodded, and Tommy followed his lead. Chris brought them into the living room where they happily climbed onto the couch next to Eric and picked up the extra controllers.

Once they were settled, he stepped into the bedroom and whistled. Jessica smiled up at him from the edge of the bed, rolling her nylons gracefully up her legs and clipping them to her white garter belt. The simple motion moved him, stirring the need for her, and he inhaled, closing the door behind him.

"Get going," she said, tilting her head toward the bathroom.

"It won't take me that long." He crossed to her, reaching out and running his fingers over her bare shoulders.

"There's no time for that."

He glanced at the clock, and his eyes widened. He only had a little more than a half hour to get ready before the car picked them up. Grabbing his clothes, he headed into the bathroom.

Chris emerged from the bedroom twenty minutes later decked out in his tailored Armani suit and a crisp white shirt open at the collar, revealing the gold chain she'd given him. The watch poked out from behind the diamond cufflinks.

He stopped in his tracks at the living room entry. His breath caught in his chest at the sight of her. Stunning was an understatement. She turned, flashing him a smile that made his legs lock in place, holding him upright against the urge to fall to his knees in front of his angel.

Her dark hair flowed in ringlets over her shoulders. Her eyelids were accented with soft shades of blue, bringing out that color from the calico combination in her eyes. Her lips looked like pink rose petals glistening in the morning dew. He couldn't remember her looking more beautiful.

"Wow," he said.

Seeing her triggered something. His eyes got a little wider, and he turned back toward the bedroom. *The rings.*

Jessica laughed. "It would not be good to forget those," she called after him.

He came out, slipping the ring boxes in his pocket and holding his camera. "I want a picture of the kids," he said. "Come on."

He rounded them up onto the balcony, sat Emily in the chair and had Eric kneel on one knee on the side facing her, positioning CJ and Tommy between Eric and Emily. With highly inappropriate jokes, he got them laughing and snapped off at least a dozen pictures, grinning from behind the camera lens, capturing the group and individual close-ups as quickly as any professional photographer.

"Now you and Mom." Eric stood, taking the camera out of Chris's hand. Eric moved the chair and pointed to the spot he wanted Chris to stand and then went inside to get his mother, escorting her to stand next to Chris in the cold air.

Chris put his arm around her, and they smiled for the camera, forever capturing the start of the most memorable day of their lives.

Chris pulled out coats for each of them from the hall closet and smiled as Jessica approached. He pulled out the beautiful white mink shawl and wrapped it around her, kissing her on the cheek. "You look more beautiful today than I ever remember you looking."

"So do you."

He escorted her out, closed and locked the apartment door behind him, and met the rest of their family at the elevator. They stepped into the lobby a few minutes later and the door attendant nodded to them as he held the door.

"Your car is waiting, sir," he said as Chris approached at the tail end of the group.

Chris smiled and hung back a moment, watching as they filed into the waiting limousine. He pulled out a tip for the doorman. "Thanks, Fred."

"Always a pleasure, Mr. Ryan." He pocketed the bill without looking. "What's the occasion?"

"I'm getting married." Chris grinned.

"Congratulations, sir."

"Thank you." Chris slid into the car. It took everything he had not to fidget in the seat. Excitement thrummed in his veins, and he couldn't wait until the last surprise was sprung on his bride-to-be.

"And what surprise would that be?" Jessica smiled from the other side of the car.

Chris grinned and exchanged a quick glance with Eric.

"I already know." Eric smiled.

"Keep that wise-ass mouth of yours shut," he warned with a small laugh.

"Yes, sir." Eric saluted, and they broke out laughing. "Does this mean that after today I have to call you Dad?"

Chris cocked his head. "You can call me anything you want." He hadn't thought Eric and Emily would call him anything but Chris.

They pulled up at City Hall, and an elderly gentleman opened the door, helping each one out.

Chris hugged the man. "It's good to see you, Sam." He smiled and held his hand out to help Jessica from the car.

Her eyebrows knit together at the stranger.

"Jessica, this is Sam Trueman. He's my lawyer and probably the closest thing to family that I've got. He's represented the Aris family for as long as I can remember." *And he believes I'm Chris.*

"It's a pleasure meeting you." Jessica extended her hand.

"The pleasure's all mine." Sam took her hand, bringing it to his lips and pasting a dry peck on the back in gentleman's fashion. "Chris told me so much about you, but you are more stunning than he described."

"Thank you." She blushed and let Sam escort her up the steps.

Chris spoke briefly with the driver and then headed up after them. He caught up and held the door for Jessica and Sam.

"The judge's office is this way." Sam led the family down the hall and into Judge Henry Sampson's chambers.

JESSICA ENTERED AND GASPED. The joy of the day increased threefold at the sight of her parents and her sister. She twirled and threw her arms around Chris's neck, kissing his cheek. Her vision distorted through tears as she blinked them away.

"Thank you," she whispered and swallowed the lump in her throat.

"Surprise." He brushed his lips against her cheek.

"Nana, Papa!" the boys yelled and ran to them, wrapping their arms around their knees in fierce bear hugs.

Judge Sampson smiled, scanning the chaos in his chamber before clearing his throat.

Chris crouched and called the boys to him, handing each one a box. "You need to give us these when the judge asks for them, okay?"

CJ and Tommy nodded, and then everyone took their places.

Jessica and Chris stood in the center, bordered by CJ and Tommy. The rest of the group fanned out behind them.

Judge Sampson began. "The step which you are about to take is the most important into which human beings can come. It is a union of two people founded upon mutual respect and affection. Your lives will change, your responsibilities will increase, but your joy will be multiplied if you are sincere and earnest with your pledge to one another." He paused and looked at the two of them. "Do any of the witnesses know of any reason why we may not legally continue with this wedding?"

Everyone shook their heads.

"Chris, will you have this woman to be your wedded wife, to love her, comfort her, honor and keep her, and forsaking all others, keep only unto her, for so long as you both shall live?"

"I will."

"Jessica, will you have this man to be your wedded husband, to love him, comfort him, honor and keep him, and forsaking all others, keep only unto him, so long as you both shall live?"

"I will." Jessica smiled up at Chris.

"Take hands and repeat after me." He waited until they were holding hands and voiced the vows.

Chris stared into her eyes, and she could see the bright sheen of tears pooling. He blinked them back, but his voice never faltered. "I, Chris, take you, Jessica, to be my wedded wife, to have and to hold, for better, for worse, for richer or poorer, to love and cherish, from this day forward."

The judge turned to Jessica and repeated the instructions.

"I, Jessica, take you, Chris"—she paused and thought *Ty*, causing his smile to widen a fraction—"to be my wedded husband, to have and hold, for better or for worse, for richer or poorer, to love and cherish, from this day forward." Her voice wavered, shaking with emotions overwhelming her.

"Do you have a ring for the bride?" Judge Sampson asked.

"Yes." Chris turned to Tommy, putting his hand out.

Tommy placed the box in his father's hand. Chris took the ring out and handed Tommy the box again, then patted his head in appreciation.

Chris slid the ring on her ring finger and looked into her eyes. "With this ring, I thee wed." He blinked back tears.

"Is there a ring for the groom?"

"Yes," Jessica replied and turned to CJ.

"Here Mommy." CJ opened the box and took out the ring, placed it in her palm, and smiled up at her.

"Thank you, sweetie." Jessica turned to Chris. Sliding the ring on his finger, she repeated the judge's instructions. "With this ring, I thee wed." Blinking didn't work for her, and a tear brimmed, and traced a hot path down her cheek.

"Let these rings be given and received as a token of your affection, sincerity, and fidelity to one another." Judge Sampson paused for a moment. "In as much as Chris and Jessica have consented together in wedlock and have witnessed the same before this company, and pledged their vows to each other, by the authority vested in me by the state of New York, I now pronounce you husband and wife."

Chris and Jessica smiled at each other.

"Son, you can kiss your bride," the judge whispered, leaning closer to Chris.

Chris leaned in and pressed his warm, wet lips to hers, and the world disappeared. His kiss, tender and sweet, filled her with overwhelming joy, more so than the words of the judge. She laid her hand on his chest, feeling the thud of his heart hammering against her palm, and when they broke apart, his blue eyes shimmered with tears.

"My wife." His husky voice gave away the emotions inside, and he blinked his eyes clear before turning toward the family. A grin spread over his lips.

AFTER THE PAPERWORK WAS signed and dotted, Chris peeled off a hefty tip for the judge. "Thank you again, Judge Sampson. I appreciate you fitting us into your busy schedule."

"Put your money away, son. This was a favor to Sam."

"Seriously." Chris put the money in his hand. "It's the least I can do." He folded the judge's fingers around the bills. "If you don't want to accept it, give it to charity, but I'm leaving this with you." He smiled and escorted his family out of the judge's chambers to the waiting limousines.

They arrived at the South Street Seaport ten minutes later and boarded a privately chartered ferry. As the boat pulled out toward the Statue of Liberty, Chris led Jessica out onto the dance floor. The light music transitioned, and he took her in his arms and twirled her around with ease, expertly navigating the small dance floor. He sang the words to "Calling All Angels" loud enough for her to hear over the piped in music.

"I must be dreaming because I believe I am holding an angel," he whispered in her ear and then dipped her before she could respond.

When he pulled her back to his chest, she whispered, "I love you."

"I know." He kissed her before twirling her off the dance floor.

"What else have you planned?" she asked.

"Dinner at Tavern on the Green, and afterwards I have cars available to take your sister and your folks home and the kids back to the apartment."

HER FATHER GATHERED THEM on the bow of the boat and took at least a dozen photographs, including one of Chris dipping Jessica and grinning into the camera. She flipped through the digital display, stopped on that particular picture, and smiled. His eyes smoldered. She glanced at him crouched between CJ and Tommy, pointing to the passing mid-town high rises.

"Thank you, Daddy." Jessica kissed her father's cheek.

The boat pulled up to the docks at the 42nd Street pier.

"For what?"

"For being here and accepting Chris," she said, and she watched her husband pick up the two boys in each arm. Happiness radiated from him, touching a special place in her heart, and he caught her staring in his direction, flashing a quick, secretive smile.

"I was surprised when he came by the other day."

"He came by?"

"He asked for our blessing."

Jessica put her fingers over her lips as her vision blurred. She blinked the tears away, but the lump in her throat persisted. She just assumed he'd called and invited them to the wedding.

"He was nervous." Russ smiled. "More nervous than Dan ever was. At least he didn't have a fire to run off to in the middle of the conversation." He winked at her.

Jessica chuckled. Dan's volunteer firefighter days had gone by the wayside soon after they married, more because they moved out of town than his desire to quit.

She glanced in Chris's direction. "Nervous?" She couldn't envision that, not for a man who was so in control of his emotions.

His eyes found hers, and a dimple appeared briefly before his attention was pulled to the boys. There was a fire all right, but not the kind her father was talking about.

"We wouldn't have missed this one. This one's forever, isn't it?"

Jessica nodded. "This is the man I've been waiting for my whole life, Dad."

"He certainly loves you and those kids," Russ said, watching his new son-in-law carry the boys off the boat and set them on the dock.

Chris turned and helped Emily off the boat, and she took the boys up to the waiting car and slipped inside. The rest of the crew followed.

Chris stopped Jessica halfway to the car and kissed her. "I still can't believe this day is real."

Dinner went by in a flash, and before they knew it, the check was delivered, and they walked outside where the cars waited.

Jessica smiled at the beautiful horse-drawn carriage. Two impeccably groomed white stallions pulled the enclosed white carriage. Mirrored windows tinted with a golden hue gave the impression of luxury, like a modern Cinderella carriage emblazoned with gold trim.

"Definitely over the top." She met his gaze, the amusement dancing in his eyes making her smile. "I assume that's for us?" She pointed as the group ogled.

"Absolutely," Chris smiled.

Hugs were given to Russ, Joanna, Julia, and Kurt and they got into the limousine that would take them home, waving madly as they went.

Chris took out his keys, handed them to Emily, and opened the door of the town car for her and the kids. "Thank you for watching the boys again tonight."

Emily nodded. "Anytime."

Eric stopped at the door, locking eyes with Chris. "Make sure that bitch pays."

"Don't worry. That's the next thing on my agenda," Chris said.

"Welcome to the family, Ty." He hugged his stepfather and hopped into the car without looking back.

End Game Chapter 25

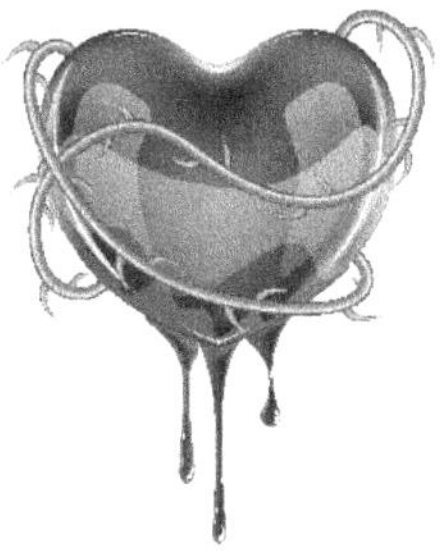

TOM STEPPED OUT OF the limousine and stood smiling at the flashing cameras. He didn't bother helping Sharon out; instead, he crossed to the designated spot and turned around, facing the swarming reporters and the street beyond. A quick glance at his watch told him they'd arrive any time, and he fielded questions, ignoring Sharon muscling her way through the crowd to take the spot next to him. She had done an exceptional job covering the bruises with make-up and a conveniently tied scarf around her neck.

She threaded her arm around his, but he jerked away, glaring at her. A wave of silence settled over the crowd for a moment, targeting the tension between them, and then the pack went into attack mode, shooting questions about their relationship one after another. He scanned the street, letting her deal with the barracudas.

Tom laughed out loud when he saw the carriage round the corner, and the crowd followed his gaze, parting like the Red Sea when it pulled up to the red carpet. Quiet settled over the crowd, and they looked expectantly at the carriage.

SHARON'S PHONE RANG, AND she looked down at the number. She answered it. "Now isn't a good time."

"I'm not on the payroll anymore," John said into her ear.

"Why not?" Sharon asked, not really paying attention.

"You don't want to fuck with the guy she's with. He can make people disappear," John said. "He said to tell you that you just unleashed Ty Aris, and he's coming after you."

Sharon shivered and closed her phone, attempting to smile at the crowd, but the heat drained out of her face, leaving her cold and frightened.

CHRIS WATCHED THE COLOR drain from Sharon's face and smiled. "Perfect timing." He glanced back at Jessica. "You ready for this?"

Jessica glanced down at the wedding band on her hand and back at him. "Yes, your wife is ready."

Chris stepped out of the carriage, and the hush that had settled over the crowd turned into a gasp. The reporters knew who he was, but he kept them at bay until he reached inside, and she stepped out.

They swarmed.

TOM GLANCED AT SHARON with a grin. "I invited them," he said. Cutting through the sea of reporters, he greeted them over their murmurs.

"You look beautiful," Tom said, taking her hands.

"Careful, that's my wife you're talking to." Chris smiled and put out his hand.

Tom shook it and gave Chris a quick hug. "She threatened the family, too," he whispered in Chris's ear. "It's good to see you," he said louder and stepped back, catching the deadly flash in Chris's eyes.

"It's good to see you, too." Chris provided the pleasantries for the purpose of the crowd and put his arm around Jessica, leading her into the building with Tom, leaving Sharon struggling to get through the human wall that formed in their wake.

"Hell of an entrance." Tom laughed when they were out of earshot. He glanced at Jessica. "I thought you hated the attention."

"I do." Jessica looked up at Chris. "But the look on her face was worth it." She smiled and glanced over her shoulder as the doors opened and Sharon stumbled in.

Tom ignored his wife and escorted Jessica and Chris inside the theater, seating them in the VIP box with him, closing the door behind him. There were only three seats in the box, just as he'd planned, and Sharon sat in the back with the producers and director, seething and glaring over at them.

He glanced at Jessica's left hand, and then over at Chris. "Congratulations," he said without enthusiasm, and took her hand to look at the ring. He put it down since touching her skin stirred more than old feelings.

"She's not going to call off the dogs. She's expanding the contract." Tom turned his head in Sharon's direction.

"I don't think so." Chris leaned back and smiled as he stretched his legs.

Tom turned back to both their smiles.

"That call she got when we pulled up was from the first assassin she sicced on us," Chris said. "And he told her she just unleashed Ty Aris."

Tom raised his eyebrows.

"And he was coming after her."

THE THEATER DIMMED TO black, and Chris took Jessica's hand in his, focusing on the front of the theater. Heat crept over his skin, and he shifted in the seat, blinking wildly. The dream from the other night barreled back, creating a low-level panic attack until his eyes adjusted.

The bright projector light hit the screen, blinding him, and he squinted as the opening credits rolled across the screen.

Jessica's hand tightened on his as the events of her captivity flashed on the screen. He kept his face stoic, trying not to let the emotions brewing in the pit of his stomach reflect in his eyes. Guilt, remorse, and sorrow swept through him at the more than accurate portrayal of the monster he once had been. Tom did an exceptional job portraying Ty, both the sick perversely twisted side and the tortured conscience, as well as reflecting the love he felt for Jessica.

He forced his body to relax and secured the floodgates against the rising tide.

He could win an Oscar for this, she thought, and he inhaled. She was right; Tom should win an Oscar for nailing the performance.

"I love you," she whispered in his ear.

Chris closed his eyes and squeezed her hand, opening them to the strawberries and cream seduction scene on screen. He felt her eyes on him and glanced at her sideways without turning his head. *I hope I made that a better memory last night.*

She nodded. *You did.*

This is fucking surreal, he thought, locking down the turmoil inside. Twirling the ring on his left hand with his thumb, he kept stealing glances at the platinum band, validating again and again that she was indeed his wife.

The only time Jessica turned away from the screen and buried her face in his chest was when the screen filled with the events leading to Mike's death. He had to hand it to Hollywood—they certainly knew how to stage a death realistically.

Chris leaned down and kissed the back of her head, and the sorrow spinning in his body took the control it was so desperately fighting for. Burning tears filled his eyes and throat and dripped into her hair, and he cast a glance at Tom, meeting his gaze and wondering how she could love someone like Ty. He pressed his lips to her hair and leaned back, drawing a shaky breath and swiping his face with his hand, erasing the wet tears. He took control of his features again.

The movie ultimately made Ty a hero, a madman redeemed, and Chris was thankful. The lights gradually came on as the ending credits rolled, and he looked around the theater. There were a lot of tears and nervous laughter. Then the clapping began.

Tom stood and waved toward the VIP box containing the actress who played Jessica along with the other actors. They bowed and so did he, with his Hollywood smile plastered on his face.

"You coming to the party?" Tom asked as the crowd shuffled out.

Chris shook his head and looked up at Tom. "Thanks."

"For what?"

Chris pointed his chin at the screen. "For making me a hero."

Tom looked at the screen and then back at Jessica. She was looking up at him with the same measure of gratitude.

"At first I didn't want to," he said, keeping eye contact with his ex-wife, and shrugged. "But then, I figured you *are* at some level."

Chris laughed.

"Along with being a son of a bitch, of course," Tom added, flicking his gaze at Chris before returning it to Jessica. "And it would be easier on you. If I had done things the way I originally wanted to, no one would understand why you loved him."

JESSICA WIPED THE TEARS away and looked down at the remaining people filtering out of the theater. Sharon glared up at her. She got on her tiptoes, kissed Tom on the cheek, and squeezed Chris's hand.

He followed her glance. "Kiss her," he said to Tom and both of them looked at him in surprise. "Let him, Jess. Trust me."

Tom didn't need to be asked twice, although Jessica had reservations. Chris let go of her hand, and her arm floated around Tom's neck. His kiss was as sweet as she remembered. Mortified, she couldn't stop, and the slow realization sparked anger in her bones.

Chris was controlling her.

But then he yanked her away from Tom. "What the hell are you doing to my wife?" His voice thundered over the remaining stragglers, including Sharon.

Play it, Tom. He sent the thought into Tom's head loud and clear. Both Tom and Jessica winced at the decibels ricocheting in their heads.

"I'm still in love with her," Tom challenged.

"She's married to me now." Chris dragged her out of the room.

"What the hell are you doing?" Jessica whispered.

"Rubbing it in," he said as he looked back at her. "Now yank away from me and run back to him."

Jessica hesitated until she heard him silently command her to do it, and against every fiber in her body, she yanked away from him and ran back to Tom. Chris looked after her with his mouth hanging open, and the devastation on his face was plain to anyone looking at him, even Sharon.

His expression almost made her legs give out.

Tom caught her. "I told you he was the best fucking actor I've ever seen." He wrapped his arms protectively around her.

"Jess," Chris whispered.

Against her will, her head shook, and she turned into Tom's chest, hiding her face in the soft silk of his shirt.

CHRIS BACKED AWAY FROM them, his eyes filling with tears, and he turned, bumping into Sharon. He looked around the lobby and then back at her.

"I can't believe her," Chris said, his voice laced with betrayal. He looked over his shoulder.

"Forget about them. Come on." Sharon grabbed his hand and pulled him back into the empty theater.

JESSICA HEARD CHRIS IN her head. *Like taking candy from a baby. Wait for me in the carriage.*

Jessica pulled away from Tom, but he yanked her back and kissed her again. This time, she pushed away. "No, Tom. I love him."

"You kissed me back," he said, and she laughed.

"Chris commanded me to kiss you." She left him standing in shock in the lobby.

She trudged out to the carriage, ignoring the questions thrown her way by the lingering paparazzi. She slammed the door on the clamor.

A few moments later, the door opened, and Tom climbed in. "I don't believe you."

Jessica lifted her hand and pointed at the ring. "I married him today."

"So." Tom reached out, grazing her knee with his fingers.

She knocked his hand away. "He's the father of my children."

"So am I," Tom replied, leaving her speechless.

End Game Chapter 26

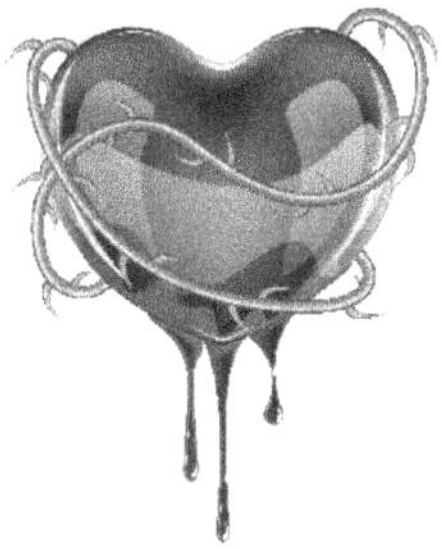

CHRIS SCANNED THE EMPTY theater and sent out his mental radar, keeping his face a mask of devastation until he was certain they were alone. Sharon's hand came to rest on his arm, and he twitched, releasing a small dose of power, locking every door in the theater.

The echo of the locks bounced off the walls. Sharon jumped, pulling her hand away like she had been burned.

Chris turned his gaze toward her, cocking his head to the side and clenching his teeth together, the fake devastation altering to the predatory glare of an angry man. "You have the audacity to put a contract out on my family?"

Sharon gulped and took a step back.

Chris smiled, pleased at the fear etched in her face.

"Who are you?"

"Your worst fucking nightmare," he replied and sent a small push out, slamming her into the wall ten feet behind her. "Now, call off the hit."

With trembling hands, she pulled out her phone and punched in a sequence of numbers—numbers he was very familiar with, numbers for the best Chinese restaurant in Manhattan.

"Don't bullshit me, bitch," he said. "I can smell a lie for miles."

Sharon's eyes widened, and she disconnected the call. She swallowed and nodded, dialing the first in a string of hit men. "It's me. I'm canceling the contract. Put the word out." Then she hung up.

"Call the rest."

She ground her teeth together. "There aren't any more."

He laughed and took a step toward her. "You really want to play that game with me?" The scarf around her neck tightened with a slight tilt of his head. He raised an eyebrow. "Really?"

She clawed at the fabric, gagging and gasping for air. "Okay," she croaked, and he loosened the scarf. Sixteen calls later, she hung up, and he was satisfied.

He closed the distance, towering over her. "I'll let you live because that's what my wife wants me to do, but you are going to divorce my friend and disappear, understand? Otherwise, I'll unleash the Angel of Death himself."

"Ty?" Sharon whispered, with a tremor in her voice.

Chris slowly smiled and nodded. "Don't ever doubt I can do that, or it will be the last thing you do."

He stormed out, the door opening in front of him without the use of his hands.

End Game Chapter 27

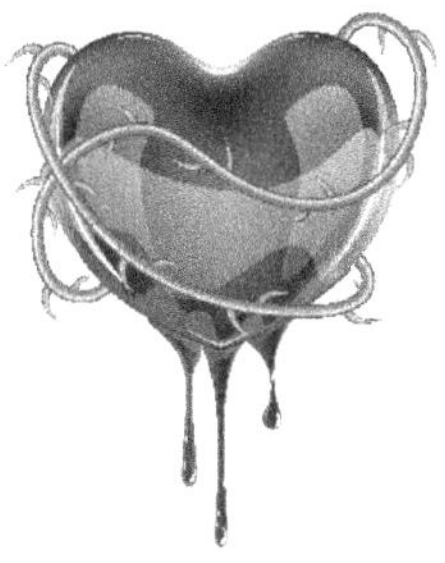

TOM SMILED AT JESSICA. "I seem to remember you like to play games." He put his hands on her knees again, and when she went to push them away, he grabbed her wrists and slammed her down on the seat, positioning himself on top of her in one motion.

"Get off of me," she snarled. Fear and anger bloomed.

"Ty doesn't have exclusive rights to take what he wants."

"What the hell happened to you?"

Tom laughed. "You. You happened to me." He kissed her.

Jessica struggled and tried to roll him off, but like Ty, Tom was too strong and held her in place.

He reached down and tugged at her dress, yanking gently against his weight.

Grim determination shined in his eyes, and her anger dimmed, replaced by both shock and sadness. This man had once protected her, made her feel safe, and he loved her as deeply as Chris. Yet here he was, reduced to a primal animal hell-bent on taking what he wanted with no regard for her.

"Please Tom, don't do this." Tears blurred her vision, crumbling her composure.

Tom closed his eyes, exhaling. "He was right."

"About what?" Tears slipped down her cheeks.

"That I would lose."

The door to the carriage opened, and Chris's expression darkened to a deadly glare. His dagger-like stare drifted to hers, softening a fraction before snapping back to the man accosting her.

Tom scrambled off her. Chris stepped inside, closing the door behind him without taking his eyes from Tom. The door latched, and Tom was lifted and slammed into the opposite side of the cabin by an invisible force commanded by Chris. The impact coincided with the sudden lurch forward as the carriage started the trek across town.

Jessica sat up, and Chris wrapped his arms around her, his gaze remaining intently on Tom and his jaw working, his teeth grinding. Anger radiated through the small carriage.

She leaned toward him. "Don't hurt him. He did nothing more than pin me."

Chris broke eye contact with him and turned toward Jessica, searching her eyes, and he inhaled, returning his focus on the unwelcomed occupant. "And to think, I called you a friend."

Tom's mouth dropped open.

"Sharon agreed to divorce you, and all the contracts have been canceled." He swiveled his gaze to Jessica. "She won't be screwing with our lives anymore."

"You don't know her like I do," Tom said. "She may not have contracts out on you anymore, but that doesn't mean she won't try to kill us, anyway."

Chris laughed softly. "I told her I would unleash the Angel of Death if she tried." He tilted his head as the smile drifted away. "Then there's you—you touch my wife again, and I will tear you to pieces."

"Chris," Jessica said softly, trying to keep him in check.

The carriage pulled to a stop in front of the Plaza Hotel, and Tom hooked his thumb toward the window. "How'd you know?"

"Lucky guess," Chris replied. He swung the door open, but Tom didn't budge.

"I want to see my son."

Jessica sucked the air in, her heart stopping a moment at the dreaded words. She wasn't ready to let him waltz into their lives, especially not on their wedding night.

"No," she said.

"Okay," Chris said at the same instant, and traded a glance with Jessica.

She couldn't believe it. Her gaze jumped to his. Heat scoured her cheeks even against the frigid breeze through the open door.

"He has the right to see him." Without waiting for her response, he leaned out and told the driver to head to the apartment, and then closed the cabin door.

"This is *not* how I wanted to spend my wedding night." Jessica crossed her arms and looked out the far window, away from the two men.

"I'll make it up to you, I promise." Chris kissed the back of the hand closest to him.

She yanked her hand from his and huffed, returning her attention to the scenery.

"Sorry," Tom muttered.

"Try to sound like you mean it next time," she snapped.

"I never thought I'd see this day." Tom waved his hand at the two of them and leaned forward. "Not in a million fucking years," he growled, his eyes blazing with aggravation.

Chris threw a right hook, connecting with his jaw, sending him back against the far side of the carriage. He flexed his hand and glanced at Jessica. "Sorry, babe, couldn't help it."

He smiled his awkward, crooked smile, the one he reserved for when he had done something she didn't approve of, and it always melted her resolve. This time was no different.

She sighed. "Just don't do it again."

Tom leaned against the back wall, rubbing his jaw. "He's got you so snowed."

Jessica glared and pointed her index finger at him. "You deserved it."

He scoffed at her, and the chariot stopped in front of their apartment building.

"I'm not bringing you up there with that kind of attitude." She crossed her arms. "It isn't fair to the boys."

Tom sighed and nodded just as the driver swung the door open for them.

"Are you going to behave?" She bounced her gaze between the two men.

"Yes," they both grumbled.

Chris hopped out and took her hand, helping her down, and a smile played on his lips as he scanned her.

TOM SAW THE WAY she looked at Chris, and his last hope of ever getting her back died. He glanced up at the apartment building and then at Central Park and the Plaza in the distance. Five years hadn't erased the sting of her betrayal, and the close proximity of his apartment to where they'd stayed the last time they were together dug under his skin, like a viper clinging to its kill.

Chris held Jessica close, and they rode the elevator in silence, casting glances at each other and then in his direction.

"You know, I always hated it when you and Eric communicated without talking, but this is ten times worse."

Jessica blushed and looked at the floor. "Sorry."

The whoosh of the elevator doors interrupted his train of thought, and he followed Jessica and Chris the few steps between the elevator and the only door on the floor. He took a deep breath when Chris swung the door open, holding it for Jessica before waving him inside.

The warmth of the apartment shocked him. Deep walnut accents and soft leather furniture, a wall of books, and a fantastic view of the city beyond—not at all what he envisioned when he thought of Ty Aris. He cast a glance over his shoulder.

Chris shrugged.

"Hi, Mom." Emily stood, turning toward the door. She froze, meeting Tom's gaze.

Five years had changed her, and damn if she wasn't the spitting image of Jessica. "Hi, Emily. It's been a while."

Eric walked in from the kitchen, glancing casually at the group. "The kids are asleep," he announced and flopped on the couch.

Tom looked at his former stepson in shock— talk about grown up. Eric, now almost eighteen, stood just shy of six feet tall, the epitome of the all-American high school athlete. Tall, good-looking, buff, and had the nonchalant devil-may-care attitude to match.

Jessica slipped away, leaving Tom standing awkwardly in the entry, shifting from foot to foot. He hadn't been this nervous since the first time he auditioned for his first motion picture.

What the hell am I going to say?

"Don't worry. My boys will talk you to death." Chris hung up his coat in the closet and crossed to the bar in the corner. "Can I get you something?"

Tom licked his lips. A drink right now sounded like the perfect stabilizer, but the sound of kids stampeding down the hall caught his attention. Two boys ran into the living room with grins, and his heart leaped in his throat.

A mirror image of his eyes stared wide-eyed up at him. He looked from his namesake to CJ, and even at four, the resemblance to his father was uncanny.

"CJ, Tommy, this is Tom Whitman," Jessica said.

"He has the same last name as you, Mommy," Tommy observed.

CJ just looked at Tom, his eyes showing the recognition of who he was, and he glanced at his father for confirmation.

Chris nodded slightly.

"Your mother was married to Tom a long time ago," Chris replied, turning his focus to his other son. "But now she has a different last name."

"Oh." Tommy looked back at Tom.

Tom crouched down so he could look Tommy in the eye. "Hello there." He put his hand out.

"Hi." Tommy shook his hand. "Nice to meetcha."

Tom returned his smile. "The pleasure is all mine, little man."

CJ tilted his head, and then his eyes widened. "You're on TV!"

Tom laughed. "Yes. I was for quite a few years."

"I saw you on a show the other day," CJ replied.

"They still play episodes of *Metropolis* on syndication." He smiled and looked up at Jessica. "Syndication is—"

"I know what syndication is," CJ interrupted.

"You do?" Tom asked, sure that the little boy had no idea.

"The rights to the show were sold so it could be played, and you receive a royalty from it," CJ replied, shocking everyone in the room except his father. "Duh," he added.

"Where did you learn such big words?" Tom smiled at him.

CJ shrugged and pointed at his father. "It's what Daddy thought when you said the word."

Tom nodded and looked back at Chris.

Tommy ran over to his father. "Daddy, he's on TV," he said, pulling on Chris's pant leg.

Chris reached down and scooped him up. "Yes, he is."

CJ cocked his head again. "You were in the movie that Mom and Dad went to tonight." He turned and glanced over at Eric. "That's why Emily and Eric were watching us."

Eric smiled. "It's been a while since you had someone in your head, hasn't it?" Eric asked Tom and stood, crossing to CJ and putting his hand on his brother's head.

"Yes, it has." Tom shifted his weight. He'd never gotten used to it, and after being away from it for five years, it really freaked him out.

"Well, this little guy can do it better than anyone I know." Eric messed up CJ's hair. "Come on, it's time for you to get some sleep." He swept CJ out of Chris's arms. "Coming, Em?"

Emily nodded and disappeared down the hall with Eric and CJ.

"I get to stay up?" Tommy asked, swinging his gaze from the hallway to Chris.

"For a little while." Chris looked over at Tom. "My friend here wanted to talk to you for a bit."

"Didn't he want to talk with CJ, too?"

"CJ doesn't talk the way you do."

Tommy considered this and then nodded.

Jessica watched Chris handle the delicate situation with ease and smiled at her husband.

"Besides, Tom here is a very special person, and we thought you'd want to tell your friends that you got to meet Superman."

Tommy's eyes went wide, and he looked over at Tom. "Superman?"

Tom did his best not to laugh. "Your Dad's exaggerating. I played Superman on television."

"Can you fly?" Tommy asked as Chris set him back down.

"No."

"Can you run really fast?" Tommy asked, and they sat on the couch.

Jessica sat in the chair, and Chris sat on the arm of the chair with his arm around her shoulder. They watched the exchange.

Tom laughed. "I can run fast, but not like Superman. That was done with special effects, same with flying."

"Oh," Tommy said. He looked at his parents. "I'm tired. Can I go to bed now?"

Jessica nodded. "Of course you can, baby." She stood up to take him to his room. "Say goodbye to Mr. Whitman."

Tommy turned and gave Tom a hug. "Bye, Mr. Whitman." He ran over to Chris and gave him a big hug as well. "Night, Daddy." Then he took Jessica's hand as she led him to the bedroom.

Tom stood and crossed to the balcony, welcoming the brittle wind ruffling his hair. He walked to the edge and looked down over the fashionable banister. The experience of seeing his son left him hollow and empty. He wanted that void filled; he wanted his son. He stared over the cityscape, ignoring the sound of the door unlatching and opening behind him.

He looked down at the light touch on his arm and then into her eyes before sweeping his gaze over the city. "Great view."

"Are you okay?"

Tom took a moment to analyze that question. "I'm not sure," he answered. "I have a son, and I don't want Ty to raise him."

Jessica drew her breath in. "You have no choice."

Tom laughed. "Yes, I do have a choice." He turned toward her.

Jessica shook her head. "As far as we're concerned, he is the son of Chris Ryan."

"Then why did you name him Thomas?"

Jessica smiled. "Thomas Patrick was his father's name." She pointed at Chris, who was watching them from the chair.

Tom raised his eyebrows. "Huh?"

"We named our sons in memory of his family," Jessica replied. "Thomas Patrick Ryan was his father, and Christopher James Ryan was his brother."

"Ty can't raise my son." Tom glared over at him, prompting Chris to stand up and head out onto the terrace.

"The name is Chris," he corrected and closed the door behind him. "And there is no way I'm letting an alcoholic have anything to do with my son on a regular basis."

"There's no way I'm letting a cold-blooded killer raise my child."

Jessica stepped between the two men. "Chris is a better father than you could possibly imagine. He loves those boys, and we're teaching them values and understanding right from wrong."

"He doesn't even know what's right and what's wrong."

"Yes, I do. I know the difference."

Tom laughed sarcastically. "Yeah right, that's about as real as me saying I'm Superman."

"He *is* a good father," Eric said from the door, shocking all of them. "Those two are the best behaved, sweetest four-year-olds I have ever met." He stepped out onto the terrace. "You were fun, but as a father goes, you don't hold a candle to him, Tom, and I will not let you separate my brothers."

"Eric, this isn't your battle," Chris said.

"The hell it isn't," Eric responded. "If he takes Tommy, I won't get the chance to be with my little brother. And CJ will go ballistic."

"Eric, please." Chris caught his stepson's gaze.

Eric went to say something else but closed his mouth as his stepfather's eyes bore into him.

"Please, let us talk."

Eric sulked back inside, glancing over his shoulder as the door closed behind him.

"Tom, you have some rights as his biological father," Chris began, seeing Jessica glare at him. "But if you even think about taking him from us…"

"What?" Tom snapped. "What are you going to do?"

"I will stop you. By any means possible." His eyes conveyed the meaning behind the words.

"Even if it means you end up on death row?" Jessica gasped.

Chris smiled. "You have no proof."

Tom's smile faded. He was absolutely right. He didn't have a shred of evidence regarding Chris's past. "People have been convicted with less."

"You would put me in jail?" Jessica said.

"No," Tom said.

"You try to pull Chris down, I go with him, and so do you," she pointed out.

Tom looked from Jessica to Chris and back.

"The only reason you are here is because of him. I didn't want to tell you about Tommy."

Her words were like a physical blow, and he took a step back. "Why?"

"I didn't want to complicate our lives. We have a very quiet, very private existence, and I want to keep it that way."

Tom digested what she'd said. "You didn't make a very quiet or private entrance tonight."

"That was all me. You're the one who invited us. You had to know I wouldn't just show up without a grand entrance. That isn't my style," Chris said.

"But a quiet, private life is?"

"Yes. Privacy is very much my style. Why do you think I insisted you put Christopher Aris on the guest list?" Chris paused. "And I wouldn't say our lives are quiet." He glanced over at his wife. "There is nothing quiet about two four-year-old boys."

Jessica smiled. "Okay, well, quiet might not be the best description of our lives, but for the last four and a half years, we have been off the media radar, and I like it that way. If you insist on trying to take your son, then he'll be thrust into the spotlight just by being related to you. Do you really want that?"

"Jessie, the spotlight never bothered me."

"I don't care. The answer is no." Jessica glared and stormed back into the apartment.

Chris looked out over the city. "And as long as you are married to Sharon, you will not come around to see us. I don't want you putting my family in any more danger than you already have."

"I thought you said she called off the hit?"

"She did. But wasn't it you that said if she ever found out you had a son, she would kill him out of spite?" He glanced over at Tom.

Tom nodded.

"I love both my boys, more than you can comprehend. I love them more than I love my wife," Chris said. "So, if you even think about putting either of them in danger by making this a public issue, I will have your head delivered to me on a platter." Chris walked into the house, leaving Tom with that morbid image.

Tom followed him in from the terrace after a few moments.

Chris stood by the front door with it open. "It's time for you to go."

Tom looked down at his feet and then over at Jessica. "I want to see him again."

Jessica shook her head. "That's not such a good idea right now."

He took a deep breath. "When?"

"I already told you. Now go," Chris replied.

"I don't even know if she'll divorce me."

"Then you won't see him."

Tom looked at the two of them and trudged out of their apartment, feeling like a knife had been embedded in his stomach. He no sooner raised his hand to flag a cab when one pulled up. Still preoccupied, he slid inside, and a jab of metal pressed to his ribs. His head swiveled in the dark interior of the cab, and he gasped, staring at his wife's glare.

"Hi, honey," Sharon said. "So, this is where they live."

Ice filled his veins, and he shivered.

"Drive," she demanded of the driver, and the cab took off.

Tom's mouth felt like a bag full of cotton had been shoved in, and his pulse quickened to an alarming rate, turning the chill into burning fear. His son was up there; he couldn't let her get to them.

"The three of you planned that little ambush. You humiliated me in public."

Tom said nothing.

"I'm going to make sure it never happens again."

"If you so much as touch them…"

Sharon slammed the gun into his temple, making him see stars. "I'm going to do much more than just touch them," she said. "And you are going to watch. You need to learn that your actions have consequences."

"I'm not a fucking child, Sharon." He glared over at her.

"I know, and your punishment isn't a spanking." She smiled and clocked him with the gun.

Blackness descended.

End Game Chapter 28

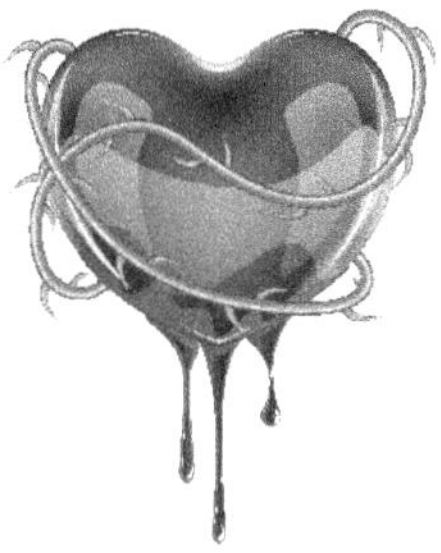

TOM BLINKED HIS EYES open and groaned. His head felt like someone had planted an axe in his temple. He went to touch his face, but his hand was stopped short. The clank of a chain sent a chill down his back. He widened his eyes, letting them adjust to the blackness surrounding him. Running his fingers over the rough surface behind him, he guessed it was brick or cinderblock. The stench reminded him of the musty mattress he'd slept on when he, Jessica, and Ty were imprisoned.

A thread of fear weaved through his blood, and he shivered. In the darkness, he could make out a few stationary shapes, but not much else. An occasional draft tickled his neck. He concentrated on breathing, keeping calm even though panic prickled his skin, stinging its way through to the bone.

He listened for anything familiar, and after a few moments, the sounds of the city streets reached his ears. He breathed a sigh; at least he was above ground, but his relief was short-lived.

Dim overhead lights flipped on, and he got a good look at his surroundings. What he saw made him wish he could be blind in the dark again.

"Jesus."

He thought that last room in Ty's prison was bad, but what Sharon laid out made that look like Disneyland. He tried to swallow, but without spit, his tongue felt like a roll of sandpaper scraping the roof of his mouth.

Sharon stepped out of the shadows, slapping her palm with a riding whip. "It's time you learn who's in control." She stopped in front of him, thrashing him across the face, leaving a welt on his cheek. She reached out with both hands and tore his shirt open with a smile, then ran her hands down his chest.

"Get away from me."

She hit him across the face with the riding whip again. "You are going to tell me you love me."

He laughed, and she whipped him again.

"Don't think so."

"What did you do with her tonight?" Sharon asked and grabbed his crotch, squeezing.

"Nothing," he said, grinding his teeth against the pain.

"What did you do tonight?" she asked, followed by a strike with the whip against his bare chest.

"Nothing."

"Did you fuck her?"

"No," Tom said, glaring at her.

Sharon studied his face. "I believe you." She released her grip and slid her hand suggestively over the front of his pants.

"Get away from me."

The whip cracked against his jaw with the full force of her fury, ripping the skin open. She slammed her knee up into his groin.

Pain exploded, and he choked with the agony filtering through every muscle in his body. The wall scraped his back as he sank as low as the chains would allow. His breath locked in his chest and his face was fire-hot. After oxygen flowed back into his lungs, a groan came out. The tinny taste of pain filled his mouth.

"Before this weekend's over, you will tell me what I want to hear." She threw the riding whip on the table and stormed away, then switched the lights off as she disappeared through the door.

End Game Chapter 29

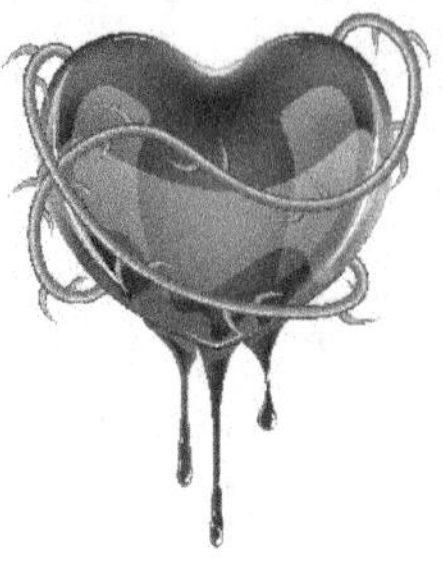

JESSICA LOOKED OVER HER shoulder at Chris following her into their bedroom. "This wasn't the ideal wedding night," she said, and he closed the door.

"Sorry you married me already?" Chris asked, dramatically covering his heart with his hands. "You're killing me." He stumbled toward her.

"Cut the shit."

Chris grabbed her arm and yanked her to him, looking into her eyes. "This wasn't the way I had planned it, either. What I had originally planned for our wedding night was moved to last night because *you* already promised *him* we would be at the premiere."

Jessica looked up at him and sighed. "Last night was wonderful. So was most of today until we stepped out onto the red carpet."

"I said I'd make it up to you." He held her face and kissed her. "What is it you desire?" he asked and moved his lips to her ear, licking the curves and sucking her earlobe. His fingers ran over the satin dress. "Hmmm?"

"You," she answered, and closed her eyes, getting lost in his exploration of her neck.

"Jessica Ryan," he said. The name rolled off his tongue and created a hunger like nothing he felt before.

"Mrs. Ty Alexander Ryan," she said deliberately and smiled as he pulled away.

"Legally, it's Mrs. Chris Ryan," he corrected, his eyes slowly taking her in as he stepped away from her. He willed the dress to flow up and over her head and watched as it drifted to the floor in front of her. He slipped his shoes off, and kicked them behind him, then stepped onto the discarded dress, taking her mostly naked body in his arms. "But I do like the sound of that much better."

"Make love to me."

He grinned. "I plan on doing that every night for the rest of our lives." He kissed her while she unbuttoned his shirt, and he chuckled. "You would think we were teenagers."

Jessica pulled away and looked at him with a sexy smile. "One would think." She unbuckled his belt and pulled it out of the loops, then tossed it across the room. "I just can't get enough of you."

"If I could spend the rest of my life in bed with you, I would die an extremely happy man."

Jessica playfully pushed him against the side of the bed, planting butterfly kisses across his chest. "You are way too talkative tonight."

"Then shut me up," he whispered and surrendered when she pushed him back onto the bed.

Her mouth found his, the kiss stripped him of air. With a glance, the stereo turned on. "If You Could Only See" by Tonic came pouring out of the speakers.

He smiled. "I love you, Jess."

"God knows how much I love you." She sighed.

He pulled her close, rolling and maneuvering them fully onto the bed. Tracing her face with his fingertips, he drank her in like never before, and his smile faded. The joy of the day was overshadowed by his past, and his eyes misted. "Is this real?"

She nodded.

A torrent of emotions hit him like a brick in the chest. He inhaled, burying his face in the crook of her neck so she wouldn't see the tears sprout. Over his whole life, whenever happiness was within reach, it was snatched from him, crushed to a pulp before his eyes. Fear bloomed. Fear of losing her, of losing his children, but most of all, fear that he'd wake and find himself alone, still working for his brother in that godforsaken prison.

She tilted his face so she could see him. "Oh, babe," she whispered.

"I don't understand why God would ever allow me to be this happy."

"Because you asked for redemption." Jessica pressed her lips to his forehead.

"Do you really believe I've been forgiven?"

"Yes."

"Why?"

"Because if I'm capable of forgiving you, I'm sure God is, too." She gently kissed him. "The only one who hasn't is you."

He looked at her for a long time without speaking. "Tom made me a hero. I am so far from a hero, it's not funny."

"You are a hero to me. You're my heart and soul."

He kissed her. "You're my everything," he whispered and slid inside of her.

Chris took his time with her, savoring every second as if this were the last time he would be one with her, feeling her emotions intermixed with his own. He controlled himself, pausing when he felt the peak coming until it subsided again, allowing Jessica to hurdle through hers over and over again. After what seemed like hours, he finally lost control over his body and exploded deep inside her.

"Okay, that made up for the rest of tonight," Jessica said as he lay spent with his head on her shoulder.

He laughed softly, propping himself up on his elbows. He traced her lips with his fingers before leaning over and playfully biting her lower lip.

"I don't have the energy for any more." Jessica yawned.

"I finally tired the Energizer Bunny?"

"Yes." Jessica nodded.

He rolled, pulling her on top of him. Jessica laid her head on his chest, falling into a peaceful sleep in his arms.

Chris absently ran his hand through her hair, a habit that seemed to put him in a deep state of relaxation. He smiled and drifted into the darkness of slumber.

He opened his eyes to a room he didn't recognize, and he was in agony. With his arms spread wide, holding his weight, exhaling seemed impossible. Pushing with his feet to lift himself far enough to exhale brought on shards of pain that shot up his legs with a force almost enough to bring on a blessed blackout.

He blinked, and his eyes finally focused on the room below him. His family lined up in different phases of torture, and the psycho bitch plotting which one was next on her hit list. They were past the point of danger, and there wasn't a damn thing he could do. He inhaled deeply and pushed himself up again despite the pain, letting out a blood-curdling cry of despair.

Chris shot up in their bed, his entire body bathed in sweat with the scream still coming from his mouth.

Jessica flew out of the bathroom, her eyes wild and darting around the room. Once her brain registered they weren't in danger, she turned off the bathroom light and climbed into the bed next to him.

The entire bed shook with the tremors coursing through him. The dream replayed itself in his head like a broken record, skipping from the end back to the beginning over and over. In the dream, he was void of the power he'd felt throbbing in his veins for the past five years.

"Chris, it was only a dream," Jessica said as she stroked her hand over his sweat-soaked back.

He nodded, but still trembled. Witnessing his own death was far from pleasant, and he couldn't shake the vision from his mind. Chris took a few deep breaths, trying to calm his nerves, but it wasn't working. What he saw in the dream was a worse death than being pulled apart by chains or bleeding to death in a chair; it was slow and agonizing and bought him more than enough time to see everything he loved destroyed.

"It was only a dream," Jessica said again. "Chris," she said louder.

He turned to look at her. "I'll be all right." He slipped out of bed. He grabbed his discarded underwear off the floor and slipped it on before heading into the bathroom.

Cold water bit at his face, and he looked up into the mirror. His eyes still held that haunted look, and he closed them, trying to shut out the vision, but it wouldn't go away. He grabbed the bathrobe on the back of the door, slipped it on, and headed for the bedroom door.

"Where are you going?"

"I need some air."

Before stepping out on the balcony, Chris filled a glass with scotch. The frigid breeze slapped at his face and his bare calves, calming the panic gripping him. He slammed back the drink, letting it warm him from the inside.

"You're going to catch a cold," Jessica said from inside the slider.

Chris laughed; that was the least of his worries. "I'll be fine. I just had a bad dream."

"I gathered that. Want to tell me about it?"

"Not particularly." He glanced over his shoulder at her. "It was much more unsettling than yours."

She went out to him, took his hand, and led him back into the warm apartment. After taking the drink out of his hand and putting it on the bar next to the table, she motioned for him to sit on the couch next to her. "Nothing is going to happen to us."

He rolled his eyes and looked at her. "You don't know that." *You weren't hanging from a cross.*

"What about a cross?"

"Don't worry about it." He leaned over and kissed her cheek, blocking her from hearing anything further. "It might have been just a carry-over from our conversation. I've had the most amazing five years with you, and I'm feeling a little insecure."

"I married you yesterday."

"I know, but still." He shrugged. "It could all end tomorrow."

"That's a little morbid."

He nodded and glanced at the clock. "We need to get some more sleep before the kids wake up." He stood and walked over to the bar, downed the remaining scotch from his glass, and closed the bottle, hiding it away.

She waited for him and took his hand as they walked silently back to the bedroom.

Chris looked around at the clothing carnage and tilted his head, exercising a bit of power to clean up the room. He glanced at her with a small smile, sliding under the covers as the last of the discarded clothes folded on the chair.

"You have no idea how much I'd like to have that back sometimes," Jessica said, burrowing under the covers next to him.

Chris's smile disappeared as the dream etched further into his consciousness. He considered her comment for a moment and then rolled her toward him and kissed her, pushing a majority of his power back into her. "Is that what you really want?" he asked, pulling away.

Jessica gasped, and her eyes widened. The power consumed her, making her entire form quake. "Holy shit."

"Didn't think so." He kissed her again, this time pulling most of the power back, leaving her with a trace, locking it deep in her subconscious as a precaution. He broke the kiss and smiled.

Jessica's eyes filled with awe. "How the hell do you control that?"

"Discipline." He shifted, spooning her. "Now get some sleep."

THE EARLY MORNING SUN woke her out of a sound sleep. He still had his arms firmly wrapped around her and his head buried in her hair, his breath tickling her neck as he snored softly. Jessica shifted, and his grip tightened a fraction before his eyes fluttered open.

"Morning, Mrs. Ryan."

"Morning, Mr. Ryan."

"What time is it?" Chris asked, still with her firmly in his grip.

Jessica pushed the edge of her pillow down so she could see the clock. "A little after nine."

"We should get up," he said, but made no attempt to move.

"We should," she agreed and wrapped her arms around his, snuggling closer to him. "What are we doing today?"

"I have nothing planned."

Jessica thought for a few minutes. "You know, I never made it to the Met."

Chris smiled. "I think the Museum of Natural History would be better suited for the boys," he said. "I can't see them being really interested in art for any period of time."

Jessica nodded. "I think they need to get out of the apartment for a while." She slipped out of his grip. "I'm going running. Are you coming?"

Chris sighed. He didn't really feel like running this morning. He just wanted to lie in bed with her.

"I know, but we can't stay in bed forever," she said, catching his thought process. "And I missed exercising yesterday."

Chris grinned. "You got a little in."

Jessica's cheeks heated, and she grabbed the sweats hanging over the back of the chair. "Not the same. I'd like you with me today, just in case Tom ambushes me again."

Chris took a deep breath and swung his legs out of bed. "I'm coming," he muttered, passing her on his way to the bathroom.

When he returned to the bedroom, Jessica was tying her jogging shoes. She watched as he pulled on his clothes and milled through the closet for his running shoes.

"Only for you," he mumbled. He slipped the shoes on and tied the laces.

"You're still muttering under your breath?"

"It's cold out there." Chris glanced up at her. "And I was real comfortable in here with you in my arms."

"Suck it up, babe." She grinned and picked up her MP3 player.

He caught her before she reached the door, spun her around, and kissed her. "I'd rather suck face."

Jessica laughed. "I'll bet, but right now, I need a run."

He gave in and let her go, following her like a scolded puppy.

"Stop sulking," she said as the elevator closed on them.

"You have to make this up to me," he said as they stepped into the lobby.

"Good morning, Mr. Ryan." The doorman smiled at Chris. "Mrs. Ryan," he addressed Jessica, much to her surprise.

"Very good morning, Fred." Chris smiled and ushered Jessica through the front door.

"Good morning," Jessica replied and smiled as Fred held the door for them. "How'd he know?" She handed Chris the earbud.

"He asked what the occasion was yesterday," Chris replied, slipping the earpiece in after they crossed the street.

The temperature had dropped significantly during the night, and the late February cold bit at both of them, the wind stinging their exposed cheeks, making them bright red from both the physical exertion and the cold. Jessica cut the run short, looping back toward the apartment building.

"Wuss."

"It's freezing," Jessica replied.

Chris just smiled. He let out a little laugh when Jessica smacked him lightly on the arm.

"You're only partially right. I still needed the run, and it feels good."

"Better than morning sex?" He nudged her as they slowed their pace and crossed the street.

Jessica laughed and looked over at him. "No, nothing is better than morning sex with you."

"Then what the hell are we doing out here?"

"I needed the run. I needed the peace it brings me."

Chris tilted his head a little, his eyes searching hers.

"I lose myself when I run. All I'm aware of is the music and the pounding of my feet, and it centers me. Kind of like karate does for you. I needed that after last night," she said as the elevator rose.

Chris put his arm around her shoulders and nodded, kissing her temple. "We have some things to take care of this morning before the banks close."

"Like what?"

"Like getting you on my accounts," he said, looking at her like she wasn't nimble-minded.

Jessica hadn't done that since she was married to Daniel. She and Tom kept their separate accounts, which made the divorce so much cleaner. She just assumed that would be the same with Chris.

He laughed at her expression. "What's mine is yours. Everything—including my homes, my cars, my kids, right down to my net worth—is yours."

"How many homes do you have?"

"This place, the place in Maine, and I have a villa on the French Riviera, and a cottage in the Caribbean."

Jessica raised her eyebrows. "Really?"

"Yes. You really have no clue, do you?"

"Clue of what?"

"How much you're worth now that you are Mrs. Chris Ryan."

"No. I didn't marry you for your money."

Chris chuckled and opened the apartment door, waving her inside. The children were up and ran to them, grasping their legs in little bear hugs as they made their way inside. He leaned over and whispered a figure in Jessica's ear.

Her gaze shot to his, and the sudden pressure behind her eyes made it feel like they would pop any minute. *Did you just say what I think you did?* Her jaw loosened, her mouth dropping wide, as wide as she imagined her eyes were. "Fifteen billion?"

"More or less," Chris managed to say through his gales of laughter. "I've done really well with my investments over the last ten years, and it's now yours. Well, technically, if anything had happened to me over the past ten years, it was always yours. You have been my sole beneficiary since the day you left the complex," he said. "Well, until the kids came along, anyway."

Jessica sat down on the floor in shock, which sent Chris into another giggling fit.

"I'm sorry, babe, but the look on your face is absolutely priceless," he said as he wound down.

"Did you say fifteen billion dollars?" Eric asked, mirroring his mother's expression.

"Yes."

"What's fifteen billion dollars?" Emily's eyebrows scrunched together.

"That's what our new stepfather is worth," Eric said.

Emily dropped the glass in her hand, and it stopped just shy of the entryway tile.

Chris caught it in his hand and raised his eyes to Emily. "You might want to sit down before you follow the glass."

All color completely drained from her face, and she took a chair as he directed.

Chris looked back at Jessica. "You really didn't know?"

"No. I knew you sold the company, but..." She shook her head.

"I got the whole shebang. Frank, Marian, and Ty had me listed in their wills." He looked at her. "So not only did I get the company, I got all the other assets as well. I sold everything. Ninety percent of the proceeds of their personal assets went to the survivors of their victims." He looked around the room. "Between the company assets and the ten percent left, I ended up with close to eight billion dollars. Ten years later and some damn good investments have made that number grow to roughly fifteen billion." He shrugged. "We live off a fraction of the interest." He smiled. "Welcome to the world of the obscenely rich."

Jessica shook her head. "You're shitting me." She covered her mouth, her gaze swiveling to CJ and Tommy, who were now laughing at her faux pas.

"I kid you not." Chris made a cross over his chest.

"But... but..."

"There is a distinct difference between being rich and acting like a rich snob. I saw enough of the rich snob attitude living with the Aris family, and there is no way I am ever treating people the way they did." He paused, and she nodded. "We could live in a palace if you wanted to, but then again, that isn't your style either." He stood and helped her up. "We can buy anything we want, but that doesn't mean that we will, got it?" He looked at the four children.

Four heads nodded, although only two really understood what Chris had said.

"And money can't replace someone's life." He glanced at Jessica and then over at Eric, and studied the floor for a moment before glancing at Emily.

"No, it can't." The color had found its way back into her cheeks. "It also doesn't mean that you are above the law, either."

Chris nodded at the barb. "I'm going to clean up," he announced. He pecked Jessica on the cheek and headed down the hall.

Jessica glanced at her daughter as she headed in the same direction, then closed the bedroom door behind her. The shower was running, and she stripped, stepped inside, and wrapped her hands around his waist while stood with his head back under the water.

He ran his hands down his face and opened his eyes. "She really doesn't like me, does she?"

"She loves you, Chris. She just has issues with the injustice of you getting away with everything that you have done."

"Injustice." He huffed and turned away from her, under the stream of water. "Money had nothing to do with that ruse," he mumbled. "If your son hadn't fixed me, I'd be dead right now." He hung his head. "And I capitalized on the opportunity." He glanced back at her.

"I know. Much more than I realized."

Chris laughed softly. "I got rich off the blood of others. Basically, I've stolen everything I have, including you." He shook his head. "Injustice just seems too mild a word."

"Ty?" Jessica whispered, and he turned toward her.

"Don't get me wrong, Jess. I am grateful for everything I have, but I believe in what goes around comes around, and my time is coming."

Jessica took a deep breath. "You have done some good things to counteract the bad."

He smiled. "That's only because of you. Everything good and pure in my life is a direct result of you." He kissed her. "But it isn't enough to balance the bad."

"Well, on the upside, I don't have to testify against you now." She smiled up at him, waving her left hand with her wedding band at him.

Chris laughed. "Leave it to you to think of something like that."

"I'm sure it's crossed your mind."

He shook his head. "Nope."

"Liar." She stood on her tiptoes to kiss him.

Well, maybe once or twice, he thought. He smiled as their lips met.

End Game Chapter 30

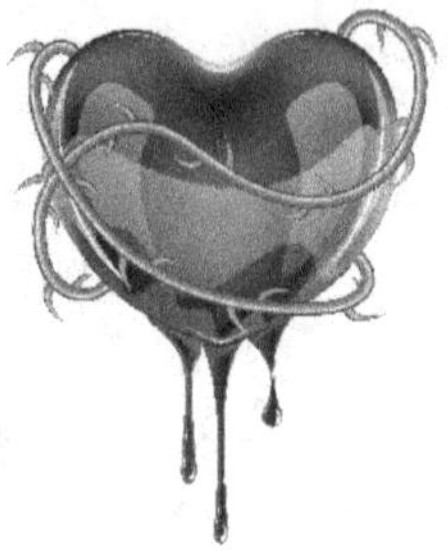

THE CLANG OF THE metal door woke Tom from a troubled sleep. He stood on aching legs. Hell, his whole body ached.

Sharon waltzed across the floor to him. "Did you have a nice night's sleep?"

"Fuck you." He tried to swallow the pasty sleep still coating his mouth.

Sharon made a quick call, sending a wink in his direction. "Don't worry, by the end of the day, you won't be alone here anymore."

Her casual manner brought both fear and anger boiling back. "Leave them out of it, Sharon. You've got me. Isn't that what you wanted?"

"It's too late for that. You humiliated me in public, and you need to pay for that. You all do."

The crazed look in her eye almost made him lose control over his overfilled, throbbing bladder. "Please don't do this," he pleaded. All he could think about was what she would do when she saw Tommy. It was hard to mistake the resemblance, just as hard as it would be to overlook CJ being Chris's son.

Her phone rang, and she turned her back on him, answering the call. "It won't be long now." She smiled and flipped the phone closed, waving goodbye to Tom as she slipped out of sight.

End Game Chapter 31

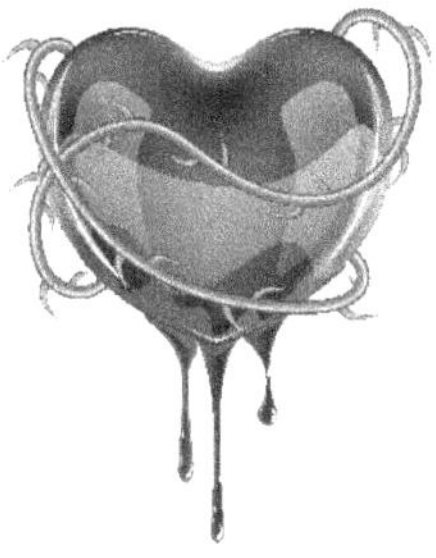

CHRIS PUT DOWN THE phone, staring at the bouquet of flowers sitting on the kitchen counter. Eric had said they arrived shortly after he and Jessica went to the bank. The card had a nice sentiment, but no signature. Sam didn't send them, and neither did Jessica's family.

Dread pressed on his chest as he glanced at her. "Do you think Tom sent them?"

"I doubt he would send flowers with that nice of a sentiment," Jessica said, inspecting the card. "This isn't his handwriting, either." She opened her cell anyway and scrolled down to his most recent call. After a few rings, the call dumped into his voicemail. "Hey, Tom, just calling to see if you sent us flowers this morning. Can you give me a yell when you get this message?"

"If it wasn't Tom, someone knows who and where we are," Chris said. "Maybe we should cut out of here a little earlier than planned. We can check into a hotel in mid-town, closer to where Eric is playing tomorrow."

Jessica nodded. "We can go after we eat lunch. That'll give the kids time to pack."

"We already ate," Eric said, crossing to the sink and depositing a fistful of empty plates.

"But we haven't," Jessica answered.

Chris opened the refrigerator. The contents were sparse, and he sighed. "Looks like you guys cleared us out." He glanced over his shoulder at Eric and then switched his gaze to Jessica. "What are you in the mood for?" As always, the question prompted his mind to launch into the gutter.

Jessica grinned, likely catching the underlying meaning in his question.

"Food, Mom," Eric said. "God, do you two ever stop?"

Color flushed her cheeks crimson.

"You're over fifty," Eric complained, rolling his eyes.

"Hey! Give your mom a break. She looks damn good for her age."

Jessica raised her eyebrows. "For my age?"

It was Chris's turn to blush, and he nodded.

"You turn forty this year, babe."

Chris grinned. "Yeah, and you're just a bit older than me."

"But I still look like I'm thirty." She put her hands on her hips.

Chris tilted his head a little as he looked at her, narrowing his eyes. "Maybe."

Bite me, she thought.

"What do you want for lunch?" He leaned against the counter. He hadn't aged much in the last ten years either. He still had a full head of hair, only a few laugh lines around his eyes, and was in superb physical shape thanks to the karate classes he taught.

Jessica shrugged. "Chinese?"

Chris walked over to the phone and placed the order. Twenty minutes later, with the kids all packed and ready to go, the food arrived. Chris and Jessica sat down to eat while the kids went in the living room to watch television.

"Maybe?" Jessica looked at him and pulled out some lo mein noodles from the white paper box.

Chris smiled. "You still look younger than I do."

Jessica slipped her shoe off and ran her foot up his leg while she sinuously slid the chopsticks between her open lips. Slowly and deliberately, she pulled them out of her closed mouth.

Chris glanced toward the entryway, and the kitchen door closed with a soft click. He slid his chair back a few feet. "I've got something for you to suck on," he whispered and pulled her from her chair and onto his lap, drowning her protests with his tongue.

"I'll bet you do. But now isn't the time."

"I beg to differ." The sound of his zipper lowering one noisy link at a time, filled the room. He grinned, his hands firmly holding her waist. "You want to tease me like that?" He pointed his chin toward her discarded chopsticks. "Tsk, tsk." His hands drifted to the hem of her skirt and underneath, finding the creamy skin of her thighs.

The lock on the kitchen door flipped with a tick, and his fingers found their objective. The soft patch of cotton between her legs soon became tacky with her juices, prompted by his gentle massage. He chuckled, his eyes locked on hers, watching the calico colors swirl in her irises. He moved the fabric aside and dipped his finger into the wetness, sliding as slow and deliberate as she had done with her chopsticks.

"God, Jessie." He sighed and stared into her strange eyes, the colors swirling ever so slightly as they always did when he was near her. "You still have no clue what you do to me."

Jessica laughed and shifted on his lap, allowing him to fill her. "I know exactly what I do to you. I've always known. From that first meeting, which was electrifying for more than one reason, wasn't it?" She smiled.

He nodded, even though that statement sent a thrilling chill through his skin. "So, I did see something in your eyes, even then."

"Yes. When our eyes first met, I felt like a lightning bolt went through me. You still have that effect on me every time I look into your eyes." She arched again, kissing him to stop the moan of pleasure from escaping.

When the kiss broke, he smiled. "It's a wonder I can breathe when you're around."

She laughed.

"I sometimes forget to when I look at you." He tightened his jaw and dug his fingers into her waist, trying to gain control as their hips slowly swirled together, but he was too far gone. The playful, sexy smile on her face combined with her lust-laden eyes shoved him over the edge. "Jess!" he whispered through clenched teeth, mindful of the kids a few yards away in the other room, even with the orgasm ripping through him and filling her with his juices.

"Ty," she whispered with the same reverie, arching into her climax, her muscles clenching and driving another wave of tremors through his spent member.

He closed his eyes and tilted his head back for a moment, taking a deep breath. He slowly opened his eyes and looked at her, sensing her shift in mood as she pulled away from him. He zipped up and watched her pull herself together, the underwear a complete loss that landed in the kitchen garbage.

The satiation of the moment faded, and he stared at her, sighing. "I don't think I would survive without you."

Jessica paused and looked at him. "If something happened to me, you would be fine. You have the boys."

He shook his head. "I wouldn't be fine."

"You'd have to be." She looked at him sharply. "With kids, you don't have the luxury of not being okay. They'd need you, and that comes first."

He took another deep breath and took her in with his eyes, slowly and completely, memorizing everything, even as something under the surface of his conscious nagged at him to remember what she looked like.

"Just smile for me, will you?" he asked softly, wanting that memory stored as well.

Jessica smiled and let out a light chuckle. "Sometimes I just don't know about you."

"It's a little late for that." He smiled and hiked his chair back to the table. With a quick glance, the kitchen door unlocked, and he picked up the chopsticks, resuming their disrupted lunch.

She took the seat next to him and finished eating the lo mein noodles and Chinese vegetables, trying not to grin like a fool.

Emily came in a few minutes later. "You haven't finished lunch yet?"

They looked at each other, grinned, and blushed. "Not yet," they replied in unison.

"We're ready to go anytime you are."

"Have Eric throw your bags into the back. We'll be a few more minutes." Chris reached into his pocket and tossed the keys to her.

"Okay." She caught the keys and disappeared, letting the door close behind her again.

"I can't wait to get home," Jessica said. "I miss the quiet."

Chris burst out laughing. "It's never quiet at home."

"You know what I mean."

He nodded. "I do." He stood and collected their plates, then brought them to the sink, leaving them on the growing stack of dishes.

Jessica looked from the mess to him.

"Maid service."

"Must be nice."

"It is. You want one at home?"

She raised her eyebrow. "Actually..."

"Consider it done."

"I don't need one every day. Just once a week would be nice."

"Whatever your heart desires, babe."

"I don't need much more than what I already have." She wrapped her arms around him, gently kissing him.

"Now you're just getting sappy."

"Bite me."

He leaned over, bit her neck, and chuckled before pulling away. "We need to pack up."

"Mm-hm," she agreed, and they headed to pack up their things.

"Do we want to sell this place?" he asked as he walked into the bedroom behind her.

Jessica turned. "Why?"

"I don't know. It's not very practical for the family."

Jessica burst out laughing. "Who cares? I'd rather stay here than in some hotel when we visit the city."

Chris thought about that. "I'd rather have room service."

"You do have room service. It's called delivery."

Chris laughed. "All right. We'll keep it."

Jessica traced the diamond necklace on her nightstand with her fingers before picking it up. "This is really beautiful. Thank you."

"I'd love it if you wore it." He crossed to her, took the necklace, slipped it around her neck, and clasped it when she pulled her hair to the side. "Pack the dress too."

She placed the dress in the garment bag and then they went into the boys' room and did a check to make sure they had everything. Chris found a game under the bed and snagged it.

"Ready?" He looked at Jessica and she nodded.

"All right everyone, ready to roll?" he asked as they walked into the living room and got nods in return.

Emily handed him the keys and they gave one last glance at the apartment before turning to catch the elevator.

Chris locked the apartment and turned. The entire family stood staring at the progression of numbers on the display. Then it hit him. This was *his* family. Joy and terror filled him, and a small shiver slithered down his spine. Of all the things in this world he wanted and never expected to come to fruition, this... this moment outshined them all. Every fantasy from his youth paled in comparison. His heart swelled.

They headed down the elevator and got the kids strapped in their car seats. Eric and Emily settled in, and Jessica clicked her seat belt. Chris opened his door as his phone rang. He dug it out of his pocket and opened it at the same time he closed the driver's side door.

"Hi, Sam, we were just getting ready to leave." He started the car.

A whir caught his attention, followed by a familiar smell. He glanced at Jessica. The same puzzled look graced her face, and then her eyes rolled back, and she slumped in the seat.

"Damn." Chris looked up.

The last thing that registered in his mind was a chloroform dispenser like the ones he'd used to capture Frank's victims. The phone slipped from his hand, and darkness settled over him.

End Game Chapter 32

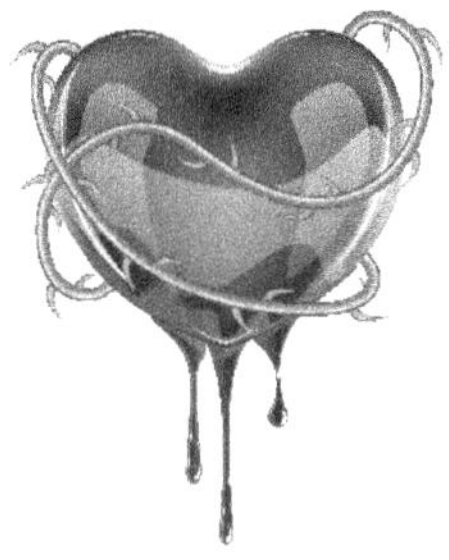

SAM STARED AT THE cell phone. "Chris?"

No answer, and a bad feeling crawled into his bones. The absence of sound, or more specifically, the absence of Chris or any of the others echoing over the sound of the engine in the receiver frightened him.

"I'll be back." He grabbed his coat, shuffling quickly toward the apartment building ten blocks away. He wrapped his coat against the frigid wind tunnel, and a few minutes later, he arrived at the garage entrance.

"Excuse me, did the Ryans leave yet,"—he looked at the nametag on the left lapel of the attendant—"Jason?"

"I haven't seen Mr. Ryan for years," Jason replied.

Sam smiled at him. "I was at his wedding yesterday. I've known Chris since he was a little boy."

Jason shifted uncomfortably. "He's not here."

"I'll tell you what. Can we take a walk to where his car is parked and see?" Sam asked, and pulled out his wallet.

"Look, Mr. Ryan isn't here."

Sam looked up at the young man. "I'm sure Chris told you to say that, but I'm an old friend. I was talking with him and we were cut off. I'm a little concerned, and I just want to ease my mind. Please, can you help me out?"

"Why don't you just call him back?"

"I've tried, and I can't get through. You can even have my card. I'm his lawyer." Sam pulled out a business card from his wallet and handed it to Jason.

Jason looked at the piece of paper and then back up at Sam, biting his lip. He took a deep breath. "Okay." He led Sam up the ramp.

"Thank you," Sam said, relief washing over him as he followed the young man.

They rounded the corner and got a full view of what lay in the penthouse parking spot. Chris, facedown with a butcher knife planted in his back.

"Jesus Christ!" Sam bolted toward his client, leaving Jason standing by the guardrail with his jaw hanging open. He dug the phone out of his pocket, stabbing 9-1-1 with his index finger, and brought the receiver to his ear, stopping short of the ever-increasing pool of blood. He skirted around, finding a dry spot near Chris's head, and crouched to press his fingers to the side of Chris's throat. "I need an ambulance," he snapped into the phone. The thread of a pulse gave him pause enough to close his eyes and say a prayer. "Someone's been stabbed, and if you don't get here soon, he'll die." He looked up at Jason's ashen face. "Yes, please send the police too."

Sam stood and put his hand over his mouth. He stepped out of the blood range and took a closer look at Chris. Tire tracks laced across both calves, and the fabric of his jeans was soaked red.

"Jesus Christ."

Someone drove over his legs, crushing them to a bloody pulp. He aimed a shaky cell phone camera and started snapping pictures, backing away from the crime scene.

The wail of a distant siren snapped his gaze away from Chris toward Jason.

"What exactly did you see?"

"I saw the truck leaving about five minutes before you came. Is he dead?" Jason's eyes remained locked on the morbid form on the ground.

"No, but if they don't get here soon, he will be."

Sirens bounced off the concrete, and the ambulance screeched to a halt a few feet from Chris. The paramedics got Chris onto a gurney and hauled him into the ambulance. Sam jumped in with them for the ride to the hospital, watching in silence as they worked on him. Once they had an IV in his arm and packing around the knife to slow the bleeding, they turned to Sam.

"Who are you?" one of the paramedics asked.

"Lawyer and family friend." He flipped one of his cards to the paramedic and received a nod in response. "Is he going to be okay?"

The paramedic glanced at Sam with uncertainty, and Sam blew air out. He looked down at the phone in his hand and shuffled through the pictures. The bloody scene transitioned to the wedding, and he shook his head, bringing his gaze back to the knife.

The paramedic grabbed a small plastic bag and handed it to Sam. "I'm sure he won't want to lose those things."

The bag contained Chris's necklace, watch, and wedding band. Sam creased his eyebrows looking between the bag and the paramedic.

The paramedic shrugged a little. "Things sometimes get lost. It happens."

Sam nodded and pocketed the jewelry for safekeeping.

End Game Chapter 33

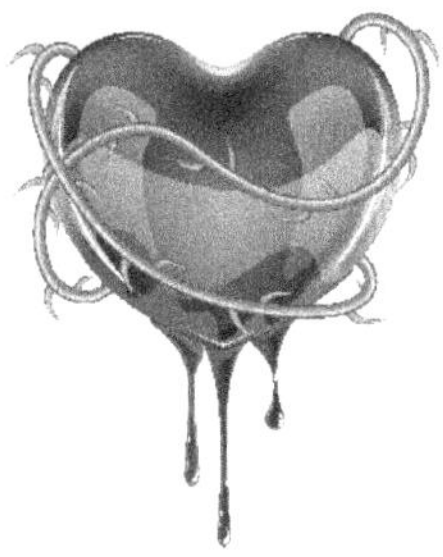

CHRIS OPENED HIS EYES to pitch black—blackness so thick he couldn't even see his own hand when it touched his face. He reached around, trying to find a reference point in the dark.

"Jessica?" The sound of his voice fell flat. His heart began to race, fear fueling it to octane level.

He froze in place, paralyzed, afraid to move in any direction.

A hand descended on his shoulder, making him jump and twirl around.

Christopher Aris stood shrouded in blackness. "Hey, bro, it's been a while."

Chris threw his arms around his little brother. "Jesus, Chris. Way to scare the shit out of me." He pulled away scanning the ambient light now surrounding them and the darkness beyond. "Am I dead?"

"Close, but not quite," Christopher replied. "I'm touched you took my name." He smiled, changing the subject.

Chris shrugged. "It was my way out."

"I know," Christopher said. "And you named your son after me too. That's quite humbling."

Chris smiled at his brother. "I married her."

"I know."

"Is Jessica okay?" Chris asked as the last coherent image drifted back into his mind.

"That's not for me to say."

Panic spread through his limbs, weighing them down. "I need to save her. How do I get back?"

"It's not that easy, Ty. You have to give up some things." He looked at his hands and then back at his brother.

"Anything for my family."

"It's actually a few things."

"Whatever it is, the answer's yes."

"You don't want to agree without knowing the terms."

"You don't understand. This is my family. I'll do whatever it takes to save them."

"For starters, you have to give up your soul," Christopher said.

"Fine, my soul is already condemned."

"That's the thing, Ty. Eric and Jessica did more than heal you, bro. They literally saved your soul."

"You mean I can actually go to heaven?"

Christopher nodded. "Yes, but if you make that choice, your whole family will die today, and they will die painfully." He paused. "You saw the dream."

Chris nodded, He remembered. "Are you in heaven?"

Christopher shook his head solemnly. "No."

His answer hit Chris hard, and he stepped back. "I'm sorry," he said, knowing he'd failed to protect Christopher. At some level, it was his fault his brother was condemned to hell for all eternity.

"It isn't your fault, Ty. I had just as much choice in what I did as you."

Chris turned his back on his brother for a moment, blinking away the sheen of tears, the crushing blow of failure derailing his thought process. He shook his head, focusing on the current situation. "Okay. What else?"

"Your powers."

Chris nodded and looked over his shoulder at his brother. "What else?"

"Sight or sound?"

"What?"

"You have to give up your sight or your hearing."

He looked at his brother in frustration.

"Do you want to see them or hear them for the rest of your life?"

"Both."

"You can't have both."

Chris closed his eyes. This sucked but time was ticking. A decision had to be made. Otherwise, he'd lose her anyway. He concentrated, seeing her in full color on his eyelids easily. But her voice... Her voice was harder to recall and always had been, but her words were what he craved since day one.

That clinched the decision. "I want to hear her say my name. Is that it?"

"Afraid not. You have to choose who dies in your place."

"Not in a million years," he replied, anger lining his flesh and clenching his fists.

"Then everyone dies."

Chris thought for a few minutes. "Tom Whitman."

"He isn't part of your family."

"Jesus, I can't make a choice like that."

"You don't want the choice to be made for you," Christopher said, his eyes conveying the message that it would be the ones closest to him if he didn't make the choice.

"Can you guarantee that the rest will be all right if I choose?"

"No, but if you don't make a choice, they all die."

Chris considered this. "What happened to me? Why am I here?" He narrowed his eyes at his brother.

"You were stabbed in the back and run over by your truck."

"Shit."

"Right now, you are on the way to the hospital, and Sam is in the ambulance with you. They gave him your jewelry, including the wedding band. He's going to find out about you, Ty."

His only hope of getting his family out alive hinged on his next question. "If I agree to the deal and make a choice, will you make sure I'm completely healed?"

Christopher thought about this for a minute and then nodded.

"Who would you choose if you were me?"

Christopher took a deep breath. He had to know that Ty loved Jessica, and without her, he would self-destruct. He had to know his children were not an option, either, so that left Eric and Emily.

"Emily," he finally said.

"Why?"

"Because she's had five more years than she should have."

"That doesn't make it right."

"Ty, if you let them choose, it will be CJ," Christopher replied.

Chris sucked the air in and closed his eyes. "Tell me where they are."

"Deserted warehouse on the water near 52nd Street on the East Side."

"Okay."

"Okay what?" Christopher asked.

"Okay, my powers, my soul, my sight… and Emily in return for sending me back completely healed."

Christopher nodded.

"Please don't let her suffer."

His brother hesitated and then nodded.

"How long do I have with them?" he asked.

Christopher shrugged. "I love you, bro. I'll see you when I see you." He smiled and began to fade.

"BACK AT YOU," CHRIS said at the precise moment the blade was pulled from his back. He felt the jolt and then the heat and pain as his body healed. He yelled out and sat up in the trauma room, his breath coming in short bursts. He looked around the room at the shocked medical staff.

"Sam, Sam Trueman," he said to the closest nurse. "In the waiting room. Get him now."

"You shouldn't even be alive," a nurse whispered in awe.

"Get me Sam Trueman NOW!" He scanned the staff, trying to read their thoughts, but his mind was blank.

"Calm down, sir," a doctor said from behind him, wiping a wet cloth over Chris's back.

"No!" Chris jumped off the table and spun toward the collection of doctors and nurses. "Get me my clothes, and get me Sam now," he said, trying to impart his influence on them.

They stared back.

"You just had this in your back," the doctor said, holding up the bloody knife. "And you have lost a lot of blood." He looked down at Chris's legs and took an unsteady step forward. "You shouldn't be able to stand on those legs."

Chris swung his gaze to one of the more lucid nurses. "Please," he pleaded.

She nodded, heading out into the waiting room.

"I need to talk to my friend alone. Can you please find me something to wear?"

The staff nodded and left the trauma room, leaving Chris alone. He took a deep breath as the weird conversation with his brother resounded in his mind.

I should have killed Sharon when I had the chance.

"Damn it," he whispered. *Jessica will never forgive me for making that choice.*

End Game Chapter 34

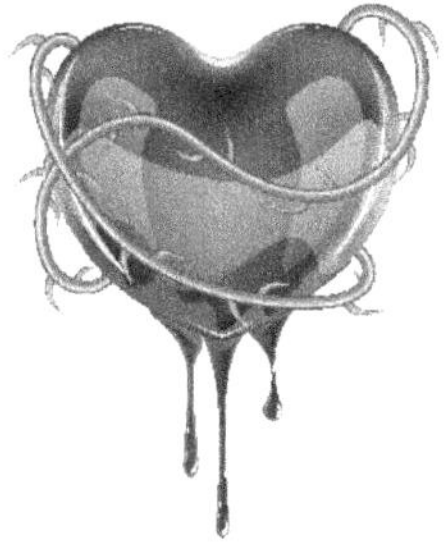

SAM STEPPED OUT OF the ambulance after they carted Chris away and followed the path of doctors and nurses until they got to a trauma room. He was blocked from entering, though, and escorted to the waiting room. Sam called his wife and let her know he would be a while. He took out the wedding ring and twirled it on his finger waiting for the news.

Sam caught a hint of writing on the inside of the ring and read the inscription.

Ty, a million years isn't long enough. Yours forever, Jessica.

The heat in his face drained as he looked up at the door to the trauma room in disbelief. "Sweet Jesus." Things began to click in his mind, and everything finally made perfect sense. The only thing he couldn't figure out was how he got rid of the scar.

"Mr. Trueman?" A very pale nurse interrupted his thoughts.

"Yes," he said, pocketing the ring again.

"Mr. Ryan is asking for you," she said, looking extremely discombobulated.

Sam stood and followed her. Chris sat on the edge of the trauma bed with a blanket draped over his waist, his legs dangling in full view and no hint of the damage he had seen in the ambulance. Although he was facing Sam, Sam knew that there would be no mark on his back if he were to turn.

"Leave us," Chris said to the nurse, and she scurried out of the room. He slowly looked up and put his hand out expectantly, his eyes not quite meeting Sam's.

Sam looked at the wedding band in his hand, put it in Chris's palm without a word, and watched as he slid it on. He looked around the room to make sure they were indeed alone.

"How?" he finally asked, and Chris put his hand out again. Sam handed over the watch and necklace.

"Are you still my attorney?"

Sam considered saying no but then thought better of it. "Yes, attorney client privilege is still in effect," he said, knowing that was what Chris was asking. "How?"

"How what? How did I not die today, or how did I not die in the complex?" He clasped the necklace around his neck and slid the watch on his wrist.

"Where is Chris?" Sam asked, his voice hissing from his throat.

"Frank blew Chris to bits along with his BMW." Chris looked up at Sam. "I have to go." He stood on wobbly legs.

"Jesus." Sam looked at the man who he'd thought he had known so well. "Is that why she did this to you, because of who you really are?"

Chris looked at him in bewilderment, his eyebrows creasing and his head cocking to the side.

"Jessica," Sam said, reading the confusion in his face.

CHRIS SHOOK HIS HEAD. "Jessica didn't do this." He looked around the room for something to wear. "I have to find her before that crazy bitch kills her and the rest of my family."

"What crazy bitch?" Sam asked and studied Chris's face.

"Sharon Whitman. It's a long story." He began to open up the cabinets. He found a cabinet full of blue scrubs with the hospital emblem, rifled through them until he found a pair of pants and a shirt in his size, and then slid them on. "Will you help me?" He turned to look at Sam. "Please," he said desperately. "My family's in danger."

Sam nodded, still staring in disbelief. The color drained from his face.

"Sam, I need you to help me. You can't pass out on me." Chris reached out to steady his only true friend outside of his wife.

Sam nodded again. "How?"

"Eric," Chris replied. "Eric and Jessica," he added. "I need to get back to the apartment and change before we go down to the docks at East 52nd Street." He led Sam out of the trauma room. His wallet and keys had been in the truck. Chris sighed as they walked out of the hospital. His feet were freezing.

"How?" Sam asked again from the comfort of a cab.

"I'm not really sure. I just know Jessica is one very special lady." He looked over at Sam. "I fell in love with her, and against all odds, she fell for me. Eric... He's the one who gave me the second chance because I saved his mom. He was only eight and so innocent. If he only knew..." Chris smiled a little.

"But how?"

Chris shook his head as they pulled up in front of the apartment building. The forensic team was still in the garage, and Chris headed in the front door.

"Hi, Fred," Chris said as he approached the front desk. "I need the spare key to the apartment."

Fred reached below the counter, opened the safe, and pulled out the spare key to the penthouse, his eyes never leaving Chris's. "But..." He handed the key over.

"I know. It was just a flesh wound." He shrugged and plucked the key out of Fred's hand, looking over his shoulder at Sam.

Sam followed him to the elevator.

"Eric and Jessica have..." He took a breath and looked over at Sam. "I know this is going to sound crazy, but they had the power to heal." *Along with other powers.* "Eric healed me."

"But he wasn't there," Sam said in confusion.

Chris shrugged. "He kind of was." He let out a laugh. "He and Jessica could..." He paused as he searched for the words. "Astral project to each other."

He shook his head as they entered the apartment. He had never told the story aloud and realized how certifiable it sounded. He glanced back at Sam and saw the expression that he expected.

"I know. I sound certifiable, but that's what happened. I will only be a minute." Chris went into the bedroom, peeled off the scrubs, and opened his closet to find what he was looking for. He pulled the black gi out of the closet and quickly threw the pants on; he was going to need all the latitude of movement that the karate outfit provided, as well as the stealth of the black color. He pulled open a drawer, found a black T-shirt, and slipped that on before putting the black karate top over it. He tied the black belt around his waist and went in search of his black sneakers. He glanced at Sam as he walked through the living room to the foyer closet where the sneakers were and then slipped them on. "Let's roll," he said, running his fingers through his hair.

"Where are we going?"

"We need your car, and then you need to drop me off down at the docks at East 52nd Street."

"Why?"

"That's where they are."

Sam's eyebrows shot into perfect arches. "How do you know where they are?"

"Chris told me when I was dead."

"We should call the police."

Chris shook his head. "And say what? That my family was kidnapped, and I know where they are because my dead brother told me? They'll put me away, and I'll lose them. She'll kill all of them." *Not just Emily.* Pain sucked the wind from his chest.

"Why?" Sam said as he followed Chris onto the elevator.

"Because Tom left her, and she blames Jess."

"That still doesn't make sense."

"Not a whole lot of what has happened in my life makes sense, Sam."

"You don't have a coat," Sam observed as they walked out the front door and took a left turn, heading toward his apartment building.

"I'll be fine," Chris said. He was on a mission, and nothing was going to slow him down.

"Ty." Sam stopped.

Chris looked over his shoulder. "What?" he barked.

"What you and your brother did—"

"Brothers. We all were involved," he interrupted and grabbed Sam's arm. "You can walk and talk, can't you?"

Sam blinked. "Chris was involved?"

"Yes," Chris said. "I wiped out any record of his involvement. There is no proof that he ever set foot down there or that I'm not him." He looked at Sam. "Even if they did forensic DNA testing on the site where Chris blew up, it would come back as a possible relative, but not as Chris. For all intents and purposes, I am Chris. Medical records, dental records, identity, and with your help, I now legally have his name."

"Jesus," Sam replied. He looked at the wedding band on Chris's hand. "Who else knows besides Jessica?"

Chris stopped. "Eric, Emily, and Tom." He looked over at Sam and then continued walking.

"Tom Whitman knows you're alive?"

Chris nodded. "Yes, he knows," he said as they arrived at the apartment complex. "Do you have your car keys on you?"

Sam nodded, and Chris steered him into the garage.

Sam unlocked the car and slid inside. He put the keys in the ignition but didn't start the car. "Tom knows and he didn't go to the police?" He looked over at Chris.

"What exactly would he have said, Sam?" Chris buckled his seat belt. "That I was Ty Aris? Look at me. There are no scars on my face, no scars where the bullets went in, no fingerprints of mine down there, no DNA to trace back. I cleaned the place down to the microscopic level before I left. Nothing recorded that could lead back to this face, back to Chris." He shrugged and smiled. "He didn't exactly like that when I pointed it out to him either. Drive, Sam."

Sam turned over the ignition. "I'm still struggling here." He backed out of the parking spot.

"I'm sure you have a million questions, but I don't have time right now." Chris took a deep breath. "At least one person is going to die today, and I have to stop her from killing the rest." He looked out the window as they headed toward the East Side Highway. "I'm not sure that I'll make it out alive either." He glanced at Sam. "If I don't come out within a half hour, you can call the cops. Deal?"

Sam nodded. "Deal," he said. "I have to know something."

"What?"

"Did you really kill your stepfather?"

Chris looked out the window. "Yeah."

"He was my friend."

"He raped Anna on a nightly basis, and I thought he killed her." Chris glanced at Sam.

Sam's head snapped toward Chris, the anger in his eyes evident. "He wouldn't do such a thing."

Chris laughed. "Sam, he did, just like he carved up my face."

"I thought that was an accident?"

"Nope," Chris said. "You weren't around very much, were you? The old man used to beat the crap out of me regularly, almost as often as his nightly adventures with my sister." The bitterness in his voice filled the car.

"Jesus," he replied. "Did he ever hit Chris or Frank?"

"He tried to hit Chris, but I always stepped in. I wasn't about to let him hurt my little brother." He looked out the window. "He never touched Frank or Marian."

"I'm sorry. I didn't know."

Chris shook his head. "Did you know he had my mom killed?"

"That was an accident. Jacob Aris loved your mother."

Chris laughed. "My mother was going to leave him."

"How would you know that?"

"I overheard her talking to Anna. She wasn't happy, and she was going to talk to a lawyer about getting a divorce." He took a deep breath. "I also overheard the fight that she had with him. The next thing I know, my mother is dead." He glared at Sam. "So, don't tell me it was an accident."

Sam pulled off the East Side Highway onto 52nd Street and stopped at the curb. He looked over at Chris and sighed. "I knew she was thinking about leaving him. But he would never intentionally kill her, Ty." He closed his eyes. "Jacob was never the same after your mother died."

"Sam, I don't want to hear it." Chris scanned the deserted warehouses around them. He looked over his shoulder across the highway and there was another one. "Shit."

Chris, help me out, which one?

He looked at the three of them again. If I were her, I would use the one on the water because of the limited access.

"Jacob was a poor excuse for what I became. I knew it was wrong, but I didn't care," Chris added as he surveyed the area again. It was getting dark, and he had to make a choice. When he glanced over his shoulder again, he saw a flash of light in one of the windows across the highway. "Until I met Jess," he finished. "Over there." He pointed at the warehouse behind them.

Sam nodded and pulled out, doing a U-turn in the road. 52nd Street went under the East Side Highway and ended in a deserted parking lot next to the warehouse. He parked, and Chris opened the door.

"Ty?"

Chris turned, the gravel crunching under his feet, and met Sam's gaze.

"Be careful."

"You too, Sam," Chris replied. "If I'm not back in a half hour, call in the cavalry."

Sam nodded, and Chris closed the door and slipped toward the building. It was dark enough so the black gi blended with the asphalt.

End Game Chapter 35

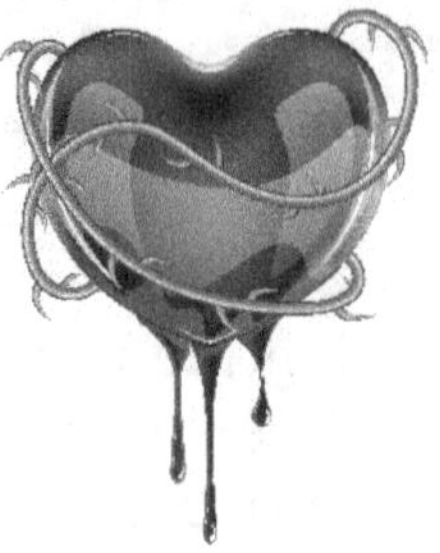

TOM STARED AT SHARON when she pushed the door open. His heart dropped at the sight of the unconscious boys being carried into the room by two thugs.

She pointed at the chairs, and they set the children down. She tightened the straps around their tiny arms and ankles.

"What have you done?" Tom stared at his son, his heart jumping into his throat, pounding hard enough to hurt with each breath.

"Christopher Aris is dead." She smiled triumphantly, causing Tom to snap his head toward her.

Fear got the better of him and his bladder let loose, filling the room with the sharp stench of urine.

Sharon laughed.

"God damn it, don't do this!" He yanked on the chains, panic overriding his senses.

The men returned with Emily and Eric, both unconscious as well, and she directed them to two more chairs.

"Please don't do this," Tom begged.

The men sent disgusted glances in his direction before they skittered out of the room.

A few minutes later, one of the men carried Jessica's body, clad in the white dress and the diamond necklace gleaming from around her neck.

Sharon whispered something in the man's ear and he nodded and left the room.

Tom fell to his knees watching his wife chain Jessica to the opposite wall. "Please don't do this," he begged, tears blurring his vision and cutting hot paths down his face.

"You have got to learn who's in control," Sharon walked over to the table, picked up a syringe, put some clear liquid in the syringe's barrel, and then walked over to the children. She grabbed Emily's arm and slid the needle in, then pushed the liquid inside her veins. She repeated this with Eric and then Jessica, leaving the two young boys alone.

JESSICA OPENED HER EYES, her vision distorted, blurring at first and then settling into fuzzy focus. Blinking, her eyes sharpened, and she scanned the layout in front of her. *Chloroform.* That had been what she smelled in the car, and that thought coupled with the clarity of what surrounded her sent icebergs through her veins.

She struggled to her feet. "Where's Chris?"

"Dead as a doornail," Sharon said, grinning like an evil bitch.

The impact of that statement was immediate and overwhelming, and Jessica fell to her knees. Her chest constricted with the pain suffocating her. "No. No!" Her scream echoed off the walls, followed by the harsh sobs ripping from her chest.

If he were alive, they wouldn't be here.

"Jessie," Tom whispered.

Eric's head whipped around at the sound of his voice. "Son of a bitch," he said, calling the attention of everyone that was conscious to him, including Jessica.

"Very interesting statement," Sharon said, staring at the four children. Her gaze fell on little Tommy like she was seeing him for the first time and then jumped to her husband and back as she approached the unconscious boy.

"Get away from him, you bitch," Emily snapped from her seat.

Sharon pulled a gun and shot Emily between the eyes, killing her instantly. She put the gun back in her waistband and returned her attention to Tommy again, ignoring the shocked silence that fell over the room.

Jessica couldn't breathe at all. The reality of her daughter being killed before her eyes was too much for her brain to acknowledge. She passed out on the floor.

ERIC INHALED SHARPLY, HIS eyes filling with tears, and he glanced at the bitch who killed his sister. He had no forewarning. No chance to try to block the shot, to put himself between the bullet and Emily. A large empty hole appeared in the pit of his stomach. The ringing in his ears finally subsided and sound returned. Her voice, grating under his skin, targeted his youngest brother.

Sharon looked over at Tom. His gaze was still locked on Emily with his mouth open, eyes wide and shocked.

"Is this *YOUR* child?"

Tom looked slowly away from Emily, his eyes meeting Eric's for a moment before meeting Sharon's. He shook his head.

"He looks an awful lot like you." She looked over at CJ. "He's a spitting image of Christopher Aris." She pointed, glanced at Jessica who was still passed out and walked over to Tom. She grabbed his face. "Is that your son?"

Tom couldn't speak. His gaze darted between Eric and his son. Fear etched in his features and Eric took a breath, praying it wasn't his last.

"Please don't hurt my brothers," Eric said, tears streaking down his face, causing Sharon to look in his direction.

Silently, he called CJ, trying to wake him, but he was still out for the count. He glanced over at his sister and stifled a sob. *Where the hell is Chris?*

"Please." He closed his eyes and hung his head. He tried to locate Chris and came up empty.

The despair that crept into his heart came close to that of his mother's. *Mom,* he thought as he looked over at her. She was slowly coming back to them.

"MY BABY GIRL," JESSICA cried as she looked over at her daughter. *Danny will never forgive me.* Her gaze landed on Eric and the two boys.

"IS THAT YOUR SON?" Sharon screamed in Tom's face.

"No, he's Chris's son," Jessica answered, the motherly instinct to protect her children coming alive again. She stood and glared at Sharon. "And so help me God, if you harm any more of my children, I will tear your throat out with my bare hands," she said through clenched teeth, her voice shaking with rage.

Sharon pulled the gun out and shot Jessica in the stomach. "Shut up, bitch."

Jessica didn't flinch as the bullet passed through her body. The path behind it healed immediately, leaving only a small circle of red on her immaculate white dress. That was two bullets. She looked at the semi-automatic gun that Sharon had and thought it held six shots in the clip.

"Fuck you," she said.

Sharon shot again, and this time, the bullet ripped through her bare shoulder. Jessica healed the bone and flesh within her body, but left the bullet hole facing Sharon still oozing She didn't flinch.

Three more.

Sharon strode across the room and put the muzzle to her forehead.

End Game Chapter 36

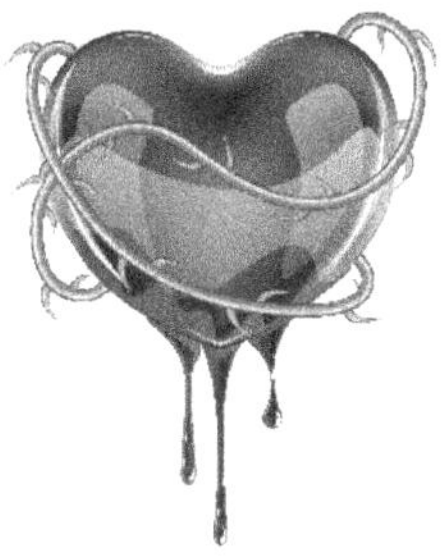

CHRIS MADE IT INTO the warehouse unnoticed and stood with his back against the wall, surveying the layout of the building. He closed his eyes and inhaled, calming his frantic heartbeat. A gunshot echoed somewhere above him. His head snapped toward the stairwell. He took the stairs three at a time and recklessly bounded toward where the sound had originated.

"IS THAT YOUR SON?" Sharon screamed.

Chris's heart jumped into his throat as he hit the landing and heard the second shot, almost immediately followed by the third one.

"Oh God," he whispered, trying to keep the shakes at bay, and slipped into the hallway. He started down the hallway but froze at the click of a hammer. "Fuck."

The barrel of a gun pressed into the small of his back.

"Move." The man pushed Chris toward the door.

Chris obeyed and threw the door open in time to see Sharon put the gun to his wife's head. "I wouldn't do that if I were you," Chris snarled.

Sharon looked at him in disbelief, turned the gun his way, and pulled the trigger.

Chris had already anticipated her move and ducked out of the way. The man behind him was not as lucky, as the bullet tore through his throat, knocking him back into the hallway.

He stepped toward the discarded gun.

Sharon put the gun back to Jessica's head and looked at Chris. "I will kill her."

Chris froze and turned his head, meeting her deranged glare.

Jessica's chest rose and fell, harnessed by fury and sorrow and she cast a glance in his direction. Her eyebrows furrowed.

"Move slowly into the room and close the door behind you," Sharon demanded.

Chris did as she said, his heart pounding so hard he thought it would barrel out of his chest at any moment. With fear alive in his veins, he scanned the rest of the room, his gaze settling on Emily. He stopped and inhaled. *My fault.* He blinked back the tears.

He looked back at Sharon, putting his game face back on. "Tell me what you want." he said, using the smooth voice he used to use on his victims. He moved farther into the room.

Jessica recognized the voice, the tone, the inflection, and stared at him. When he finally glanced over at her, he sent one thought her way, and she gasped.

No more power, babe. It was the only way I could come back.

Sharon smiled. "I want Tom to see her suffer and die." She looked back at Jessica and pulled the gun away, moving it slowly around the room until it fell back on Chris. "Now move over there." She pointed to a pole that had wrist shackles hanging from it. "Take off your shirt and hook yourself in." She walked over to CJ and pointed the gun at his head. "Or your son dies."

Chris didn't hesitate. He walked over to the pole, stripping the top of the karate outfit off and the black T-shirt underneath. He hooked his hands into the shackles and looked over at his wife, dread filled every fiber, but better Sharon take out her anger on him than anyone else in the room. It would buy them time. Time for CJ to wake up and set things right.

Sharon placed the gun in the back of her pants and picked up something that looked like a whip with several strands on it, but at the end of each strand was a small, spiked ball. She laughed as she walked over and stood behind him. She ran her hand over his back.

"My, my, if I had known just how sexy you were, I might have chosen you instead of Tom," she purred. She smiled at Jessica as she reached around him and ran her hand over the front of his pants.

Chris turned his hips away from her and sent a glare over his shoulder. "Not in this lifetime, bitch."

She toyed with him, waving the spikes in his field of vision and running her hand over his ass. "What if I gave you a choice? The end of the whip or the opportunity to fuck me?"

"That's easy. I'll take the whip any day over your twisted cunt."

She stepped back and cracked the whip against his back.

Chris put his head against the pole but didn't cry out even though the spikes ripped through his flesh. He glanced over at his stepson. *Can you wake CJ?*

Eric shook his head.

Chris closed his eyes as the next deluge of pain tore through his back.

"Stop!" Jessica screamed

Sharon pulled the gun, firing another shot at her. This one barely missed her heart, and she healed the path again. Chris's pained gaze met hers.

Crack after crack and he didn't utter a sound, the pain as acute as any of the horrors he'd experienced. He clung to consciousness, forcing his legs to hold him as long as he could. They needed time, even if it meant trading his life.

The speed and power increased, and Sharon growled with each hit. He was getting to her, his silence frustrating her, taunting.

He caught Tom's gaze and he stretched his lips into a sadistic smile, one Tom was very familiar with. Then Chris's legs gave out. He fell, his knees not quite reaching the ground, and he bit the yelp back, breathing through the sudden ripple of pain as his back muscles tightened to hold his weight.

A sudden flare bloomed in his temple and blackness engulfed him.

THE BUTT OF THE gun slammed down into his temple along with a guttural cry of frustration. Chris slumped, unconscious.

"Sharon, please don't," Tom said, wondering why Chris hadn't stopped her.

"He can't," Eric answered in a whisper, glancing over his shoulder at Tom. "He gave up more than just his powers too." A tear slipped down his cheek.

Sharon unclasped the cuffs and dragged Chris to the cross beam laid out on the floor. She tied Chris's arms to the wood and left him there, then crossed to the table and picked up three large nails and a hammer. "This was supposed to be for you," she said to Jessica as she passed. "But I think it's better if you watch him die like this."

"Sharon, stop this right now!" Tom struggled against the chains, watching her line the nail to the middle of Chris's wrist.

Sharon slammed the nail with the hammer, and it slid easily through the flesh and bone. Chris groaned but didn't wake up. She pounded the hammer down until the nail had embedded deep in the thick wood. She repeated this with his other wrist and then walked to his feet to take his shoes and socks off. She lined his feet up on the small wooden wedge before glancing at Jessica with a smile.

"Crucifixion is such a nasty way to die. You suffocate to death, slowly." She hammered the nail through his feet and pounded it in as far as the others.

Her breath wheezed from exertion when she stepped back, dropping the hammer on the floor.

"That ought to do it." She crossed to a switch hanging near the door and pushed the button, watching as the chains holding the cross slowly lifted. She pressed the stop button when the base of the cross reached eight feet off the floor.

CHRIS HITCHED HIS BREATH in as pain enveloped him. He didn't have to look to know. This was his dream. He was going to die, and there wasn't a damn thing he could do about it.

He tilted his head back and screamed in pain and frustration, causing all eyes in the room to fall on him. "You fucking bitch!"

She pointed the gun at Eric. "Eeny,"—the gun moved to CJ—"meeny,"—she pointed it at Tommy—"miney,"—she landed on Jessica—"mo." She grinned.

Chris fell silent, watching her. Tom was right—she was crazier than Frank.

"You aren't Christopher Aris, are you?"

"No."

"You're Ty Aris, aren't you?"

"Wrong again." Chris smiled and slid his glance to Jessica, pushing with his feet to give his arms a break. Weakened by both blood loss and pain, what was supposed to be a slow suffocation accelerated. It became increasingly harder to exhale. The pain made him swoon a little. He shook his head to keep from passing out. He needed to wake CJ, so he closed his eyes, concentrating all his thoughts on waking his son. He couldn't project them like before, but he hoped somehow, his son would hear his father calling and react.

When he opened his eyes, Eric flinched and glanced over at his brothers. CJ was still out, but Tommy was waking up. He looked back up at Chris.

"What else?" Eric whispered

Pain flashed deep within him, and it wasn't because he was nailed to a cross. His gaze drifted over to his dead stepdaughter.

My powers and my soul, Chris answered Eric. He glanced over at his wife. *My soul, babe. I traded my soul for you.*

Jessica let out a sob.

"Daddy!" The scream tore through the room making everyone jump a mile. Tommy's wide blue eyes stared up at his father hanging from the cross. They had been in enough Sunday school classes for him to have an inkling of what was wrong.

Chris focused on his youngest child. "Daddy is going to be just fine." He smiled, lying to his son.

"Daddy, Jesus died like that," Tommy's chin quivered, and tears brimmed and slid down his cheeks.

"Don't cry." Chris pushed with his feet, allowing his voice to come out without being laced by the pain racking his body. He smiled again. "See, it isn't so bad."

Tommy turned his head toward Eric.

"Tommy," Chris called, pulling his attention back. He didn't want Tommy to see Emily.

Jessica let out a shaky sob. "Tommy, baby."

Sharon suddenly understood what they were doing and walked behind Tommy. She unhooked him and yanked him up by his hair, making him cry out. She pulled the knife out of her pocket and put it to his throat.

Fear laced Chris's mouth with a tinny taste. He clamped his jaw together, glaring a warning. The bitch just smiled back.

Sharon dragged him in front of Emily, holding a handful of hair and directing his gaze toward Emily. "You won't be as lucky as your sister."

"Mommy!" Tommy cried, sobbing and squirming in Sharon's grip.

Chris couldn't see his face, but the fear in his voice shot straight to his heart. He was going to kill her, even if he had to come back from the dead to do it. Before he could voice his vow, Tom growled words that struck ice in his veins.

"He's mine, all right! He is my son and I swear to God, I will kill you if you hurt him." Tom strained against the chains.

Chris closed his eyes again and sent the scream out for CJ. He opened his eyes settling his gaze on Eric.

Eric's left hand spread wide, and his forehead broke out in sweat, his face a mask of concentration. Chris swallowed, and his eyes snapped to Sharon and the knife against his son's throat. His gaze flitted back and forth between Eric's now-bleeding hand and his son.

"Jess," he whispered. *Unchain Tom. I left some of the juice in you. Unchain him!*

Jessica's eyes went wide as she caught his thought. She closed her eyes and concentrated.

"I thought you were sterile." Sharon tilted her head.

"I got myself fixed. There was no way in hell I was bringing a child into this world with you."

Sharon gasped. "You son of a bitch." She sliced what she thought was Tommy's throat.

Eric cried out as the blade tore through his hand.

Chris blinked the edges of darkness away and tried to push himself up with his feet. Pain traveled up his legs, flaring almost enough to make him pass out again. His wrists ground from his weight every time he lost the strength in his legs, sending excruciating pain through his shoulders. His eyes finally focused on the room again. He needed to wake his son. After inhaling deeply and pushing himself up again despite the pain, he let out a blood-curdling cry, causing everyone in the room except Jessica to turn their attention on him.

"Christopher James!" he screamed, both aloud and in his head. He looked down in time to see his son's eyes flutter open and then all went black.

JESSICA FELT THE POWER jump out of her at the same moment Tom lunged. His eyes widened when the chains didn't stop him. He reached her, yanking Tommy from her grip and pushing him to safety.

The sixth bullet tore through Tom's side, but that didn't slow him down. Fury filled his features, turning his ruggedly handsome face into a ferocious growling mask.

"You tried to kill my son." He flung her across the room.

Jessica tore her gaze from his predatory advance and looked up at Chris. He hung limply from the cross, his head hanging and blood dripping from the wood, pooling on the floor below. Thin red tendrils rolled down his arms and sides, the wounds in his wrists leaking small droplets every few seconds. She glanced down at the pool, her heart hammering in her chest, drowning the sound of her hitching breath. *How much blood has he lost?* Her eyes snapped back up at him, searching, praying, but not finding any motion in his chest, no rise and fall, no groans of pain, just silence. Fear choked his name from her throat.

"Mommy?" CJ said, and she turned towards him. He broke eye contact and looked up, his eyes going wide at the sight of his father nailed to a cross.

"Let me out, CJ, and get your father down."

The chains fell from her wrists and ankles just as Tom caught a handful of Sharon's hair and pitched her into the wall. The nails creaked and shot out from the wood, releasing Chris. Jessica watched him fall, time flashing like a shutter, his descent a progression of snapshots. His broken, battered body bounced in the puddle of blood and then went still.

She was across the room before his name finished barreling from her lips, and both Eric and CJ stood at her side.

TOMMY'S EYES WIDENED AT the sight of his father falling through the air and splitting into two people. One lay on the floor where his mother and brothers gathered, and the other... The other scared the shit out of him.

He glowed and had a scar on his face, but his eyes belonged to the man who raised him, who loved him and tucked him in every night, promising to keep him safe from harm. The ghost's gaze met his, and he nodded before turning his sights on the scary woman.

Tommy swiveled his gaze between the ghost and his father's body. His mother cried over his still form, kissing his forehead, his chest— anything to bring him back to life—and something inside Tommy clicked.

He bolted toward the ghost, grabbed its wrist, and dragged the spirit back to his father's body where he slammed it down, watching as it fused with his father's skin. "Mommy, hurry, I can't hold it in much longer."

She leaned over and kissed his father on the forehead. Light danced across his skin, and he gasped under her lips. Tears ran in a steady stream down her face, and she glanced at Tommy.

He smiled back at her as his father's eyes fluttered open.

CHRIS'S EYES BLINKED OPEN, and he glanced at his wrists before looking up at his family. "Thank you, babe," he said, and then his gaze went to his two boys. He reached up and touched Tommy's cheek, blinking back the tears. He knew the boy saved his life by pushing his spirit back into his body.

"Thank you, Tommy," he whispered.

Tommy nodded.

He turned his gaze to CJ and sat up. CJ threw his arms around his father's neck and kissed his cheek. A fraction of his power flowed into his father.

"Now you have what you need," CJ said.

Chris reeled from the sheer strength of the power coursing through his veins. "Did you give me all of it?"

"No, just a tiny bit," CJ said.

If this raging flow of energy was just a tiny bit of his son's power, Chris wondered how the child contained it within his little frame. It ran rampant in his blood, his muscles, fusing, morphing, growing.

Chris stood on shaking legs and met Jessica's gaze. *Our boy could change the trajectory of the sun and moon if he wanted to.* He looked back at his son.

"CJ, keep them safe." He stalked toward the mêlée in the center of the room.

Tom lumbered after Sharon and stumbled, weakened by blood loss. Sharon kicked him square in the groin, and he dropped to his knees.

"She's mine," Chris growled passing by Tom, trying to catch her before she reached the table of weapons.

She beat him to the table, grabbing something and then spun in his direction.

The distinct hissing sound of an aerosol can hit his ears at the same time the spray covered his eyes. Burning pain gripped him. He staggered back a few steps with his hands out in front of him, blocking some of the spray but the damage was done. The acid-laced mace gouged his eyes. He reeled into the center of the room.

Sharon kicked Tom in the face on her way by, knocking him out. "You will never see her again," she said to Chris.

But I will still hear her. He shifted into karate form with his head held low. "Game on," he growled.

She's behind you. Jessica's blessed voice echoed in his mind.

He turned toward Sharon. "You really didn't believe me when I said I could bring him back, did you?" He looked toward where he thought she was standing with the skin around his eyes still sizzling from the chemicals.

"No, I didn't," she replied.

He laughed. "Just for the record, my name is Ty Alexander Ryan," he said, and although he couldn't see a thing, he accurately zoomed in on her, looking at the spot where she stood. "And I am going to make you wish you were never born."

Rustling fabric behind him caught his attention and Chris tilted his head. "Looks like Tom's with us again."

Tom's gasp masked her movement, but Chris caught a wisp of fabric to his right and focused back on her.

Hush, I need to hear her.

"I can still kill them," Sharon said.

Chris slowly turned toward her voice. It was closer than before.

"I dare you to try." A second later, an electrical buzz snapped, and a distinct ozone odor filled the room. He pointed in CJ's direction. "Keep that in check, CJ. This isn't your fight. Your job is to keep your mother, Tommy and Eric safe, understand?"

"Yes, Daddy," CJ answered.

"Jess, get them out of here." He focused back on Sharon.

You have it back, Jessica said in his head.

He nodded. He felt her power alongside CJ's. "Go. Now. And take Tom with you."

Eric crossed the room to Tom. "You just unleashed hell," he said to Sharon. Then picked Tom up and shuffled back to the family and out the door.

Chris chuckled. CJ would see to it that they got out of the building intact, vaporizing anything in his way. The door slammed as Chris willed it. He was giddy with the power flowing in his veins. Christopher said he would lose his power; he never bet that Jessica and CJ would give him theirs.

"Now, let's see…What should I do with you?" Chris contemplated, tapping his index finger on his lips.

She had circled around behind him again. He heard the click of an automatic weapon above him.

"Dive." Chris sent out the command.

The shooter obediently dove from the rafters two stories above and landed headfirst on the concrete floor a few feet behind Sharon. The wet thud of a skull cracking open spread a smile over Chris's lips.

Sharon gasped, backing away from the dead man she'd hired. "What the hell are you?"

"I'm your worst fucking nightmare." Chris smiled. He heard the clip fall from the gun she held and another slip in. "Not happening. Toss me the gun." He put his hand out, and she tossed the gun in the air to him. It landed in his hand. "I bet the look on your face is absolutely priceless."

"Why won't you just die?" she whispered.

"I'm not in a hurry to go to hell. Although right now, I'm sure the devil is having a royal fit, and my brother is laughing so hard he's rolling on the ground with tears coming from his eyes."

She lunged toward him with the knife. Chris spun, grabbing the wrist that held the weapon and spinning around so his elbow connected with her face. He tossed her away.

"Did you know I'm a third-degree black belt?" he asked.

"You son of a bitch, you broke my nose."

"I guess Jess and I have another thing in common now."

Sharon lunged at him again with a roar, announcing her whereabouts.

Chris blocked her arm as she swung the knife and thrust the heel of his hand into her chest, sending her sprawling back on the ground. "You know, I don't really like the fact that you hung me on a cross today," he commented, hearing her get to her feet. "Or that you shot my wife three times." He lowered his head, listening. He heard her breathing hard and smiled as she ran at him again.

This time, the knife grazed his skin, drawing blood. He grabbed her arm and twisted it, snapping it like a twig. The knife went flying. Sharon screamed. He let go and stepped back into the center of the room.

Sharon stumbled to the table and grabbed another weapon. The whir of the barbs clued him in, and he ducked, spinning out of the way. He guessed she had donned the same torture mechanism she'd used to rip his back to shreds. The same sound he heard before the whip cracked his back whizzed inches from his face.

Chris heard her lumbering gait coming for him again. He jumped in the air, and did a powerful roundhouse kick that caught the side of her head as the barbs hit his leg, tearing the fabric of his pants and the skin beneath.

Sharon went flying and hit one of the chairs, toppling over with it.

Chris stood in the center of the room, his eyes closed, concentrating and gritting his teeth against the familiar pain. The chemical burns around his eyes faded, and the cut on the inside of his thigh disappeared. When he opened his eyes, the chemical burns on his corneas were gone, leaving the perfect blue they had always been, the only difference being he still couldn't see a thing. Chris looked in her direction, not seeing her, but giving the illusion he could.

"What are you?" she asked again, witnessing the transformation.

"Would you believe the Angel of Death resurrected?"

"I'd believe just about anything right now," Sharon said, slowly getting up.

"You killed Emily," he growled, looking straight at the spot where she stood, which happened to be right next to his stepdaughter's dead body.

"Tom needed to learn his lesson."

"And that meant destroying my family?" he asked, tilting his head, sharpening in on her exact location.

"He loves your wife."

"So what? You've been blackmailing him for the last five years."

"I wanted him."

The whisper of fabric and scuff of shoes told him she'd moved but he didn't know in what direction. But her thoughts were murderous.

"I don't need to see you with my eyes. I can see you with my mind, and if you think you can tag me with that thing again, go for it." He shifted into ready pose with a smile.

She took the bait and attacked, swinging it at his head.

Chris ducked. The barbs whistled by his face. He and he lunged forward and sent a powerful punch into her solar plexus, using the power of his crouch to his advantage. He felt something snap under the pressure of his fist, and a spike grazed his arm as she flew backwards screaming in pain.

Hinges creaked, and Chris turned toward the door, listening for movement and turning his attention away from her to scan the mind of the intruder.

TOM SURVEYED THE ROOM, his gaze landing on Sharon, and his hatred flared. He wanted to squeeze the life out of her. He wanted her to feel the same kind of pain and fear she reined on Chris, on Jessica, and on his son. He wanted her dead.

"Get out, Tom," Chris said, pointing at the door. "Killing her will destroy you."

"And it won't destroy you?"

"No, it won't." Movement caught his attention, and he whipped his head in her direction. "Park your ass," he commanded.

She sat back down on the floor obediently.

Tom's jaw dropped. "I thought you didn't have your powers."

"I didn't. Left that at the gates of hell." Chris looked back toward Tom. "Along with my soul and apparently my eyesight." He smiled. "But the devil never guessed Jess had some of that power left inside her, or that she would give it back to me. And he sure as shit didn't bet on CJ." Shuffling sounds interrupted him, and he swung his head in Sharon's direction. "Sit," he said, and she promptly sat back on the ground. "Your son has a touch of it, too." He smiled back toward Tom. "Hell of a thing to be shoved back into your own body. If it weren't for Tommy, I'd be down under getting my ass whomped by Frank right now."

Tom shivered at the mention of Frank's name.

Chris's smile faded. "Too bad Tommy wasn't awake when Emily was shot. I wasn't able to save her after all." He looked toward Sharon, and his jaw tightened.

With his first step toward her, the transition completed, and he became the Ty Tom remembered near the end, soul-less, cold, and frightening.

"Beg." The growl rolled off his tongue, and he reached his hand out, squeezing the air as if he had his hand around her neck.

With one hand, Sharon clawed the invisible grip around her throat, stumbling to her feet. In the other, she gripped the handle, looping the spikes in a small arc. "Please," her restricted voice whimpered.

Careful, she's up and moving to your right side.

Chris squared his shoulders in the direction Tom indicated. "Please what?" He tilted his head, lowering his arms.

"Die," she screamed and swung the barbs at his face.

Chris moved at inhuman speed, grabbing the strands of the whip, yanking it from her hand, and lobbing it across the room. His bloody hand curled into a fist and slammed into the middle of her face, shattering bones beneath the raw force of his punch. She died instantly. Her body flew across the room and landed on her back, staring blindly at the rafters.

Chris waited a moment. "I think that about does it." He turned back toward Tom, shaking his hand and sending blood across the floor. "Damn, that hurts." He closed his eyes. The cuts on his hand and wrist disappeared.

"I will never get used to that," Tom said.

"Are they all gone?"

"Is what gone?"

"The burns around my eyes?"

"Yeah."

"You still bleeding?"

"Yeah."

"Come here," Chris said. Tom went to him, and Chris put his hand on Tom's arm. "Show me where."

Tom took his hand and put it next to the bullet hole.

Chris smiled awkwardly. "This doesn't mean I like you, okay?"

Tom laughed, and the minute Chris's lips touched the skin above his hand, hot pain flared, and he sucked in his breath. "That hurts like a bitch." He stepped back.

"Sorry, but I guess it comes with the territory." Chris stood straight, wiping the back of his hand across his mouth. "Where's my family?"

"RIGHT HERE," JESSICA SAID. Feet shuffled across the floor, and then her arms wrapped around him. "I thought I lost you today," she sobbed.

"I thought so too, babe." Chris lifted his hands to her face and felt for her lips, then leaned over and kissed them, pushing the lion's share of the power back into her, where it belonged. He pulled away from her. Tears formed in his eyes. He looked down at the floor, seeing nothing but darkness as he waited for her voice, and when it came, he closed his eyes letting the tears fall.

"Ty, I know. I know what you gave up for us."

"No, honey, you don't really know." He took a deep breath. "I had to choose." He put his head on her shoulder. "I had to choose which one would die so I could come back."

She stiffened in his arms. "Then you shouldn't have come back."

"Everyone would have died if I didn't come back, Jess," he whispered and opened the door to his dream so she could see the alternative.

Jessica gasped at the image he showed her. All of the kids dead, each by a different, horrible method.

"I even asked them to take Tom instead, but they said no. I had to choose one of them. I couldn't let you watch Sharon torture and kill each of the kids before she killed you. So, I made the choice. It's my fault Emily is dead." His voice cracked, and he pressed his lips together, dipping his head. "I'm so sorry."

Jessica closed her eyes. "Why didn't you offer me up instead?"

"That wasn't an option. I had to give up one of the kids in addition to everything else. I gave up eternity with you to come back and save our family. Heaven was laid out at my feet, and I could have made that choice instead, but the thought of our children dying painfully..." He shook his head. "The cost was just too high." He kissed her cheek and pulled away, wiping his face with his hands. "I will understand if you don't ever want to see me again."

He lied—that would crush him.

"Why her?" she asked, her words encased in a sob.

Chris closed his eyes. "Because she was given five more years than she was supposed to have. They would have taken CJ if I let them choose."

Silence blanketed the room.

"Did she suffer?" He prayed Christopher had kept his end of the bargain.

"No, Emily didn't suffer," Tom answered. "What happened here today isn't your fault. It's mine."

"Tom, I made a deal with the devil."

Tom laughed. "I married the devil, and I put your lives in jeopardy when I walked out on her." He absently pointed at his wife's dead body. "It's a miracle that any of us survived." He paused. "It's not his fault, Jessie. It's mine."

When her hands slipped into Chris's, relief washed through him, erasing the fear of losing her heart. Fresh tears fell from his eyes.

"I should have let you kill Sharon when you had the chance," she whispered, her voice raw with emotion.

He hung his head, reaching up to touch her face, feeling the wet tears on her cheek. He felt the pain in her heart and was glad he couldn't see it in her eyes. "I should have just done it anyway," he replied and shivers took hold of him. "Can you get me my shirt?"

Tom retrieved both the T-shirt and the top to his karate uniform, and Chris pulled the T-shirt over his head. He pulled the gi on and laced it up. "My belt?"

Tom handed him the thin strip of fabric.

Sirens wailed in the distance, and Chris raised his unseeing eyes. "I want to see my family."

End Game Chapter 37

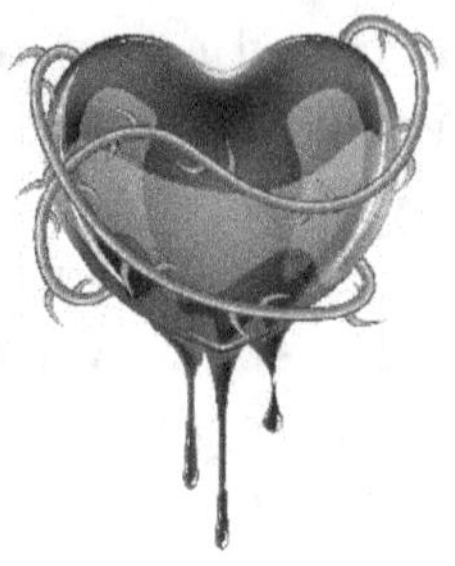

THE TWO BOYS RAN to their father and wrapped their arms around his knees. Chris let go of Jessica's hand and gently peeled them from his legs, kneeling down and sweeping them into his arms in a powerful hug. Jessica put her hand on his shoulder to let him know she was still there with him. He reached his hand out for Eric, not knowing where he was.

Eric took Chris's hand and closed his eyes. He knew Chris had sacrificed his sister to save them. "Why didn't you sacrifice me?"

Chris shook his head and looked in the general direction of the voice. "I couldn't," he whispered. He clung to his two children and squeezed Eric's hand before letting go. "My brother made the choice for me, and I agreed to it." He hung his head.

THE DOOR AT THE end of the hall pushed open enough for a rifle barrel to slip through. Tom caught sight of it just as it spit fire. He launched himself in front of the bullet path.

"Jessie!" His yell was drowned by the rifle. Their eyes met.

The bullet entered his back, shattering his spine, catapulting through his heart, and blasting out the front of him, spraying the family with his blood.

The bullet grazed Chris's temple and buried into the wall next to where he knelt.

JESSICA JUMPED, CATCHING TOM'S gaze just before the bullet tore him apart and missed her by mere inches. Her head whipped toward the door and a spark flew from the barrel, announcing another bullet, but it never reached them.

The air rippled, and a wall of sheer power thrust down the hallway at Mach speed. The force of the explosion blew a hole the size of a dump truck through the building, showering debris a hundred yards into the Hudson at the far end of the warehouse, and annihilating the bullet and the sniper in the process.

Her head swiveled, at first looking at her husband, but the pure shock on his face told her he wasn't the one to do the damage. Her gaze fell on her son.

CJ stood with his head tilted, chin to his chest and his little fists clenched. Rage bled into his muscles, his clenched jaw, and narrowed eyes, profiling the destructive force coiling inside him.

Chris tightened his grip on his son, and Jessica turned her eyes to Tom's motionless form, the reality of his sacrifice sinking in.

"No," she screamed and dropped to his side.

"Jess," Chris said, panic lacing his voice.

"I got him, Dad," CJ said.

Jessica sobbed, repeating "no" as sadness layered over her like a suffocating blanket.

"Eric?" Chris whispered.

"Not me. Tom," Eric said from close to Chris. "He's dead."

It took Chris a moment to understand. He pulled both Tommy's and CJ's shaking forms closer. "Tom?" he asked Eric.

"He jumped in front of the bullet," Eric said, and he put his hand on his mother's shoulder.

"Jesus."

"FREEZE!"

Jessica's head snapped. Her brain instantly registered the uniform, and she turned toward CJ, sending the silent warning. *Don't! It's a police officer!*

CJ's chin quivered, and tears sprang from his eyes. He turned and buried his head in his father's chest.

The police descended on the gruesome scene like a hawk swooping in on its prey.

End Game Chapter 38

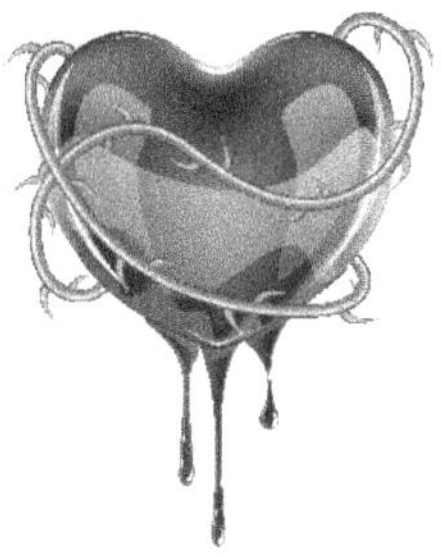

CHRIS SAT IN THE room as the EMT worked on the cut on his temple. Jessica spoke to the police a short distance away.

"Are you okay?" Chris said, sensing Eric looking at him. He glanced over to where he thought Eric might be.

"Please don't move," the EMT snapped.

"I will be," Eric said. "What about you?"

Chris sent an awkward smile toward his stepson. He wasn't sure how okay he was, not with everything that happened today. "I'm alive."

Feet shuffled closer. "They want to talk to us." Jessica's voice shook.

"Are you finished?" Chris asked the technician.

"Just about," the EMT replied.

Chris waited patiently. Jessica could have fixed the cut, but Chris didn't want her to. He wanted a reminder of what he'd lost today. Even though he would never see the scar, he would feel it. It went from his eyebrow to just under his hairline and it would fade to a very thin line with time, but he would know it was there.

When the EMT left the room, Chris looked toward Jessica.

He stood on shaking legs, letting Jessica lead the way, and promptly stumbled over something on the ground.

"Sorry, I keep forgetting you can't see," she said.

"You suck as a guide."

"Sorry, babe." She led him to the chair at the table in the make-shift interrogation room.

"Hello, Mr. Ryan. My name is Detective Sanders."

Chris nodded his acknowledgement in the general direction of the voice.

"You've put us in quite the predicament here," Detective Sanders said, and a chair scraped close by.

"Is there a problem?" Chris asked after the silence grew.

"I've got a few questions," he said.

"I'd like to have my lawyer present," Chris replied and sat in the chair.

"What's your lawyer's name?"

"Sam Trueman," Chris replied.

"I'm afraid that will be impossible. Mr. Trueman is dead."

Chris closed his eyes, lowering his head.

"You already knew he was dead, didn't you?"

"I was hoping he wasn't," Chris said. He thought he heard a rifle shot when he faced off against Sharon, but he wasn't sure, and the only logical conclusion was he got too close.

"He was the one who called us," Detective Sanders said.

That impacted Chris more than the fact that he was dead. It meant that he'd suffered.

"Shit." Chris lowered his head again. Wetness streaked his cheeks, and he wiped his tears with his knuckles. "I'm sorry, he was like family. He was supposed to stay back and wait for me."

Jessica slid her hand into his. "I'm here, babe."

Chris nodded. He took a deep breath and focused on the detective. "What are your questions?"

"Do you want a lawyer?"

Chris shook his head.

Detective Sanders's chair creaked. "That was a very shrewd way to get information."

Chris shrugged. "You wouldn't have told me if I asked outright."

"When did you get married?"

"Is it still Saturday?"

"Yes."

"We got married yesterday. Judge Sampson married us."

"Judge Sampson?"

"Yes, he performed the ceremony as a favor to Sam." Silence settled over the room and Chris waited.

"Why don't you have any cuts outside of the one on your head?"

"I don't know. Divine intervention?"

"What I don't get is how you can walk out of this unharmed."

Chris let a bark of a laugh out. "Unharmed? My closest friend is dead, I'm blind as a fucking bat, and my wife lost her daughter. Never mind the psychological damage to my boys. They saw their father beaten and crucified, their sister murdered, and their mother shot. My kids have her ex-husband's blood all over their clothing because someone tried to shoot her, and he just happened to throw himself in front of the bullet." The flare of anger radiated from him.

"Unharmed? You have got to be a sadistic son of a bitch."

"Calm down, Mr. Ryan," Detective Sanders said.

"Calm down?" Chris laughed. "I don't think so."

"You killed that woman."

"Self-defense," Chris snapped back.

"You had every intention of killing her," Detective Sanders said.

Chris didn't reply.

"She was going to kill all of us..." Jessica started, but Chris put his hand up to quiet her.

"You toyed with her," Detective Sanders said.

"She blinded me. How did I toy with her?"

"You are a third-degree black belt, Mr. Ryan. She was at a disadvantage even with the weapons."

"Normally I would agree with you. However, I couldn't see her, so therefore she had the advantage. Besides, every strike I made was defensive. I never went on the offensive. If I had, it would have been over like that." He snapped his fingers.

"Why did she give you the gun?"

Chris tilted his head, his brain catching up to the line of questioning. "How'd you know she gave me the gun?"

"Closed circuit video."

He raised his eyebrows.

"What'd you say to her to get her to toss it to you?"

Chris shrugged.

"And why didn't you use it?"

"For all I knew, she could have loaded it with blanks to screw with me."

"Then there's this guy… Where did he come from?"

Chris looked toward Jessica for assistance.

"The video showed someone taking a dive from the rafters."

"Huh?"

"Looks like someone jumped from the rafters," Detective Sanders replied.

"Really?"

"What the hell did you think that noise was?" Detective Sanders asked.

"I was too busy trying to survive to analyze the noises I was hearing. I was focused on where Sharon, was because if I'd let myself get sidetracked by anything else I'd be dead now."

"Did you kill Sharon Whitman?"

"Yes."

"Did you go to the warehouse today with the intent to kill Sharon Whitman?"

"No."

"Did you want to kill Sharon Whitman?"

Chris took a deep breath. "She killed my stepdaughter, shot my wife, and then tried to slit my son's throat. She had every intention of killing us all slowly and painfully."

"You didn't answer my question."

Chris looked square at the detective, giving the illusion he actually saw him. "What would you have wanted if that was your family?"

Detective Sanders didn't say anything for a few moments and then a chair creaked. "What happened to the shooter in the hallway?" he asked. "It looked as if a bomb went off."

Chris shook his head and closed his eyes. "I don't know. I didn't see anything." His hand went to the stitches in his temple. "Can we go?" he asked. "It's been a hell of a day."

"I don't want you leaving the city just yet."

Chris glanced in Jessica's direction. "When can we take Emily home?" Just saying her name caused tears to sprout. The reality of having to bury her hit him hard, and he flashed back to the first time he saw her, scared, pale, shaking in one of Tom's guest rooms in California. That night, he'd promised to protect her from the evils in this world and beyond... and he'd failed.

Jessica squeezed his hand.

"It will be a couple of days," Detective Sanders said. "Once the autopsy is complete."

"Is my car here?"

"I'm not sure," he answered. "What would a blind man want with a car anyway?"

"It has all of the clothing we need for the rest of the weekend."

"What's the make and model?"

"It's a blue Hummer."

"We have it. The forensic team is going over it now."

"Can we have our bags?" Chris asked. "And can someone call us a cab?"

Silence draped the room.

"I can't see, remember?"

"Yes, you can have your bags, and we will call you a cab. Where can we get a hold of you?"

Chris gave the detective the address and phone number for the apartment and let Jessica lead him out of the room.

BACK IN THE APARTMENT with the boys cleaned up and tucked into bed, Chris stood in the master bedroom with his head down in shame.

"This is my fault." He turned to head into the bathroom, slamming his foot into the dresser on the way. He swore under his breath as he felt for the shower knobs and turned on the water. He stripped and stepped into the shower, then let the water wash the dry, caked blood off his back.

Jessica stepped in moments later. She reached for the soap and ran it gently over his back. Sobs ripped through her with each stroke. "You died twice today."

Chris nodded.

"You came back to me twice."

Chris nodded.

"You saved me again."

Chris shook his head. "No, I didn't save you. Tom did." He took a shaky breath. "And CJ did." He put his forehead against the cool tile, and the shakes started.

"Ty, you saved us."

He shook his head. "I failed. Not everyone walked out of there alive, Jess. I failed, and I lost my soul in the process." Tears, hot and bitter, burned his throat.

Jessica turned him toward her and took his face in her hands. "Did you ever wonder why we were soul mates?"

"Every fucking day of my life."

"We balance each other. Your soul is not lost because I won't let it be."

"You don't have a choice," Chris said, and his hands found her waist. "I told you a long time ago that my nature is much darker than yours, and I'm going to pay for my sins whether you want me to or not." He leaned over and kissed her, feeling her skin under his hands, the feel and smell of her setting him on fire. He needed her more at this moment than he ever did before.

She let out a little laugh.

"What?" he asked.

"Your eyes still smolder," she said as she touched his face, her tears mixing with the shower. She kissed him.

End Game Epilogue

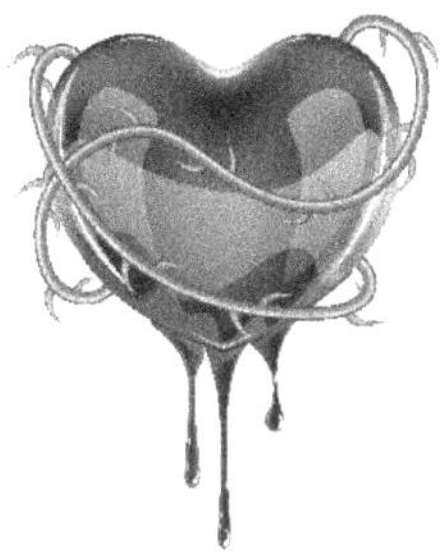

CHRIS SAT ON THE end of the dock in cut-off shorts, feet hanging over the edge in the cool water, stroking the head of a beautiful German Sheppard as it lay on his lap. The sunglasses on his face were for show. Six months after the horror in the warehouse, he still couldn't see a thing.

The funerals had been more of a nightmare than he expected. He knew Emily's would be hard, but never fathomed how difficult Tom's would be. Not just because all of Hollywood came out to pay their respects, but because he felt personally responsible for his death. For all the hostilities between them, Chris knew Tom was truly a good guy and didn't deserve to have his life cut short like that.

Sam's funeral was equally as emotional. After all, Sam had been his only real friend, and saying goodbye was a bitch. Sam's daughter Lynn was a partner in Sam's law firm, and she had impressed both Chris and Jessica enough that they decided to keep their legal affairs within the Trueman family.

After the reading of Tom's will, Lynn became paramount to diffusing both the media hype and the police questions. As sole heir of his estate, Jessica endured close scrutiny, but ultimately,

Sharon's death was deemed as self-defense and the case was closed.

Jessica sold the Malibu property but kept the syndication rights to the television show, movie royalties, and some personal items she thought Tommy would want some day. Tom received an Oscar for his work in *Survival Games*, and she was asked to accept it on his behalf. She had cried on national television when they handed her the golden statue. The speech she wrote turned the amphitheater into a standing ovation, the likes of which Hollywood hadn't seen in years. That had touched her beyond words. She kept the Oscar in Tommy's room, telling him that his real father earned that for playing the part of Chris' brother.

Chris adjusted to being blind, but he missed the way she looked, the sensuous curve of her waist in a silk dress, the line of her calves as she lay on the beach reading a book, all the little things, all the snapshots stored in his head. The snapshots he could retrieve at will. He thanked God he chose sight instead of sound, because, while he missed seeing her, he relished the sound of her and the way she whispered his name at night when he held her.

He felt the vibrations as she walked down to the end of the dock and sat next to him, then took his hand in hers.

"Looks like Sam is falling asleep on the job," she said, and Sam's head lifted from his lap.

"He's just taking a break with me. Where are the kids?"

"Unpacking the groceries. Eric's with them."

Chris nodded.

Eric spent a significant amount of time with the boys, spending most of July with them at the lake. Boston College offered him a full ride basketball scholarship, and he had already packed to head to the campus at the end of the week.

Jessica sighed. "I'm going to miss him."

"Me too." Chris took a deep breath and put his arm around his wife. "Is the sun setting?"

"Yes."

"Tell me what it looks like."

Her words painted a vivid sunset across the back of his eyelids.

The End

Continue Ty and Jessica's story in

HUNTING SEASON, the third book in

THE STEVE WILLIAMS SERIES.

Check out the HUNTING SEASON excerpt on the

following pages!

About J.E. Taylor

J.E. Taylor is a USA Today bestselling author, a publisher, an editor, a manuscript formatter, a mother, a wife, a business analyst, and a Supernatural fangirl. Not necessarily in that order. She first sat down to seriously write in February of 2007 after her daughter asked:

"Mom, if you could do anything, what would you do?"
From that moment on, she hasn't looked back.

Besides being co-owner of Novel Concept Publishing, Ms. Taylor also moonlights as a Senior Editor of Allegory E-zine, an online venue for Science Fiction, Fantasy and Horror, and co-host of the popular YouTube talk show Spilling Ink.

She lives in New Hampshire with her husband and during the summer months enjoys her weekends on the shore in southern Maine.

Visit her at https://books.JETaylor75.com to check out her other titles.

An Except from Hunting Season:

SATURDAY ROLLED AROUND, AND Steve found solace in the library while Eric entertained his girl for the night. It was the first time Eric left him alone for more than an hour's time and with no new information on Kyle and no change in Jennifer's condition, Steve focused on his new partner, pilfering through the archives, digging up everything he could on Eric Connor and his family.

He accessed the New York City police department database, pulling up the video of Eric's family under siege at the warehouse incident five years before. After repeated viewings, he concluded that the only ones who should be alive today were Eric and one of his younger brothers.

Besides his sister's death, his younger brother should have bled to death when the crazy bitch raked the knife across his throat, but nothing happened to him, nothing, no mark, no blood, nothing.

Eric was another story—at that same moment, his right hand split open to the bone, as if he somehow put his hand between the knife and his brother's throat, saving the kid's life.

The gunshot wounds Eric's mother sustained should have killed her, but according to the medical reports; she only had one shallow lesion in her shoulder. He re-read that part, switching between the video and the medical notes again, and again, and again.

"No fucking way." He sat back in the seat, wiping his mouth with his hand.

Eric's stepfather was something different entirely. With so much that didn't add up, Steve wondered how they could close the case so quickly. *But then again, having more money than God must have helped.* Filthy rich didn't begin to describe it. Eric's stepfather was one of the wealthiest men in the world.

The shitty quality of the tape didn't diminish the horror of Chris Ryan's beating and the crucifixion that followed. The blood loss alone, three quarts according to the forensic notes, would have killed a normal man. Yet he somehow lived and had the strength to kill the bitch with his own hands.

"Shit." Steve muttered, biting his lower lip and concentrating on a frame-by-frame analysis. Some frames were warped static and he couldn't make out a thing, but the clear ones made him shiver.

Frame by frame, Chris Ryan fell from the cross and just before he disappeared from view, Steve swore he saw the man split in two. He rewound to see it again, printing the frame.

He rubbed his eyes and watched a third time. "Was that a fucking ghost?" Steve leaned back, his jaw slack, and he watched yet again. That meant Eric's stepfather actually died in that warehouse. "Holy shit."

A dozen frames later, Eric's stepfather stepped back into view. Steve froze the frame and stared at the man's back. Bloody, but smooth—not a trace of the raw shredded welts it had been when she finished the flogging.

"Jesus Christ almighty!" He rubbed his sweaty palms on the soft fabric of his jeans, swallowing the rock that formed in his throat. After a deep, calming breath, he rewound to the full frame of the ghost.

His heart lurched in his chest.

The ghost wasn't Eric's stepfather.

This face was familiar for very different reasons and Steve's blood shifted, braised by an arctic wind that attacked his veins, chilling him to the core.

"Ho-ly shit." He pushed his chair, shot to his feet, and paced back and forth, staring at the monitor like it was a cobra ready to strike. "No fucking way."

He took a seat again, pushing the heel of his palm to his good eye, sucking air in to calm his racing pulse. He slammed his index finger on the print button, lifting the color photograph off the printer, studying it. A shiver bit his neck and he shuddered, dropping the photo in his backpack with the others.

He played the rest of the video in slow motion. Slowing to frame by frame as the woman blinded Eric's stepfather with chemical mace. Chemical burns scarred the skin around his eyes in one frame, but in the next, it was gone.

Steve shook his head, rubbed his eyes, and played the scene again. The same results, impossible becoming possible, and Steve exhaled, suddenly aware he had been holding his breath.

Eric's stepfather insisted he killed the woman out of self-defense, and from what Steve saw—it looked valid even with the rest of the inconsistencies on the tape. He burned the video to disk and slid it into his backpack.

Steve picked up the print of the ghost. The case analysis they had done on this one still gave him the creeps. Kidnapping, rape, murder, all for what? Underground porn and snuff videos?

He plugged in a name and the picture that came back was identical to the picture of the ghost in his hand. He tossed the picture in his backpack and brought up the archive of the still open case. The file included ten years' worth of videos, violent and bloody mixed with steamy and hot. Steve pulled up the last one. The one aired on national television after the story broke. He burned it to a disc and went through the gruesome scene frame by frame.

Steve stopped the video when an image in the mirror gave him pause. It was a little boy holding his mother's hand. Not the image of the room. He rewound a few frames and played the tape again.

It wasn't his imagination.

A little boy was holding the woman's hand in a long hallway. Not the horrifying reflection of Ty Aris stretched by chains, like the frame before and after the anomaly.

Steve pushed the chair back. He wiped his face with his hands and glanced up.

ERIC STOOD AT THE head of the stairs, looking down at Steve, his heart hammering in his throat. He had been there long enough to know Steve had figured out his family secret.

Steve didn't move. He just sat in the chair looking up at Eric, his hands frozen halfway down his face. His eye glanced back at the frame in front of him and back up to Eric as a new thought echoed in his mind. *That's you, isn't it?*

"Yes."

Steve winced at the volume of the voice invading his mind.

Leave it alone. Eric's voice boomed again.

"Stop doing that," Steve said aloud.

Eric smiled at Steve's discomfort. *Not until you forget everything you just spent the last twelve hours sorting through.*

"Bullshit!" Steve raised his voice. It echoed through the nearly empty library.

Eric trotted down the stairs and approached the table. He took a seat opposite Steve, his swirling eyes hard and intense.

Steve blinked and looked at the screen, the images converging together in his mind like a storm. His mind grappled with the unimaginable, processing the information he gained from all the reports—the inconsistencies. The miracles.

"Jesus!" The exclamation accompanied a sudden epiphany, and he knew what Eric was hiding. He shook his head, glancing between the screen, his backpack, and Eric. His eyes narrowed as everything slammed into place. "Why are you here?"

"To uphold the law."

Steve laughed. "You've been aiding and abetting a fugitive, for what, fifteen years?"

"You have no idea what you are talking about." Eric sat back.

Steve leaned forward. "Your stepfather is Ty Aris," he whispered.

"His name is Chris Ryan." Eric said. "Ty was his brother."

"Then why did Ty's ghost split off from your stepfather in that warehouse?"

It was Eric's turn to blink. He couldn't cover the surprise fast enough. "You've got no proof."

"That's where you're wrong." Steve pulled the copy paper out of the bag and handed it to Eric.

The picture was a blur. Eric looked at it and handed it back to Steve, the crease between his eyes deepening. "Are you sure you're all right?"

Steve looked at the photograph, and his mouth dropped. He clamped it shut and looked at the screen. Only the reflection of the room was visible in the mirror. He glanced at Eric, filled with both fury and self-doubt. "I know what I saw."

"I'm sure you do," Eric allowed. "But understand this: if you come after my family, you will never get the chance to get the bastard who destroyed yours." He stood and left the library, leaving Steve gaping at him.

STEVE LOOKED BACK AT the computer, and the image was there, blazing on the screen, and burned in his memory.

You can find HUNTING SEASON along with all of J.E. Taylor's books at https://books.JETaylor75.com

www.ingramcontent.com/pod-product-compliance
Lightning Source LLC
Chambersburg PA
CBHW060640310726
48982CB00003B/822